There's ta...
village but...
are prom...
we...

Secrets in the Village

A stunning collection brought to you by
Kate Hardy, Gill Sanderson,
Melanie Milburne and
Margaret McDonagh

There's talk of secrets in the
village but the loudest whispers
are promises, proposals and
words of love!

Secrets in the Village

Kate Hardy Gill Sanderson
Melanie Milburne Margaret McDonagh

MILLS & BOON

> **DID YOU PURCHASE THIS BOOK WITHOUT A COVER?**
> If you did, you should be aware it is **stolen property** as it was reported *unsold and destroyed* by a retailer. Neither the author nor the publisher has received any payment for this book.

All the characters in this book have no existence outside the imagination of the author, and have no relation whatsoever to anyone bearing the same name or names. They are not even distantly inspired by any individual known or unknown to the author, and all the incidents are pure invention.

All Rights Reserved including the right of reproduction in whole or in part in any form. This edition is published by arrangement with Harlequin Enterprises II B.V./S.à.r.l. The text of this publication or any part thereof may not be reproduced or transmitted in any form or by any means, electronic or mechanical, including photocopying, recording, storage in an information retrieval system, or otherwise, without the written permission of the publisher.

This book is sold subject to the condition that it shall not, by way of trade or otherwise, be lent, resold, hired out or otherwise circulated without the prior consent of the publisher in any form of binding or cover other than that in which it is published and without a similar condition including this condition being imposed on the subsequent purchaser.

® and ™ are trademarks owned and used by the trademark owner and/or its licensee. Trademarks marked with ® are registered with the United Kingdom Patent Office and/or the Office for Harmonisation in the Internal Market and in other countries.

Mills & Boon, an imprint of Harlequin (UK) Limited, Eton House, 18-24 Paradise Road, Richmond, Surrey TW9 1SR

SECRETS IN THE VILLAGE
© Harlequin Enterprises II B.V./S.à.r.l. 2012

The Doctor's Royal Love-Child © Pamela Brooks 2008
Nurse Bride, Bayside Wedding © Gill Sanderson 2008
Single Dad Seeks a Wife © Melanie Milburne 2008
Virgin Wife, Playboy Doctor © Margaret McDonagh 2008

ISBN: 978 0 263 89669 5

024-0112

Harlequin (UK) policy is to use papers that are natural, renewable and recyclable products and made from wood grown in sustainable forests. The logging and manufacturing processes conform to the legal environmental regulations of the country of origin.

Printed and bound in Spain
by Blackprint CPI, Barcelona

The Doctor's Royal Love-Child

KATE HARDY

Kate Hardy lives on the outskirts of Norwich with her husband, two small children, a dog—and too many books to count! She wrote her first book at age six, when her parents gave her a typewriter for her birthday. She had the first of a series of sexy romances published at twenty-five, and swapped a job in marketing communications for freelance health journalism when her son was born, so she could spend more time with him. She's wanted to write for Mills & Boon since she was twelve—and when she was pregnant with her daughter, her husband pointed out that writing Medical Romances™ would be the perfect way to combine her interest in health issues with her love of good stories.

Kate is always delighted to hear from readers—do drop in to her website at www.katehardy.com

For Sheila, my wonderful editor

CHAPTER ONE

'FANCY seeing you here, Dr Lovak,' Melinda said with a grin as Dragan wound down the window of his car. 'Anyone would think I had matched my call lists to yours.'

Knowing that she'd done exactly that when she'd phoned him after her morning's surgery—except his first call had taken a little longer than he'd expected, which was why he was arriving at the boarding kennels just as she was leaving—Dragan smiled back. 'Tut-tut, Ms Fortesque. Suggest things like that and people might start to talk.'

'If they do, I'll just tell them I wanted to check on my favourite patient and see how her leg's doing. Isn't that right, Bramble?' Melinda looked over Dragan's shoulder at the flatcoat retriever they'd rescued a few months before, who was lying on a blanket in the back of his car.

The dog's tail thumped loudly, and she gave a soft answering woof.

'Hear that? Bramble says she'll be my alibi.' Melinda leaned in through the open window and stole a kiss from Dragan. 'Though I think people might have already started to guess, *amore mio*. Do you know how many people this last month have told me what a wonderful doctor you are?'

'Funny, that. People have been singing your praises to me, too.' He stole a kiss right back. 'But that's the thing about living in a place like Penhally. Everybody knows everything about everyone.' Or nearly everything. So, despite the fact that they'd kept their relationship low-key, he was pretty sure that everybody in Penhally knew that the vet and the doctor were an item.

For a moment, he could've sworn that worry flashed into Melinda's gorgeous blue eyes. But then the expression was gone again. No, he must be imagining things. What did Melinda have to hide, anyway? She'd come to England on holiday years ago, had fallen in love with the country and decided to settle here and train to be a vet.

Not so very different from himself. Although holidays had been the last thing on his mind when he'd walked off that boat seventeen years ago, he too had fallen in love with England. And he was as settled here in Cornwall as he'd ever be anywhere. The wild Atlantic wasn't quite the same as the Adriatic, but at least the sound of the sea could still lull him to sleep at night.

'Do you have time for lunch?' she asked.

He shook his head. 'Sorry. I'm already behind schedule. And I really can't keep my patients waiting.'

'Of course you can't.' She stroked his cheek. 'I'll cook for us tonight, then. Your place.'

He turned his head to press a kiss into her palm. 'That would be lovely. Though you don't have to cook for me, Melinda. I'm perfectly capable of doing it.'

She scoffed and put her hands on her hips, shaking her head at him as he got out of the car. 'Dragan Lovak, you know as well as I do that you *never* cook. That if I let you, you'd live on bread and cheese and cold meats and salad—even in the middle of winter.'

He flapped a dismissive hand. 'Well. Food doesn't have to be hot. It's fuel.'

'It's much more than that,' she told him. 'You don't just shovel down calories like a Ferrari taking on petrol at a pit stop. Food is a *pleasure*. Something to be enjoyed.'

Since Melinda had been in his life, Dragan was beginning to appreciate that. Not only because she was a fantastic cook: her enjoyment of food had taught him to notice flavour. Texture. Aroma. Things he'd blocked out in the dark days and that he'd more or less trained himself to ignore since then.

'Are you on call tonight?' he asked.

'No. It's the turn of the other practice to cover tonight. What about you?'

'No. And I'm not on late surgery, either.'

'So we have the whole evening to ourselves. *Bene.*' Her eyes sparkled. 'I'll pick up something at the Trevellyans' farm shop and bring it over to cook when I've finished surgery, yes?'

Recently she'd spent more nights at his little terraced cottage in Fisherman's Row than at her own flat above the veterinary surgery, just round the corner. Maybe, Dragan thought, it was time that he gave Melinda her own key. Time that they took their relationship to the next level. Time that he asked her to move in with him.

Though it was taking one hell of a risk. Since his family had been killed during the war in Croatia, he'd kept people at a distance—just close enough to be polite and pleasant and easy to work with, but far enough away to keep his heart safe. He reasoned that if he didn't let people too close, he wouldn't get hurt if he lost them, or if they walked away.

He'd kept his private life extremely private—until Melinda Fortesque had entered his life. With just one smile, the Italian vet had cracked the fortress round his heart wide open, and she'd walked straight in.

But although part of him wanted it so badly—to ask her to live with him, be his love, make a new family with him—the fear flooded in and stopped the words before he could say them. What if it all went wrong? What if he lost her? He didn't think he'd be able to pick up the pieces again. Not this time.

He shivered.

'Dragan? You are cold?'

On a sunny spring day like this? Hardly. He summoned a smile. 'No. I'm...' No. This wasn't the right time or the right place for that particular discussion. 'Late for my appointment,' he finished wryly. 'I'll see you later.'

'OK. *Ciao*.' She blew him a kiss. '*Zlato*.'

His mouth must have dropped open, because she laughed. 'You're not the only one who can speak several languages, you know.'

Italian was Melinda's native tongue and he knew she also spoke French and Spanish as well as English, albeit with a slight Italian accent.

But she'd just called him 'darling' in his own tongue.

Croatian.

How many years had it been since he'd heard that word spoken?

'Dragan?' She was looking worried. 'What's the matter? I said it wrong—it doesn't mean what I think it means and I've just mortally insulted you?'

'No.' He forced himself to smile. 'You said it perfectly. I wasn't expecting it, that's all.' And it had brought back memories he usually kept locked away.

She shook her head. 'I can see it in your eyes. I hurt you. I didn't mean to—'

'Hey.' He got out of the car and slid his arms round her, held her close. Rested his cheek against her soft, silky hair and breathed in the sweet scent he always associated with her. 'I know you didn't, *piccola mia*. It's all right.'

'I looked it up on the internet. How to say "*amore mio*" in Croatian. I just wanted to...well, to please you,' she said softly.

'You did. You *do*.' He was so close to telling her how much she meant to him. How he really felt about her. Just how much he loved her. But the first time he said those words, he wanted it to be perfect. Romantic. At the top of the cliffs, with moonlight shining over the Atlantic—or maybe at sunrise. A new dawn, a new beginning. He hadn't quite worked out the details. But the middle of the car park of the local boarding kennels really wasn't the right place for a declaration of love.

Especially when he was supposed to be working. And so was she.

He let her go. 'I'll see you later. Have a nice afternoon.'

She lifted herself on tiptoe and kissed him. 'You, too.'

The touch of her mouth against his made him forget his good intentions. He wrapped his arms round her again, let the kiss deepen. Lost himself in the warmth and sweetness of her mouth.

Until a polite cough interrupted them.

'My apologies,' he said to Lizzie Chamberlain, the owner of the boarding kennels. 'I, um…' What could he say? He was meant to be here to check on her mother and talk about the consultant's report she'd just received. Yet here he was, kissing the vet stupid in the middle of the car park.

Lizzie just smiled. 'It's nice to see you both looking so happy.'

Melinda's face was bright red and his felt as if it were a matching shade. And he couldn't think of a single word to say.

Luckily Melinda's brain cells seemed to snap in a little more quickly than his. '*Grazie*,' she said.

'We've thought for a while that you two were more than just good friends,' Lizzie commented. 'But you kept everyone guessing.'

Melinda's fingers twined around Dragan's. 'It's very new,' she said softly. 'Dragan and I…we both like a quiet life.'

'And you want time to get to know each other properly without the village grapevine interfering and people asking you when we're going to hear the bells at St Mark's,' Lizzie guessed.

'*Essattamente*.' Melinda beamed at her. 'I knew you would understand. Thank you, Lizzie. We appreciate your kindness in keeping it to yourself.' Her fingers tightened briefly round Dragan's, and then she let his hand go. 'I need to go and see a man about a dog.'

She meant it literally as well, Dragan knew; he liked her sense of humour.

Melinda smiled. '*Ciao*.' And then she was gone.

'She's such a lovely girl,' Lizzie said as Melinda drove out of the car park. 'And a brilliant vet. She's got such an affinity with animals.'

'So she was here because you're worried about one of your rescue dogs?' Dragan asked.

'A kitten, actually.'

He blinked. 'A kitten—*here*?'

'You know Polly, who helps me in the mornings? Her son Jamie was out with his friends last night when he heard this tiny mewing sound at the side of the road. They spent half an hour searching with the lights from their bikes and their mobile phones, and they found the kitten. Tiny little thing— about three weeks old, Melinda reckons. It was dehydrated, had a terrible cut on its head and its nose was rubbed raw. Jamie didn't think the vet would come out at that time of night, so he brought it over to me.' She smiled. 'Melinda said I did the right thing. Washed the cut out, fed the kitten with a dropper and nursed it for most of last night.'

'And Melinda thinks the kitten will pull through?'

'With good nursing and a bit of luck, yes.'

'Jamie brought the kitten to the right place, then,' Dragan said. Lizzie's work with rescue dogs was legendary in the area, and he was sure she'd give the kitten the attention it needed. And Melinda, no doubt, would find the kitten a home.

Just as she'd done when they'd rescued Bramble, just before Christmas. Despite being bitten, Melinda had made a fuss of the dog, calmed her down and then taken her into Theatre and set to work fixing the dog's broken leg.

Lizzie smiled. 'Your Melinda's wonderful, you know. She's so good with people. Since she's let Tina help her out on Saturday mornings, there's been a world of difference in her attitude—I don't get those surly teenage grunts and glares any more, and she does her homework without complaining. Your Melinda's taught her a lot—she's given Tina the time the teachers just can't nowadays and answered all her questions. And she's lent Tina some books about poultry since Turbo Chick arrived.' The chick had got its name because it was enormous and nobody believed it could possibly have come out of an ordinary chicken's egg—except Tina had been videoing the eggs as part of a school project and had actually filmed the chick bursting out. 'She's a gem.'

His Melinda.

Funny how that phrase made him feel all warm and fuzzy inside. A feeling he'd never thought to have again. Dragan smiled. 'I don't suppose I could persuade you that we're just good friends.'

'After seeing you kiss her like that?' Lizzie teased. 'And you've changed, too. You've smiled a lot more since she came to the village.'

Dragan raised an eyebrow. 'My name's pronounced Dra-*gahn*, not Dragon.'

Lizzie laughed. 'You know what I mean. Mum adores you but she worries that you're a little too quiet. Too serious.'

'But if I started roaring around on a motorbike or bought a Maserati like Marco had, or wore trendy clothes and had my ear pierced, everyone would say I was having a midlife crisis,' Dragan said with a smile.

'I think,' Lizzie said, 'if you started roaring round on a motorbike, you'd have all the teenage girls in the village mooning over you.'

He laughed it off. 'Flattery. At thirty-five, I'm practically double their age. Much too old.' Then he sobered. 'Before we go in to see Stella—how is she really, Lizzie?'

Lizzie grimaced. 'Up and down. Sometimes she's bright and interested in what's going on. Other days, it takes her an hour to get dressed, she can barely walk from the sitting room to the kitchen, and you can hardly understand a word she says.'

Dragan nodded. 'I had the consultant's report through yesterday.' It was the reason he was doing a house call today—to discuss it with Lizzie and Stella, knowing that Stella would find it hard to get down into the village and Lizzie simply couldn't drop everything and ferry her mother about. 'It annoys me when these consultants think they have to write in medical jargon all the time. Especially when they're sending their report to a patient. I know they have to be accurate because they worry about lawsuits, but this is ridiculous.' He shook his head in exasperation. 'I swear they'd call a spade "an implement for displacing an admixture of organic remains".'

'I did look some of it up,' Lizzie admitted. 'But "hypophonia" was beyond me.'

'It means the voice is very quiet—"phonia" refers to the voice and "hypo" means "under". Literally, under-voicing. Stella's pronouncing her words properly, not slurring them, or they would have called it "dysphonia". It's the volume that's the problem,' Dragan explained.

'And "retropulsion"?'

'Movement backwards. They're concerned about how easy Stella finds it to walk or move about. That was the test where they asked her to walk forwards and backwards along a line, yes?'

Lizzie nodded, looking worried. 'The consultant said that I should think about Mum's care needs. But we've had the occupational therapy team out and they said there wasn't much more that they could do. They've put grab rails in her bedroom and the bathroom and a seat on the bath, and they've raised the level of her chair so she can get out of it more easily.' She bit her lip. 'I don't want her going into a home. She's my mum and I want to look after her.'

'Nobody's saying she has to go into a home,' Dragan said gently. 'But I did notice what the psychologist said in the report about the mood swings—as you know, depression's common in Parkinson's.'

'But she's not going mad.'

'Of course she's not,' Dragan said. 'That bit about perceptual problems means she doesn't necessarily see things how they really are. Which can be a strain on you.'

'I'm fine,' Lizzie said.

He wasn't so sure. Lizzie's smile was a little too bright for his liking. 'I think that the odd bit of respite care might help you both. A morning at a day centre once a week, where Stella would get a chance to make some new friends and have some outside interests and have some fun—and it would give you a break, too, a few hours where you don't have to worry about your mum as well as everything else.'

'I'm fine,' Lizzie repeated, shaking her head. 'No need to worry about me.'

'You've got a lot on your plate, Lizzie—and, yes, you do it brilliantly, but even Wonder Woman would have days when she struggled with *your* workload,' Dragan said softly. 'Running a business—and not just any old business either, because you do the rescue work with the dogs as well as the boarding kennels—plus bringing up Tina on your own and being a full-time carer to your mum…It's an awful lot to ask of someone.'

'I manage.'

'I know. You more than manage. But I also want you to know that you don't have to do it all on your own. The help's there whenever you need it. I'm not going to push you into something you don't want, but I also don't want to see you struggle when you don't have to.' He squeezed her shoulder. 'Don't be too proud.'

'Are you bringing Bramble in? Mum'd like to see her.'

He noticed the change of subject, but he realised that now wasn't the right time to push Lizzie. He'd deliberately parked in the shade—as he always did when he took Bramble on house calls—but some of his patients liked to see the dog, including Stella Chamberlain. And there was evidence that petting an animal helped to lower blood pressure and increase the general well-being of patients. His ready agreement to Lizzie's suggestion had nothing to do with the fact that he loved having a dog again and hated being parted from Bramble.

Much.

'Come on, girl.' He opened the boot of his estate car, and lifted the dog out so she wouldn't bang her injured leg. He knew he was being overprotective, but the leg had been slow to heal and he didn't want to take any risks.

Stella was delighted to see Bramble and made a huge fuss of her. Though Dragan could see that she was having one of her 'off' days—she was definitely struggling to get out of the chair, despite the fact the legs had been raised, and by the end of every sentence her voice was so soft that he could barely hear her. She listened intently to what he had to say about the consultant's report and the changes in her medication to help with the stiffness in her gait and her memory lapses, but Stella, like Lizzie, completely rejected the idea of day care.

'I'm not spending my days stuck in a home with a load of daft old bats. This is where I live, and this is where I'm staying,' Stella said, lifting her chin.

'You won't be stuck anywhere. It's a…' He struggled to think of something that might entice Stella. 'A bit like a coffee morning where you sit and chat, or you have someone to give a demonstration of something and you all have a go afterwards.'

'I don't want to sit and chat with people I don't know,' Stella insisted.

Time to back off. 'It's just a suggestion. Nobody's going to force you to do anything you don't want to do,' Dragan reassured her.

'Good. Because I'm *not* going.'

Maybe he'd talk to Melinda, Dragan thought. Not about Stella's condition—he would never break patient confidentiality—but she was good with people. She'd got Tina to open up to her, confide her dreams of becoming a vet, and had then talked to George about giving the teenager some work experience at the practice. Perhaps Melinda would have some ideas about how to persuade Stella and Lizzie that a weekly session of day care could help them both. Because, the way things were going here, he could see Lizzie ending up having a breakdown.

'Remember, call me any time you need to,' he said to Lizzie as he lifted Bramble back into the car. 'That's what I'm here for.'

'I will.'

Though he knew she wouldn't. She'd straighten her backbone and just carry on.

He took his leave, then headed out to see his next patient.

CHAPTER TWO

DRAGAN had been home half an hour when the doorbell rang. Bramble barked—just in case he'd missed the fact someone was on the doorstep—and pattered behind him as he opened the door.

'Dinner will be approximately thirty minutes,' Melinda announced, holding up two brown paper bags.

Not take-away food either, Dragan knew as he followed her into his kitchen. Melinda liked to cook from scratch.

'First of all, this needs to go into the freezer.' She retrieved a tub of ice cream from one of the bags and put it in the coldest part of the freezer. 'And next, for you, because you're beautiful.' She bent down and made a fuss of the dog, then took a handful of treats from her pocket and fed them to Bramble one by one.

From the blur of her wagging tail, Dragan knew that the dog loved having Melinda around as much as he did. 'You spoil that dog,' he remarked.

'And you don't?' she teased.

'Never,' he deadpanned. 'So where's my treat, then?'

She grinned, reached up and slid her arms round his neck, then kissed him thoroughly. 'Better?'

He smiled. 'Much better. Want a hand making dinner?'

'Absolutely not.' She shook her head. 'It's wonderful being

able to work in a proper kitchen. The one in the flat over the surgery isn't even big enough for a hamster wheel.'

And she looked good in his kitchen, he thought. At home. So much so that she didn't hesitate to switch on his iPod and pick out some of the tracks she liked, by an opera-pop crossover artist that she'd downloaded for him the previous week. He'd never heard of the singer before, but he liked it, especially when she was singing along to it, half humming and half singing the lyrics. She was as good with the Spanish lyrics as she was with the Italian ones, and he loved the sweetness of her voice.

It wasn't just the music. He loved having her around, full stop.

Because she made his house feel like *home*. She had done ever since her second visit to the cottage, when she'd brought him the iPod, complete with a set of speakers for his kitchen, and insisted that he accepted the gift. 'You can't cook properly without music, Dragan. You can't *live* without music.'

Melinda was always singing. And she always took over the CD player in his car. Since she'd been around, there had been a lot more music in his life.

A lot more everything.

Maybe he'd ask her tonight. Maybe he'd take her for a walk on the beach and kiss her under the stars and ask her to stay. For always.

He enjoyed just watching her as she chopped and stirred and tasted and stirred a bit more.

Then she looked over at him and the corners of her eyes crinkled. 'You can lay the table, if you like.'

The small bistro table was set in front of the French doors that overlooked the garden; although it wasn't like the huge rambling garden he'd grown up with, he enjoyed his little patch of green. Right now it was full of spring flowers, with a carpet of blue squill underneath the apple tree. He set the table, took a bottle of white wine from the fridge, poured two glasses, and sat down as she brought over two plates.

Bramble immediately settled on the floor between the two of them, and Melinda laughed. 'Ah, no, you can't have any of this, *bellissima*. The chilli sauce won't be kind to your stomach.'

'And she's already wolfed down half a dozen prawns while you were preparing this,' Dragan pointed out.

'Of course. She's my official tester.' Melinda waited until he'd taken his first mouthful of the avocado with prawns and chilli sauce. 'So do you like it?'

'It's fabulous,' he said honestly. Trust Melinda to come up with a combination he would never have thought of.

The lemon chicken with broccoli, carrots and new potatoes was equally good. And although he didn't have a sweet tooth, he was content to watch her eat the hazelnut meringue ice cream that was a speciality of the Trevellyans' farm shop and which she absolutely adored.

'So you admit now that food is not just fuel?' Melinda demanded when they cleared the table together.

'Yes, I admit it. You are right and I am wrong, *carissima*.'

She laughed. 'And therefore you owe me a forfeit.'

He laughed back. 'Indeed. It's in the cupboard next to the fridge.' He never ate chocolate, but Melinda loved it, so he'd taken to buying some just for her. Rich, dark chocolate flavoured with spices and a hint of orange.

She found the bar of chocolate within seconds. 'For someone who never touches the stuff, you have amazingly good taste, Dr Lovak.'

Her little 'oh' of pleasure as she snapped off the first square and slid it into her mouth sent desire flickering down his spine. A desire he could see matched in her beautiful blue eyes.

He made them both coffee, strong and dark, and placed the mugs on his low coffee-table before sitting on the sofa and pulling her onto his lap. He loved having her near. And he loved it even more when she kissed him spontaneously, cupping his face and nibbling at his lower lip to deepen the kiss. He loved the silky feel of her hair against his skin, her sweet floral scent, the warmth of her body against his.

He tipped her back on the sofa and was halfway through undoing her shirt when she groaned. 'Dragan. You should've been born in Sparta.'

'What?' He frowned. 'I'm not with you.'

'Your *sofa*. It's like a bed of nails.'

It wasn't the most comfortable in the world, true, but it did him. He didn't actually spend much time on it anyway—he was either out walking with the dog or somewhere with Melinda or sitting at the little table, working on some notes on his laptop. He smiled and stroked her hair back from her face. 'Don't be such a princess.'

She stiffened, then pushed him away and sat up, buttoning her shirt again.

He frowned. 'Melinda? What's wrong?'

'Nothing.' Her face shuttered. 'I ought to be going.'

What? A few seconds ago they'd been kissing. Undressing each other—she'd completely unbuttoned his own shirt. And now she'd gone all frosty on him. He couldn't think of anything he'd done wrong. 'What? Why? Neither of us is on call. I thought we were spending time together?' Then the penny dropped. He'd accused her of being princessy. 'This princess business—I was teasing, *tesoro*. You know the story of the princess who can still feel the tiny pea through fifty mattresses—that's like the way you complain about my sofa.'

'Uh-huh.'

He didn't understand why she was reacting so badly—Melinda had a great sense of humour usually, and it was rare for her not to have a smile on her face—but he hated the idea of her being hurt and him being the cause. He slid his arm round her and hugged her. 'You're not like that at all—you don't have any airs and graces, and your four-by-four isn't like that dreadful woman's next door.'

'What woman?'

'I didn't catch her name—I wasn't paying attention,' he admitted. 'Natalie or Natasha or Na...I don't know. It's not important.' He flapped a dismissive hand. 'She's staying next door in the holiday cottage. Hopefully not for too long. Now, *she's* the princessy type. Hair cut in the latest fashion, designer clothes and shoes, a four-by-four that's probably never been within a mile of an untarmacked track in its life. Whereas yours is covered in mud outside and animal hair inside.'

Her mouth tightened. 'So now you're saying I look a mess.'

'*No*. I'm saying you're the most beautiful woman I've ever met, you don't need make-up to emphasise how lovely you are and you'd manage to look stylish in a...oh, in a potato sack.' He made an impatient gesture with his hand. 'I don't have a clue why we're fighting—I don't want to argue with you, Melinda.' He sighed. 'Actually, I wanted to talk to you about something tonight.'

'What?'

'When you look as if you want to slap me?' He shook his head. 'No way.' There was no point in asking her. She'd reject him straight out, and then their relationship would slowly start to fall apart.

'I don't want to slap you. But I don't like what you said.'

'Then I apologise. Without reservation.' Clearly he'd touched a raw nerve. He had no idea why his throw-away comment had upset her so badly; or maybe he'd accidentally repeated something that an ex had once said to hurt her. 'I really didn't mean to hurt you, Melinda. I'd never do that. You mean too much to me.'

She remained perfectly still for a moment, then she nodded, as if reassured, slid her arm round his waist and leaned into him. 'Apology accepted. So what did you want to talk about?'

'The idea was to go for a walk. Up on the cliffs, or barefoot on the sand. In the moonlight or maybe watching the sun rise.'

She pulled a face. 'You want me to get up before dawn?'

'Yes—No.' He raked a hand through his hair distractedly. 'Melinda. Today, when you called me *zlato*—did you mean it?'

She frowned. 'Why?'

'I asked first.'

'Yes. And it upset you.'

'Only because it's been a long, long time since anyone used that word to me. Remember, I've lived in England for half my life now.'

'Didn't you ever want to go back to Croatia?'

'There's nothing there for me any more.'

His face and voice were both expressionless. And Melinda knew without a doubt that this was what haunted Dragan. What caused the shadows in his eyes. And that night she'd stayed here last month and had woken up in the middle of the night to find him standing by the window, staring out at the sea with such a bleak expression that it had almost broken her heart...He'd refused to talk about it, but she had a feeling this was to do with the same thing.

And she also had the feeling that this was the last tiny barrier between them.

Ha. As if she had the right to push him to talk, when she never talked about what had driven her to England. But how could she talk about it? She knew from experience that the minute people knew about her family, they started treating her differently. Either they withdrew from her because they secretly thought that she was just slumming it and didn't really want their friendship, or they started seeing her as a passport to high society.

Except she didn't hang out with high society. She'd never fitted in—and although her parents hadn't actually taken the step of disowning her, they didn't approve of her life here. On the rare occasions she went back to Contarini they never talked about her job, almost as if ignoring it meant that it wasn't really happening. To listen to her parents, anyone would think that she was merely living abroad for a while to broaden her life experience, and spent her days shopping and sightseeing.

Most of the time Melinda managed to put it to the back of her mind and get on with her life. And she was happy: she'd never been particularly close to her parents, she loathed her brother Raffi's playboy friends, and she had nothing in common with her sister Serena's Sloaney mates, so it didn't worry her that she was pretty much on her own here.

Whereas Dragan, she thought, was different. Like her, he felt there was nothing for him in his old home but, unlike her, he missed it and it hurt so much that it was like a fracture right across his heart—a fracture she wanted to heal.

She took his hand and pressed a kiss into it. 'Why not?'

'I'd rather not talk about it.'

'Keeping things bottled up inside isn't good for you,' she said quietly. Even though she knew she was being a hypocrite. The longer she went without telling him the secret she'd been keeping ever since she'd first come to England, the harder it was to bring up the subject—and the more scared she was about his reaction. He wasn't the social-climber type, but she really didn't want him to reject her—to see her as Princess Melinda, second in line to the throne of Contarini, instead of the girl practically next door who'd fallen in love with him.

But this wasn't about her. She pushed the thoughts away and squeezed his hand. 'You need to talk.'

'Whatever.' The flippant, dismissive drawl did nothing to disguise his pain.

'Dragan, I mean it. Talk to me.'

'There isn't much to tell.'

'Then tell me anyway.' She tightened her fingers round his. 'You trust me, don't you?' Even as she said it, she winced inwardly. A trust she hadn't given to him. But this was different. She could live with her secret because it didn't hurt her; whatever he was keeping locked inside was slowly eating him away.

'Ye-es.'

'Then tell me,' she insisted softly.

He was silent for such a long time that she didn't think he was going to talk. And then finally he spoke, his voice very low.

'We lived in a little village on the Adriatic coast. My family had a boatyard.'

She could see it in his eyes—there was more to it than that. Much more. And she guessed that the only way she'd get him to tell her was to ask questions.

'So you weren't always going to be a doctor?'

He shook his head. 'I was going into the family business when I'd finished my education.'

'Sailing boats?'

'In my spare time. My elder brother studied marine engineering and he was good with his hands—he designed and built the boats, just like my father. And I was the one who was good at languages and figures.'

She knew about the languages and could've guessed about the maths. Dragan was bright—in her view, he'd be good at absolutely anything he chose to do. 'So you would be the finance director?'

'For a while, then the idea was that I should take over from my father as managing director. He was going to retire and spend more time with my mother while he was still young enough to go out and about and enjoy their leisure time.'

She knew all about parents wanting to retire and expecting their children to take over. And she thanked God every day that she wasn't the one who'd have to take over from her father. Being a girl and being second-born meant that she'd been able to choose her life—to do the job she loved instead of one that would have stifled her. 'It sounds a good plan,' she said. Even though she had doubts about the way it would work in her own family. She'd always thought Serena, her baby sister, would make a better job of ruling than her older brother. Rafael had too much of a wild streak.

'So you were going to study economics?' she guessed.

'International law,' he said. 'In Zagreb—but I planned to spend the holidays at home in the boatyard.'

Clearly he'd loved the family business, had wanted to be part of it. He'd fitted in. Had been happy.

So what had gone wrong?

There was another long pause.

'And then the war happened.'

Five tiny words. Spoken so quietly that she could almost hear his heart breaking in the silence that followed. And all she could do was hold him. 'I'm here, *amore mio*,' she said softly.

'It wasn't just our village. It was all over the country. The fighting, the bombs, the bullets. Such a mess. Such a *waste*. Dad and I had gone to Split for a couple of days on business. Everything was fine at home when we left. And we came back to…' His breath shuddered and his jaw tightened.

She stroked his face, willing the tension to ease. Wanting him to speak. Let out the pain that was eating him away from the inside.

'Everything was gone,' he said finally, his voice flat. 'The boatyard was in ruins. My brother had been killed, my mother, the people who worked for us. All dead. And others, too, in the village. Smashed glass everywhere from the bullets. Holes ripped in buildings by bombs. And…' He swallowed. 'It's something I hope to God I never have to live through again.

I know I should be working for Doctors Without Borders. Helping people, the way I wish my own people had been helped when we needed it most. But, God help me, I just couldn't do it.' He closed his eyes. 'I'm such a selfish bastard. I couldn't bear to go back into a war zone. There are too many memories.'

'There's no "should" about it, and you're not selfish,' she told him fiercely. 'Some people want to do it—they have their own reasons for doing it. Just as you have a very good reason for *not* doing it. And you *do* help people, Dragan. You help them here. Where they need you just as much.'

'I still feel guilty.'

She kissed him gently. 'What happened wasn't your fault.'

'Not the war. But my father…' His voice trailed off.

'What happened?'

He dragged in a breath. 'The shock was too much. He collapsed. I know now it was probably a stroke, but back then my first aid was pretty basic. I could do mouth to mouth and I knew what to do if someone was drowning, but I really didn't know what to do with a heart attack or a stroke. The phones lines were out so I couldn't call an ambulance.' Back then, mobile phones hadn't been widespread, Melinda knew—that wouldn't have been an option. 'I managed to find someone with a car that could still be driven, borrowed it and took him to hospital.'

She knew from the bleakness in Dragan's eyes that his father hadn't made it.

'He died in the queue for the emergency department. And I vowed then that I'd get the medical skills. It was too late for my family, but I could stop other people losing what I'd lost.'

'Dragan, if it was a stroke, you probably couldn't have done anything for him anyway.'

His jaw tightened. 'I could've done more than I did.'

It wasn't true, but she knew that this was an argument she

wasn't going to win. And she didn't want to hurt him even more by pushing the issue and forcing him to confront it. Instead, she asked softly, 'So you went back to university, switched your course from law to medicine?'

'My father's last words to me—he told me to go to England. Where I would be safe. Where I could carry on and know my family would be proud of me, whatever I chose to do.'

'They're proud of you,' she said softly. 'I believe people still look out for you when they've passed on. Like my *nonna*—my father's mother. She supported me when I said I wanted to be a vet.' The only one of Melinda's family who'd accepted her choice of career. The only one who'd admitted that Melinda just wasn't princess material and was far happier—not to mention better at—treating sick animals than she was schmoozing with foreign dignitaries and trying to remember the finer points of etiquette. 'She died before I graduated, but I knew she was there on the day, applauding as I stepped onto the stage and accepted my degree from the chancellor of the university. And you—look at you. The village doctor. Everyone looks up to you because you're a good man and you're really good at your job. Your family are proud of you, Dragan.'

'I hope so.'

'They *are*.' She hugged him. 'So then you came here?'

'Eventually. I needed to sort out the business first.' He sighed. 'The insurance didn't cover acts of war. And there was nothing left of the boatyard. But I wasn't going to let my family name be blackened, for people to say that Lovak Marine was bankrupt and defaulted on its debts.'

She could understand that. Honour was important to Dragan. And duty.

The thought pricked her conscience: she hadn't exactly been a dutiful daughter, had she? Melinda Fortesque,

MRCVS, had chosen the much lighter responsibilities of a village vet rather than helping to shoulder the burden of running the kingdom of Contarini. Some people would see that as absconding, avoiding what she'd been born to do. 'So what did you do?'

'I sold the land. Used the proceeds to settle the mortgage and the outstanding debts.'

'And then you bought a ticket to England?'

He shook his head. 'I didn't have enough money after I'd paid the creditors, and our debtors were never going to be able to pay me what they owed. The debts had to be written off.'

Though he'd refused to let his family's debts be written off. It wasn't *fair*, Melinda thought. 'So how did you get here?'

'I bartered my way onto a ship—I would crew for them in exchange for my passage to England. And this country has been good to me, Melinda. The authorities let me stay. I had nothing—no proof of who I was, no proof that I had any qualifications in my homeland. I spent a year working as a waiter by day and studying for exams at night, until I had the qualifications I needed to study medicine.'

He'd worked his way up from nothing. Worked longer and harder than anyone else she knew. And her heart ached with pride in him. 'You're amazing,' she said softly, stroking his face. 'I don't know anyone else who would have had the strength to do all that.'

He shrugged it off. 'It wasn't that big a deal.'

Yes, it was. 'Some people, in your shoes, would be hard and bitter and never give anybody an inch. But you...you understand people. You *care*. Your family would be so proud of you. *I'm* proud of you.'

His dark eyes glittered, and he said nothing.

The strong, silent type. That was her Dragan. But now he'd opened up to her, she didn't want him to close in on himself again. 'So when you qualified, you came here?' she asked.

'I worked in London for a while. But I missed the sea. And then some friends brought me to Cornwall for the weekend. I fell in love with the area.'

'Me, too.'

'And I'm very, very glad I decided to stay. That I met you.' He rested his forehead against hers. 'I am sorry, *piccola*. I didn't mean it to get this heavy. It's not something I talk about.'

She could tell that. And how much it had stirred up his emotions. It was rare that his English slid from being perfectly accentless to having a strong Croatian accent. 'But I hope talking to me helped,' she said softly.

He brushed his mouth against hers. 'So, *zlato*. You looked up Croatian phrases on the Internet, then?'

'How else was I going to learn?'

'You could have asked me.'

'And you would have told me?'

He smiled. 'Let me teach you something now. *Volim te*.'

'What does that mean?'

'The same as *ti amo*.' He paused. 'And I do. I love you, Melinda.'

It felt as if the room were full of butterflies, the sunlight dancing on their wings. Dragan loved her. And he loved her for who she was: Melinda Fortesque, country vet.

Then the butterflies went straight into her stomach. She really ought to tell him the rest of it. He'd told her everything, and she was holding out on him. But now really wasn't the time or the place. And if she told him...would he stop loving her? Would he back away, feeling that she'd look down on him—even though she didn't?

'There was something else I wanted to say. But it's too late for sunrise.'

'Tell me anyway.'

'I've never said this to anyone else. Ever.'

'Now you're worrying me.' She kept her tone light, but fear flickered through her anyway. Had he found out about her family?

No, of course not. How could he possibly know?

But he looked so serious, so intense, that it scared her.

'I wondered...' And he tailed off.

No, no, no. She had to keep this light. Tease him out of seriousness. 'Dragan Lovak, your English is perfect—if I didn't know you came from Croatia, I'd think you *were* English. Please, don't tell me you're turning completely English on me and developing a stiff upper lip.' She fiddled with his short dark hair. 'And then this is going to go floppy and fall in your eyes. And you're going to start saying "um" a lot.'

To her relief, he smiled. And the haunted look in his eyes lessened. 'Hardly. And I'm never going to be posh anyway.'

Oh, *Dio*.

'Nothing wrong with that. I like you just how you are.' Now was definitely not the moment to tell him. Because if he was even the slightest bit worried about his background...the last thing she wanted was for him to think she was slumming it.

She'd have to work out the right way to tell him. But there was something else important he needed to know, something far more important than who she was: how she really felt about him. 'Actually, "like" is probably the wrong word.' She traced his lower lip with the pad of her forefinger. *'Volim te, zlato. Ti amo, amore mio,'* she added in her own language.

'Melinda...' He paused. 'No. It sounds wrong.'

'Try me.'

He took a deep breath. 'Move in with me.'

'Move in with you?' Now, that she hadn't been expecting.

His eyes were very dark. 'I told you it sounded wrong. Wrong time, wrong place.' He grimaced. 'I wanted to ask you somewhere romantic. "Come live with me and be my love",' that sort of thing.'

'You want me to live with you.'

'Not *just* live with me. I thought maybe we could go and talk to Reverend Kenner.'.

She blinked as what he'd just said sank in. 'You're asking me to marry you?'

'If we'd done this my way,' he pointed out, 'it'd be somewhere romantic. Not on my bed-of-nails sofa.'

'If we'd done this your way, it'd be at the crack of dawn and I wouldn't have had enough coffee to be awake enough to answer you.'

'So that's a no, then.'

'You really want to marry me?' A man who loved her for herself. A man she loved all the way back.

'Why are you so surprised? Melinda, you're like sunlight. You make everything around you seem better. And you make me a better man.'

How, when he was already a better man than she could ever wish for? 'I… Dragan, I don't know what to say.'

'I'm sorry. Forget I said anything. I'll take you home.'

'Take me home?' She stared at him, not following his logic. 'Why?'

'Because I've upset you.'

'Upset me?' She shook her head. 'How could asking me to marry you upset me? I said yes!'

'No, you didn't,' he pointed out.

'I didn't?' She stared at him. 'But I…' Then the penny dropped and she smiled. 'Ask me again. Properly.'

He stood up and pulled her to her feet, then dropped to one knee in front of her. 'Take the sunrise as read. We're on a cliff overlooking the sea and it's a bright new day ahead.' He smiled. 'Melinda Fortesque, I love you. Will you do me the honour of becoming my wife?'

'Yes. Yes, please.'

He whooped, stood up, then picked her up and spun her

round. And then kissed her, hot and sweet and slow. Telling her with his body as well as his mouth that he loved her. 'I did this all the wrong way round. I should've bought you a ring.' He dropped a kiss on the ring finger of her left hand.

'It doesn't matter. We can choose one together.' She blinked back the tears. 'Dragan. You really want to marry me?'

He nodded. 'Though I really should have asked your father for his permission first.'

Her father. Oh, lord. How could she tell Dragan that he'd have to ask the king of Contarini for his permission?

And would he even want to ask her father once she told him who she was? That thing he'd said about being a better man…Would knowing the truth about her background make him want to walk away?

This was getting messier and messier. She didn't want to lose the man she loved. She couldn't keep lying to him, but how could she tell him the truth? 'No need,' she said quickly.

He frowned slightly, and she flinched inwardly. How tactless could she get? He'd just told her that he'd lost his family—and it would sound to him as if she was dismissing hers. Which she wasn't… But her family came with complications. *Major* complications. 'It's the twenty-first century and I'm a modern woman,' she said softly. 'I can make my own decisions. And I choose to accept your proposal.' She stroked his face. 'I would be honoured to be your wife, Dragan.'

'Then we'll talk to Reverend Kenner,' he said. 'Unless you'd prefer something less traditional?'

'No. I'd like nothing more than to marry you at St Mark's.' The beautiful little parish church with its lych-gate—so different from her own parish church and all that heavy, overpowering gilding. Tourists loved her family church in Contarini, whereas Melinda had always found it oppressive.

She much preferred small, quiet, simple English country churches like the one here in Penhally. 'With all the spring blossom around. Like confetti falling on us—but we can't have confetti.'

'Why not?'

'Because foil isn't biodegradable and it can choke birds, and the paper sort contains dyes and bleach.'

He smiled. 'Trust you to know that sort of thing.'

'I'm a vet. Of *course* I know that sort of thing.' She thought for a moment. 'Dried flower petals are fine. Or the stuff that contains seeds for the birds.'

'Whatever you want, *carissima*. So when do you want to get married? Summer?'

'Spring,' she said, stroking his face. '*This* spring. Because I can't wait to be your wife.' She reached up to kiss him. 'I love you, Dragan. I really, really love you. I hope you know that.'

'I do. And I love you, too.' He held her close. 'But I do need to buy you a proper ring. I was going to suggest going shopping this weekend, but I'm doing Saturday morning surgery.'

'Me, too—but I'm not on call in the afternoon. Are you?'

'No. OK, we'll go and choose a ring together then. And move your stuff across from the flat to here. If you want to, that is,' he added diffidently.

'Of *course* I want to.'

He smiled. 'I never knew life could be so perfect.'

'Me, too.' There was a definite stormcloud ahead, in the shape of her family—but then again, they'd had to accept that she had the right to choose her job. They'd have to accept that she had the right to choose her own life partner, too. That she'd chosen the man she loved—and that he loved her right back.

As long as Dragan knew she loved him, that who she was really didn't matter, everything was going to be just fine.

She'd find the right words to explain.

Soon.

CHAPTER THREE

DRAGAN'S estate car wasn't parked outside the little terraced cottage. It didn't necessarily mean the doctor was out, Nick thought. It might be that he hadn't been able to find a parking space on Harbour Road. Although it wasn't yet peak season, the tourists had already started to trickle into the village.

Nick rapped on the door and waited.

No reply.

So obviously Dragan was either still out on house calls or he'd gone somewhere—probably with Melinda, if the village gossip was correct. The Croatian doctor was always so close-mouthed—in over two years of working together at the practice, Nick still really didn't know him that well. Dragan wasn't one to sit in the staffroom and chat over coffee and Cornish fairings with the rest of the team. He was brilliant at his job, and the staff at the practice adored him because he was always even-tempered and polite and remembered everyone's birthdays, but as to what made the man tick...It was anybody's guess.

Nick shrugged, resigned. Never mind. He could catch Dragan tomorrow morning before surgery.

And then the front door of the cottage next door opened.

'Well, hel-*lo*,' a voice drawled.

Nick looked across at the woman leaning against the door.

Her jeans did nothing to disguise her curves—or just how long her legs were. Her green eyes held the most sexy comehither look he'd ever seen. And her long blonde hair was slightly tousled, as if she'd just got out of bed—despite the fact that it was late afternoon.

His body tightened at the thought.

'I'm Natasha Wakefield,' she said.

'Nick Tremayne.' He smiled at her. 'Are you new to the village?'

She shrugged. 'Maybe, maybe not. I'll see how it goes. It was time for a change of scene.'

A woman with complications, then. So maybe he'd better squash the impulse to ask her out to dinner. Complications were the last thing he needed. In his eyes nowadays it was fun or nothing. So he brought the subject back to what he really wanted to know. 'Do you know if Dragan is in?'

'Dragan?' she asked, mystified.

Clearly—despite living next door to her—Dragan hadn't introduced himself. Which didn't surprise Nick in the slightest: Dragan really guarded his privacy. 'The man who lives here,' Nick explained.

'Oh, *him*.' She waved a dismissive hand. 'He's off somewhere with Blondie and Hopalong.'

It took Nick a moment to realise that Natasha meant Melinda and Bramble. And although he didn't like the idea of anyone making fun of the quiet, serious doctor he'd come to rely on more and more since Marco had gone back to Italy, he acknowledged the aptness of her remark. Melinda's hair was striking, and the dog was still limping slightly despite the pins and plate that held her broken leg. 'Never mind, I'll catch him at the surgery tomorrow.'

'You're a doctor?' She looked surprised. 'You don't look like one.'

He knew she was angling but he couldn't resist it—this

might be fun. And he could do with some fun in his life right now. 'What do I look like?'

'The kind of man who sails fast boats.'

He laughed. 'I haven't done that for a long time.'

'Maybe,' she said, 'you ought to. I know someone with a boat. Come out with me tomorrow.'

Her mouth was incredibly sensual. If they weren't so short-staffed at the practice, he could've been tempted. Seriously tempted. 'Sorry, I'm on duty.'

'Ah. The kind of dedicated doctor who won't play hookey.'

'Is that such a bad thing?' he asked mildly.

'Maybe not.' She looked at him through lowered eyelashes, and he noticed again what an intense green her eyes were. 'But if you work hard, you need to play hard to balance it out.'

A definite offer. And if there were no strings—why not? 'Have dinner with me tonight, then.'

'That,' she said, 'might be...interesting.'

Nick felt his libido stir. A pub meal at the Penhally Arms would hardly be to the tastes of a woman like Natasha. 'There's a nice little restaurant in Rock.'

She wrinkled her nose. His surprise must have shown on his face because she added, 'I'm from Rock. I eat there all the time. *Bor*-ing. How about somewhere different—somewhere local?'

The Anchor Hotel, then: the most upmarket that Penhally had to offer. 'Sure. I'll pick you up at...' he glanced at his watch '...seven.'

She smiled. 'It's a date.'

Melinda's mobile phone rang. She made an apologetic face at Dragan as she answered it. 'I'm on call. Sorry,' she mouthed.

'It's fine. I know what it's like,' he reassured her quietly.

'Melinda? Oh, thank God. It's Violet Kennedy. I'm sorry to bother you, but it's my Cassidy. He's not at all well.'

Even though the parrot was the elderly widow's closest companion, Melinda knew that Violet wasn't one to panic. For her to call out of hours, the parrot must really be ill.

'Try not to worry,' she said quietly. 'I'll come out to see him. Now, if you tell me his symptoms, if I'm not sure what's wrong I can talk to one of my former colleagues, who's a specialist in birds, and he'll give us advice.'

She took a notepad from her handbag and scribbled down the list of symptoms. 'I'll be with you very soon, I promise.' She ended the call, then turned to Dragan, who had pulled into a layby. 'Sorry, I don't think we'll be having dinner out after all. Do you want to drop me back at the surgery?'

'You don't have the same patient confidentiality rules that I do—I'll come with you, if you like,' he suggested.

She smiled. 'You'll be my assistant?'

'Well, I can drive you while you're talking to your colleague. Do you need me to take you back to the surgery for your contact book?'

She waved her phone at him 'It's all here. But you are an angel. Do you know Violet Kennedy?'

'She's one of my patients, actually—so, yes. And I know the quickest way to get to her house from here.'

'*Bene*.' She leaned over and kissed him. 'You will be the perfect vet's husband.'

He smiled. 'And you'll be the perfect doctor's wife.'

Dragan turned the car round and drove them back to Penhally as Melinda rang her former colleague. 'Hello, Jake? It's Melinda Fortesque. How are you?'

'Fine. Long time, no hear.'

'I know. I'm terrible. Listen, Jake, I'm sorry to bother you, especially out of hours, but this is your field and I need a specialist in exotics.'

Jake gave a resigned sigh. 'Hit me with it, then.'

'African grey parrot, we think about forty years old. He's

being sick and has diarrhoea—and I think his owner's panicking a bit about bird flu.'

Although Dragan wasn't consciously listening in and he was concentrating on driving, he couldn't help overhearing the conversation. And Melinda was just as he'd expected her to be with her colleague—warm, friendly, open—and her answers were concise and thorough. No longwindedness.

'No, it's just him and his owner,' Melinda said. 'No, just his normal diet—bird seed, apples, bananas and sweetcorn.' She paused. 'Yes, I have some at the surgery. Crop needle? Oh…' She grimaced. 'Yes, you did teach me. OK. Yes. I'll do that. Thank you.' Another pause. 'Are you sure?' She smiled. 'You are a wonderful man. I will make you my chocolate and hazelnut torte. Really, I will. Thank you.' She ended the call. 'Dragan, can we go back to the surgery so I can pick up some powders and some equipment?'

'Of course.'

'Jake was the head of my old practice in Exeter. He specialised in exotics—there's nothing he doesn't know about parrots. He thinks the bird's probably eaten something when his owner wasn't looking.'

'So what are the powders you were talking about?'

'Electrolyte replacement.'

'The same sort of thing I'd give a child with sickness and diarrhoea to stop dehydration,' Dragan said thoughtfully. 'Except the dose would be different.'

She nodded. 'It's good stuff—it helps to flush the kidneys into proper working order again.'

When they'd collected the equipment, he drove them out to Violet Kennedy's towards the edge of the village.

Violet opened the door, her face lined with worry. 'Thank you so much for coming, Melinda.'

'That's what I'm here for. I have an assistant with me,' she said with a smile. 'I believe you know him.'

Despite her obvious worry, Violet smiled at him. 'Dr Lovak, how nice to see you.'

'And you, Mrs Kennedy.'

The parrot, which was usually strutting on its perch, showing off its glorious black and crimson tail feathers or throwing a toy around, and which greeted all visitors with a piercing whistle and ''Ow do, m'dear?' before shocking them with a barrage of ripe language, was hunched in the corner of the cage, absolutely silent. Dragan cast a worried look at Melinda. If the bird died, he really wasn't sure that Violet Kennedy would be able to cope. Since her husband's death, she'd lavished most of her love on the parrot; her children and grandchildren lived in London, so she didn't see anywhere near as much of them as she'd like.

'Oh, Cassidy, *tesoro*, what have you done to yourself?' Melinda crooned, and rubbed his poll. She gently lifted him out of the cage and felt his feet. 'Violet, do you have a hot-water bottle, please? I need to keep him warm and that's the best thing. I need some hot water, too, please. And two small cups, a bowl and a spoon, if I may?'

Violet looked grim. 'I'll put the kettle on. So do you think it's bird flu?'

'No, I don't,' Melinda reassured her. 'There haven't been any reports of dead wild birds in the area, there are no problems at the local poultry farms, and to be honest he's an indoor bird, not kept outside in an aviary—so even if there were problems outside he'd be at very, very low risk.'

'So what's wrong?' Dragan asked, keeping his voice low.

'His feet are cold. That's not good. I'll need to start treatment for the dehydration now, but Jake said if his feet are cold I'll be better off looking after him at the surgery in a heated cage.' She bit her lip. 'Violet really isn't going to like this.'

'She'll understand if it's best for Cassidy.'

Violet returned with a hot-water bottle. 'Where do you want the other things?'

'In the kitchen, please. I need to mix up some powders—they'll help replace the salt and sugar in his blood and make him feel better.' She paused. 'Has Cassidy eaten anything other than his normal diet? Could he have, I don't know, taken something from your plate while you answered the phone or something?'

'I don't think so.' Violet looked thoughtful. 'The grandchildren were visiting until yesterday and they had one Easter egg I'd given them.'

'And they fed some chocolate to the bird as a treat?'

Violet shook her head. 'I don't think they would. And they know I keep chocolate in the drawer, but...no, they wouldn't have done that.'

'Can Cassidy open drawers with his beak?' Melinda asked.

Violet was silent for a moment, her brow crumpled. 'He's a clever old bird. Maybe.' She pulled open one of the dresser drawers. 'Oh! The children wouldn't have ripped open a packet of chocolate buttons and left them like that. They're little monkeys but they're not bad kids.' She shook her head. 'Well, I never. He must have opened the packet, eaten some, and closed the drawer again.'

'As you say, he's a clever bird,' Melinda said. 'And chocolate buttons could well be what's making him feel so ill now. One thing my colleague told me, parrots can't eat avocados or chocolate. They're both poisonous for parrots.'

'Poisonous?'

She nodded. 'It doesn't take much—only fifty grams of chocolate, just one small packet of buttons, could be fatal. So I'd keep them locked away in future, if I were you, or in an airtight container you know for sure he can't open.'

Violet went pale. 'Is he going to die?'

'Not if I can help it. Because I promised to teach him Italian—did I not, *tesoro*?' She rubbed the bird's poll again. 'Come on. Let's get you feeling better.' She smiled at Dragan. 'I wasn't joking about you being my assistant, by the way.'

He spread his hands. 'Just tell me what to do.'

'OK. We're going to make up some powders for Cassidy, and I'm going to feed him through a crop needle and a syringe so I can make sure he gets enough.'

'A bit like when babies are too sick to eat and they need feeding by a tube,' Dragan added, seeing the worry on Violet's face. 'It's a very common procedure and it doesn't hurt.'

'*Essatamente*,' Melinda said. 'And just to make sure—do you have any olive oil, Violet?'

'I've got sunflower oil,' Violet said.

'That will do nicely. I need to put it on the needle—he's dehydrated and his throat will be dry, so the oil will lubricate the needle and make sure it doesn't hurt him.' She nodded to the bowls on the table. 'Dragan, can you put the hot water in the bowl for me? And, Violet, I need you to cuddle Cassidy with the hot-water bottle. *Bene*, just like that.'

Dragan noticed how she involved Violet and talked her through the treatment without being patronising. She would've made a fabulous doctor for human patients too, he thought.

She was gentle with the bird, but even so when she'd finished the old lady was clearly only just holding back tears. 'My Cassidy. What will I do without you?' she whispered.

'I want to take him back to the surgery with me,' Melinda said gently. 'It will take him a few days to get over this. He needs to be in a heated cage so he doesn't get cold, and we'll need to feed him this mixture twice a day until he's able to eat normal food again. And then I'll bring him home safely to you, I promise.'

'Cassidy's been with me for years,' Violet said. 'My husband got him for me when he was in the navy. I...I can't imagine not having him.'

'I'll bring him home to you as soon as I can,' Melinda reassured her, 'and you can visit any time you like.' She rubbed the bird's poll. 'We'll have you back with your *mamma* soon.

And while you're at the surgery I can teach you some words of love in Italian—then you can charm people instead of swearing like a sailor and making your *mamma* turn red every time the vicar calls round, yes?'

The bird—which Dragan knew from experience would usually tell her where to go in extremely colourful language—made no response.

And he could see just how worried Violet looked. He squeezed her hand. 'Try not to worry. Melinda knows what she's doing.'

'I know you'll do your best,' Violet said, her voice slightly shaky.

'Normally I'd suggest transporting him in a cage,' Melinda said, 'but as he's so ill and so cold, he's not going to move around much. He can sit and have a cuddle on my lap on the way to the surgery, if you don't mind lending me that hot-water bottle until tomorrow. And Dragan will drive us very, very carefully. I'll call you when we're back at the surgery so you won't have to worry. And I'll call you tomorrow morning to let you know how he's doing.'

Exactly the same kind of care and reassurance that he gave his own patients, Dragan thought. And he could've hugged her for it. Just as Lizzie had said the previous day, Melinda was a gem. She recognised that the family had needs as well as the patient.

He drove them back to the surgery, and followed Melinda inside. She sorted out a heated cage and made the parrot comfortable, then called Jake for a quick confab about the treatment plan.

'It always surprises me how small your theatres are compared to ours,' Dragan remarked when she'd finished.

Melinda smiled. 'My patients are usually a lot smaller than yours. I don't really need a seven-foot-long table for a Jack Russell.'

'No, I suppose not.'

'Poor Cassidy. I never thought I'd see the day when this bird was quiet,' Melinda said, looking at the parrot. 'I really want to keep an eye on him for a while.'

'Do you want to stay here tonight?' he asked. With her flat being just above the surgery, it made sense.

'If you don't mind sharing a single bed.'

'Now, I'm the one who's meant to be Spartan,' he teased. 'Of course I don't mind. I'll go and get us some fish and chips, shall I, while you call Violet and let her know how Cassidy has settled in?'

She kissed him. 'Most men would not be this understanding, Dragan. You are...' she smiled '...*meraviglioso.*'

'Tell me that when I'm on call and the phone goes at two a.m. and I have to go out to a patient,' he said dryly.

'That, I won't mind. But then you'll come back and warm your feet on me.'

'When you're all warm and soft and irresistible.' Dragan kissed her. 'I'll be back in ten minutes, *piccola.*'

Melinda had just finished reassuring Violet when her mobile phone rang. She glanced at the screen and grimaced. Her mother. Please, don't let this be another call about duty and how she really ought to stop playing at being a country vet and come home. Because it wasn't going to happen: she was staying right here where she belonged. Melinda Lovak, country vet and doctor's wife.

Which was something else she needed to tell her parents. Though she'd need to choose her words very carefully—which meant maybe not tonight. If she made the call rather than took it, she'd feel more in control and not so much on the defensive.

She pressed the answer button. '*Buona sera, Mamma.*'

'*Buona sera*, Melinda. I am sorry to call you so late. But I have some bad news.'

CHAPTER FOUR

MELINDA went cold. '*Papà*?'

'No, he is fine.' Her mother sighed. 'It's Raffi.'

Here we go again, Melinda thought. Her older brother Raphael had done something stupid and she was expected to come to the rescue—because it seemed she was the only one who could ever get through to him. Raffi ignored whatever Serena said because she was the baby; though most of the time he didn't listen to Melinda either. 'What is it this time? He was caught *in flagrante delicto* with someone and she's sold her story to the press? He's in debt at Monte Carlo? He raced his new boat against someone and lost it in a bet?' Raphael had done all three over the last two years, and he never seemed to learn from his mistakes. Sometimes Melinda thought he actually *enjoyed* repeating them. He'd talked about sailing over to see her, but she'd been quick to give him the impression that Penhally was a complete backwater and he'd be bored, bored, bored within two seconds—the last thing she wanted was for him to cut a swathe through the female population of Penhally and leave her to pick up the pieces afterwards.

'No.'

There was a pause in which Melinda thought she detected a sob—then again, Viviana Fortesque would never lose that much control. Melinda must've imagined it.

'He's dead.'

Dead? The word seemed to be coming from the far end of a long, long tunnel. She couldn't take it in. Raffi, her brother who was much larger than life and more than lived every minute to the full, dead? 'No. There must be some mistake. He can't be.'

'He died yesterday afternoon.'

'What?' She dragged in a breath. 'What happened?'

'He was driving.'

Too fast, the way Raffi always did. She didn't need to be told that. Even losing his licence for three months hadn't stopped him speeding the second he'd got his licence back.

'He spun off the road and hit a tree.'

'Oh, *Dio*. Was anyone else hurt?'

'He was on his own in the car.'

Which was a good thing, in one sense: at least no other family was going to have to go through this aching loss, this misery at losing a loved one too soon. But all the same, her heart ached for him. There had been nobody to hold his hand at the end, nobody to tell him they loved him. And even though he'd been a selfish, spoiled brat and sometimes she'd wanted to throttle him, nobody deserved an end like that. 'Poor Raffi. So he died all alone,' she said softly.

'No, your father and I were with him at the end.'

'But…' Melinda frowned, not understanding. 'You said he was alone in the car.'

'He was.' Viviana's voice was dry. 'It's been touch and go for the last couple of days whether he would pull through.'

It took a moment to sink in. And when it did, Melinda was furious. 'Hang on, it happened a couple of days ago? My brother was in hospital—in Intensive Care—and you didn't call me?'

'There was no point. You wouldn't have come.'

Oh, this was outrageous. Not only had her family kept the

news of Raffi's accident from her, now they were trying to make her feel guilty about it. Thinking for her instead of letting her make her own decisions. Just the way it had always been.

And they'd taken away her chance to say goodbye.

She'd never forgive them for this.

And how come she hadn't read about in the papers? Unless her parents had hushed it up. Come to some agreement with the press so Raffi wouldn't be hounded in hospital by the paparazzi.

'Of course I would have come,' she said through gritted teeth. 'He's my brother.'

'Apart from the fact you two barely speak when you do see each other,' Viviana pointed out, 'you're still playing at being an English country vet.'

'I am *not* playing.' She twisted the end of her hair round her fingers. 'This is my life now, Mamma, my career, and—' The twisted hair started to hurt, and the pain brought her back to her senses. What was she doing, letting her mother get to her like this? 'I am not going to argue with you. Not with Raffi dead. It's the wrong time.' And surely even her mother would see that. 'When is the funeral?' She just about managed to bite back, *Or weren't you going to tell me about that either?*

'Two days' time.'

'Then I will come back to Contarini.'

'*Bene.* I will send the jet tonight to your nearest airport. Which is…?'

'I can't fly out tonight. *Mamma*, I have responsibilities here.'

'You have responsibilities to your family, Melinda,' Viviana said, her voice like cut glass.

'I can't just drop everything and leave George to sort out my patients and my surgery tomorrow. It's not fair. We need time to sort out a locum for me.'

'Locum?' There was a shocked pause. 'You mean, you are actually planning to go back again?'

'Of course. It's my job. My vocation, *Mamma*.' Not to mention the fact the man she loved and was going to marry lived here in Cornwall. Though now was most definitely not the time to tell her mother about that.

'While you were the middle child, we were prepared to let you play.'

Play? A degree in veterinary sciences meant long hours and hard work. Years and years of study and exams. She twisted her hair again, and the sharp pain made her pause instead of saying something she knew she'd regret. She'd let that 'play' comment slide. For now. 'Nothing has changed.'

'Raffi is dead. You are the eldest now. Which means that you have responsibilities and duties here, Melinda. You are the next in line to the throne, and you need to come back to Contarini for good.'

'I'll come back for Raffi's funeral and to see you, *Papà* and Serena. But I'm not promising any more than that.'

'Why must you be so difficult? So headstrong?' Viviana demanded.

Headstrong? Melinda nearly laughed. She wasn't the one who drove fast cars and fast boats and fast planes, who went through money as if a fresh supply could be printed every day, or whose champagne bill was legendary. She was the one who'd always been quiet, bookish, who'd spent her time in the stables and the kennels. Raffi was the headstrong one and Serena was the one who wore pretty dresses and had beautiful manners and charmed people. Melinda was the odd one out, and everyone knew it. A very square peg whose corners just couldn't be rubbed off to make her fit the role they wanted her to take.

A role she didn't want.

A role she'd *never* wanted.

'*Mamma*, I am too tired to argue. I can't fly out tonight. I'll talk to George, then I'll catch a flight from here to London tomorrow and from London to...' She thought rapidly. Palermo was nearer to Contarini, but Naples was probably a little more discreet. 'To Napoli. I'll text you to let you know my flight times, *d'accordo*?'

'Then we will see you tomorrow.'

And that was it. The line went dead. No 'I love you'. No warmth or affection. Just as it had always been when she had been growing up—her parents had always been too busy and their duty had come first.

Maybe, she thought, if Viviana and Alessandro Fortesque had spent more time with their children, Raffi would have learned to control his impulses.

Gritting her teeth, she dialled her boss's number. She knew the burly vet would be understanding, but she still hated the fact that she was letting him down.

'George? I'm sorry to bother you on your night off.' She took a deep breath. 'My mother just called. I need to go home for a few days.'

'Something's wrong?'

'My brother...died. In a car crash.' It felt weird, saying it. And she felt cold, so cold. She really needed Dragan. Needed to feel his arms round her.

'Oh, love, I'm so sorry. Of course you have to go. Look, I can cover for you tonight. Go now. Don't worry about a thing.'

Dear George. She could have hugged him. 'I can't get a flight until tomorrow anyway. I'll still do tonight on call. But if I could leave first thing in the morning—and I'll write down a list of my patients and what have you—that'd be...' She swallowed hard. 'That'd be really appreciated.'

'Are you on your own? Do you want me to come over, or do you want to come over to us?'

George, his wife and four children lived in a sprawling old farmhouse just outside Penhally. At the Smiths', you could always be sure of a warm welcome, a cat to curl on your lap in the big farmhouse kitchen and a dog to sit by your feet.

'No, no. I'll be fine. I'm, um…Dragan is keeping me company this evening. I'm hoping I don't get another callout because I have Cassidy here.'

'Violet's parrot? Why?'

'I think he ate some chocolate and his system's reacting to it.'

'Chocolate's poisonous to parrots—as well as to dogs,' George said.

'*Essatamente*. So he needs nursing here in a heated cage for a few days. I've given him the electrolyte powders tonight, but he'll need them twice a day and a gradual return to his normal diet.'

'Leave me your treatment plan and I'll ask Sally to come in early tomorrow and take over,' George said.

Melinda was happy that the practice nurse would follow the treatment plan exactly. And she was so experienced that she'd probably seen a few sick parrots in her time: Melinda often thought Sally knew as much as the vets did. 'George, thank you so much. I really hate it that I'm letting you down. And if I'm not back by Saturday—'

'Then young Tina Chamberlain can shadow *me* for the morning. She might like to come and see what we do with the livestock, so she sees the other side of the practice and not just the small-animal work,' George finished. 'I'll clear it with Lizzie first. Don't worry about a thing. Just ring me if you need me or there's anything I can do, all right? And we'll see you when we see you.'

'Thank you, George.'

She'd just put the phone down when the doorbell rang.

Dragan.

She went down to meet him and unlock the door; he followed her back up the stairs to her small kitchen, carrying two wrapped parcels. 'Sorry I was so long. There was a queue, and then I had to wait for fresh chips. But at least they're really hot,' he said with a smile. And then he frowned, taking in her expression. 'What's wrong, Melinda? Cassidy's worse?'

'No.' She dragged in a breath. 'My mother called. My brother...' She rubbed a hand over her face. She still couldn't quite believe it. 'He died yesterday after a car accident.'

'Oh, Melinda.' He put the fish and chips on the worktop and held her close. 'I'm so sorry.'

'I have to go back.'

'Of course you do. How are you getting there?'

'I haven't booked a flight yet. But I'll take the first one I can get tomorrow from Newquay to Gatwick, and then Gatwick to Naples.'

Dragan could remember the feeling. The black hole inside when he realised he'd lost his entire family. That he was the only one left. And although he realised that Melinda wasn't close to her own family, he knew she would do the right thing. She'd go back and help her family with the funeral, comfort her parents.

Though it was a tough thing to do on your own. Especially when you felt you didn't fit in—the one thing she *had* admitted to him over the last few months.

'Do you want me to come with you?' he asked, stroking her hair. 'For support?'

'Bless you for asking, but no. I can do this.'

But her expression was grim. She was clearly dreading this. 'Melinda, you're not on your own,' he said softly. 'You have me. And if there's anything I can do, all you have to do is say so.'

'Right now, just hold me. Please.' Her voice sounded hoarse, broken—as if she was trying to hold back her tears. Typical Melinda, being brave and not leaning on anyone else.

'Let the tears come, *piccola*,' he said softly. 'They will help.'

She dragged in a breath. 'Right now I feel like the most selfish, horrible woman in the world.'

'Why?' He really didn't follow. Ignoring the fish and chips, he led her over to the sofa and settled her on his lap.

'Because you…you've lost your family. And you were close to them. I'm not close to mine—and I feel horrible telling you that, because I have what you've lost and I don't want you to think I'm just…oh…not appreciating it, throwing it all away like a toddler having a tantrum with her toys.'

'Of course I don't. I'd already guessed you weren't close to them. But it doesn't make me love you any less. Not all families are like mine—I see plenty of difficult relationships in my job,' he reminded her. 'Let me go with you, *tesoro*. So at least you have someone on your side.'

For a moment he thought she was going to say yes. But then she shook her head. 'I won't drag you into all this mess. And I…I could strangle Raffi for being so reckless, so stupid. And my parents, for not letting me say goodbye to him. The accident happened days ago. He died yesterday. And they didn't tell me until *today*, until after he was dead and it was too late for me to say goodbye.'

'Maybe it was grief,' he suggested. 'Maybe they couldn't find the words to tell you.' It had been hard for him to tell people after his family had been wiped out. Most of the time it had hurt too much to articulate. And when he had managed to say it, the pity on other people's faces had choked him.

'It's not just them. I'm so angry with him.'

Anger was one of the stages of grief, he knew, along with denial and bargaining and depression. And finally there would be acceptance. But she really needed to talk about this. As she'd said to him so recently, bottling things up made them worse. 'Why?' he asked softly.

'He always had to have the fastest car. And he always drove like a maniac. He knew *Papà* was expecting him to take over—but would he be careful? No. Scrape after scrape after scrape. And I always had to bail him out.' She shook her head. 'The day before my Finals started, he expected me to go back to Contarini and sort things out with our parents. He'd been stupid and lost a lot of money in a card game.'

So her parents were wealthy? Dragan wasn't that surprised. She had an air of breeding about her. Though he'd just bet she'd been like him and worked her own way through college—not because she'd had to but because she was too independent to rely on a silver spoon.

Maybe that was why she'd reacted so badly to his teasing 'princessy' comment.

'But I said no. I'd worked too hard for my exams to give it all up for something I knew would just happen again and again—because Raffi only ever did what he wanted and he never stopped to think things through before he acted.' She gritted her teeth. 'And he barely spoke to me afterwards, because I made him stand on his own two feet for once.'

'He probably still knew you loved him.'

'And that's another reason I don't like myself. Because I'm not so sure I *did* love him.'

'You can love someone without liking them,' Dragan pointed out, stroking her hair.

'I don't fit in with my family. I never have. And I know the second I step off that plane the pressure's going to start.'

'Pressure?'

'To go back to Contarini. To do what they want me to do. Give up being a vet—but I can't. This is who I *am*, Dragan.'

'Then let me come with you. Take some of the flak for you.'

'You can't.' She shook her head. 'That's really not fair to you.'

'*Carissima*, you didn't ask. I offered. Look, I've lived

through a war. Nothing scares me any more because I know there is always a light at the end of the tunnel, no matter how dark things seem at the time. And I can help you through this.'

'You *can't*,' she repeated. 'We've got that appointment lined up with Reverend Kenner tomorrow.'

'He won't mind putting it back. Besides, I can't discuss the wedding without you.'

'Yes, you can. Otherwise it holds everything up.'

He frowned. 'What difference does a couple of days make? Why the hurry?'

'Because I don't want to wait for the rest of my life to start.'

Something was going on here, and he really wasn't sure what it was.

'Dragan. I love you,' she said softly. Urgently. 'I want to marry you and I don't want my family interfering.'

He didn't understand why they'd interfere. At twenty-seven, Melinda was more than capable of making her own choices. 'So you haven't told them yet? About us, I mean?'

She shook her head. 'And now isn't the right time. Not with Raffi's funeral.'

'But if you want to get married as soon as we can, you'll have to give them some notice. Surely they'll want to come to the wedding?'

'I'll tell them when we've set a date. Which you and Reverend Kenner can sort out tomorrow.' She twisted her hair round her fingers. 'At least I'll be able to come home to you and to happy news.'

He rested his cheek against her hair. 'All right. If that's really what you want me to do. But at least let me drive you to the airport tomorrow. And I can pick you up when you get back.'

'Thank you.' She held him tightly, almost as if she were drowning and he was the only thing keeping her afloat. 'Dragan. There is something I should tell you about, something we need to discuss. Something…'

She sounded worried sick, and he dropped a kiss on her forehead. 'Not now. You've just had a horrible shock. Whatever it is, it can wait until you're back from Contarini. Everything's going to be fine.'

'I love you. And I don't deserve you.'

He scoffed. 'Of course you do.' Or was this why she wasn't close to her family? Was this why she'd chosen to move to another country, because they were always putting her down and telling her she wasn't good enough? Wealthy parents were often ambitious for their children—and if she'd resisted going into a long-standing family business, that was probably the root of the difficulties between them. A career that would make any other parents proud might disappoint hers because they'd expected something else for her. 'And I love you, too. You need to book that flight—but eat first.'

She grimaced. 'I can't face anything. Not now.'

'And the chips are probably cold by now. I could put them in the microwave,' he suggested.

'Dragan Lovak, and you a doctor!' She shook her head in apparent disbelief. 'Tut-tut. Think of the bacteria. Reheated food that hasn't been chilled properly in between...it's an absolute breeding ground. And, besides, the chips will go soggy if you put them in the microwave.'

'Perhaps you're right.' But at least he'd made her smile again.

Though the look in her eyes disturbed him. The desperation. Would it really be so bad for her, going back? 'I'm here,' he said softly. 'And nothing's going to hurt you while I'm around.'

If only that were true. As soon as he found out about her family...Oh, *Dio*. She had to tell him, she really did. But now wasn't the time or the place. And he'd said it could wait...

Coward that she was, she was relieved. The risk of losing

the man she loved right on top of losing her brother was just too horrible to contemplate. She knew he'd be hurt that she hadn't told him before—and maybe angry that she hadn't trusted him—and she felt bad about it. Guilty. But she just hadn't been able to find the right words or the right time.

Though she'd tell him the truth about herself tomorrow morning. First thing.

CHAPTER FIVE

'I'LL go and check on Bramble,' Dragan said, 'while you sort out your flights.'

'You can bring her back here, if you like,' Melinda said. 'She's no trouble.'

Having a dog to make a fuss of might help her, he thought.

Even though he lived just round the corner, to save time in the morning he drove over to Melinda's and left his car in the surgery car park. If people talked—well, let them. After his meeting with Reverend Kenner tomorrow, everyone would know anyway.

Melinda had given him her key; he unlocked the door to her flat and carried Bramble up the stairs. Strictly speaking, he knew she could manage it herself, but he also knew what a lively dog she was—and her leg still hadn't healed properly. If she slipped on the stairs and cracked a bone or shifted the pins again, she might have to lose the leg. And he really wanted to avoid that if possible.

The dog took full advantage of her position to lick his face, and he laughed. 'You horrible mutt. What are you? Horrible!'

She licked him again, clearly hearing in his tone of voice how much he loved her. She reminded him of the dog he'd had as a boy. So when Melinda had been looking for a home for the dog she'd rescued, a few months before, he hadn't been able to resist offering.

'How did you get on?' he asked Melinda as he set the dog back on her feet.

'I've done some notes for George and Sally, and there's a flight to London at twenty past seven tomorrow morning. I can pick up my tickets from the desk, but I need to be at the airport an hour before my flight.'

'Crack of dawn start, then.' He shrugged. 'Not a problem. I'll just go and fetch my clothes and Bramble's basket from the car.'

When he returned, Bramble was settled very comfortably, thank you, on the sofa, and Melinda was making a fuss of her.

'Don't think you're sleeping there tonight, dog,' he warned.

Bramble just thumped her tail, as if she knew perfectly well that Melinda wouldn't mind.

'I'll make us something to eat,' Dragan said. 'And, no, Bramble, you are not scoffing all the cold, soggy chips,' he added at the dog's hopeful look when he carried the paper parcel over to the bin. 'They're bad for you.'

'Don't do anything for me. I'm really not hungry,' Melinda said with a grimace.

'You need to eat,' he said gently. 'Trust me, low blood sugar on top of the bad news you've just had will only make you feel worse. Now, you go and check on Cassidy, and I'll make you an omelette.' At her raised eyebrow, he smiled. 'I make a very good omelette, I'll have you know.'

When she came back from checking on the parrot and the large, fluffy omelette was cooked, he divided it into two and slid it onto their plates.

She ate about three mouthfuls before pushing her plate away.

'It's that bad?' he asked.

'No, no.' She shook her head. 'I'm sorry. I just... It feels wrong to eat somehow. My brother's dead and here I am, stuffing my face. It's...*wrong*.'

'OK. I won't force you.' He scraped the contents of her plate into the bin and made short work of the washing-up. 'Come on. Let's try and get some sleep.' He looked at the dog, who was still curled happily on the sofa. 'Bramble, in your basket.'

'Oh, leave her,' Melinda said, her voice weary. 'It doesn't matter.'

He remembered that feeling, too. As if nothing mattered any more. And he ached for her.

'Come on, *cara*,' he said, and shepherded her into the bedroom. She used the little en suite bathroom first and by the time he'd had a quick shower and cleaned his teeth, she was curled up in bed.

'Have you set your alarm?' he asked.

She nodded.

'Good.' He slid his arm round her waist and drew her back into the curve of his body. Melinda was a bright, independent woman who was more than capable of standing on her own two feet—but tonight he felt very protective towards her. He wanted to be the barrier between her and the world, make sure nothing else happened to hurt her.

Clearly her family was nothing like his own had been. The trace of bitterness in her voice when she'd spoken about not fitting in... Well, she fitted in just fine with him. And together they'd make a new family. A family where she was the centre.

Ha. He hadn't even thought about children before. But now the idea had slid into his head, he liked it. And he could imagine their daughter—a small, stubborn version of Melinda, with his own dark eyes and hair and Melinda's beautiful smile. She'd wrap her daddy right round her little finger.

'*Volim te*,' he said softly, and kissed Melinda's bare shoulder.

He really hadn't intended to pressure her into making love with him. But when she twisted round in his arms, slid her arms round his neck and kissed him back, he couldn't help responding.

Her hand slid down over his shoulder, squeezed the firm muscles of his upper arms. 'You feel so good,' she whispered. And her mouth traced a path over his jawline, down his throat; her tongue pressed against the pulse point beating hard and fast in his neck.

'Ah, *bellissima*,' he muttered, and tipped his head back against the pillows, offering himself to her. If she wanted to take comfort from him, that was fine by him. He would tell her with his body that he was there for her, any time she needed him. That he loved her, wanted her, always would.

He dragged in a breath as she kissed her way down his breastbone. Her mouth was so soft, so sweet, and her hair felt like warm silk against his skin. He couldn't resist sliding his hands into the blonde tresses, urging her on. 'Melinda. You're driving me just a little bit crazy here.'

She lifted her head and her blue, blue eyes crinkled at the corners. 'Did you know, when you get turned on, your accent comes back a bit?'

'My accent?'

'Normally you sound very English. But when we make love…'

'I lose control,' he admitted.

'That's what I want. I want to make you feel the same way I feel.' She shifted to straddle him. He could feel the warmth of her sex against his erection and it made his pulse ratchet up that little bit more.

'I need to be inside you, Melinda,' he breathed.

'*Si?*' she teased, wriggling just enough to make him gasp.

In retaliation, he cupped her breasts, stroked the soft undersides and rubbed the pads of his thumbs against her nipples until she gave a sharp intake of breath.

'Dragan. I *need* you.'

He lifted his upper body from the bed so he could take first one and then the other nipple into his mouth, sucking hard. Her hands fisted in his hair and he could feel little shivers of desire running through her.

'Please, now,' she whispered. 'I need you now.'

'Let me get a condom.'

'No.' She leaned forward and kissed him hard. 'I don't want any barriers between us tonight.'

'Melinda, we should—' he began.

She pressed her forefinger lightly against his lips. 'It's OK. It's my safe time.'

The doctor in him knew there was no such thing as a safe time. Though he also knew exactly why she was asking him to do this: it was a way of fighting back against the spectre of death, of proving to herself that she was alive and kicking.

He shouldn't do this.

She was vulnerable.

And he was taking advantage of her. This had to stop.

'Tonight I need you close, Dragan.' She dragged in a breath. 'I want nothing between us. Just you and me.'

His heart overruled his head. How could he stop now, push her away and make her feel even worse? She needed comfort. She needed him. And if they made a baby tonight…then so be it. They were getting married in a few weeks in any case. He would've liked more time with her on his own, but if they made a child tonight he'd love their baby. Always. Just as he'd always love Melinda. She was the one who made him feel complete.

'I want you so badly,' she said, her voice hoarse. 'I need you. I love you. *Ti amo.*'

'I love you, too. Always. *Siempre.*'

She shifted slightly and slid her fingers around his erection, guided him to her entrance; he rocked his hips, easing inside her. Lord, she felt good, so warm and wet. Her eyes were almost black in the lamplight, her pupils dilated so he could barely see the iris. As turned on as he was. Needing this as much as he did. Right now they were as one—body, heart and soul.

And he never wanted this moment to end.

Her mouth opened in a soft sigh of pleasure as he began to move, a pleasure echoed in his own body as her muscles tightened round him and her movements mirrored his, lifting herself until he was almost out of her and then pushing down hard as he pushed up, taking him deeper than he could ever remember.

His fingers laced with hers and they gripped each other tightly as the tension ratcheted higher and higher.

'Dragan!' Her body started to ripple round his, and he could feel the tension in his own body reaching snapping point.

And then he was falling with her.

Over the edge, into a starburst.

She collapsed forwards onto him and he wrapped his arms round her; he could feel her heart beating rapidly against his chest, just as he knew she'd be able to feel the answering beat of his heart.

'I love you,' she whispered.

'I love you, too. And everything's going to be all right.'

'Is it?'

'Everything's going to be fine,' he promised her. 'Look, it's not too late to change your mind—I can maybe ask Lizzie Chamberlain to look after Bramble for me and come with you tomorrow.'

'No, I can't ask that of you—and you're short-staffed at the practice as it is.'

'They'll manage. We can get a locum. You're more important to me, *tesoro*. More important than anything else in the world.'

He could feel dampness against his chest and realised she was crying. Silently, with no shudders, as if she didn't have any strength to hold the tears back any more and they were just leaking out.

'Let it out, honey,' he whispered. 'Let the tears wash away the pain.'

She sobbed against him. 'I don't even know why I'm crying for him. Raffi was a selfish bastard and most of the time we didn't get on. He could be charming and good company—but most of the time he was a pain in the backside and he drove me demented with his thoughtlessness.'

'He was still your brother, still of your blood—there was still a bond between you, even when you fought.'

'I just don't want things to change between you and me. *Ever.*'

'Hey, why would they do that?' He lifted her slightly and kissed away her tears. 'I won't insist that you take my name, if you choose not to. Though I think it sounds nice. Melinda Lovak.' He kissed her gently. 'Beautiful. *Bellissima.* Like you.'

Her smile was wobbly, but at least it was a smile, he thought with relief. 'Of course I'll take your name, Dragan.'

'It's not a problem if you want to keep your maiden name for professional purposes.'

'No. But thank you for giving me the choice. For understanding.'

Her words were heartfelt, he could tell—but he had no idea what she meant. Giving her the choice? But...why wouldn't she have a choice? This was the twenty-first century. He wouldn't expect her to give up her career. If they were blessed with children and she wanted to be a stay-at-home mum, that was fine; but if she wanted to combine a career and children, that was also fine. They'd work something out between them.

Maybe the root of this was in her relationship with her family. The fact they hadn't wanted her to be a vet—they'd wanted her to be part of the family firm, even though she was clearly born to be a vet. And she obviously felt guilty about the fact she had a family she wasn't close to, whereas he'd lost the ones he'd loved so much. Maybe when she came back from Contarini he'd persuade her to tell him about it. Get the bad memories out of her heart and replace them with happiness.

It took a while, but at last Dragan could tell from the regularity of Melinda's breathing that she'd fallen asleep. Though sleep eluded him. He was too worried about her.

He'd talk to Nick tomorrow morning, see if they could arrange a locum to cover him at the practice. Then he could go over to Contarini to give Melinda his support.

Then again, if her relationship with her family was that strained, this would be a seriously bad time to meet them. No way would her parents want to hear news of their daughter's wedding just before the funeral of their son.

Which left Dragan torn between being Melinda's support and abiding by her wishes: whatever he did, it didn't seem enough. For now all he could do was hold her while she slept. And when she came back to England he'd do his best to make her world a brighter place. Give her the happiness she deserved.

CHAPTER SIX

It was still dark when Melinda's alarm beeped.

'Urgh. I am so not a morning person,' she grumbled. Especially today, knowing what she was going to face in Contarini.

And today, when she had to tell Dragan exactly what she was going back to. Why she was dreading it so much.

'I'll put the kettle on while you have a shower,' Dragan said.

By the time she'd dressed, he'd already made her a cup of coffee—strong and dark, just how she liked it—and he took a quick shower himself before he carried Bramble down the stairs to let her out. The dog, clearly sensing Melinda's need for comfort, insisted on sitting with her nose on Melinda's knee when Dragan brought her back up to the flat.

'All right, *cara*?' he asked.

No. Definitely not. But she tried to force a smile to her face. Be brave for him.

'Come on. You have to eat something.' He looked at the toast she'd crumbled onto her plate.

'I'm not hungry.' She felt too sick to eat. Sick with tension and guilt and misery and worry.

She had to tell him.

Now.

You're not just marrying the village vet. You're marrying...

'And we have to leave in ten minutes,' he warned her, after a quick glance at his watch.

'And I need to check on Cassidy before we go.' Which meant no time to talk. She couldn't neglect her professional duties. But she didn't want to neglect the love of her life either.

'Do you want me to hold him while you get the formula into him?'

She gave in. He was being so kind, so sweet—so caring. She couldn't tell him and expect him to cope with everything in the space of ten seconds before he helped her with her patient. 'Yes, please.'

They'd just finished when Sally walked in. Melinda gave the nurse the rundown on Cassidy's treatment plan and made sure she had Jake's number for queries.

And then it was time to go.

Dragan carried Bramble down to the car first, then brought Melinda's small flight bag and slid it onto the back seat. She locked the flat behind them and climbed into the car. Although she normally fiddled with his radio or the CD player, today she wanted silence. Silence to work out the right words to tell him. And Dragan was in tune with her mood enough not to push her to chatter.

She still hadn't worked out the right words by the time they got to the airport. Every time she tried to speak, it felt as if her tongue was glued to the roof of her mouth.

He left the window open enough to give Bramble some fresh air—he wouldn't be that long at the airport and, besides, it was still early morning and cool, so the car wouldn't become hot and uncomfortable for the dog.

'I'll carry this,' he said, hoisting Melinda's bag over his shoulder, and he walked hand in hand with her into the airport. He waited while she checked in at the reception desk and picked up her tickets, then walked with her to the departure lounge.

'Send me a text when you get there, so I know you've arrived safely,' he said, holding her close. 'I won't have my phone on during surgery, but I'll pick up your message as soon as I switch the phone on again.'

'OK. I'm not sure when I'll get a chance to ring you.' Her face was white. 'I really don't know what…' Her voice faded. Now. She had to tell him now.

Dragan, clearly oblivious to the real reason for her silence, squeezed her hand. 'Look, I'll call Nick. I'll sort out a locum and go back to Penhally to get someone to dog-sit Bramble and then I'll follow you straight out to Contarini. You don't have to face this on your own. I'll be there beside you.'

She swallowed hard, hating herself for being a liar and a fraud and hurting the man she loved. 'You are a good man, Dragan. I really don't deserve you.'

'Of course you do. Come with me and we'll sort out my tickets.'

'No, Dragan. I have to…' She dragged in a breath. 'I appreciate your offer, but I have to stand on my own two feet.'

'Sometimes,' he said with a sigh, 'I wish you weren't quite so independent. But I hope you know you can lean on me—that I'll never let you down.'

Oh, *Dio*. How could she do this? 'Dragan, I need to tell you—'

'Later,' he said, pressing a finger lightly against her lips. 'Don't worry about whatever it is. Everything will work out OK in the end. You have a flight to catch.'

And she hated herself even more for letting him talk her out of telling him. This was important. And the longer she left it, the more hurt he was going to be when she finally told him.

Please, please, don't let this be too much for him. Don't let it make him walk away from her. Don't let her lose him.

'You know you can call me any time,' he reminded her.

'Even if it's three in the morning, it doesn't matter—if you need me, just ring me.'

'I'm not going to disturb your sleep. But thank you. It helps to know you're there.' Her face was white. 'I love you with all my heart, Dragan.'

He stroked her face. 'Are you scared of flying, or something?'

Or something. 'I just want you to know that I love you.'

He smiled. 'I know. Just as I love you. And we're going to make that promise to each other in front of everyone the day you walk down the aisle to me.'

If he still wanted to marry her, once he knew the truth about her. 'Tell Reverend Kenner I'm sorry I couldn't make our meeting,' she said.

'He'll understand.' Dragan paused. 'Look—I won't ring you because it might be awkward timing for you. But call me when you can, OK?'

'I will.' She'd call him the second she got to Contarini.

And she'd tell him she loved him.

And she'd tell him what she was going home to. Exactly who she was.

'I love you. *Ti amo. Volim te,*' he added.

'I love you, too,' she whispered. '*Siempre.* Always.'

Dragan watched her as she walked through the scanner. All clear.

And then she was gone.

The way she'd kissed him goodbye had almost made it feel as if it was goodbye for ever. He pushed the thought away. Of course it wasn't. She'd be back in a few days. And maybe then he'd be able to take the sadness from her eyes, make her realise just how much she was loved. That it didn't matter if she didn't fit into her family, because she had him and their future children—and they'd be all the family she needed.

He drove home in complete silence. Parked in the road outside his cottage, lifted Bramble out, and let them both in. He had enough time to have a cup of coffee, make a fuss of the dog and change into a suit for morning surgery, and then it was time for work.

And right now Melinda would be on her way to London.

He walked over to the surgery. The village seemed to be busier than usual—clearly the tourist season had started early this year. Quite a few people had cameras. Well, Penhally Bay was picturesque, with the smattering of pagan memorials in the surrounding countryside, the wreck of the seventeenth-century Spanish treasure ship *Corazón del Oro* and the smugglers' caves, and the cliffs overhanging the Atlantic. Maybe these people were all from some camera club and they'd come to find inspiration for a competition or something.

'Morning, Dragan,' Hazel, the practice manager, said as he walked in.

'Morning, Hazel.' He smiled at her and headed for his consulting room. He'd just settled in when there was a rap at the door and Nick—as usual, without waiting to be asked—opened the door.

'Quick word,' he said—more of a statement than a question.

'Sure.' Dragan gestured to the chair next to his desk.

'We need to think about locums,' Nick said.

So now would definitely not be a good time to say he needed leave for a few days. Dragan carefully kept his expression neutral. 'We could do with a long-term one to keep us going through the summer. I know Adam's here now and he's taken over Marco's list, but we still need cover for Lucy while she's on maternity leave,' he said. And maybe longer, if Lucy decided she wanted a break before returning to medicine. 'We can just about manage for now, but we'll really need someone to help us next month when the tourists start arriving.'

'Good point. I'll get Hazel onto it,' Nick said. 'I did call to see you yesterday, but you were out. Interesting neighbour you have.'

'Cruella De Vil, you mean?' Dragan said before he could stop himself.

Nick's eyes widened in surprise. 'I thought she was rather fun, actually. We went out for dinner last night.'

'Uh-huh.' Dragan gave him a polite smile. Natalie or Natasha—or whatever her name was—wasn't his idea of fun. Nick was lonely, and Dragan could understand that, but why bother going out with someone so shallow when he could find himself someone genuine and warm? Someone more like...well, more like Kate, Dragan thought, the midwife who'd been their practice manager before Hazel had taken over.

'I'll see you later, then,' Nick said, and to Dragan's relief the senior partner left him to see his first patient.

Dragan just about managed to keep his mind on his work during the morning. But the second his last patient left his consulting room, he grabbed his mobile phone and checked it for messages.

There were two—both from Melinda.

In London. Love you. M.

Napoli. Love you. M.

It wasn't until after he'd finished his house calls that he had the text he'd really been waiting for.

Contarini. Love you. Call you soon. Something I need to tell you. M. xx

Something she needed to tell him? He frowned. She'd tried to tell him something earlier, but he'd told her it could wait. Well, whatever it was, it probably wasn't as bad as she thought. Things often seemed worse than they really were after you'd just had bad news.

Although he was itching to call her, see how see was, he

kept the desire under control. The last thing she needed was for him to ring her in the middle of something awkward. And at least he had something positive to do that evening. Knowing that Reverend Kenner liked dogs, Dragan was perfectly comfortable taking Bramble with him for a walk along the harbour down to the rectory, next to the church. Though it was with some relief that he passed Nick's house and saw that the senior partner's car wasn't there. He was probably out somewhere with that atrocious woman—which was a good thing. Then Nick wouldn't be asking just why Dragan was calling in on Reverend Kenner, who wasn't on his patient list. Until Melinda was back and wearing his ring, Dragan wasn't ready to discuss his plans with anyone else.

'Ah, Dragan. You've brought Bramble with you.' Reverend Kenner bent down to pat the dog. 'How's her leg?'

'This time round, hopefully, it's healing nicely. And I'm not letting her off the lead until we've got the X-rays back after her next check-up.'

'Would you like a cup of tea?'

English tea was one thing Dragan definitely hadn't learned to love. 'Thanks, but I'm fine,' he said with a smile.

'So, what can I do for you? You were quite mysterious on the phone.'

'Melinda's agreed to be my wife,' Dragan explained.

'Congratulations! I'm so pleased—you make a lovely couple. And people have been wondering, you know.'

Dragan smiled wryly. 'Nothing's ever secret for long around here, is it? Melinda would have been with me today, but she had a call from her parents last night and had to go back to Contarini. Her brother's been killed in an accident.'

'I'm so sorry. Do give her my condolences when you speak to her, won't you?'

'Of course.' Dragan paused. 'About the wedding—we wondered if you'd marry us in St Mark's.'

'I'd be *delighted*,' Reverend Kenner said warmly. 'Though you should expect the whole village to turn out.'

'That's fine by me. Um, I haven't done this sort of thing before, so I don't have a clue what the procedures are. I assume we have to fill in some sort of paperwork?'

'Yes. Strictly speaking, I *should* see you both together,' Reverend Kenner pointed out.

'Melinda will come to see you as soon as she's back in Cornwall,' Dragan promised.

'So have you any date in mind?'

'As soon as possible.'

Reverend Kenner raised an eyebrow. 'Should I be concerned about your reasons?'

Dragan shook his head. 'Not at all. It's just that now we've decided to get married neither of us wants to wait any longer than we have to. So what happens now? Do you read the banns or something?'

'Hmm.' Reverend Kenner frowned. 'Are you both British nationals?'

'I've spent nearly half my life here,' Dragan said, 'and I obtained British citizenship when I qualified as a doctor. But I'm not sure about Melinda.'

'Then we're probably safest to get a common licence— that's permission from the bishop for non-British nationals to marry here.'

Dragan blinked. 'We have to go and see the bishop?'

'We're quite a way from the bishop's diocese, but the good news is I'm one of the bishop's surrogates—I can sort out your application for the licence,' Reverend Kenner reassured him. 'I have copies of all the forms you'll need to fill out. You'll need proof of your nationality—your passport will do fine—and maybe a letter from the embassies saying that the marriage will be recognised in Melinda's home country.' He frowned. 'Is Contarini part of the European Union?'

'Probably.'

'If it is, I won't need a letter from the embassy, but check with Melinda. If it's not, I'll need the letter.' He smiled. 'I'm just so pleased for you both.' He checked in his diary. 'As soon as possible, you say. We need to allow a couple of weeks for the paperwork to go through, so we're looking at the end of the month... Ah, yes. We have a slot at three o'clock on the last Saturday in April, if that suits you both?'

'That'd be perfect.'

'You've sorted out your best man and bridesmaids?'

'Not yet. But now we've got a definite date, we'll work on it.'

Reverend Kenner handed him a sheaf of forms. 'Obviously we'll need to have a little chat—I always do with couples who want to marry—but it's nothing too onerous.'

'We don't mind,' Dragan said. 'We just want to get married. Properly.'

'And the whole village will be celebrating with you,' Reverend Kenner said warmly.

On the way home, Dragan remembered the hot-water bottle. Melinda had promised to return it to Violet Kennedy. Well, that was one small thing he could do to help: collect it and deliver it for her. It would give Melinda one less thing to worry about; being the conscientious vet she was, she was probably fretting about it. And she had enough to deal with right now.

The tourists were still hanging about outside the café—probably waiting for the sunset, he guessed. He unlocked the door to Melinda's flat, carried Bramble up the stairs, retrieved the hot-water bottle, and had just set the dog back on her feet and locked the door again when he realised he was surrounded. By the tourists. Who were busy taking photographs—of *him*.

'What's go—?' he began.

'So who are you to Princess Melinda?' one of them cut in.

'I beg your pardon?' He stared at the man. Princess Melinda? Was the guy talking about *his* Melinda?

'Princess Melinda. The heir to the throne of Contarini, now her brother's died,' one of the others said.

'Right stunner, she is. Blonde and...' One of the others lifted two hands, as if cupping curvaceous breasts.

They *were* talking about his Melinda. Dragan just about managed to contain the urge to punch him—no way was this grubby louse going to get his paws anywhere near Melinda!

'Give it a break, man. She's never going to look twice at you. Beauty, brains and royal, to boot—she's way out of *your* league,' one of the others said, nudging the mouthy photographer.

A camera flashed in Dragan's face. 'So you've got the key to her flat, then,' one of them said conversationally.

'I'm just a friend,' Dragan said. Though right now he was beginning to wonder. How could Melinda possibly be a princess and not have told him something so important about herself? She'd agreed to marry him, for goodness' sake. For better or worse. No secrets.

'Friend, hmm?' Another flash. 'So what's the hot-water bottle for?'

'It belongs to the owner of a patient she treated on call yesterday,' Dragan said shortly.

'And she didn't have time to return it before she went back to Contarini for the funeral?' one of the paparazzi said. 'Right. Good of you to help out. A *friend*, you say.'

'Hang on, you're the local doctor, aren't you?' another asked.

'Yes.'

'And you live just round the corner. Handy,' another one remarked.

How did they know he lived nearby? Had they been watching him?

'So what do you make of King Alessandro, then?' one of the others asked.

King Alessandro? Presumably he was Melinda's father. Dragan spread his hands. 'Can't help you, I'm afraid. Sorry. Excuse me.'

To his relief, they let him go, but his brain was whirring as he walked back to Fisherman's Row. Melinda was a princess? Heir to the throne, according to the paparazzi—and that meant she'd be Queen Melinda on her father's death.

And hadn't she said something about her father wanting to retire?

Oh, lord.

This changed everything.

He'd asked the local vet to marry him.

And it turned out that she was of royal blood. The heir to the throne.

No wonder she'd reacted so badly when he'd teased her about behaving like a princess—because that was exactly what she was.

But why hadn't she told him the truth about herself? Why had she lied to him? She'd agreed to marry him, yet she'd kept something this big from him. That didn't bode well for their marriage—if she'd be allowed to marry him in the first place. Her Royal Highness Princess Melinda Fortesque was hardly likely to marry a commoner. Especially when she was about to become Her Majesty, Queen Melinda.

Oh, hell.

Even if it was possible for her to marry him, they couldn't base a marriage on secrets and lies. No wonder she'd wanted to keep things low-key between them. It was nothing to do with avoiding being the top subject of the village grapevine—she'd probably been terrified that the press would ferret it out.

Well, they had now.

And if this was the 'something I must tell you'—she was too late.

* * *

Dragan's mobile phone—which he'd forgotten to take with him when he'd gone to see Reverend Kenner—was ringing as he walked in the door. He picked it up and glanced at the screen. Melinda.

What the hell did he say to her?

Although he was tempted to leave it and get his head round the situation before she called back, at the same time he needed to know the truth. From her. 'Hello?'

'Dragan? *Carissimo*, I rang and rang and you weren't there,' she said, sounding worried. 'Are you all right?'

No, he wasn't. 'Sure,' he lied. Even though she'd kept the truth about herself from him, she was in an awkward situation. Hundreds of miles away with a family who didn't accept her for who she was, preparing to go to her brother's funeral. Now wasn't the time to make a big deal out of it—though that didn't mean he was going to let her off the hook. 'Are you?'

'Sort of. But I miss you so much. Dragan, there's something I need to tell you.' She'd slipped into Italian and was speaking so rapidly that he had to concentrate to follow her. 'It's important and I know I should have told you before I left, but it was all such a mess, and there was no time, and I'm sorry, and...' She paused for a moment. 'Dragan, about my family. There isn't an easy way to say this, so I'll say it straight. My father's the king of Contarini.'

'King Alessandro. I know.'

Melinda was stunned. He *knew*? But who'd told him? 'How?'

'I went to get Violet Kennedy's hot-water bottle from your flat to take it back to her and save you the job, and the paparazzi were there when I came out.'

'And they hassled you? Oh, no!' He must be so hurt and angry—learning that she'd kept this from him for so long. And hearing it from someone else instead of from her...

'Dragan, I'm so sorry. I really didn't want you to find out that way. I wanted to tell you myself.'

'Bit late now.' He was clearly trying to keep his voice toneless, but even he could hear the hurt and anger seeping through.

'Are you all right? The paparazzi didn't—'

'It doesn't matter about them,' he cut in. 'Why didn't you tell me before?'

'Because I couldn't find the right words. I know I should have told you. But I was…' She paused, trying to find the right word. One that wouldn't make things even worse. 'I was scared.'

'Scared?'

'That I'd lose you.' She dragged in a breath. 'Once people know I'm Princess Melinda, they treat me differently. And I didn't want things to change between us.'

'You think I'm that shallow?'

'No, of course I don't! But it's human nature that people see the title—it gets in the way of seeing the person. I didn't want to lose you, lose what we have. All I wanted was to live a normal life, just like any other person.'

'But you're not just any other person, are you? You're next in line to the throne. You're the heir in waiting.'

'Yes and no.'

'What's that supposed to mean?'

'Officially I'm the heir at the moment. But I don't want to be queen. And I'm not going to be either.' She swallowed. 'My father wants to retire—abdicate, call it what you want. He's got high blood pressure, so it's sensible that he starts to take things easier now he's older. And at least nowadays there is the option to abdicate—in the old days he would have been king until he died and the job would have killed him. If he hands it over to me…then he's free. It will be better for his health.'

'So you're staying in Contarini.'

'No.' She bit her lip. 'I don't belong here, Dragan. I belong in Penhally, with you. I'm just Melinda Fortesque, the local vet. And I'm getting married to the love of my life.'

His silence told her that he didn't believe her. That he was hurt and angry and didn't know how to trust a single word she said.

She hadn't actually *lied* to him.

But then again, she hadn't told him the whole truth either. And lies of omission were still lies.

'Dragan. I love you, I love Penhally and I love my job. I don't want to be the Queen of Contarini. I don't want to run the kingdom. I have no interest in politics and I'd be a rubbish head of state. I'm not what Contarini needs.'

'What about your duty to your family?'

He'd stayed in the village in Croatia during the war to pay off his family's debts—debts that hadn't been their fault at all—to make sure his family honour stayed intact. He'd put his duty before his own safety. And in her shoes she knew he'd do the dutiful thing. He'd give up the woman he loved and the job he loved for his family's sake.

But her family wasn't like his.

And giving up the life she loved to be the Queen of Contarini would be the biggest mistake she'd ever make.

She had to convince him of the truth. 'I'm not the only child. My younger sister Serena's everything I'm not—she enjoys politics and diplomacy, and she's good at it. She'd make a brilliant queen and she'd love every second of it. Whereas my heart won't be in it, and that would make it wrong for me and wrong for the country.' She closed her eyes for a moment. 'I have to do the right thing, Dragan. The right thing for everyone.'

'So that means it's over between us.'

'No! I'm still the same woman I was when you asked me to marry you.'

'Are you? Melinda, you're of royal blood. You're never going to be allowed to marry a commoner.'

'Yes, I am.'

'And then what? If you're married to a commoner, the law means you can't become queen?'

She sucked in a breath. Did he really think...? 'I'm not using you to get out of being queen, if that's what you're thinking. *Dio*—I fell in love with you, Dragan, almost the first moment I saw you. You're everything I want in a man. Apart from the fact that I go up in flames every time I look at you, it's who you *are*. You're honest and you're honourable and you do what's right. You're compassionate and you're kind and you're clever and I...I'll be so proud to be your wife. And I'm stuck here, hundreds of miles away from you, where you can't see my face or my eyes and know for yourself that I mean every word I'm saying, that I'm not lying to you or using your or...' She swallowed hard. 'Look, I'm coming home. I'll call you from the airport and let you know when my flight's due in.'

'Melinda, you can't. You went back to Contarini for your brother's funeral,' he reminded her.

'Which is tomorrow.' She closed her eyes for a moment. 'And it's going to be horrible. My parents didn't let me say goodbye to him in private. Saying goodbye in public isn't the same.'

'I know, but you still need to say goodbye. Or you'll feel there's unfinished business.'

Was that how he felt? Had he even had the chance to say goodbye properly to his family? She hadn't asked—and she couldn't ask now, not without ripping his wounds open again. She'd hurt him enough today—enough for a lifetime. 'I'm sorry,' she whispered. 'This is all such a mess.'

'Go to the funeral, Melinda,' he said softly. 'You owe it to yourself and to your family. Don't turn your back on them.'

'I...'

'Things will work out, Melinda. For the best.'

He sounded all calm and reassuring, but there was an undercurrent. An undercurrent that told her he was having doubts—about her, about the way she felt about him. She needed to get back to Penhally and straighten this out. She'd stay for the funeral, but then she'd be on the first possible flight back to England. She'd go home to the man she loved—and make him see that she loved him. 'I'm coming home as soon as I can after the funeral,' she said. 'We'll talk when I get back.'

'Sure.'

'I love you, Dragan. And I'm so, so sorry.'

'Uh-huh.'

He hadn't said he loved her, too. Her stomach turned to water. Please, don't let her lose him. Don't let him walk away from her under some misguided notion that he was helping her do the right thing—because ruling the country would be so very much the wrong thing for her and for Contarini. 'And, Dragan? About the press—'

'I told them I was your friend,' he cut in. 'Your neighbour.'

'They drag things up,' she said. 'So don't believe whatever you read in the papers or what they say to you. It might not be true. There might be a spin on it to make a story. And don't let them rile you either—just smile politely and say "No comment" to absolutely everything, and they'll leave you alone pretty quickly because they'll realise they won't get anything. Otherwise they'll hound you and push you into doing or saying something you'll regret. But I'll be home soon and I'll take the heat off you. I promise. And I love you.'

'OK.'

One tiny word. Two syllables. And it was untrue: everything was very far from being OK.

And he hadn't said he still loved her.

She had to get home to Penhally and fix this.

Fast.

CHAPTER SEVEN

DRAGAN was halfway through his breakfast the following morning when his mobile phone beeped.

Melinda.

He flicked through to the message.

Am flying home tonight. I love you. M x

He loved her, too. But he'd spent a lot of the previous night thinking. And he still didn't have any answers. It was her duty to go back to Contarini and rule. Her family needed her. But he would have no place in the life of Queen Melinda: he was standing in her way. It wasn't fair to make her choose between him and her family. He was going to have to do the honourable thing.

Even though the thought of losing her ripped his heart into shreds.

Be thinking of you today. D x, he texted back.

His phone beeped again within seconds. *I miss you. M x*

He missed her, too. But playing text-tennis wasn't going to help either of them right now. *Due in surgery. Turning phone off now. D x*

As soon as he left the house, he saw the paparazzi. And he was well aware that he was being followed all the way to the surgery.

There were stares from the patients, little speculative

murmurs and whispers behind hands as he walked in to the waiting room.

'Well, well. You and Melinda,' Hazel said, a knowing look on her face.

Oh, great. So Nick had spotted him last night, leapt to conclusions and speculated in the staffroom. Just what he could do without this morning. 'What did Nick say?'

'Nick?' She looked surprised. 'Nothing. He's too busy with that pushy bottle blonde to notice anything.' She shook her head. 'That woman's no good for him.'

'He needs someone with a heart,' Dragan agreed.

'Someone like our Kate. She's such a lovely girl.'

'Absolutely.' Dragan's smile was genuine; he liked the midwife. 'Though maybe we shouldn't be matchmaking.'

'Matchmaking.'

Uh-oh. Wrong choice of word. He'd clearly just reminded Hazel about a choice piece of gossip, because the practice manager tapped the side of her nose. 'You kept it quiet about Melinda.'

He sighed. 'Because we both prefer things to be private. Not that there's much chance of that around here,' he said ruefully. 'And the village grapevine's not on form because that's very old news.'

'No, not about you two seeing each other. Everyone's known that for *ages*,' Hazel said impatiently. 'I mean about who she really is. Of course, the papers got some of it wrong because it's not a secret about you two around here.'

Papers?

Even as it sank in, she fished under her desk and handed him the paper. The headline was enormous.

ROYAL VET'S SECRET LOVER

Underneath, there was a picture of him—a photograph that had clearly been taken outside Melinda's flat the previous evening.

'I had no idea she was royalty,' Hazel said, looking interested. 'I mean, she's always had that air of quality about her, but I thought she was the Penhally vet.'

'She is,' Dragan said. 'Hazel, forgive me for being rude, but I really don't think this is the time or place discuss this.' And he most definitely didn't want any speculation getting back to the paparazzi. 'Excuse me. I'm keeping everyone waiting. I'll be ready for surgery in five minutes.'

He managed to field awkward questions from his patients, but the paparazzi were still there when he left the surgery at lunchtime, posing as tourists: sitting at one of the little pavement tables outside the café, looking out to sea or reading a newspaper; browsing in the window of the surf shop or the little souvenir place; apparently studying the collection times listed above the post box set in the post-office wall.

If he ignored them, they'd probably follow him to all his house calls and compromise his patients' confidentiality. But he couldn't *not* do his house calls and compromise his patients' health.

Just smile politely and say 'No comment' to absolutely everything, and they'll leave you alone.

He'd never had to deal with the press. So he'd have to rely on Melinda's advice for this one.

For the first time ever, he found himself sympathising with the celebrities who complained about the invasion of their privacy. He'd had barely a day of it, but it was already grating on his nerves.

'What's wrong with these people, Bramble?' he asked. 'I'm just an ordinary man.'

The problem was, his girlfriend wasn't ordinary.

He gave the paparazzi polite smiles but said nothing as he lifted Bramble into the back of his car, although he realised before he'd driven to the end of Bridge Street that he was being followed on his way out of the village. Part of him was tempted to lead his pursuers on a wild goose chase and lose them in the maze of narrow Cornish lanes with their high stone walls. But then again, Melinda had said that if he didn't react they'd realise there was no story. So let them follow him. They'd soon find out what a GP's life was like. And it wasn't the media version of a doctor raking in the cash and dumping their patients on an out-of-hours call system either—at Penhally Bay Surgery, they did their own calls.

He noted after his first three calls that his pursuers tended to hang about in gateways with maps—obviously they could pretend to be lost tourists if anyone challenged them. But he forgot about them completely when he did his fifth call of the afternoon, at the riding stables a few miles south of Penhally.

Georgina Somers came out to meet him. 'Thanks for coming, Dr Lovak.' She leaned through the car window to stroke Bramble. 'Hello, you. So when are you going to be fit enough to chase rabbits again, then?'

'Soon. Provided she doesn't overdo it and skid round a corner and crack the bone again, like she did the last time I let her off the lead.' Dragan smiled at her. 'So what can I do for you, Georgina?'

'It isn't me.' She kept her voice low. 'It's Luka. I'm worried about him.'

Dragan frowned. Luka was one of the stablehands, who lived in a caravan tucked away in a quiet corner of the stable grounds. George Smith, Melinda's boss, had always said that Luka was brilliant with horses and he'd give him a job like a shot. 'What's wrong?'

'He says he's just got a virus, that's why he's got a sore throat and a bit of a temperature. But I'm not so sure. He caught himself on some barbed wire last week. He says I'm fussing, but he just doesn't look right and nobody else has come down with a sore throat and a temperature. I think it might be blood poisoning or something because he wouldn't let me treat his hand last week either.' She sighed. 'I know, it's awful of me to call you out for a cut hand—but you know what Luka's like.'

Along with the rest of his family—Romany travellers—Luka Zingari was incredibly suspicious of the medical profession. And out of all of the doctors at the Penhally practice, Dragan knew that he was the one they were most likely to respond to: the stranger in a strange land, like them. 'I'll have a word with him,' he promised.

'I'll take you over.'

Was this just a concerned employer worrying about her stablehand? Dragan wondered. Had Georgina's father called him, it would be more a case of an employer worrying about being sued—Malcolm Somers was very much of the old school and believed in paying his staff as little as possible for the maximum amount of work. Malcolm had finally handed over the running of the stables to his only child the previous year—although he interfered all the time, according to Melinda.

Something about Georgina's expression alerted Dragan. It wasn't the face of a concerned employer. It was more like a girlfriend who was worried sick.

Were Georgina and Luka…?

He chided himself even for thinking it. Who was he to speculate? Especially as the press were speculating about him and Melinda. He should know better. It was none of his business. But it would explain a lot.

Georgina rapped on the caravan door. 'Luka? It's me. Can I come in?'

There was a muttered croak from inside the caravan, and she opened the door. 'I know you said not to fuss, but Dr Lovak's here. He was calling on Mum…' her quick glance pleaded with Dragan not to expose the lie '…and when I told him you'd been ill he asked if he could drop in.'

'I don't need a doctor. She's fussing,' Luka said.

But the sardonic grin on his face worried Dragan. Luka was a typically handsome gipsy—again according to Melinda, half the girls in the village fancied him—and that grin definitely wasn't his normal expression.

An alarm bell rang in his mind. Luka worked at the stables. He'd cut his hand on barbed wire. If Luka's tetanus vaccinations weren't up to date, that could be a pretty nasty combination. 'So how are you feeling?' he asked.

'It's just a virus. Sore throat, headache, bit of a temperature. It'll go.'

'But you're having problems swallowing.'

'Only because of my sore throat.'

'Then you won't mind me checking your pulse, will you?' Before Luka could protest, Dragan checked the pulse at his wrist. 'Your heartbeat's pretty rapid.'

'Because I've got a bug.' Luka rolled his eyes. 'Georgie's fussing.'

'Have you had any pains in your arms or legs or stomach?'

'It's just a bug.'

Dragan knew Luka was going to evade any other questions along that line, so he changed tack. 'How's that hand you hurt the other week?'

'Fine.'

'Can I take a look?'

Luka looked at Georgina, sighed, then held out his left hand. Dragan gently unwrapped the slightly grubby bandage. 'Have you put anything on this?'

'It'll heal.'

Dragan raised an eyebrow. 'Well, I reckon you've got a bug all right.'

'See?' Luka glanced at Georgina. 'I told you it was all right.'

'Actually, it's not. You haven't got flu. It's a bacteriim called *Clostridium tetani*,' Dragan said.

'Oh, lord. You mean he's got *tetanus*?' Georgina looked shocked.

'When was the last time you had a tetanus vaccination?' Dragan asked Luka.

'No idea. I don't like needles,' Luka admitted.

'Most people don't. But it's not worth taking the risk of skipping a vaccination, especially with what you do for a living. Stables are one of the most common places to find *Clostridium tetani*.' Dragan looked at him grimly. 'Get a puncture wound from a nail—or in your case have an argument with some barbed wire—and then muck out a stable, and the bacterium's just found its dinner.'

'So what does tetanus do—*if* I have it?'

Lord, the man was stubborn. Even more so than Melinda.

'It's a disorder of the nervous system. It gives you muscle cramps—and that sometimes makes it hard to open your mouth, which is why tetanus is also known as lockjaw. In the early stages, you might get muscle spasms around the site of the infection—but when it hits the bloodstream it tends to affect your facial muscles,' Dragan explained.

'So when the bug's out of my system I'll be fine.'

'That's the thing,' Dragan said softly. 'If you don't treat it, you're pretty likely to die.'

Luka blinked. 'You what?'

'You're likely to die,' Dragan repeated. 'And it's not a nice way to go. You can't breathe properly, your muscles go into spasm and you suffocate. Or maybe the next muscle to go into spasm is your heart—it stops, and that's it. We probably won't get you back because your heart muscle won't respond to being shocked. Then there are your kidneys, there's the possibility of septicaemia... So you need treatment, Luka.'

'You don't know I've definitely got tetanus.'

Dragan had met Luka before and knew the man wasn't being awkward just to be macho—the chances were that Luka was terrified of hospitals, and denying that anything was wrong with him meant he wouldn't have to even consider the idea of going near one.

Georgina clearly thought the same, because she begged, 'Make him see sense, Dr Lovak. Luka, if I lose you…'

Luka's right hand reached out to grip hers. 'You're not going to lose me.'

'Then you need treatment, Luka,' Dragan said softly. 'You need to go to hospital. For Georgina's sake, if not your own.'

Luka shook his head. 'I'm not going in an ambulance. They're meat vans.'

'You don't have to go in an ambulance. I'll take you myself,' Dragan offered.

'I hate hospitals.'

'So do a lot of people. But you've got a three in five chance of dying if you don't have treatment.'

'Which gives me a two in five chance of being fine. Forty per cent's reasonable odds,' Luka said.

Dragan shook his head. 'This is going to get a hell of a lot worse before it gets better. *If* it gets better.'

'What does the treatment involve?' Georgina asked.

'I'm not going to lie about it. It involves needles. But you'll need some antibodies against the bacteria, Luka—they're called tetanus antitoxins. And some antibiotics, as well as something to stop your muscles going into spasm. This kind of treatment's best done in hospital, where there's a sterile environment.'

Luka scoffed. 'You see it in the paper all the time, people going into hospitals and catching a superbug because the place isn't clean.'

Luka's caravan, although small, was absolutely spotless.

'Often things make the news simply because they *are* news, not the norm. You need medical attention, Luka. Attention I can't give you.' Dragan sighed. 'As well as the medication, they're going to need to get plenty of protein into you and a lot of calories to fight the infection, so they'll probably put you on a drip. Once the needle's in, it doesn't hurt, and it's the best way to get the right fluids into you.'

'So you're saying I'll have to *stay* in hospital?' Luka's eyes widened.

'It won't be for that long.'

'No. No way. I belong *here*.'

He'd heard that before. Very recently. From someone just as stubborn.

Except she wasn't here now.

'I belong with the horses,' Luka insisted.

'Then the sooner we get you to hospital, the sooner we can get you back here with the horses again.'

Luka was silent for a long, long time. Only the way he gripped Georgina's hand gave any clue to what was going on in his head. Finally, he looked at Dragan. 'All right. I trust you.'

Melinda hadn't. The thought skidded into Dragan's mind before he could stop it. He pushed the idea away. Now wasn't the time to start thinking about the way his life had been turned upside down. He had a duty to his patients. 'Let's go, then,' he said quietly.

'Can I come with you?' Georgina asked.

'Better not,' Luka said. 'Your dad will go mad. You're not even supposed to be seeing me. And with your mum ill…She doesn't need the stress of your dad in one of his moods.'

'Dad's just going to have to accept it,' Georgina said, lifting her chin.

'His daughter moving in with what he calls a "dirty bloody gyppo"?' Luka shook his head. 'Don't push it, Georgie. You don't break a horse by smashing its spirit. You get it to trust you and work with you as a partner, so you're a team.'

'And you think you can make Dad change his mind?'

'It just takes time. Softly, softly. The more he gets to know me, the more he'll realise that true Romanies aren't thieves or liars or unclean—that he's got the wrong idea.'

'Dad never admits to being wrong.'

'He will this time.' Luka squeezed her hand. 'I'm not going to kiss you. I don't want you to get this. But everything's going to be all right.'

The irony wasn't lost on Dragan. It was the same situation as his own: Malcolm Somers, the owner of the riding stables, might just as well be the king of Contarini. Just like Melinda's father, Malcolm Somers wasn't going to want his daughter seeing someone he considered to be of inferior social status.

Whether Luka would be able to work a charm offensive on Malcolm and make the older man realise that there was no disgrace—that Luka was Georgina's equal and would treat her with the love and respect she deserved—Dragan didn't know. But he seriously doubted that he'd be able to do that with Melinda's family. Which meant they'd cut her off. She'd be isolated from her family.

So he was going to have to do the right thing and let her go. Let her be what she was born to be: a princess.

CHAPTER EIGHT

DRAGAN wasn't answering his phone. Melinda frowned. He'd probably left it at home while he took Bramble for a walk. *Dio*. She missed the dog pattering around. She missed holding Dragan's hand while they strolled down to the cliffs. She missed Cornwall. And, oh, how she missed Dragan.

But soon she'd be home. And she couldn't wait to see him. She quickly tapped in a message. *On way home. Will call you from Newquay.*

'Your Highness, are you sure about this?' the pilot asked when she boarded the small plane. 'Your mother...'

She smiled at him. 'Don't worry. She'll be angry with me, but I'll make sure you won't get into trouble. I just want to go home.'

The pilot gestured out towards the airfield. 'Contarini is your home, Your Highness.'

She shook her head. 'Not any more. Please, can we go?'

'No, you jolly well can't,' a voice said from the doorway. 'You're supposed to say goodbye first.'

'Rena! What are you doing here?' Melinda asked, surprised to see her sister.

'Just making sure you're all right.' Serena boarded the plane and sat next to her sister. 'Are you sure you're doing the right thing? This isn't...a...well...'

'Fling?' Melinda supplied.

The pilot withdrew to a discreet distance.

'No.' Melinda was very definite. 'Dragan is the love of my life. For the first time I can ever remember, I belong somewhere. With him. And I want to be with him, Rena.'

'Well, if his personality's as gorgeous as his looks...'

'It is,' Melinda confirmed.

'And he makes you happy?'

Melinda nodded. 'Happier than I've ever been in my life.'

Serena hugged her. 'Then follow your heart. I wish you both all the best. And I'm most definitely coming to the wedding—and I expect to be a bridesmaid—so you ring me as soon as you've sorted out a date.'

Melinda bit her lip. 'I don't think *Mamma* and *Papà* will be there.' Her mother had expressly decreed that morning that there would be no wedding. And Melinda had finally snapped, telling her mother a few things she should have said years ago.

The ensuing row had practically blistered her ears.

They'd presented a united front at the funeral, for the sake of the media. But Viviana Fortesque had made it very clear that if Melinda went back to Cornwall it should only be to sort things out. 'And then you will come back here, to your rightful place. You are next in line to the throne,' she'd said coldly. 'And you know your father needs to abdicate, to take things easier and leave the running of the kingdom to someone else. You *cannot* walk away from your duty.'

What about her duty to her patients, to her colleagues? Melinda refused to leave them in the lurch. And, most of all, she refused to leave Dragan. And she'd made that just as clear to her mother—who'd responded with the stoniest, iciest silence Melinda had ever encountered.

'*Mamma* will calm down. In a week or so,' Serena said. '*Papà* will talk her round, like he always does.' She grinned.

'Though I never thought I'd see the day you got the headlines above Raffi.'

'It's not funny, Rena. The timing was atrocious.' And it had taken every ounce of backbone she'd had that morning, to face her mother's fury as she'd banged the newspaper onto the table. ROYAL VET'S SECRET LOVER

'*Mamma* would've had a fit whatever day she'd seen that headline,' Serena said wryly. 'Though yes, today was probably not the best of days for it to happen.' She hugged her sister. 'Be happy, Lini. And I'll speak to you soon. Let me know you've arrived safely.'

'I will. And thank you, Rena. For being there.'

'It's how families are supposed to be,' Serena said softly. 'How I wish ours had been when we were growing up. And how I hope yours will be now.'

So do I, Melinda thought. So do I.

The flight back to England seemed interminable. But finally they landed. As soon as she was through customs, she rang Dragan. And how good it was to hear his voice.

'I'm in Newquay. I missed you so much, *amore mio*.'

'Do you want me to come and pick you up?'

'Better not—there are paparazzi everywhere.' And she didn't want her reunion with Dragan all over the front pages. She wanted that to be very, very private indeed. 'Have they been bad to you?'

'They've followed me everywhere. But I took your advice: I just smiled and said nothing.'

'Good. We'll draft a statement to the press and it will quieten down.' She bit her lip. 'Dragan, I'm so sorry it happened like this.'

'You can't change the past.'

He sounded calm, but she could hear the hurt seeping through his stoicism. 'I'm still sorry. Because I never meant to hurt you.' She paused. 'I'll sneak into yours the back way, yes?'

'Won't they follow you?'

'Believe me, I've had a lot of practice in avoiding them,' she said dryly. 'I could have a PhD in it by now.'

'I'll leave the French doors unlocked.'

'Thank you.' She paused. 'Dragan? *Volim te.*'

'I'll see you soon.'

Hell, hell, hell. If he wasn't responding when she used his own language…this was going to be hard. Knowing Dragan, he was still thinking about her duty and he was putting distance between them to make it easy for her to go back to Contarini.

But that wasn't what she wanted.

She'd fight for her man.

Because he was worth it.

The drive back from the airport dragged on and on and on. But finally the taxi drove into Penhally—and how good it was to see the bay spreading out in front of her. *Home*.

The driver dropped her by the Higher Bridge; she knew that the paparazzi, even if they had information that she was on her way back, would be camped outside the veterinary surgery and she would be shielded from their view by the houses in Gull Close. Any other photographers would be stationed at the front of Fisherman's Row; they wouldn't expect her to cut round the back of the houses in Bridge Street and through the little alley at the back of Dragan's house.

She could see him sitting at the table in front of the French doors, reading some medical journal or other. And just the sight of him made her catch her breath. She tapped softly on the glass, then opened the door, locked it behind her and closed the curtains. Just in case.

And then she was in his arms. Holding him so tightly, as if she'd never let him go again.

She had no intention of ever letting him go again.

'*Volim te.* I've missed you so much.' She reached up to draw his head down to hers, brushed her mouth against his.

She could feel a reserve there—well, he'd learned the truth about her in the worst possible way, so of course he'd be hurt and wouldn't quite be sure of her—but please, please, just let him kiss her back. Let him give her the chance to show him exactly how she felt. Skin to skin, body to body, no barriers between them. Let her tell him without words how much she loved him, make him believe the truth: that she was completely his and nothing was ever, ever going to change that.

She pulled back slightly to look into his face. His dark eyes were unreadable. 'Dragan?'

'I'll put the kettle on.' He untangled himself from her arms.

The kettle? She hadn't seen him for days, he hadn't kissed her back, and he was talking about making a cup of *coffee*?

This wasn't the man she'd left in Penhally.

And she wanted her man back. Right now.

She followed him to the kitchen and, after checking that the blinds were drawn, slid her arms round his waist and rested her cheek against his back. 'I've missed you, *zlato*.'

Gently, he prised her arms away.

'Dragan? What is it?'

He turned round to face her, leaning back against the kitchen worktop. 'I can't do this.'

'Can't do what?' Ice began to trickle down her spine.

'You and me. I...don't think this is a good idea.'

She stared at him. 'But...only a few days ago you asked me to marry you.'

'I asked our local vet to marry me,' he corrected her. 'But you're Princess Melinda. A stranger. I don't even know what I should be calling you. Your Majesty? Ma'am? Your Royal Highness?'

'Ma'am and Majesty are for queens. And don't you *dare* start on that "Highness" rubbish. It's an accident of birth that my parents are who they are. I'm just Melinda. The same as you've always called me.' She dragged in a breath. 'I haven't changed, Dragan.'

'Yes, you have,' he corrected quietly. 'Because I don't know you at all. The woman I asked to marry me—I thought I knew her. But I was wrong. You're a princess.'

'I'm sorry. I *know* I should have told you the truth about me, a long time ago. I should have prepared you properly for what it would be like, not left you to the mercy of the paparazzi. I just didn't think they'd be here so soon. Stupid of me.' She shook her head. 'I just want to be like any other woman. I want to marry the man I love. Work among people I care about. Be *myself*.'

'But you have duties, Melinda. Responsibilities.'

Now, this she'd expected. She'd prepared her arguments. 'I've talked to my parents about this. I'm not going to be queen. This stuff with the paparazzi—it'll last a few more days, maybe, and then it will all go away and we can get on with our lives as normal.'

'But what's normal?' he asked.

'You and me. Penhally. Seeing patients. Matching up our call lists so we can grab half an hour to ourselves at lunchtime.' She shook her head. 'Dragan—look, I know I hurt you and I'm sorry for that. I know I was wrong not to trust you with everything—but it isn't you. It's my own stupid fault, for being too scared that you'd walk away if you knew who I was, for letting my fears blind me to the kind of man you are. I didn't want to lose you—I *don't* want to lose you.' She gritted her teeth. 'I hate this royal stuff. I always have. When I was younger, it was like growing up in a fishbowl. I couldn't open my mouth or do anything without people analysing what I did or said—and most of the time they put completely the wrong interpretation on it. Every mistake I made, the press blew it way out of proportion. I couldn't do anything like a normal person, and the paparazzi were there every minute of every day, telephoto lenses poking into my life.'

Dragan could understand that. He'd had a taste of that the past few days.

'Everything I did was in the public eye,' Melinda continued. 'And my days were one long round of protocol, protocol, protocol. Even when I knew someone was a devious, lying snake and I wouldn't trust them a millimetre, I had to be gracious to them at official receptions or it would turn into a diplomatic incident and undo years and years of work.' She shook her head. 'No, it's not a fishbowl, it's a straitjacket. I loathe politics and all the politeness and the lies and the spin and the protocols. That's not the world where I want to be.'

But it was the world she'd been born into.

'I can't live in your world, Melinda.'

'My world is *your* world,' she said softly.

'How? I'm the village doctor here in Penhally and you're a princess—the heir to the throne of a Mediterranean island.'

'I haven't called myself "princess" in years.'

'That doesn't stop you being one.'

'I've never felt like a princess, Dragan.' She took a deep breath. 'You told me about your family...now let me tell you about mine. You want to know the truth, why I don't talk about my past? Because I was unhappy, and I don't want to dwell on all that misery.'

Her eyes were sparkling with anger and pain, and he could tell just how strongly she felt because her accent had deepened. 'My parents were always distant, too busy with affairs of state to see what was happening with their children. My brother Raffi was left to grow up like a wild child. When he was just fifteen, he was photographed by the paparazzi in a bar, drinking alcohol, despite being way under the legal age limit. It snowballed from there. He followed our Uncle Benito—my father's younger brother—in being a playboy, except Benito at least worked hard to balance it out. Raffi...well, he just laughed and said it didn't matter, because he was the heir to the throne and the favourite and he'd do whatever he liked.' She spread her hands. 'He had no self-discipline, no thought for others. Which was why he ended up wrapping his car round a tree last week. Thank God he was the only one involved and didn't hurt anyone else.' She shuddered. 'I think that's why my father didn't suggest abdicating before—because he knew Raffi was too young and irresponsible to make a good king.'

Dragan looked at her. 'You're the heir to the throne now. And you have the self-discipline your brother lacked.' Studying for a degree in veterinary sciences wasn't an easy option, and doing it in her second language would have made it even harder.

'But I don't have the rest of the princessy accomplishments. I was never the elegant young debutante who was happy with her ballet lessons and piano lessons and deportment and whatever else a princess is supposed to learn—the only thing I enjoyed out of that lot was riding, and that was only because I could escape to the stables and could learn how to look after the horses. The number of times my mother dragged me out and told me that I shouldn't be playing around in all the mess—how I should act like a princess instead of having straw in my hair like a stablehand. And I couldn't do it. I never fitted in.' She sighed. 'You know, most girls spend their time dreaming they're princesses in disguise—like the princess and the pauper. For me it was the other way round. I wanted to be the ordinary girl, not the princess.'

That was what she'd been when she'd met him. An ordinary girl. The newcomer to the village—a stranger in a strange land, like himself.

But all the time she'd been playing a part. Pretending to be someone she wasn't.

Was she playing a part now? He couldn't help wondering.

'You're not an ordinary girl. You're Princess Melinda of Contarini.'

'I'm Melinda Fortesque, MRCVS. Soon to be Melinda Lovak.' She paused. 'Unless you've changed your mind.'

It was breaking his heart to do this, but he had to do the right thing. Families were important, and he couldn't let her cut herself off from hers. 'It can't happen. I don't fit into your world—and you know it, or you would have asked me to go with you.'

'You think I asked you to stay because I was ashamed of you?' She shook her head. 'Far from it. I'm *proud* of you. But you have to understand, my mother is a cross between Queen Victoria and Attila the Hun. She's a terrible snob. I didn't want her being rude to you and hurting you.'

'Your parents are never going to accept me,' he pointed out softly. Just as Georgina's parents would never accept Luka. Different class, different culture.

'They *will*.'

Typical Melinda. Stubborn. But for her own sake he had to make her face the truth. 'So how did they react to that newspaper story?' he asked.

'Not well,' she admitted.

'Exactly. No way will they let you marry a commoner.'

'I don't want to marry some prince or other they've chosen for me. I want *you*,' she said.

'The papers brought out all the stuff about me being a refugee.'

She spread her hands. 'So? Dragan, it wasn't your fault there was a war. And you have nothing to be ashamed of. Nothing! You had a horrible time that wasn't of your making, but you came through it. You've worked hard and you've made something of yourself. You haven't just taken and taken—you've given back. You're a good man. And that's exactly what I told my mother. That you're kind and compassionate, that you're a brilliant doctor, that you're clever—for goodness' sake, you were going to study law and you speak more languages than I do! I told her that every day is better for me now when I wake up because I know you'll be there. I love you, Dragan.'

She paused and looked straight at him.

He knew what she was waiting for. And how he wanted to tell her that he loved her all the way back. That, yes, he felt hurt and angry and betrayed that she'd kept the truth from him, but they'd work it out together because he loved her.

But he had to do the right thing. Which meant denying it.

'I can't forgive you for keeping me in the dark—for agreeing to marry me when you know it can't happen.'

'Yes, it *can*.'

How? They were worlds apart. And Melinda was destined to rule her country. 'Marry me, and you'll cut yourself off from your family.'

She raked a hand through her hair. 'Dragan, I know family's important to you. I know you miss yours. And if mine were even the slightest bit how you described yours to me, there wouldn't be a problem. But they're not. And I've barely been back to Contarini since I came to England to study veterinary science. My parents didn't even come to my graduation. That's how close we are. So cutting myself off…' She shrugged. 'There's nothing *to* cut off. My sister's the only one I'm close to, and I don't really fit into her social circle either.' There was the tiniest sparkle in her eye. 'Though she liked your picture in the paper. And she told me to follow my heart.'

Follow your heart. Good advice. Except…sometimes you had to put your duty first. Melinda's father was ill and needed to retire. Her family needed her—and in his eyes family should always come first. He knew she was planning to put him before her duty—which was wrong, wrong, wrong. Whereas if she thought there was nothing for her here, it might make it easier for her to leave. To go back and do the right thing.

For her sake, he was going to have to say something that hurt him bone-deep. 'We're not getting married,' he said. 'It's over.'

Her eyes widened. 'No. You don't mean that. Please, Dragan. Tell me you don't mean it.'

'I can't marry someone who doesn't trust me. Someone I don't trust any more.'

'But, Drag—'

'It's over,' he said, not looking into her eyes because he didn't trust himself not to crumble. 'I'm sorry. You'd better leave through the back door—there are paparazzi out the front.'

She stared at him for a long, long moment.

Then she left the room. Closed the French doors behind her.

And Dragan discovered that the pain he'd known as a teenager, when he'd lost his family, had just come back. With a vengeance.

CHAPTER NINE

YEARS of training let Melinda walk down the little alley at the back of Dragan's house and through to the other side of Harbour Road with her back straight and her expression neutral. Even though she wanted to bawl her eyes out, she made absolutely sure that the paparazzi couldn't detect her thoughts—no way was she going to let them have a picture they could use with a speculative caption.

But the second she was back in her flat with the door closed behind her, she slid down the wall to the floor, drew her knees up to her chin and wrapped her arms tightly round herself.

It was all over.

Dragan had called off the wedding.

Now he knew who she was, he didn't want to know—her worst nightmare had just come true.

As she'd told him, if you were royal and you made a mistake, it would be all over the papers. Talked about. And just when people had started to forget, the whole thing would suddenly blow up again. It would go on and on and on.

She could see the headlines now. DR LOVE-AK DUMPS PRINCESS

About the only people who'd be pleased about it were her parents.

But it didn't change things. Even if Dragan didn't want her, she still had a life here in Cornwall. And she wasn't going back to rule Contarini.

'Backbone,' she reminded herself. 'Keep it straight.' *Like a princess.* And she was well aware of the irony.

She picked up the phone and dialled her boss. This was another call that was way overdue. Someone else she'd lied to by omission. 'George? It's Melinda.'

'How are you, love?' he asked.

My heart's just cracked right down the middle. 'I'm fine,' she lied. How could he be so nice to her when she'd behaved so badly? 'And, George, I'm really sorry that you've had a hard time from the press.'

He laughed. 'Once they realised that the only time I'd talk to them was with my arm up a cow's backside and plenty of manure around, it rather put them off.'

'Even so. I'm sorry. I really should have told you who I was. As my boss, you had a right to know.'

'You had your reasons.'

She had.

Her boss was a damn sight more understanding about it than the love of her life had been. But, please, don't let this princess business have wrecked her job, the way it had wrecked her relationship with Dragan. Dragan hadn't even been able to look at her; he'd never be able to forgive her for hiding the truth from him. For not trusting him when she should have done. 'Do I still have a job?' she asked in a small voice.

'Of course you do. Being a princess doesn't get you out of your job without at least a month's notice, you know.'

His tone was light and teasing, but she could hear the warmth and concern in his voice and it hurt. Because right now she felt so alone. So isolated. So *empty*.

'Then I can come back to the surgery tomorrow morning?'

'Bright and early, usual time,' he said. 'You'll be pleased

to know Cassidy's ready to go home tomorrow and he's back on his usual diet. We had a bit of a scare with him while you were away, but Jake sorted us out. He's a good contact to have for exotics. Well done, you.'

'I didn't exactly do much.' She'd brought the parrot into the surgery—and then she'd abandoned him along with the rest of her job and caught the next flight to London. Some vet she was.

'You treated the bird before he was too far gone to help. If you'd left it until the morning, he wouldn't have made it and Violet would have a broken heart. Don't do yourself down, love.' He paused. 'Or should I call you Your Highness from now on?'

She strove for lightness. 'Melinda will do just fine.'

'I'll see you tomorrow, then, love.'

'See you tomorrow, George. And thank you.' She cut the connection, replaced the phone, took an apple from her fruit-bowl and headed down into the practice.

Cassidy perked up as soon as he saw her. ''Ow do, m'dear?'

'Pretty rubbish, actually,' she told him.

The parrot swore a blue streak, and she smiled wryly. 'Saves me doing it, I suppose. But I was meant to be teaching you something nice.' She made a kissing noise. '*Ti amo, tesoro.*'

The bird responded with something pithy.

She cut him a piece of apple with a scalpel and fed it to him. '*Ti amo, tesoro.*'

This time there was no response at all.

She checked that he had enough water, scratched his poll just the way he liked it—and clearly he'd picked how to purr like a cat since he'd been in the surgery—then walked out of the room. As she turned off the light, she heard a very quiet kissing sound. '*Ti amo, tesoro,*' Cassidy informed her.

Something Dragan would never say to her again.

And somehow she had to learn to live with it.

Kate walked through the door of the practice a moment after Dragan the following morning. She looked hot and bothered, although she didn't appear to be out of breath; he had a feeling that her high colour was due to anger rather than rushing. 'What's up, Kate?' he asked.

Kate pulled a face. 'Nick and that wretched clippy-clop woman.'

'Clippy-clop?' Dragan asked, mystified.

'The one who thinks it's practical to wear high-heeled mules in a Cornish seaside village.' Her scowl deepened. 'Horrible woman. She dresses at least fifteen years too young, too. Nick must be going through the male menopause to think it makes him look young, having *her* on his arm. Maybe she looks young from a distance—but up close you can see she's trowelled on her make-up to cover up the lines.'

Nick had never, ever heard Kate make a bitchy remark about anyone; their former practice manager, who'd recently done a refresher course and returned to the practice as a midwife, was always calm and unflappable and friendly. He stared at her in surprise. 'What did she do?'

'Oh, nothing. Just made some stupid remark about Jem's name, and I shouldn't let her get to me.' She flapped a hand. 'I was just taking Jem to meet Mum in the café—it's the school holidays and she's looking after him while I'm here this morning—when we bumped into them outside the post office. She couldn't have got much closer to Nick if she'd stripped off the little she was wearing.'

Kate wasn't normally that vehement or judgemental; then again, she was very protective of her son. Which didn't surprise Dragan that much, as she was a single parent and Jem was all she had. 'Natasha's staying in the holiday cottage next to me,' he remarked.

Kate rolled her eyes. 'Oh, don't tell me *you* think she's gorgeous, too.'

'No,' Dragan said mildly.

'Good. At least one of the men around here has some common sense, then.'

'Don't be too hard on Nick. He has his faults but he has a good heart.'

Kate pulled a face. 'Well, at the moment he's acting like an *idiot*.'

There was much more to this than met the eye, Dragan was sure, but he didn't push it. He hated people interfering in his life, so he'd give Kate the space she clearly needed.

Kate grimaced again. 'Hazel, I'm sorry I'm late. Give me three minutes and I'll be ready.' She patted Dragan's arm. 'Sorry for being grouchy. Are you all right? Those photographers must be making your life hell.'

He shrugged. 'I'll survive.'

'Well, if you need to escape, you know where I am.'

He smiled ruefully. 'And then the headlines will no doubt claim I'm cheating on Melinda with you. Thanks for the support, Kate, and I really appreciate the offer—but I'm not going to put you or Jem through that.'

'With any luck they'll find someone else to bother soon.'

'With any luck,' he agreed. But he knew it was going to run for a bit longer yet—and either way he was going to come out of this badly. Either the papers would denounce him as the love rat who'd dumped the princess, or they'd denounce him as the loser who wasn't good enough for the princess and she'd dumped him.

He managed to get through the morning's calls, deflecting all speculation and questions with a smile and bringing the conversations right back to his patients' health worries, but in the afternoon he was called out to Mrs Harris, a neighbour of the Chamberlains.

'I was cycling home from my friend's when I saw her milk was still out on the front doorstep. So I went round the back and found her,' Tina explained. 'She's fallen and she says her leg hurts.'

'Don't move her,' Dragan said. 'But get a blanket and put it over her to help keep her warm. I'm on my way.' Mrs Harris was one of his patients, and he knew she had osteoporosis. The chances were she'd cracked at least one bone and she'd need X-rays and hospital treatment. St Piran Hospital was a half-hour drive away; although he could drive her there himself, given her condition it would risk making her injuries worse, and she'd find the ambulance much more comfortable. He rang through to the ambulance station and explained the situation, agreeing to call them from her house if her injuries weren't as severe as he expected.

But the examination confirmed his worst fears. 'You've broken your hip,' he said gently. 'I'm going to give you some pain relief now, but you need to be treated in St Piran.' And, given her osteoporosis, fixing the fracture could turn out to be a real problem. Not that he was going to worry her about this now. 'An ambulance is on its way.'

'Hospital? But I can't! What'll happen to Smoky?'

The cat—which was almost as elderly as Mrs Harris—was sitting in her basket. She lifted her head on hearing her name and miaowed softly.

'We could take her in and look after her until you're home again,' Tina suggested.

'That's sweet of you, love, but she's terrified of dogs. No, I'll have to stay with her.'

'You need to go to hospital, Mrs Harris,' Dragan said gently. 'You need specialist treatment, something I can't do for you here.'

'I can't leave Smoky,' Mrs Harris said stubbornly.

'Leave this with me,' Tina said, and pulled her mobile phone out of her pocket.

Dragan assumed she was going to call one of her friends and concentrated on treating Mrs Harris, examining her to make sure he hadn't missed any complications and to make sure she wasn't going into shock from loss of blood, then giving her pain relief.

It was only when the door opened and he heard a soft voice saying, 'Hello, Mrs Harris. Now, Smoky, shall we reassure your mum that we can find you somewhere nice to stay while she's in hospital?' that he realised who Tina had called.

Melinda.

Every nerve-end was aware of her. And how desperately he wanted to hold her close.

He glanced up. 'Ms Fortesque,' he said, as coolly as he could.

'Dr Lovak,' she responded, her tone equally cool.

She scooped up the cat and sat on the floor with Smoky on her lap, near enough for Mrs Harris to be able to touch her cat.

Yet more proof of why she was a brilliant vet. She understood her patients *and* their owners and she was sympathetic to both. When she left to rule Contarini, she'd leave a huge hole behind in the community as well as in his heart.

'How long will you need to stay in hospital?' Melinda asked.

'Dr Lovak says it depends on how long it takes to heal,' Mrs Harris said, her voice slightly shaky. 'Am I going to be stuck on a bed in traction?'

'Not with your hip—it's usually treated by an operation,' Dragan said. 'The ambulance is already on its way, and they'll take you to the emergency department at St Piran. They'll give you an X-ray to see what the break looks like, and then they'll decide how best to treat it. They might put a special pin in your thigh bone to fix it, or they might have to replace the head of your thigh bone with a special metal head. Or if the break is very bad, they might need to replace your hip completely. But they'll get you up on your feet again as soon as possible, walking with a frame, and as soon as they think you're able to look after yourself, they'll let you come home again.'

'They won't put me in a home?' Mrs Harris bit her lip. 'Nursing homes don't take pets, and I can't be without my Smoky.'

Dragan took her hand. 'They won't put you in a home,' he said. 'The occupational health people will come out to see you, but not to put you in a home—they'll want to see what help they can give you to make life easier, especially while you're recovering. They can fit rails and change the height of your chair to make it easier for you to get out of it.' They'd also check the flooring and the layout of the house to reduce the risk of her falling again, Dragan knew. The important thing was to make sure that Mrs Harris didn't lose any of her confidence or independence; they didn't want her ending up trapped in the house. 'And Lauren from the practice will come and see you about physiotherapy to help you get your leg working properly again.'

'Lauren's lovely—she's really kind. And don't worry about Smoky,' Melinda said. 'I know several people who don't have dogs who would be able to look after her for you until you're back.'

'And I can come in and help you with Smoky when you're home again,' Tina said. 'Mum and I will keep an eye on your bungalow until you're home, and I'll call the milkman and sort everything out for you.'

'And I'll take pictures of Smoky in her holiday home and

bring them to show you in hospital. That's the difference between Penhally and the city,' Melinda said, giving Dragan a speaking look. 'People here *care* about others.'

That one had been aimed specifically at him, he knew.

He cared all right.

But he was trying to do the right thing for Melinda's family. Putting her before his own wants.

Determined not to rise to the bait, he concentrated on reassuring Mrs Harris until the ambulance arrived, then gave a handover to the crew, telling them what he'd given her and advising them about her osteoporosis.

Tina locked up. 'I'd better get back, or Mum'll be worrying about me.'

'Thanks for all your help,' Dragan said. 'You were brilliant.'

'And I'll let you know about Smoky,' Melinda said, gently putting the cat into a travelling basket.

And then it was just the two of them.

There were dark shadows under her eyes. She'd clearly slept as badly as he had last night. 'How are you?' he asked.

'I feel as bad as you look.'

Straight and to the point. That was his Melinda.

Except she couldn't be his Melinda any more. 'I'm perfectly fine,' he lied.

'You are *such* a liar.'

He coughed. 'Isn't that the proverbial pot calling the kettle black?'

'I've already apologised for that. It was wrong of me not to tell you the truth. But what you're doing right now is just as wrong. Dragan, you know we're right together. I love you and I know you love me. Why torture us like this?'

'Because,' he said, 'sometimes you have to put your duty first.'

She shook her head. 'My future is with *you*, not in Contarini.'

'And your family? You're just going to abandon them when they need you?'

'No. There's a way through all this. We just have to find it.' She bit her lip. 'So what do I tell the press? They're expecting an official statement.'

'Tell them you're going back to Contarini.'

'No.' She looked exasperated. 'Dragan, I love you, but right now you're driving me crazy. The best way for me to protect you from the press is to give them a statement, otherwise they're going to keep following you and hounding you until you crack.'

'You said they'd go away when they realised they wouldn't get a story from me.'

She grimaced. 'They will—but they'll try their hardest to get their story first.'

'Then tell them it's over.'

'That's the thing about a newspaper story. "Who, what, where, when and why?" They've already got the who, where and when—that's us, here and now. If we give them a "what"—that we're not together—that leaves one question unanswered. "Why?" And they won't rest until they've got an answer.' She spread her hands. 'So telling them it's over is only going to make things worse. And it's also not true anyway.'

'It's *over*,' Dragan repeated.

'Look me in the eye and tell me you don't love me any more,' she challenged.

He looked away. 'I don't love you any more.'

'Yes, you do,' she said softly. 'Dragan, you're hurting both of us. I understand you're angry with me for keeping things from you. I messed up. But how long are you going to make both of us pay for my mistake?'

'It's not just that. How do I know you're not keeping anything else from me?'

'I'm not.' Her eyes narrowed. 'So you're saying you don't trust me any more?'

'Right now,' he said quietly, 'I don't know what I feel. Except mixed up. A few days ago everything was simple. Now it's a minefield. Whatever I do suddenly has all sorts of consequences. I'm in a world where I don't belong.'

'I don't belong there either.'

'You were born into it,' he reminded her. 'That is who you are.'

'No, it isn't.' She sighed. 'This is getting us nowhere. Dragan, when are you going to see—?'

His mobile phone rang, cutting into her question.

'I'm on call,' he reminded her. He glanced at the screen. 'It's the surgery.'

'A patient needs you.' She frowned. 'You'd better answer that. We'll talk about this later, when we have more time. *Ciao.*'

CHAPTER TEN

DRAGAN didn't ring Melinda that night. He didn't want another of those circular arguments; right now he needed some space. Time to think.

Bramble lay at his feet, nose on her paws, staring at the door and clearly waiting for Melinda to appear.

'I know I'm hurting you, too, and I'm sorry,' Dragan said ruefully. 'But she's not ours any more. I was stupid to let her close to us in the first place—I should've learned by now that if you let people too close, you lose them. And somehow we both need to learn to stop loving her.'

The dog blew out a breath, and continued staring at the door.

Melinda didn't ring him—clearly realising that he needed some time—and Dragan spent most of the night watching the minute hand on his alarm clock drag slowly round. When he got to the surgery the following morning, tiredness meant he wasn't in the best of tempers.

'A word,' Nick said, leaning against the doorjamb.

I'm really *not* in the mood for you this morning, Dragan thought, but forced himself to smile at the senior partner. 'What can I do for you, Nick?'

'All this royal stuff. I'm worried that it's going to affect the practice.'

'It's not going to affect the practice.' So far today the paparazzi had left the surgery alone. But that might be because they were camping outside the veterinary surgery, he thought wryly.

'I just want to make sure that nobody's going to have any problem doing their job.'

The holier-than-thou attitude stuck in Dragan's throat. And before he could stop himself, he snapped, 'I'm not the one who affects the practice by screwing up relationships with the staff.'

'What's that supposed to mean?' Nick demanded.

'Get your own house in order before you start trying to organise mine.' Dragan knew he should shut up, and shut up now—but the pent-up anger of the last few days was too much for him. 'That girlfriend of yours, Natasha, is upsetting the staff every time she expects them to be her personal secretarial service. And look at the way you behaved towards Ben and Lucy, look at how things were between you and Jack— and I bet they're not much better between you and Edward. Then there's the way you never date anyone more than half a dozen times, with the excuse that you don't want to get close to anyone after you lost Annabel.' He ignored the fact that he'd made exactly the same decision after losing his family. 'Do you really think she'd want you to live like this?' Dragan shook his head. 'You're brilliant with patients but your personal life is a complete mess, so *don't* you tell me what to do, Nicholas Tremayne.'

Nick's jaw dropped and he just stood there, clearly lost for words and looking shocked.

Probably because Dragan was always quiet and professional. Well, today he'd had enough of being quiet. He'd had enough, full stop.

'Now, if you will excuse me, I have patients to see. And we are trying to stick to our ten-minute slots, are we not?'

To Dragan's relief, Nick took the hint.

Though he also banged Dragan's door very hard as he left.

The morning surgery calmed Dragan's temper, and by the

end of his session he was feeling thoroughly guilty. He'd overstepped the mark. Big time. He checked on the computer that Nick was free, then walked across the corridor to the consulting room opposite his and knocked quietly on the door.

'Yes?' Nick snapped.

Dragan opened the door and leaned against the doorframe. 'I owe you an apology. What I said was out of order. Your personal life is none of my business.'

'Apology accepted.' Nick raised an eyebrow. 'Though it's the first time I've ever known you lose your temper.'

'I'm sorry. It was unprofessional of me.'

'It was human,' Nick said, surprising him. 'You've been under a hell of a strain these last few days. And you can't exactly go and punch one of the paparazzi or the pictures will be splashed all over the tabloids.'

'Sadly, Nick, you're absolutely right.' Dragan shrugged. 'It'll die down. I'm only sorry that it's making people's lives a bit difficult around here.'

'Hazel told me one of them had been in here the other day, giving her a hard time—and you sorted it out. Thank you.'

'It's my job,' Dragan said. He wondered if Hazel had also let slip about Kate's reaction to Natasha—a reaction that had made Dragan wonder just what the midwife's feelings were about Dr Nicholas Tremayne.

'Even so. I should've been here.'

'You weren't on call,' Dragan pointed out. 'And you were busy with, um...' He just about managed to stop himself using Kate's nickname for the woman—or the one he'd bestowed himself, Cruella De Vil.

'Going to lecture me again?' Nick asked.

'No. All I will say is that families are important. And I don't think someone that shallow and self-centred will fit in with Lucy and Ben or Jack, Alison and Freddie.'

Nick didn't correct him, Dragan noticed. So clearly he

knew what Natasha Wakefield was really like. He looked thoughtful. 'Anyone would think you have someone else in mind for me.'

Someone like Kate with her warmth and her calm, common-sense attitude towards life. Though Nick would probably deem her not glamorous enough. And it wasn't any of his business anyway. Dragan shook his head ruefully. 'With the mess I've made of my own personal life, I'm in no position to give advice.'

'I think,' Nick said wryly, 'you were right about what you said this morning. I'm not giving advice either. Except I could do with a pint and a spot of lunch—and you look as if you could do with one, too. Smugglers Inn?'

'I have house calls this afternoon,' Dragan said.

'They sell non-alcoholic beer.'

It was an olive branch. Probably one he didn't deserve. So, despite the fact it was something he wouldn't normally do—he couldn't even remember the last time he'd had lunch with Nick—Dragan nodded. 'You're on.'

'We'll look out to sea and set the world to rights. *Without* the complication of women,' Nick said.

Melinda stared at the computer screen in dismay.

Bramble was on her list of patients for the late afternoon surgery.

And although she adored the dog—she'd been the one to rescue the flatcoat retriever in the first place—right now she had a major problem with the dog's owner. He was being so pig-headed, and even though she could understand why he was behaving that way, it drove her crazy. Half a dozen times the previous night she'd picked up the phone and started to punch in his number. But every time she'd stopped part way through and replaced the receiver. Pushing him would only make him more determined. Maybe he needed time to miss her as much as she missed him—so much that it physically hurt. He'd talk to her when he was ready.

She just about managed to get through the first three cases on her list. Check-up and first vaccination for a kitten, followed by an annual booster and a check-up for a springer spaniel called Rusty who had a slight heart murmur.

'I can hear it,' she said when she removed the stethoscope from her ears, 'so I think it's upgraded to a three rather than a two, as it was last time.' Heart murmurs fell into six classifications: anything up to three was fine, but more than that needed medication.

The owner looked dismayed. 'But he hasn't seemed ill. I would've brought him in if I'd noticed anything different. He pants a bit in the evenings, but no more than he used to.'

'Any coughing?' Melinda asked.

'No.'

'OK. Just keep an eye on him—if he's panting more or he starts coughing, then we know he's struggling. You can help relieve some of the strain on his heart by keeping him on the lean side.'

'I know our last spaniel was overweight, but we've been careful not to give Rusty any snacks between meals.'

'You're doing fine,' Melinda said. 'He's not overweight at all. But being a little tiny bit lighter—say a kilogram—will make it a lot easier on his heart.' She checked the dog's teeth and ears, then made a fuss of him. 'Well, Mr Beautiful. You can take your owner home now.' She smiled up at the owner. 'You're doing a great job with him. He's a lovely, lovely dog.'

Next up was a dog who'd been limping. She showed the owner the claw that had almost curved back into the pad of the dog's foot.

'What's happened here is that this tendon doesn't work properly, so his toe's lifted up and the claw doesn't come into contact with the ground when he walks,' Melinda explained.

'You'll need to keep an eye on the toe and either bring him here for clipping, or do it yourself when you check his dew-claws.'

'Is it going to hurt?' the owner asked.

'No, it's like clipping your own fingernails—though obviously if you go too far you'll hurt him. Most of them don't like it, so I'd suggest it's a two-person job. And give him lots of praise and a reward afterwards.' She talked the owner through the procedure. 'Slip the nail into the opening here, keep reassuring him, try to distract him a bit, and—there. Done. He might limp for a day or two, but that's because he's sore from the claw going into his pad—having the nail clipped hasn't hurt him. But if you don't like the idea of doing it yourself, you can always bring him in. Just keep an eye on the claw because it needs cutting before it starts to touch the pad.'

'Thank you so much.'

And then she had to face Dragan and Bramble.

It was a real effort to be professional when all she wanted to do was run into his arms and tell him how much she missed him, how much she wanted him back.

'How are you?' she asked.

'Fine.' There was a pause. 'You?'

'What do you think?'

He didn't answer, but he looked incredibly embarrassed. Obviously he realised she was 'fine' in the same way that he was. As in *not*. Melinda wasn't sleeping, she wasn't eating, and she was as miserable as hell.

She forced herself to be professional. Bramble was, after all, her patient. 'How's Bramble? I see she's not limping as badly.'

'No.'

'Still lifting her?'

'To be on the safe side.'

Bramble's leg had been slow to heal, and then the dog had

chased after a rabbit. When Dragan had called her back, she'd skidded, twisted slightly, and then had been in such obvious pain that Melinda had X-rayed the dog and discovered the movement had loosened the pins in her leg and the bone had cracked again.

'Would you like to lift her up onto the table?'

He did so, and Melinda felt the dog's leg. 'No flinching or guarding—that's good. And the wound has healed nicely.'

Bramble licked Melinda's face, and Melinda swallowed hard. 'Ah, *bella ragazza*, I miss you, too. I miss going for walks along the harbour with you. I miss having you curled on the sofa with me while a certain person is doing paperwork. I miss feeding you scraps of chicken in the kitchen when I'm cooking and he can't see me sneaking you a treat.' She gently stroked the dog's head. 'I wonder, does he miss it, too? Does he find the bed's way too wide, that the seconds drag, that the sun's stopped shining?'

'Melinda.' Dragan's voice sounded tortured. 'Don't do this.'

So he missed her, too.

Good.

With any luck, he'd come to his senses soon and stop making both of them so miserable.

'One more X-ray, I think,' she said. She ruffled Bramble's fur. 'I know you hate needles, *carissima,* but this is just one tiny, tiny one to sedate you for the X-ray and make you comfortable.'

A second later it was done. She carried Bramble over to the X-ray area. 'I'll have the results back tomorrow.' And it was a brilliant excuse to talk to him.

'Hopefully she'll be fine and the next time you see her will be for her booster vaccination,' Dragan said.

'The next time I see her in a professional capacity, you mean.' The words were out before she could stop them. She rubbed a hand over her eyes. 'Sorry. But I miss her.' And she missed him. 'Dragan. We really need to talk about this.'

'Not here. You have a queue of patients building up.'

'After surgery, then. Are you on call tonight?'

'No. Are you?'

'Yes.' She walked over to her desk and pressed it hard. 'But, touch wood, we'll have at least some time to talk. Is half past seven good for you?'

He nodded. 'Your place or mine?'

'Neither. Let's escape from the paparazzi. You know that little pub we used to go to?' The one just outside Penhally where they'd met up in the early days of their relationship, when they had still been keeping things quiet from the village grapevine.

'OK. We'd better take separate cars,' he said. 'In case you're called out.'

'And if we both take different routes, it should put the paparazzi off our trail.'

'Fine. I'll see you then.'

For a moment she thought he was going to kiss her goodbye. He even swayed towards her. But then he pulled back without touching her. 'Thank you for seeing Bramble.'

'*Prego.*' She bit back her disappointment. She couldn't expect too much, too soon. But maybe tonight, when she'd talked to him, he'd understand. He'd hold her. And they could start taking those important steps back towards each other.

As soon as Melinda pulled into the car park that evening, she saw Dragan. He'd opened the boot of his car and was sitting on the bumper, making a fuss of Bramble.

The man she loved.

The man she wanted to be her family.

Her heart felt as if it was doing a back flip when she saw him smile at the dog. Please, please, let him smile at her again. Let things go back to how they'd been before Raffi had died.

'What can I get you?' he asked.

'In a moment. Let's walk on the beach first.'

Bramble's tail wagged madly at the word 'walk', and Dragan just about caught her before she jumped out of the car. 'Steady, girl,' he said softly.

They walked down the rocky path to the bay; once, Melinda stumbled, and Dragan automatically put a hand out to steady her. She wasn't quite sure how it happened, but then they were holding hands. And it felt so good, she wanted to cry with relief. Maybe they still had a chance. Maybe she hadn't wrecked this completely.

She didn't say a word, not wanting to break the spell and make him pull his hand away from hers. And, to her relief, the beach was deserted. Everyone was probably having their evening meal in the pub.

They stood in silence near the edge of the lapping waves, looking out to sea. When Bramble flopped onto the sand, Melinda smiled and dropped to a sitting position, tugging Dragan down with her.

Although in some respects she didn't want to break the silence, she knew they had to get this out in the open before they could move on. 'I've been thinking,' she said softly. 'I know you think I have a duty to go back. And I know you think I'm being selfish.'

'Aren't you?'

She turned to face him. 'Dragan, I know you'd give anything for the chance to be able to go home and help your family. That they came first with you. But the difference is, your family loved you right back. And they wouldn't have expected you to give up being a doctor for them.'

'I was going to be a lawyer,' he reminded her. 'And then manage the family firm.'

'But supposing you'd hated boats? Supposing you'd discovered...oh, say, that you were a brilliant artist? Your family would've encouraged you to follow your dreams. To follow your vocation, yes?'

'Yes,' he admitted.

'There's the difference. My parents never did. They only ever noticed me when they wanted me to do something for them. Right from when I was very small, I wanted to work with animals. I wanted to be a vet. And I've worked hard to make it happen.' Her jaw tightened. 'Only my *nonna* understood that. Remember I told you that my parents didn't even come to my graduation? They treat me as if I'm a spoiled child who's just playing dress-up—that this is some kind of *hobby* for me.'

He shook his head. 'You're a professional, and you're good at it. But the thing is, Melinda, there are other people who can do your job. There aren't other people who can rule Contarini.'

'Actually, there are.' She dragged in a breath. 'Do you want to know what I spent last night doing—apart from trying very hard not to come over and see you? I read the constitution of my country—I got Serena to scan it and email it to me. And there are ways around this. My father could pass an act of parliament so the title goes to his brother instead of to me. Or I could be crowned and then abdicate—and then Serena can take over, because she's next in line after me.'

'Have you asked Serena how she feels about that?'

'She was born to be queen, Dragan. She's everything Raffi and I weren't. She's diplomatic, she's good with people—'

'You're good with people,' he cut in.

Melinda shook her head. 'Not in the same way.'

'All the same, have you asked her?'

'Not *exactly*,' she admitted.

'So aren't you just doing the same as your parents? Expecting someone else to fall in with what you want?'

She felt the colour burning through her cheeks. 'I'm not being manipulative, Dragan. Of course I'll talk to Serena about it—it has to be what she wants, too. And if she does…then there's no reason why I can't stay here. With you.'

'And if she doesn't?'

'Then it's back to the drawing board. We'll think of something else.' But at least he was still holding her hand. Her fingers tightened around his. 'Is it so much to ask? Just to live my life like any other woman, be with the man who makes me feel as if I really belong somewhere for the first time I can remember?'

He was silent for a long, long time. Finally, he raised their joined hands to his mouth and kissed the back of her hand. 'I don't know. I would always put my family first, do the right thing. But, as you say, our experiences are different.' He paused. 'And I'm still trying to get my head round the fact that you didn't trust me.'

'I *do* trust you, Dragan. I just panicked—I acted with my head instead of my heart. I remembered the way people had reacted to me in the past, and although I know you're not like any of them I couldn't help myself.' She grimaced. 'The irony is now you don't trust me.'

'Can you blame me? Our whole relationship was based on secrets and lies.'

'Not lies,' she corrected. 'There was one thing I hadn't told you.'

'I'm very glad,' he said dryly, 'that you didn't call it "just one little thing". Because it was a *big* thing.'

'I know, and I'm sorry. But it was the *only* thing I didn't tell you.' She held his gaze. 'And everything else I've told you has been the truth.'

'The truth, the whole truth, and nothing but the truth?'

She smiled wryly. 'Yes. And I'd swear that in a court of law. I never wanted to hurt you, Dragan. You mean everything to me.' She swallowed hard. 'So where does that leave us?'

'This whole thing has hurt us both,' Dragan said, 'so let's just take it slowly. Get to know each other again. This time no secrets.'

'No more secrets. I promise,' she said.

'*Bene.*' He kissed the back of her hand again.

She coughed. 'Up a bit.'

He shook his head. 'Too soon. We're taking this slowly.'

'And that means what…dating?'

'It means taking it slowly and learning to trust each other,' he said, standing up and pulling her to her feet. 'Come on. Time to go back.'

CHAPTER ELEVEN

'SLOWLY' meant frustratingly slowly, Melinda discovered. She'd drafted a statement for the press, with Dragan's agreement, that they were 'just good friends'. Which meant that in Penhally they couldn't even hold hands or kiss each other goodnight. In a way, it went with Dragan's insistence on taking things slowly, getting to know each other again—but she ached for their old, more physical relationship. She missed waking up in his arms, having breakfast with him.

Well, maybe not so much breakfast.

She'd lost her appetite, and even the scent of toast had turned her stomach.

Or maybe it was her period coming. She'd always been peculiarly sensitive to smells just before—

She stopped dead.

No.

She couldn't possibly be pregnant. She and Dragan had only made love without protection that one time—the night before she'd gone back to Contarini. And it had been her safe time. Some couples tried for years and years to get pregnant; the chances of her falling pregnant on just that one night were low.

All the same, she couldn't shift the thought from her head.

Thank heaven today was Saturday and she was only working in the morning—which meant she could drive out to Newquay in the afternoon, where she could be safely anonymous. There was something she most definitely didn't want to buy in the village—the last thing she needed right now was gossip.

After surgery, she deliberately took a route through the back roads, knowing she'd be able to lose the paparazzi in the high-walled narrow lanes with all their twists and turns and little by-roads—months of living and working here meant she knew the roads so well that she no longer needed the map she kept in the glove box. Once in Newquay, she parked and browsed through a few shops, just in case she was still being followed. The second she was sure she was alone and unwatched, she bought a pregnancy test in the supermarket. The little cardboard box felt as if it was burning a hole in the boot of her car all the way back to Penhally. And she was careful to keep a very tight hold of her shopping bags when she carried them up to the flat—if she dropped them and the test spilled out, the paparazzi would go bananas.

Results in one minute. Just what she needed.

She read the instructions swiftly and did the test. And watched as the first line turned blue: good, the test was working.

And then she watched in horror as a blue line appeared in the second window.

Positive.

She was pregnant.

Expecting Dragan's child.

Oh, *Dio*.

Two weeks ago, if someone had told her she and Dragan were going to have a baby, she would have been shocked but delighted. But now life was a whole lot more complicated. Her relationship with Dragan still wasn't quite what it had been before she'd returned to Contarini, and she wasn't sure how he'd take the news. Would it make things right between them again when he learned that they were going to have their own family?

And then there were her parents. She had no idea how they would react to the news. Would her mother be like a normal grandmother, forgive everything the second she held the warm weight of the baby and breathed in that special newborn scent? Or would her parents decide she was bringing shame on her royal lineage—for being pregnant and unmarried?

And when the press found out about this they'd have a field day.

She needed to tell Dragan first.

But she needed to know for sure before she told him. Because this would really rock his world—they hadn't talked about having children, so she had no idea how he'd react. Delight at the idea of having a family of his own again? Or would it send him running scared?

She had to take this carefully.

Maybe the test was wrong. Maybe she'd done something incorrectly.

Luckily she'd bought a double pack. She drank water. Lots of it. Repeated the test. And watched the two blue lines slowly, slowly appear.

OK. Definitely pregnant. But *how* pregnant?

There was one person who might be able to tell her. One of her best friends in the village was a midwife: and Melinda knew Chloe would be discreet. She dialled the number. It rang and rang, and Melinda was just about to give up when she suddenly heard a familiar voice. 'Hello?'

'Chloe? It's Melinda. Um, are you busy?'

'Nothing I can't can a break from. Are you all right?'

'Ye-es. I don't really want to talk about this on the phone.'

'Got you. I'll be there in a minute.'

'You're wonderful. Thanks. I'll put the kettle on.'

But when Chloe arrived and noticed that Melinda was drinking water rather than coffee, she raised an eyebrow. 'This isn't just a girly chat, is it?'

'No,' Melinda admitted. 'Though can you promise me you won't say a word to anyone?'

Chloe's eyes widened. 'Of course I won't! Apart from patient confidentiality, you know I'm not like that.'

Melinda winced. 'I'm sorry. I know you won't. I didn't mean to...to make you feel bad. It's just this paparazzi thing getting to me and my mouth isn't acting in synch with my brain.' She dragged in a breath. 'I'm pregnant, Chloe.'

'Are you sure? When's the baby due?'

'I don't know. That's what I was hoping you might be able to tell me.'

'When was your last period?' Chloe asked.

'Two weeks ago.'

'Then you can't be pregnant, Melinda—you're only halfway through your cycle.'

'That's what I thought. But lately I've been feeling as if I want to howl my eyes out—and I've never been the leaky tap type.'

'You're under a lot of stress right now,' Chloe reminded her, 'what with your brother dying and these photographers following you about. It's not surprising you want to cry.'

'And I've been feeling sick. And I'm off my food.'

'Also symptoms of stress,' Chloe said calmly.

'And my sense of smell—it's much stronger than usual.' Melinda grimaced. 'The thing is, Dragan and I... We took a risk once. The day before I went to Contarini. So I did a pregnancy test, just in case.'

'And?'

Melinda took the test sticks from the worktop and handed them to her friend in silence.

Chloe stared at them. 'These are just as reliable as the ones I can do, so that's pretty conclusive.' She took Melinda's hand and squeezed it. 'Well. Congratulations.'

'I hope. Things still aren't that good between me and Dragan. We're taking it slowly.' Melinda swallowed hard.

'And you know what they say about people having a baby to patch up a relationship. It never works.'

'Firstly, that's not why you're having this baby. And, secondly, Dragan loves you. He's just a bit...well...mixed up at the moment. Not that I've said anything to him.'

Chloe was a total sweetheart and she'd never interfere, Melinda knew.

'I need to tell him. But not until I know for sure how pregnant I am.'

Chloe looked thoughtful. 'Your last period...was it lighter than usual?'

'Yes.' Melinda frowned. 'Now I come to think of it, the last two were a bit light.'

'Some women have a very light bleed for the first couple of months—it's all to do with hormones settling down,' Chloe said, 'so you could be three months gone already. Did you have any spotting before the first light period?'

'I'm really not sure. Why?' Melinda went cold. 'Does that mean there's a problem?'

'No, it just happens sometimes as the egg implants into the lining of the womb,' Chloe explained. 'Nothing to worry about at all.'

'Can you do a scan?'

'We don't have the equipment at the surgery. You'll have to go to St Piran for the ultrasound,' Chloe said. 'I can get you an appointment—and because you're not sure of your dates and you might be three months already, they'll fit you in pretty quickly. I'll ring first thing on Monday morning and book you in—that is, if you want me to be your midwife?'

Melinda hugged her. 'I'd *love* you to be my midwife— you're one of my best friends and I know I'll be in safe hands. Thank you, Chloe. I really appreciate this.'

'Hey. That's what friends are for.' Chloe hugged her back. 'Don't worry. Everything's going to be fine.'

Maybe.

But Melinda still felt the prickle of doubt all the way down her spine.

No more secrets.

Guilt flooded through Melinda. But this wasn't a secret, exactly. Nobody knew, apart from Chloe—who wouldn't say a word. Melinda was going to tell Dragan as soon as she knew when the baby was due. She'd make sure the time and the place were right—and she'd tell him.

But even so, she found herself picking at her meal when she went to a restaurant not far from Penhally with him on Sunday night.

And he noticed.

'Are you all right?' he asked.

'Just not that hungry,' she prevaricated, pushing her plate away. 'Sorry. I'm just a bit tired.'

'I'll pay the bill, then walk you back.'

It wasn't exactly far. Just round the corner.

'Do you want to come in for a coffee?' she asked.

'Better not.' He moved his head very slightly in the direction of the photographer who was loitering in view of the door to her flat, reminding her that they were being watched.

It was a good thing, in a way, she thought. The smell of coffee really made her feel sick. But she missed the old days when Dragan would have carried her up the stairs to her bed. Or to his.

'Dragan…' She stopped. No, now wasn't the time or the place.

'What?'

'Nothing. Just I'm sorry I'm not good company tonight.'

'Still not heard from Serena?' he asked softly.

'Yes. But there's nothing to tell. *Papà* seems OK with the

idea of finding an alternative solution, but *Mamma*...' Melinda shook her head in exasperation.

Dragan smiled. 'Could this be where you get your stubbornness?'

'Very funny. I'm nothing like her.' But she smiled back. 'So do I get a kiss goodnight?'

'"Just good friends" don't kiss each other goodnight,' he reminded her softly. 'And we've already talked long enough for that photographer to get very interested. He's just moved a bit closer.'

An added pressure on their relationship she could well do without. She sighed. 'Goodnight, then.'

'Goodnight.'

He waited while she unlocked the door, then smiled at her. 'Get some sleep. You'll feel better tomorrow.'

True. Once she had a date for her scan. And once she'd had the scan itself, it would be even better. 'I have a day off tomorrow.'

'Sleep in. It'll do you good,' he advised. 'I'll call you in the morning.'

Melinda had just stepped out of the shower the following morning when the phone shrilled.

She wrapped a towel around herself and hurried to answer it. Dragan? Or was it Chloe, with the news of the appointment? 'Hello?'

'Melinda, just *what* is all this about?' Viviana asked crisply.

Melinda grimaced when she heard her mother's voice. She really wasn't in the mood for another fight. 'Serena's already told you. We worked it out between us.'

'I don't mean that. The *headlines*, child,' Viviana said impatiently.

'What headlines?'

'You know very well which ones.'

'*Mamma*, I haven't seen a newspaper this morning.'

'How long have you known that you are pregnant?' her mother snapped.

'I…' Melinda was suddenly, horribly awake, as if someone had thrown a bucket of icy-cold water over her. 'Pregnant?'

'Unless the headlines are untrue, in which case we will be suing for libel.'

'But…' Melinda dragged in a breath. 'I don't understand how they could possibly know. I only found out myself the day before yesterday.'

'So you *are* pregnant? How *could* you be so stupid?' Viviana demanded.

Melinda put a protective hand on her abdomen. So much for Viviana being a delighted grandmother.

'Unmarried and pregnant by a Croatian refugee!' Viviana made an exclamation of contempt. 'Well, you have your wish. We cannot *possibly* crown you queen of Contarini now. Even if you get rid of the baby, the scandal will stick to you and damage the monarchy. I thought Raffi was the reckless one, but you—you have gone even further!'

No 'How are you feeling?', Melinda thought. No 'When's the baby due?'. No 'How's the morning sickness?'. No interest in anything except the wretched monarchy.

Exactly the same way it had been for her entire life.

'As far as we are concerned,' Viviana said, 'you are no longer our daughter.'

Melinda blinked. Had she just heard that right? 'You're disowning me?'

'Given how little loyalty you have shown to us, why do you sound so surprised?' Viviana said scornfully. 'You are no longer part of our family. And I wish you well with your Croatian *refugee*.' She spat the word as if it were an insult. And then she hung up.

Melinda stared at the phone in disbelief.

Her family had just disowned her.

And then something really horrible occurred to her.

If her mother had seen the papers... She had to reach Dragan before he saw them. She had to tell him the news before the paparazzi scooped her.

She glanced at the clock. Half past eight. Would he still be at home? Please, please don't let him have left for the surgery yet. She called his mobile.

'The mobile phone you are calling is switched off. Please leave a message or send a text.'

She couldn't tell him the news by voicemail! 'Dragan? It's Melinda. If you pick this up before I speak to you, please ring me urgently. I need to talk to you. It's really, really important.' She hung up and tried the surgery number.

Engaged.

As it always was at this time on a Monday—the rush time after the weekend, when people who'd been feeling rough over the weekend rang to get an appointment to see the doctor.

Well, she'd redial as many times as she had to until she got through.

And she'd have to hope that she caught him before his first appointment.

The waiting room was practically silent.

This definitely wasn't normal, Dragan thought. People usually chatted to each other; Penhally was a warm, friendly place, and the surgery here wasn't the inner city waiting rooms full of silent strangers avoiding each other's eyes.

'What's happened?' he asked.

'Nothing,' Hazel mumbled, but she wouldn't look him in the eye.

'Have the press been harassing you again?'

She shook her head.

He glanced round at the waiting room; people shuffled in

their seats and looked away. But the second he looked back at Hazel, he was aware of people staring at him. 'Why is everyone staring at me?' he asked softly.

She looked really embarrassed, and handed him the newspaper in silence.

The headline on the front page screamed at him: THE DOCTOR'S ROYAL LOVE-CHILD

And suddenly he couldn't breathe.

It took a huge effort and every bit of concentration he possessed to walk into his consulting room. He stared at the page and read it over and over again, but he couldn't take the words in.

Melinda was pregnant.

With his child.

And once again the press knew all about it before he did.

Why the hell hadn't she told him?

So much for her promise of no more secrets.

She'd lied to him yet again.

Or was this some elaborate bluff, some excuse to get her out of being the queen of Contarini?

Or—even worse—had she planned the whole thing? Was this why she'd asked him to make love to her without protection the night before she'd gone away, knowing what her family would ask of her? She'd been so emphatic about it being her safe time. Had it been yet another layer of lies? Had she deliberately tried to get pregnant by a man she knew her family would never accept?

Feeling used and angry—and convinced now that Melinda had never really loved him at all—he picked up his mobile phone and speed-dialled her number.

It was engaged.

Great. Just great. His world had been turned upside down and shaken like a child's snowglobe, and he couldn't even talk to her about it.

To hell with the paparazzi and playing nice. He wanted answers. If he had to kick her door down to get them, he damned well would. Grimly, he keyed in a short message—a message he knew would get a reaction—and sent it to her mobile phone.

He flicked the intercom to let Hazel know he was ready for his first patient.

And then, after surgery, he'd have it out with Melinda.

CHAPTER TWELVE

'I'M SORRY, Melinda, he's with a patient,' Hazel informed her. 'Oh, and congratulations, by the way.'

Oh, no.

Oh, no, no, *no*.

If Hazel knew, that meant everyone in the surgery knew.

Including Dragan.

She was way, way too late.

And he was going to be so hurt and angry because he was the last one to know. After she'd promised him no more secrets, too—just to rub salt into his wounds.

But how on earth had the paparazzi found out?

'Thank you,' she muttered. 'Um, could you tell him I called?'

'Of course, love. And I've got this lovely pattern for a little matinee jacket—I'll knit you some in lemon and white. Because we don't know if you're having a girl or a boy yet, do we?'

'Thank you, Hazel. That's very kind.' It was a real effort to chat and be nice when all she wanted to do right now was get off the phone.

Her mobile phone beeped, telling her that someone had sent her a text.

'Um, Hazel, I won't hold you up because I know how busy the surgery is on a Monday morning,' she said quickly.

'Well, I'm sure I'll see you soon, dear,' Hazel said.

With relief, Melinda said goodbye, hung up and switched to the message.

New message from Dragan flashed onto the screen.

She flicked into the message. It was very short and to the point. *No more secrets?*

Even though a text message was just words and it was impossible to tell the sender's tone, she knew from his choice of words that he was absolutely livid. And she couldn't blame him: this was news he should have heard from her and nobody else.

He'd be hurt, too. Because she'd let him down. She'd promised him no more secrets—and then this had happened.

But she'd tried to get hold of him. Hadn't he heard her message?

Maybe his voicemail was having problems. She'd text him instead. And Hazel was bound to tell him that she'd phoned, so he would at least know she'd tried to get hold of him.

Sorry, not meant to be like this. We need to talk. Please call me.

She had no idea when he'd pick up the message. Maybe during his break or at the end of surgery—and despite the fact that consultations were only supposed to take ten minutes, Dragan never rushed his patients. Sometimes his surgery overran slightly, cutting into his lunch-break, and he'd been known to fit in extra patients, too, not wanting them to have to wait until the next surgery.

Wait.

Ha.

All she could do right now was *wait*.

She didn't dare venture outside. Given that the press had the news of her pregnancy, the place was probably crawling with paparazzi, and she really didn't feel up to answering questions. But there was another call she had to make.

She rang the surgery. 'Hi, Rachel, it's Melinda. Is George around?'

'He's just finishing with a patient. Want me to grab him before his next appointment and get him to ring you?' the receptionist asked.

'Yes, please. Is, um, is everything OK down there?'

'We had a few people in but George got rid of them,' Rachel said. 'Are *you* all right, Melinda?'

No. Far from it. 'Yes,' she lied.

Five minutes later, George called her back. 'This is getting to be a bit of a habit,' she said wryly. 'And I apologise. I take it you've seen the papers today?'

'Yes.'

'Things are a bit messy,' she said.

He laughed. 'We've got siege conditions outside. I hope you've got your blackout curtains up.'

'George, I would've told you. But I only found out myself two days ago. I don't even know when the baby's due. I'm waiting for my ultrasound appointment.'

'It's all right,' he reassured her. 'Legally, you don't have to tell me yet anyway. But I'm glad I do know, because I need to make sure your job conditions are suitable.'

'I'm a vet, George. And the surgery's just had a refit.'

'Not *those* sorts of conditions. In our profession, you know as well as I do there are cases you need to avoid during pregnancy on health and safety grounds. So there are some rules, and they're not breakable under any circumstances. Number one, you don't go anywhere near lambs; number two, you're meticulous about hygiene; and, number three, you wear gloves if you go anywhere near a cat. Understood?'

'I know. Because of the risks of chlamydophilia, listeria and toxicarosis.' Organisms that could all be harmful to unborn babies—and to their mothers.

'Exactly. You don't take any risks. You don't take any of my calls to large animals. And if there's a heavy animal in the surgery that needs to be up on the table, you get help—you *don't* do the lifting yourself. Got it?'

'Got it,' she said.

'Good. Now, try and get some rest today. Everyone in the practice is under instructions to say "No comment" to just about anything. But if you need anything, you just tell us. Rachel can nip out to the shops for you if you need something and she can bring it in to you through the back.'

'George, you're a wonderful man and I don't deserve you as a boss. I owe you your body weight in chocolate,' she said feelingly.

'I might just take you up on that,' he teased. 'Still, at least your other half's a doctor. He'll keep a good eye on you.'

'Mmm.' Though right now she wasn't too sure Dragan was still her other half. Far from the baby drawing them closer together, overcoming the last hurdles between them, the news could be the thing to shatter their relationship for good.

She waited all morning. And finally, at lunchtime, Dragan called her. His voice was like ice when he said, 'It isn't very nice discovering through the newspapers that you're going to be a father.'

'I'm sorry. It wasn't supposed to happen that way.' She hadn't even begun to think how she'd tell him, but she'd never intended him to find out like this. She sighed. 'Look, I really don't want to talk about this over the phone. Can I see you?'

'With all the paparazzi swarming round? The surgery's besieged.'

'It's bad here, too.'

'I doubt if we can both give them the slip. So it's the phone or risking more speculation. Your choice.'

'Believe me, *you* won't be the one in the news tomorrow,' she said dryly. 'That will be me. And then, as an ex-princess, I'll cease to be news and they'll go away.'

'Ex-princess? What do you mean, ex-princess?'

'I'll explain when I see you.' She swallowed hard. 'So do I come over to you or are you coming here?'

'I'll come over.'

The few minutes it took to walk from the surgery to the vet's felt like hours. Cars were parked everywhere—including on the double yellow lines—and people were shouting at him.

'Congratulations, Dr Love-ak!'

Lord, how he hated the way they'd mangled his name for the headlines.

'How does it feel to be a soon-to-be dad?'

How the hell should he know? He hadn't really had time to take it in.

'Are you going to be king of Contarini?'

Absolutely *not*.

'Give us a smile!'

Yeah, right.

He resolutely ignored them. And he wasn't leading them to Melinda's back door either; he walked through the front door into the vet's.

'Dr Lovak!' Rachel looked up from the reception desk at him, surprised. 'I didn't think Bramb— Oh.' Her voice tailed off as she realised that, for once, the dog wasn't with him.

At least there were no paparazzi here; he knew everyone in the waiting room. Though the sympathetic smiles mixed with speculative looks made him uncomfortable. He lowered his voice. 'Can I nip through the back way to Melinda's? I want to avoid the posse outside.' He raised an eyebrow. 'How did you manage to keep them out?'

'George told them the next person to step inside was the one who'd help him sort out the next gelding, with no anaesthetic—and he'd be standing between the stallion's back legs, holding the relevant bits.'

Despite his anger, Dragan couldn't help smiling back at her. 'George has quite a way with words.' Not to mention that he was the same height as Dragan and much broader in the shoulders—if he drew himself up to his full height he could look very intimidating. 'Maybe I should take a leaf out of his book. I could borrow an epidural kit from Kate and threaten them with the syringe.'

'Ah, but then they'd have your picture all over the front page, captioned "Doctor Doom" or something like that,' Rachel said.

'Which might be marginally better than Dr *Love*-ak.' He grimaced. 'Thanks, Rachel.'

He went through the back of the surgery to the lobby, which also contained the door to Melinda's flat, and knocked on the door.

When she answered, he could see how pale and unhappy she looked—and although his first instinct was to wrap her in his arms and hold her close and tell her everything would be all right, he held back.

Because he was extremely angry with her. For keeping this from him. For letting him find out something important through the press yet again. What else had she kept from him? All the secrets and lies... He didn't want a life based on that, and he was beginning to realise that that was exactly what he'd get with Melinda. A life of subterfuge. Of keeping the stiff upper lip she'd once teased him of developing. And he really, really didn't want that. He didn't want their love for each other chipped away until he began to resent her and she started to despise him.

Without comment, Melinda stood aside and beckoned him in. She closed the door and followed him up the stairs.

Ah, hell.

Last time he'd been in this flat with her, he'd made love with her. Had that been the night they'd made the baby?

He clenched his fists. Why had it all had to go so wrong? Why did life have to be so bloody complicated?

'So when were you going to tell me?' he asked.

'I only found out myself on Saturday afternoon.'

'You saw me last night. Why didn't you tell me then?'

'Because I don't know how pregnant I am. I wanted to wait until I knew the due date.'

He shook his head. 'I don't understand. No more secrets, you said. So how come the press knew?'

'I have no ide—' Her voice faded, and he could see the worry on her face.

'What?' he asked suspiciously.

'Chloe wouldn't have said a word. So they must have gone through my bin and found the test kit or the packaging. *Dio.* I can't believe I was so stupid. What was I thinking?'

It took a moment for her comment to penetrate his brain. 'Hang on. *Chloe* knows? You told *Chloe* before you told *me*?'

'I needed professional advice,' Melinda defended herself. 'And apart from being a midwife, she's one of my best friends.'

'Don't you think that the baby's father should have been the first to know?'

'What was I supposed to tell you? I'm pregnant but I have no idea *how* pregnant?'

'I'm a GP, for pity's sake.' He stared at her. 'Don't you think *I* could've helped you?'

'I'm not your patient—and it's not ethical for you to treat me.'

'*You're* pulling me up on ethics?'

'I didn't mean it like that! I'm sorry.' She raked a hand through her hair. 'Look, I needed time to get used to the idea before I told you.'

Being pregnant was a huge life change, and of course she needed time to get used to the idea. And if she hadn't been Princess Melinda, it wouldn't have mattered. She would have had that time, and it wouldn't have been spread all over the press before she was ready to talk to him.

Though he was still hurt that she'd told Chloe first. And there was the issue with the scan: she was pregnant with their baby, and she hadn't asked him to go to the dating scan with her, as any normal man would want to do. It felt as if she'd pushed him out—that they were making a new family between them and she'd cut him off before he had a chance to be part of it.

'So what are you planning to do? About the baby, I mean?' When she didn't answer immediately, he continued, 'That is, I assume there really *is* a baby? It's not just a way of forcing your parents' hand?'

He regretted the question the second he'd asked it, because her face lost all colour.

'I can't believe you just said that.' Her voice was a cracked whisper.

'There have been so many secrets and lies flying about, I don't know what's true and what's not any more.'

She swallowed hard. 'I'm pregnant, Dragan. I did the test twice. Just to be sure. But I don't know when the baby's due—Chloe thinks I might be as much as three months already.' A muscle twitched in the side of her cheek. 'She's got me an ultrasound appointment for next week. She's coming with me.'

'It didn't occur to you that *I* might want to go with you?'

'For pity's sake, Dragan. You've kept me practically at arm's length since I came back from Contarini. I didn't know what to think, how you'd react. We never talked about having kids—I don't know whether being a dad is going to bring back all the memories of your family and make you unhappy, or whether you're pleased, or what.'

'So you're blaming me?'

'No, of course I'm not! I'm trying to work out what's in

your head, and failing miserably.' She groaned. 'This is all going hideously, hideously wrong.'

'It's not very nice from this side of the fence either.'

'No? Well, you try being pregnant and completely on your own.' She glared at him. 'Not only does my baby's father doubt every single word I say, my family have disowned me.'

He remembered what she'd said about being an ex-princess. 'What do you mean, they've disowned you?'

'My mother saw the papers this morning. So that's how I found out the press knew. She rang me when I was in the shower. And as from this morning I'm no longer part of the Contarini royal family,' she said dryly.

'I suppose that solves one of your problems, then. If you're no longer Princess Melinda, they can't make you rule Contarini.'

She stared at him. 'Are you suggesting I did this *deliberately*?'

Had she? Right now, he really didn't know. He didn't have a clue what was going on in her head. 'I remember a certain night when you talked me out of using a condom.'

Melinda flinched. 'Apart from the fact I'm almost certainly more than a couple of weeks pregnant... If you can believe that of me, then I suggest you leave. Right now. Because I'd rather bring up our child on my own than be with someone who has such a low opinion of me.'

Memories of his family flashed before his eyes. How his older brother had planned to marry his childhood sweetheart. The way his parents had talked about having grandchildren, reliving their memories of their own children with such happiness. The nursery furniture his brother and father were going to build together. His own role in the family as best man and godfather and uncle.

All gone, because his brother had died before the wedding could take place.

And now Melinda was putting a barrier between him and their child. He'd lost his new family before it had even begun.

'I can't deal with this,' Dragan said, and walked out. Before the bitterness in his throat choked him.

CHAPTER THIRTEEN

MELINDA spent the next few days as if she were in a trance. As she'd expected, the headlines were screaming about the royal vet being kicked out of the monarchy. But that would die down soon enough—at least now she had one less problem to deal with.

The only saving grace of that particular mess had been the call from her younger sister. 'Lini? It's me. I've just seen the papers and I could murder our mother! I've told her that, whatever happens, I still love you and you will always be my sister. And I've also told *Mamma* exactly what I think of her behaviour.' Serena's tone was caustic. 'She wanted to know if you'd taught me the swear words I used.'

'Oh, no.'

Serena laughed. 'I told her that I'd been the one to teach them to Raffi, actually, and she went off to get the smelling salts, muttering about how disgraceful my generation is. She's going to be in for a shock when *Papà* hands over to me, because I'm dragging Contarini into the twenty-first century, whether it likes it or not.' She paused. 'Well, I'm looking forward to being an auntie. And to meeting your Dragan properly.'

Melinda swallowed hard. 'You've seen the papers. I don't think he is my Dragan any more.'

'Don't be silly. Of course he is. I remember everything that you told me while you were over here. It's obvious that you love him and he loves you.'

'It's not as simple as that.'

'Everything's simple,' Serena said crisply. 'People just think too hard and then they complicate things. He loves you and you love him. You're expecting his baby. The only thing that was standing in your way was the monarchy. And now that hurdle's gone, there's no reason for you not to be together.'

'He walked out on me, Rena.'

'So you had a fight. Patch it up. Don't be too proud about it,' Serena counselled softly. 'Go and see him. Tell him how you really feel about him.'

'Maybe.'

'Stop messing about and just *do* it.'

'Hey, you're not queen yet. You can't order me around,' Melinda said, trying to keep it light.

'I can try.' Serena's voice grew serious. 'Lini, I meant what I said. Just forget what *Mamma* said. It's not true. You'll always be my sister. And I'll always be there for you—just as you've always been there for me. If it wasn't for you, I'd never be able to do this job, because you're the one who's shown me I can do anything if I try. Look at you—you left home at eighteen and went to study in a foreign country. And veterinary science is hard enough in Italian, let alone in a different language. So you showed me how to reach for the stars—how something might seem impossible but I could do it if I tried hard enough.'

'I really am going to cry now.'

'Don't. Call Dragan and tell him you love him. And when you get the first picture from the scan, if you don't send me a copy right away I'll have you chucked in the palace dungeons.'

'Noted, Your Highness,' Melinda said.

Serena just laughed. 'Don't think I don't mean it. Look, I have to go, *cara*. But you call me if you need me, OK?'

'I will. And thank you, Rena. I thought...' Melinda choked back the words.

'You think too much. Now go and do as your sovereign-to-be orders.'

But Dragan wasn't answering his phone. Melinda assumed that he was out somewhere with Bramble. But the longer she left it, the harder it was to make the call, until she didn't make it at all.

Work kept her busy the next day.

And then she had a callout to the caravan park. There had been a dogfight, and one of the animals had been badly bitten. 'I know I should've told them to bring the dog down here,' Rachel said, 'but the girl was hysterical.'

'OK. I can always bring the dog back myself, if need be,' Melinda said.

But when she pulled in to the caravan park, she recognised one of the other cars in the car park. Dragan's. Rachel could have warned her that a doctor had been called out, too.

Well, Penhally wasn't that big a place. She'd have to face him some time. May as well be now. She lifted her chin, straightened her spine and went over to where he was treating a teenage boy whose arm was bloodstained. Next to him, a girl was on her knees beside an elderly Yorkshire terrier lying on a picnic blanket, stroking its head and crying her eyes out.

Dragan looked at her, unsmiling.

She might not want to talk to him on a personal level, but she'd show him she could be professional. 'Dr Lovak,' she said, giving him a cool nod of acknowledgement.

'Ms Fortescue,' he responded.

'I'm Melinda, the vet,' she said to the girl. 'You're Colleen, who rang about your dog?'

The girl nodded. 'My mum's going to *kill* me,' she quavered.

'What happened?'

'I was taking Bruiser for a walk. Except I wasn't looking after him properly.' She flushed. 'I was talking to Micky.'

Micky being the boy with the bloody arm. Clearly a holiday romance, Melinda thought with a pang. One that the poor girl would remember for all the wrong reasons.

Without meaning to, she caught Dragan's eye. And she could see from his expression that he was thinking exactly the same thing.

It was a mess.

Just like their relationship.

'And this dog came out of nowhere,' Micky said. 'It attacked Bruiser. And when I tried to get it off him it bit me, too.'

'Micky was so brave.' Colleen sniffed.

'Where's the other dog now?' Melinda asked.

'The police have got it,' Micky said. 'It ought to be put down.'

'Make sure the police have your details—and that they've made a note on the Dog Bite Register. That way, if that dog routinely attacks other dogs, they can do something about it. Now, let me have a look at Bruiser here.' She dropped to her knees and let the dog sniff her hands for reassurance that she wasn't going to hurt him, then gently examined the dog. 'There's one pretty nasty bite here. Are all his vaccinations up to date, Colleen?'

The girl nodded.

'That's one good thing. How old is he?'

'Nine. We got him when I was six.'

'OK.' Gently, she cleaned the wounds, talking to the dog and reassuring him as she did so—just as Dragan was irrigating the boy's wounds. Again, she couldn't help glancing at him, and discovered him looking straight at her, his expression unreadable.

He looked away first. 'I'm going to need to take you back to the surgery, Micky,' Dragan said. 'I need to give you some antibiotics, just to make sure there was nothing nasty in the dog's bite.'

'I'm going to need to give Bruiser antibiotics, too,' Melinda said. 'And I'm not going to stitch the wounds closed because there's more of a risk of infection with puncture wounds.'

'Same with you, Micky,' Dragan said. 'I'm going to cover your wounds with a light dressing, and you'll need to come back to me in a couple of days for stitches.'

'Snap,' Melinda said to Colleen with a smile.

'Is Bruiser going to be all right?' she asked. 'He's not going to die?'

'He's going to be a bit sore for a few days. And you need to keep an eye on him—if you notice anything unusual about his breathing or if he seems hot or uncomfortable, call me straight away.' She gave the girl one of the practice business cards. 'So where's your mum?'

'She's gone shopping in the village.'

'OK. When she gets back, ask her to ring me and I'll explain. It wasn't your fault that Bruiser was attacked. If she'd been with you, it would still have happened,' Melinda reassured the girl.

'You probably saved the dog's life,' Dragan told Micky. 'Though next time you might find a bucket of water's more effective and less painful for you in breaking up a fight. Better let your parents know where you're going—I'll drop you back here when I've sorted the antibiotics.'

'Are you all right?' Melinda asked Colleen.

The girl nodded and continued to stroke the dog. 'I'm just so sorry he got hurt.'

Yeah. Melinda knew how that felt. Again, she glanced at Dragan—and met his unfathomable dark gaze.

'It'll work out,' she said to Colleen.

Though she was none too sure if the situation between her and Dragan could be fixed. They'd worked as a team here, sorting out a problem. He was a brilliant doctor and she knew she was good at her job, too. They were both good at reassuring others. So why couldn't they reassure themselves?

She had no idea where they went from here. All she knew was that she missed him. And she had to find a way to get through to him, to prove to him that she loved him and she'd never hurt him again.

Later that evening George rang her, sounding anxious. 'Melinda? When's your dating scan again?'

'Wednesday afternoon.'

'And you're not sure just how pregnant you are.'

Ice trickled down her spine. There had to be a reason why he was asking. And from the tone of his voice, it was a serious reason. 'Why?'

'You know when you helped me at Polkerris Farm when lambing went mad a few weeks back?'

'Ye-es.' Usually Melinda dealt with the small-animal work at the practice, but that particular week there had been more lambs than George could deal with on his own, and she'd gone over to the farm to help him out.

'I asked you before we started if there was any possibility you were pregnant, and you said no.'

'I didn't think I was.'

George dragged in a breath. 'Then you need to see your midwife and ask her to do some tests.'

Melinda's mouth felt almost too stiff to move. 'You're telling me that some of the ewes are losing their lambs?'

'It's definitely EAE.' EAE stood for enzootic abortion in ewes, and it was every sheep farmer's worst nightmare at lambing time. The infection could also be transferred to humans, so pregnant women were advised to avoid all contact with lambs, ewes who were lambing and even the boots and clothes of people who'd been involved in lambing.

'I'm taking samples,' George said. He paused. 'Look, is there anyone who can be with you?'

Dragan.

No. Not after this afternoon. His coldness had made his feelings clear. 'I'll ring Chloe.'

'Do that. And actually she's probably the best person to give you advice. Let me know how things go—and if there's anything you need, you only have to say, OK?'

'I will. Thank you, George.'

Melinda cut the connection and pressed the speed-dial button for Chloe's number. Please, be there, she begged silently. Please be there.

The phone rang.

And rang.

And rang.

By the time it was finally picked up, Melinda was frantic. 'Chloe? It's Melinda. Can I come over? Please?'

'Melinda?'

What was Dragan doing at Chloe's place? And why was he answering her phone?

She must have asked the questions out loud because he said, 'You didn't call Chloe. You called *me*.'

It must've been her subconscious dialling the wrong number. Because when George had broken the news, she'd wanted Dragan with her so badly.

'What's wrong?' he asked.

She'd tried so hard to be strong. But hearing him sound so warm, so concerned—the way he used to be—was too much for her. She couldn't handle this, not when they weren't together any more. The weight of all that had happened suddenly hit her. She dropped the phone and sobbed.

Three minutes later her doorbell rang. As if someone was leaning on it. Hard. And it didn't stop ringing until she stumbled down the stairs and opened the door.

He closed the door behind him and wrapped his arms round her. 'It's all right. Calm down. Deep breaths. It's OK.'

Sobs racked her.

'Is it the baby?' he asked.

'N-no. Y-yes.' She couldn't get the words out.

'Are you bleeding?'

'N-no. It's…it's…'

'All right, *carissima*. I'm here. I've got you.' And he lifted her bodily, cradling her against him with one hand under her knees and the other supporting her back.

Just as if he were carrying her over the threshold.

Which wasn't going to happen.

She shivered, even more miserable now—wanting him to go away and yet wanting him close at the same time.

This was all such a mess.

And if she lost the baby…

He gently placed her on the sofa and disappeared for a couple of moments, returning with a glass of water. 'Here. Small sips. Slowly.' When her breathing had slowed, he stroked her face. 'Now tell me what's wrong.'

She dragged in a breath. 'I've been exposed to EAE.'

He frowned. 'I thought you only did the small-animals side?'

'I do. But George was run ragged, so I helped him out on Polkerris Farm. He just called to tell me…' She shuddered. 'He says the flock's got EAE.'

'And when was this that you helped out?'

'A few weeks back. There wasn't any sign of it then.' She shook her head. 'And George asked me if I was pregnant before I started helping. I said no—because I didn't think I was. I swear I had no idea. I would never, ever risk our baby like that.'

'I know you wouldn't.' He held her close. 'First we need to take a blood sample for testing. Has Chloe booked you in yet, done the usual tests?'

'No. We were going to do that just before the scan.'

'Right. Well, we can sort that out now. And we need to find out just how pregnant you are. Right now I'd say try not to panic because there's a very good chance everything's going to be fine.' He shifted her very slightly so he could retrieve his mobile phone from his pocket, then dialled a number and waited. 'Maternity department, please.'

Clearly he was ringing St Piran Hospital.

'Hello? It's Dr Dragan Lovak from Penhally. I have a pregnant mum who's been exposed to EAE, but we're not sure of her dates. Yes, a few weeks back. No, no bloods or scans yet. That's great. Forty minutes? That'd be perfect. Thank you so much. Yes. Her name's Melinda Fortesque. Thank you.' He cut the connection and looked at Melinda. 'They're going to give you a scan to check your dates, and do the blood test. It's a half-hour drive from here to St Piran, so you've got time to wash your face if you want.' Then he went all inscrutable on her. 'Would you rather someone else took you? Shall I call Chloe?'

'No.' She wanted him. Though right now she didn't want to move: she was in his arms, just where she belonged.

'All right. Wash your face while I go and get my car.'

'What about the press?'

Dragan said something in Croatian that she couldn't translate but she was pretty sure it was extremely rude. 'You're more important,' he said.

She dragged in a breath. 'Thank you. It's more than I deserve after the way I've treated you.' Yes, he'd walked out on her, but she'd told him to leave. And she'd kept him in the dark about too many things.

He made no comment.

'We can take my car, if it would save time.'

'OK—but I'll drive,' he said, 'because you're really not in a fit state.'

She didn't argue. And she washed her face and cleaned her teeth, then managed to keep herself together while they got to the car.

To her relief, no paparazzi were around. Or, if they were, they kept well hidden.

'So how can they tell if I've been affected by the lambing?'

'They'll do a blood test,' Dragan explained. 'It's what they call complement fixation testing, but that on its own won't tell them if you've been exposed to an ovine strain or an avian strain. They'll do immunofluorescent testing to sort that out.' He looked grim. 'Have you had any flu-like symptoms?'

'No.'

'That's good.'

'Is it?' She remembered the leaflets she'd read. 'I thought it was asymptomatic in humans.'

'It can be,' he admitted.

'How's it treated?'

'Antibiotics—usually a two-week course of erythromycin.'

She frowned. 'But aren't antibiotics bad during pregnancy?'

'Let's not cross that bridge just yet. We don't know you've definitely been infected and we don't know how pregnant you are.' He took his left hand off the wheel for a moment to hold hers. 'If it helps, most reported cases of problems are in the period from twenty-four to thirty-six weeks, and I'm pretty sure your dates aren't in that area. And it's also very, very rare for someone to lose a baby because of it nowadays.'

'Because everyone knows the guidelines. If you're a vet or you work with sheep, and someone in your family's pregnant, you stay away from them during lambing—you don't even let them near your clothes or boots, because they can pick it up from there. And it can cause problems with the baby's development. I've seen the leaflets and the advisory notes, Dragan. I know what it can do. And I know what it can do to me, too. DIC.'

'Disseminated intravascular coagulation is an extremely rare complication.'

'But it's a possibility.' One which could kill her, if the heavy bleeding went along with shock and infection. She'd once heard Chloe talk about it and it had shocked her that in this century women could still die in childbirth. 'So are complications of the liver and the kidneys. And EAE can lead to a woman losing the baby.'

'In the severe form of the disease. And the chances are very high that you don't have that.'

'But what if I do? What if I've got it and I don't have the symptoms?' She dragged in a breath. 'I didn't know I was pregnant when I went out to the farm. I swear I didn't.'

'Nobody's blaming you, *carissima*. And it's going to be all right.'

'Is it? You can't give me a guarantee, can you?' She released his hand and wrapped her arms round her abdomen. 'I can't lose this baby, I can't.' Her breath came out in a shudder. 'It's all I have left of you.'

As the words penetrated his brain, Dragan was stunned.

Melinda was so upset that clearly she was speaking from the heart instead of playing a role.

And what she'd just said…

It's all I have left of you.

She wanted the baby because it was *his*, not to get her out of being queen of Contarini.

So these past few days of hell, when he'd thought she'd used him and had never really loved him—he'd been completely wrong. Paranoid, stupid and just plain wrong.

Because Melinda loved him.

She really, really loved him.

And she wanted this baby because it was his.

Right now she was vulnerable. Her real self, not hiding. And she needed him to be strong for her. Needed him. Wanted *him.* After all, when she'd thought she'd been calling Chloe, she'd rung *his* number. He was the one she'd needed.

He swallowed hard. 'You're not going to lose our baby.' He hoped to hell she wasn't. It all depended on whether she'd been infected by the bacterium and what stage the pregnancy was. 'And you haven't lost me either. I'm sorry. You gave me a hard time—but I've given you a hard time, too. We're as bad as each other.'

'I never meant to hurt you.'

'And I never meant to hurt you.'

Again, he reached across to hold her hand. Her hand gripped his so tightly, she was close to cutting off his circulation, but he didn't care. And he was glad that they were on a straight bit of road right now with no roundabouts or traffic lights ahead—because he would really, really resent having to loosen her hand to change gear.

'It's going to be all right,' he promised softly. 'And I'm going to be there with you every single step of the way.'

They made it to the hospital with five minutes to spare. Just enough time to get to the maternity department—and Dragan kept his arm round Melinda the whole time.

It was the first time she'd felt warm since her return to England.

Until they reached the maternity ward and Melinda saw the whiteboard with her name on it, in the column marked EMERGENCY. '*Porca miseria!*' She clapped a hand to her mouth, sounding horrified.

'It's written up there because they're expecting you in and I asked for an emergency scan,' Dragan said quietly. 'All it means is that you didn't have a pre-booked routine appointment. There's nothing to worry about, *cara*. I promise.'

He led her over to the reception desk, where one of the midwives was busy writing notes. 'I've brought Melinda Fortesque for a scan and to see Mr Perron.'

The midwife looked up and smiled. 'Have a seat. I'll let him know you're here.'

The wait seemed endless. And Melinda was still shaking even as the consultant came over and introduced himself, then took them into a small treatment room.

'I understand you're a vet,' he said.

She nodded. 'I didn't know I was pregnant when I helped out with the lambing. It was a few weeks ago, and my boss tells me the farm's been hit by EAE. We don't know the cause yet, but as chlamydiosis is the most common...' Her voice faded.

'You've done the right thing in coming here,' Mr Perron said. 'I know it's hard, but try not to worry. It's pretty rare that women are affected by chlamydiosis, and even rarer that the baby's affected—there are fewer than ten cases a year nowadays.'

'Because people are aware of the risks.'

'Even so. Try not to worry,' he said gently. 'And this is your doctor?'

'Her partner,' Dragan corrected.

'Sorry.' The consultant checked the notes. 'Must be crossed wires. It's down here that you're her doctor.'

'I'm a GP, yes,' Dragan said, 'but not Melinda's. I just rang through to save time.'

Mr Perron nodded. 'So you know what we're going to do.'

'Blood test and an ultrasound to give us some dates,' Melinda said.

'We'll do the nasty bit first,' Mr Perron said. 'Can you make a fist for me, Ms Fortesque?'

'Melinda.'

'Melinda,' he said with a smile, checking for access to a vein in her inner elbow. 'Pump it for me... That's good. Now, sharp scratch...' She flinched, and he took the blood sample and then labelled it. 'The results won't be back for a couple of days, but do try not to worry. Have you had any flu-like symptoms at all?'

'Nothing. No chills or fever, no cough, no headache.'

'How about a sore throat or any joint pains?' Mr Perron asked. At her shake of the head he added, 'Any problems with bright light?'

'Nothing.'

'Sickness?'

Melinda dragged in a breath. 'Oh, *Dio*. I thought it was morning sickness. And it's only been this week.'

'Then it probably *is* morning sickness, and it affects women in very different ways,' he reassured her. 'There's no guarantee if you have morning sickness in one pregnancy you'll have it in the next—and vice versa. Now, let's have a look at the scan. Can you get onto the couch for me and bare your tummy?'

She did so, and Dragan sat next to her, holding her hand tightly.

'I'm going to put some gel on your stomach—I'm afraid this is the portable scanner so the gel's going to feel cold. The gel's always warmer in the ultrasound department than it is here.' He smiled at her. 'Right. Then I'm going to stroke this over your abdomen—you might feel a little bit of pressure, but it shouldn't hurt at all. Can you both see the screen?'

'Yes,' Dragan said.

'And... *Voilà*.'

Dragan gazed in wonder at the screen.

Their baby.

Two arms, two legs, a head. Definitely alive and kicking. And he could see the heart beating.

Mr Perron did some measurements. Without even needing to look at a chart, he smiled. 'I'd say from this you're about ten weeks.'

'And everything's all right?'

'Two arms, two legs, a head, a nicely beating heart.' He

moved the scanner round. 'Your placenta's in the right place, too, so nothing to worry about there.'

Dragan couldn't take his eyes off the screen. A little life. Something he and Melinda had created. The beginning of their family. His fingers tightened round hers.

'Could we...? Is it possible to have a picture, please?' Melinda asked.

Mr Perron shook his head regretfully. 'This is the portable scanner and it's not hooked up to a printer. I'm afraid you'll have to wait until your dating scan. Unless...' He paused. 'Do you have a mobile phone?'

'Yes, and I switched it off before we came into the hospital,' Dragan said.

'Does it have a camera?'

'Yes.'

Mr Perron spread his hands. 'Well, then. There's the solution.'

'But—I thought you weren't supposed to use mobile phones in hospitals? In case it interfered with the equipment?' Melinda asked.

'It really depends on the area. I'd stop anyone using one in Intensive Care, the special baby care unit or where there's a lot of equipment being used—places where there's a high risk of electromagnetic interference or where a ringtone might sound like an alarm tone on medical equipment and there's a chance it might be missed.' Mr Perron gave her a rueful smile. 'And I have to admit, it drives the staff crazy if phones are going off all over the place, disturbing patients' rest or drowning out a discussion about someone's health-care plan. But you're taking a photograph of your own scan so it's not breaching patient confidentiality—and you're far enough away from any other equipment that it's not going to hurt anyone. Go ahead.'

'Thank you,' Dragan said, pulled his phone from his pocket, switched it on and took a couple of photographs.

'I'll be in touch with the blood results,' the consultant said. 'I think the chances are that you'll be fine, but if there is a problem we can start treatment immediately.' He handed Dragan some paper towels.

Dragan cleaned the gel off Melinda's stomach and restored order to her clothes. When she sat up, he held her close.

'I'll give you a minute or two,' Mr Perron said softly. 'It's always emotional, the first time you see the baby on a scan.'

Melinda had no idea how long they stayed like that, just holding each other. But when they pulled apart and she looked at Dragan, she could see that his eyelashes were wet, too. The scan had moved him just as much as it had moved her.

'I've missed you so much,' she said. 'And I didn't do this on purpose, Dragan.'

'I know that now—and I'm sorry. I thought you were using me.'

She shook her head. 'I'd never do that. And besides, we didn't make the baby that night. It was long before then. I know we used condoms, but you know as well as I do that the only one hundred per cent reliable method of contraception is abstinence.' She looked at him. 'I wouldn't use you like that. I love you.'

He stroked her face. 'I love you, too. *Volim te*.'

'Do you?' She wasn't so sure. He'd walked away from her.

'Yes.' He brushed his mouth against hers. 'These last few days rank among the most miserable of my entire life. When I thought I'd lost you—and the baby—it felt as bad as when I lost my family.'

'So why did you walk out on me?'

'Pride. Stupidity, because I let my pride get in the way. I should've stayed to fight for you.'

'Me, too.'

'Let's go home,' he said softly.

'Home?'

'To hell with the papers. They can print what they like. You and the baby are the only ones who matter. Before you went back to Contarini, we were planning to move in together. Get married. So let's do it.'

'You still want to marry me?'

'I never stopped wanting to marry you,' he said softly. 'But I tried to do the right thing. To let you go back to Contarini so you weren't cut off from your family.'

'They chose to do that anyway.' She closed her eyes.

'We can sort it out. Because I'm on your side,' he reminded her.

'My mother—'

'Will be fine. She'll be reconciled with us. I have a plan.' He stroked her hair. 'Your official dating scan is…when?'

'Wednesday.'

'And your next time off is…?'

'The weekend after.'

'Mine, too,' he said. 'I'll book Bramble in with Lizzie and we'll fly over to Contarini. Pay your family a visit. I think it's time your mother discovered that family is more important than duty. And, faced with you and a certain photograph, I think she'll soften.'

Fear tricked down Melinda's spine. 'What if she doesn't?'

'She will. Trust me.'

'Because you're a doctor?'

He laughed. 'Or so the saying goes. *Sve ce biti okej.* Everything will be OK,' he translated. 'And we've got a wedding to plan. Last Saturday of April.'

Her eyes went wide. 'You what?'

'Unless you've talked to Reverend Kenner to call it all off, the wedding's booked for the last Saturday in April.' He smiled wryly. 'That's the one thing I didn't think to do. Speak to the vicar to say it wasn't going to happen any more. I suppose subconsciously I still hoped it would work out.'

'It's going to work out. Because I'm never, ever going to keep anything from you again.'
'No?'
'No.'

CHAPTER FOURTEEN

MELINDA'S booking-in appointment and scan went as planned. She'd just finished evening surgery on Wednesday when Chloe dropped into the vet's.

'I wanted to tell you in person,' she said with a smile. 'Mr Perron just rang your results through. You're clear.'

Melinda hugged her. 'Chloe—that's so...I...'

Chloe smiled. 'Hey, you're meant to start forgetting your words a bit later on in pregnancy than this!'

'I'm just so relieved—so happy.' Melinda hugged her again. 'You must come and celebrate with Dragan and me tonight.'

'No.' Chloe patted her arm. 'It's lovely of you to ask me, but this really should be just the two of you. At least you can relax and enjoy your pregnancy now.'

'Definitely.'

She locked up the surgery and walked with Chloe towards Fisherman's Row. 'Are you sure you won't come in?' she asked when they reached Dragan's door.

'I'm sure. This should be between just the two of you. Now, go and put him out of his misery. See you later.' Chloe walked further down to her house, while Melinda opened the door with the key Dragan had given her two days previously.

The key to his house.

Which he'd told her was now *their* house.

It might be small, but it was home—and she loved it here. Close to the sea, with a little patch of garden. And, best of all, Dragan was here.

Bramble bounded over to her, wagging her tail.

'Oh, you bad dog—you're supposed to be taking it easy, still, not leaping around,' Melinda scolded.

Bramble completely ignored the telling-off and licked her.

Dragan saved the file on his computer, then pushed his chair back and walked over to enfold her in his arms. 'Good day?' he asked.

'Better than good. Mr Perron just rang through to Chloe. We're in the clear.'

Dragan whooped, picked her up and twirled her round. 'That's fantastic. So now we can relax and just look forward to October.' He kissed her. 'I'm just so happy.'

'Me, too.'

They ended up celebrating in bed.

And the following evening they went late-night shopping in Newquay. For just one item. Melinda steered him away from the more expensive jeweller's shops.

'I can afford it, you know. The upside of living like a Spartan is that I have a fairly decent savings account,' Dragan said.

'I'd rather spend the money on the baby than on me.'

'There's enough for both of you.'

She sighed. 'I love you, Dragan, and I'd happily marry you with a plastic ring from a Christmas cracker. You don't have to make a fuss about precious metals and gemstones.'

Dragan laughed. 'I think we can do better than a plastic ring. Just have a look around. And we're not looking at prices—we're looking for something you *like*.'

He knew the second she'd seen the one because her eyes lit

up. A plain platinum band with an emerald-cut solitaire diamond.

And when she tried it on, it was a perfect fit.

'This was meant to be,' he said, bought it, and slipped the velvet-covered box into his pocket.

He considered giving her the ring over dinner, but it didn't feel right, getting officially engaged away from Penhally. The place that had brought them together.

'You know when I asked you to marry me, I said it should've been at sunrise?' he said conversationally when they were back in the village.

Melinda groaned. 'No. Please tell me you're not planning to make me get up before dawn tomorrow.'

'That was plan A,' he teased. 'But I'll settle for plan B. Bramble needs a walk. Coming?'

'I'm a little tired.'

'That was a rhetorical question,' he informed her. 'And we'll take it slowly.'

'Slow? With Bramble?' she teased. 'She's a husky in disguise!'

It was a clear evening, and the sky was full of stars. Better still, there were no paparazzi around as they strolled down the harbour towards the lighthouse. Everything was quiet; there was just the swish of the ocean as the waves lapped against the short.

'Lie down and wait,' Dragan told Bramble, who promptly did his bidding.

Then he turned to Melinda and dropped to one knee. 'Now I'm going to ask you properly. Melinda Fortesque, will you be my wife, my love, for the rest of our days?'

'Yes,' she whispered.

He took the ring from its box, slid it onto her finger, then stood up again, pulled her into his arms and kissed her. 'Thank you,' he said softly when he broke the kiss.

They strolled back home hand in hand, the dog trotting along beside them. As they passed the church, Dragan said, 'This is where we'll be, the last Saturday of the month.' He paused. 'Do we really have enough time to organise this wedding?'

'All we need is each other and a ring.'

He smiled. 'This is Penhally. Whether we like it or not, we're going to have a church full of friends. Even if we have the tiniest reception, we're going to have a huge wedding.' He looked at her. 'If it's too much for you, we can put it back a bit.'

Melinda shook her head. 'My sister Serena says that everything is simple until people complicate things.'

'Wise words,' Dragan said. 'Though we need to see your family before we can get married.'

'You don't have to ask my father's permission.'

'No, but I would like his blessing. Families are important, *cara*. And I want our marriage to start on the right note.'

'It will.' She squeezed his hand. 'And your family will be there in spirit. I hope they would have approved of me.'

Dragan had to swallow the lump in his throat. 'They would've *loved* you, Melinda. Just like I do.'

His family would have taken her straight to their hearts. But he had a feeling that her family wouldn't react to him in the same way. After all, she was a princess and he was just an ordinary man.

'That's something else I wanted to ask you, Dragan. The baby... If it's a boy, I'd like to name him after your father. And a girl after your mother.'

The lump in his throat grew even larger. 'Are you sure?'

She nodded.

'What about your parents? It's not fair to name a baby after one set of grandparents and not the other.'

Melinda smiled. 'That's one of the things I love about you, *carissimo*. Your sense of fairness. But I was thinking we'd have more than one baby...'

* * *

On Saturday morning Melinda and Dragan caught the early flight to London, then a connecting flight to Naples. The nearer they got to Italy, the quieter Melinda became. And Dragan noticed that she didn't talk at all during the flight to Contarini. He laced his fingers through hers.

'All right?' he asked softly.

'*Mi sento male*,' Melinda muttered. *I feel sick.*

His heart missed a beat. 'The baby?'

She shook her head. '*La mia famiglia.*'

So she was sick with nerves at facing her family? He noticed that she'd slipped back into her own tongue. He smiled reassuringly at her and squeezed her hand. '*Va bene, bella mia.* It will be all right.'

She sighed. 'I'm not so sure.'

'Your sister is on your side. And I am here. Trust me.'

Finally they landed. 'I booked a taxi. It was supposed to meet us here,' Melinda said when they'd gone through customs. She shook her head in annoyance. 'Maybe they're running late. I'll check.'

But before she could take her mobile phone out of her handbag, a woman sashayed towards them. She was slightly taller and thinner than Melinda, Dragan noticed, and her hair was worn back in a smooth Grace Kelly–type style rather than loose and wild, the way Melinda wore it—but the family resemblance was unmistakeable.

This had to be Melinda's younger sister.

'Did I hear someone asking for a taxi?' she said with a smile.

'Rena?' Melinda stared at her in obvious surprise. 'What are *you* doing here?'

'Meeting you, of course.'

'But—I had a taxi booked.'

'I know. I cancelled it. Carlo's outside.'

Melinda blinked. 'You brought the limo?'

'It makes life less complicated. Welcome home, *carissima*.' The woman hugged her, then stood back and looked at Dragan.

He gave her a tiny formal bow. 'Your Royal Highness.'

She made a small impatient gesture and hugged him. 'Don't be so formal. You're going to be *mio cognato*, my brother-in-law. So there's no need for any of this "Your Royal Highness" business. My name is Serena. Or Rena, for short.' She grinned. 'I must say, you're dishier than your photograph.'

'Rena!' Melinda said, sounding shocked.

Serena laughed. 'And *you* look a million times happier than the last time I saw you, Lini. Let me see the ring.' She held Melinda's left hand and peered at the stone. 'Now, that's pretty,' she said, her voice full of approval.

'Not quite in the league of your family jewels,' Dragan said dryly.

'But this was given with love. Which makes it sparkle an awful lot more,' Serena said, her voice utterly sincere.

He smiled at her. 'I think I'm going to like having a sister-in-law.'

'Pity you have the demon mother-in-law to go with it,' Serena said.

'Rena!' Melinda said again.

Serena laughed. 'I'm only saying what you're thinking, *sorella mia*. Dragan versus the dragon…'

'Stop it. I'm worried enough about this.'

'Chill. It will be fine.' Serena gave an exaggerated wink. 'If *Mamma* misbehaves, the second I am queen I can chuck her in the dungeons.'

'You'd never believe she was always the demure one, would you?' Melinda asked Dragan as they followed Serena to the limousine. 'This queen business is going right to her head.'

'The phrase, *sorella mia*, is "Off with her head",' Serena corrected, laughing.

The journey was an easy one, and then Carlo drove through the gates to the palace. It was a huge mellow stone building, clearly several hundred years old. When they went inside, Dragan noted that the carpets were so thick he sank into them as he walked, and the curtains were of heavy velvet and brocade. Portraits hung close together on the walls: generation after generation of people who'd lived there.

Old money.

Breeding.

Tradition.

Royalty.

A million miles away from his little cottage in Penhally. This wasn't the kind of place where he belonged.

It wasn't where Melinda belonged either. And all of a sudden he began to understand how she'd felt on the plane. Because he was feeling exactly the same way right now—with adrenalin tingling through him.

Alessandro and Viviana were seated on couches in one of the formal rooms. And Dragan suddenly wished he'd thought to ask Melinda about etiquette. How did you behave around royalty? Both Melinda and Serena were down to earth and didn't stand on ceremony—but he knew their parents wouldn't be the same.

'*Mamma. Papà.*' Serena curtseyed before them both, and kissed both of them on the backs of their left hands.

Lord. He'd never, ever been anywhere so formal. Didn't these people greet their children with a hug and a kiss, like normal parents?

Then again, they weren't normal people. They were the king and queen of Contarini.

'*Mamma. Papà.*' Melinda also made a small curtsey, but there was no kiss.

And then all eyes were trained on him.

OK. He could do this. If Melinda and Serena had to

curtsey, it followed that he would have to bow. 'Your Majesties,' he said, first bowing to Melinda's father and then to her mother.

They nodded graciously.

And then it was the most awkward pause he'd ever experienced in his life.

'Be seated,' Viviana said, giving an imperious gesture towards one of the sofas.

No wonder Melinda had wanted to escape all this. It was *stifling*. Like going back in time a hundred and fifty years.

Alessandro looked at Dragan, his arms folded. 'So you are the man who wishes to ask for my permission to marry my daughter.'

What now? Was he supposed to say certain things in a certain way?

He didn't have a clue what the traditions were.

But the one thing he could do was to speak from his heart.

He stood up. 'Your Majesty, I love your daughter,' Dragan said quietly. 'She is the sunshine in my life. And I asked her to marry me before I found out she was a princess—before I discovered that she was expecting our child.'

Viviana gave a sharp intake of breath. 'You—'

Alessandro lifted one hand. 'Allow him to speak without interruptions.'

Viviana glowered, but to Dragan's relief she fell silent.

Dragan took a deep breath. Melinda's mother definitely wasn't going to like this next bit. But it had to be said. 'Thank you, Your Majesty.' He paused. 'I'm not asking for your permission to marry your daughter. I'm asking for your *blessing*.'

'My blessing?'

'It would mean a lot to Melinda—and to me. But if you choose to withhold your blessing, I will still marry her. Because we are meant to be together.'

Alessandro looked thoughtful. 'She is a princess. She is used to the finer things in life. Can you afford that?'

Dragan smiled. 'She has royal blood, but at heart Melinda is a country vet. I admit that I wouldn't be able to keep her in the kind of thing you have in mind—jewels and haute couture—but that's not what she wants anyway.'

'No?'

'No,' Dragan affirmed. 'I would have paid a year's salary for her engagement ring, if that's what she'd wanted—but I know Melinda. She'd have taken it back to the shop the next day, picked something much smaller, got a refund for the difference and given the money to an animal charity.'

Alessandro raised an eyebrow.

OK. So this was where he would be thrown out of the palace.

And then, to his surprise, Alessandro burst out laughing. 'That sounds like *exactly* what she would do. You know my daughter's heart, then.'

'Yes. And I can tell you now I will be a good husband. I'll love her and cherish her—and our children—for the rest of my days. Sometimes my hours are long but, then, so are Melinda's.'

'You expect her to work after your marriage—after the baby arrives?' Viviana asked sharply.

Dragan met her stare without flinching. 'I expect Melinda to do what makes her happy. She loves her job and she's very, very good at it. If she chooses to work full time or part time, she has my support. We'll work out what's best for us as a family.' He paused. 'And that's the most important thing—family. Without that, all the property in the world means nothing. You can't put a price on love.'

There was a long, long silence.

And then Alessandro nodded. 'My daughter says you are a good man. And we had you investigated.'

'You did what?' Melinda asked, sounding appalled.

'I did what any father would do. I found out just who the man was who wanted to take my daughter—to see if he will make her happy.' He inclined his head towards Dragan. 'You worked to make sure your family's honour remained intact before you left Croatia. And you went to England with nothing—took nothing, expected nothing, and you have worked hard to make a good life. You are a man of honour. And I know you love my daughter. So, yes, you have my blessing.'

Melinda stood up and took Dragan's hand, then looked at her mother. 'And yours, *Mamma*?'

'You should have been queen,' Viviana said, shaking her head. 'But you have always known what you wanted to do. And if your father is happy to give his blessing, I will not stand in your way.'

'Families are important,' Dragan said softly again. 'And we have something for you.' He glanced at Melinda, who took three small envelopes from her handbag and handed one to each of her parents and her sister.

'What is this?' Viviana asked.

'I think I know,' Serena said with a broad smile. 'Open yours first, *Mamma*.'

Viviana frowned, but did so. Opened the card. And her eyes widened as she took in exactly what was inside the card.

The picture from Melinda's scan.

'The first photograph of your grandchild,' Dragan said. 'And I would like very much to know that our son or daughter will have a *nonno* and *nonna* who will come to visit.' He smiled at Serena. 'I know already our children will have an aunt in a million.'

Serena turned bright pink, stood up and hugged him. '*Grazie*, Dragan. And welcome to our family.'

Then Viviana shocked him completely by doing the same.

'My daughter is right. Welcome to our family. I know you have no family, Dragan, so *il bambino* may only have one set of grandparents—but we will do our best to be as good as two.'

CHAPTER FIFTEEN

BACK in Penhally, Dragan brought a tray of cold drinks and biscuits through to the living room, where Melinda, Lauren and Chloe were talking non-stop.

'I'm leaving you lot to it,' he said. 'I'm taking Bramble out—but I'll have my phone on if you need me.' He gave Melinda a lingering kiss. '*Ciao, tesoro*.' He whistled to Bramble, and a few moments later Melinda heard the front door close.

'I asked you both over tonight for a reason,' she said to Lauren and Chloe. 'You know I'm getting married at the end of the month...well, I need bridesmaids. Which is where you come in.'

'You want *us* as your bridesmaids?' Chloe asked, looking shocked.

Melinda rolled her eyes. 'I wouldn't have asked you if I didn't.'

Lauren looked worried. 'I don't know, Melinda. I'd hate it if I tripped over your train or something and fell flat on my face in the middle of the aisle. You know how clumsy I am. I don't want to spoil your wedding.'

'And you're a princess, Melinda. It's a royal wedding.' Chloe bit her lip. 'I can't be a royal bridesmaid.'

'Yes, you can. Because it's not a royal wedding, it's *my* wedding,' Melinda reminded them. 'We need to get a few things straight here. Lauren, you *won't* fall flat on your face in the aisle. You can wear flat shoes and the dress can be ballerina-length if that'll make you feel more comfortable. Look, you two are my best friends. I really want you as my bridesmaids, along with my sister. And my wedding day just won't be the same if you're not.'

Chloe and Lauren eyed each other doubtfully.

'If you're sure…' Lauren began.

She hugged them each in turn. 'Of course I'm sure. And I hope you realise you're top of our godmother list, too. Along with my sister Serena, or she'll have us thrown in the dungeons.' As her friends' eyes widened, she laughed. 'Figuratively speaking. I think it's actually against the law for her to chuck anyone in the dungeons. She just likes saying it. Anyway, I'm under instructions to measure you tonight for the dresses.'

'So we're not going shopping?' Lauren asked.

'Yes and no,' Melinda said. 'Serena has this friend who's a brilliant dressmaker. She's emailed me half a dozen designs—we pick the ones we like and her friend makes them, then comes over for the fitting. We get to choose colours, too.'

'I've never had a dress made just for me,' Chloe said quietly.

'Nor me,' Lauren said.

'Well, now's your chance. And it'll be by someone who Serena reckons is going to be one of the hottest designers in Milan by next summer.'

'You're really sure about this?' Lauren asked.

'Absolutely.' Melinda fetched her laptop from her briefcase. 'Let's sort out our dresses.'

Later that evening, Melinda was aware that Dragan had gone really quiet. 'What's wrong?' she asked.

'I was thinking about the wedding.'

She went cold. 'Have you changed your mind?'

'No, of course not.' He hugged her. 'It's just that tonight you were sorting out bridesmaid stuff. And that reminded me, it's traditional for the groom to have a best man.' He looked away. 'I always thought I'd be my brother's best man at his wedding, and he would be mine.'

Melinda stroked the hair back from his face. 'Oh, *zlato*. I'm sorry.'

'Not your fault.' He sighed. 'But it leaves me with a problem. I have no family. And I don't know who to ask.'

'What about Nick Tremayne?'

'Nick?' Dragan looked surprised.

'He's your friend as well as your colleague, isn't he?'

'We're not that close...but you're probably right. Nick would be a good choice.'

'Then ask him, *caro*.'

The following morning, before surgery, Dragan knocked on Nick's door, opened it and leant against the jamb. 'A word?'

The senior partner looked up from his desk. 'That's my line.'

'I know.' Dragan coughed. 'Nick, I need a favour.'

'What sort of favour?'

'I'm getting married. And I need someone I can trust to hold the ring for me and make a half-decent speech at the reception.'

Nick's brown eyes widened. 'Hang on. You're asking me to be your best man?'

'Got it in one.'

'Good lord.' Nick smiled, and suddenly looked younger than Dragan had seen him for a long, long time. 'I'd be delighted. Thank you.'

'Good. Oh, there is one tiny little thing.'

Nick's voice was full of suspicion. 'What?'

'I'd rather you didn't bring Cruella as your wedding guest.'

Nick's frown deepened. 'Why?'

'She's upset half the people in the practice—Kate, Alison, Hazel. She's rude about my dog. And she was rude to Melinda before she realised that she was speaking to Princess Melinda Fortesque—since then, she's been driving Melinda crazy, trying to be pally with her and swapping fashion tips. I can't get through to her that Melinda hates all this royal stuff.'

'Ah.' Nick grimaced.

'I don't want an atmosphere at the wedding. Melinda's mother is, um…' Dragan searched for a diplomatic expression '…a strong character. And if someone wasn't particularly careful about what she said or who might overhear her, it could make life difficult.'

'Point taken,' Nick said. 'I'll come on my own. Actually, I think Natasha's planning on going back to Rock anyway.'

Dragan knew a few people who'd correct that to 'crawling back under the rock she came from', but held his tongue. 'Thank you.'

The last days of the month sped by. Serena came over from Contarini to help with the wedding plans, and Dragan was impressed by how quickly and easily the future queen of Contarini managed to organise everything and took all the stress off Melinda—and at the same time she still managed to make the bride feel that she was completely in control. Melinda simply said what she wanted and Serena organised it.

Serena also had things to say about the press.

'If we have a deal with syndicated rights, we get a wedding photographer who's desperate to take the best pictures of his life, and you'll get a measure of privacy—well, as much as any royal wedding will. The papers will be happy because they get brilliant pictures, and the paparazzi won't hassle us because the deal is done and dusted. Everybody wins.'

'And for syndicated rights, we get money,' Melinda said thoughtfully. 'Which I'd like to donate to charity.'

'You took the words out of my mouth,' Serena said. 'Do you have anything special in mind?'

'Local ones who do animal rescue, plus something towards church funds,' Melinda said.

'And the primary school and village nursery,' Dragan added. 'They could do with some new play equipment.'

'And something to the lifeboats,' Melinda said.

'Good idea,' Dragan said. 'Kate, one of the midwives at our practice, was married to the man who ran the lifeboat station. He died in a rescue at sea—and Nick, the senior partner at my practice, lost his father and brother in the rescue too.'

'I read about that. Such a tragedy.' Serena looked serious. 'Right. Give me a list of contacts and I'll sort it out.'

'You're going to be an excellent head of state,' Dragan told her. 'You've got the right touch with people.'

'Melinda's good with people, too,' Serena pointed out.

'But her heart wouldn't have been in the job, so it wouldn't have been right for her. Whereas you—you'll make an excellent queen because your heart is in it.'

'And my sister's heart is with you.' She smiled. 'And so it should be. I know you're right for her.'

'You thrive on all this wheeling and dealing, don't you?' Melinda asked with a smile.

Serena grinned. 'You bet I do. And this wedding is going to be a day the whole of Penhally's going to remember for a long, long time—with a lot of love and affection.'

On the Saturday morning, Dragan woke early. It felt odd not to have Melinda curled in bed beside him, but there had been much insistence from both Melinda and Serena on sticking to tradition. According to them, it was bad luck to see the bride on the day until she arrived at the church, so Melinda and Serena had spent the night at Chloe's house.

He went over to the window and peered out. It was a perfect spring day, with the sun shining and the sky a rich deep blue.

His wedding day.

There was just one shadow in his heart—that his family weren't there to share the day with him. But Melinda's words echoed in his head. *Your family will be there in spirit.*

'I hope so,' he said softly. 'Because I miss you so much. But I'll see you in my children's faces. And your love still goes on in my heart.'

He drove Bramble over to Lizzie Chamberlain's. 'I think Melinda would've liked her at the wedding,' he confided to Lizzie.

Lizzie laughed. 'You can imagine what kind of chaos a flattie would cause at a wedding—they like to be the centre of attention. Don't you, girl?' she said, bending down to cuddle Bramble. 'What you and Melinda did—donating that money—thank you. It's going to make a real difference to the rescue work,' she said.

'That's what we wanted,' Dragan said simply. 'We're part of this community.'

'That you most certainly are,' Lizzie said feelingly. 'Have you got time for a cup of tea?'

'Make that coffee, and you're on,' Dragan said with a smile. 'And while I'm here, I can have a chat with your mum about how it's going with the new drugs and exercise routine.'

Lizzie tutted. 'It's your wedding day. You're not supposed to be working.'

'You'll be doing me a favour,' he said. 'Keeping me busy so I don't have time to think or get nervous.'

Lizzie tapped the side of her nose. 'Got you.'

Meanwhile, at Chloe's house, the wedding preparations were going ahead at full steam. Vicky had come over to do the bride's and bridesmaids' hair and make-up. At first she'd been a little overawed by the thought of being official hairdresser and beautician to two of the Contarini royal family, but as soon as she'd met Serena she was back to being her normal chatterbox self.

'Doorbell!' Lauren yelled. 'Want me to get it, Chloe?'

Chloe, who was busy making yet another round of tea, put her head round the door. 'Isn't a bit early for the flowers?'

'You stay put,' Serena warned Melinda. 'Vicky, stick pins in her if she moves. And if that's Dragan I'll shut the door so they don't see each other.'

Lauren walked back into the living room a few minutes later, carrying a single red rose. 'Not Dragan. But I'd guess this is from him,' she said, handing the rose to Melinda.

Melinda opened the card and read the message. *Six hours until you make my life complete.*

'Oh-h-h,' she breathed.

Serena grabbed the card and read it. 'Don't cry. You'll smudge the make-up.'

'It's waterproof,' Vicky chipped in.

'Don't give her the excuse.' Serena shook her head impatiently. 'And, Lini, I can read your face like a book. You can't go and see him. It's bad luck.'

'To *see* him, yes.' Melinda grabbed her mobile phone. 'It doesn't mean I can't talk to him.'

'It's bad luck,' Serena insisted.

Melinda sighed and put the phone away.

But when a second rose arrived an hour later—and another one an hour after that—Melinda grabbed her phone again. 'I need to talk to him.' When Serena was about to protest, she said softly, 'I have my friends and family around me. Dragan's on his own, once he's taken Bramble over to Lizzie's.'

Serena sighed. All right. 'Leave this to me.'

* * *

A few minutes later, Dragan opened the door and his eyes widened in surprise when he saw Serena there. 'Is Melinda all right?'

'Yes, but I have a message from her.'

He went cold. 'You'd better come in.' He closed the door behind her. Please, don't let this all go wrong now. He could barely force the question out. 'She's changed her mind?'

'*Idiota*! Of course she hasn't. But it's bad luck for the bride and groom to see each other before church, and...' Serena flapped an impatient hand. 'She says she loves you and she loves the red roses—and she's counting the minutes until she's your bride.' She gave him a hug. 'That was such a romantic thing to do.'

'There should be two more. We're on a countdown,' Dragan said.

'That's so *sweet*.' She paused. 'And, actually, there was something I wanted to say, too. When you marry Melinda, she'll be your family—but so will I. And *Mamma* and *Papà*. My father really likes you, you know.'

The lump in his throat was so big he couldn't say a word. He just hugged her right back.

'I'll see you in church,' she said. 'And just so you don't worry, Melinda will be precisely three minutes late.' She smiled. 'It's tradition. If she had her way, she'd be three minutes early!'

And finally everything was ready. The flowers had arrived, along with one last rose from Dragan. Everyone's hair and make-up was pristine, and Vicky had gone to get changed for church.

And then the doorbell went.

Serena glanced at her watch. 'That must be *Mamma* and *Papà*, with the cars. Ready?'

'Ready,' Melinda said softly.

Chloe answered the door and did as much of a curtsey as she could in her bridesmaid's dress. 'Your Majesty.'

'You must be...Chloe? Lauren?' Viviana asked.

'Chloe.'

'Serena has told me what a good friend you are to my daughter. *Grazie, tesoro.*'

'Um, my pleasure,' Chloe said, looking slightly awestruck.

Viviana swept in. 'And you are Lauren, yes?'

'Yes, Your Majesty.' Lauren also curtseyed, and nearly tripped.

Viviana took her arm for support. 'No more curtseys.' She surveyed the four women. 'You look lovely.' She came to stand in front of Melinda. 'And you...*mia bambina. Che bellissima,*' she said softly.

'Stop it, *Mamma*. You'll make her cry and spoil her make-up. Hormones,' Serena reminded her swiftly. 'And that goes for you too, *Papà*—you only say things to make Melinda smile. Now, we must all go to the church and wait for Melinda just inside the lych-gate.'

'Bossy,' Alessandro grumbled, but he was smiling.

When the girls had left, he took Melinda's hand. 'You look beautiful, Melinda,' he said, 'and I am very proud of you. You are a true royal because you always stand up for what you believe in—and your Dragan is a good man. I am proud to give you away to him, and to know he will treat you as the heart of his heart.' And then he looked worried. 'Please, no tears. Serena is scarier than your mother.'

She didn't think he meant it—not quite—but it made her smile.

'Shall we go?' he asked.

She locked the door behind her and gave the key to her father for safekeeping and transfer back to Chloe during the reception. He helped her into the vintage Rolls-Royce convertible outside, and they slowly made their way to the church. People seemed to be lined up all the way along Harbour Road, throwing flowers and confetti.

Alessandro raised an eyebrow. 'Weren't you and Serena banning confetti?'

'This is biodegradable,' Melinda explained with a smile. 'And we've said we want the bird-seed type in the church grounds.'

Alessandro laughed. 'You've thought of everything.'

He helped her out of the car when they reached the church and ushered her through the lych-gate. Serena, Chloe and Lauren were all there, holding their bouquets.

Just before Alessandro gave Melinda her bouquet, Viviana hugged her. 'I wish you so much happiness, *figlia mia*,' she said.

'*Grazie*.' Melinda could hardly speak for the threatening tears.

'*Mamma*! Church, now,' Serena ordered. 'Go and give Reverend Kenner the nod that we are ready.'

Viviana gave her younger daughter a speaking look, but did as requested.

'Deep breath. And smile,' Serena directed. 'You're going to marry the man you love.'

And then Melinda walked through the church door on her father's arm, with her bridesmaids behind her, to the strains of 'Jesu, Joy of Man's Desiring'.

She glanced around quickly. The church was absolutely packed—standing room only. And she knew absolutely everyone there. They'd all come to wish her and Dragan luck and love and happiness.

As she passed the front pews, she saw her mother, her Uncle Benito and a space for her father—and behind them she recognised more aunts and uncles and cousins. The entire royal family of Contarini had turned out—how on earth had Serena done this without her so much as guessing? And there were all the friends she and Dragan shared from Penhally.

And then Dragan turned and smiled at her, his dark eyes full of love—and nothing else mattered.

The music stopped, and then Reverend Kenner was smiling at them both. 'Dearly beloved, we are gathered here today…'

* * * *

Nurse Bride, Bayside Wedding

GILL SANDERSON

Gill Sanderson, aka Roger Sanderson, started writing as a husband-and-wife team. At first Gill created the storyline, characters and background, asking Roger to help with the actual writing. But her job became more and more time-consuming and he took over all of the work. He loves it!

Roger has written many Medical Romance™ books. His ideas come from three of his children—Helen is a midwife, Adam a health visitor, Mark a consultant oncologist. Weekdays are for work; weekends find Roger walking in the Lake District or Wales.

> To my midwife daughter, Helen,
> who has helped me so much.

CHAPTER ONE

'WILL you marry me, Maddy? We'll live in my big white house on the hill and have strawberries for breakfast every morning.'

Nurse Madeleine Granger smiled. 'Sounds a good idea, especially the strawberries. I'd love to marry you, Mr Bryce, but people might say I was after your money.'

'It's my money, I can do what I want with it. And I'd do anything to stop the Chancellor of the Exchequer getting it all. Ow!'

'I'm sorry. I know it hurts, but...'

'It doesn't matter. My fault for tripping up the stairs and scratching my leg.'

'This was more than a scratch. I've been treating it for ten days now—and it's only just starting to heal.' Maddy dusted antiseptic powder over the ulcerated shin, then reached for a dressing. Sometimes old people's wounds took a long time to heal, especially when there was little flesh between skin and bone. And Malcolm Bryce was an eighty-five-year-old widower. But he was alert, sprightly and had made more new friends than anyone else on the ship.

'So you won't marry me? I'm going to be terribly disappointed.' She loved the mischievous sparkle in his eyes when he teased her.

'I'd certainly marry you if I wanted to marry anyone. But I don't. For me marriage is out. O-U-T.'

There was a keenness in his faded eyes. 'You seem very certain of that.'

'I am.' Her reply was gentle, but firm.

'Ah, well. Rebuffed again. But I will be strong. So what should I do with the Bryce millions?'

'Spend them. Come for another cruise to the Indian Ocean on the good ship *Emerald*.'

'Well, I have enjoyed it. Didn't you say it was your first trip as a cruise-ship nurse? Have you enjoyed it?'

Maddy smiled. 'It's a lot more luxurious than the hospital A and E department I came from. Yes, I have enjoyed it, I've made a lot of new friends. Now, for the past few days you've come to the medical centre for treatment. But today you phoned and asked me to come to your cabin. Any special reason why?'

In fact, she had noticed that he didn't look his usual healthy self. He was still lying in his bed, unknown for him at this time of day. He was pale, there were beads of sweat on his forehead. Although he tried to keep up their normal cheerful chatter, his voice was noticeably weaker.

'I feel a bit feeble,' he said. 'When I woke up this morning my left arm was numb and tingly. Then I went back to sleep again and I never do that.'

'Did you have palpitations? Could you feel your heart beating harder than usual?'

Mr Bryce considered. 'Sort of,' he said. 'It seemed queer—irregular. But I still went back to sleep.'

Maddy tried not to show the concern she was feeling. 'You're probably a bit excited at the prospect of getting back home,' she said. 'It affects some people that way. Still, I'll check your blood pressure and listen to your heart.'

His BP was too high and his heartbeat seemed unsteady. Well, he was a man of eighty-five but... 'I think you'd better stay in bed today,' she said. 'In fact, you might as well stay in bed till we dock. Then I'll get a doctor to come and look at you. I'll get a steward to fetch you your meals—nothing heavy and no alcohol. And I think I'll prescribe aspirin as well.'

Mr Bryce nodded. 'I've had a minor stroke, haven't I, Maddy? A transient ischaemic attack.'

'What do you know about transient ischaemic attacks?' Maddy was shocked at the way he guessed what she was thinking.

'A temporary reduction of blood and oxygen to the brain, probably caused by a minor blood clot. My wife had several of them before she died and I got to recognise the symptoms. But mostly, Maddy, I'm upset because you won't marry me.' The smile was still there but the voice was getting weaker.

'Perhaps I'll think about it,' she said gently. 'Now, rest. The steward will come to see to you and I'll drop in again later.'

'Looking forward to that,' said Mr Bryce.

Maddy's next call was two decks further up. Another phone call asking for a cabin visit. It was unusual as most people much preferred to come to the medical centre. Maddy's suspicions were growing. She knocked, and a weak voice asked her to come in.

Entering the cabin, the smell was unmistakable, and a glance at the white-faced patient confirmed that Mrs Adams was feeling very unwell indeed. Maddy's heart sank as she realised what she could be dealing with. This wasn't the first stomach upset she'd treated in the last twenty-four hours. 'How are you feeling, Mrs Adams?'

'Nurse, I feel like I'm dying. I've been sick and I...I don't think I can get out of bed.'

'Well, let's take your temperature for a start. And we'll check your pulse and BP. When did you start to feel ill?'

'It happened so suddenly! I didn't much feel like my meal last night. I thought I'd be better in the morning, but in the middle of the night I...' And Mrs Adams was sick again.

Reassuring the poor woman, who kept apologising weakly, Maddy cleaned her up and made her as comfortable as possible. 'There you go, Mrs Adams, and you're to stay in bed all day. Whatever you do, don't leave your cabin. Don't try to eat anything, but if you can, drink plenty. I've got some special stuff here. No tap water and especially nothing sweet. And take these pills now. I'll put a couple of bottles near you. And I'll be in to see you later.'

'I don't think I've ever felt as bad as this in my life,' Mrs Adams whispered.

'We'll do what we can to get you better. Now, just rest.' Maddy wondered if she looked as confident as she sounded.

She walked back to the medical centre, washed her hands again, made herself a coffee and sat down to think. Late last night it had been just a vague suspicion, but now it was turning into a certainty. This was going to be trouble. And it could be big trouble.

There had been plenty to occupy her during the cruise. Many of the passengers were quite elderly and had the usual ailments that come with age. But mostly it had been small stuff. The medical staff had coped easily.

And until yesterday morning she had been just one member of a medical team—the least important member. There had been a doctor on board, and another nurse. But a launch had met them as they'd approached the British coast, taking off the doctor and the other nurse. There had been an illness, and the doctor and nurse were needed urgently on a cruise ship about to depart. And since the *Emerald* was practically in British coastal waters, due to dock in two days, it had been decided that one nurse would be sufficient.

She now thought that was doubtful.

Last night there had been two complaints about upset stomachs. This morning she had treated another person—and it looked like there would be more. In an enclosed environment like a cruise ship, illness could spread like wildfire.

She winced. She thought that these were cases of acute gastroenteritis, sometimes known as cruise ship fever.

It was important that the captain be informed at once—he had to make the big decisions. But to a certain extent he'd have to rely on her medical advice. She knew he'd be fair—but he wouldn't be happy.

Especially when she told him that the port authorities might not let them dock.

She picked up her phone and told Ken Jackson, the captain's steward, that she needed to see the captain urgently.

'Urgently?' Ken asked. 'He is pretty busy now, arranging docking, and—'

'Ken, I said urgently and I meant it.'

He caught her tone. 'I'll ring you back,' he said.

She sat down to wait, to get her thoughts in order. Captain Smith would want precision. She'd give it to him.

In fact, she only had to wait five minutes before the phone rang. She picked it up at once. 'Captain Smith, I—'

'Hello, Maddy? Have you missed me?'

She had been expecting to hear from the captain and this was not his voice. She knew she recognised it but who could…? And then she realised and stiffened with horror. It was a voice she had never wanted to hear again.

It was Brian Temple, her ex-fiancé…the cause of so much pain. It was the man who was responsible for her giving up the A and E work she had enjoyed so much. The man who had ruined her life. The man responsible for her taking on this job—just to get away from him.

'Are you there, Maddy? I know it's you.' There was that faint alteration in tone. Brian always needed attention at once.

'What do you want, Brian? I thought I made it quite clear I never wanted to hear from you again. You seemed to get the message, to accept it. We agreed that everything between us was over.'

As ever, he paid no attention to what he didn't want to hear. 'You know you didn't mean that. A pal of yours told me that you were docking tomorrow, so I thought I might meet you off the ship. We could get together and go and have a chat and a drink.'

'No! We've been through all that. Brian, we are over!'

His voice took on that whining, angry tone that she

knew so well and hated so much. 'Maddy, I love you! We love each other, we both know that.'

'We don't love each other. I'm not seeing you, Brian. I wish you well but you're out of my life for ever.'

'You can't say that!'

She could feel genuine pain in his voice so gently she asked, 'Are you taking your medication regularly?'

'I don't need it so I stopped.'

Maddy sighed. This was likely to go on for ever.

He paused a moment and his voice took on a totally different, more unpleasant tone. 'I suppose you've found somebody else. A fancy ship's officer or some rich old man. Well, I told you before, I won't have it.'

Suspicion. Was there anything more hateful than constant, unprovoked suspicion? Their entire relationship had been tormented by it. For a moment she was angry, and was tempted to lie to him, to tell him that she had indeed met a man. But she knew better. It would only cause more trouble.

'After you, I never want to meet another man,' she said. 'Now, don't ever ring me again.'

But she knew as she replaced the receiver that it was a forlorn hope.

She went into her cabin and took out the folder of personal papers in the bottom drawer of her desk. For some reason she had kept the last message Brian had sent her when she had set off on the cruise ship. She reread it—it was half pleading, half threatening. And he reminded her of the good times they had had.

She supposed there had been some good times. Trips to the coast. A weekend in London. Meals she had cooked for him. And their plans for the future—she wanted at least two babies. But then it had all gone bad. She had been unlucky in love—always. Every time she had met a man something had gone wrong.

She took a couple of deep breaths to calm herself. She looked out of the porthole, trying to take some comfort from the English coastline she could see slipping past. It looked beautiful in the sun but she was not glad to be back in Britain. There were going to be problems. The terror was coming back.

She could see cliffs, green moors behind them, the odd white-painted or grey stone cottage. Four years ago she had worked here as a practice nurse for a summer. She'd worked for a Dr Tremayne—Nick Tremayne. He'd been a good doctor. They still exchanged Christmas cards but that was all. In one card he'd told her that he'd moved to a village in Cornwall called Penhally Bay. It must be around here somewhere. She hoped he was happy. Somebody ought to be.

Her phone rang again and she looked at it apprehensively. It might be Brian...but it was Ken Jackson. 'Could you come up to see the captain now, please, Maddy?'

She glanced in the mirror, made sure her shoulder-length hair was tied back, her uniform neat. Captain Smith was very keen on tidiness. 'Untidy dress suggests an untidy mind which suggests untidy work,' he had told her. 'That's how I run my ship.' She liked him for it.

She took a deep breath, picked up her case notes and walked up to his cabin.

Captain Smith was a giant, white-bearded man. Maddy knew he'd had a distinguished career in the Royal Navy—

on the walls of his cabin there were photographs of the ships he had commanded. He smiled at her, invited her to sit down. 'You need to see me urgently, Maddy?'

This was a job she didn't want. She had never dealt with anything like this before. Most of her nursing career had been in A and E rather than dealing with infectious diseases. But, still, it was her duty to report what she suspected.

'I think we may have an outbreak of an infectious disease,' she said. 'Exactly what I don't know, but it seems to be gastroenteritis. You might think it necessary to inform the port authorities. And they might want to quarantine the ship.'

Captain Smith kept his emotions under strict control. But Maddy could see how much this news dismayed him. Still, he wasn't going to panic. 'I see. How many cases so far?'

'Four. But this kind of thing spreads very rapidly. I suspect there'll be more as soon as I get back to the medical centre.'

'I can believe it. You know that gastroenteritis is sometimes known as the cruise ship disease?'

'I've heard it called that.'

Captain Smith thought for a moment. 'And you are the only medical staff I have.'

'Quite a few of the stewards have a little medical training. I have a list of them. They are a willing crew and they could act as orderlies. But that is all.'

'True. But we lost a doctor and a nurse yesterday.'

Maddy could see that had angered him, but he was not going to say so.

'Just how serious is this outbreak?'

It was necessary here for her to be absolutely accurate. 'I'm not an expert. But I do know that gastroenteritis can vary tremendously in seriousness. And because many of our passengers are old, they'll be particularly vulnerable. To find what has caused it, we need someone who can carry out laboratory investigations. I doubt there'll be any deaths but it will be extremely unpleasant. And, quite frankly, although I feel quite competent to deal with the condition, I need more professional help. There could be just too many cases.'

'I can see that. And when I find out who authorised the removal of two-thirds of my medical team…' The captain looked thoughtful. 'Of course, we have to report this to the port authorities and they'll not let us dock until we know more about the situation. I'll be in touch with our head office, but they tend not to move too fast in cases like this. So this is my problem.'

'I have a suggestion,' Maddy said hesitantly, 'if you don't mind.'

'I don't mind. If you can be of help, that is fine by me.'

'There's a doctor I used to work with who lives on the Cornish Coast near here. If he's available, he'd come out. And I know he's quite an expert in his field. He might give you the advice you need. His name is Nick Tremayne. Tell him I'm the nurse here.'

'Telephone number?'

Maddy shrugged. 'I only know that he has a surgery in Penhally Bay.'

Captain Smith took up his phone. 'Jackson? There's a Dr Tremayne who works in Penhally Bay, which is a few miles away. See if you can get him on the phone.'

Surprisingly quickly, the phone rang back. 'Dr Nick Tremayne? I'm Captain Smith, captain of the large ship you might see a couple of miles off shore. We have a medical problem.'

Unashamedly, Maddy listened in to the conversation. 'Recommended by a Nurse Madeleine Granger...suspected outbreak of gastroenteritis. This would be a private consultation... So quickly? I'd be much obliged.'

He turned to Maddy. 'Your doctor's coming out at once. He says that perhaps I don't understand how quickly this can spread to become an epidemic. But I do.'

Dr Ed Tremayne always rose early. He never slept very much. Those early morning half-sleeps, when you weren't sure of what was real and what was imagined. Or remembered. And then you woke to reality. It made you vulnerable and Ed didn't like feeling vulnerable. He liked to feel he was in control.

For England at the beginning of May, it was a very hot early morning. And it was close too, not like the dry blast of African heat that he remembered so well.

He parked his car by the beach, kicked off his trainers and tracksuit. Most days he came to this little cove for his early morning swim. He loved it. He loved the solitude and he liked the feeling of freedom in the water.

He stretched, then carefully looked round him. An old habit that he couldn't lose. He liked to know where he was, if there was anything he ought to be aware of. There were thick clouds on the horizon, and his experienced eye told him that there would be bad weather later in the day. He also saw a small tent half-hidden in the bushes. In summer a lot of young people came down here, sleeping wherever they could.

He ran to the sea, glad that no one was around. They'd stare, not at his well-muscled body, but at the scars.

He swam straight out of the cove mouth. He swam hard and fast, there was pleasure in pushing himself. And when he was in the open sea he stopped, trod water for a moment and again looked around him. Then he frowned.

A hundred yards away there was a rubber dinghy holding two young people, aged seventeen or eighteen, splashing, enjoying themselves, with two tiny paddles. Ed trod water nearby.

'I don't think you know these waters,' he warned. 'There's a rip tide out there and if you get caught in it you'll be pulled out to sea. Better get back into the cove. You'll be safe there.'

'We know what we're doing,' the lad said. 'We'll get back when we're good and ready.'

'I do suggest you go back now,' Ed said quietly. 'I know these waters. We have a few people drown every year. You want to be one of them?'

'Yeah, drownings, right. Tell you what, you be careful you don't drown yourself. At least we've got some kind of boat.'

Ed swam closer. 'Paddle this thing back into the cove,' he said mildly, 'or I'll turn it over and you can swim back.'

'You'll kill us!'

Ed's voice was calm but firm. 'I'm trying to stop you from killing yourselves.'

Suddenly the girl spoke. 'Kieran, he might be right. And I'm fed up with being out here anyway.' She looked at Ed. 'We're going back now.'

'I'll hang around until I see you in the cove.'

He thought he saw that the lad might still be willing to argue, so he said, still in a calm voice, 'See that shelf of rock over there?'

The two looked to where he was pointing. 'Yeah.'

'We found a drowned tourist there two years ago. He'd been in the water two days. He wasn't a pleasant sight. Now, start paddling back.'

They did. They paddled hard.

Ed finished his swim and when he got back into the cove he discovered that the couple, the rubber dinghy and the tent had gone. He shrugged. He knew he'd been hard on them. But better to lose face than be dead.

He looked round again. On the horizon he saw a cruise ship—not a big one. And close behind it were the dark clouds that meant a storm was coming.

CHAPTER TWO

HE'D only just bought his cottage. Was still working on it slowly, trying to decide what sort of home he needed. Which meant, of course, what sort of life he wanted to lead. So the cottage seemed somehow half-finished.

He'd never owned a house before so he loved it. And he knew that in time he'd turn it into the kind of home he would love even more. But something was missing. He knew what it was but he wouldn't let himself dwell on it. He had made plans, but those plans had been wrecked. Now he had to go forward; the past was gone.

He had a shower, a quick breakfast and drove up to the surgery. He was not yet a proper partner in the practice, but his father was anxious that he should join them as quickly as possible. There was plenty of work.

Officially, he was still on sick leave after leaving the army. But that would soon be over. Anyway, he felt well. More or less.

He loved the work of being a GP, loved the variety, the chance to meet and to know his patients. But in that case…why was he not more happy than he was? He shook his head, angry with himself. Troubles were there to be overcome.

He was early at the surgery as usual. He walked to the staff lounge. The door was open and there was Nick, his father, talking cheerfully to Kate Althorp, a midwife at the practice. It wasn't like his father to look so relaxed. His head was bent low over some papers on the table and Kate's head was close to his. The two were laughing at something.

Just a bit odd, Ed thought. There seemed to be a togetherness there that he hadn't noticed before. Then he decided he was imagining things.

They hadn't heard him arrive so for a minute Ed stood and looked at them. His father was a tall, lean, imposing figure, made more imposing by his habitual reserve. He tended to command instant respect—but not instant love. Ed had seen little of his father in recent years, and had never really been close to him. As a man he was hard to get through to. But Ed was trying. The trouble was, they were both reserved men.

He coughed, feeling almost like an intruder. Both looked up and smiled. Kate's was the friendly warm smile that made everyone take to her. His father's smile was, well, genuine, but cautious.

'You're early, aren't you?' Nick asked. 'And I thought you didn't have surgery this morning.'

'I don't. I'm going up to Clintons' farm. I want to see Isaac Clinton and I called in to check through his notes.'

His father was interested. 'Are there problems?'

'I don't think it's anything too serious—not yet. His daughter phoned last night, and asked me to call some time today. She thought her father might have had another angina attack in the afternoon, but she persuaded him to lie down and it passed.'

Kate collected the papers on the table and stuffed them into her briefcase. 'I think we've finished here, Nick, and I've got things to do. I'll leave you two to talk business. Bye, Ed.' Another happy smile and she was gone.

Nick looked after her for a while. Ed wondered what he was thinking. It was not like his father to be pensive so early in the morning. But then Nick shook himself and said, 'Isaac Clinton is an awkward old so-and-so. He thinks that farm will fall to bits if he isn't always on the lookout. And he's got a great farm manager in Ellie, that daughter of his. Would you like me to—'

'My patient,' Ed interrupted. 'There's no need for you to bother. I'll talk some sense into him. I promise you, if I need help I'll ask for it.'

'Of course, of course. I've got every confidence in you. You know before his heart attack Isaac had a history of injuries? I spent no end of time up there sewing him together. He just wasn't safe anywhere near farm machinery. Good farmer, though.'

'I've looked through his notes,' Ed said with a grin. 'If he'd got that many injuries in the army, he'd have had a dozen medals by now.'

His father smiled back. 'And I'll bet when you first met him he told you about every injury?'

'In great detail.'

Conversation between them was easier now they were discussing medicine, but it had always been like this. They avoided talking about feelings and there was seldom any obvious show of affection. Personal relationships, especially with those they loved, just weren't their best point. Even though they both tried. Ed suspected that the feelings were there, they were just never shown. He felt it was a pity.

He drove high onto the moors, enjoying the sunshine. But the air was still close; there was an unpleasant stickiness to it. He knew that some time soon there'd be a storm. Everyone in Penhally kept an eye on the weather.

Clintons' farm was well kept. Ed drove into the farmyard and was met at the farmhouse front door by Ellie Clinton. She must have been looking out for him. She smiled, a smile of welcome rather than relief—obviously she was not too worried about her father. Ed had met her several times before. Even though she was the farm manager, she always seemed to be around when he called to see Isaac.

'Dr Tremayne, it's good to see you. You must be warm—can I get you a glass of lemonade? I made it myself. Or tea or coffee?'

'Nothing, thanks. How is your father?'

Ellie stood back from the door, waving him inside. 'Well, you know. He's as awkward as ever. Yesterday I caught him loading stones into a cart, he looked dreadful. After an argument I got him to go to bed. And I phoned you. Are you sure you wouldn't like some lemonade?'

He knew it was probably the wrong thing to do. He wanted the relationship with Ellie to remain strictly doctor-patient, not hostess-guest. But it was hot and she obviously wanted him to try some. 'Perhaps a small glass,' he said. 'Thanks, Ellie.'

He was a guest now so he had to sit down to drink his lemonade and make conversation. He looked at Ellie. She was definitely very attractive, dressed today in a sleeveless, rather low-cut blue dress. She was wearing more obvious lipstick, her hair freshly washed and gleaming. A bit different from the usual farmer's boots, jeans and T-shirt. 'Going out somewhere?' he asked.

She did a little pirouette, the skirt swirling round her calves. 'Do you like the dress? It was such a lovely day, and I had to wait in for you, so I thought I'd try it on. It's new, I bought it for the hospital benefit ball. It's next Saturday. You know, St Piran Hospital. You are going, aren't you?'

Ed frowned. 'Somebody mentioned something about it at the surgery. I think quite a few of them are going but I'm not.'

'But you must! It's a very good cause, they're trying to buy a new scanner. And if the doctors can't support it, well, that's a pity.'

She looked at him, elaborately casually, as if she had just thought of something. 'In fact, I have a spare ticket. I was going with my cousin but she can't make it. You could go as my guest if you liked. The hospital has done a lot for Dad, I'd like to pay a bit back.'

For a moment Ed was tempted. Ellie was an attractive woman, intelligent, and had a great sense of humour. Any man would enjoy her company and be proud to be seen with her. But...why start something that he knew could never have a happy ending? He shook his head, smiled and said, 'It's just not my thing. I don't like big parties. But I approve of the scanner so I'll buy a book of raffle tickets at the surgery. Now, tell me about your father.'

Ellie smiled sadly and said, 'He's not been too bad today. He's waiting in his room to see you. Do you want to go up?'

Isaac was sitting by the window in his bedroom. He looked up as Ed entered and said, 'I'm all right, there's nothing wrong with me. That daughter of mine—'

'Is too good for you. She's concerned about you and by the look of you, she has cause to be. Now, do you want to lie on that bed and let me have a look at you?'

Just the usual examination. At first Isaac seemed reasonably healthy, but when Ed eventually listened to his heart he didn't like the murmurs he could hear.

'Are you taking your pills regularly, Isaac?'

'Well, yes, more or less, but they don't seem to do much for me. I don't feel any better for taking them.'

'They do plenty for you. And they're not meant to make you feel better. They're to ensure that you don't get any worse. Listen, Isaac, it's hard to take but you have to face up to it. You're not the man you used to be. You can't be, you're getting old. And that happens to all of us. You go out into that farmyard of yours again, pretend that you're a man of thirty instead of sixty-six and one day…'

'I'll be ready for the knacker's yard,' Isaac said with relish. 'Don't wrap things up nicely do you, Doctor?'

'You don't need nice, Isaac, you need truth. Now, we're not stopping you from taking a gentle walk around the place, keeping an eye on things. I've told you exactly what you can and what you can't do. And keep taking the pills regularly!'

Ed nodded at the view across the fields that Isaac had been surveying. 'You would miss this place if you had to spend months in a nursing home, wouldn't you?'

It was hard but it was necessary if he was going to get through to this stubborn old farmer. 'Could it be that bad?' Isaac asked. He was obviously shaken by that, if nothing else.

Ed patted him on the shoulders. 'We don't want to find out,' he said.

There was a tap at the door. Ellie came in with a jug of lemonade and two glasses. 'Have you talked sense into him?' she asked. But there was an obviously fond look at her father.

Ed smiled. 'He's got you to keep an eye on him,' he said. 'So he should be all right. Now, Isaac, you're to keep to the house for the next three days. No further than the front door. Plenty of bed rest. Then take it easy, a step at a time after that. Ellie, if there's any change you can ring me at any time, OK?'

'OK,' she said. And added hopefully, 'Are you sure I can't persuade you about the ticket?'

'It's just not my thing,' he repeated. He saw the disappointment in her eyes.

Driving back to Penhally, he wondered why he had turned Ellie down. He doubted if there was an unattached woman as attractive as her anywhere in the little town. And he had been attracted. So why had he refused her invitation?

Partly, he knew, it was because he wanted to be fair to her. He knew he could never give her what she wanted. A purely physical relationship, that was fine—but she deserved more than that. He knew the closeness she wanted, because once he had had it himself. He had lost it. And he was not going to risk more pain by looking for it again.

* * *

When Ed got out of his car to walk into the surgery he found his shirt sticking to his back. He'd already discarded his tie and jacket. Even moving slowly was like wading through warm water. He looked up at the grey skies and frowned.

As he walked past the reception desk his father came to the door of his room, phone clasped to his ear. He waved at Ed to come and join him. After Ed entered the room, his father promptly shut the door behind him. Ed heard him say, 'OK, Captain, you sort things out with your head office. I'll make arrangements to come out to you at once... No, I can do it quicker myself... Fine, we'll call it a private call.'

He put down the phone, looked at Ed and said, 'There's an emergency. There's a cruise ship just off shore and they need a doctor.'

'I thought all cruise ships had doctors.'

'They did have one. He was taken off the ship yesterday. And now they need him more than ever.'

'Always the way,' said Ed. 'What's the problem?'

'A virus—it's spreading like mad, turning into an epidemic.'

Ed was aware that his father was studying him, and he knew why. But he managed to keep his neutral expression and said nothing.

His father went on, 'It's gastroenteritis, but we've no idea what has caused it. Could be mild, it could be severe.'

There was a moment's pause and then Ed said, 'Well, I'm available this afternoon, and I'm the obvious one to go.'

He knew what his father was going to say next, but he waited for him to say it.

'I think I ought to go,' Nick said after a while. 'I know

the nurse who's reporting it, we've worked well together in the past. She thinks it might be quite serious.'

'But you've got surgery all afternoon and this evening. I'm available.' Ed paused a minute and then said, 'Come on, Dad, I know what you're thinking. So say it.'

Nick smiled, though it wasn't a very happy smile. 'Don't have much time for the niceties, do you? But I appreciate it. All right, I'm not sure you're fit to deal with a possible large-scale infection. It will bring back memories.'

'But I am the man who has dealt with an epidemic. In this case, I'm the expert. I know you're the best man to do the lab work, to work out what strain it is. But for the hour-to-hour medical care, the general organisation, I'm the best. And I can cope with my memories.'

'Can you?'

'I have to.'

They stared at each other, aware of the tension rising. Ed wondered if it always would be like this between them. And what made it worse was that each was trying to do the best for the other. Both knew it.

'All right,' Nick said eventually. 'The best thing will be if we go together. I can hand over my surgery. You get ready, meet me down at the harbour in half an hour and I'll find a fisherman to take us out to the ship.'

As he spoke there was the first rattle of rain against the window-panes.

'Get a good one,' said Ed. 'There's a storm brewing.'

'They're all good. Now let's move.'

Ed went first to the surgery dispensary, where he signed himself out a large quantity of antibiotics. He knew there would be antibiotics on board, medical centres on cruise ships were always well equipped, especially with anything needed to deal with gastroenteritis. But he liked to make sure. Then he drove home, packed a small bag with whatever clothes and toiletries he might need for a two or three day stay. Practice again. It wasn't the first time he'd had to pack in a hurry.

Then down to the harbour. The rain had slowed a little but now the winds were starting. Ed looked at the sky, at the sea. This was going to be a really bad one.

His father was at the end of the jetty, waving to him. A fishing boat danced madly up and down below him. As Ed strode down the jetty he wondered how his father was feeling. In 1998 there had been a disaster in Penhally. During a storm like this a sea rescue had ended in tragedy. Among others, Nick's father and brother had both died that night.

So how did Nick feel now? Ed wondered. For that matter, how did he feel himself? His uncle and his grandfather, both remembered, both loved, and both dead.

He reached the end of the jetty, climbed carefully down an iron ladder and jumped aboard the heaving fishing boat. The fisherman grabbed his arm, helped him into the tiny cabin. 'Going to be a bad one,' he said, echoing Ed's own thoughts, 'and it's going to get worse.'

They were taken to the lee of the ship where the boarding platform had been rigged. It was still a hard job, jumping across. But both Ed and Nick were fit, and soon they were being taken up stairs and along companionways to the captain's cabin.

Ed took to the captain at once. He recognised the

military training, the ability to see a problem and try to sort it out, no matter what the cost.

'My first concern is the safety of the passengers,' the Captain told them. 'And their safety comes before their comfort. I will do whatever you think fit. I've been in touch with the port authorities, and the ship in effect is now quarantined.' He looked at Nick. 'Dr Tremayne, they'd like you to send them a report. My head office is not very happy—they're losing money.' He smiled without mirth. 'Well, that's just too bad. Since I spoke to you I've spoken to the passengers and explained the situation. All ill or possibly ill passengers will be confined to their cabins, where food and medical attention will be brought to them. I've ordered a VSP—a vessel sanitation programme—and had as much of the ship as possible disinfected. At my nurse's suggestion I've stopped self-service at meal times.'

'You obviously know what to do in cases like this,' Ed said approvingly.

The captain's smile was bitter. 'We've been to the Indian Ocean. When passengers and crew return from a visit on shore, each one of them is handed a napkin and told to rub their hands with it. It contains a disinfectant that is supposed to kill all known germs and viruses. My crew constantly wipe down and disinfect all handrails in the ship. And I've made sure these precautions have been carried out thoroughly! And then this happens when we're nearly home.'

Ed nodded. 'You seem to have done all you can, Captain.'

'There's more. I don't know if you realise it, but all medical attention has to be paid for. The one exception is stomach upsets. Passengers are told very clearly that if they have any suspicion of a gastric problem they are to phone the medical centre and all medical care will be free.'

Ed was impressed. 'With all these precautions it seems unfair that you should be struck down like this. But you are prepared.'

'An old military rule. Hope for the best, plan for the worst. Now you'll be taken down to the medical section and I leave you to do what you can. Please, let me know at once if there's anything you need.'

'I like a man who knows what he wants,' Nick muttered to him as they were led along companionways.

'You can always tell a military mind,' Ed muttered back. 'But I'm desperately trying to lose mine. I'm a doctor, not a soldier.'

Ed still felt a little uneasy. He knew his father was watching him, looking for any sign of weakness. But he had been in large-scale disease outbreaks before. The fact that he had lost... He forced himself to keep his memories and his feelings in check. But he knew it would be hard.

There was no one in the medical centre when they arrived and the steward left them there to find the nurse. Both took the opportunity to look around. There was a reception area and two treatment rooms, one of which could double up as an operating theatre. It even had X-ray facilities. There was a minilab, a pharmacy and five tiny wards. To one side was a corridor with the staff's living quarters leading off it. It was a hospital and GP surgery combined and in miniature.

Behind him Ed heard a feminine voice say, 'Nick! It's good to see you again.'

'Maddy, it's good to see you, too. You were the best nurse I ever had.'

Ed turned to see his father stooping to kiss the cheek of a petite woman in nurse's uniform. Then Nick stood aside and said, 'Maddy, I'd like you to meet another Dr Tremayne. My son Ed.'

Ed held his hand out. 'Pleased to meet you, Maddy.' And then he looked at her properly. She was about his own age, and had shoulder-length light brown hair, now carefully tied back. Her body was curvaceous. She was very attractive. Then he tried to distance himself from that thought. He was only a doctor here!

Maddy smiled at him, and he found himself looking into her eyes. They were large, hazel-coloured and rather beautiful. But for the moment it was the expression in them that concerned him. There was apprehension there, but that was to be expected in someone who was faced with an outbreak of illness. And something more. Ed had a sense that something was haunting her, a fear perhaps, or a memory.

He thought that he'd like to know more about Maddy, perhaps help her get over whatever it was that was troubling her. He could feel her anguish—after all, he had suffered anguish himself.

But first he had his duty to attend to! 'So how can we help you, Maddy?' he asked.

'I'd like you to tell me I'm wrong. But I know I'm not. I've now got fifteen people confined to their cabins and there are more who're about to go down sick. At the moment I'm the only trained medical staff but there are stewards who've been on an elementary course and they can act as orderlies. They've been very good. The illness is…' She corrected herself. 'I think the illness is caused by Norovirus. Acute gastroenteritis. But it seems to be much more serious than normal.'

'Is that possible in this country?' Ed asked. 'I thought that for Europeans, who are reasonably well fed, it was nasty but not too dangerous.'

There was a pause. Then Nick said, 'I'm afraid there are variations. Some quite recent mutations. And some of them can be very unpleasant indeed.'

'You've dealt with them before?'

'Only in the lab,' Nick said.

Maddy was pleased to have Nick and Ed there. She felt confident that she could have coped with the outbreak alone somehow. But with the Tremaynes helping her work, coping would be easier.

She could tell the two were father and son. It was not just the physical resemblance—though that was there. The were both big, tall, handsome men. More important was the feelings they inspired, their attitude. They seemed calm, competent, tough.

Or was that just the way she remembered Nick? He didn't seem to have changed much since she'd last seen him. His dark hair was perhaps a little more grey, there was the odd extra line on his face. But he was as lean, as erect as ever.

Ed was different. His hair was blond, cut very short. His eyes were blue, unlike his father's brown ones. And he moved differently, lightly, almost on his toes. Maddy recognised it as the action of a well-trained athlete.

They were both very different from the men she had been mixing with recently. Apart from the crew, most of the men were old. Dr Coombs was short, a bit tubby and was never going to die of overwork. She was feeling more confident by the minute.

'So what have you got for us, Maddy?' Nick asked.

She gave a quick summary of what had happened so far. 'The captain is doing what he can, confining the sick ones to their cabins, taking all possible precautions. The passengers here have been well fed, well looked after. But a lot of them are old, or have come on this cruise to convalesce. I've dealt with gastroenteritis before, I know it's not supposed to be too serious. But the vital signs in some of them are very worrying.'

'Might I glance through the case notes?' Nick asked. She had them ready and handed them to him.

He passed half of the pile of notes to Ed and both started to skim through them. After a while Nick muttered, 'This does seem to be more serious than…'

'May I see the rest of the notes?' Ed asked him, and the two exchanged piles. Then there was silence for a moment and Maddy felt her confidence ebbing. It was good to be proved right…but she didn't want to be right.

Ed spoke first. 'I agree with you, Maddy. This is bad. I've come across an attack like this before. People think that gastroenteritis has just one cause but there can be many. In this case, onset seems far too rapid to be normal, dehydration far too advanced. It looks like a particularly effective bacterium or virus.'

'Most likely a virus,' Nick put in.

Ed shrugged. 'We'll have to find out. To be more exact,

you'll have to find out. But my experience says that it is a bacterium. Note the consistent high temperatures. More in line with bacterium than virus.'

'A viral infection is more common.'

'True. But I intend to use antibiotics until you tell me definitely that this is a virus.'

Maddy realised that this was a small trial of strength between the two men. Between father and son—both doctors. There was a difference of opinion and she knew that Nick didn't like being contradicted.

There was a silence and then Nick said slowly, 'We agreed that you are in charge. You must do what you think best.'

Ed nodded. 'I'd like you to do the necessary tests and let me know the results as quickly as possible. Analysis is one of your strengths.' He looked at Maddy. 'How busy were you before this outbreak? You've obviously got more cases than these.'

'I've been kept busy,' she said. 'There's the usual small stuff—minor injuries, conditions that need an eye kept on them. This morning I had a man who'd had a TIA—I think.'

'Would you like me to have a look at him?' Ed asked.

She appreciated being asked. 'I'm reasonably happy but, yes,' she said. 'If you don't mind.'

'I don't mind, I'm a doctor. I'll be happy to.' He smiled at her then—she realised for the first time. And it made his face, the sometimes stern Tremayne face, look so much more attractive.

'One good thing,' he went on, 'is that this condition tends to burn out very quickly. Only a forty-eight hour isolation period is needed. Now, shall we go and check on the patients so far?'

They agreed that Nick should visit the male patients with a steward, and she would visit the female patients with Ed. They set off at once.

As they paced along the corridor she was aware of an odd sensation. At first she didn't recognise it, it just seemed that the world might not be as bad a place as it had seemed a few minutes ago. There was promise in it. Then it struck her, so suddenly that for a moment she stopped walking. It was Ed Tremayne! He was…she was…she was attracted to him! This was ludicrous!

Her felt her stop, turned to her. 'Everything OK?'

'Just something I thought I had forgotten,' she mumbled. 'Nothing important.'

She tried to examine what she was feeling. It was just relief, she decided. There was something solid and dependable about Ed. Whatever attraction there was, it wasn't sexual. Was it? But he was attractive—both physically and in his personality, And there was something hidden about him—she couldn't work out quite what it was…

'Which branch of the armed forces were you in, Ed?' she asked, hoping her voice sounded normal.

He laughed. 'How did you know that I'd been in the armed forces?'

That was an easy question to answer. 'Well, there's the short haircut. But more than that, I've had dealings with soldiers before. There's something about the way they behave that I recognise. It's the way they look round, assessing everything. Then the certainty that they are right. Often the way they are ready to take charge.'

A small smile. 'So you expect me to take charge? Maddy, I've no intention of doing that. I've said it and I meant it—we're partners. And I've always thought of myself as a doctor far more than a soldier. As to being certain that I'm right, well, no. I've been wrong, very wrong. And later I've realised it.'

His voice went quiet as he spoke, as if an unwelcome memory had flashed across his mind. For a moment she wondered what he was thinking, but she decided it wasn't the right time to ask. 'We all make mistakes,' she said. 'It's part of the human condition.'

'True.' His voice was mild as he went on, 'but I do have to own up. I am an ex-soldier and some of the happiest days of my life were when I was in the army.' He paused a moment and then said, 'But not necessarily because I was in the army.'

'Right,' she said.

CHAPTER THREE

ED HAD skimmed through her notes and decided that this was the patient he wanted to see first. She had been one of the earliest to fall ill, and her condition appeared to be one of the worst.

Miriam Jones was a widow of sixty-eight. She was not happy with her condition. 'I paid a lot of money for this trip, Dr Tremayne,' she said after Ed had introduced himself. 'I do not take kindly to having to spend the last two days of it lying on a bed in my cabin.'

But her voice was weak. Maddy could see that a lot of the strength had gone out of someone who had previously been a tough lady. She was trying to survive—but she was failing.

Ed examined her. Maddy had already set up a giving set to get fluids into the patient but Ed suggested a more rapid rate of flow. He also prescribed a larger dose of the antibiotic that Maddy had already given her. Then he took Mrs Jones's hand.

'I'm not going to hide anything from you, Mrs Jones,' he said. 'You're seriously ill. But I've got confidence in you, I know you've got the strength to pull through. And I know you won't be as much trouble as some others we're seeing.'

Mrs Jones's pale face lit up. 'No, I won't,' she said.

'Then I'll be in to see you later. Anything really serious, phone us.'

The next call was totally different. Miss Owen—the new Miss Owen, having previously been Mrs Dacre and now very satisfactorily divorced—had come on this cruise to 'rebuild her confidence'. Contracting gastroenteritis had shaken this confidence.

Maddy saw Ed handle this patient in a totally different fashion. He joked with her. Even got a smile. And when they left the cabin, Miss Owen was a slightly happier person.

They worked their way through the rest of the cases. Most cabins were occupied by couples. Maddy noticed that when this was the case, Ed was as charming as ever with the sick person. But then he took the husband or wife to one side and had a quiet word with them. She managed to listen to one conversation and was intrigued by it. Ed's words were partly reassurance and partly a clear statement of what he expected. Ed knew what the patients needed and was going to see that they got it.

Finally they had seen all the cases and were walking back to the medical centre to meet Nick again. Maddy felt that this was going to be a good partnership. 'I'm glad you've come on board,' she said. 'I feel that things aren't too bad now.'

He glanced at her, smiled. 'So, for the moment, have you got over your bitterness at the military mind? Tell me, was it the army as a whole or one particular individual?'

This took her aback. Ed was an astute observer, far more perceptive than she had realised. 'Sorry if I was a bit short with you,' she muttered. 'I'm sure we'll work well together.'

She wasn't going to answer his question about her being upset by one particular individual. She waited for him to ask again but he didn't. He knew she didn't want to answer and that made her even more cautious.

She didn't want to reveal herself, to be vulnerable. And Ed was getting close to making her feel exposed.

They turned a corner and saw a mother and child coming towards them. The little boy, aged about seven, ran towards her, yelling, 'Nurse Maddy! Look, I'm a pirate again.'

And a pirate little Robbie Cowley was. He flourished a large plastic cutlass, had a skull and crossbones on his large plastic hat. His T-shirt didn't quite match, though. On it was the picture of a devil, cheerful rather than frightening. There was a dressing on his right arm.

Laughing, Maddy was about to pick him up then remembered where she had just been. The less contact between people the better.

'Just stay there, Robbie,' she said with a smile to reassure him. 'There might be some nasty stuff on me.' Then she turned to the mother and smiled. 'Don't tell me, Mrs Cowley, he's still a handful.'

Mrs Cowley, a buxom blonde in her early thirties, smiled and shook her head. 'I thought when he cut his arm that it would quieten him down a bit. You told him he had to be good, not to run around so much or he might hurt his arm even more. And he was good, didn't run around. For about twenty minutes.'

'That's little boys for you,' Maddy agreed. 'You just have to be there with them all the time.' She turned and said to Ed, 'This is Mrs Cowley and her son Robbie. I've seen quite a bit of young Robbie.' She twinkled at the little boy. 'He's been a regular customer—that devil on his T-shirt says it all.'

'I'm a pirate now, not a devil,' Robbie shouted. 'What nasty stuff on you? I'll hit it with my cutlass.'

Ed stopped a cutlass swing with his arm, and crouched down to face Robbie. 'That's a fine weapon you have there, Captain,' he said, 'and a fine hat, too. What's the name of your ship?'

'The Hisp...the Hisp thingy,' Robbie said. 'After Nurse Maddy had bandaged up my arm she read me a bit about it. It was good!'

'She's a good reader. I'll get her to read to me. Now, you will be careful with that deadly weapon, won't you?'

Maddy watched curiously. Ed had work to do but from his body language it was obvious that he was clearly taken with the little boy. There was regret in the way he straightened himself, became a doctor again.

'I'm going to capture a ship,' Robbie told him. 'One of those white ones on the top deck.'

'I wish you luck. A pirate's life is a hard one.'

There was time for a few polite words with Mrs Cowley and then they moved back to the medical centre. 'You seemed to quite take to Robbie,' Maddy suggested.

'Typical little boy. I like them.' A clipped reply. 'Is his father on board?'

'There is no father. And Mrs Cowley has just been diagnosed with adult-onset diabetes. She has the pills, she knows—or she should know—how to control her diet. But she relapses. I've kept an eye on her, tried to get her to discipline herself. But if you like eating then a cruise ship is the last thing you want to be on.'

'So Mrs Cowley has spent quite some time resting in her cabin? And Robbie has been allowed to run riot?'

'There are two big children's playgrounds and staff always on duty. But no way can they keep track of every child. Robbie was trying to climb onto a lifeboat but he fell and gashed his arm. Before that he tumbled down some stairs and trapped his fingers in a door.'

'But a cheerful child?'

'He's lovely,' Maddy agreed.

There was a message from the captain waiting for them when they got back to the medical centre. The storm had got worse and the forecast was that over the next twelve hours it would get worse still. It would be extremely difficult, probably impossible, to try to move ill people from the ship to land. A helicopter landing was out of the question, a boat trip would be highly dangerous.

'I don't think we want to start moving old sick people anyway,' Nick said, 'but we'll have to decide if it's necessary. What do you think, Maddy, Ed?'

Maddy was pleased that she was included in the decision-making. But she decided to remain silent for a while. Perhaps she was too close to the problem.

'It's gastroenteritis all right,' Ed said, 'but it's a very nasty strain. I still suspect it's bacterial in origin.'

Nick shook his head. 'We can't be certain until I've done tests,' he said. 'I've collected samples, and we'll know more when I've been inside the lab for a while.'

He looked at his son, a glance half compassionate, half assessing, Maddy thought. There was something here that she didn't know about. And she wanted to know what.

'We're agreed that Maddy needs help—that one of us should stay aboard?'

'We're agreed. There's just too much work for one person. And I'm the obvious one to stay.'

'Are you sure you'll be all right?' Nick asked.

'I'll be fine.'

Another silence. Maddy wondered what was happening. There seemed to be some silent exchange of messages between the two men. She could read it in their body language. Nick was relaxed, trying to be helpful. Ed had the taut look of a man who was expecting an argument. Finally Nick said, 'Right, then. Still, remember, a good doctor will ask for help if he needs it. Now I'm going to see the captain, explain the situation and tell him what we think it's best to do. Then the final decision will be his. But unless he objects, Ed, you stay, do what you can, and remember that the next twelve to twenty-four hours will be the hardest.'

'I've dealt with that before,' Ed said.

'Good. Oh, the patients I've just seen, there's one, a Mr Simmonds. He's got gastroenteritis all right and I've given him a thorough examination—he's an old man but there's nothing seriously wrong with him. Nothing physical, that is.'

'But mentally?' Ed asked.

'Well, I noticed he's on antidepressants—mild ones. When I asked him about them he said they did little good, he'd stopped taking them and he felt better. But...I've got a feeling about the man.'

Ed shook his head. 'I'll keep an eye on him,' he said, 'but I suspect there'll be nothing we can do. We just have to hope.'

'Sometimes that's all a doctor can do,' his father said. Then he turned to Maddy. 'Been good to see you, Maddy. Hope you and Ed get on well together. I've every confidence in the pair of you.' And then he was gone.

Maddy and Ed looked at each other. 'This morning we didn't even know the other one existed,' Maddy said hesitantly, 'and now we're thrown together like this.'

'Strange, how things happen. But I'm looking forward to working with you. Getting to know you better.'

That was a statement that could be taken more than one way, Maddy thought. But as they looked at each other he didn't say anything more. There seemed to be some kind of understanding flowing between them that, just for the moment, didn't need words. His blue eyes stared at her. She could see puzzlement there, as if he didn't really know what he was feeling. But finally he jerked them back into the present.

'Let's get started,' he said. 'Now, are there any scrubs I could borrow?'

She pointed to a cupboard. 'One thing about being on a cruise ship, the laundry is done fast and well.'

'It's going to need to be that way,' Ed said. 'During a gastroenteritis outbreak, cleanliness is all important. Now we need to see what resources we—'

The phone rang. Maddy picked up the receiver, listened for a moment. 'Cabin B52? We'll be right there.' She looked at Ed. 'Another case. It's going to be like this nonstop now, isn't it?'

'It is. And there's your regular work, too.' He smiled again. 'But we'll manage together.'

He decided to change into scrubs before they set off.

When he came back in the green shapeless garments she noticed the muscles on his forearms. And she noticed something else. He was wearing a wedding ring.

For some reason she was disappointed, which was silly. She should have known. A good-looking man like Ed would obviously be married. He would have been snapped up years ago. What was she thinking of? Anyway, she was off men. It was foolish on her part, harbouring even the smallest feeling for him. They were just colleagues for a while.

They went to Cabin B52 and examined the patient—a man this time. There was the usual initial assessment. A high temperature suggested bacterial infection rather than viral. Hypotension—low blood pressure—was another indicator. There would be tachycardia—a fast pulse, and often it would be thready. The most obvious signs were of dehydration. A dry mouth, no tears, skin that tented when it was pinched, poor capillary return, tested by pinching the fingernails. There would be mild discomfort to the abdomen—but it didn't get worse when palpated. Either she or Ed would take a blood sample and test it in the medical centre.

And there was always the chance that it could be some other condition. It would be foolish to assume that any illness was automatically gastroenteritis.

To avoid dehydration each patient had to be given a saline and dextrose IV line. The amount given depended on physical state, body weight and the blood count. Since Ed had decided that this was a bacterial infection, not a viral one, antibiotics could be used. But the kind and the amount and the frequency depended on the patient's state.

And the seriousness of the attack. Some people were more susceptible than others.

As before, after this assessment Ed spoke to the man's partner and told her what to expect, what to do. Again, as before, Maddy was impressed by the clear way he spoke, by the manner in which he made it clear that he expected his suggestions to be carried out. The passengers certainly seemed calmed by him.

But Maddy still felt a little unsettled. Working with Ed was not as satisfying as it had been before.

As they walked back to the medical centre she asked, as casually as she could, 'Ed, will your wife mind you being away for a while?'

'Why do you think I have a wife?' The question was abrupt, hostile even.

'Well, it's just that I saw you were wearing a wedding ring. I'm sorry if I upset you.'

'You didn't upset me.' But his tone contradicted his words. 'My wife is dead.'

She wondered if he was going to say any more, then wondered if she ought to say she was sorry again. But he said nothing, pacing more quickly down the corridor so she had to hurry to keep up with him.

Obviously she had upset him. She wondered if all relationships had to result in pain.

When they got back to the medical centre Ed became his normal efficient self again. 'We know the situation is going to deteriorate,' he said, 'and we need to get on top of it now. I'd like to check on all supplies. If necessary, we might have to get in some more. Somehow.'

'I'll write out an inventory of the most needed drugs,' Maddy said, 'we can mark them off as we use them, so we know when we're getting low.'

'Good idea. And shall we have a list of the stewards we can call on and work out a rota? If you want to pencil in any personal comments, I'll see them but they'll go no further.'

'You've done this kind of thing before, haven't you?' she asked.

'I have.'

She noticed he didn't give her any details. For a moment there was a hunted look on his face, as if there was a painful memory. But when he spoke he was as clear and forceful as ever. 'What's very useful is to have a wall chart, marking off each patient we have, the stage of development of the illness, the treatment. It's important that we can see at a glance just what the situation is. A set of patient's notes that you have to page through just isn't good enough.' He thought for a moment. 'In fact, could we have a steward or someone in here to act as ward secretary?'

'I'll phone the captain, see if he can find someone for us. I'm sure he will.'

'Good. Is there anything special that you—?'

The phone rang again. This tine it was Ed who answered it, who took the number of the cabin and then said, 'I'll be right there.'

He looked at Maddy. 'Looks like another case. I'll take this one on my own—you've got plenty to do here organising the logistics of this operation. I'll be back to liaise as soon as I can.'

Back to liaise? Maddy thought as soon as he had gone. Had she joined the army without knowing it? Then she realised. Everything Ed had done made perfect sense. This was an emergency and he was treating it as such. He was concerned about the welfare of his patients. Then she remembered something else. There had been a set expression on his face as he'd talked about the organisation necessary. As if this was—or had been—painful. What was he hiding?

She had finished the paperwork when he returned and told him that the captain was sending them down a purser's assistant to act as ward clerk. He nodded approvingly. 'I hate paperwork,' he said, 'but I know it's vital to keep it up. Now we can concentrate on the important work. Maddy, did you tell me that you thought that one of your patients had a TIA this morning?'

She nodded. 'Mr Bryce. I got a steward to keep an eye on him, but I'd like to go and see him myself.'

'Let's go together. Are the case notes handy?'

He scanned the notes and she saw him frown. 'If we were on shore, I'd send this man to hospital,' he said.

'So would I. But this morning I thought that shipping him ashore might be more of a risk than keeping him in his bed. That was when I thought that we'd dock tomorrow. And now, with the disease and the storm, it's impossible.'

'You still made the right decision. Let's go and look at him.'

So they went. And it was obvious that Mr Bryce was a very sick man indeed. Now his speech was slurred, he was much weaker. Maddy watched helplessly as Ed listened to Mr Bryce's heart, took his blood pressure, talked gently to him.

'You've enjoyed the cruise, then, Mr Bryce? Thinking of coming back on another one?'

'If I'm alive, yes.' Maddy saw a tiny smile on her friend's face. 'And if Maddy there is on the ship.'

'Maddy is a star. I've only just met her but I can tell that.'

'That's a nice thing to say. Yes, Maddy is a star.' Mr Bryce's eyes closed.

Ed changed Maddy's prescription of aspirin for warfarin—a much more effective anti-coagulant. Then he shook Mr Bryce's hand and told him that they'd be back to see him.

'How is he?' Maddy asked, knowing and dreading what the answer would be.

'He's an old man and I think there's a danger of a stroke,' Ed said. 'But, Maddy, no one can tell. He has a fighting chance and he looks like a fighter. Was he a particular friend of yours?'

'Sort of,' Maddy said. 'I've seen a lot of him. Ed, you were kind to him.'

'I try to be kind to all my patients,' he said. 'When it's possible.'

After that cases came in with predictable regularity. Ed saw each one first, made an initial diagnosis—which was usually not difficult. More difficult was assessing the seriousness of the attack and deciding on the medication. This was a task Maddy was pleased to hand over. After Ed's initial visit, Maddy took over the nursing duties.

Here again, things weren't as normal. Ed had to warn her. 'Maddy, this is an emergency, you can't give each patient the time you would in a normal nursing situation. You're a specialist and you must learn to delegate. Whatever a steward can do, get him or her to do it. You're needed for the special nursing jobs.'

She didn't like what she had to do, leaving patients who needed and wanted her skills. Needed her care. But she knew that Ed's apparent ruthlessness made sense.

As the day wore on the situation got worse. More and more people were falling ill. The captain came down to see them. He said, 'I'm not going to stay, not going to interfere. Whatever you need, just ask for it. If it's available, you can have it.' And he was gone.

'Good man, the captain,' was Ed's remark.

They were coping—just. But they knew that they'd have to be up all night. 'Don't worry,' Ed told her, 'whatever happens, we'll manage. We'll manage because we're a team, we're working together.'

She liked him for this. She wasn't exactly enjoying herself—but Ed made her feel as if her work was worthwhile, he gave her a sense of purpose. She liked working with him.

They worked together until the evening. Maddy was sitting in the medical centre, checking over the supplies. Ed had gone what he called wandering. 'Just ambling about, dropping in here and there,' he said. 'Getting the feel of things.'

Then after fifteen minutes, she was buzzed. 'Hi, Maddy, Ed here.' It had only been ten minutes since she had seen him. But she was surprised at how welcome his voice was. What was happening to her? Then she recognised the tone of his voice, quiet, regretful. This wasn't good news.

'Who is it, Ed?'

'It's Mr Bryce. He's...very ill but he's asking for you.'

'Mr Bryce?' An old man but the one true friend she had made on the voyage. 'How is he, Ed?'

There was a hesitation, then the usual careful doctor-speak. 'He's very ill, very weak. There's nothing more we can do for him. But he's lucid—now.'

Maddy got the message. Her friend Malcolm Bryce was dying. She had managed to visit him twice that day, though if she had not been so busy she would have stayed with him much longer. But she just hadn't had time! And now he was dying. Maddy bit her lip, trying to stop the tears squeezing from beneath her lids. Why did it have to happen to her friend?

'All right if I come to see him?'

Ed understood what she was asking. 'Of course. If you'd like to stay with him a while, I have other things to do.'

'I'm on my way.'

She only needed one glance at Malcolm to know that he didn't have very long. To a trained nurse the signs were obvious. But he was still awake, he recognised her and smiled when she took his hand.

'Something to say to you, Maddy,' he managed to whisper. 'I don't think I'll have the chance again. When I asked you to marry me—I know it was a joke, but I half meant it.'

She smiled sadly at the old man. 'I told you, Malcolm,

just now I don't want to get married. But if I did, you'd be the man I'd pick.'

'I don't think I can wait. But if I'd been forty years younger then I would have waited. But, Maddy, you'll make some other man very happy.'

'Perhaps,' she replied, and squeezed his hand. Then she watched as his eyes closed and he lapsed into unconsciousness. She knew he wouldn't open them again.

She was tired, she needed to go to bed. But Malcolm had been her friend, she did not want him to die alone. So she sat in a chair and listened to his laboured breathing. The nicest man she had met in a long time—and he was going to die. She couldn't help it. Silently, the tears came.

It didn't come as a shock when there was a quiet tap on the door, and Ed came in. He said nothing, glanced at Mr Bryce then raised his eyebrows at her. She shook her head. Nothing could be done. But he was still a doctor, he made a quick but gentle examination—and apparently agreed with her.

'I'm going to stay with him for a while longer,' she said.

'Well, I'm entitled to a bit of self-indulgence. I'll stay, too.' He sat by her, looked at her as she sat there with her head bowed. 'Was he a particular friend?'

'Perhaps he was. He had to come to the medical centre quite a bit, he'd hurt his leg—and this morning he asked me to marry him.'

'He what?'

Maddy managed to smile. 'It was only a joke. Or perhaps half a joke. But I liked him a lot.'

Both of then looked up as the sound of Mr Bryce's breathing altered. Cheyne-Stokes breathing. An alteration from very rapid to very slow breaths, with pauses between them. In a man of Mr Bryce's condition it meant that death was near.

'He was the first man to be nice to me for quite a long time,' she said.

Ed looked surprised. 'The first man to be nice to you? I would have thought that there was no shortage of men interested in you. You're very attractive, Maddy, you must know that.'

She felt a small pleasure at hearing him say this, but at the moment she had other things on her mind. 'Perhaps so. You know this morning—was it only this morning, it seems so long ago? I got a phone call. It was from my ex-boyfriend, ex-fiancé if you like. For a while I thought I was going to marry him. I wanted to have babies with him. Anyway, he wants to pick up with me again. And I don't want to... I just can't... Though I do feel guilty.'

'Why should you feel guilty? Better to decide early that you're not suited.'

'I'm a nurse, I'm supposed to heal the sick. And he was sick.'

She wasn't surprised when Ed took her hand. 'Why don't you tell me about it? I'll try to help if I can. Or help you to understand.'

She laughed, without humour. 'That might be possible. The two of you have things in common.'

He raised his eyebrows again, but all he said was, 'I'd like to help.'

She sighed. 'We got engaged. It was a lightning courtship, he was a hard man to resist. He was a soldier, he went off on active service and he came home with PTSD—

post-traumatic stress disorder. And after that things got so bad that I had to get away from him. It was classic mental abuse—but I suspected that if I married him the mental abuse would have turned physical in time. I was...scared. In fact, at times I still am.'

'Did he have any treatment?'

'He went to a clinic a couple of times at first. Then he said it was a waste of time and that he was cured. He wouldn't take the medication he was prescribed.'

'Tell me more about him. What had he in common with me?'

'He was decisive like you. He knew what he wanted, was going to get it because he thought he was right. It's good if you want to get something done. It's not so good if you're the one being done to. He just can't or won't accept that we're finished. And we are!'

'Have you a family to offer you support? Are your parents alive?'

'I've got no one. My parents died a while ago now, before this happened, and they had no relations. You said I was attractive, well, apparently I am. And because of that, I found that too often men were out for just what they could get. I had a couple of rotten experiences. Then I met Brian. And at first he was different. At first.'

'I see,' he said. Then, with a small smile, 'Maddy, you might not like it but I'm going to be decisive. Obviously your ex-fiancé needs treatment. I'm a doctor, I've had experience of army cases. I can make some phone calls, see that he's picked up and given proper attention. He obviously didn't get it before. But some of the army psychiatrists are very good indeed. They can help.'

There was something odd in his tone, at first she couldn't work out what. But then she realised. It was pain, the pain of memory. She lifted her head to look at him and said, 'You say that as if you know it from personal experience.'

There was a hesitation before he said, 'I was sent for psychological assessment. I had to have a couple of consultations, whether I wanted them or not.'

'Sent because you were showing signs of some kind of mental problem?'

He laughed, but there was no humour in his laughter. 'Just the opposite. It was thought that…that I had suffered things that ought to produce mental problems, but I showed no signs of them.'

'What kind of things that ought to produce mental problems?'

His reply was definitive. 'I don't talk about them.'

But she still wanted to know more. 'So why didn't you show signs of them?'

'I could say because I was tough,' he said. 'But I know that I was just lucky.'

She thought she could believe that. 'And you were given a clean bill of health? No psychological problems found, no irrational fears or phobias?'

'None.'

Just one simple, curt word. But for some reason it didn't convince her. 'Are you sure?'

He lifted his arms, in a gesture almost of surrender. 'Psychology isn't like medicine. It isn't true or false, right or wrong, good or bad. There are great grey areas. And if a psychologist digs hard enough, he's bound to find something not quite right.'

'Are you going to tell me what they found that was not quite right about you?'

'No,' he said.

'Are you going to tell me what things you suffered that caused these problems?'

'No.'

Apparently he thought that the conversation had run its course. But there were more things Maddy wanted to know. She thought that she was getting close to the real Ed, and she wanted desperately to hear more. She started…

It wasn't a sound, it was a lack of sound. Both were trained, both knew what had happened. They turned to look at their patient. Mr Bryce had stopped breathing altogether.

Neither Maddy nor Ed spoke or moved for a while. Then Maddy moved over to look at her friend, bent to kiss him on the forehead.

'You're tired,' Ed said. 'And there's nothing more you can do. I'll do the paperwork and see to everything, it's better if you don't do it. He was your friend, his last few minutes were made happier because you were here. Just go back to the centre, try to close your eyes, relax a little.'

She looked at him through tear-shrouded eyes. 'You're a kind man, Ed.'

'I'm just doing my job,' he said gruffly.

It was eleven o'clock at night, and they were lucky—there was a slight lull in things. She made herself a mug of tea and sat and thought about Ed. He was like her. There was some burden he was carrying—and she wanted to know what it was. She'd only known him a few hours, but during that time she'd seen enough of him to know he was a caring and sensitive man. She could even come to... No, she couldn't. The fear was still deep inside her.

He walked into the medical centre a few minutes later and smiled at her, a weary smile. 'We're getting there,' he said.

'We're getting there because we're working together.' She stood, walked up to him, touched his arm. Just a gentle indication of her liking. 'I couldn't have managed without you.'

'I suspect,' he said, 'that you could.'

Afterwards she wondered, didn't exactly know how it had happened. They were both tired, of course, perhaps not entirely certain of what they were doing. Perhaps it was a purely spontaneous act, something that happened without either of them knowing why.

He looked down at her hand on his arm. Very slowly, he slid his other arm round her waist. It was warm, comforting, she leaned back against it.

His eyes were very blue. She could see them clearly, they were looking down at her with a half curious, half intent expression. Beautiful blue eyes. Why hadn't she noticed how beautiful they were before?

His lips touched hers. So tentatively she knew that she could break away in a second. But she didn't want to. In fact, she reached up, slipped her arm around his neck. At first a gentle kiss. Then it deepened. It turned into something much more than she had anticipated. His body pressed closer to hers. But she was only half-aware of it, all she could think of was the kiss and how it made her head spin, and how Ed was like no man she'd ever met and—

The phone rang and they sprang apart.

Ed picked up the phone, no sign of emotion in his face as he listened intently. 'You're sure? Yes, that sounds right. OK, I'll be there in five minutes.'

'Work calls,' he said to Maddy. Then he shook his head, looked puzzled. 'I'm sorry that happened,' he said. 'It was my fault. I shouldn't have kissed you. We're working hard, we're stressed, we daren't get involved with each other. Emotion and this kind of situation... I've been here before and it's...it's bad.'

Things were different now, but Maddy was still trying to make sense of what had happened. Above all, make sense of how much she had enjoyed it.

'You might be right,' she said, 'and I don't know why we did that. It must be because we are both tired. I don't usually kiss—I mean, kiss like that—people who I've only just met.'

'And I don't go around kissing people like that either,' he said. 'But this is a time apart. And it's a world apart—being on a cruise ship is fundamentally unreal. We've both got lives to go back to. Then we'll forget this.'

'Of course we'll forget it,' she agreed. But as she looked at him, she wondered if either of them believed her. The kiss had been so wonderful.

There was one thing she had to add. 'But, Ed, whatever it was, it wasn't bad.'

CHAPTER FOUR

IT WAS at half past eleven that they were called in to Mrs Jones's room. She had fought valiantly, but now her body was weary. The steward observing had called Ed, and Ed took Maddy with him.

Ed thanked the steward, then nodded for her to go. Then he examined Mrs Jones and then said to Maddy, 'She still has a chance. A small one. All we can do is wait.'

They sat together in silence. Then she thought that this was the man who not fifteen minutes ago had kissed her. And had apparently enjoyed it. Where had he gone now?

He moved over to Mrs Jones, leaned over her and checked her condition. 'Perhaps a bit of an improvement,' he muttered, 'but we'll see.'

Maddy realised that he was calming himself by acting as a doctor. But there were things she wanted to know, he couldn't just leave her with half a story.

'So is all this extra-hard for you?' she asked. 'Does it bring back memories?'

'No. It's not extra-hard. But it is hard. The memories I can deal with, I have to deal with. Now I've got a job to do, I'll do it.' He walked over to their patient, studied her for a minute. 'Maddy, it looks as if Mrs Jones might have rallied a little. I'm going to check on a couple of our other patients, you stay here a while.' He was gone before she could object.

So her chance of questioning him, of learning more about him, had disappeared. She suspected he had left so he didn't have to answer any more of her apparently innocent queries. But when he'd left she found herself wondering. This sudden interest in a man had never happened before.

She had met him for the first time only about twelve hours ago. And twenty minutes ago she had kissed him. Or he had kissed her. Whatever, she knew she had enjoyed it. And this was just not the way she normally behaved. With the departed Dr Coombs and the other nurse she had got on well enough. She'd been popular among both passengers and crew, and she'd enjoyed the dancing in the evening. But she'd only really made friends with Malcolm Bryce, who had been no threat to her heart. And being aboard ship made it easier for her to be pleasant to people and yet be safe. She was never any distance from help, the ship protected her.

So why was Dr Edward Tremayne different?

She felt uneasy. No way was she going to become closely involved with a man again. Not even a man like Ed Tremayne. He seemed to be...different.

She checked Mrs Jones who's condition appeared to be stabilising.

While she was thinking about this, Ed came back. He looked at Mrs Jones and nodded.

She smiled. 'Ed, she's going to be OK. You're doing a really good job.'

She thought at first that he wasn't going to answer, he took so long to reply. But then he said, 'Thanks for being there Maddy. I'm sorry if I'm… It's just this is bringing back so many memories.'

'Even doctors are entitled to feelings,' she told him gently. 'Don't be ashamed of them.'

There was another pause and then he said, 'I just wanted Mrs Jones to have that chance. But I'm sorry if I was a bit short with you.'

Maddy paused for a moment and then said, 'So you're obviously used to emergencies like this. Where were they?'

'Africa.' A curt, one-word answer. But after a moment he said, 'I was an army doctor, went out there expecting to deal with trauma, war wounds, the diseases that a fit soldiery might catch. And I finished up spending most of my time with a starving native population.' He looked at her. 'Come on, there's more patients to see.'

They worked together through the night. Steady but exhausting work. But they knew they were doing a good job.

Maddy was glad she had Ed with her. He seemed to know almost instinctively what was the right dose, the right treatment. She knew she would have done what she could. But Ed was able to do it better. 'You're saving lives,' she told him.

'I've learned how. I've watched other people lose them,' was the flat reply.

She wondered what he was really thinking.

At two in the morning there seemed to be another lull. They both knew it wouldn't last—but it was there. Maddy pointed to her watch. 'This is going to be a long haul,' she said, 'we both know that. You've sent half the stewards off to have some sleep, now you need some yourself. Go to bed, just for a couple of hours. You'll be a better doctor when you wake up.'

'I'd rather you took a break first.'

She shook her head. 'You're showing signs of fatigue now. What time did you get up this morning?'

'I'm an early riser, I was in the sea at six this morning. But I don't need much sleep.'

'I was up a lot later than that and now you need it more than me. Just look at yourself in the mirror.'

She saw him do so, knew he couldn't miss the darkness around his eyes. 'Don't act the macho male with me,' she urged. 'You've got more sense than that. Exhausted doctors make mistakes. Just a couple of hours will improve you no end.'

She could see that he was reluctant to agree but that he had to accept her argument. 'All right, then. But only two hours!'

'After two hours I'll wake you up,' she promised.

She took him to her cabin, pointed to her bed. 'Sleep there. It's my cabin but there's no time to find you somewhere of your own to sleep. And there's a bathroom there if you want it.'

The phone rang. She left him, went to answer it.

He was tired, he had to admit it. And the temptation was just to take off his shoes, lie on the bed and go to sleep.

But he decided not to. He'd have a shower first. Just five minutes would make no end of difference.

He had to smile when he walked into her tiny bathroom. Maddy had not been expecting visitors. On a couple of strings stretched across the shower there were three sets of underwear drying. So far he'd seen her as a nurse, in a rather severe uniform or scrubs. And it suited her. But the knowledge that underneath she wore the flimsiest of coloured lace rather intrigued him.

He had a swift shower, cleaned his teeth. He had brought toiletries with him, in anticipation of his stay on board.

He was still tired but felt considerably better when he climbed into her bed. He decided that he could allow himself another five minutes—but no longer—to think about what he was doing here.

So far he was surviving. He knew he was being efficient, organising the treatments, doing the best possible for his patients. He thought—he hoped—that people felt confident in him.

No one suspected the memories, the terror that swirled underneath. And as he got more fatigued he knew it would get worse. But he would do it. He had to. Only his father would guess what he was going through.

Or had Maddy guessed, too? He had noticed once or twice the thoughtful way that she had looked at him. Her seemingly casual questions had been probing, too. Maddy was quite a woman.

So far he had been thinking about her solely as a colleague. Or had tried to. Now he could think about her as a person. She was so attractive! He was becoming increasingly aware of the generous curves of her body, for some reason emphasised by the plainness of the uniform covering it. When they touched—accidentally, of course—there was that slight electric shock. And the sheen of her hair and the way that it brushed against her cheek when she leaned forward. And he had kissed her! What had possessed him? It was the fact that he was enjoying just being with her and he wanted to— Stop it!

To his horror he realised that he could fall for her. It wasn't just that she was beautiful—though he was coming to appreciate that she was. Ellie Clinton was just as beautiful. Well, nearly as beautiful. And Ellie had nothing like the effect on him that Maddy had. Maddy had some power—a combination of her voice, her figure, her actions, her face... Her face. He remembered that look deep in her eyes... She had been hurt. Like him.

Then he remembered when he had been in a situation like this before. Working in a closed environment with someone he loved. It wasn't good! The risk of tragedy was too great.

Perhaps it would be better if they left each other alone. If they could.

She had intended to leave him for two hours, but after an hour she had to go into her room to wake him. Now she herself was really tired—but she felt that alertness that sometimes came with extreme fatigue.

She switched on the light. She saw his clothes neatly piled, saw him in her bed. The sheet had ridden down, there was a naked shoulder, part of his bare chest. He was muscular—well, she had known that. And was that the end of a scar? Not a medical scar, though.

For a moment she was captivated by the sight of him. He was asleep in her bed, not exactly in her power but something like that. She could look at him, dream, not worry that her feelings might be showing on her face. He was asleep. Then she told herself not to be ridiculous, this was only fatigue. She was not interested in men.

He rolled over onto his back, the blue eyes opened. Briefly she had a glimpse of what he must have looked like as a child as he hovered for a brief moment between being asleep and awake. Innocent, unscarred by life. He would have been a beautiful baby. But he wasn't beautiful now, not exactly. Life had scored lines on his face, made it harsher. And more interesting.

He blinked and intelligence returned to his eyes at once. He was looking at her, recognising her, assessing the situation. However, he was still not fully awake, still not quite his usual guarded self. She thought she saw his pleasure at seeing her. For a moment they just looked at each other, and perhaps some non-verbal message passed. But both seemed to agree that this was not the time to talk about it. Or even to consider it.

'Sorry to wake you early,' she said, 'but we've got an emergency, something quite different.'

'OK, I'm rested.' He sat up, swung a bare leg out of bed and grinned. 'If you wouldn't mind turning your back just for a moment?'

'Oh, yes, of course.' He was naked in her bed! Why did the thought give her a sudden tiny thrill?

There was the rustle of clothes and then he said, 'What's the emergency, then?'

Just the sound of his voice gave her some confidence

but… 'It's the last thing you'd expect, the last thing we need. We're supposed to be coping with an outbreak of gastroenteritis here! Isn't that enough?' The thought of even more work was shocking her.

'Old saying, quoted to us by the captain. "Hope for the best, expect the worst." What's happened?'

'A woman has just gone into labour, I think. She claims the baby's about four weeks premature.'

This did shock him. 'What the hell is a heavily pregnant woman doing on a cruise?'

'Tell me then we'll both know. It's the first I've heard of it. She must have deliberately kept quiet about it. Worn those long floaty dresses. The cruise firm doesn't allow passengers on board who will be over twenty-eight weeks pregnant during the holiday, and for good reason.'

'Right. But she decided she knew best and now we're faced with the problem.' He frowned and Maddy was surprised.

'Childbirth isn't an illness, Ed,' she said gently. 'It's a perfectly normal healthy process.'

She saw him take control of himself. 'Of course. Now we've got her, we'll have to cope. Just how up to date are you with childbirth, Maddy?'

'I'm no midwife. I've watched a few births, been on take a couple of times. If it's straightforward, I could manage. But mostly I've worked in places with a midwifery section. How about you?'

'I did a bit when I was a medical student but nothing much since then. When I was in Africa the people had their own midwives so I was rarely requested for help.'

'That makes sense. Now, I've already phoned the

captain. It's protocol, he has to be informed of events like this. He says he hopes we can cope. The storm has got really bad—nearly hurricane-force winds. If he has to ask for a boat to come out, he will. But he doesn't advise it.'

'No way can we put a pregnant woman into a boat in this weather. It's up to the home team, Maddy.'

She smiled. 'Right. And we've got to be extra-careful not to get the poor little blighter infected. We're still dealing with a gastroenteritis outbreak.'

'I remember,' he said. 'Let's go and see what we can do.'

Maddy was surprised at the bleakness in his voice. True, Ed had worked a full day, and had then had only an hour's sleep. But when she had woken him up he had seemed fine. Only when she'd told him that this was an emergency birth had he seemed upset. She wondered why.

Mr and Mrs Flynn were having their first baby. They had calculated exactly when it was due to be born, worked out that they could have that long-awaited holiday before it was born. There was a month to go. They knew that if they'd told the cruise company that Mrs Flynn was pregnant, they'd never be able to book the cruise. So they hadn't told anyone.

'We never expected this,' Mr Flynn wailed as Maddy and Ed walked into their cabin. 'We thought everything would be all right. I think that it's the storm that's brought it on. All that shaking.'

'Very possibly,' Ed said. 'Now Mr Flynn, if you'd just sit over there and stay calm, we will examine your wife.' He went to Mrs Flynn's side and spoke to her quietly and reassuringly. 'Have your waters broken, Mrs Flynn?'

She nodded, and Maddy sighed. She had had a last hope that it might be a false alarm, that there were just contractions which might slow down and stop. No such luck. The waters had broken.

Ed had taken the usual readings, was now timing the contractions, trying to decide roughly when the baby might be born. Then he placed his hand on the woman's distended belly, gently palpated it.

Maddy was watching his face, saw the quick flash of alarm. He felt again. Then he said, 'Maddy, would you like to palpate?'

She did, and found at once what he was concerned about. This was something that she'd only read about, never experienced. Not that it was too uncommon, but it was to her. She managed to keep calm and said to Ed, 'Yes, I see.'

Ed stood back, peeled off his rubber gloves. 'Well, Mrs Flynn is certainly in labour. It's going to take quite a while before the actual birth, so you should be all right for an hour or two. Now, we are going to get things ready, if there's any sudden problem, phone us. Mr Flynn, on no account are you to leave the cabin. We still have people suffering from gastroentiritis, and we don't want it in here.'

'Is my baby going to be all right?' Mrs Flynn sobbed.

Ed's face softened and he nodded. 'I've never lost a newborn baby yet,' he said firmly. 'I don't see any problems. Now, try to stay calm because you'll need all your energy. We'll be back shortly.'

Maddy walked down the corridor with him. 'You've never lost a newborn baby because you've never delivered one outside hospital,' she said.

'I lied, Maddy. I have lost a baby.' A short, flat statement, delivered without emotion. Ed went on, 'But we had to reassure Mrs Flynn. Now, what did you feel when you palpated?'

Maddy was shocked by his statement that he had lost a baby, she wanted to know more. But yet again this was not the right time to ask. 'I've never felt one. But I thought the baby's head was in the wrong place. The baby is upside down—I mean the right way up. It's going to be a breech birth.'

'I think so, too. Can we cope with a breech birth?'

'We've got medical textbooks in the centre. Let's go and look it up.'

When they reached the medical centre they found the captain waiting for them. Maddy thought it typical—it might be the middle of the night, but the captain had dressed properly, formally. 'I need to know the situation, Doctor,' he said. 'Then I will make a decision. It'll be an informed decision as I will be guided by you. But the decision will be mine.'

Maddy saw that Ed approved of this attitude.

'We have a woman going into labour, about four weeks prematurely. There might be complications, though small ones. On shore I would recommend she be taken to hospital at once. Moving her from here by boat or helicopter could be dangerous. But, of course, it would no longer be your responsibility.'

Maddy smiled to herself, she knew Ed had slipped this in on purpose. She also knew what the captain's response would be.

'Everyone on this ship is my responsibility until they

are safe on shore. Can you and Maddy deal with these complications?'

'Probably. Any risk would be small.' Maddy thought it interesting to see how precise Ed was trying to be. 'But there is a risk. However, I have a suggestion.'

'Which is?'

'We have a very experienced midwife at Penhally Bay. There may be a storm raging but we also have fishermen there who could probably get her here.'

'Would she take that risk? It's a lot to ask.'

For a moment Ed was silent. Then he said, 'Perhaps not. Her husband died during a sea rescue some years ago. But I could always ask her.'

The captain thought a moment, then said, 'Will you try her, please? And make it clear, to her and the fisherman, that price is not a consideration.'

'The fisherman might need paying but Kate won't,' said Ed. He picked up the receiver, flicked on the speakerphone and dialled.

Maddy was sitting next to Ed. She heard the phone ring, then heard a sleepy voice say, 'Kate Althorp here. Whose baby is being born in the middle of the night?'

'Middle of the night and the middle of the sea. Kate, it's Ed Tremayne here. I'm on the cruise ship.' His voice was a bit diffident, and Maddy guessed that he didn't know Kate too well.

'And you've got a birth out there?'

'A primigravida, about four weeks premature. And a breech presentation.'

'How far is labour advanced?'

'I calculate at least three or four hours to go.'

'You need a midwife,' Kate said. 'And you're in luck. Jem is spending a fortnight at a friend's house.'

Ed winced. What a thing to forget! Kate had an eight-year-old son. Still, it turned out he wasn't a problem. 'So do you fancy coming? Kick Jerry Buchan out of bed and ask him to bring you here? His boat is the safest one for miles and there'll be good money for him.'

'That'll bring Jerry. I'll come.'

Maddy saw Ed hesitate. 'Kate, this is the worst storm for years. It's dangerous. Are you sure you want to...to risk it?'

There was a pause. Then a flat voice said, 'I'll risk it. Other people do. Other people have done. What kind of equipment have you got there?'

'We've plenty of high-class medical stuff. Drugs, bandages, sutures, instruments and so on. We've got a very well-equipped theatre you can use. Specific midwifery kit—none. It's not supposed to be needed.'

'I can bring what I need. I'm on my way. I'll be perhaps an hour, an hour and a half. Oh, and, Ed, tell the mother that she's probably going to have an awful backache and the best way to deal with it is to be on all fours.'

'I didn't know that. I'll tell her.' Ed replaced the receiver, looked at the captain. 'You heard that, Captain?'

The captain nodded. 'I'll have the lights on, and a good crew on the landing platform. And I'll be there.'

'Right.' Maddy saw Ed thinking. 'Maddy, we've still got the gastro to deal with. But for the moment I'll see to that. How about if you arrange to get Mrs Flynn transferred to one of the wards here—with her husband—and then keep an eye on her until Kate arrives?'

'Seems a good plan.' She was glad that as usual he had asked her instead of directing her.

'Let's get started. Captain, we'll keep you informed. But for the moment I feel happier.'

'I never had problems like this when I was Captain of one of Her Majesty's frigates,' the Captain said gloomily.

After arranging for Kate to come aboard, Ed had little to do but check up on mostly sleeping patients, see that the stewards were happy with their work. And they were. There were no more new cases, no sudden crises.

He felt responsible for bringing Kate out to the ship, so when he heard that the fishing boat was nearing the landing platform, he went out on deck. He knew that probably the most dangerous part of her trip would be the jump between fishing boat and platform. So he wanted to be there. Perhaps he might be able to help.

It took an effort to push open the door that led to the deck. And when he did step outside, the wind whipped across his face, pushing him violently against the railing.

He had lived by the sea for much of his life. But he had never seen, or heard, a storm like this. The waves were breaking as they did on the shore. There was the hiss of them as they smashed against the side of the ship. And above all the howl of the wind screaming through the ship's rigging.

He could make out the dancing lights of the fishing boat as it approached the landing platform. The landing platform itself was brightly lit, showing the chaos of waves beating at it. He'd asked Kate to come out in this! Just for a moment he wondered how he would feel if there was an accident. If Kate were injured—drowned even? What would his father say?

Interesting that he thought of his father first.

Then he decided that he was being foolish. Sometimes decisions had to be made. If necessary, he would make them.

He saw the captain approaching him, clutching the railings as he did so. 'Dr Tremayne? Not expecting to go down onto the platform, are you?'

'I wondered if I might be of help.'

'You'd only get in the way. My crew are trained. Leave them to do their job.'

Probably—certainly—true. He'd stay here, where he could do no harm. He noticed the captain did the same.

The fishing boat came alongside the platform, tossed by the waves so that sometimes the two were level and sometimes the boat was a good six feet lower. Ed saw a fisherman on the boat wave to one of the crew waiting on the platform and then throw a bag across. The crewman caught it, ran to take it to safety. The boat sank again below the platform level.

Ed saw two of the crew poised right on the edge of the platform. Each was fitted with a safety line, controlled by another crewman further back. Ed saw the boat rising—and there was Kate, balanced on the edge of the fishing-boat deck, a fisherman holding her from behind. A wave swept the fishing boat upwards, Kate jumped. She landed on her knees on the landing platform, where the two crewmen grabbed her.

She was safe. She was half hurried, half dragged back into the ship. The fishing boat stood off at once, with just a wave from the fisherman.

'A good competent job,' the captain said to Ed.

Ed wiped his forehead. It was cold out here—but he had been sweating.

A crewman brought Kate up to them, and the captain escorted her inside the ship. Then he said, 'I'm Captain Smith. Mrs Althorp, welcome aboard. I don't need to tell you how thankful I am to have you here, I think you know. Anything you need, just ask for. Now I'll leave you to Dr Tremayne.'

Ed smiled his relief. 'I'll keep my distance from you, Kate, just in case, but you don't know how glad I am to see you. I know it was a lot to ask.'

'Because of my husband being killed in a storm?'

He had not expected her to be as forthright as this. 'That's right. You must have been terrified.'

She shook her head. 'Not so. This is my way of fighting back.'

'Good. And you're not too tired to work?'

Kate looked at him sardonically. 'Since when did babies come only in the daytime? Midwives are on twenty-four-hour call. Anyway, how are you coping with this outbreak Nick told me about?'

He shrugged. 'We're coping. There's a nurse here.'

'So I heard. Is one nurse enough? How good is she?'

'She's very good. We've bonded, we're a team, she knows what I want before I do.'

He felt Kate look at him again. 'So quickly,' she commented casually. 'What is she like as a person?'

He had wondered about this and then decided that this wasn't the time or place for any such thoughts. 'She's professional,' he said, 'which is all I need right now.'

'Of course,' Kate said.

CHAPTER FIVE

STILL keeping his distance, Ed took Kate to the medical centre. Then he told her to go inside, introduce herself to Maddy and the mother, and do what was necessary. 'There's clean scrubs available, you'll want to get out of those wet clothes. You're in charge, Kate. Maddy will give you a buzzer, you can contact me if you need me.'

Kate nodded. 'I'll probably need you when we deliver. It might be an idea to have both of you. But before you get inside my delivery room, you make sure you're clean!'

'Shower and new scrubs on us both,' he promised her. Then he set off on his rounds again.

Maddy joined him fifteen minutes later. When he saw her smiling at him he felt his spirits lift. It was good to see her, even though it had only been a couple of hours since he'd seen her last. Why do I feel this way? he wondered. Then he decided it was just a side effect of fatigue.

'How have you got on with Kate?' he asked.

'Wonderfully. She inspires instant confidence, doesn't she? Are all the members of your practice like that?'

'Of course. Do I inspire instant confidence?'

She pursed her lips. 'I'm afraid you do. But I still have

to be convinced that it's genuine medical ability and not just a con trick.'

'It was a weekend course I went on, just for GPs. How to inspire instant confidence and thus cheer up patients even if they are dangerously ill. Is Kate happy with her patient?'

'Very happy. And the patient is happy, too. Even Mr Flynn is happy. Kate took him to one side and gave him a short but intense lecture on the duties and functions of a father-to-be in a delivery room.'

'Kate has her own way of doing things,' Ed said.

'I'm glad that she's come,' Maddy said after a pause. 'But if it hadn't been possible, could we have managed on our own?'

Ed thought for a moment. Then he said, quite honestly, 'Together we would have been fine. But I'm not sure I could have managed. It's not something I'd want to do on my own.'

His face went blank and just for a moment Maddy had the impression that some memory had returned to haunt him. And she remembered how earlier he had said that he had lost a baby. But then he smiled and said, 'Anyway, the problem's over now. I think we have a good team.'

'We do,' Maddy said.

Together they looked in at six patients, had quiet conversations with the stewards. The lull was continuing. But they still had to work and they knew that nearer morning, things would get worse.

'Aren't you tired yet?' she asked him. 'You only had an hour's sleep.'

'It refreshed me. And a situation like this brings its own momentum. It drags you along with it. But how about you? Aren't you tired? You've had no sleep at all.'

'I'm fine,' she told him. Then she said something that suggested that she was not as in control as she'd thought. 'And I really like working with you.'

There was a pause, a long pause. 'It's mutual. I really like working with you,' he said eventually. 'I think you're a very fine nurse.'

She thought that she would have liked something a little more personal than that.

But it was a start.

His buzzer sounded. He listened to the message and said, 'I see. We'll be right there.'

'Mr Simmonds,' he said to Maddy. 'Remember my father was worried about him? I've dropped in to see him a couple of times, he's not doing too well.'

'He was one of the first to fall ill. He didn't send for me like the others. One of the stewards asked me to call round. When I called in he didn't complain, just said that these things happen, that we had to put up with them.'

'Hmm. A fatalist. Anything more you know about him?'

'He kept very much to himself, didn't look for company. Apparently he booked this trip six months ago with his wife—but she died three months later. He told me that they had planned the trip together so he was going to come on it in memory of her.'

She thought Ed looked uneasy. 'That seems an odd thing to do to me,' he said. 'However, let's see how he is.'

They went to the cabin and Maddy knew at once that

things weren't good. Neither the drip nor the drugs had been able to control his fever. His skin was hot and dry, and he was shivering. His temperature was far, far too high, and he was delirious. 'Biddy,' he mumbled, 'is that you, Biddy?'

'Who's Biddy?' Ed asked, though Maddy suspected he knew the answer.

She pointed to a photograph by the head of the bunk. It showed a younger Mr Simmonds and a laughing woman by his side. Looking as if they didn't have a care in the world. 'That's Biddy. She was his wife.'

Ed took up the photograph and stared at it. Then he replaced it, shook his head and when he spoke his voice was unnaturally calm. 'We've done all we can. It's up to Mr Simmonds now. Do you want to wait with him, make sure he's comfortable?'

Maddy knew her voice was shrill. 'What about trying the mammoth injection? Like you did for Mrs Jones? It worked for her. She's recovering.'

'It wouldn't work for this man.' Ed shook his head. 'He wouldn't survive it. Look, I'll leave you here for a while and check on some of the other patients. When it happens—and it won't be long—then buzz me.'

And he was gone.

Mr Simmonds died quietly, and Maddy wondered if there was a smile on his face. Certainly he looked at peace. And before she had time to buzz Ed he came back into the room. 'Mr Simmonds is dead,' she told him. 'Just as you said would happen.' She couldn't keep a thread of anger out of her voice.

His voice was gentle. 'I've seen a lot of deaths through

gastroenteritis,' he said, 'which is unusual, I know. In the West it's usually not a killer, whereas in the developing countries it often is. You learn in time to tell just who will survive and who won't. It's a feeling rather than a medical technique.'

'I thought you didn't like feelings. But you say that you've seen a lot of deaths through this. How many is a lot?' Her voice was abrupt. For some reason she had to keep pushing him. He had upset her.

He didn't reply at first, but then he said, 'A lot is over two hundred deaths in three weeks through gastroenteritis. That's not counting those who died for other reasons.'

Maddy winced. How could he carry on having seen so many deaths? Perhaps this was the time to back off. 'I'm sorry,' she said. 'And, Ed, before, I was a bit…a bit personal. I'm sorry.'

Perhaps there was a touch of humour in his voice. 'You don't have to be sorry. I like straight talking. Now I'd better pronounce death. Do we tell the captain now or let him have some sleep?'

'We ought to tell him, but there's absolutely nothing he can do. Let him sleep a little longer.'

Ed looked at Mr Simmonds's still form, looked at Maddy. 'Are you all right, Maddy?'

'I'm a nurse, I've seen death before. Don't worry about me, Ed.' She was glad they were OK again. 'Now I'll have to—'

Her buzzer sounded. Kate's voice said, 'Things are moving faster than I had expected here. Want to come and lend a hand? And can you get Ed to come, too? Is it possible?'

'He's here with me. We're both on our way.'

'Make sure you've showered, scrubbed yourselves and put on something clean. I like my delivery room sterile.'

'Right,' Maddy said.

They left Mr Simmonds's cabin, locking the door behind them.

Breech births were often faster than normal births, Maddy learned. The ideal position was supported squatting, which made it easier to perform an episiotomy.

The second stage occurred just as it was described in the textbooks. As it was a breech presentation it seemed to be faster than normal. The mother cried out one last time as Kate's capable hands busied themselves. Then Maddy saw the midwife smile.

'It's a little girl!' And then they heard that first tiny cry.

The parents had opted not to be told the baby's gender in advance.

Kate wrapped the little pink form in a blanket, clamped then cut the cord. She offered the wailing bundle to Ed so he could give her to her mother, to be put straight on the breast.

Ed shook his head, stepped back and indicated that Maddy should hand over the baby.

Maddy was happy to do it. She thought it was a magical moment when a mother saw her child for the first time. Unlike a lot of medicine, childbirth usually produced a happy ending. And as ever, the mother was overwhelmed, the pain now largely forgotten as the reward was so great.

'Have you thought of a name yet?' she asked Mrs Flynn.

She smiled weakly, exhausted but euphoric. 'No. We were going to wait and see what we got. No good picking a name if you're not going to use it, is it? But I think I'd like something to do with the sea.'

'We'll all have a think,' Maddy promised with a smile.

There was still the placenta to be delivered, the Apgar score to be recorded and Mrs Flynn checked for excessive bleeding. But although it had been a breech birth it had been largely trouble-free.

'Think you could have managed it?' Maddy whispered to Ed as Kate busied herself with her tasks.

'Not on my own. But I think perhaps that we could have managed it together. Though I think you would have been better at it than me. But in medicine it's always when you think that you can more or less manage that things go seriously wrong. Like I said, hope for the best, prepare for the worst.'

'There's the planning mind again. That's your slogan, isn't it? And I suppose it's quite a good one.' Maddy looked across the little theatre. 'Kate, I'll stay but do you need Ed any more?'

'No. But, Ed, once you've been out in that corridor, exposed to things, just to be on the safe side you're to keep out of the baby's ward. From now on it's an isolation ward. In fact, you keep out too, Maddy. Mother and baby are now my concern, I don't need you.'

'Bossy people, midwives,' Ed said.

They had decided that the mother and baby should be moved from the theatre to one of the small wards. Kate had already prepared it. She had also arranged for food to be delivered, for Mr Flynn to get what was necessary from their cabin and for him to have somewhere to sleep.

'You go and do the rounds,' Maddy suggested to Ed.

'Come back when we've got mother and baby settled and we'll have a drink to celebrate.'

'Champagne at half past five in the morning?'

'I thought that tea might be more sensible.'

'Then I'll be there.' Ed went to congratulate the mother again and left the room.

He came back three-quarters of an hour later to join Kate and Maddy. Kate had been given the now absent doctor's cabin. Mother and baby had been settled next door but an alarm ran from the ward to the cabin.

'Celebratory tea,' Maddy offered, 'and a special meal of chocolate biscuits.'

'Sounds good.'

'We'll have our little party and then Kate can sleep here for a while. Someone dragged her out of bed in the middle of the night.'

'I'll just doze,' Kate said, 'so I can listen out for my patients.'

Ed accepted a mug of tea and a chocolate biscuit. 'You didn't tell my father you were coming out here, did you?' he asked Kate.

Kate grinned at him. 'I did not. And you didn't ask him either, or he'd have been at the harbourside with a few things to say about the idea. He likes to be kept informed, so he's not going to be very pleased when you tell him.'

'That's something I'll have to deal with. Did you mind coming out here without his permission? Will he be angry at you?'

'Nick has been angry with me in the past—and I've been angry at him,' Kate said serenely. 'Somehow we've both got over it.'

Maddy couldn't quite make out the expression in Kate's eyes when she spoke about Nick. It wasn't just affection, there was a feeling of...wistfulness? Then she shrugged. It was the middle of the night, and Kate was obviously tired.

'What about a name for baby Flynn?' she asked. 'The mother thinks she'd like something to do with the sea.'

'The obvious one is Marina,' Kate said promptly. 'Or there are variations. Maris or Marnie or Rina.'

'I quite like Marina,' Maddy said. 'Are there any other sea-type names?'

'Dorian means child of the sea.' Kate was obviously an expert on names.

Maddy winced. 'You couldn't send any child out into the world called Dorian Flynn.'

Kate shook her head. 'Parents can do anything. Thank goodness this was a little girl. If it had been a boy, they might have called him Errol.'

Maddy had seen this happen before after a birth or a successful operation. If the staff had time they would sit together feeling excited, successful. They might have a half-joking conversation, like this, it was all part of sharing. And for the first time in some hours she was feeling relaxed.

'I want a baby some time,' she said. 'There was a time when I thought it was possible, when I could see a future with a husband and a baby, living in a house with a nice garden. I even bought a book of names. I rather fancied calling my daughter Hannah or my son Luke. But it never happened.'

'Plenty of time yet,' said Kate. 'Your chance will come.'

'Perhaps. Or perhaps I'll concentrate on my career and finish up the matron of a vast hospital.'

'Matron? You mean Senior Manager,' Kate snorted. 'Whatever that might be.'

Although he was sitting there, a half-smile on his face, Ed wasn't joining in the conversation. He didn't share in the excitement, the elation. Perhaps he was tired, Maddy thought. But, then, they were all tired.

Ed's buzzer sounded. He took the call, and Maddy heard him say, 'You were right to call me, I'll be right there.' He looked at Maddy. 'Mrs Gillan, cabin D35. The steward says she's very weak, panicking a little. I'll go and see how things are.'

'I'll come, too,' Maddy said. 'And Kate can stay here and doze.'

In fact, Mrs Gillan was over the worst of the infection. Her fever was down. But she was very tired, still afraid, more in need of reassurance than anything else. Ed examined her, told her that she was over the worst and gave her something to help her sleep. Then he said that he and Maddy would stay with her for a while. He chatted to her but Maddy thought that his usual good humour wasn't there, his words seemed a bit forced. Perhaps she should join in the conversation…

'We've just delivered a baby,' she told Mrs Gillan. 'Not what you expect on a cruise ship—but these things happen.'

Mrs Gillan looked vaguely interested. 'I'm expecting my first grandchild in two months,' she murmured. 'I'm quite excited.'

'It's something lovely to look forward to,' said

Maddy. 'Now, close your eyes and think of babies' names like we did.'

Shortly afterwards Mrs Gillan was sound asleep but Ed showed no wish to move from her cabin. Maddy looked at him, concerned. 'You seem a bit low,' she said. 'Is going without sleep getting to you?'

'I don't need sleep, Maddy. I'm fine.'

She noticed that he didn't deny that his spirits were low. 'Mrs Gillan here is fine and we've just had a very nice surprise with baby Flynn. The successful birth of a baby is usually one of the more enjoyable bits of medicine.'

'So I understand.'

'You understand? Is that all? Ed, what is the matter with you? In the past couple of hours you've changed. Something is hurting you—can't you tell me what? We've shared a lot so far. Can't you share this?'

His voice was bleak. 'All right, I'll share, though it's not something that usually I like doing. I'll tell you but I don't want to talk about it afterwards. Is that OK?'

She felt that she'd achieved something with him. A barrier between them was coming down. 'That's fine,' she said.

They were talking in whispers as they didn't want to disturb Mrs Gillan. 'You guessed I'd been in the army and I've told you that I worked in Africa, that I supervised a so-called hospital where there was an epidemic of gastroenteritis.'

'I know that,' she said. 'It must have been horrific. How could you cope? And how do you cope now?'

'Same answer to both questions. Because I'm a doctor, it's what we do.' He paused, and she wondered what might come next, what could come next.

'It's the feeling of inadequacy,' he said. 'The anger at knowing that with a little more help you could do so much good. People around me were dying for the want of a few pounds' worth of drugs. Especially children. I started off strong, determined to do what I could and knowing that I'd have to be satisfied with doing my best. But it was a poor best. And as the days passed and I got more and more tired and the death rate didn't go down…well, it hurt. When I left that place I vowed that never again would I go back to an epidemic like it. But when I heard of this outbreak, I just had to come to see if I could cope.'

'But you're doing a fantastic job!' She frowned and said, 'But the memories are hurting, aren't they?'

'Something like that.'

She thought over what he had told her. 'But there's more isn't there?'

The answer came back too quickly to be true. 'No!'

There was silence for a moment and then she said, 'I'm interfering again, I know. But, please, would you tell me more about it some time? It would help me to know you better and I…I want to do that.'

Another long silence and she stared at his forlorn face. Then he took one of her hands, squeezed it and then somehow managed to smile. 'You're the only person I've ever been tempted to talk to about it. Perhaps some day I will tell you. But now you stay here with Mrs Gillan while I go to check on a couple more patients.' And he was gone.

Maddy made a quick nurse's check on Mrs Gillan and then sat down to think about what Ed had told her. Now she could understand him better. Every moment he had been on board he must have been reminded of that camp in Africa. She knew about battlefield trauma but she realised there was similar trauma for those who were not actually fighting.

Now she knew so much more about his life. Only she had a feeling that he had held something back. And that he wanted to tell her, but he couldn't let himself.

The next question was why did she want to know more about him? She'd already decided that he wasn't the kind of man she ought to care for. She didn't really want to care for any man. Or did she?

She remembered their kiss. How many hours ago had it been? Six, seven? Had it been as long as that? She had thought about it so often since. He had kissed her—without any encouragement at all. No encouragement? Well, she had put her hand on his arm. In a sense she had made the first overture. Just a little one, though.

There was the gentlest of taps on the cabin door then Ed came in. She looked at him almost in surprise, as if he was the last person she had expected. She had just been thinking about him!

'If Mrs Gillan's OK, I could do with a hand on the next deck,' he said quietly.

'She's asleep and she'll stay that way. I'm coming.'

They walked out of the cabin, along the deserted companionway, They came to a porthole, and for a moment both stopped to look at the dark raging sea outside.

Once again, she put her hand on his arm. 'You have to know I'm not like this,' she said. 'I'm off men, I don't want any new relationship, I don't really even know you. But we agreed. This is time out. We're on a ship, what we do here doesn't count. So I want you to kiss me again. Just for comfort, for you as well as me.' She stopped a moment, looked up at him and asked hesitantly, 'That is, if you want to kiss me.'

She could tell that he did want to kiss her. One arm round her waist, one hand holding the back of her head, gently he leaned towards her. When their bodies were touching it felt so…so right. As if she were coming home, as if she belonged here. And there was no hurry. She wrapped her arms round his waist.

He was stroking her, his fingertips caressing the soft skin of her throat and cheek. It was gentle but it felt so good.

Then his lips touched hers. Softly at first, then, when she offered no resistance, harder, stronger, more demanding. What had started as gentle, cautious turned into something far more desperate, more passionate. She could feel her need for him growing within her. Suddenly her breasts were taut, her body feeling a warmth that had nothing to do with the air around them. And she knew he felt it, too, his need was all too obvious. And she liked it. Perhaps they could…

And then he eased them apart. She whimpered softly, she didn't want him to go. His reluctance was obvious, too. So why was he doing this?

They stood facing each other, heads down, linked only by their still clasped hands. Her voice trembling, she said, 'Remember, this is not serious. It's a time apart, we're both weary, we needed respite. It was so good—but it stops here.'

'As you wish,' he agreed. 'We'll forget it happened—or try to. Now, we have patients to look at.'

She was confused, saddened a little. Did he have to agree so readily?

* * *

An hour before dawn Ed told her to go to bed. 'You're flagging,' he said gently. 'You've worked hard and now you need a break. Maddy, don't argue, go to bed and sleep. I can cope.'

'But you need—'

'I need you refreshed and alert, so go to bed. I can spare you for three hours.'

She couldn't help it, she yawned. 'All right. I will go,' she said, 'providing you promise to wake me after exactly three hours.'

'I promise. I need you.'

She saw that he meant it and it made her feel good.

She went to her cabin, decided to do as he had and have a quick shower. Then she heard movements from next door, wrapped a towel round herself and peered into the corridor. There was Kate, coming out of the little ward. 'Everything all right?' Maddy asked.

'Everything is fine. Though I'd like to get off this ship. It's not the right place for a newborn. But mother's doing well, the baby's going to be called Marina and I've spent a fair amount of time reassuring the husband. It's a good thing that men don't have to have babies!'

'You're not the first midwife I've heard say that.' Maddy yawned again. 'Ed's sent me to bed. Just for three hours.'

'That man is a good doctor. Sometimes he reminds me of his dad, sometimes not.'

'So you and Nick are good friends?'

'We've known each other for years.'

Maddy thought there was a peculiar inflection in Kate's

voice, but perhaps she was tired. 'So, bed for me,' she said. 'Goodnight.'

'Good morning.' Kate grinned.

The minute Kate got into her bunk she realised that she was sleeping in the same sheets that Ed had slept in. Mind you, he had slept in the sheets that she had… What did it matter? These weren't easy times. But she thought she could detect just the faintest smell…as if his warm body were still in the bed. The thought excited her.

Ed Tremayne. Eighteen hours ago she had never met him. Now they were colleagues, friends even. He had kissed her twice and she had enjoyed it, much to her surprise. She had to stop thinking! Ed Tremayne was just…

She had only just shut her eyes—she thought. But there was a gentle hand on her shoulder and an enticing smell of coffee. Eyes still closed, she asked, 'Three hours?'

'To the minute,' came Ed's voice. 'There's coffee by your bed and…oh, there's a message for you sent down from the radio office. Now I'll leave you to get dressed.'

She opened her eyes then stared at him. He seemed entirely undisturbed by his night awake. Perhaps the lines around his eyes were a little deeper, but he still looked confident, in charge of the situation.

She sat up. Then she remembered that when she had gone to bed she hadn't bothered with a nightie. Hastily, she scrambled under the sheets again. But not before she had seen the gleam of appreciation in his eyes.

'I'll go and talk to Kate until you're ready,' he said. 'Or, more likely, I'll shout down the corridor at her so as to keep things sterile. See you when you're ready.'

She drank half her coffee and then reached for the message. Who could it be from? She'd never had a cable before.

Her morning was spoiled at once—the message was from ex-boyfriend Brian. Why couldn't he leave her alone? She skimmed the contents, though she knew what they'd be. *I can't believe what you said to me... Remember what we had? Remember you telling me you loved me? This will go on for ever...I love you and that is all that matters... Need to get together so we can sort things out... You know you'll have to see me... I'll get a job and then... Madeleine, I am serious...*

The message was timed—how could he have sent a message at three that morning? Then she remembered that one of the things he did was to sleep during the day and contact her in the middle of the night. Just because he felt like it.

She felt resentment and fear welling up in her. This was what happened when you put your trust in men. In love. One sad thing was that she did remember what they'd had. It had been so good and it had turned out so bad.

So, back to her resolve. No more contact with men. Then she thought about Ed. Like Brian, he was determined, too. But Ed was different. He could see another person's point of view. Couldn't he?

She screwed up the message, slid it into her bedside cabinet. Then she finished her coffee, though it didn't seem so good now. She dressed and then felt the beginnings of a slight headache. Strange, she hadn't had one before. Still, there was work to be done.

She found Ed in the corridor. He turned to her and smiled but she couldn't work up any enthusiasm to greet him. 'What do you want me to do now?' she asked.

She might have guessed—he detected her change in mood at once. 'Are you sure you're all right?' he asked. 'You seem a little out of sorts.'

'There's nothing wrong with me,' she snapped. 'I've just got a job to do.'

'Not bad news from your message?'

'I told you, Ed, I'm fine, really. The message was from…an old friend. He wants to get in touch. Perhaps I'm just a bit tired still.'

But she knew he didn't believe her.

They worked steadily for the next four hours and after a while she thought she saw some progress. Just a little, not much. Fewer people were now falling sick. One or two of the first to fall ill now appeared to be recovering. It was encouraging—just.

They were still a good team but the old camaderie with Ed had gone. The message from Brian had scared her. She knew that no one could be less like Brian than Ed. But she had decided to abandon all hopes of an emotional relationship with a man and Brian's call had reawakened this decision. So she and Ed worked well together, but there was no longer the old feeling of joy in their joint work.

They ate when they could, apparently surviving on a diet of coffee and chocolate. And then, midmorning, Ed said, 'I think we can take a fifteen-minute break. Things are easing up. We've been spending too much time in sick-rooms and air-conditioned corridors. We need real air. We'll go on deck for a while.'

So they went on deck and it was exhilarating. The waves were breaking against the ship's hull and the wind was as strong as ever. A gust made her stagger, and he put his arm around her back to steady her. It was just a friendly gesture, but his arm felt warm and strong and she liked it. And it seemed to stay there a little longer than was strictly necessary.

'Look,' he said, pointing to where there was a little gathering of white buildings on the coastline. 'That's Penhally Bay.' Then he pointed to a little boat being bounced about in an alarming fashion by the waves. 'See that fishing boat? Well, I'll bet my father's on it. It'll be Jerry Buchan bringing him out, the man who brought Kate last night.'

'Is it a good idea, coming out in this weather?'

Ed grinned ruefully. 'Probably not a good idea. And he could have done everything necessary by phone. But being Nick Tremayne, he has to come out in person. Especially as Kate is here.'

'And you respect him for it, don't you?'

'I suppose I do. And I also suppose that in his shoes I'd have done the same thing. Look, he won't be long getting here. Let's go down to the landing platform and meet him.'

As before, they were told by the crew to wait safely on deck, while crewmen helped Nick out of the wildly pitching fishing boat and up the steps towards them. Then Maddy witnessed the apparently emotionless meeting between the two men.

'How's the job going, Ed?'

'We're coping. We've had two deaths, one unrelated.'

'Right. You're tired?'

'I'm still on top of things.'

A curt nod from his father. 'What I would have expected. Now, I've got to see the captain. Want to come with me?'

'Maddy comes, too,' said Ed. 'This has been a joint effort.'

'Of course she comes, too. Now, let's go.'

Maddy wondered if the two knew just how much they were alike. She also wondered if they ever showed the deep love that she suspected was between them. For the Tremayne family, it seemed that emotions were to be kept strictly under control. But she was sure they were there.

But was it her business? Did she want to know more about Ed's emotions?

CHAPTER SIX

NICK knew that probably it shouldn't have been, but his first thought was for his son. Nick was one of the few men who could guess what Ed had just been through. Who could guess what hurt he must have felt. A gastroenteritis outbreak. The sights, the smell, the sounds, all must have come crashing back on him. Not a lot of men could have stood that.

A small smile of paternal pride touched Nick's lips as he looked at his obviously weary son. Ed might be weary but he was confident and he was in charge of the situation. He was a Tremayne. Of course, Nick was not going to say anything. But he was proud of his son.

They were now sitting in the captain's cabin. They were handed coffee and then the captain said, 'I've been in touch with our head office and with Dr Tremayne here. Dr Tremayne, I'd like you to review the situation.'

Nick said, 'I've been phoned by the relevant port authorities, and the ship must remain in quarantine for another forty-eight hours at least. Yesterday, last night and this morning I worked on trying to identify the cause of the disease. Ed was right. It is bacterial in origin, not a virus. But it's a completely new strain, a very powerful one, there'll be a lot of people taking an interest in it. Still, this makes no difference to the treatment. Now, I've come here in person to look around, help if possible and then accompany my midwife back to shore. The midwife I didn't know had come out here.'

He looked severely at Ed, who looked serenely back.

Nick went on, 'The Met Office has said that the gale has almost blown itself out and conditions should rapidly improve. The navy has offered to help. They've liaised with the cruise line and later this afternoon one of the navy's smaller boats will come and take off the new baby and her parents. At the same time they'll bring out a small team of nurses and another doctor.'

'Who's the other doctor?' asked Ed.

'A Dr Wyatt. Apparently she's not long out of medical school, but she gained an excellent pass.'

'What is her experience of dealing with an epidemic?'

'As far as I know, none at all,' Nick said flatly. 'I didn't procure the doctor. The cruise line did.'

'This isn't work for a new doctor.' Ed said. 'I think I should stay in charge for a while longer.'

There was a silence and then the captain said, 'I would like you to stay. It'd be foolish to change responsibilities in the middle of the situation. As head of the practice, do you agree, Dr Tremayne?'

'I do,' Nick said after a short pause. 'Ed should stay a while longer. You can arrange this with the line?'

'The line left me without a doctor—and look what happened. They'll do whatever I say.'

'Right. In that case, Captain, I'll go down to see how I

can help in the medical centre. I'd really like to take a good look at this new baby.'

'Keep me informed of everything,' the captain warned.

As soon as they reached the centre Maddy was called away. Kate was asleep, and Nick decided not to wake her up. For the first time since he'd boarded the ship he was alone with his son. And there were things he wanted to say to him.

'You should have consulted me before bringing Kate out here in the storm,' he said reproachfully. 'Surely you know about her husband being drowned? How do you think she felt?'

'I thought she might have been terrified but, in fact, I don't think she was. But terrified or not, I would have wanted her here. She was the best available person for the job so I asked her to come. You'd have made exactly the same decision, wouldn't you?'

'I still would have liked to have been consulted,' Nick said, avoiding the answer he knew he'd have had to give. 'Couldn't you have managed without her?'

'Possibly. Probably. But she made a better job of it than either Maddy or I could have done. It was safer to have her there. Why don't you ask her what she felt about being called out in a storm?'

'I don't need to.' Nick scowled. 'I know exactly what she'd say.' Then he smiled. 'I like to have good people working for me. Now, how're you getting on with Maddy?'

'She's a brilliant nurse,' Ed said, turning away for the moment and rummaging through a pile of forms. 'We've worked well together.'

'Just a brilliant nurse? I thought I saw some attraction there between you.'

'I like her. But I don't do attraction. I've been married once and that's enough for me. I doubt I'll ever see her again when I leave the ship.'

'I see,' said Nick.

'I've got a patient I want to look at now,' Ed went on. 'Kate's in the second cabin down the corridor. Why don't you go and give her a shake? She'll take you to see Sarah and Marina Flynn. You know she'll be mad at you if she finds out you've been here for a while and not woken her.'

'Good idea,' Nick said.

He waited until his son had left and then went into the corridor. There was Maddy taking something from a store cupboard. 'You need something, Nick?' she asked. He thought she looked flushed. Tired? Or upset?

'Ed's gone to see to a patient,' Nick said. 'We were having a chat when I saw you pass outside. He didn't see or hear you. It just struck me that you might have heard something of our conversation.'

'Nick, I do not eavesdrop! I heard a mumble, that was all.'

He lifted his hands placatingly. 'Of course not.' But he was an experienced doctor and he knew when people weren't telling the entire truth.

'In fact, I was telling him that I thought I'd seen an attraction between the two of you. He said he didn't do attraction, that he'd been married once. He doubts he'll ever see you again after he leaves this ship.'

'I'm sure that's true,' Maddy said, turning away. 'As for attraction, well, we work well together, that's all. Like I worked well with you.'

Whatever feelings she had seemed to be under control, Nick thought. And he had always tried to make it a rule never to interfere with the personal lives of his children. Whenever he had broken that rule and interfered, it had never worked out. But… 'Ed and I have been apart a lot,' he said. 'We've never been really close, which is a pity. But he is my son. Perhaps I know how he feels, and I think you mean a bit more to him than he realises.'

There, that was it, he had said it. He could do no more.

'I doubt that's true,' Maddy said in an offhand voice. 'He's off relationships and I certainly am.'

But Nick could tell that she was pleased—or at least intrigued.

Nick was alone in the medical centre now. He wandered around, admiring the fittings, peering into the ward where the mother and new baby were peacefully sleeping. He wanted a closer look at them—but not until he was with Kate. And then he went into the cabin where he had been told Kate was asleep.

There was a low light left on by the head of the bed, partly illuminating Kate's face, making it a thing of planes and shadows. She was a handsome woman. He had known her since his youth, so many years ago. And now he was having difficulty in reconciling the mature woman he was looking at with the teenager he had once known.

It wasn't like him. Usually he was certain, knew what to do, what to think. But now he wasn't sure. Possibly it was the storm outside but it brought back memories of that evil night when the Penhally lifeboat had been launched and Kate's husband, James, and Nick's own brother and father had all died during the rescue of a party of schoolchildren. So much had happened that night, so many emotions, of grief and fear and despair. Intense emotions that had overwhelmed Kate and himself that fateful night. Leading to something that had never been acknowledged by either of them since.

Kate and he went back a long time. They had been teenagers together, with that fizzing off-on relationship that was so common in the young. But then life had come between them. He went to university and married Annabel, she had married James. Both Annabel and James were now dead.

Was Kate happy? he wondered. She seemed serene enough as she went about her work. Was he happy? That was a question he, a busy GP, shouldn't even try to answer. In fact, he shouldn't even ask it.

He and Kate were colleagues—friends, he supposed. But they were wary of each other. Sometimes he caught her looking at him and he wondered what she thought.

He slipped into the cabin, sat on a chair and looked at her. It had been years since the storm. He had fought against thinking of that night, had tried to push it out of his mind, certainly never mentioned it. But now he did think of it. And the memory was as vivid as if it had all happened yesterday.

For a while he didn't want to do anything. He was content just to sit there, to gaze at her sleeping face. But it didn't last long. Perhaps the very intensity of his gaze was felt by her. He saw her eyes twitch open and then focus.

'Nick! What are you doing here?'

'I had to see the captain, sort out a few things. And I

wondered about you. I wanted to see if one of my staff was all right.'

It was important to emphasise that he was concerned because she was a member of his staff. Safer that way.

'I would have liked to have been more involved last night,' he went on. 'I should have been told.'

Kate was as practical as ever. 'I left you a note explaining things and details of who would handle my work today. There was no need for you to go without sleep.'

'Perhaps not.'

Unlike Ed and Maddy, Kate had not bothered to undress when she'd lain down on the bunk. Now she sat up, waved at Nick. 'Wait outside for me. I need a couple of minutes to freshen up. I take it you've come to look at Marina and Sarah Flynn?'

'Just a quick check.' Then he remembered that Kate was always particular about the relative functions of a doctor and midwife, so he added, 'If that's all right with you.'

'It is.'

'The storm seems to be dying down a bit. This afternoon we've got a navy boat coming alongside, bringing nurses and another doctor. They've offered to ship you, the baby and her mother back to Penhally Bay. What do you think?'

'They're both doing fine. I'd certainly like to get them off this ship.'

'Your decision.'

She seemed short with him, and he now realised why. He had seen her asleep, almost defenceless. And Kate always had her defences in place. 'I'll organise you a drink,' he said. And then, wanting to say something pleasant, something that might bring them a little closer together, he added, 'You've done brilliantly, Kate.'

'I know,' she said.

He was a doctor. He was a scientist who believed in empirical proofs, who disdained what he called the mumbo-jumbo of astrology, of sixth senses, of the supernatural. But for a moment he wondered if what he had been remembering had somehow communicated itself to Kate. He would really like to know.

A quick inspection and it was obvious that mother and baby were doing fine. In fact, they were thriving. So what was now most important was to get them away from the ship. Kate agreed that they should move out with the navy boat. 'Now you can go and help Ed,' she told Nick. 'I can cope here very well.' He thought that Kate could always cope. On her own.

Ed, glad of Nick's help, handed him a list. 'I've given you these fifteen people to check over,' he said. 'It's just a case of making sure that the right drugs are given, the right IVs set up. The stewards are pretty good now but it's as well to keep an eye on them. You know where everything is?'

'I'll manage,' said Nick.

It felt just a little unusual, taking orders from his son, but he knew that in a case like this there could only be one leader. And he had to admit that Ed was good at it. He looked as tough as ever—but his eyes were getting bloodshot. Maddy, too, was showing signs of fatigue. But Nick could tell that there was no way she would ask for respite. Not while Ed was still working.

The disease on ship was peaking. There were now forty-eight people on board infected with it. That was forty-eight people falling ill, being ill or recovering from illness. They needed constant care and attention. But they should all survive.

Then the news came down from the captain. The pinnace was on its way. And the storm had nearly blown itself out. Ed said, 'Dad, why don't you go and scrub up and then get ready to help Kate move the Flynns?'

'Good idea,' said Nick. 'When will I see you on shore again?'

A short answer. 'When I think my job's done.'

A good answer, too, Nick thought.

They all look clean, energetic and above all awake, Maddy thought. Whereas she felt weary, crumpled and apathetic. She had watched as the new medical team had come aboard, each carrying a small bag. She had watched as one of them had helped Kate and Nick transfer the Flynn family to the pinnace. She was glad the family had gone.

Now they were sitting, crammed into the medical centre, listening to Ed. Three nurses in uniforms. They were all about her own age but for some reason she felt older than them. And there was the young doctor, Dr Ellen Wyatt. Slim, pretty, vivacious. Maddy suspected she was just out of medical school. She was also suspicious of the way the young doctor looked approvingly at Ed. It was more than just professional curiosity. She had moved her seat deliberately to sit next to him.

And Maddy had to admit that Ed still looked good. So long without sleep didn't appear to have affected him too much. There were lines round his eyes—now bloodshot eyes. And his mouth was more grim than before. But he looked better than she felt.

She was sitting at the side of the room while Ed briefed the nurses and the doctor. He had arranged things with the captain and herself, organised cabins to sleep in, meals, treatments, the nurses' roster. She had been consulted but it was obvious that this was something that Ed was expert at. Even the captain had listened. Ed was a superb organiser. And he made it clear that he was in charge.

'If there are any nursing problems, first buzz Maddy. I'll not give her any cases, she will be on call here for the next few hours. If you need a doctor, buzz Dr Wyatt first. If necessary, she'll liaise with me. Now, there are times when you'll have to work fast. But, remember, you don't cut corners. And records are all-important! Don't let them slip.'

Then he smiled, and Maddy could feel the stirring of interest. 'Last thing, everyone. Thank you for coming at such short notice. Now! We have work to do!'

Maddy realised that in a weird way Ed was enjoying himself. He was forcing himself to the limit, losing himself in work. She now knew why. He was causing himself so much present pain to try to push past pain out of his mind.

Just for a moment she wondered what life would be like when this was all over. Would they ever see each other again—even casually? Would he move out of her life, forget her? As he had told his father he would do?

Or would she forget him? She had to be honest and admit it. She didn't think she would forget him. In fact, a life in which she didn't see something of Ed—it would be hard.

CHAPTER SEVEN

INEVITABLY there were problems but most of them were quickly sorted out. The new team didn't yet know where to find things, what the protocols were, what the right relationship with the stewards was. But they learned, and Maddy had to admit that they were conscientious, hardworking. She worked for a few hours. And then at midnight Ed came into the medical centre and said, 'Things are running smoothly now so you go to bed.'

Bed! She could think of few places she'd rather be. Taking the strain off her eyes, her legs, her back. Blissful just to lie there. 'All right,' she said. 'Aren't you going to sleep too?'

'I am. I've arranged with Dr Wyatt for her to take the next six-hour shift. If it's desperate she will wake me, but I doubt it will be necessary. I've got twenty minutes' more work to do then I'll sleep for those six hours, just as you are going to.'

'Right. And you're in the other nurse's cabin, which is next to mine?' For some reason, the question seemed very important to her.

'That's right. I'll sleep well there.'

'I'm tired but I won't sleep at once,' she told him. 'You know the stage when you've gone beyond being weary?'

He nodded, his eyes never leaving her face.

'Well, that's where I am. So instead of going straight to bed, I'm going to shower, wash my hair and then have a mug of tea with a shot of whisky in it. I feel like pushing the boat out a bit.'

She paused, afraid of the enormity of what she was going to say next. Staring at the floor, she said, 'If you want, you can come into my cabin and...have some tea and whisky, too.'

She felt his hand on her chin. With the most delicate of touches he lifted her head so they were looking at each other. He eyed her meaningfully, and unspoken messages passed between them. 'Are you sure?' he asked eventually.

'I'm sure. I'm certain. It's more than that, I want you to come for a drink with me.'

'Then I'd like to join you. Just for a while, of course.'

'Of course. I'll go now.' As she walked down the corridor she knew she had made a decision. Exactly what she had decided she didn't know.

She showered, shampooed her hair, and it was as wonderful as she had anticipated. She put on a clean nightie. Then she climbed into bed.

He knocked then came into her room twenty minutes later. 'Everything OK?' she asked.

'Everything is fine. They're a good team and I don't expect to be disturbed. You look...refreshed.'

'I am. Why don't you have a shower, too? There are spare towels in my bathroom.'

This was a lunatic conversation, she thought as he disappeared to shower. We're sidling round what we know we both want and neither of us dare say anything about it. Then she blinked, rethought things. Was this what she truly wanted? Or was she just blinded by fatigue? It wasn't too late to change her mind now.

Then she decided it was too late. Anyway, she knew what she wanted.

He came out of her bathroom, wearing only a towel wrapped round his waist. She winced as she saw scars on his naked chest. 'What are they?' she asked. 'You must have been terribly hurt.'

'Not too terribly. They're just flesh wounds. It's a danger that comes with being near a battlefield. Even if the war is unofficial.'

'I'd like you to tell me about it some time. But not now. I want to be calm and happy now.'

'Calm and happy. Sounds a good plan.'

She felt happy, but detached from herself. As if she could look down on what she was doing and judge it as an independent. She knew this was partly the result of fatigue. She also knew she'd want this even if she had slept all night and recovered.

They drank the tea she had made. He sat on the edge of her bed. 'You can sit there till you finish your drink,' she told him, 'but then you're to get in bed with me.'

He hesitated. 'Maddy, I do want to get in bed with you, desperately. But I don't want you to be hurt if...'

'I'll be hurt if you don't get in bed with me. Now, finish your drink.'

Was this her talking? she wondered. This just wasn't like her. She didn't do things like this, talk like this. She was throwing herself at a man—when she had promised herself that never again would she let a man take advantage of her. Well, it was done now. She'd made up her mind.

They sipped their drink in silence, finished almost together. She leaned over, switched off the overhead light so there was only the dim glow of the bedside lamp.

Now he was only a half-seen figure. He stood up and the towel round him dropped away. Another moment's hesitation, then he lifted the cover and slid into bed beside her.

She was really tired but in spite of this all her senses seemed extra-alert. She could hear and feel the hum of the shipboard machinery. She could smell the faint scent of whisky on his breath—or was it on hers? When he got closer to her she smelt the scent of her own soap. But it seemed different on him. Why would that be?

It was a bed rather than a bunk, but it was designed for one person. There was only just room for the two of them side by side. He didn't move or try to touch her, this seemed to be something that they had to do step by step. Perhaps it was her turn to do something. She wriggled upwards a little, crossed her arms and pulled her nightie over her head. Then she leaned across him to toss it carelessly onto the floor. As she did so she felt her breasts trailing over his naked chest. She smiled as she heard his sudden intake of breath.

When she was lying by his side again she let her fingers trail across him, gently touch the scar. 'Tell me more about this,' she said. 'There's a lot I don't know about you. And I want to know.'

She felt him shrug. 'It was an explosion. A mortar bomb lobbed into the camp hospital. A bit of white-hot metal gouged lumps out of me. It could have been a lot worse.'

'Which war was that?'

'No war had been declared. It was just people killing each other for no good reason.'

She could hear his bitterness, and decided it was better to move on to something else. 'Forget all that, I shouldn't have asked. But you're here with me now.'

His voice was urgent. 'Maddy, I am here with you now and it's wonderful but I don't know if we're doing the right—'

'You're trying to make sure that I know what I'm doing?'

'Yes.'

'Well, I do. Now, don't you really want to stay here with me?'

'Of course I do! But…'

'You've kissed me twice and it was wonderful. Both times we agreed that this was a thing apart, nothing serious, almost a shipboard romance. If you want, we'll carry on like that. For the moment that suits me.'

He said nothing. After a moment he slipped his arm around her shoulders and eased her back onto the pillow. 'Maddy, I—'

She laid a finger on his lips. 'We've gone beyond words. There are to be no promises, no confessions, no protestations. Let's face it, we're both damaged. We've both got pasts that hang over us. For now we'll forget the past and the concern that this could have no future. There's just the present, just you and me. And we can make each other happy. That would be so wonderful.'

Then she thought of something, something she should have thought of before. For a moment she was anxious. 'Last words—do you have precautions?'

He laughed. 'I stole something from your pharmacy. You have everything needed there.'

He leaned away from her, she heard the crackle of paper. For a moment she lay there, eyes closed, listening to the sound of his breathing. A last fugitive thought—was she making a mistake? But then he leaned over her, his face came down on hers and she closed her eyes.

She wasn't a virgin, of course, but neither was she vastly experienced. She was apprehensive now, her mind made up but not knowing what to expect. And Ed... She knew something of his character, how determined he was. What kind of lover would he be? Considerate, thoughtful, loving? He rolled onto his side, bent his head over hers and kissed her. A delicate kiss, his lips just touching hers. She had been kissed by him twice already. And the same magic worked as before. What started as something simple became suddenly something serious and exciting. It was still only his lips, her lips, meeting. Nothing more.

She was content for now—but where was he taking her? She was aware of his body, so close to hers and yet not touching. It was exciting. Tantalising. Now he leaned over her, his body above hers but still not touching. She could feel the warmth of him and knew that she had to do something. Reaching up, she slid her arms around him and eased him down so their bodies were now together, fully together. There seemed to be a lot of him. He seemed to cover her entire body, arms, legs, breasts all pressed against him. She felt that her body was owning his, he was paying the same tribute to her as she was paying to him.

They were still kissing. But the kiss was more passionate. And after a moment of bliss he took his lips from hers and kissed the rest of her face, her ears, the corners of her eyes, even the tip of her nose. Then he returned to her mouth again and she felt the strength of his desire as she met his probing tongue with hers.

He stopped, she whimpered, it had been so wonderful. Then he threw off the sheet that covered them. And his lips strayed downwards, touching the throb of the pulse in her neck, the edge of her arm and shoulder, the valley between her breasts. Then, after moments of almost unendurable expectation, he kissed her breasts. She moaned with ecstasy as he took each thrusting peak into his mouth. Her back arched, urging him onwards. It was the most exciting of caresses. She could feel it throughout her entire body, felt that dampness below that told her how ready, how quickened she was.

Now…he wasn't going to… He was… She sensed his head travel down her body, felt the touch of his tongue in that most secret of places. It made her cry out loud as he moved her towards a rapture she had never experienced before, never even dreamed of. Not long now.

Something told her that his need was as great as hers. Her hands slid down, grasped him and pulled him up to kiss her lips again. And her hips surged against his in silent longing and invitation.

It was so obvious, so perfect, like coming home. He was in her, part of her, they were joined body and spirit. A movement that both of them felt, a joint knowledge of something burgeoning, growing. It was something that could only be done when the two of them were together and then that moment of exaltation as they both cried out their pleasure.

Afterwards there was calm and contentment. She felt she could speak now. 'You are so good to me,' she murmured.

'And you are good to me, too,' he replied softly.

She slept through the night, the deep sleep of the completely exhausted. Then she half woke; she didn't know who she was, where she was, whose arm was round her. She only knew that she was warm, happy and safe, and that all the world was good to her. The man next to her would see to that. Perhaps she could sleep a little more and— A buzzer sounded and she was fully awake. Now she knew who, where and what she was. And who she was in bed with. But she was still happy.

Ed took his arm from under her, leaned out of bed and picked up the phone. 'Dr Wyatt? Of course not, I told you to... Yes, I'll be there in five minutes. Don't do anything until then.'

He rolled out of bed, she looked up at him and he bent over to kiss her. 'Maddy, I've got to work but...'

She held up her hand to stop him. 'It's OK, we don't need to talk about it. That way I'm certain there'll still be some...magic.'

He thought for a moment then nodded. 'Perhaps that is best. Carry on as if nothing had happened. But, Maddy, I think that—'

'Off you go! Back to your own cabin.' She glanced at the clock. They had had just over five hours' sleep. 'I'll be up soon and will come and help.'

He looked at her a moment, then turned to go.

She decided that she could stay in bed for a further fifteen minutes, but she knew she wouldn't sleep. She felt at a bit of a loss. He said they were to carry on as if nothing had happened. Was that the answer she really wanted? She wasn't sure.

She thought of yesterday and the time spent without sleep. She had worked harder than she had ever worked in her life before. She had been hounded by her ex-fiancé. She had watched the death of a man who had asked her to marry him. And she had slept with Ed and it had been wonderful. What more could the future bring? She didn't like to think. But there was no time to think now. She got out of bed.

The work went on. They now had two doctors and four nurses and assistance from the stewards. But Dr Wyatt and one of the nurses were taking a six-hour sleep break. And the work didn't get any less.

For some reason she didn't spend much time with Ed that morning. But they saw each other from time to time. She had been wondering just how the two of them would react when they were first working together again. All right, they had agreed to say nothing. But when they met it was impossible. There was an understood acknowledgement of what had happened, a special smile or a brief touch of hands, unrecognised by anyone else. It was only a little but it meant so much to her.

She was sneaking a quick lunch with one of the other nurses when Ed came and sat beside her. He had been insistent that they all have regular meals and had arranged for food to be brought to the medical centre. 'You need all the energy that you can get,' he had told them. 'Eat lightly but eat well.' And they had done so.

He sat opposite her, took a glass of orange juice and a plate of salad. Maddy felt uneasy as he looked at her. There was an expression on his face she didn't understand. Like nothing she had seen before. Fear? Horror? But his voice was calm as he said, 'I'd like you to come back with me when you've finished. I've got a case that's concerning me. Penny Cox. Do you know her?'

Maddy shook her head. 'No. I don't think she's ever been to the medical centre.'

'Probably not. She looks to be young, fit, apparently healthy. But she's had a splenectomy, the result of a motorcycle accident years ago.'

Penny Cox's condition had deteriorated, but she was strong and now Maddy was relieved to see that she seemed to be over the worst of it.

'I think she's OK now, Ed. I can call you if things change.'

Ed frowned. 'No, I'll stay, just to make sure she doesn't relapse. I'll be buzzed if I'm wanted.'

'Well, there's not too much I can do here. It's just a matter of waiting. Shall I go?'

He looked alarmed. 'No! No, I want you to stay. You can… You might be…'

It was then that she realised that there was more to this case than appeared. It meant something to him. 'Did you know this lady before?' she asked.

'No. Never met her before in my life. Never even heard of her.'

'It's just that…you seem especially interested in her. I know you've done your best for all of our patients, but this one seems to mean more to you than the others, you're more involved. Will you tell me why?'

It was the first time she had ever seen him at a loss, not been in absolute control of himself. He shook his head fretfully, then walked over and stared down at Penny Cox's white face.

Maddy wondered if she should walk over to him, perhaps put her arm around his waist to comfort him. She decided not to. Whatever demon he was wrestling with, he had to fight it on his own. But it was hard just to sit there, to know he was suffering.

The silence between them lasted for perhaps ten minutes, during which neither of them moved. And then there was a change. The only sound had been Penny's breathing, no longer heavy and laboured. Now Maddy felt she could go over to stand by Ed. 'Penny's over it, Ed,' she said. 'The worst has passed, now she stands a good chance of recovering.'

'I think you're right. This one stands a good chance of recovering.'

This one? Maddy thought. Who was he comparing her with?

She took his hand, and led him to the far side of the cabin. There was a bench there where they could sit together. Perhaps now was the right time. 'You're to tell me what's wrong,' she said, 'why you are suffering. You've given me hints but now I need to know everything. You told me about working in the hospital in Africa but I think there's more. I've already told you my story, told you things about my relationship with Brian that I've told no one else. Ed, we have to share. I know it's hard for you, you like to keep feelings locked up. But it's good to tell. And it's not bad to feel!'

He looked at her as if puzzled. 'Why are you so concerned about me, Maddy?'

'Because you're like me—you're carrying a load of memories that hurt. I'm offering you the chance to share that load.'

He still seemed puzzled, looking at her as if she had not fully understood him. 'But it's just not me to talk about things like that.'

'There are bits of you that I very much admire. And there are other bits that I don't. This keeping quiet is one of them. Ed, please, tell me.'

He stood quickly, walked over to look at Penny again. 'Better and better,' he muttered. 'Maddy, she's going to be fine.' Then, just as quickly, he came back to sit by her.

'We've got a minute,' he said. 'This will be hard for me—but I will tell you. I might regret it afterwards but I will tell you.'

Now Maddy was nervous. What was she going to hear?

'Penny Cox was double trouble,' he started. 'Because of the splenectomy she had an immunodeficiency problem and then she caught gastroenteritis. She could have died, but she's been very lucky. Some few years ago, in a hot and sweaty part of Africa, another Penny had exactly the same symptoms but with a further problem. She was four months pregnant. And she died. That was Penny Tremayne, my wife.'

Maddy winced. Never had she suspected his story could be as tragic as this. 'So this...brought it all back?'

'It did. We were in a desperate bit of Africa, I was running a bush hospital. There was an outbreak of gastroenteritis there and it spread like wildfire. The people there were mostly refugees from a neighbouring country and no one except us cared about them. They were malnourished, weak, they died like flies.' He pursed his lips, as if considering. 'But we did save some. We did some good.'

'Go on,' said Maddy.

'I had a tiny team of orderlies, not enough drugs, not enough helpers. This wasn't what I had joined the army for...but there were political considerations.'

Maddy found it hard to ask, but she had to. 'Was your wife in the army, too?'

'No. She was a nurse, working for an African charity. When she heard where I had been posted to she pulled a few strings and got leave to come to work with me. I didn't want her there, but she just turned up and refused to leave. How I wish I'd forced her back!' He paused and then said bitterly. 'But there weren't a lot of volunteers for the job.'

'She sounds a...fine woman, ' Maddy said carefully. 'You must have been proud of her.'

'It's wonderful being proud of a dead woman!'

For a moment there was raw emotion in his voice, and Maddy flinched. How could she ever have thought that this man was without feelings?

He went on, 'She had immunodeficiency problems from an earlier illness, she was pregnant, and I was working a twenty-hour day. Then she caught gastroenteritis. A day later we both knew she was dying. I sat by her bed, held her hand and wiped the sweat off her face.

We had so much planned together! Then an orderly came, saying there was a major problem that only I could solve. She knew this. She told me to go and get on with my job, there was nothing more I could do for her but I could save other people. So I left her—and perhaps I did save other people. But she died alone.'

He stopped a moment. Then, almost whispering now, 'I was leaving the army because my father had offered me a job. We were going to come back to Penhally, buy a house and settle down. I was so looking forward to being a father.'

That last sentence was the hardest thing to bear. Maddy knew there was nothing she could say. On impulse she wrapped her arms round him, rested her head against his chest. And, as she knew they would, the tears came.

He stroked her hair, the back of her neck. 'It's a long time ago,' he said. 'Don't be sad.'

He was comforting her!

So much made sense to Maddy now. 'That's why you weren't as pleased as Kate and I when the baby was born?'

'Possibly. But it would be mean-spirited to be envious of the parents' happiness.'

Maddy sighed, her heart aching for his pain. 'Ed, how you must have been suffering! All those memories flooding back. How could you bear it?'

'I was the best man for the job,' he said. 'But you're right. The memories have been...hard, especially seeing Penny here. It brought back all the agony, all the misery and the pointlessness of things, all the long waiting for life to seem better. And it never did. I was in love with my wife, I was enthralled with the idea of being a father and within twenty-four hours it all disappeared.'

His voice altered, became more curt. Now he was once again the professional, ex-military doctor, not used to talking about his emotions. 'I made a decision then. I never wanted to love like that again, because there was always the chance of loss. So I've avoided...emotional entanglements ever since.'

'Is that why you don't want to get too close to me?'

'It is. We agreed that this is just a shipboard fling and it doesn't count. I'm happy to be with you, Maddy, because I know it will end.'

'I see,' she said flatly.

He stood. 'You were right about one thing. It does help to tell someone else. But now that's over. Let's have a last check on Penny here and then we'd better get on our rounds again.'

So, back to business. There was work to be done, she had to concentrate on it. But she also had to think about Ed. Now she thought she understood him so much better. But did he have to be so certain about how he would live his life in the future?

It was a hard day but by the end of it things were obviously easing off. There were no new cases. More than a few people were still seriously ill but the medical team was coping.

Late that evening Ed called a meeting of all his little staff, thanked them for what they had done so far and said that he thought that things would be considerably better by the next day. The staff smiled. It felt good to know that you were on top of things. Ed went on to say that unless there were any objections they would stick to the same shift pattern. This would mean that he and Maddy would get to sleep for six hours again that night. Though either could be buzzed if there was an emergency.

Two hours later it was time for bed and Maddy met Ed outside her cabin. 'You look tired,' she said. 'It's getting to you at last.'

'No one can go on for ever.'

She looked at his unyielding face and said, 'I'm looking forward to my bed, but if you'd like a tea and whisky first, then I'll be making one.'

Rarely for him, he made a confession. 'I was so hoping you'd say that. But I thought it would be forward of me to ask.'

'I think we two are beyond being forward with each other,' she said tartly. 'Will you shower in your cabin or mine?'

'I'll shower in yours if I may. It makes it all seem a bit more…intimate.'

'It does indeed,' she agreed with a little smile.

So, shortly, they were sitting side by side in her bed again and tonight she hadn't bothered with her nightie. But she didn't feel like being too obvious. She tucked the sheet around her shoulders.

She looked at his face, trying to work out what he wanted from her. Simple sex? She didn't think so. If anything, she thought he needed companionship. It suddenly struck her that, in spite of being part of a large family, he might also be a lonely man. A man who seldom confided in anyone, who kept his feelings to himself. But he had revealed himself to her. The thought made her happy.

'Ed, what you told me in Penny's cabin. I'm glad I

know more about you. Sometimes you come across as being brilliantly professional—but there's always a reserve there. And I think I've got beyond that reserve.'

'There are things one needs to keep to oneself,' he said. 'Apart from anything else—why should I trouble other people with my problems?'

'Because they want you to trouble them,' she told him. 'Because they…I…think a lot of you.'

'Perhaps. Maddy, I think I…think a lot of you.'

'Good,' she said. 'And I think a lot of you, or we wouldn't be doing this.' A small part of her brain wondered if that was the most passionate declaration he was capable of. Still, she supposed it was something.

He smiled at her. Then he drew her to him and kissed her and she felt that whatever their problems, they could be solved. But now was not a time for problems in the future. Now was for now.

The night before their love-making had been at first tentative and then a desperate seeking for solace. It had been over quickly, because that had been what both of them had wanted—had needed. Tonight, even though they were more tired than ever, it was different. It was a gentler, more giving love-making. And she felt that it was love. He didn't use the word, but all his actions were those of a man who would do all that was possible for the woman he was with. They fitted together so well! They could both anticipate, knew what the other wanted, knew what would give most pleasure. And then there was a final climax that seemed to roll on and on for ever.

One final kiss and then it only was a moment before she could feel his chest rising and falling under her arm, hear the deep breaths of a man whose exhaustion had led him instantly to sleep. She felt exhausted, too.

Perhaps it was this fatigue that allowed an idea to surface, a thought that she had not permitted herself even to consider. Ed Tremayne. She admired his medical skill, she enjoyed being with him, sex with him was wonderful. But there was more than all that.

Now she knew she loved him.

She thought of what she had decided, or what had been revealed to her, and then slept at once. It was a deep sleep, but somehow the knowledge of the love was with her and it comforted her.

CHAPTER EIGHT

IT WAS a mistake, a big mistake.

Next morning was different from the morning before. This time she woke up first, checked the time. They had twenty more minutes together. For a moment she just lay there, looking at him. He was still asleep, and his face had that peaceful innocence that she had noticed before. It was the face of a new, different Ed. An Ed who had been hidden from her before. The lines drawn by pain had disappeared.

She remembered the night before, an almost startling realisation. Had it happened so suddenly? She loved him. More than that, she now felt capable of love again and that made her so happy.

She just couldn't resist. She knew he needed every minute of sleep he could get but... She leaned over him, just brushed his lips with hers. And his eyes flicked open immediately. She was so filled with happiness, filled with the realisation that her life had changed so much for the better, that she said it without thinking. It was so obvious to her.

'I love you, Ed.' It shocked her to hear herself say it. But, still, she waited for his reaction.

He had been asleep. But when he woke up he was alert at once. She saw him frown when he grasped what she had said. Why didn't he smile? Why didn't he say something?

He pushed himself up in bed, looked at her. 'What did you say, Maddy? I must be still asleep. I thought I heard you say you loved me.'

It was the wrong reaction, she thought. If you told someone you loved them, they should say it straight back. Or kiss you or something. Not ask foolish questions. Faltering, she said, 'Well, after last night... And it was so wonderful... I just thought that...' And then it hit her. They had made an agreement. This affair was to take place on board only—then it was to end. Yes, they liked each other, yes they had learned each other's secrets. But that had only been for a couple of snatched days.

She had made a terrible mistake. Shaking her head as if confused, she said, 'Sorry, I was just waking up. Not knowing what I was saying, dreaming really. Forget it.'

Even to herself this sounded lame but she managed to press on. 'Now it's time to get up. I'll go first in the shower and then we can...'

They were sitting side by side in her bed, he put his arm round her, pulled her towards him and kissed her on the cheek. On the cheek? This was a kiss you'd give your child or your grandmother. Not your lover.

His voice was kind, which made things worse. 'Maddy, you weren't dreaming. You said you loved me and you meant it. And I'm so sorry.' He shook his head in distress. 'I never intended this to happen. I knew what I was doing was wrong, I took advantage of you. When you're working in a stressed situation like we are, you do not start love affairs.'

This made her angry. 'No one took advantage of me. There were two of us involved—if anything, I made the first moves.'

'Then I should have resisted them.'

Silence for a moment. 'Thanks,' she said. 'That makes me feel great. Now, you stay in bed, I need the first shower.'

'But, Maddy, I…'

She slid out of bed, ran to her shower and locked the door. She turned the shower on full blast so the sound of it would hide her sobbing. And then anger took over and she stopped crying. She had made a fool of herself and she hated it.

From outside she heard the sound of a door clicking shut. He had got up and left her cabin. Well, she might as well carry on with getting ready for the new day.

When she left the bathroom, wrapped tightly in her dressing-gown, he had, of course, gone. Perhaps that was the best thing. Perhaps it would be best if she just forgot what she had said to him, just carried on as if nothing had happened. Shortly he would leave the ship and they would stick to their agreement—what they had was for on board the ship only.

But she knew she couldn't just forget Ed Tremayne. She did love him.

She had come on board this ship to be away from marauding men. She had never wanted to think of love again. But she had found a man and she had fallen in love with him and he didn't want her. What to do?

She shrugged, smiled a bitter smile. There was nothing she could do but suffer.

She dressed, stayed in her cabin until she heard the sounds of the other staff coming into the medical centre. It was time for handover, the reports of staff who were coming off duty to those who were coming on. She'd be happier meeting Ed again if they were in company.

She went out, saw Ed talking to Dr Wyatt. 'Morning,' she said pleasantly. 'How are things going?'

She saw the faint relief in Ed's eyes, knew that he realised she was going to remain professional. Well, of course, she was going to remain professional. At the moment it was all she had going for her.

'Things are now definitely improving,' Ed reported. 'There are no new cases, the worst are improving, those who are nearly better are complaining about not being able to go on shore. I think we can congratulate ourselves.'

'In that case, may I have the morning to deal with the few patients who have problems other than gastroenteritis?' Maddy asked him. 'There are some dressings to be checked and changed, some injections to be given. A few people I just like to keep an eye on.'

'Good idea. It's too easy to forget that there might be problems other than the gastro.'

She wondered if there were also the faint signs of relief in his voice at her suggestion. This way they wouldn't have to spend time together.

It was good to get back to her old job, good to be able to do it well. Apart from the medical attention she could spare the time to chat for a few minutes, instead of being in the vast hurry she'd been in recently.

Most of her patients were eager to get ashore now, some were quite annoyed. Maddy managed to calm most of them, making them feel relieved that they hadn't been infected themselves. It was all part of a cruise ship nurse's job.

But as the morning wore on she felt worse and worse. At first she thought that it was misery because of her mistake with Ed. Then she wondered if she was going down with the illness herself. That wouldn't be fair! She had been so careful with the necessary precautions. But then she decided that she was not showing any of the initial symptoms. She just felt dreadful.

Her last call was to Mrs Cowley's cabin. Robbie's dressing ought to be changed. Robbie's dressings got dirty faster than anyone else on the ship.

He wasn't in the cabin. 'His friend Joey just came to call,' Mrs Cowley explained. 'Came with his dad and asked if Robbie wanted to go to the play area with them. Well, he'd been getting restless and I felt a bit tired so I said he could go. They'll bring him back in time.'

'Feeling tired?' Maddy questioned. 'You are sticking to the diet, aren't you?'

'Well, sort of...'

For what must have been the tenth time Maddy went through the dangers of binge eating if you were diabetic.

Finally she left, telling Mrs Cowley that she'd find Robbie some time later. She still felt dreadful, so she decided to go back to the medical centre and have a drink of water. Was she dehydrated? She didn't think so. Perhaps it was just fatigue catching up on her.

Just as she thought this Ed came into the room. He looked at her and frowned. 'You don't look too good,

Maddy,' he said. His tone was medical, professional, but she thought she could detect some touch of personal feeling there.

'I'll be all right. It's catching up on me, I just need to sit down a moment.'

'We'd better make sure you're not coming down with the bug as well. Come into your cabin and I'll examine you.' There was a pause and then he said, 'Do you want a chaperone?'

She managed a small smile. 'I think it's a bit late for that now.'

They went into her cabin so he could examine her. She noticed that he took rubber gloves out of his bag—and then dropped them back in. 'You should wear gloves to examine every patient,' she told him.

'On this occasion I'll manage without.'

She knew why. The last time his hands had been on her body they had... To touch her again with rubber gloves would be an insult to them both.

He said, 'You know, Maddy, we have to talk and—'

She cut him off. 'Not now,' she said. 'I just can't deal with it. Perhaps not ever. Just get on with your work.'

It didn't take long and she knew what the result would be. 'Nothing too seriously wrong with you, Maddy. Nothing physical, that is. You've just done too much. A body can't take stress indefinitely. Now, pay attention to me. You're going to rest now. Just for three hours; I promise I won't leave you longer than that.'

'But, Ed, I'm needed.'

'Things are a lot better. You're not needed now.'

Telling her she wasn't needed was the wrong thing for

him to say, she saw that he recognised this at once. But he said nothing and neither did she. 'I'll do as you say,' she said.

The moment he had gone she remembered her last task—finding Robbie and re-dressing his arm. Well, it would only take a minute. She'd do that now and then have her rest.

First she went back to Mrs Cowley's cabin. No Robbie there. And Mrs Cowley was asleep. Having checked that she hadn't fallen into a diabetic coma, Maddy went up to the children's indoor play area. It was a large, glassed-in room with the usual games. There were ship attendants there and children being watched by their parents. The children's room was busy. The storm had abated slightly but it was still too cool and windy for anyone to go out on deck.

But no Robbie. Maddy said hello to a few people she knew, and asked about Robbie. Everyone knew Robbie. She was told he had been there playing with Joey Billings and his dad but he had left half an hour ago.

Maddy was now feeling slightly worried. But probably Robbie was in the Billingses' cabin. She went down to ask.

'Left the play area with us about half an hour ago,' Mr Billings said with a big smile. 'The boys had a great game of pirates. I took him down to his corridor, saw him walking to his cabin.'

'Did you take him into the cabin?'

Mr Billings looked uncomfortable. 'Well, no. I've been in there before... Often Mrs Cowley doesn't like to be disturbed.'

'So you didn't actually see him go into the cabin?'

'No. But he was only three doors away.'

Maddy thanked Mr Billings and left. Somewhere Robbie was wandering. There were an awful lot of attendants on the ship so he couldn't really get into mischief, could he? Possibly, yes. Robbie was gifted that way.

It would cause an awful lot of trouble and alarm to broadcast a request for people to look for a small boy in a pirate's outfit. She might have to in time, of course, but where could he be? Then Maddy remembered. Robbie wanted to be a pirate. And the pirate ship he wanted was one of the lifeboats—he'd been stopped from climbing on them before. He had pointed out to Maddy that if the cruise ship sank, this would be the best one for a pirate.

Maddy climbed to the lifeboat deck, and went out onto the deserted companionway. The wind wailed around her, pushing her back against the railings. There was absolutely no sign of Robbie. She walked closer to the lifeboats. From a distance they looked small but nearer they were quite alarmingly large. She spotted the one that Robbie wanted and went to stand underneath the lifeboat, looked up at the davits, the complex gear for swinging the boat out and lowering it into the sea. One last look around—no Robbie. She'd go back to the play area.

The biggest noise was still the wind but suddenly Maddy thought she heard something else. A cry, a whimper? But from where? Then she remembered that Robbie had had to be stopped from trying to climb on top of this lifeboat. Had he succeeded this time? 'Robbie,' she shouted, 'it's Nurse Maddy.'

'Nurse Maddy, help, I'm frightened,' a little voice came.

'Where are you?'

'I'm on top of the boat. And I'm slipping.'

Maddy looked up at the launching gear, saw how a determined little boy could have climbed up. Quickly she climbed onto the railings, reached up to where there was a handhold, a place to wedge her feet. Then somehow she wriggled upwards and came to where she could see the top of the lifeboat. There was a covering over it, two smooth sloping surfaces. And on one of the surfaces Robbie was stretched out. He had boarded his pirate ship. But there was nowhere to hang onto and he was in danger of slipping off the edge and falling. Possibly even bouncing into the sea. He knew it and he was terrified.

Somehow Maddy struggled a bit further upwards—Robbie must have been like a monkey to get up here with a bandaged arm! She mustn't alarm him, mustn't let him panic. 'How's the pirate chief, Robbie?'

'I want to get down!'

'All right. Now, you just stay there and I'll reach forward and grab your hands. Then I'll slide you towards me. But keep still till I reach you!'

Robbie nodded.

Maddy looked down. She was in a difficult position, her feet braced on a rail, one hand clutching a thick wire cable, the other hand stretching out to Robbie. Robbie grabbed for the outstretched hand, missed it and started to slip. Maddy lunged, just managing to get a hand to him, to grip him by the collar of his jacket. But with only one hand she didn't have the strength to pull him to safety. And now both she and Robbie were starting to slip. But she wouldn't let him go!

What to do now? It was something she had never done before. She cried out for help, hoping someone would hear her over the wind and sea.

Dimly she was aware of the rattle of feet on the deck below her. The strain on her arm was getting to be too much, she could feel her grasp on the cable loosening. She had to hang on!

CHAPTER NINE

ED'S morning had not been good. For once in his life he had absolutely no idea of what to do. And he didn't like being in doubt. It was driving him crazy.

He had just sent Maddy to bed—the bed he had climbed out of not four hours before—and walked away from the medical centre with his feelings in turmoil. Of course, he'd realised how hurt Maddy had been but as usual he'd managed—he thought—to hide his own feelings.

He thought back over the past two days. What decisions had he made and why? First, why was he on the ship at all? He knew his father could have dealt with the situation just as well as him. But he had insisted. This job had to be his.

The worst time of his life had been spent dealing with an epidemic, so why had he wanted to experience it again? In fact, he knew why. He had to face up to things, he couldn't go through his life knowing that he was afraid of something. And it had been hard but he had managed somehow.

Now he knew the crisis was almost over. He wasn't needed any more. He could go ashore knowing that he had done a good job And he had faced down his devils. Well, some of them.

But while the fear of the outbreak was behind him there was another, bigger problem. No, not a problem! Maddy was the best, the most exciting… No way could he call her a problem. But what should he do about her?

He had tried to be fair to her by telling her there could be no future in their affair. And later he had tried to explain why—how, after his wife had died, he'd never wanted to fall love again. Because of the risk of being hurt again. And this was unusual. He'd never felt the need to explain his actions to any other woman. So why Maddy?

And why had he felt some kind of peace or relief when he had told her? They had had a hard couple of days— probably it was good that the work had been so hard because so many memories, feelings had been dragged to the surface. The outbreak itself, the birth of a baby which had reminded him of his own unborn child. Penny, who had the same name and fatal combination as his dead wife—gastroenteritis and a compromised auto-immune system. But this Penny had survived and there had always been someone with her.

He had tried to insulate himself against these negative feelings. He couldn't, wouldn't suffer again.

He realised that he was going round in circles, not facing the big question. Could he give Maddy up? Always supposing she wanted to see more of him. Halfway along the corridor he made a decision and turned back to the medical centre. He had to see her. Never mind if she was tired, she must help him. He wasn't sure of what he was going to say to her, he just knew he had to say something.

Then he realised what he was trying to do. He was handing over responsibility to her. What did she think he ought to do? He had never done this before in his life. He was asking, not deciding. But he felt he had made some kind of a decision.

Back in the medical centre he tapped on Maddy's door then peered inside. No Maddy. A nurse came in to collect some more medicines, and when Ed asked her she said that she had seen Maddy two minutes ago on her way to the children's playroom. And she had looked terrible.

Ed nodded, rushing off to the playroom. There he was told that Maddy had just been in, asking for Robbie, and someone had seen her climbing up to the next deck. They didn't know what she was doing there. Ed wondered, too. There was nothing for her up there except lifeboats. Then it struck him. Robbie the devil who wanted to be a pirate. Who had already picked out the lifeboat he wanted as his pirate ship. Who had fallen off it once.

Ed ran up the stairs and out onto the lifeboat deck. It was windy, cold and there was no one about. No sign of Maddy or Robbie. He looked up and down and down and something flapping in the wind caught his eye. A scrap of blue—the colour of the scrubs Maddy was wearing. What was it doing halfway up a lifeboat davit? That was dangerous!

He ran along the deck, looking up to see Maddy precariously balanced, leaning over the lifeboat. She shouldn't climb in the state she was in! He shouted to her, then climbed up behind her, seeing her half-spreadeagled over the lifeboat canopy. She held Robbie by his jacket collar to stop him sliding off the edge of the canopy and into the sea. Her face was twisted with pain.

He was bigger, stronger, more fit than Maddy. He lunged forward, grabbed Robbie and dragged him under one arm. The three of them were balanced there. What should he do next?

'I'm all right for a minute,' Maddy gasped. 'I can hang on. You get Robbie down.'

He looked at her, thinking frantically. Was he abandoning another woman he loved? Then common sense took over. Carefully he climbed back down to the deck, keeping a tight arm round the little boy. For once, Robbie had the sense to stay still.

Robbie was now safe on deck, scared but otherwise fine. Ed looked up again to see the woman he now knew he loved.

Maddy's grasp loosened. He saw her plummet and desperately he dived to catch her but he just couldn't manage it. Her head hit the deck. And he recognized the sound that sickened him—Maddy had a fractured skull.

Feelings that he had hoped to forget rushed back so strongly that he had to choke back a cry of despair. This couldn't happen again! He loved Maddy!

It was nearly the hardest thing he had ever done. He was a doctor. Maddy was someone injured. What was needed now was professional skill, not emotion.

Calling to Robbie to stay where he was, he checked Maddy's vital signs. She was still alive. ABC—airway, breathing, circulation. All seemed, well, adequate. Still alive. The gentlest of palpations of the skull—yes, fractured. A delicate touch at the back of the neck. There appeared to be no damage to the spine but it was hard to tell.

He needed help! He buzzed the medical centre. Dr Wyatt

was there. 'I'm up on the lifeboat deck, starboard side. Come up yourself and get two stewards to bring up a stretcher. Maddy has a fractured skull. I want you here now!'

'On our way,' said Dr Wyatt. 'I'll bring some stuff and a hard collar.'

A distant bit of Ed's brain told him to remember to congratulate her on her quick thinking. He needed a hard collar and had forgotten to ask for one!

Now the captain. Ed buzzed again, told Ken, the captain's steward, to interrupt the captain, whatever he might be doing. This was an emergency. And while he waited for the captain to come on the line he looked at the sky. Yes, it looked possible.

'Yes, Dr Tremayne? Captain Smith here.'

It was good to hear that calm efficient voice. He would be calm, efficient himself. As much as he could. 'Captain, Maddy Granger has just had a bad fall and has a fractured skull. This is serious, far beyond my expertise. I'm taking her to the medical centre for now but she needs to go to hospital urgently. Is it possible now to get a helicopter to the ship?'

'I think so. I will see to it at once as a matter of extreme urgency. I'll ring down to the medical centre as soon as there is news.'

'The nearest competent hospital is St Piran's,' said Ed. 'The head of A & E is Ben Carter. I'll contact him.'

'Good. I'll arrange the helicopter transport.'

There was the rattle of feet on the deck and a horrified Dr Wyatt and two stewards ran up. Ed detailed one steward to take the now crying Robbie back to his mother. Then, with help, he slid Maddy's neck into the hard collar. Then they gently lifted their unconscious patient onto the stretcher and took her down to the medical centre.

Ed looked at her white face. Another white face kept flashing into his mind, and there was the memory of a death. Please, this couldn't happen again. But he had to concentrate!

In the medical centre Maddy was examined for other injuries. There didn't appear to be any. Just the skull. Just!

He looked down and his heart rate suddenly surged as Maddy's eyes fluttered open. She looked at him, blinked and waited for consciousness to arrive. 'Hello, Ed. I fell, didn't I? Is Robbie…?' and then she lapsed into unconsciousness again.

Twenty minutes later there was a phone call from Captain Smith. 'The chopper is on its way. Can you prepare to load the patient in half an hour?'

'I can.'

'How is she?'

'Holding her own,' Ed said. 'So far anyway. Captain, I want to go with her.'

'Of course. I think your work here is more or less done. Dr Wyatt can take over.' There was a tiny pause to show that the captain was moving from professional to personal and then he said, 'Ed, I want know what happens. Maddy—we all think a lot of her.'

'I'll keep you posted,' Ed promised. Then he turned to stare down at her.

Ten minutes after that there was another call, this time from his friend Ben Carter at St Piran's. 'You have a patient for me, Ed?'

For now this wasn't the woman he loved, this was a

patient. There was no time for emotion. 'She fell and smashed her head. Obviously she's concussed and she's drifting in and out of consciousness. Blood pressure up, slow pulse. I've taken X-rays, there's a depressed fracture and some fragmentation. I suspect a subdural haematoma, and I've got an IV line in to deal with any dehydration through blood loss.'

'Sounds like I need to see her urgently. I understand there's a chopper bringing her in?'

'That's right.'

'Well, I need to have a look at her and we need CT and MRI scans. Once I've got those we'll have her in Theatre. I'm getting the team together.' There was a short pause and then Ben said, 'Your voice is cracking, Ed. Is this girl a personal friend of yours?'

'I hope so,' Ed said quietly.

This was silly, Maddy thought. No, not silly, weird. She knew she was floating in and out of consciousness. The odd thing was, when she was conscious she was able to have quite intelligent conversations. Well, she thought they were intelligent. They just suddenly…stopped.

Her head hurt. But if she turned it slightly she could see an IV giving set dripping blood into her. Yes, she must have lost quite a lot of blood. That would be why she felt quite so weak and…

She knew that her injury was serious. Possibly extremely serious. She had seen it in the faces of Dr Wyatt and the nurses. Dr Wyatt had told her that this wasn't her area of expertise. She wondered what expert they might manage to find and if it would be in time. And where was Ed?

The odd thing was that this should have happened just when she was beginning to be able to feel again. Feel emotionally, that was. It was as if a black cloud had lifted. She could see possibilities all around her, saw that there were chances that she ought to take. Ought to have taken.

Ed Tremayne. She had started to feel something for him. Perhaps she should have fought harder against letting him go. Though where would that have got him now? More misery? She knew that this injury was serious. It would have been a pity if he had... She drifted off again.

Somehow she knew that quite some time had passed since she had last been conscious. And when she came to she knew that her condition had deteriorated. But she could still think clearly, even though it was an effort to open her eyes, to turn her head. And there was Ed. The man she loved!

He looked different. The old iron face had gone, she now could tell exactly what he felt. Of course, he was terribly worried. But there was something else that she wasn't quite certain of. A new expression on his face that she had never seen before.

He took her hand, lifted it to his lips and his eyes never left her face. 'You weren't here when I woke up before,' she said. She was amazed at how weak her voice sounded.

She thought he was fighting to keep his feelings under control. 'Did you think I wanted to leave you here to be injured on your own? It was so hard, leaving you! But there were things I had to arrange. We've got a helicopter coming to take you to hospital.'

'You're coming, too!' She didn't want to be parted from him.

'Of course I'm coming, too. You're going to see a friend of mine, Ben Carter. He's a surgeon.'

'So I need a surgeon? I'm that bad?'

'Ben had a look at your X-rays, we had a video connection. He wants to have a closer look.'

'You mean open up my head. So you know what's wrong with me?'

It was strange how weak she felt and yet how alert. Something to do with her injury? No, nothing like that. But she saw the doubt and fear in Ed's eyes and she guessed what he was not telling her.

'We're not sure yet. It'll all be clearer when Ben has operated.'

'Ed! The two of us have always been honest with each other. At least, we've tried, though I'm not sure how well we have succeeded. Now, never mind about reassuring the patient. Tell her honestly what her chances are.' She paused a moment to get her breath, and then went on, 'There are definite reasons I need to know.'

She saw him debating, wondering whether to tell her or not. She was glad when he decided to be honest.

'There is pressure from fragments of broken bone in your skull, causing bleeding into the brain. We don't know how serious the bleeding is, but it's got to be stopped soon. Ben needs to drill through to try to relieve the pressure, tie up the leaking blood vessels and deal with the bone fragments. He won't know how hard the job will be till he gets inside.'

'What are my chances?'

He didn't answer.

'Listen, Ed! I've been a theatre nurse in A and E, I know what skull fractures are like. I've seen enough road accidents. And you've turned into a terrible liar—you couldn't convince anyone. It's really important that I know the worst possible thing that could happen to me.'

He gave up trying to hide things from her, she was too certain about what she wanted. 'There's a risk that you could slip into a coma and never come out of it.'

She held his gaze. 'So what are the chances of that happening to me?'

He didn't answer at first. She could see his pain was even greater. But then she knew he would act like the doctor he was, the man who could do whatever was necessary, whatever it cost him. 'The chances of success are about fifty-fifty. Ben thinks that we daren't wait any longer. He's been talking on the radio to some expert in London, and the man agrees we need to operate at once. Your condition is deteriorating every minute.'

Strange how detached she felt, she thought. This was like talking about someone who wasn't her. 'That's more or less what I had guessed. Don't worry, I can take it.'

'You can take it! What about...?' Once again she saw the giant effort he had to make to calm himself. Then he went on, 'For the moment I'm your doctor. I have to ask you if you agree to this operation. You know the risks involved. I have to ask you if you are willing to sign the consent form.'

'I'll sign it now. Can you get it and fetch me a pen?'

She had a moment alone while he fetched the form. She considered, made a decision then wondered if it was the right one. 'Life's too short to spend changing my mind,' she muttered to herself. Life was too short? It could be even shorter now her decision was definite. But the prospect of the operation really didn't alarm her. It was something else.

Ed came back in the room held out a pen and paper. 'Read what it says,' he urged. 'I don't want you to…'

She scrawled her name across the bottom of the sheet. 'I'll read it afterwards,' she said. 'Just out of curiosity. Ed, sit down, there's something I want to say to you.'

He sat, took her hand again. 'Maddy, don't waste your strength. We can—'

'No. I need to talk. I have to because I might doze off again and that would be terrible. You said I had a fifty-fifty chance of pulling through. Well, in case I don't, there's something I want to say to you. If I might die, I think that I have licence to say it. I don't need to worry about whether it's proper or not. And, Ed, you don't need to say anything.'

She took a breath. Now she had decided, she had to hang on, just for a while longer. She could feel unconsciousness creeping up on her, but she had to say this first. 'Ed, I meant what I said this morning. I do love you. Forget all that rubbish about shipboard romance, about this being out of time, not to be thought about. I love you.'

Why that funny way he was looking at her? As if he'd just heard news that surprised him. As if something odd had just occurred to him.

He shook his head, as if not certain. Then he did jerk her into full consciousness. 'And I love you, Maddy,' he said. And, almost as if it was an afterthought, 'Will you marry me?'

But after that first wonderful shock she felt the clouds gathering in her head again. His face seemed to blur, she was sinking into something deep and warm and comforting. 'You certainly know how to make a girl feel good,' she managed to whisper. 'Now I've got something to dream about. Marry you? Of course I will.'

She knew she was smiling as she fell asleep.

For a moment Ed stared down at the unconscious Maddy. He'd just asked her to marry him and he knew that it was what he wanted. More than anything. He would marry Maddy and they would be happy together—if she survived. And suddenly fear hit him, stronger than ever. A fifty-fifty chance. How could he cope? He had lost one woman he loved—how could he bear to lose another?

Then he told himself not to be a coward. He had tried to avoid falling in love because of the pain that loss might bring. But now he knew that the risk was worth taking. He was in love. And it was wonderful.

'Not quite as bad as I had feared,' said Ben. 'X-rays are good but they don't tell the whole story. Can't be certain yet, of course, but I feel…reasonably hopeful.'

Ed supposed that this was the best that could really be expected from a surgeon. He watched as Ben stripped off his blood-spattered scrubs and threw them into a bin.

'They're bringing her to now,' Ben went on. 'You can go in if you like. She might just recognise you.'

Ed went into the recovery room. A nurse smiled at him and left them alone. Ed looked down at Maddy's pale face, half-hidden by a turban of bandages. There was a sudden surge of pity for something that wasn't really too important. When it wasn't fastened up for work, Maddy's hair was light brown, shoulder length, and he thought it beautiful. He suspected she was rather proud of it. But now much of it would have been cut away. It would take months to grow back. Well…things could have been much worse.

There were tubes in her arms and behind the trolley there were monitors giving a constant flow of information. Automatically he scanned them. No obvious cause for alarm. Things seemed to be fine.

He bent to kiss her cheek. He couldn't see much of her forehead. She didn't smell like the woman he had kissed so passionately the night before. Now there was the smell of antiseptic and that unforgettable theatre smell. No matter. It would pass.

He straightened, looked down at her. And her eyelids flickered. She saw him, her eyes opened fully. 'Hi, Ed,' she whispered. Then her eyes closed again.

'You made it,' he whispered. That was good enough.

CHAPTER TEN

THIS was a lovely room, Maddy thought. She had the room to herself and at the bottom of the bed she could see French windows that opened out to the garden, and beyond that the sea. In time she would be able to sit outside on the terrace and watch the boats sailing in and out of the harbour.

She wasn't really sure how things had worked out this way. As she had no family, no close relations, the captain had arranged with Ed for her to be transferred from St Piran's to this nursing-home in Penhally Bay. The company would pay for it. She had been asked if this was what she wanted. Maddy had been content to leave all the decisions, arrangements to Ed. He was good at this sort of thing.

That was…what was it?…three days ago. She had been sedated most of the time. She had seen Ed twice every day. But she hadn't been able talk to him, to make sense of what he was saying. She had just held his hand. But now she was recovering, she didn't have to sleep quite so much. And she could look about her. Think of the future.

She had been told that she was to expect a visit from

her doctor. Good. She was feeling more herself now, she was still weak, her head still hurt an awful lot, and when a nurse had brought her a mirror, she had thought that she looked terrible. How long before her hair would regrow? What kind of style could she try? Whatever, she thought having her hair half cut off might be bad—but things could have been so much worse.

Where was her doctor? She was waiting to see Ed.

She had thought about him and when she had been asleep she had dreamed about him. But she wasn't sure about him. She knew she was still weak, emotionally as well as physically, but soon she knew she would be her old confident self. Able to make her own decisions and to think about what had happened to her. Able to think about what she had said—and about what had been said to her. Everything might be different now. But she was looking forward to seeing Ed again.

A nurse came in, smiled and said, 'The doctor's coming to have a look at you now. Ready for him?'

Well, she was. Sort of.

But it was a definite disappointment when the doctor who came in was Nick. She couldn't stop herself. She said, 'I thought Ed was my doctor.'

Nick smiled at his patient. 'No. I told him that I would be the physician in charge. I'll tell you why in a minute. Ed can be a visitor, and I'm sure he'll be in to see you soon. And Ben Carter will be over to see you tomorrow—he'll want to admire his good work. Now, we'll have the medical examination first and then perhaps chat a while.' He turned to the nurse. 'Janice, could you remove…?'

It seemed odd to be examined instead of examining. It

was weird to have your records looked at, instead of looking at them. She wasn't sure she liked it. But Nick was a professional. If nothing else she could admire his skill.

Finally the examination was over, her head was bandaged again and Nick told the nurse she could go. Maddy looked at him thoughtfully. He seemed to have relaxed. Now he was her friend. 'So why not Ed as my doctor?' she asked him. 'I thought he was very efficient.'

'He is efficient and I'm proud of him and his ability. But he's better not being your doctor because he can't keep the necessary distance. Because of the relationship between you two.'

'I'm not sure there is one,' she said. 'Things said in…in emotional moments aren't always true when you think about them dispassionately. You get over-eager.' Then, wanting some kind of encouragement, she asked cautiously, 'But if there was any kind of relationship, would you approve?'

'It's not my place to say. But I do find you a very competent nurse.'

Maddy felt just a little irritated. 'Thanks for the compliment—I think. Nick, are you always so guarded about what you say? It must be hard when so many of your patients are known to you. Are your friends, in fact.'

She was a bit surprised at the strength of his answer. 'Of course I'm guarded. Doctors aren't like most people, Maddy, you should know that. You have to keep some distance, if only because you learn so many secrets. Now, let's move onto something else. You can't go home alone so you're to stay here until we think you're fit to be discharged, and that'll be a while. You don't recover from cranial surgery quickly. So what do you see as your future?'

'I just haven't thought about it,' she said honestly. 'I suppose I could get another job with the cruise line. But I only signed on for one trip.'

'After your operation that won't be a good idea for several months. You need to be on dry land, within easy distance of a hospital. Not that I see any trouble ahead. But it's good to be cautious.'

He paused a moment, then said. 'I've been very impressed by you, Maddy. And when you worked for me before, you were excellent. Would you like to think about a job in the Penhally Bay practice?'

She looked at him in amazement. The thought had never crossed her mind. 'Is there a vacancy?'

'There will be shortly. We're expanding rapidly.'

She thought some more. 'Did Ed put you up to this?'

'No, it was entirely my idea. And I didn't ask him. I'm always on the lookout for good staff. Don't answer now, just think about it.'

He stood, picked up his doctor's bag. 'Ed's working this morning but he said he'd be in to see you this afternoon. You might like to talk about my offer to him. Bye, Maddy.' Then he smiled, taking her hand. 'It's good to see you looking so well. When I heard about your accident, I was worried.' And he was gone.

Maddy lay back on her pillow, wondered if the thinking she now had to do might make her head hurt even more. The offer of a job in the Penhally Bay practice. Working with Ed. Suddenly life seemed more complicated. Or more simple?

When she had only known Ed for three days she had told him that she loved him. Well, perhaps she hadn't been in her right mind, she had been about to have a possibly life-threatening operation. The trouble was, now she had had her operation, now she had been told that she was going to recover, she still knew that she loved him. And she had decided that she loved him before her accident. All right, sane, professional, reasonable nurses didn't make that kind of decision after three days. But she had. And she meant it.

She had told Ed that she loved him and he had promptly asked her to marry him. But had he only done it to aid her recovery, to make her feel better? In that he had been successful. She was sure that the proposal had helped her pull through. But had he really meant it? Had it just been the agony of the moment, a sudden rash decision to be later regretted? He wasn't ready for the consequences. And he was still upset over his dead wife, he just wasn't capable of making big decisions. Not for the rest of his life, it seemed to her. She was thinking clearly now, it was all so plain. He hadn't really meant it. No way could she hold him to a promise made so quickly.

What to do now? Ed was an honourable man. He had asked her to marry him. She thought she had said yes but she wasn't really sure. So he would want to do the proper thing—marry her. She must tell him that agreeing to marry him had been a mistake.

So the decision was made and the tears flowed again. But when they had passed she found herself stronger, determined. She knew what she had to do.

He came into her room that afternoon. It was a warm day, he was dressed in fawn chinos and a dark blue, open-necked, linen shirt. The blue of the shirt contrasted with his tanned face and he looked absolutely gorgeous. In one hand he had a bunch of flowers, in the other hand a silver-wrapped box that she guessed would hold chocolates. She didn't think she'd ever seen a more wonderful sight come into a patient's room.

He laid the flowers and the parcel on her bedside table, kissed her on the cheek, took her two hands and sat on her bed. 'So how are you?' he asked. 'You look so much better than when I last looked at you. It's good to see you improving.'

'I'm fine. I'm still weak but I'm getting better by the minute. And it's good to see you, too, Ed.'

'Know what day it is? It's Tuesday. Exactly a week since we first met.'

A week? Was that all? Half her life seemed to have been crammed into those few days. 'It seems longer,' she said. 'But only a week? We hardly know each other.'

'We've known each other since the moment we met.'

'No, we haven't. You were decidedly cautious with me when we first met. And I was cautious with you, felt that I'd met men like you before.'

'We got over that caution quite quickly. I kissed you. And you kissed me back.'

He didn't need to remind her. She remembered so well!

'But we were busy most of the time. What time did we have to get to know each other?'

'Two wonderful nights in a small bed,' he told her. 'Remember those?'

She did remember. How well she remembered. 'I'd blush if I could,' she said. Then, because she had to be honest, she said, 'I don't think I'll ever forget them.'

'Nor me.' He looked at her cautiously. 'What do you remember about what we said after you'd fallen and cracked your skull?'

She had to be careful here. 'I was confused,' she said. 'I just remember talking to you. You were comforting but I can't remember quite how.'

'I was comforting. In fact, you told me that I knew how to make a girl feel good. That pleased me.' He was looking at her with a half-smile on his face. 'It's not like you to be coy, Maddy. One of thing things I love about you is that you're direct and honest. So tell me, how did I make you feel good?'

No way could she lie, pretend she couldn't remember. Apart from anything else, it was a memory she wanted to cherish. 'You asked me to marry you,' she mumbled.

'I did.' He leaned over and kissed her again. 'One of the best things I've ever done in my life. And then you said that you would marry me. Proposal and acceptance. We're an engaged couple.'

From his pocket he took a tiny leather box, held it out to her. 'Open it. It's for you. Just until we can decide upon something better.'

The excited half of her desperately wanted to open the box, the wary half knew that it wasn't a good idea. The excited half won. Inside the box was a cushion of red silk and set into the cushion was a ring. It was worn with long use, but the stones—a pattern of emerald and jade—were as bright as ever. 'It's lovely,' she cried.

'It was my great-grandmother's engagement ring. This morning I asked my father if I could have it and he said yes.'

'Did he know you wanted it for me?'

'Well, I haven't been seeing any other woman recently,' Ed said mildly. 'I think he must have guessed.'

Maddy started to take the ring out of the box and then thrust it back. She knew that if she tried the ring on then she would never want to take it off. She gave the box back to Ed. 'You don't like it?' he asked in some surprise. 'Well, no matter. We can—'

'Ed! We've got to talk. It's so lovely but I can't take this ring. We just can't get engaged. I know you asked me to marry you and I said yes, but we were both over-emotional. We weren't thinking right. Things are different now.'

He looked surprised. 'Some things are different. I'm now not terrified that you might never come to after the operation. But the important things are still the same. I love you. And you love me—don't you?'

There was no way she could bring herself to say that she didn't love him. But she didn't have to answer the question directly. 'We were both tired, both emotional. I'm not going to take advantage of something you said when you weren't…when you weren't…'

'I think you're entitled to because I took advantage of you,' he said, with a grin that almost made her melt. 'I knew you were emotional and tired—but I still got into bed with you. Maddy, no way are you taking advantage of me. Don't you think that I don't know what I want?'

It was a hard thing to do but she felt she had to hurt him—even if it mean hurting herself more. 'Ed! You're still in love with your wife! You think of her all the time!'

She didn't get the reaction she had expected. He looked thoughtful rather than hurt or angry. 'I loved Penny,' he said after a while. 'I always will. But she's gone now and I can accept it. I've mourned her but now I'm over it. You helped me get over it. And, Maddy, I know she'd not have wanted me to spend the rest of my life just clinging onto a memory.' Almost as an afterthought he added, 'I also know she'd have liked you.'

That was such praise. For a moment Maddy was overwhelmed, didn't know what to say. One last argument. 'You also told me once that you'd felt such pain when your wife died you never wanted to risk it again.'

'How do you think I felt when I saw you go into Ben's operating theatre? I discovered then that any pain is worthwhile for someone you love. And I love you, Maddy. Being apart from you would hurt me so much.'

She could think of no further arguments. Gently, she lowered her head onto the pillow, stared at the flowers he had brought her. They were beautiful. What should she say now?

'You're tired.' His voice was tender. 'And you've been ill. It's wrong of me to push you. You need to sleep. I'll leave you now.'

He leaned over her, his lips brushed hers. 'Shall I leave this ring with you? Just so you can think about it?'

'Better not. It's too beautiful. The temptation to put it on might be too great, and then I'd never want to take it off.' She decided to make one last appeal. 'Ed, why don't we not talk about it for a year? Just carry on as friends. You can ask me to marry you in a year's time, when we've got to know each other better, when I'm fully well.'

'I don't want to wait a year. I love you now. And you love me, don't you?'

She couldn't bring herself to lie. 'Yes, I do love you and that's why I won't marry you. Not yet anyway. '

He sighed. 'Right, then. Maddy, I'm not allowed to bully helpless patients, it's against the doctors' code. But don't think I won't ask again! Now, I can't come to see you tomorrow, I'm going to London on a week's course. It was arranged months ago. But could I ring you tomorrow night?'

She reached for his hand, took it to her lips and kissed it. 'I'll be sad if you don't ring,' she said.

Ed drove up onto the moors. He didn't know how to deal with the turbulence of his feelings. Over the past week he had suffered a greater excess of emotions than at any time since—well, at any time since his wife had died. He realised that since then he had been coasting along, only half living. He had deliberately cut himself off from feelings—doing his job, taking a mild pleasure in the sea and countryside, occasionally taking out a girl who knew right from the beginning that it was nothing serious. Now none of that was good enough. He had started to feel again. And discovered that feelings could bring great joy.

He had promised to drop in at the Clintons' farm, to see how Isaac was getting on. Once again he was met at the farmhouse front door by Ellie. But this time she was in working clothes, boots, jeans and a decidedly scruffy-looking T-shirt. But he thought she looked well. There was a smile on her lips, a sparkle in her eyes.

'Dr Tremayne, how are you? The gossip is that you've been saving lives out on a cruise ship.'

'All part of the day's work, Ellie. Tell me, how was the St Piran's Ball?'

'It was wonderful! Do you know a Dr Peter Hunter who works there? He's a junior registrar in the orthopaedic department.'

'Don't think I know him,' Ed said cautiously. 'You met him there?'

'I spent most of the night dancing with him. Oh, and other people as well. But…he's driven over to see me a couple of evenings.'

'Be careful of forming a relationship with a junior registrar,' Ed warned her. 'They work even longer hours than farmers.'

Ellie laughed. 'Early days yet. But I'm glad I went. Come inside, I'll get you a drink. You've come to see Dad?'

'Just a casual visit,' Ed said, skating around the truth. 'I was in the area and I thought I'd drop in.'

'He'll be pleased to see you but there's no real need. Since you talked to him last week he's been perfect. Done everything you told him to. He grumbles, of course, but he wouldn't be my father if he didn't.'

'Sounds like one of my successes,' said Ed.

In fact, he didn't really need to examine Isaac. The old man was obviously looking after himself and was feeling much better for it. Ed spent a quarter of an hour chatting to him and then set off for home.

He thought about Ellie as he drove down into Penhally. About how happy she seemed to be with her new doctor friend. Why couldn't he be as happy as that? He realised what he had lost or would lose if he couldn't marry Maddy.

He loved her. He thought she loved him—but she had this idea in her mind that they had to wait. He didn't want to wait. So…

He had a military mind so he would consider this a battle. The first thing you did when fighting a battle was look for allies. Allies! Now he had a plan.

CHAPTER ELEVEN

MADDY had no clear memory of Ben Carter. She knew he had operated on her, had been there when she had come round, but that was all. Now she met him properly. A tall, lean, smiling man with brilliant blue eyes. Were all the men in Penhally Bay gorgeous?

'Basically I'm a general surgeon, not a brain man,' he told her as he examined her next morning. 'Done a bit of skull work, of course, wondered about specialising in it at one time. But mostly it's general. Good thing you were out of it when I came to see you. You might have objected otherwise.'

'Ed seemed to think you were the best there was.'

'The best there was available. He was in a hurry—which incidentally was necessary.' He smiled. 'By the way, did you know you were operated on by television?'

'What? Television how?'

'I was linked up with a surgeon in London. I had a headset on while I was operating with a camera showing what I was doing. He offered advice.'

'I've heard of that kind of thing.'

'Set up by your friend and mine, Dr Ed Tremayne. He thought it might be a good idea. You know, the ex-military mind can be very impressive. Possibly you owe your life to Ed. He decided what needed doing, organised it at once and then saw it through. I wasn't the obvious choice to operate on a skull but I was the nearest, the most available. And time was running out for you. So he decided, coolly, logically, just like a machine. But he can feel, too. I've never seen him look so desperate. I had to send him out of the room while I operated. Are you two close?'

'Sort of,' Maddy said.

'He's a friend of mine but he's a good man,' said Ben. 'And he deserves a good woman.'

The nurse had unwrapped the bandages round her head and Maddy could feel the cool air on bare skin where there shouldn't be bare skin. She must look a mess!

Ben seemed to guess what she was thinking. 'We had to shave some of your hair off,' he said. 'But you know it'll grow back. You'll be as beautiful as ever. And though I say it myself, I did a pretty good job. You're going to make a complete recovery, Maddy.'

Ben stepped back while the nurse began to put fresh dressings on Maddy's head and started to write up her notes.

'Take things easy for a while,' he said. 'Nick Tremayne will keep an eye on you and I'll be back in a few days just to check up that all is well. But you can get up for a while...say tomorrow. Nothing too energetic. Just a short trip outside. Remember, Maddy, you were lucky. Be glad that you had Ed Tremayne on your side.' And he was gone.

Maddy lay back on her pillows and considered. Two things that she had not quite thought about yet. One, she possibly owed her life to Ed. Two, he had been desperate when he'd seen how ill she had been. She was not sure what to make of the two facts. But she thought about them.

An hour later she had another visitor. 'Hi, fellow midwife,' a voice called out, and there was Kate Althorp. She came over, kissed Maddy on the cheek. 'Can't say I care for the new-style headdress.'

Maddy smiled. She liked Kate, she was uncomplicated. The two of them had got on well when they had worked together on the ship. They had bonded as a team. She had hoped to see her again.

'I would have come to see you sooner,' Kate explained. 'But a mum-to-be came in with antepartum haemorrhage, Nick and I looked at her and diagnosed placenta praevia. But we got there in time. With any luck she'll go full term and the baby should be okay.'

She pulled a letter out of her pocket. 'And I wanted to see you anyway. I've got something to show you, something we did together.' She handed Maddy the letter.

There were two pictures of a baby—tiny but perfect. And a letter from Sarah Flynn. Quickly Maddy read it. Sarah apologised for sneaking onto the boat while she had been pregnant, said that baby Marina was now fine and thriving and that it was due entirely to Maddy and Kate. Many thanks. And she was writing to the chairman of the cruise line to congratulate him on the quality of his nursing staff.

'Nice to be thanked, isn't it?' Kate said. 'It's one of the reasons I took up midwifery. You usually get a happy result.'

'You're a local midwife and this is quite a small town,' Maddy said. 'You must see a lot of the children you brought into the world.'

Kate grinned. 'I do. And sometimes I regret having done so.' Her eyes twinkled. 'Now, what I thought was—'

The door opened, and there was Nick Tremayne. He looked from Maddy to Kate, obviously surprised. 'Kate? What are you doing here?'

'Maddy and I were midwives together, remember? I called in to say hello.'

Maddy saw an exchange of glances between the two, wondered if there was some hidden message that was not for her to know. Then she decided she was imagining things.

'I've just had a word with Ben,' Nick said. 'He's happy with your progress and suggests that you might like to get out of bed, perhaps tomorrow. I'm happy with that.'

'I was going to offer to take Maddy for a ride,' said Kate. 'She needs some fresh air.'

'As long as she takes it easy.' Nick turned and left.

For a moment Kate stared at the door through which Nick had left and Maddy was puzzled the odd expression she saw on Kate's face. 'I know the two of you work at the same practice,' she said. 'I mentioned before, you seem to be more than just close friends.'

Kate shrugged. 'We've known each other for years. In fact, we were teenagers together and...quite close. But then we went our different ways. Both of us married and both of us were happy. And then his wife died and my husband was killed.'

'Ed's wife died, too,' Maddy said. 'And none of you remarried. Is there anything between you and Nick?'

Kate tried to laugh. 'There's nothing between us,' she said. 'We are friends and we do work together. Anyway, he can be a grumpy old so-and-so when he wants to be.'

Maddy realised that this wasn't something Kate wanted to talk about. Then she forgot her interest when she heard what Kate had to say next.

'I had a phone call quite early this morning from Ed,' Kate said. 'He didn't want to disturb you but the message is for you. He'll phone tonight but he wanted you to know this at once. About a Brian something who you once knew.'

'Brian Temple. I knew him all right.' Maddy had forgotten telling Ed about Brian. Now his name brought out new worries. Brian would find it easy to discover what had happened to her, easy to discover where she was. He would come here, she knew it! And then… 'What did Ed say?' she asked in a panic.

Kate put a reassuring hand on her shoulder. 'There's no cause for alarm, Maddy. Ed said that you weren't to worry, it was all under control. He's been in touch with an army psychologist and Brian was offered treatment, which he's accepted. Ed says that all will be well.'

'Just like that? That man spoiled my life for months.'

Kate smiled. 'The Tremayne family tends to get things done.'

It was good to be among friends, Maddy thought. And she knew she could confide in Kate. 'I thought I was in love with Brian,' she muttered. 'He was a very determined man, ex-army like Ed. He got things done too, and at first I liked him for it. But then he came back from some mission with PTSD—post traumatic stress disorder—and there was just no living with him. I thought he'd turned into a monster, then I realised he'd always been one. He was madly jealous of everything I did, every friend I had.

There was no end of mental abuse, and I knew in time that it would turn physical. So I left him and he stalked me and made my life a misery. So much for love.'

'Love is wonderful,' Kate said after a while, 'if you get it right. But getting it right isn't easy. Now, Nick's signed your pass so would you like to come out for a ride for a couple of hours tomorrow?'

'I'd love to,' said Maddy.

There had been a lot of excitement during the morning. In the afternoon Maddy was taken out onto her terrace, put in the shade and told to rest. She decided that she was getting better. So that meant she couldn't be an invalid much longer, she had to start thinking about her future. Then she decided, not yet. She couldn't put up with it yet. There was too much to worry about.

That evening the telephone trolley was wheeled to her bedside, she was told that there would soon be a call for her and she was left on her own. When the phone rang she had to stop herself from grabbing for it. No need for Ed to think she was desperate for a call.

'Hi, sweetheart, how are you?' It was Ed. And her heart bounded.

'Hi, Ed. I'm fine. I'm improving. I've had visitors—Ben Carter, Kate Althorp and your dad.'

As so often there was a smile in his voice. 'Living the social round without me. It's all happening in Penhally Bay.'

'So how was your day?' she asked.

'Long but interesting. There's a new treatment for diabetes. It looks good and I'll try to persuade the practice to try it out.'

It was good to sit and chat to him. But suddenly she wanted him by her, she wanted his physical presence. Just so she could see him, hold him if she wished. 'Tell me where you are,' she said rather sadly.

'I'm in my hotel room. I should be looking through my notes, but...don't laugh. I'm reading *Pride and Prejudice*.'

Maddy couldn't help a little giggle. 'You!'

'Yes. And I've just got to the bit where Darcy has apparently given up the idea of marrying Elizabeth. But I've not given up. I still want to marry you right now. But I know you're ill so I won't push you.'

'Ed, for the good of both of us, forget it for a while. I may be ill but I'm not mad. Let's wait for a year and see how we feel then.'

His voice was serious. 'It's how I feel now that's important. How we feel. I love you, Maddy.'

'I love you, too,' she said. 'But I'm not going to change my mind about marrying you.'

It was sunny again next day. Well, she was entitled to a few sunny days after the storm the week before. In the afternoon a nurse helped her dress. It seemed strange to be putting on clothes that she hadn't seen for so long. Her clothes? How had they got there?

'Dr Tremayne organised it all,' said Samantha, the nurse who was dressing her. 'Dr Ed Tremayne. He got a lady doctor on the ship to pack for you.'

Organisation. She might have guessed.

It wasn't what she wanted but she was taken in a wheelchair to the front door, where Kate was waiting for her in her car. 'My hours tend to be irregular,' Kate said. 'Babies arrive to suit themselves. So I can often take time off when I need to. We'll take a couple of hours and you can look around Penhally Bay and the countryside.'

They went up onto the moors first, saw the great sweep of green, the blue of the sea beyond. Maddy felt that it was wonderful to breathe fresh air again, something different from the all-pervasive hospital smell she was so used to. Then they drove into the little town and she was shown the harbour, the walk along the beach. Then up to the surgery. It was a beautiful white building.

'We could go inside and have a look around,' Kate suggested. 'Who knows? You might find yourself working there.'

'Why do you say that? Has Nick said anything to you?'

'No. He keeps his ideas to himself a lot of the time.' Kate shrugged. 'But we are expanding, Nick is always on the lookout for good staff and I know he thinks well of you. Anyway, what are you going to do when you've recovered? Off on a cruise ship again?'

'I just don't know! At the moment my life seems all over the place.'

There must have been stress in her voice, because Kate patted her hand comfortingly. 'Don't worry about it. You've still not recovered. But all will come out well in the end.'

They drove on, came up to the church and saw a line of cars outside. But there were only one or two people about. Kate pulled up where they could have a good view of the church gate. 'I love a good wedding,' she said. 'The bride must be just about to arrive. Let's watch.'

Maddy was quite happy to sit and watch. They saw a

vintage, open-topped car draw up, two bridesmaids help the bride out of the car, smooth down her dress and adjust her veil.

'She looks good in plain white,' Kate said in a judicious voice, 'it suits her colouring. Would you get married in pure white, Maddy?'

Maddy shook her head. She was rather enjoying herself. She hadn't had a girly conversation about clothes in months. 'Pure white makes me look washed-out. I'd go for ivory. What's that material? I like it.'

'It's raw silk. Creases easily but hangs beautifully.'

They watched as the bride took the arm of her father and walked towards the church. Dimly heard organ music swell to greet her.

'I know the girl,' Kate said. 'Rowenna Pennick. Her father's a fisherman. She met a visitor last summer, a solicitor from London, and now she's marrying him.'

'And going back to London to live?'

'No. He's found a job down here. It's surprising how often that happens.'

They drove on, slowed as they passed another handsome stone building. 'That's Nick's house,' Kate said.

Maddy wondered at her flat tone. 'It's lovely. Does he live there all on his own?'

'Yes he does now. Whether anyone else will ever move in, I just don't know. Now. See what we have here. One bit of the family hasn't moved very far.'

They pulled up outside a whitewashed cottage and Maddy fell in love with it at once. 'Whose is it?' she asked, although she already had a good idea.

'It's Ed's cottage. Like to look inside?'

'But we can't. He's in London somewhere.'

'He always leaves a spare key in the surgery. I phoned him last night. There are some notes I need to see and he has them in his desk. I'm going to pick them up. Come and have a look.'

Maddy so much wanted to. She thought that you could tell a lot about a person by their home and she wanted to know more about Ed. Just out of curiosity, of course. 'Won't he mind?' she asked.

'Not at all. If I can go in, then you can, too.'

'Maybe just the front room,' Maddy said. In fact, she wanted to see the whole house, spend a couple of hours dreaming there. But the front room would do.

Kate helped her out of the car and she walked cautiously to the front door—through a tiny hall and then into the front room.

'Sit down,' said Kate. 'It'll take me a minute to run through these papers.'

So Maddy sat and looked about her. The room was even more lovely than the outside suggested. A through room, with the front facing the road and French windows at the back, overlooking a tiny patio and then the sea. It had a black wood-burning stove set into an alcove.

The room itself was fine, but...it needed something.

'He hasn't been here long,' Kate said, noting Maddy's interest. 'He hasn't really moved in, has he? It's all a bit bare.'

'Did he buy the curtains and the carpet?' Maddy asked. 'Did he decide on wallpaper rather than paint?'

Kate chuckled. 'Who's a little nest-builder, then?' she asked. 'You're right—wallpaper, curtains and carpet all came with the cottage. They need replacing. What this place needs is a woman's touch. Now, I've found my papers. We'd better get you back.'

Maddy had really enjoyed her outing with Kate. It had left her pleasantly tired—but in some ways strengthened. Now she could think. Decide on things.

She loved what she had seen of the moors, of Penhally Bay. She could be happy here. She had loved Ed's cottage and there was so much she could do to it. Kate was right, it needed a woman's touch. New carpet and curtains, redecoration. The furniture was fine but the room needed vases with flowers in them, pictures, photographs. She wondered what the kitchen, the bathroom were like. The bedroom…

This was silly! She was daydreaming when she ought to be making decisions about her future. What was she to do?

She had accepted it, she loved Ed. She had lost all her old fears. Ed could be the man for her, she would be happy with him. And she knew he loved her. Or he thought he loved her. That was the problem. Would he be happy with her?

The trouble with Ed was his sense of honour, his determination to do whatever was right. His dying, pregnant wife had told him to leave her side to help those he could save. And he had done it. He'd listened to her. And had suffered for it ever since.

She couldn't allow him to make another mistake. To discover after a few months that the woman he had married was not the one he needed. He was in too much of a hurry. He had to have time, whether he knew it or not.

Could she give him time? One thing was certain—she couldn't live here with him, just waiting. She'd have to get on with her life to give him time to get over her—if he wanted to.

So, she had made her decision. She knew it was the right one. And she hated it.

Samantha came back into the room. Maddy asked her if there was a copy of the *Nursing Times* she could borrow. Time to look for a new job. Did she want to go back on a cruise ship? No. She had enjoyed it but she knew it would never be the same again. A large city A and E department? Possibly. But after looking around Penhally Bay, large cities had lost their attractions. But she had to carry on looking.

That night the trolley was wheeled to her bedside again, and Ed phoned almost at once. He asked after her, was pleased she had gone out with Kate. Maddy didn't tell him that she had been in his home. He might ask what she thought of it, how it could be improved, and she didn't want to go into that.

He was good company, even on the phone. He told her a story about one of the delegates falling asleep and snoring during a lecture. The lecturer had said that he could accept a subtle hint that he had gone on for long enough. She loved listening to him, talking to him.

But there were things that she had to say. 'Ed, I'll tell you now so as not to hurt you. Your dad offered me a job and I would love it. But I've decided definitely to leave Penhally Bay. We need to be apart for a while.'

His voice was gentle. 'Maddy, I want to marry you. I feel that way now and I'll feel that way in a year's time and in fifty years' time. But not if you're unsure. So just don't decide anything yet. I'll be back soon and I'm so much looking forward to seeing you.'

There were plenty of tears when she rang off.

Next morning there was a message that Kate was coming to take her out again. Good. Maddy felt that she needed to be with a friend. After a while, even the best of nursing-homes got a little claustrophobic. And she could gossip about the Tremayne family, though it was a bitter-sweet experience. Not just Ed, of course. All the Tremayne family.

She managed to dress herself but with a nurse hovering near, in case she was needed. Then she insisted on walking to the front to meet Kate—but once again with a nurse in attendance. It would be great when she could look after herself again!

Kate was waiting, kissed her on the cheek again. 'You look better every day,' she said. 'Now, we'll try something a bit more exciting today. We're going to meet Angie, an old friend of mine. She's a dressmaker, just set up in business but doing very well for herself. It's your birthday soon, isn't it?'

Maddy was surprised. 'Yes, it is. But how did you know that?'

'There was a phone call to the practice from your Captain Smith. The cruise line and he want to give you a birthday present. Something a little bit different, a bit special. They asked my advice—I said an evening dress. It always cheers a woman up.'

'But I never get the chance to go out in evening dress!'

'The odd thing is, once you get the gown then opportunities to wear it mysteriously appear. So let's go and see what Angie can do for you.'

They drove across the moors again. Maddy wasn't really interested in a new evening dress. She looked a mess, her head was half-shaved and covered in bandages. She couldn't wear an evening dress looking like this. But Kate's enthusiasm was infectious and so she decided she'd enjoy the trip out.

Angie was tall, thin, serious and dedicated. She worked from the ground floor of a large house. There were lots of fabric samples on view, patterns and pictures on the wall. She looked at Kate with a critical eye and said, 'You've got the perfect figure for a long dress. Just enough fullness, enough curves in the right places.'

'Thank you,' said Maddy, wondering if she'd been complimented.

'Have you any style in mind?'

Maddy hadn't. 'I'm not sure,' she said. Then, not wanting to disappoint anyone, she said, 'I'm not quite myself, you know. But in general I like flowing lines and an absolute minimum of decoration. And not too low-cut.'

'Hint but not state,' Angie said approvingly. 'Look at these patterns here.'

It was fun, the three of them looking through the patterns. But eventually Maddy decided on one, and the other two agreed that it would be a perfect choice. It was simple but elegant. Maddy's mood changed a little. She wanted to wear this dress.

'Now fabric and colour,' said Angie. 'I've got some swatches here.' She looked at Maddy's face with the same considering expression and said, 'You've an autumn colouring. Look at these shades, warm with a touch of darkness.'

Maddy looked. And eventually she decided on a heavy

bronze silk-linen mixture. Because it was a mixture there was a subtle change in colour as she moved. It matched her hazel eyes beautifully and would go well with her hair. When her hair was on show.

She thought there had been times in the past when she would have loved this. But now wasn't the time. It would be nice to have the dress, but when could she wear it? Who would be her partner?

Now she had to stand in the middle of the floor with her arms outstretched as Angie took her measurements. It didn't take long. Then Angie stood back with a satisfied expression and said, 'That's all I need for now. And I gather this is to be an express job? I'll have it ready for fitting in a couple of days.'

Maddy looked at her in bewilderment. 'That fast? It usually takes weeks.'

'Only if you hang about,' said Angie.

Maddy was getting better, and every day now she felt stronger. Ed phoned each night and they chatted about what he had done, how she was feeling. But he never asked her about her future plans and she never told him. He didn't mention marriage again, and she didn't bring up the subject either. Perhaps he had given up the idea completely. Had decided to accept what she said?

That thought made her feel strangely unsettled.

After two days she was called for by Kate and taken to Kate's home. Another lovely cottage, but with the little extras that Maddy had thought that Ed's cottage lacked. This was a home.

Angie was waiting there. 'Take your dress off and stand in the middle of the floor, please,' she said.

Maddy did as she was told, standing still as the bronze silk was carefully lowered over her head. Angie walked round her, pulled at a sleeve, adjusted the hang at the back. 'Not bad,' she muttered. 'Just a bit of alteration.' Like all dressmakers she put pins in her mouth then started to take in here, let out there. And then eventually Maddy was told, 'Now you can turn and look at yourself.'

Kate had brought a full-length mirror into the room. Maddy did as she was told. And she thought she looked wonderful. The dress was simple, elegant. It brought out her figure and enhanced her colouring. But the bandages on her head spoiled the overall effect.

'I know what you're thinking,' Kate said. 'Don't. The bandages will go, your hair will grow again.'

Maddy smiled ruefully. 'I know. It's a truly gorgeous dress and the cut is absolutely wonderful.' She meant it. But she couldn't sound too enthusiastic. When would she need an evening dress? Never in the foreseeable future.

So the week passed and she continued to improve. Nick came in, said how pleased he was with her progress. But he didn't mention his job offer again and she wondered why.

The dressing on her head was now much less obvious and she could feel the faint itching that said that her hair was beginning to grow again. But she still felt a mess. Who could possibly fancy a woman with half her head shaved?

She now went out every afternoon or evening with Kate. Although there was a difference in ages, they had become firm friends. She thought that working with Kate would be fun. But that would mean working with Ed. And she couldn't do that. Not if they didn't... And she hadn't found a job she fancied either. What was she to do?

Then it was the night before Ed was due to come back. She was both dreading and looking forward to seeing him. She had missed him so much! But she had also decided that Ed could not be held to a promise that he had made so thoughtlessly. What could she say to him?

Kate picked her up later that evening. 'Your dress has arrived,' she said as they drove down into Penhally. 'I've been desperate to see you in it, so we'll have a fitting at once. Angie asked if she could have a photograph of you in it.'

'Not with my hair like this,' Maddy said.

The car slowed, and Kate turned off the engine. Maddy peered out of the window and blinked. 'This isn't your house,' she said, her voice rising. 'It's Ed's cottage. What are we doing here?'

'Slight chance of plan,' Kate said briskly. 'Not important. You're still going to try the dress on. Now, out you get.' She helped Maddy from the car.

'But it's Ed's cottage!' Then she noticed there was a light on inside. 'Is Ed in there?'

'Let's go and find out.' There was a conspiratorial smile on Kate's face.

Maddy was instantly suspicious. 'I'm being set up here, aren't I?'

'I'm your friend, Maddy! No way would I set you up!' Kate didn't knock on the door, just pushed it open and then pushed Maddy into the cottage. 'I forgot something,' Kate went on. 'I'll have to fetch it. I'll be back in a quarter of an hour.' And she was gone.

Maddy stood there and looked at Ed. He was dressed in a white T-shirt and dark blue chinos. She had missed him so much. She had spent most of the past week thinking about him, remembering him, visualising him and his body and his smile... Now she saw him and there was a slight shock. He was more wonderful than she had thought. She just couldn't move.

He came over to her, put his hands on her shoulders and drew her to him. Gently, tentatively, he kissed her on the lips. Maddy waited a moment. It was all she could do. Then she threw her arms round him, pulled him to her and gave him the kiss that she knew he wanted. And that she wanted to give.

After ageless minutes they parted and he led her to the couch. He put his arm round her shoulder, she leaned against his chest. It was so warm and comfortable there! As if it was meant to be.

'I should be angry with you,' she mumbled, 'angry with you and Kate. You tricked me. Right now I'm too happy to be angry but I might get angry later.' Then she shook her head. 'Why am I talking this rubbish? First, why are you back early?'

He shrugged. 'Tomorrow is the plenary session. That means that people talk, argue and get nothing except the pleasure of hearing their own voices. I decided I had much better things to do here. I didn't want to spend an extra day without you so I came home.'

He eased her head away from him, stared at her. 'I want to look at you. You look so much better. How do you feel?'

'I'm not fully well but I'm getting there.' Then she had to be honest. 'I'm better just for seeing you. But—'

He held up his hand. 'No need for buts. Just sit here with me and I'll hold you and kiss you.'

'Seems a good idea for now. But there will be buts.' She didn't know how it was possible. She felt both at peace with the world and excited by it. Certainly she was happy. Later there might be the need to talk, to make decisions, to suffer even. But not yet. Surely she was entitled to a few minutes of worry-free happiness?

It seemed a short quarter of an hour, but when a knock came at the door she glanced at the clock she saw that, in fact, it had been nearer half an hour.

'Better let her in,' said Ed, and stole one last kiss before going to the door.

Kate came into the room, clutching a large purple paper bag. 'Girl stuff,' she said to Ed. 'You wander off somewhere and wait. We'll call you when we need you. Did you get a mirror, like I asked you?'

He went to the side of the room, turned round a large sheet of wood propped against the wall. On the other side was a full-length mirror. 'I took the door off my wardrobe,' he said. 'If you want anything, I'll be in the kitchen.'

'And don't peek!' Kate called after him.

Getting the dress was very nice, Maddy supposed, and she had to try it on. But she'd rather just be with Ed. Still, a lot of time and work had gone into this. She pulled off the dress she was wearing and hoped Ed was not peeking. Her underwear was decidedly practical.

Kate stood behind her. She put her arms over her head. There was a rustling sound and then the fabric slipped over her head and downwards. When the dress was sitting loosely on her shoulders she looked down in amazement.

This was not the bronze silk she had ordered, tried on. This was a much lighter colour—ivory. What was happening? She felt Kate zip up the back, pull at the shoulders and waist. She heard her mumble that it really needed a slip—but for now it didn't look too bad.

There was a tremor in Kate's voice. 'Maddy, you can look at yourself now,' she said. 'Ed! Come on out.'

Ed came out of the kitchen and Maddy stared at herself in the mirror. This wasn't the bronze dress she had been measured and fitted for. This was an ivory dress in raw silk. She realised that it was exactly the same pattern as the bronze dress had been, and it fitted her just as well and it was just as...well, more beautiful. But this wasn't an evening dress, it looked like a... 'This is a wedding dress!' she burst out.

'Well, so it is,' said Kate. 'How strange.' She and Ed exchanged complicit glances.

Maddy felt... What did she feel? A maelstrom of emotions.

'You planned this between you!' she cried. 'You got me a wedding dress when I hadn't asked for one.'

'It wasn't Kate, it was all me,' said Ed quietly. 'It's all my fault. Kate had doubts—but I had hopes.'

'You got me a wedding dress! By deception!'

'True. Do you like it?'

She didn't know what to think, to feel. So in the end, after a long silence, she answered honestly, 'I couldn't think of anything more wonderful. If I was going to get married, that is.'

'Ah,' said Ed. 'Well, now we have to have a little talk.'

Maddy was still too dumbfounded to say anything. But

from behind her she heard Kate say, 'You know, I really want to stay here and listen. But reluctantly I'm going to go. Ed, you can take her back to the nursing-home later. Maddy, will you phone me some time tonight. Please?'

It seemed the smallest of her problems but she said, 'Who will help me out of this dress?'

'I will,' said Ed. 'It's something I've always wanted to do.'

'No,' Kate put in. 'This is a woman's job. Back into the kitchen for a moment.' As she unzipped Maddy she said, 'It works just as well in raw silk as in the other fabric, doesn't it? And I knew you liked ivory because you said so when we were watching Rowenna's wedding.'

'What about the bronze dress?'

'You've got that as well. For your next ball.'

Maddy thought it odd but she felt reluctant to take off this glorious ivory dress and put back on her rather ordinary blue one. But she needed to feel ordinary for a while. Still, she looked sadly at Kate who was carefully packing the dress back in the purple bag. 'Kate, I can't cope with all this. I don't know what I'm doing, whether to be blazing angry or tearfully happy. I just don't know.'

'That's your problem now. I'm out of things.' She kissed Maddy on the cheek. 'Just one bit of advice that life has taught me. If you find the man that you need, grab him at once. And don't forget my phone call. Bye!' And she was gone.

Ed came back into the room, carrying two mugs. 'I occupied myself by making us tea,' he said. 'I couldn't just stand still, I felt a bit...nervous about things.'

'So you should. Ed, how could you...? Why did you...? It's a wedding dress. Why a wedding dress?'

'It was my idea. I was talking to Kate on the phone and she told me about the evening dress. I thought, if one dress—why not two? Kate told me how you liked the colour ivory and how you liked raw silk. And about the style looking so good on you. Kate was doubtful but I persuaded her. I commissioned an extra dress. A wedding dress.'

'Just in case I needed it?'

'In case you needed it. And I'm afraid there's more.'

'More? How could there be? What more?'

'Let's start with one thing. You said you loved me?'

Maddy felt she was being drawn into something. But she found that she didn't really mind. Just where was Ed taking her? She answered his question honestly. 'Yes, I did say I loved you. Mind you, I thought I might be going to die. It does make a difference.' But after an internal struggle she told him the absolute truth. 'I still do love you.'

'Good. And I told you I loved you and I wanted to marry you. But you thought I might have changed my mind. You thought I had said it in a moment of high emotion and I might want to rethink it. You thought I felt trapped. Right?'

Well, it was sort of what she'd thought. 'I thought you might feel trapped,' she agreed.

He grinned, then leaned over her and kissed her. When he took hold of her hands she could feel the tension there. 'Maddy, I told you there was more. The more is...I trapped you back. I've got you a wedding dress. I know the groom isn't supposed to see the bride's dress until the ceremony but I decided to ignore that. I was breaking lots of other rules.'

From his pocket he took out the little leather box that she remembered. 'Here's the engagement ring I offered you.' He put it on the table in front of her. 'In a moment I want you to put it on. I phoned the local vicar, he's a friend of mine. He's booked us the church for the very end of May. I've circulated the information to everyone who knows us and told them to keep the date free.'

He smiled, but she could tell that there was hope and fear as well as confidence there. 'Maddy, you have to marry me. All the arrangements are made. You're trapped just as you imagine I was trapped. And we do love each other so much.'

He opened the little leather box, took out the ring and offered it to her. 'Will you marry me, Maddy Granger?'

She still hesitated. Could she marry a man like this? A man so determined? Then she saw the depth of his love in his eyes, an emotion that matched her own. 'Of course I'll marry you,' she whispered softly, reaching out a hand to stroke his beloved face.

He placed the ring on her finger, then pulled her into his arms and kissed her, a kiss that seemed to last an eternity. When he finally broke the spell, Maddy whimpered in protest and snuggled deeper into his chest.

'I think Kate is waiting for your phone call, my love.' He smiled.

EPILOGUE

It was a wonderful wedding. Even the weather was right, warm but not too hot. The bride wore an ivory raw silk dress. She wore a veil, her head was covered with a little cap. Few people realised how artfully her hair had been arranged to look entirely normal. After the ceremony three girls asked Maddy for the name of her dressmaker.

The groom wore his military uniform. Maddy had never asked him the name of the regiment he had been attached to. But in the scarlet tunic that had been worn before the Battle of Waterloo, he looked magnificent.

Kate was a fantastic matron of honour, and looked beautiful in a new outfit made by Angie. Holding her hand was little Robbie, this time in a page-boy outfit, looking as pleased as anything as Mrs Cowley looked on proudly from her pew. Unusually, the best man was the groom's father. Ed had asked Nick, who had been at first surprised and then quietly honoured. But, of course, he didn't say so.

And Captain Smith gave the bride away, dressed in his naval uniform.

The reception was wonderful too, on a pretty white yacht moored in the bay. There was a great meal, there were witty speeches—including one by the bride—and afterwards a dance and party. But the bride and groom left early for their honeymoon. No one knew where. Ed was a great organiser.

After the guests had waved goodbye to the couple they trooped back into the hall and the music started up again. Time to have a good time! To celebrate!

Kate and Nick stood side by side on the deck, away from the music and laughter for a moment. For some reason they didn't want to go straight back in. Kate felt happy, as if a job had been well done. She wanted to dance, but not just yet. It had been an exciting but an exhausting day.

'Walk with me for a minute,' she said to Nick. 'I'd like some fresh air. It's lovely to see so many friends together but I'd like five minutes' peace.'

'Good idea,' said Nick.

She took his arm as they strolled along the deck. 'Are you happy for them?' she asked. 'Or, better, do you think they will be happy?'

'I think they will,' said Nick, cautious as ever. 'Ed is my son, but surprisingly I don't know him all that well. I realize he's had problems. That stretch in Africa, losing his first wife—they could have scarred him for life. And I don't mean only physically. Maddy had problems, too. But I think they'll be good for each other. And you helped bring them together, Kate. I have to thank you for it.'

Kate smiled. 'They're a lovely couple and what little I could do to help, I was happy to do. And didn't they look gorgeous together?'

Nick smiled his customary guarded smile. 'They say that the bridesmaids mustn't look more glamorous than the bride. Well, as matron of honour in that pink dress, you came close. You look beautiful.'

Kate was shocked—and then delighted. This was not the reserved man she knew. 'Nick? A compliment? Are you feeling well?'

'Never better.' They paced a few more yards and then he said, 'I was remembering when we two were young. Teenagers together. We were happy then.'

Now Kate was apprehensive, even bewildered. This was forbidden ground. They never talked about their past. As they walked on she tried to take her hand from his arm and he took her hand, put it back where it had been.

'On the ship,' he said, 'when Ed had sent for you and I came aboard later, I was angry because I hadn't been consulted. However...I looked in your cabin when you were asleep. You looked just as you did when we were young. And I realized we can't keep ignoring what happened the night of the storm years ago. The guilt we both feel has been poisoning our relationship.'

Now Kate was upset. 'Nick, this is a happy day, don't spoil it. It's not the time to drag out old memories. We get on well enough now. Besides, we had an agreement never to talk about that night.'

'We never made an agreement!'

'We never needed to! It was there, it was obvious.'

He stopped, took hold of her other arm so they were facing each other. She could feel the tears in her eyes, knew that he could see them.

'Kate, that night we made love! Don't you think we need to talk?'

'Perhaps,' she said quietly. 'Not now—but soon.'

* * *

Maddy and Ed hadn't moved too far for their honeymoon. Both had travelled a lot, they didn't need to go to foreign parts. Now they were sitting on the balcony of a gorgeous boutique hotel, watching the sun go down over the sea. On the table between them was the traditional bottle of champagne.

'It was an amazing day,' Maddy sighed as Ed popped the cork and pale champagne fizzed into her glass. 'Everyone seemed to have a great time. I even saw Kate and your father dancing. They seemed to enjoy being together. Do you think they are happy, Ed?'

'I think perhaps they could be happier.' Ed said. 'If they could find out how.' He put down the champagne bottle and smiled at his wife. 'But are we happy, Mrs Tremayne?'

'Very happy, Mr Tremayne.' She held up her hand, admired the new gold ring next to the antique one. 'Everything is wonderful. Everybody is happy, but mostly you and me.'

'That's true,' Ed said as he bent to kiss his beautiful new bride. 'And I don't think I could be happier.'

Single Dad Seeks a Wife

MELANIE MILBURNE

Melanie Milburne says: 'I am married to a surgeon, Steve, and have two gorgeous sons, Paul and Phil. I live in Hobart, Tasmania, where I enjoy an active life as a long-distance runner and a nationally ranked top ten Master's swimmer. I also have a Master's Degree in Education, but my children totally turned me off the idea of teaching! When not running or swimming I write, and when I'm not doing all of the above I'm reading. And if someone could invent a way for me to read during a four-kilometre swim I'd be even happier!'.

A very special thank you to Dr Robert Kelsall MB BS (Adelaide) FRCPA MB BS(Perth) *Ad Eundem Gradum*, whose extensive forensic experience was invaluable in the researching of this novel. Rob, I literally could not have done it without you. Also to Sergeant Iain Roy Shepherd who, like Rob, is always just a phone call or e-mail away. My heartfelt thanks to you both.

CHAPTER ONE

'I'M VERY sorry, Dr Hayden, but your luggage seems to have gone missing without trace,' the baggage official informed Eloise as he looked up from the computer in front of him. 'There's no record of it even being loaded on your flight.'

'Missing?' Eloise glared at the young man. 'What do you mean, it's missing? I was supposed to be in Cornwall twenty-four hours ago. I can't hang about here waiting for my things to arrive on another flight from Sydney. You'll have to send them on to me.'

'That won't be a problem, Dr Hayden,' the young man answered, reaching for a pen and the necessary documentation. 'The airline will pay for delivery under these circumstances. Do you have the address of where you will be staying?'

Eloise suppressed a frustrated sigh and rummaged in her handbag for the name and address of the guest-house she had been booked into in Penhally Bay. As far as rating stars went, Trevallyn House looked like it was missing a few, but, then, that was the Australian Health Department budget for you, she thought cynically. Her superiors had told her a month in a Cornish seaside town should more than compensate for any discomfort from staying in a building that looked as if Captain Cook himself had dropped in on his way to Botany Bay in 1770.

She gave the man the brochure with the address on it, and also her own card, and tapped her foot impatiently as he took the relevant details. 'How soon do you think it will be located?' she asked as she took back the guest-house brochure.

The man gave a little shrug. 'It could be a day or two, maybe longer. It's hard to tell. It must have been put on the wrong flight in Sydney. It happens occasionally.'

Eloise mentally rolled her eyes. 'Well, it's nice to know my luggage gets to do a round-the-world tour, but I really would like you to do what you can to locate it and quickly. I've been in these clothes for close to thirty-six hours. I'm on official business so I need to have access to my luggage as soon as possible.'

'I'll do everything I can to speed things up but, as I said, it might take time,' he said. 'The increased security at airports has eased some problems but created others, as I am sure you will understand.'

Eloise gave him a small tight smile. 'Thank you for your help,' she said. 'I will look forward to hearing from you.'

She made her way out of the busy terminal to the hire-car pick-up area where after another long wait she was finally assigned to one of the tiniest cars she had ever seen.

'I'm going to kill you with my bare hands, so help me, God, Jack Innes and Co,' she said under her breath as she drove out of the parking lot. 'Just as well my luggage didn't arrive. Who knows where I would have put it.'

Penhally Bay was a typical Cornish village. There were picturesque houses and shops lining the streets overlooking the harbour and there were loads of tourists milling about, taking advantage of the warm summer weather. There was a lifeboat station at one end of the bay and a lighthouse at the other and as Eloise looked out to sea she could see several boats and their crews enjoying the calm conditions.

She found Trevallyn House on Harbour Road. It was similar to the other houses except it was slightly bigger, but what it made up for in space it clearly lacked in maintenance. The white paint was cracked in places and one of the shutters on the downstairs window was hanging lopsidedly by its rusty hinge.

She made her way to the front door with flagging spirits but before she could even search for the doorbell, the door opened with a loud creak and a round figure appeared in its frame.

'You must be Dr Hayden, the police doctor from Australia,' Mrs Trevallyn, the elderly guest-house owner, greeted her warmly. 'Welcome to Penhally Bay. I'm sorry things are in such a mess but one of my cleaning girls left me in the lurch a couple of days ago. I haven't found a replacement yet. I'll get Davey to take your luggage upstairs for you. I've put you in room seven. It has the best views of the bay.'

'Er...I actually haven't got my luggage with me just now,' Eloise said with a tiny grimace. 'It's coming...later.'

'Oh well...then,' Mrs Trevallyn smiled cheerily. 'No bother. I expect you'll want to freshen up in any case. There's a bathroom on the landing. You have to be careful with the shower—it can scald you if someone turns a tap on somewhere else.'

Just you wait, Jack Innes, Eloise thought as she made her way up to her room. However, she was pleasantly surprised when she opened the door of room seven. It was quaintly decorated in pink and cream and there was a vase of colourful summer flowers on the dressing-table, the heady fragrance of a single red rose in the centre of the arrangement drawing her like a magnet. She stood in front of the vase, and almost without realising she was doing it she reached out and touched one blood-red velvet petal with her finger. She slowly lifted her hand and looked at the end of her finger, her heart beginning to thud, her hand visibly shaking until she realised there was no trace of blood there.

Eloise stepped back from the flowers and gave herself a mental shake. 'You've been in forensics way too long, my girl,' she said, and went to the window overlooking the bay. She opened it, closed her eyes and breathed in the tangy salty air.

Chief Inspector Lachlan D'Ancey closed the folder with a little snap as he faced his junior colleague. 'I still believe this is going way over the top,' he said. 'I don't see why we need to have an Australian forensic pathologist coming to review something we've already dealt with. We handled this death as we would that any other high-profile person.'

Constable James Derrey gave a little nod of agreement. 'Yes, I know, but apart from the family it looks like someone else down under is asking a lot of questions about the death of this celebrity surfer, Chief. Ethan Jenson was expected to win the World Surfing Championship. The Aussies just don't accept that a surfer of his calibre could accidentally drown. I understand our orders to allow an external case review have come from very high up.'

Lachlan raked a hand through his dark brown, hair making it stick up at irregular angles. 'Yes, they have, but I just hope this forensic pathologist they're sending will see that we've done a first-rate investigation and just go back home and let us get on with doing our job.'

'Yes, sir, I couldn't agree more.'

Lachlan leaned back in his chair with a weary sigh. 'Going through this case file yet again is certainly not my preferred way to spend the next month.'

'Mine neither but this Australian woman will want you present for the whole review to answer questions, no doubt,' James said. 'Have you met her yet?'

Lachlan shook his head and glanced at his watch. 'She was supposed to be here yesterday but maybe something more important cropped up.' He suddenly looked up and grinned as he added, 'Or maybe she got lost. She's probably halfway to Scotland by now. You know what Aussies are like—they drive further for a litre of milk than we do for our annual holidays.'

James smiled back. 'And I bet she has a chip on her shoulder the size of Stonehenge. They always do. Remember that bird that came up from London that time? What is it about career-women anyway?'

There was an awkward little silence.

James had the grace to blush. 'Sorry, Chief,' he mumbled. 'That was in poor taste. I forgot about Margaret and the divorce and all…'

'Forget it, James,' Lachlan said. 'I'm over it. I admit it's been tough, but to tell you the truth we should have split up years ago. In fact, we shouldn't have got married in the first place but Poppy was on the way and, well…' He blew out another sigh and continued, 'I thought it was the right thing to do at the time.'

'How is your daughter?' James asked. 'I heard she was pretty upset about Jenson's death. She was a big fan of his, right?'

Lachlan gave a wry smile. 'You know teenage girls, James, they're all celebrity crazy. There wouldn't be a woman under forty around here who doesn't go weak at the knees when a bronzed surfer with a six pack walks past.'

James got to his feet. 'Yeah, that's true enough. Well, I'd better get back on the job. I've got to check on a possible theft out at Henry Ryall's farm. He thinks some of his sheep are missing but it's more likely he wants some company for a cup of tea. You know what he's been like since Mary died.'

'Poor old chap,' Lachlan said. 'It's probably time he moved closer into town but I don't see that happening in the near future.'

'He'll die with his work boots on for sure,' James agreed. He moved to the door and added, 'Good luck with the forensics lady. You never know, she might be a bit of all right.'

Lachlan didn't answer. He waited until James had left before he opened the file again and looked down at the features of the dead man for a long moment, a small frown bringing his brows closer together...

Eloise found the local police station without too much trouble, although when she opened the front door she was a little surprised there was no one seated at the small front desk. Penhally Bay was so quiet she could hardly believe it had a police station and certainly not one where a chief inspector had been appointed.

She looked over the counter to find a bell or buzzer to push, located a small brass bell and gave it a tinkle. She hovered for another minute or two before she called out, 'Hello? Is anyone there?'

No answer.

She gave the bell another rattle, feeling a little foolish as she did so. But then she had to admit she had never felt more ill prepared for a professional appointment in her life, let alone her first international assignment. It seemed ironic to have been so churned up with nerves only to find the station she had been assigned to work from was far from a high-tech law-enforcement agency.

She was glad now she hadn't wasted precious time trying to find somewhere to buy a new outfit. Somehow turning up in her well-worn jeans and close-fitting vest top with a cotton shirt over the top didn't seem quite so out of place now. Admittedly, there was a coffee stain on her top on her right breast, where the mid-air turbulence had caught both herself and the flight attendant off guard during dinner, and her jeans felt as if they could have stood up all by themselves. As for her face...well...what could she say about her face? At least it was clean—the scalding blast of hot water in the shower a short time ago had not only lifted off thirty-six hours of make-up but what felt like the first layer of skin as well. Her fine blonde hair hadn't appreciated the detergent-like guest-house shampoo, and without her radial brushes and high-wattage hairdryer it was now lying about her scalp like a straw helmet instead of her usual softly styled bob.

She whooshed out a breath and raised her hand to the first door she could find, but before she could place her knuckles on the wood the door suddenly opened and a tall, rock-hard figure cannoned right into her.

'Oh...sorry,' a dark-haired man said as he looked down at her, his strong hands coming down on her arms to hold her upright. 'I didn't realise you were standing there. Did I hurt you?'

Eloise blinked a couple of times, her heart doing a funny little stumbling movement in her chest.

She swallowed and gave herself a mental shake. She was dazed by the sudden contact, that's what it was.

Of course it was, she insisted firmly.

It had nothing to do with intelligent brown eyes the colour of whisky and it had absolutely nothing to do with the feel of male hands on her arms for the first time in...well, a very long time indeed.

'Um...I'm...er...fine....' she said hesitantly. 'I rang the bell but no one answered. I was just about to knock when you opened the door.'

He gave her a smile that lifted the corners of his mouth, showing even white teeth, except for two on the bottom row that overlapped slightly, giving him a boyish look, even though Eloise calculated he had to be close to forty.

'I'm sorry the front desk is unattended,' he said. 'The constable on duty left on a call half an hour ago and the other constable is off sick. What can I do for you?'

Eloise ran her tongue over her lips in the sort of nervous, uncertain gesture she had thought she had long ago trained herself out of using, but without the armour of her clean-cut business suit and sensible shoes and carefully applied but understated make-up she suddenly felt like a shy teenager.

And it didn't help that he was *so* tall.

She decided she would definitely have to rethink the sensible shoes thing in future otherwise she would be seeing a physiotherapist weekly if she had to crane her neck to maintain eye contact with him all the time. He was six feet one or two at the very least, his shoulders were broad and his skin tanned, as if he made the most of the seaside environment.

'I'm Chief Inspector Lachlan D'Ancey,' he said offering her his hand.

Eloise's stomach did a complicated gymnastics routine as she blinked up at him in surprise.

He was the chief inspector?

Somehow she'd been expecting an overweight, close-to-retirement balding man with a packet a day nicotine habit, not a man who looked like he could run two marathons back to back and not even break a sweat.

Eloise put out her hand to meet his. She was well known back home for her strong, one-of-the-men handshakes, but for some reason this time she couldn't quite pull it off. She felt a faint but unmistakable shiver of reaction shimmy up her spine as his long tanned fingers curled around hers, the slightly calloused feel of his skin against her softness making her feel utterly feminine.

'Er...Eloise Hayden,' she stumbled gauchely. 'Dr Eloise Hayden...from Australia. Sydney, actually. I live there...in the city...near the beach...' *Shut up*, she chided herself. Y*ou're rambling like an idiot.*

One of his dark brows lifted slightly. '*You're* the forensic pathologist?'

Eloise wasn't sure what to make of his tone or his expression. His gaze swept over her again, lingering pointedly on the coffee-stain on her top right over her left breast before returning to meet her eyes.

'Yes,' she answered a little stiffly, removing her hand from his. 'I am.'

A hint of amusement lit his gaze and the edges of his mouth lifted again. 'They must train them very young down under,' he said. 'I was expecting someone much older and with a bit more experience.'

She straightened her spine and eyeballed him as she clipped out, 'I am thirty-two years old and I can assure you I have had plenty of experience.'

This time his expression was far easier to read: it contained a generous measure of mockery. 'Well, then, Dr Hayden from Australia, I hope you will put that experience to good use while you are with us in Penhally Bay,' he said, his lip curling ever so slightly over the words.

Her hands gripped her handbag hanging over her shoulder and her mouth pulled tight as she replied, 'I intend to, Chief Inspector.'

His eyes roved over her again. 'I'm a pretty easygoing chief, but I was expecting someone dressed a little more formally for our first meeting. Or have you been moonlighting in covert operations?'

She lifted her chin, her eyes shooting sparks of livid blue fire at him. 'Actually, I've come straight from an international flight that was delayed for more than twelve hours and my luggage failed to arrive with me—it's probably somewhere over the Middle East by now. So if you have a problem with what I'm wearing, Chief Inspector D'Ancey, perhaps you'd better take it up with my airline, not me.'

Lachlan suppressed an inward smile at her little show of insurgence. She was as Constable Derrey had predicted: a career-woman with a chip on her shoulder, clearly resentful she had to take orders from a man.

She was, however, far more attractive than he had expected in a hard-nosed career-woman. She looked like she could strut along the catwalk with her slim-but-with-curves-in-all-the-right-places figure. Her short chaotic hair was almost but not quite platinum blonde and her eyes a startling clear china blue, in spite of her recent long-haul flight. Her mouth was set in a prim line right now but there was a suspicion of sensuality about it in its soft contours which made him wonder just how much experience she had had and who had enjoyed it with her.

His eyes went to her left hand to see if she was married but her finger was bare. She was wearing a silver watch on her left wrist, an expensive one by the look of it and somewhat at odds with her faded jeans and stained vest top, but he wasn't going to apologise for his comment. Dr Eloise Hayden looked like she needed taking down a peg or two and he was happy to be the one to do it.

'Where are you staying?' he asked.

'Trevallyn House.'

His brows lifted again and his mouth twisted sardonically. 'So your forensics department is cost-cutting, is it?'

Eloise felt like slamming him up against the nearest wall. He was deliberately baiting her, she could tell. She had met so many men like him in her line of work that she had lost count years ago—power hungry, and resentful of a younger woman taking command of an investigation. But she hadn't travelled all this way to be treated like a novice. She had a job to do and woe betide anyone who stood in her way. This was her first international appointment and the success of it would secure her reputation as one of the best forensic pathologists Australia had to offer.

She met his whisky-brown eyes with a level stare even though it made her neck protest. 'I am quite happy with the accommodation I have been assigned,' she said in a curt tone. 'It's right in the centre of the village and I'm used to roughing it whenever necessary.'

'Well you'll certainly be roughing it at Trevallyn House,' he said with a crooked smile. 'Last I heard there was only one toilet working.'

Eloise unclenched her jaw and returned, 'I see no point in wasting taxpayers' money on luxury accommodation when this case could very well go on for longer than first expected.'

Something flickered in his brown gaze as it held hers, but she didn't have time to identify exactly what it was for he masked it so quickly.

'We've done a first-rate investigation, as my briefing showed,' he said. 'I hardly think you will uncover anything that would prolong the investigation any more than a week at the most, no matter how impressive your CV.'

The look she gave him was imperious. 'My review could be straightforward, but there are a few things I do have questions about. I guess that's the whole point of an external review, isn't it? To get a fresh perspective.'

He gave her a cool little smile as he pushed open his office door. 'Let's get started, then,' he said, and indicated for her to precede him inside.

CHAPTER TWO

ELOISE moved past him in the doorway, keeping her arms close to her body in case she inadvertently touched him, but even so the subtle notes of his aftershave drifted towards her, an intoxicating combination of sharp citrus and moody musk that made her nostrils flare involuntarily.

She took the chair opposite his cluttered desk and it was only when she was seated with her legs pressed tightly together that he took his own chair, his brown gaze watchful as it connected with hers.

'So, Dr Hayden,' he began in a seemingly polite tone. 'Was it your choice to come all this way to Penhally Bay or were you the only one available at the time?'

Eloise felt her lips pursing in annoyance. 'There were other people available but my boss thought I had the best mix of skills for this review,' she said. 'It will also be beneficial to my career to take this posting.'

'Is this your first international assignment?' he asked.

'Yes, but that doesn't mean I—'

'This is a small close-knit community,' he interrupted her without apology. 'If you come here with the intention of stirring up a hornet's nest just for the heck of it to score brownie points back home, forget it.'

'I wasn't intending to do any such thing. I just—'

'The autopsy report showed that Ethan Jenson died by drowning,' he cut her off again. 'I doubt very much if you will find out anything more, no matter how talented your boss thinks you are.'

Eloise had trouble containing her anger. She wasn't normally the hot-headed type but something about his manner towards her made her skin start to prickle all over with irritation. She could see what he thought of her in the derisive line of his mouth and the glint of scorn in his gaze every time it came in contact with hers.

She sat up straighter in her chair, her eyes glittering as they held his. 'That was my first question, actually,' she said. 'I'm not happy with the autopsy. The diagnosis of drowning was made mostly on external pathologic findings, but the circumstances of the case don't add up in my mind. How could a world-class surfer drown on a shallow beach? There was only one lung biopsy taken, and that didn't show any oedema. I want to redo the autopsy, and I want more lung tissue and tracheal and bronchial tissue to examine.'

'Are you calling our local pathologist incompetent?' he asked. 'And have you considered the impact of this on the victim's relatives—his mother and father, for instance, or his three younger brothers?'

'I understand that it is a difficult time for the family,' she said. 'But from the autopsy report that I've seen, I could not definitively rule out suicide, or even murder. The finding of accidental death is not conclusive.'

'This is Penhally Bay, not somewhere violent crime is commonplace,' Lachlan said with a heavy frown. 'As far as I'm concerned, the autopsy was carried out by a senior pathologist, the diagnosis was drowning, and there simply were no suspicious circumstances. The closure the family needs right now is to fly their loved one's body home for burial. This has gone on for a week as it is. I see no point in prolonging their agony by performing another autopsy, which will no doubt come up with nothing of significance.'

'But surely you know that the request for another autopsy came via the Jensons' legal advisors in Sydney?' Eloise responded tightly. 'Ethan Jenson had several high-profile sponsors who, along with the family, want firm answers about what happened.'

She snatched in a quick breath and, trying her best not to be intimidated by his laser-like stare, continued, 'You must know yourself the diagnosis of drowning is one of the most difficult in forensic pathology. Sure, there were external signs that the body was in water for some time, but that doesn't mean that death was from drowning. From the report I saw, there was no description of froth in the airway—maybe he was dead first and was then put in the water. The one lung biopsy didn't show emphysema aquosum or pulmonary oedema. And I'm not happy that the diatom test was thorough enough. I want to repeat it on new cardiac, blood, lung, liver, bone marrow and brain tissue, because the diatom report reeks of fresh-water contamination of the samples. And it was qualitative, not quantitative. I want samples of the water at the site where the body was found for a proper comparison.'

Lachlan shifted his lips from side to side as he considered her angle on things. She had made several good points certainly, but he had every faith in the local pathologist and didn't like to rock the boat, so to speak, by openly supporting another autopsy. He understood where the family was coming from in requesting a review of the verdict. A lot of relatives of accidental death victims did the same. It took them time to accept their loved one wasn't coming back. It had only been a week—their pain was still so raw they were still struggling to cope with it all.

'And that brings me to question two,' Eloise said into the taut silence. 'The toxicology results—I noted there was no carbon monoxide assay, yet the victim's hands were noted to be cherry red.'

He returned her direct look with an unblinking stare. 'You're making the autopsy report I received sound completely incompetent, Dr Hayden. I know the pathologist who did the autopsy. He's extremely reliable. I've worked with him many times before. I have the greatest admiration for him.'

'I am sure you do,' she said. 'But no one is perfect and even the best of us miss things at times.'

A corner of his mouth lifted slightly. 'Are you admitting you sometimes get it wrong, Dr Hayden?'

She stared back at him, her lips pulled tight once more. 'Not often but I'm not arrogant enough to assume I never will.'

His mouth was still tilted in a half-smile. 'Let's hope for your sake this is not one of those times, although if what you are telling me is correct, I would have to support a re-examination of the body.'

'Thank you, Chief Inspector D'Ancey,' Eloise said, having trouble concealing the effect his stomach-flipping smile had on her. Every time she looked at him her chest felt as if a tiny moth had landed inside the cage of her lungs and was now fighting for a way out.

She crossed and uncrossed her legs and then added in a businesslike tone, 'And that brings me to question number three. Was Mr Jenson a known drug user?'

'Not that we could ascertain,' he answered as he leaned

back in his chair, his gaze still locked on hers. 'The toxicology report isn't in yet and won't be for another couple of weeks. Why? Do you have additional information on him that we weren't sent?'

'No,' she said, moistening her lips with a darting movement of her tongue. 'I have been given the same files as you have. Ethan Jenson had a couple of DUI charges when he was in his late teens but there has been nothing since. Did you know him personally?'

Lachlan mentally kicked himself for not anticipating her question. He wasn't used to being caught off guard but he had only recently become aware of his daughter's infatuation with the surfer and hadn't yet made up his mind if the rumours currently circulating the village were true. Poppy had admitted she had met the victim on the beach and that he had given her his autograph, but she had denied any other involvement with him, although James Derrey's comment made him wonder if he should have another little private chat with his daughter. But while he knew it wasn't too late for him to be taken off the case, he also knew speculation would increase if he stepped down from the inquiry.

He wondered if Dr Eloise Hayden already suspected something. She had a look of sharp intelligence about her. Those china-blue eyes had been busily assessing him from the word go, her features schooled into cool impassivity while she quietly made up her mind about him.

He leaned back in his chair and idly flicked his pen on and off, the tiny click-clack prolonging the tight-as-a-violin-bow silence.

'As I said a moment ago, Dr Hayden, this is a small close-knit community,' he said. 'The presence of a celebrity surfer in our midst was a big thing. Ethan Jenson was hardly able to walk down the street without someone stopping him for an autograph every few paces.'

'Did you ask him for one?'

He frowned at her. 'No, I did not.'

One of her finely arched brows lifted. 'So you weren't exactly a fan of his, Chief Inspector D'Ancey?'

Lachlan felt like grinding his teeth but somehow he managed to give her a cool smile instead. 'I am usually too busy keeping order in Wadebridge. I have only been assigned this case while you are here as I happen to live locally.'

'I did wonder why someone with your senior ranking would be operating out of such a small community,' she put in. 'Who else is assigned to this station?'

'PC James Derrey and PC Gaye Trembath,' he answered. 'They are the local officers and along with me will help you in any way you require during your stay.'

Eloise privately wondered if Lachlan D'Ancey was going to be more of a help or a hindrance. There was something about his manner that alerted her to an undercurrent of tension running through him. He was good at hiding it, she had to admit, but she'd been working alongside cops long enough to know how much they liked playing their cards close to their chests. He was all cool politeness but behind the screen of his brown eyes was a studied watchfulness that made her suspect he was more than a little uncomfortable with her presence in the village.

Her eyes went to his long-fingered hands, the right one still clicking his pen in that annoying little way that she assumed was meant to intimidate her.

Click. Click. Click. Click.

Her gaze zeroed in on the narrow band of lighter-toned skin of his left hand ring finger, the absence of a ring suggesting he had either lost it recently or that he had been married but was no longer. Somehow she automatically presumed the latter rather than the former. Although his desk was cluttered, everything about him suggested he was an organised and meticulous officer. She couldn't imagine him losing anything or indeed much escaping his notice; he had an aura of quiet but steely authority about him and she couldn't help feeling those whisky-coloured eyes hinted at dark secrets lurking just below the surface.

Her eyes collided with his in the silence, and a sensation like a feather being brushed over the back of her neck made her shift restlessly in her seat again.

'You mentioned your luggage didn't arrive,' he said. 'Is there anything you need for tonight or tomorrow? I can organise some clothes for you. I have a sixteen-year-old daughter who is much the same height and build as you.'

Eloise was surprised at how much his features softened as he spoke of his daughter. The hard set to his mouth relaxed and tender warmth entered his gaze momentarily. He might have been recently separated or divorced from his wife, she thought, but quite clearly not from his offspring.

'That's very kind of you but I'm not sure I will be taken seriously by the locals if I turn up in a sixteen-year-old's attire,' she responded, and after a tiny pause added with a deliberately pointed look, 'I made a bad enough impression on you, turning up in jeans.'

Again a small smile lifted the edges of his mouth. 'Are you expecting an apology from me, Dr Hayden?' he asked.

'No,' she said with a level stare, but her chest cavity started fluttering again. 'But, then, you don't seem the type to hand them out all that frequently.'

He held her look with enviable ease. 'You consider yourself quite good at reading people, don't you?'

There was a tiny almost imperceptible lift of her chin. 'I've hung around cops for a long time, Chief Inspector D'Ancey, so, yes, I am pretty good at it, as I imagine you are too.'

He leaned back in his chair in an indolent manner. 'What do you make of me so far?' he asked.

She pursed her lips for a moment as she considered her reply. 'You like control.'

His expression remained slightly mocking. 'What police officer doesn't?'

'You are also unhappy about me being here to investigate Ethan Jenson's death,' she said, 'but I haven't yet ascertained why.'

His gaze locked on hers again but Eloise couldn't help noticing the way his right thumb began clicking the pen again. 'Maybe I have something against Australians,' he offered dryly.

She tilted her head. 'Or maybe you have something against women—professional women in particular.'

She was good, Lachlan had to hand it to her. She was perceptive but far too attractive for his liking. Not to mention her attitude. She stood up to him in a way few people did, which both intrigued and irritated him.

'I have no problem with career-women as long as they play by the rules,' he said.

'Those would be your rules, I take it?' she put in pertly.

His mouth tightened before he could stop it. 'I am used to being in charge, Dr Hayden,' he said. 'It comes with the title of Chief Inspector. What I say goes.'

'I am here to review the findings of what has been an unexpected death of an Australian citizen,' she said. 'I don't anticipate there being any compromise over protocol. I know how to conduct myself both professionally and personally.'

A taut silence thickened the air for a few pulsing seconds.

'I also know how to deal with difficult colleagues,' she added when he didn't speak.

One of his dark brows lifted. 'You are suggesting I am going to be a difficult colleague?'

She resettled in her chair. 'You are showing all the classic signs of being one.'

His mouth twisted as he held her look. 'And those signs would be?'

Eloise sat silently fuming. Just like so many of the men in the force back home, he was deliberately trying to make her feel inadequate and uncertain. 'You are certainly not what I was expecting,' she said through tight lips.

'And what exactly were you expecting, Dr Hayden from Australia?' he asked. 'A welcoming committee with a brass band and fanfare for your arrival?'

This time Eloise didn't bother disguising her anger. 'No, but the very least I had hoped for was a chief inspector who had an open mind on the case, which clearly you do not. You seem intent on alienating me when hopefully all I will end up doing is to add credence to the results of your own investigation.'

He leaned forward across the desk. 'It seems to me all you are here for is a fast track to promotion,' he ground out. 'This is just the sort of case to do it, isn't it? An Australian celebrity surfer who suddenly turns up dead on Penhally Bay beach.' He leaned back in his chair. 'That could earn you some serious favours with the boss if you raise a whole lot of unsubstantiated allegations and suggest foul play.'

'An alternative finding of possible murder or suicide will be decided on the basis of the results of the fresh autopsy I perform,' she clipped out.

He gave a little snort of derision. 'He'd been in the water for hours. You'd have to be better than good to find anything on him that our guys didn't find, diatoms and airway froth notwithstanding.'

'It never hurts to have an independent review.'

'It never hurts to respect the family either,' he said. 'But apparently you and your superiors have completely missed that angle on things.'

'That's not true,' Eloise said. 'I've already told you it's the family who want to know what really happened to their son and brother. Hugh Jenson, Ethan's father, is an influential person in Australia. He has called in a lot of favours to pull off an uninvited external review of your findings. Surfers do drown, but not usually on calm beaches. The surf report that day noted a meagre one-metre swell, hardly the conditions for a very experienced surfer to drown in.'

His brown gaze became steely. 'Sounds like you've already made up your mind about your review findings. You haven't even examined the body and yet you've reached a conclusion.'

'That's not the case at all,' she insisted. 'I'm trained to keep an open mind, that's imperative in my line of work.'

'Are you, now? Exactly how long have you been a forensic pathologist?' he asked.

Eloise tried to stare him down but it took considerable effort on her part. 'I trained in medicine and then took four years to qualify in general pathology. If you must know, I developed an interest in forensic pathology when I was asked to do histopathology for a string of murders that eventually led to the conviction of a serial killer. I am now employed by the Central Sydney Health Board where I've subspecialised in DNA profiling. Cases that had been cold for ten or more years are now being solved with the new technology. It's meant justice has been served when the victims' families had given up hope of ever finding out what happened.'

'So you're hoping to achieve the same thing for Ethan Jenson's family?' he asked.

'Well, of course,' she answered. 'A review will give them more certainty about what happened to him.'

His gaze bored like a very determined drill into hers. 'What if your trip over here turns out to be a complete and very expensive waste of time?'

Eloise pursed her mouth again. 'I don't see how a second opinion can be a waste of time, Chief Inspector D'Ancey,' she said. 'Or are you worried I might actually prove your local people wrong?'

He held her challenging look. 'Not at all, Dr Hayden,' he said with one of his enigmatic half-smiles. 'I would, however, like you to keep a relatively low profile while you are here. There are many people who have been upset by the death of Ethan Jenson. If you go at it like a bull at a gate, you will hinder any subsequent investigation. The locals will be less likely to co-operate if or when the time comes for our people to interview witnesses.'

Eloise sat back, turning her head slightly to break from his intense gaze.

'I understand from the report faxed to me that Mr Jenson was found at dawn by some local surfers,' she said.

'Yes, he was dead and had been for several hours,' he answered. 'You have a copy of the statements taken individually from the three young men.'

'Where was Mr Jenson staying while he was in town?'

'At one of the pubs—the Penhally Arms. It's on Harbour Road. You would have passed it on your way here.'

'I think I may have seen it,' she said, recalling a blue and white building with colourful baskets of lobelia and petunias hanging outside.

A small silence crept on tiptoe into the room. Eloise wondered if he was deliberately letting it stretch and stretch to make her feel as uncomfortable as possible. She sat up straighter in her chair and trained her eyes on his, although the distinctly audible sound of her stomach rumbling lost her some ground.

Lachlan discreetly cleared his throat and, breaking his gaze, glanced at his watch. 'Oh, is that the time?' he said, and with a forced smile added, 'I'm afraid I'll have to bring our meeting to a close. Duty calls, as they say.'

Eloise got to her feet, not sure if she was being fobbed off or let off the hook. 'That's fine. I have to go too. We've gone way past our scheduled half-hour. I want to introduce myself at the medical clinic.'

'Why's that?' he asked, frowning slightly. 'You'll be based here.'

'I realise that but your report indicated one of the local doctors...' she glanced down at her notes to check the doctor's name '...Nick Tremayne, was called to the scene. I have some questions about his examination of the body, that's all. Where will I be working from here?' Eloise asked glancing pointedly around the cramped office. 'This seems a rather small station.'

'It is,' he answered, 'but we've assigned you a small office out the back. If it proves inadequate, arrangements can be made for you to travel back and forth to the main station at Wadebridge.'

'I'll probably move between the two,' she said. 'I wouldn't want to get under anyone's feet.' *Or at least not yours*, she thought.

'I'll show you the way to the clinic,' he said, and came from behind his desk, hooking his jacket off the chair with one finger.

'There's really no need,' she said. 'I can find it myself. Mrs Trevallyn at the guest-house gave me a tourist map.'

'It's fine,' he said holding the door open for her. 'I'm heading that way myself.'

Eloise moved past him in the doorway, this time not quite managing to keep from touching him. It was the briefest brush of her arm against his but it was enough to send a shock wave of reaction right through her body.

Careful, she reminded herself sternly as she followed him outside. Mixing business and pleasure had never worked for her in the past and she had sworn after what had happened with Bill Canterbury that she'd never be tempted to do it again.

And she hadn't been, not even once.

Until now…

CHAPTER THREE

'THAT offer of a change of clothes is still on if you change your mind,' Lachlan said as he led the way to the clinic. 'There are a few shops locally but they probably won't have much more than T-shirts, swimsuits and sarongs at this time of year.'

Eloise bit her lip as she thought about how she was going to cope without her luggage. She needed a toothbrush and a change of underwear at the very least. She could probably spin another day out in her jeans but the vest top *had* to go.

'I'm sure Poppy won't mind,' he added. 'She's got too many clothes as it is. I'm forever picking them up off the floor.'

She gave him a sideways glance. 'I wouldn't like to put her out or anything. Perhaps you should ask her first to see if it's all right.'

He suddenly frowned as he looked towards the clinic entrance. 'Looks like you can ask her yourself,' he said.

Eloise followed the line of his gaze and saw a beautiful-looking girl with long blonde hair coming towards them. She was tanned and slim, her brown eyes made up with smoky eye-shadow and eyeliner making her look much older than sixteen. She had a rather serious look on her face, and in spite of the carefully applied eye-make up Eloise suspected she had been crying recently, but as soon as the girl saw her father her expression turned from serious to surly.

'I thought you were working until seven tonight,' she said, and then with a quick glance at Eloise turned back to her father, her mouth twisting sarcastically. 'What's going on? Are you arresting her or dating her?'

Lachlan opened his mouth to reprimand his daughter but Eloise got in first. She gave the girl a polite but distinctly cool smile and introduced herself. 'Hello, Poppy, I'm Eloise Hayden. I'm afraid I've come to ask a favour of you.'

Poppy looked a little startled, making her look more like a small child instead of an in-your-face teenager. 'You...you have?' she croaked.

'Dr Hayden's luggage has gone missing,' Lachlan explained before Eloise could get another word in. 'I thought you might be able to tide her over for a couple of days with something out of your extensive wardrobe.'

This time the young girl's expression changed from frowning worry to a sneer. 'I hardly think anything of mine will fit her,' she said, folding her arms across her chest. 'She's much bigger than me.'

Catty little girl, Eloise thought behind the screen of her deadpan expression, although she automatically sucked in her tummy and wished not for the first time that she hadn't inherited her mother's generous breasts.

'She's got a beautiful figure, just like you,' Lachlan growled. 'Now, stop being so appallingly rude to her.'

You're a fine one to talk, Eloise would have been tempted to say normally, but she was still reeling from his assessment of her figure as beautiful.

Poppy's lip curled. 'So you *are* dating her, then, are you?'

'Er...no,' Eloise said quickly, hating it that she was

blushing and that Lachlan was witnessing every agonising second of it. 'I'm here on official business.'

The worried frown came back. 'Is it something to do with Ethan Jenson?' Poppy asked.

'Yes,' Eloise said. 'I'm a forensic pathologist from Australia, appointed to review the investigation into his death.'

Poppy's brown gaze flicked to her father's. 'I thought it was already sorted out—you know, that he drowned and no one else was responsible.'

'Dr Hayden will no doubt come to the same conclusion,' he said with a challenging little glint in his eyes as he looked at Eloise.

Eloise gritted her teeth and turned back to his daughter. 'Did you know him, Poppy?' she asked.

The girl's eyes fell away from hers. 'Not really,' she mumbled. 'I met him once or twice but that was ages ago.'

'Ages ago when?'

'Dr Hayden, this is neither the time nor place to conduct an interview with my daughter even if you were authorised to do so,' Lachlan said firmly. 'Come on, Poppy, we have an appointment, remember?'

Poppy looked confused. 'We do?'

'Yes. You asked me to take you to Fiona's place.'

'But that's tomor—'

'We'll leave some clothes for you at the guest-house,' Lachlan said to Eloise as he ushered his daughter away with a firm hand at her elbow.

Eloise stood watching them until they disappeared around the corner. Chief Inspector D'Ancey quite clearly didn't want her talking even casually to his daughter about Ethan Jenson, which made her wonder if the girl had been lying about how well she had known the surfer.

'Are you looking for somebody?' a female voice said from behind her.

Eloise turned to see an elegant-looking woman in her mid to late forties standing at the entrance to the medical clinic. 'Oh, yes, sorry I was just coming in to introduce myself,' she said. 'I'm Eloise Hayden from Australia, I'm here to—'

'We've been expecting you,' the woman said with a warm smile. 'I'm Kate Althorp, one of the midwives here. Come inside and I'll introduce you to the practice manager, Hazel, and Sue, the head receptionist. Dr Tremayne is with a patient but he'll be out shortly. I'm afraid the other doctors have either left for the day or are out on calls, but you will probably meet them over the next few days.'

Eloise followed the woman inside the two-storey building, taking in with interest the comfortable-looking waiting room with a children's play area in one corner and the neat reception area on the left.

After exchanging greetings from the two women behind the reception desk, Kate looked up as a tall man with dark hair peppered with grey came out of the first room off the waiting area.

'Ah here's Dr Tremayne now,' she said. 'Nick, this is Eloise Hayden, the forensics specialist from Australia.'

'How do you do?' Nick said, offering Eloise his hand for the briefest of handshakes. 'Welcome to Penhally Bay.'

'Thank you,' Eloise said. 'I was wondering if I could ask you some questions about Ethan Jenson. You were the one who examined him at the scene, I understand?'

'Yes,' he answered somewhat brusquely.

'Is now a convenient time, or can we make another time soon?' Eloise asked. 'It won't take too long if you've got a minute or two available.'

His brows moved closer together. 'I am extremely pushed at the moment,' he said. 'I still have a house call to make.'

'Mrs Griggs won't mind waiting for you,' Kate interjected. 'She understands when you get caught up.'

Nick Tremayne exchanged a quick glance with Kate before turning back to Eloise. 'Come through to my room,' he said. 'But it will have to be quick.'

Eloise followed him into his consulting room, sat in one of the two chairs available and quietly observed him. She couldn't help noticing he seemed on edge and impatient as he took his seat.

'Right, fire away,' he said, folding his arms.

'Was the body still in the water when you were called?' she asked.

'No,' he answered. 'The deceased had been dragged onto the beach by the three boys who had found him.'

'So how long after he had been removed from the water did you see the body, Dr Tremayne?'

'The body was found at six a.m. and I saw him around seven-thirty so it was about an hour and a half.'

'Was the body covered by anything in that time?' she asked.

'Yes,' he said. 'When I arrived a blanket had been placed over the body as there were quite a few people gathering on the beach at that time.'

'Do you remember what type of blanket, what colour, what it was made of?' Eloise asked.

'Wool, I think…brown, if I remember correctly.' His deep brown gaze narrowed slightly as it returned to hers. 'Is there some query about my assessment of the body?'

'No, there's no specific query about your assessment at all,' she said. 'It's just that there are some aspects of the case that are puzzling, and I'm just trying to clear them up. The

Australian authorities have been invited to carry out an external review of the death. There's no question of competence—more a fresh look to see if anything surfaces that might not have come to light so far.'

Eloise waited a beat or two and when he didn't respond, she continued, 'So he'd been out of the water for one and a half hours before you saw him and you are quoted as saying at the time you thought he had drowned. Can you tell me what made you so sure that drowning was the actual cause of his death? Could he have died from another cause and been placed in the water later?'

His brows moved together. 'Murdered, you mean?'

'It happens in the quietest villages as well as the biggest cities, Dr Tremayne.'

He held her direct look. 'There were no other obvious causes for his death. He had no external marks of trauma. He was in the water and as far as I could see he had drowned. I believe the autopsy bore out my assessment.'

'It did, yes. But, still, there are a couple of features I need to clarify.'

'Such as?'

'Well, for one, I notice in your statement that the hands and feet were somewhat pinkish—that's not quite consistent with the cyanosis you would expect after a drowning. Also, the deceased was a world-class swimmer and the ocean swell was relatively calm that morning. Why would someone who has faced some of the world's most challenging waves drown on a calm beach?'

'Surfers do occasionally drown,' he pointed out. 'They're human, like everyone else. They're not immune to freakish accidents.'

'Yes, but if Ethan Jenson had met with an accident of some

sort, one would expect to see some sign of it on his body—a head wound, for instance, if his surfboard had rendered him unconscious, but your report did not identify any such signs of injury or trauma.'

'That is because there weren't any,' he stated with an air of impatience as he glanced at his watch. 'The pathologist, Peter Middleton, didn't find any either.'

Eloise held her ground and continued, 'I'm not actually all that happy with some of the tests done at the autopsy—some of them were not as complete as I would have liked, and there were a couple of tests I would like to have seen done which weren't.'

He frowned darkly. 'Has another autopsy been authorised?'

'Yes. His family, along with his sponsors, requested it via their lawyers. The coroner has been informed and I've been given the go-ahead.'

'That's going to delay getting this matter cleared up, isn't it?' he commented, still frowning slightly. 'Still, you're the forensic specialist, Dr Hayden. I wish you well in clearing up your doubts. But as far as I can ascertain, the victim looked as though he went to the beach for an early morning swim and for some reason got into difficulties and drowned. I'm no Sherlock Holmes, but that was my clinical assessment and that's what the local pathologist decided was the case. Now, I really must be off. If I can be of further assistance, Hazel or Sue will make an appointment for you to see me.'

'Thank you for your time,' Eloise said, and got to her feet.

Kate caught up with Eloise once Nick had stalked out of the practice, mumbling something to the receptionist on his way past. 'Don't take his offhand manner personally,' she said with an expressive roll of her eyes. 'He's like that with everyone.'

'This village seems to have its fair share of difficult men,' Eloise remarked with wryness.

Kate gave her a speculative look. 'So you and the chief inspector didn't quite hit it off? I saw you together earlier.'

'I'm not here to make friends but to find out the truth about a young man's death,' Eloise said firmly.

'Lachlan D'Ancey is a pillar of this community,' Kate said as she walked Eloise to the front entrance. 'I'm sure you'll change your opinion of him when you spend more time with him. Nick, however, is another story. I've known him a long time and he's as arrogant and aloof as ever.'

Eloise couldn't help feeling there was a hint of regret in the other woman's tone. Kate Althorp carried herself with natural elegance, but every now and again her warm brown eyes seemed sad, as if life had not turned out quite the way she had hoped. 'There are three other doctors here, aren't there?' she said. 'Including Dr Tremayne's son, Edward.'

'Yes, he's just got married and he's on his honeymoon at the moment,' Kate answered. 'But with the workload increasing all the time, we're taking on a new doctor, Oliver Fawkner, in a week or two. We also have two nurses, Gemma and Alison.'

'It sounds like a busy practice,' Eloise offered.

'It is,' Kate said. 'The closest hospital is St Piran, half an hour away, so we service quite a large area, although I imagine not as large an area as some places in your country.'

'Yes, indeed,' Eloise agreed. 'Before I specialized, I did a short locum in the outback where we had to fly everywhere to see patients on remote cattle stations. It was certainly very different from working in the city.'

'Has anyone come over with you?' Kate asked once they were outside. 'A partner or your husband perhaps?'

'No,' Eloise answered with a rueful look. 'I'm not currently attached. I guess I've been too busy concentrating on my career.'

'It's a lonely life without a partner to share the highs and lows. I should know—I lost my husband some years ago.' She let out a little sigh and added, 'A rescue went horribly wrong during a storm. I lost James and Nick lost his father and brother. It was a terrible time.'

'I'm so sorry,' Eloise said, 'how very tragic for you all.'

'I have a son Jem, short for Jeremiah,' Kate said with a smile of maternal tenderness. 'I don't know how I would have survived without him.'

'Have you lived most of your life in Penhally Bay?'

'Yes,' Kate said. 'I trained as a midwife but after James died I felt I needed a change and sort of drifted into administration and eventually became Practice Manager here. But I went back to midwifery, which is my first love.'

'How old is your son?' Eloise asked.

'He's just turned nine,' Kate answered, and with a wistful smile added, 'Still a little boy but not for much longer, I expect…'

'It must be a lovely place to bring up a child,' Eloise said as the breeze brought the salty tang of the sea towards them. She glanced out of the open window and looked at the wide view of the sparkling blue of Penhally Bay below. 'I read in one of the tourist brochures that there's a seventeenth-century Spanish wreck in the bay and smugglers' caves. That would hold considerable appeal for many a young boy, I imagine.'

'Yes…' Kate said, her expression gradually becoming sombre again. 'I really feel for Mr and Mrs Jenson. They were here yesterday. Nick spent over an hour with them. I can't imagine the hell they're going through, wondering if their son was murdered or committed suicide.'

'So you don't think he just drowned?' Eloise asked, phrasing her question carefully.

Kate's creased brow indicated she hadn't quite made up her mind. 'It's hard to say,' she said after a little pause as she looked out over the bay before turning back to face Eloise. 'He was a brilliant surfer—some say he had the potential to be one of the best ever. My son showed me a photo in a surfing magazine of Ethan riding at Shipstern's Bluff in Tasmania, reputedly the largest and most dangerous waves in the southern hemisphere. Like his family, I find it hard to believe he could come to Penhally Bay in Cornwall and drown. It doesn't make sense.'

'The local authorities seem convinced otherwise,' Eloise returned before she could check herself, 'Chief Inspector D'Ancey in particular. He seems to think my presence here is only going to make things worse for the grieving relatives.'

Kate frowned. 'Yes, there is that, I suppose, but if it had been my son I would want to know for sure what had happened to him. What if it *was* foul play?'

'Was he popular amongst the locals?' Eloise asked.

'He was *very* popular with the girls,' Kate said. 'I guess that might have annoyed some of the local lads a bit, but not enough for anyone to want to get rid of him, I wouldn't have thought.'

'What about his surfing rivals?'

Kate pressed her lips together for a moment. 'I guess if someone wanted to win the next surfing round enough, they might be tempted to eradicate the running favourite, but unlike some sports, where fans take their allegiance to extremes, the surfers all know each other very well and any rivalry is generally friendly.'

Eloise knew she was probably overstepping her professional boundaries but she didn't see the harm in getting some background on the victim and how he had been accepted in the village. 'So you can't think of anyone who would want Ethan Jenson dead?' she asked.

After a brief pause Kate met her questioning gaze levelly. 'There are probably dozens of fathers of teenage girls in the district who are secretly glad Ethan Jenson is out of the way. He had a bit of reputation, if you know what I mean.'

'So he was a bit of a player locally?'

'Very much so,' Kate answered. 'But it comes with the celebrity status, doesn't it? Mind you, young women these days seem to want to play around just as much as the men. They crow about which high-profile person they've bedded and how often. Times have certainly changed.'

'Yes, they have,' Eloise said, thinking of her staid and conservative foster-parents' views on dating.

'Where are you staying while you are here?' Kate asked.

'Trevallyn House. It seems very comfortable and close to everything.'

'Beatrice Trevallyn is a real sweetheart,' Kate said with a soft smile. 'She'll make sure you're well fed and her son is quite a character. He's got learning difficulties but he's lovely. You'll often see him about the village, doing odd jobs for people. Bea's done a good job keeping things going as long as she has since she lost her husband. The place is a bit run down and could do with a lick of paint but I don't think she has the money to do it. She'll be tickled pink you've chosen to stay there.'

'She's made me very welcome,' Eloise said. 'She gave me a lovely room overlooking the bay.'

'How long are you staying in Penhally Bay?' Kate asked.

'I've been assigned a month but it depends on whether I find anything that changes the verdict on Mr Jenson's death. If that should be the case, I would be called on to give evidence if there's an inquest or trial.'

'What the poor Jensons need to do is lay their son to rest,' Kate said with another sombre look.

'I understand how difficult it is for them at a time like this,' Eloise said. 'I've been involved in other cases that dragged on for several weeks in order to identify the bodies of victims after a bomb attack or fire. It's hard on everyone.'

Kate grimaced. 'I don't know how you do it, handling dead bodies all the time. I still struggle to hold myself together when we have a stillborn. I have to be strong for the parents but inside I feel nearly as devastated as they do.'

'I've had to toughen up a lot,' Eloise admitted. 'After my first autopsy I didn't eat meat for a year. I still can recall the smells of my first murder scene. But it's worth it to see justice served. The families can at least draw some measure of comfort that the person or persons responsible are locked away for good or for a very long time.'

'The chief inspector's not long ago gone through a drawn-out and particularly harrowing divorce,' Kate said. 'I think he might be finding being a single dad of a sixteen-year-old daughter quite a steep learning curve. Poppy's a bit of a handful, she's at that difficult age. All hormones and moods and missing her mother, no doubt, although she'd never admit to it, of course.'

'Did you know the chief inspector's ex-wife well?' Eloise asked, with what she hoped sounded like mild interest.

'Margaret D'Ancey didn't have much time for the locals,' Kate said. 'Or at least not since she was promoted in the financial investment firm she works for in London. I often wondered why she got married in the first place—a career always seemed to be more important to her than her husband and daughter. She was always leaving Lachlan to look after Poppy while she went off to some high-powered seminar. I don't know how he managed to juggle it all, given the stresses and strains of his job.'

Eloise found it difficult to know what to say in response. She valued her career above everything else in her life so far. Marriage and babies was something she tried not to think about too much. Years of dealing with crime and death had made her realise how tenuous life really was. The thought of bringing a child into the world only to lose it through an accident or a random act of murder was so terrifying she had more or less ruled it out as an option for her life. Besides, no one had entered her life who she had felt she could spend the rest of her days with. Her forensics colleague Bill Canterbury had been the closest she'd come to considering the possibility, but the fallout from their brief interaction had taught her to keep her private life separate from her professional life. She hadn't been in love with anyone so far, or at least not the sort of love that novels and movies portrayed as permanently life-changing. She wondered, given her background, if she ever would trust anyone enough to love them.

Kate gave her a searching look. 'I hope I didn't offend you. You've gone very silent. I didn't mean to suggest there's anything wrong with having a career or anything.'

'No, of course you didn't offend me,' Eloise said with a re-assuring smile. 'My career is a high priority at the moment but that's not to say it will always be so, although to be honest I don't really have any great desire to settle down right now.'

'You don't want children at some point?' Kate asked.

'I've thought about it once or twice but I haven't met a man I respect and trust enough to be the father of my child,' Eloise said truthfully. 'Most of the women I know are doing it single-handedly, having been deserted and left holding the baby, so to speak. Their chances of finding a new partner are pretty bleak with a couple of kids in tow. It looks like too much hard work if you ask me.'

'I know,' Kate said with a rueful look. 'A lot of men don't want the baggage of another man's child. Besides, it's hard on young kids, having people come and go in their life. I want my son to feel secure, it's so important at his age.'

'It's important at any age,' Eloise said, thinking of her various stints in foster-care after her mother had died of a drug overdose. It had taken years for her to settle down with June and Charles Roberts, and even now she still wondered if they had regretted their decision to parent the nine-year-old daughter of a heroin-addicted prostitute and a father registered as unknown.

Kate glanced at her watch. 'I have to get going—Jem will be wondering what's happened to me. Is there anything you need from the clinic or will you just be interviewing Nick?'

'Thanks, but I think Chief Inspector D'Ancey's organised all the equipment I'll need at the station at Wadebridge. I'll be performing the autopsy tomorrow and will then have to process some tests in the lab—the results may take a few days. Normally they take several weeks but this is a high-profile case so it will be given top priority.'

'It's still all a bit of a waiting game, though, isn't it?' Kate said.

Eloise let out a little sigh. 'Yes, it is, but that's life, right?'

Kate's small world-weary smile seemed to say it all. 'Yes, it certainly is.'

CHAPTER FOUR

'DR HAYDEN, there's a bag of things for you here,' Beatrice Trevallyn said as Eloise came downstairs later that evening. 'Chief Inspector D'Ancey dropped them off a few minutes ago. I asked him if he wanted to see you but he seemed in a bit of a hurry. I expect it's that daughter of his,' she tut-tutted, and added, 'That Poppy is going to be trouble, I can tell. She's far too grown up for her age. If she's not careful she'll have the reputation of Molly Beale.'

Eloise was inclined to agree with Mrs Trevallyn on what she had seen so far of Lachlan D'Ancey's daughter. Poppy certainly wouldn't be an easy teenager to manage. She came across as street-wise and moody. She also had the body of a woman, even though she was little more than a child. The chief inspector would have his work cut out for him, keeping some semblance of control, she imagined, especially without the close back-up of the girl's mother.

She took the carrier bag from the elderly lady's hands and asked, 'Who is Molly Beale?'

Beatrice's mouth was pulled tight. 'My cleaning girl—you know, the one I told you left me without notice? I let her have one of my rooms on the cheap because her mother kicked her out when she got a new man herself, but I wish I hadn't now. Molly was no better than she should have been, if you know what I mean.'

'Have you found someone else to help you in the house?' Eloise asked, out of politeness rather than any real interest.

'I'm interviewing a couple of women tomorrow,' Beatrice said, and then glancing around to see if any of the other guests were within earshot she said in an undertone, 'Davey saw them together, you know, down at the beach.'

Eloise found herself whispering back. 'Saw who?'

'That man that was drowned,' Beatrice said with an air of puffed-up authority. 'It wasn't the first time either. Poppy D'Ancey was seeing him behind Robert Polgrean's back.'

Eloise could feel her intrigue building. 'Who is Robert Polgrean?' she asked.

'Her boyfriend,' Beatrice answered. 'Or at least he was until that surfer came to town and lured her away from him. Robert was devastated and still is, mind you. He and Poppy had been going out since their first year at secondary school.'

'Sixteen is rather young to be thinking of permanency in a relationship,' Eloise felt obliged to say in the girl's defence. 'Kids of that age fall in and out of love almost weekly.'

Beatrice's bird-like eyes narrowed disapprovingly. 'And in and out of bed almost daily, if what Davey saw is to be believed. That girl has been running amok since her mother left. Of course, the chief inspector does his best but he's got to work full time to provide for her, doesn't he? Margaret should have stayed at home and been a proper mother to the girl, instead of gallivanting off, trying to prove how clever she is.'

Eloise had to bite her tongue to stop herself launching into one of her well-used feminist soapbox speeches. She suspected that, like her conservative foster-parents Beatrice wouldn't be all that impressed with her line of argument.

Instead, she tactfully changed the subject. 'I thought I might go out for a walk along the bay. I've got my key with me so don't wait up.'

'It's a lovely evening,' Beatrice said. 'If I wasn't so troubled with my rheumatism, I'd join you. It's been many a long year since I've been able to get down to the water. But it's a fair walk to the surf beach.'

'I love walking and I live near the beach at home,' Eloise said. 'I never really feel my day is complete unless I dip my toes in.'

One of the other guests came down the stairs at that moment and Beatrice turned to speak to them. 'Good evening, Mr Price. Do you fancy a cup of tea or are you on your way out?'

'A cup of tea would be absolutely marvellous, thank you,' a man in his early seventies said with an interested glance in Eloise's direction.

'This is Dr Hayden from Australia,' Beatrice said. 'She's investigating the death of the surfer.'

The man's bushy grey brows rose over his faded blue eyes. 'Oh, really?'

Eloise smiled politely. 'I'm pleased to meet you, Mr Price. Are you holidaying in the area?'

'Yes and no,' he answered with a somewhat quirky smile. 'I'm a writer. I take my work with me wherever I go.'

'Mr Price writes crime fiction, don't you, Mr Price?' Beatrice said.

'Yes,' he said, still smiling.

'Mr Price comes here every year, don't you, Mr Price?' Beatrice said with a fond look.

'I do indeed,' he answered. 'I love the sea air and Mrs Trevallyn's Cornish pasties. They are the best I've ever tasted.'

Eloise hadn't heard of him but, then, she'd never been much of a crime fiction fan, and even less so since she'd been working in forensics. The thought of reading about the sort of stuff she dealt with on a daily basis was not exactly her idea of relaxation, but she didn't like to burst the man's bubble too brutally. 'I look forward to reading one of your books soon,' she said with another polite smile.

Mr Price gave her a sheepish look. 'Um...I'm not actually published just yet but I have a manuscript with an agent in New York as we speak.'

'Isn't that exciting?' Beatrice's round cheeks glowed. 'We'll be able to say we knew Mr Price before he became famous.'

'I also have another manuscript I'm working on with me upstairs.' Mr Price smiled at Eloise. 'I know it's probably a dreadful imposition on my part, but if you had time, would you mind reading the first couple of chapters for me to see if I've got the police procedure right?'

'I'm not sure if I'm the right person to help you,' Eloise said, relieved she had thought of a valid excuse in time. 'Even though I'm called a police surgeon, I'm not really a police officer. I'm employed by the Health Department. Besides, the police have different ways of doing things in Australia. They even call their officers of the same rank different names.'

Mr Price began to beam from ear to ear. 'But my work in progress is set in Australia, in the outback actually, and the main character is a forensic doctor. Isn't that fortuitous?'

Eloise felt like rolling her eyes. Instead, she smiled a smile that felt like it had been stitched to her face with fencing wire. 'In that case, Mr Price, I'd be happy to look over it—perhaps Mrs Trevallyn could drop it into my room,' she said. Excusing herself, she made her way back upstairs with the carrier bag Lachlan D'Ancey had left for her.

Once in the privacy of her room she took out the various items of clothing and laid them on the bed, grimacing ruefully as she thought of her neutral coloured, businesslike skirts and jackets still in transit somewhere between Cornwall and Sydney.

She picked up a brightly flowery patterned skirt and matching sleeveless top and absently rubbed the silky fabric between her fingers, her thoughts automatically drifting to the last time she had seen her mother. She could still remember the garish colour of her mother's silk dress that day, and the cloying scent of her perfume, and the way her mouth had been a red slash of lipstick, the end of a cigarette jutting out from her lips as she'd mumbled something about being a good girl while Mummy went to work.

Eloise let the fabric drop to the bed and, turning on her heel, left the room and the ghosts she'd summoned locked safely inside.

Eloise saw Lachlan D'Ancey as soon as she walked past the café on Harbour Road. He was standing talking to a local fisherman, the smile on his face easy and relaxed, his casual jeans and black polo shirt taking nothing away from his naturally commanding presence.

He looked up and locked gazes with her and then, turning back to his companion, politely excused himself and sauntered over. 'Out for an evening stroll, Dr Hayden?' he asked.

'Yes,' she said. 'But I'm glad I ran into you as I have a couple of questions for you.'

'Professional or personal?'

'A bit of both, actually.'

If her answer rattled him he showed no sign of it. His face remained an indifferent mask as he held her gaze. 'I suppose back home you would be just starting work for the day,' he commented as he glanced momentarily at his watch. 'Or are you so career focused that you work around the clock?'

She gave him a brittle look. 'If the case calls for it, I put in whatever hours are necessary.'

'You know what they say about all work and no play, Dr Hayden,' he said with a teasing glint in his eyes.

Eloise lifted her chin. 'And you know what they say about people getting away with murder, Chief Inspector.'

The corners of his mouth lifted. 'What *do* they say, Dr Hayden?' he asked.

Eloise felt a hot little spark of attraction set fire to her insides. She could feel the flames slowly but inexorably spreading, heating her in every secret place. Her breasts felt tight and tender, her mouth felt dry and her heart felt as if it had forgotten its normal rhythm entirely. She sent the tip of her tongue out to run over the surface of her lips, her stomach feeling as if a miniature pony had begun kicking inside her as Lachlan's lazy brown gaze followed the path of her tongue.

She tried to drag her mushy brain back to the conversation at hand. 'Um...'

He cocked one brow in enquiry. 'Um?'

She moistened her mouth again. 'I forgot what we were talking about...'

'We were talking about people getting away with murder.'

'Oh... Yes...' She looked down at the map in her hands to escape the slow burn of his gaze. 'I was hoping to have a look at the place where the body was found. Could you point me in the right direction?'

'I'll come with you,' he said, and led the way down Harbour Road towards a church that was situated above the lighthouse.

He glanced down at her flat but thinly strapped sandals after a moment or two. 'Will you be all right on the steps down to the beach in those?'

'Of course,' Eloise said, hoping he couldn't see the blister on her left little toe that was growing bigger by the minute.

The swell was rough, with dumping waves stirred by the stiff onshore breeze. She pushed her hair back out of her eyes and soldiered on, stopping when he did at the edge of the foamy waterline.

'He was found floating out there,' he said, pointing to just beyond the first breakers.

Eloise stepped closer so she could follow the line of his arm, her nostrils widening as she smelt his freshly showered smell.

'I've organised some new water samples for you,' he added. 'They'll be at the lab tomorrow.'

Eloise looked out at the rolling ocean and wondered yet again what circumstances had led to the surfer's death. Dr Tremayne was right in saying surfers were not immune to drowning, but she still felt something was not quite right about the way the case had been handled, especially since Ethan Jenson had been a celebrity. As far as she understood it from her experience back home, the normal protocol on high-profile people was extensive testing on autopsy and yet only the most basic tests had been performed. It was a sensitive process: by coming here she would be at risk of offending the local pathologist, questioning his verdict, and yet she felt compelled to leave no stone unturned no matter what egos were dented in the process.

She was still deep in thought when she felt Lachlan's hands suddenly grasp her upper arms. 'What the—*Oh!*'

The foamy water of a larger wave caught her off guard and in spite of his attempts to get her out of the way, her feet and ankles were soaked, her jeans clinging damply to her lower legs.

'Sorry, I should have warned you earlier,' he said with a wry grimace. 'It got me, too.'

She looked down at his feet but, being so much taller, the water had barely come over the top of his shoes.

'Do you want to take your sandals off?' he asked.

Eloise knew that if she took them off she'd never be able to put them on again with that blister throbbing the way it was. 'No, they'll dry on the way back,' she said, and trudged on.

Lachlan walked alongside her, his fingers still feeling the tiny electric aftershocks of touching her bare arms as he'd pulled her out of the wave's way. He made a determined effort not to brush his shoulders against hers each time they came upon one of the narrow sections of the pathway, but he felt the magnetic pull of her all the same.

He was quite surprised to realise he quite liked her take-no-prisoners attitude. For, unlike his ex-wife who had ridden roughshod over everyone she could to get to where she wanted to go, Eloise's brusque, businesslike attitude was looking more and more like a façade. He saw it now and again when she thought he wasn't looking. A shadow of uncertainty would flicker in her eyes, like a gull suddenly flying past the sun, momentarily blocking the light.

'You're limping,' he said as they came back to the start of Harbour Road.

Her chin went up and she straightened her shoulders. 'No, I'm not.'

Lachlan suppressed a little smile. *There, what did I tell you? Nothing but a façade.*

Eloise stiffened when he bent down in front of her and began to inspect her feet. She scrunched up her toes, hoping it would hide the evidence, but it seemed he hadn't been appointed Chief Inspector for nothing.

'You've got a blister,' he said. 'I can see it.' His finger

brushed ever so gently against her foot, sending a jolt of awareness right up her leg.

Eloise looked down at his head, which was at her waist height, and her stomach gave a flustered little quiver. He had such thick, dark wavy hair that her fingers ached to feel its springiness. 'I—It's nothing. I can hardly feel it...'

He straightened and locked gazes with her. 'Do you fancy a drink?' he asked after a tiny pause.

Eloise stared up at him wide-eyed, her mouth opening and closing, although no sound came out.

He suddenly grinned. 'You're looking at me as if I've just asked you to swim the English Channel.'

His gaze shifted from hers to look back at the ocean for a moment. 'Have you got someone back home waiting for you?' he asked.

'No.' Eloise immediately wished she hadn't been so quick to answer. Even in such a liberated age there were few women over the age of thirty who liked admitting they were without a partner. 'Not at present,' she added lamely.

He turned and gave her a speculative look. 'So, like me, you're in between relationships.'

'Sort of...I guess.'

'So there'd be no harm in having a drink now that we both know where we stand,' he said. 'Besides, you need to rest your foot for a while. That blister looks painful. What do you say?'

She examined his expression guardedly. 'I wouldn't want you to get the wrong idea...'

His smile was crooked and Eloise thought perhaps a little self-deprecating. 'You're going to have to help me out here, Dr Hayden,' he said. 'It's been years since I asked a woman out for a drink. If you refuse my very first attempt, it might permanently damage my ego and you know what they say about the fragility of the male ego.'

Eloise made a little moue with her lips. 'Yes, but I've never had cause to believe it was true,' she said, still trying not to smile. 'Anyway, I'm sure your ego will bounce back quite rapidly and robustly if I say no.'

His brown eyes gleamed. 'You said *if*, so does that mean I'm still in with a chance?' he asked.

Eloise felt herself wavering, even though she wondered if his rather endearing desperate and dateless act was exactly that—just an act. But she reasoned a drink at one of the nearby pubs was a good way to get a feel for the local area, perhaps even meet a few of the regulars.

She blew out a little sigh. 'All right,' she said. 'One drink but one drink only.'

He stood looking down at her with that lopsided boyish smile of his. 'Tell me something, Dr Hayden from Australia. When was the last time you were asked out for a drink by a man?' he asked.

Eloise hated it that she had to really think about it before answering.

Had it been *that* long?

'Um…a few months,' she said. Two years more like, but she wasn't going to admit that to him.

He paused and then smiled again, liking the fact that he was getting to see a little bit of the real Eloise Hayden.

'What about a kiss?'

She gave him a wary look. 'What about a kiss?'

His smile was still tilting up one side of his mouth. 'Have you been kissed by a man in the last few months?'

'Of course,' she said, thinking of the slightly embarrassed peck on the cheek she had received from her foster-father at the airport.

Reaching for one of her hands and securing it in the warmth of his, Lachlan asked, 'How many months?'

She gave him a back-off stare but for some reason couldn't quite summon up the strength to counteract his gentle but firm hold. 'I don't see that it's any of your business.'

He shrugged. 'What if I said I'm making it my business? I'm interested in getting to know you, Dr Hayden,' he said, his fingers burning like fire against hers.

'Um...I'd tell you that I...that I...'

His thumb began to stroke along the sensitive skin of her blue-veined wrist. 'How long?'

She ran her tongue over her lips, her stomach doing that little pony-kick thing again. 'I—I can't remember...'

He smiled a white-toothed smile. 'That makes two of us.'

She wrinkled her brow at him. 'You can't remember the last time you kissed a woman? What about your ex-wife?'

He gave her a rueful look. 'You know what they say about married couples.'

She stared, mesmerised by the movement of his lips as he spoke. He had such a beautiful mouth, the top lip sculpted and the bottom lip sensually full. There was no doubt in her mind that if that mouth took it upon itself to kiss hers, she was going to be in serious trouble. His thumb on her wrist was doing enough damage as it was; her belly was flip-flopping all over the place and her inner thighs already dampening with desire.

'Um... What do they say?' she managed to finally croak.

His gaze went to her mouth again. 'They say that once a couple is married, they forget how to kiss.'

She gave him a disbelieving glance. 'I'm sure that's not true.'

'Do you know any married couples who kiss like there's no tomorrow?'

Eloise couldn't help thinking of her foster-parents, who

hadn't even exchanged a quick peck on the cheek in the whole time she had been living with them. She had learned early on that they were uncomfortable with public shows of affection. Any attempts on her part had been met with stiff formality; she had felt at times as if she was leaning into a brick wall. They had held her at arm's length, as if frightened that too much affection would have her craving more than they could give.

'Er...no, but that doesn't mean they don't when they're in private,' she said. 'Kissing is a very intimate thing.'

'So you don't think we should do it right here where everyone can see us?' he asked ruefully.

'I'm not going to kiss you, Chief Inspector D'Ancey.' The sensible side of her knew it was a bad idea, but even so she could feel her heels lift off the back of her sodden sandals to bring her mouth within a breath of his.

'Not even once, just to see what happens?' he asked softly, his warm hint-of-mint breath skating lightly over the surface of her lips.

Eloise knew exactly what would happen. It would be fireworks and earthquakes and she knew she'd enjoy it. She couldn't afford to let it happen. It was madness to even think about the possibility.

But it was so tempting, so very tempting.

She could feel herself starting to cave in, the mingling of their breaths making it even harder for her to resist him.

It had been a very long time since she'd felt a man's arms around her—in fact, anyone's arms around her.

Standing in front of her was the most attractive man she had met in a very long time. And besides, she was a modern woman. Sex was a normal part of life in spite of what her foster-parents had preached.

But sex has consequences, a little voice inside her head

reminded her, especially for women. The emotional investment in a physical relationship was nearly always greater for women. If she fell in love while over here on assignment, where would that leave her?

She took an unsteady breath and forced her eyes away from his mouth to meet his gaze. 'Not even once to see what happens... Sorry...'

'Pity,' he said, releasing her hand and stepping back from her. 'You know what they say about missed opportunities.'

Eloise rolled her eyes and hoped he couldn't see her lips twitching in reluctant amusement. 'I'm not even going to ask.'

He grinned at her. 'Come on, you owe me a drink for providing you with emergency clothes. Did they fit, by the way?'

'I didn't try them on but, yes, I think they will, in spite of what your daughter thinks of my figure.'

He gave her another amused glance. 'So that pressed a few of your buttons, did it?'

'I know how to handle difficult teenagers.'

'Good, then maybe you can give me a few hints,' he said with an element of wryness in his tone. 'Sometimes I can't believe it's the same little girl I used to cradle in my arms when she was a baby.'

Eloise found her eyes wandering to where his hands were hanging by his sides, a vision of him holding a little baby sending a warm river-like sensation through her belly. He had nice hands, large and long fingered with a dusting of dark hair running over the backs right up his arms.

'It must be hard learning when to let go,' she said into the sudden silence.

'It is,' he said. 'The world is a dangerous place, especially for young women. They think they're invincible but you and I both know they are not.'

Eloise exchanged a grim look with him. 'I know.'

Another silence passed as they walked towards the Penhally Arms.

'You're not going to wear the clothes, are you?' he asked.

She gave him a sidelong glance as she passed him in the doorway. 'I'm not really a bright colour person. I guess that comes from too many years at a convent school where inward beauty was encouraged over outward.'

'You know what they say about hiding your talents under a bushel.'

Eloise couldn't stop her smile this time. 'You really like your sayings, don't you?'

His brown eyes twinkled as he pulled out a chair for her. 'Chief Inspector Cliché, that's me, or so my daughter thinks.'

Eloise waited until he was seated opposite before she said, 'Why don't you want me to talk to her?'

His eyes instantly lost their sparkle and a small frown crisscrossed his forehead. 'It is not your responsibility to interview the locals—that is my job and that of my colleagues. But in any case I would prefer her to be kept away from the investigation. It's got nothing to do with her. She barely knew the guy.'

'Not according to one of my sources,' she said, watching him closely.

He held her probing look but the line of his mouth tightened. 'You want to have a drink with me or play detectives?'

'I don't seem the harm in a bit of both.'

His top lip curled. 'I can see what you're doing, Dr Hayden. Your acceptance of a drink with me is all about pumping me for information, isn't it?'

'I'm sure you don't need me to remind you that if you're withholding information pertinent to the case, you could get into serious trouble,' she said. 'Poppy may be your daughter but if she's somehow involved in the suspicious death of Ethan Jenson, you'd better tell me now.'

'I told you she barely knew the guy.'

'I have reason to believe you're lying.'

His gaze hardened as it challenged hers. 'You think so?'

'You know what they say about gut feelings, Chief Inspector D'Ancey.'

'Hasn't anyone told you gut feelings don't stand up in court, Dr Hayden? If you want to solve this case then you'll need solid evidence and cold, hard facts.'

Eloise forced her chin up. 'I know that, you don't need to tell me how to do my job.'

'Tread carefully, Dr Hayden,' he warned in a low deep tone in case others nearby were listening. 'You might be after the biggest promotion of your career, but you're dealing with real people here and one of them happens to be my daughter. I won't allow you to use her as a stepladder to get where you want to go.'

'This isn't about my career,' she said, 'or your daughter for that matter. It's about a young man in the prime of his life who suddenly turned up dead. I want some answers for his family as well as the Australian government. That's what I'm being paid to do and forgive me if I've somehow got this wrong, but I was under the impression you were supposed to be helping me.'

Lachlan let a stiff silence pass before he sent one of his hands through his hair. 'Look,' he said on a tail end of a sigh, 'how about we drop the subject? Work takes up enough of my time and yours as it is. We're both off duty and can surely for the space of an hour or so talk about something else.'

Eloise felt one of his legs accidentally brush against hers. 'OK,' she said, tucking her legs well back. 'What shall we talk about?'

'Chief Inspector D'Ancey?' One of the barmaids rushed over with a worried expression on her face. 'There's some trouble with the some of the lads outside. Can you come and sort it out?'

Eloise suddenly became aware of the sound of jeering and swearing and glass breaking. Exchanging a brief glance with Lachlan, she followed him quickly outside.

CHAPTER FIVE

THE first thing Eloise noticed was the blood. There were great splotches of it on the cobblestones in the alley and even on one of the rubbish bins. She had to fight down her reaction. It had been several months since she'd attended the murder scene of a twenty-two-month-old girl and yet the sharp metallic scent of blood in the air brought it all back in an instant. Her skin felt clammy, her stomach churned and her head felt as if it had been placed in a vice.

'Quick! Cops!' A young male voice called out from further down the alley.

The gang of youths dispersed in all directions, one flying past Eloise so fast he very nearly knocked her from her already unsteady feet.

She watched as Lachlan caught another one in three fast strides, holding him up against the stone wall of the building. 'What's this about this time, Brian?' he asked. 'Do you want another assault charge on your record?'

The youth scowled at him. 'He started it,' he said, pointing to the young man who was now getting to his feet not far away from where Eloise was standing, blood pouring from a head wound.

Eloise went towards him. 'Are you all right?'

The young man wiped at his face, grimacing as he saw the blood. 'I'm fine,' he said. 'It was Davey I was worried about.'

She frowned and looked up and down the now deserted alleyway. 'Davey? Do you mean Davey Trevallyn?'

He nodded. 'The gang were hassling him. They do it all the time.'

'Where is he now?' she asked, handing him some tissues from her bag.

He mopped at his face, wincing slightly. 'I managed to get him out of the alley before the boys set on me.'

'I think you might need that wound looked at,' she said when he removed the tissues from his face. 'It might have some glass in it.'

'Yeah, I will. It feels like something's in there,' he said, wincing again as he dabbed at it. 'I'll see Dr Tremayne in the morning.'

'I think you should call him now,' Eloise said. 'Wounds like that can turn septic very quickly.'

'She's right, Robert,' Lachlan said, coming over to where they were standing. 'It looks nasty. Do you want to press charges?'

Robert shook his head. 'No, it won't do any good.'

'Brian's got it coming to him,' Lachlan said gravely. 'I let him go but I'll call on his parents tomorrow. He needs taking in hand.'

'It wasn't just him,' Robert said. 'You know what Gary Lovelace and his gang are like. They give Davey a hard time just for sport. It's sickening.'

'I know but it takes all types in this world,' Lachlan said. 'Come on, let's get you to the clinic and cleaned up. I'll give Dr Tremayne a call to meet us there.'

Eloise followed them out of the alley, listening as Lachlan

spoke to Nick Tremayne in his quiet but authoritative manner, his gaze flicking now and again to the young man by his side.

'You're the Australian police doctor, right?' Robert asked Eloise once they were on the Harbour Road. 'Poppy told me about you.'

Eloise smiled. 'You must be Robert Polgrean. Mrs Trevallyn told me you were Poppy's boyfriend.'

'"Was" being the operative word,' Robert said with an embittered look. 'We're not seeing each other any more.'

Eloise ignored the diamond-sharp look she was getting from Lachlan. 'Did you know Ethan Jenson at all?' she asked.

Robert's expression turned sour. 'He was a show pony if ever there was one,' he said. 'He changed girls more than he changed his board shorts.'

'Dr Hayden,' Lachlan interjected. 'Robert is bleeding, in pain and probably dazed from the roughing up he's had.'

'I do feel a bit faint...' Robert said, and before Eloise could reach him he crumpled to a heap on the pavement.

'Where's a doctor when you need one?' Lachlan said as he knelt down beside the boy and placed him in the recovery position.

'*I'm* a doctor,' Eloise said, feeling more than a little affronted.

'When was the last time you treated a live patient?' he asked.

'A fair while back,' she answered, 'but I haven't forgotten any of my resuscitation skills.'

'You might want to run those skills past him now,' he suggested. 'It's about four hundred metres to the clinic and I don't fancy carrying him.'

Eloise checked that Robert's airway was unobstructed and that his breathing was even. His pulse felt strong and about normal rate. 'Is it possible to call an ambulance?' she asked.

'No point,' he said, reaching for his mobile phone. 'They

would be half an hour coming from St Piran. I'll give Nick another call and get him to come this way.'

Within a few short minutes Robert had woken up and Nick arrived almost simultaneously. Robert was bundled into Nick's car and taken to the clinic, with Eloise and Lachlan riding in the back.

'I'm sorry about this,' Robert said as they entered the clinic. 'I don't know what came over me. I never faint.'

'It happens to the best of us,' Nick said, as he led the way into the clinic. 'I fainted at my first anatomy lesson. It was damned embarrassing.'

Eloise was expecting Nick put the young boy's mind at ease by chatting to him about inconsequential things while he cleansed the wound, as most doctors did, but instead he barely said a word. He injected some local anaesthetic and carefully removed a shard of glass embedded in the skin and inserted three stitches before he spoke again.

'I'll give you a short course of antibiotics to prevent infection. Your record here says you haven't had a tetanus booster for seven years, so I'll give you one now,' he said as he took off his gloves. 'I'll check the wound in a day or two, but in the meantime take it easy.'

'I will, Dr Tremayne, thank you. And thank you, Dr Hayden and Chief Inspector. You turned up at a good time,' Robert said.

'No problem, Robert,' Lachlan said patting him on the back. 'Do you want us to walk you home?'

'I'm going his way,' Nick said as he reached for his keys. 'You and Dr Hayden can get back to what you were doing.'

'We weren't doing anything,' Eloise said, and then blushed furiously as three male gazes turned to her. 'I mean…er… nothing important… Just work stuff…sort of…'

Nick gave a stiff on-off smile before turning back to his patient. 'Come on, Robert. Your mother will be wondering what's happened to you. How's your father, by the way? He hasn't been back to see me after his accident. Is he doing the exercises I gave him?'

'I think so,' Robert said, as he followed Nick outside.

Eloise glanced at Lachlan on their way out. 'This is all your fault, you know.'

'What's my fault?'

She pointed to Nick and his young patient a few steps ahead of them. 'It will be all over the village tomorrow and you know it,' she said in low whisper.

'What will be?'

She rolled her eyes at his innocent look. 'We were seen having a drink at the Penhally Arms.'

'I hate to contradict you, but we didn't actually get around to having a drink.'

Eloise had to look away from the temptation of his mouth. 'Yes, well, the service was a little slow,' she grumbled.

'We didn't have a drink because you were too busy trying to cross-examine me,' he said. 'The bar staff were probably too frightened to come over to take our order in case they were suddenly whipped up onto your makeshift witness stand.'

She gave him a droll look. 'The truth is, Chief Inspector, *you* were too busy trying to withhold information from me.'

'Actually, I was too busy thinking about how it would feel to kiss you.'

Eloise stared at him for a moment, her mouth opening and closing like that of a fish. 'I'm going to pretend you didn't say that.'

'It's true, Eloise,' he said. 'Or do you prefer being called Ellie?'

She turned away. 'No, I don't.'

'You have something against shortened names?'

'I have something against men who won't accept no for an answer,' she said. 'I'm here to work. I'm not interested in taking the place of your ex-wife.'

'I wasn't exactly offering you marriage.'

She turned around to look at him. 'Just what is it you are offering, Chief Inspector D'Ancey? A quick fling to pass the time until someone more suitable comes along?'

His rueful smile totally disarmed her. 'I'm not very good at this, am I? Too long out of the saddle, isn't that would you would say back in Australia?'

She pursed her mouth at him. 'I'm sure it's like riding a bike, you never forget the steps.'

'Have you had dinner?' he asked.

Here we go again, Eloise thought. Did this man not understand the word 'no'? 'You're asking me to have dinner with you?' she asked.

'Just dinner,' he said, with another one of his stomach-tilting smiles. 'I wouldn't rule out a kiss, though, but maybe just one to be on the safe side.'

'What about your daughter?' she asked, trying her best to ignore the way her heart was jumping about in her chest at the thought of feeling that mouth pressed against hers. 'Shouldn't you be at home, looking after her?'

'Poppy is staying with her friend tonight,' he said. 'I'm a free man.'

She gave him a probing look. 'Have you checked that she is actually where she says she is?'

A small frown creased his brow. 'Listen, Dr Hayden, my daughter isn't out all the time neither does she sleep around if that's what you're thinking. I admit she's young and wilful but, then, she hasn't long witnessed her parents going through a difficult divorce. I also admit she's no angel, but if she says she's staying at her friend's house, I see no need to check up on her. It's tantamount to a betrayal of trust.'

'It's also your duty as a parent,' she pointed out. 'Do you know how many parents I have met who thought their kids were safe at a friend's house, only to have to go and identify them at the morgue the following day?'

His jaw tightened. 'You've been in forensics too long, Dr Hayden. You're seeing everyone as a potential victim.'

'I thought you said I didn't have enough experience?' she said with a little jut of her chin.

'The experience you've had has obviously coloured your judgement,' he said. 'Is that why you put your hand up for this job—to get away from something too distressing for you to get to sleep at night?'

Eloise blinked at him, her mouth going dry as little Jessica Richardson's features swam before her eyes. The last autopsy she'd done before she'd left, she would vividly remember that tiny body, still dressed in a pink fairy costume, her skin porcelain pale in death.

'Are you all right?' Lachlan asked, touching her on the arm.

She bit her bottom lip, struggling for control. 'Jet-lag,' she said, blowing out a ragged breath. 'I guess I haven't adjusted yet.'

His hand was warm and solid on the bare skin of her forearm. She looked down at it, her whole body registering the tingle of his flesh where it connected with hers. What would it feel like to have his mouth and tongue rub and stroke against hers? What would it feel like to have his hands shape her breasts, or slide down her thighs, or even delve into that secret place between them that had been empty for so long?

'You need some food,' he said. 'If you're not comfortable

with eating in public with me then why not come back to my house and have something with me there? It's not far from here, if you think your foot will manage it.'

Eloise could feel herself weakening. She didn't feel like spending her first night in Cornwall on her own. She had spent far too many nights alone with pink fairy wings flapping inside her head to torment her. 'I can get something back at the guest-house…' she said.

'Yes, like food poisoning,' he said with one of his sudden and totally disarming grins. 'Bea Trevallyn isn't the best cook in the world and certainly not the most hygienic. The place was almost closed down a few months back after a salmonella outbreak.'

Eloise gave a whole-body shiver. 'You're seriously starting to tempt me,' she confessed.

'Good,' he said. 'I'm not quite up to celebrity chef standard or anything but I can rustle up something to get by.'

'Are you sure you don't mind?' she asked, reluctantly removing her arm from the comforting hold of his.

His smile this time revealed his two crossed bottom teeth. 'You know what they say about rejecting an invitation the first time around.'

'OK, what *do* they say?' Eloise asked, as she fell into step beside him, a small smile beginning to tug at her mouth.

He glinted down at her. 'You might not get another chance. The invitation might not be repeated and you could have missed a golden opportunity that you might end up regretting for the rest of your life.'

'I make a point of not dwelling on regrets,' she said as she looked away. 'They don't change anything.'

Lachlan glanced at her bent head, taking in her pleated brow and the downturn of her mouth. Dr Eloise Hayden may be a career-woman on a mission but she had a soft side that she valiantly tried to keep hidden. He couldn't help wondering what she had faced so far in her career to make her present such a tough, suffer-no-fools-gladly exterior. He knew it was a tough call, being a forensics specialist. He had seen many a colleague turn to alcohol to try and block out the images of gruesome murder scenes or heavily decomposed bodies. Their relationships suffered as well. It was hard to deal with distressed relatives of victims while trying to maintain their own family relationships. Divorce rates were high in the force and higher still amongst top-level officers. He often wondered if his career had had more to do with his divorce from Margaret than anything else. She hadn't really understood the demands of the job and had come to resent the unpredictable hours he had worked. He had learned the hard way to loosen up a bit. He didn't want to do what so many did and burn out completely.

'What do you think of Nick Tremayne?' he asked as they walked up a slight incline to his house.

'He's seems very competent,' Eloise answered. 'But I have a feeling he's not comfortable dealing with me. I spoke to Kate Althorp earlier and she said he's like that with everybody.' She sent him a quick glance. 'Is there something going on between them?'

Lachlan gave a could-mean-anything shrug. 'Hard to tell,' he said. 'Nick is a bit of a closed book. He lost his wife Annabel to peritonitis a couple of years back. He blamed the surgeon at St Piran Hospital for her death. Nick's a hard nut to crack—pretty much keeps to himself, if you know what I mean. I guess it's understandable really. He still feels he would have been able to save Annabel if he'd got there in time, but Ben Carter did his best. Ben's his son-in-law now so things have settled down in that quarter. Nick of all people should know it happens like that sometimes. Cases go horribly wrong and no one's really to blame. The human body is not something you can predict the outcomes of in regard to medical intervention. Patients and relatives still expect things will turn out perfectly every time.'

Eloise glanced up at him again. 'You sound like you really understand the life of a medico.'

He gave her a brief smile before looking away. 'My father was a doctor, an O and G specialist, actually.'

'Was?'

His smile faded a little as he stopped outside a white house, his hand going to the back pocket of his jeans for the keys. 'He died a few years back,' he said. 'A ruptured aneurysm. My mother has never really come to terms with it. A bit like Nick, she feels guilty that she didn't see the signs in time.'

'Doctors make the very worst patients,' she said as she followed him into the cottage. 'They think they're bullet-proof. I guess it comes from years of diagnosing everyone else's ailments. You think it will never happen to you.'

'What about your background?' he asked, as he closed the door of the cottage. 'What do your parents do?'

'I don't have parents,' she said and looked away from his penetrating gaze. 'Or at least not real ones,' she added with a rueful twist to her mouth. 'I was brought up by foster-parents.'

'Tough call.'

She turned to face him, the empathetic warmth of his expression making her chest feel as if something similar to rapidly rising bread dough had been placed in it. 'Yes,' she said. 'It was.'

'And still is?'

Eloise had to look away from that all-seeing gaze. 'I'm over it,' she said. 'My foster-parents have been good, better than good actually. They have made it their life's work to ensure I was kept on the straight and narrow.'

'And have they succeeded?' he asked, as he reached for a bottle of red wine and two glasses.

She couldn't help a small wry smile as she took the glass of wine he poured for her, meeting his dark eyes in the process. 'They would be shocked to see me right now,' she said, indicating the glass in her hand. 'They're staunch teetotallers.'

He smiled one of his spine-loosening smiles as he raised his glass to hers in a toast. 'To the moral corruption of Dr Eloise Hayden from Australia,' he said.

She twisted her mouth at him. 'I'm not sure I should drink to that.'

He smiled at her over the top of his glass. 'You have some other suggestion?'

She touched her glass against his, the sound of it a little loud in the silence. 'To finding out the truth about Ethan Jenson's death,' she said.

He brought his glass to his lips, his eyes still holding hers.

Eloise felt the irresistible pull of his gaze and took another sip of wine to distract herself. She was a little stunned by her reaction to him. It was not her style at all to become infatuated with someone so quickly. She wondered if it was her hormones or something. He was undoubtedly one of the most attractive men she had encountered in a very long time but that didn't mean she had to fall into bed with him. Her fosterparents would be appalled to think she was considering having an affair with a divorced man. According to their beliefs, such a union was taboo and the fact he had a teenage daughter would make it a million times worse.

Not that she was considering having an affair with him or anyone, she quickly reassured herself. She was here to work, that's all. After all, a month was hardly long enough to get to know someone enough to make such a commitment.

She took another sip of wine, enjoying the black cherry and hint of cinnamon taste on her tongue, wondering if she should say something to break the little silence, but before she could think of something work related and safe, Lachlan swooped in under her defences and asked, 'So what happened to your real parents?'

CHAPTER SIX

ELOISE did her best to disguise the slight tremble of her hand as she lowered her glass to the kitchen counter. 'They died a long time ago.'

'How old were you?'

She tucked a strand of her hair behind one ear and lowered her eyes from the probe of his. 'I was eight...almost nine.'

'An accident?'

She met his eyes briefly. 'I'm not sure about my father,' she said, looking away again. 'I've never met him. I don't think my mother even knew who he was, actually.' She paused for a moment before adding, 'She died of a drug overdose.'

'That must have been a hard thing to deal with as a small child,' he said. 'Were there no other relatives to take you in?'

She gave him an embittered movement of her lips. 'Yes. I had grandparents but they hadn't spoken to my mother for years. They weren't interested in taking in her child. They considered me the spawn of the devil and wanted absolutely nothing to do with me.'

Lachlan frowned. 'You were an innocent child, for God's sake. How could they blame you for your mother's actions?'

'My mother dabbled with drugs during her teens and had me just after she turned eighteen. I think I was the result of a one-night stand with a dealer,' Eloise said in a tone stripped of emotion. 'She was a heroin addict by the age of twenty-one, Chief Inspector. I'm sure you've met plenty like her in your line of work, just as I have done. She slept with anyone she could to feed her habit. She died at the age of twenty-seven. She was three times my age at the time of her death but I always felt as if I was the adult.'

'How did you survive such an upbringing?' he asked.

She gave a little shrug. 'How does anyone survive?' she asked. 'You and I have both dealt with the other victims of crime—the relatives of the perpetrator. They live with the shame of what their loved ones have done. They become outcasts, untouchables if you like. My maternal grandparents considered me beyond redemption, having been exposed to such depravity for so long. They assumed I would turn out just like their daughter so to spare themselves further heartbreak they cut all ties with me.'

'Is that why you're on the other side of the law?' he asked. 'To prove a point to them so to speak?'

She let out a tiny sigh. 'I guess to some degree—yes. I wanted to show that no matter what background you come from you can rise above it if you have enough determination. I loved my mother but she had a problem that was too big to fix and I was far too young to help her. Knowing what I know now about addiction, and if I'd been even a little bit older, I could have got her into some sort of programme. It might have helped. I know it doesn't always but I like to think it would have in her case. I think she really wanted to get straight. She hated her life. She hated putting me through it but she was caught in a cycle of addiction that was too strong for her.'

In the small pause that ensued Eloise felt the warm pressure of his brown eyes on her. He didn't offer any useless platitudes but listened in a respectful silence that somehow gave her the courage to reveal more than she had ever done before—to anyone.

'My grandparents didn't want anything to do with her,' she carried on after another beat or two of silence. 'They were both well-to-do academics with high-profile lecturing positions at a Sydney university. They just couldn't cope with the shame of having their once academically brilliant daughter dropping out of her studies to have a child out of wedlock, let alone to go on to sell herself to get her next high. She stole from them and some of their friends so many times they eventually placed a restraining order on her.'

'I admire you for what you've achieved,' he said, his voice deep and gravelly. 'It must have taken a lot of guts to get where you've got.'

'My foster-parents were determined to do their bit to salvage me,' she said. 'They took me on as a sort of project, I think. I resented them for years, out of loneliness and frustration, I expect, but deep down I think they wanted the best for me, even if they didn't always feel entirely comfortable about my background.'

'Are you close to them?'

She gave another little shrug. 'No... I don't think anyone can ever take the place of your mother. My mother would never have made the first-round criteria of mother of the year or anything, but she loved me. I never doubted it. The trouble was, heroin got there first. It was her first priority and was until the day she died.'

'And here I am worrying about Poppy,' he said wryly. 'I need to get a grip or, as she says, take a chill pill.'

Eloise met his warm gaze. 'You have every right to worry about her,' she said. 'She's your daughter and you love her. She needs protecting. She's at that terribly vulnerable age—not quite an adult, not really a child. It must be hard, doing it alone.'

He gave her a twisted smile. 'To tell you the truth, I've often felt as if I've always been doing it on my own,' he said. 'Margaret never really wanted a child. We got caught out while we were dating. Contraception isn't always foolproof and certainly back then even less so. We were faced with the agonising decision of terminating or carrying on. I was twenty-three years old, she was twenty-two. We didn't have two pennies to rub together but somehow I managed to convince her to keep the baby.'

Eloise was surprised it had been him to do so. So often it was the man in the relationship who wanted the easy way out. It made her realise there was more to Lachlan D'Ancey than she had given him credit for.

'We got married later that summer,' he went on. 'It wasn't a happy marriage from the word go. Margaret had had her career path all mapped out and never let me forget it was my fault it had been thwarted. It was a difficult pregnancy and Poppy was an unsettled baby. We lived a long way from any relatives who might have helped out a bit. And of course my shift work didn't help. I never seemed to be there when she needed it most.'

'I'm sorry,' Eloise said. 'It must have been very hard for both of you. Are you on better terms now that you're divorced?'

He leaned back against the counter, cradling his glass in one hand. 'The bond of a child is not something you can sign away on the piece of paper that dissolves a marriage. Margaret sacrificed a lot in agreeing to go through with the pregnancy. She could have just as easily ignored my wishes and got on with her life, but she didn't and I will always admire her for that. But as for being friends…' He let out a breath that sounded as if it had come from deep within him. 'We're friends but not particularly close. Besides, it wouldn't be appropriate now that she has Roger as her partner.'

'How does Poppy get on with her mother's boyfriend?'

'She doesn't say much,' he answered. 'I think she worries it might upset me or something.' His mouth lifted in a smile as he added, 'I know she was a bit rude towards you this afternoon but I think she's really pretty keen on finding me a replacement.'

Eloise could feel her cheeks warming as he held her gaze. 'Why is that?' she asked. 'Most girls her age would prefer not to have to compete for their father's attention with another woman. I hear horror stories all the time over blended families and the rivalry that goes on. It can get pretty ugly, or so I'm told.'

'I know, I've seen it myself and, as you say, it can be *very* ugly.' He let out a little sigh and added, 'I've often thought Poppy might have been happier if she'd had a brother or sister, especially now that Margaret and I aren't together any more. She begged her mother for years to have another child but Margaret wouldn't hear of it.'

'What about you?' she asked, surprised yet again at her audacity at asking him such a personal question. 'Would you have liked another child?'

Lachlan gave the contents of his glass a little swirl, watching as the wine left a light film higher on the bowl of the glass. 'I grew up with two siblings, a younger brother and sister. We had a great time, playing in the back garden, building tree-houses, playing cricket or swimming in the stream at the back of the village green. I would have liked Poppy to have had a similar childhood, but it wasn't to be.'

'It's not too late,' she said. 'You could easily have another child or two.'

His eyes came back to hers, a mischievous twinkle lurking in the brown depths. 'Are you auditioning for the job, Dr Hayden?'

Eloise felt her cheeks flame all over again and to disguise her discomfiture said in a dismissive tone, 'And give up my career? I don't think so. I've worked too hard and for too long to stand in some man's kitchen barefoot and pregnant.'

'You know what they say about women who put their careers ahead of having a husband and family,' he said.

'Yes, I do, actually,' she answered curtly. 'They have freedom and lots of money and luxurious holidays without tears and tantrums.'

'They also end up lonely in their old age.'

'That's funny because I know plenty of married women with children who are desperately lonely,' she argued. 'They've spent their lives giving everything to their families, only to have them leave without a backward glance. Then to add insult to injury their husbands exchange them for a newer version. It totally stinks.'

'So you're not prepared to risk it?' he asked.

She let out a little almost inaudible sigh. 'I thought about it once...but it ended in tears.'

'Yours or his?'

Her eyes came back to his. 'I'd been warned before that dating a colleague was asking for trouble,' she said. 'I foolishly thought I could get away with it but it backfired horribly. As soon as word got out in our department that we were seeing each other, life became unbearable for both of us. I bailed out first.'

'How did he take it?'

She gave him a jaded look. 'He married a hairdresser three months later.'

He winced. 'That must have hurt.'

'Not as much as it probably should have,' she said. 'I guess if I'd really been in love with him I would have been devastated, but I wasn't. I went back to work the next day and sat down at the desk three away from his and carried on.'

'Have you ever been in love?' he asked, as he reached to top up her glass. 'As in weak-at-the-knees-heart thumping-can't-think-of-anything-else type of love?'

Eloise felt her whole body react as his hand briefly brushed against hers as he held her glass steady. She avoided his gaze, trying to get her heart rate to return to somewhere near normal, her stomach leaping and diving as she breathed in his male scent. That alluring hint of musk and citrus, the warmth of his body, the sheer bulk of it so close to hers, the impulse to reach out and touch the peppery shadow of evening growth on his lean jaw almost more than she could bear.

It must be the wine, she thought, eyeing it suspiciously as he poured it into her glass. Red wine was lethal when it came to self-control. It made people do things they wouldn't normally do. The relaxation of inhibitions, she saw it all the time in her line of work. Perfectly rational intelligent people did outrageous things under the influence of alcohol. She was clearly no different and would have to watch herself in future, especially around someone as seriously tempting as Lachlan D'Ancey.

'No,' she finally managed to croak out as she raised her glass to her lips. 'What about you?'

He held her gaze for several pulsating seconds. 'No,' he said. 'I'm a bit ashamed to say I didn't love Margaret in that way. I cared about her, I still do and very deeply, but I never felt like I couldn't live without her or anything. As I said, we got caught out and in another time and place we would never have ended up together.'

'But you have Poppy.'

He smiled a smile that totally transformed his features. 'Yes, I have Poppy.'

'And you would do anything to protect her, wouldn't you?'

Lachlan's brows came together in a wary frown. 'What exactly are you saying, Dr Hayden?'

'I'm saying that I am here to investigate a suspicious death,' she said. 'A death of a person it is alleged your daughter had an intimate relationship with in the days before he died.'

He put down his glass with a sharp little crack. 'That is hearsay, not a substantiated fact.'

'Not according to Robert Polgrean.'

'Robert is an eighteen-year-old boy who has fancied himself in love with my daughter for years,' he bit out.

'Davey Trevallyn saw Ethan Jenson and your daughter on the beach together,' she said. 'Beatrice told me.'

He threw his hands in the air in disgust. 'Beatrice Trevallyn believes everything her son tells her, but it doesn't mean a word of it is true. He's has learning difficulties, Dr Hayden. Please don't misunderstand me, I'm not discounting him as a person or even as a reliable witness, but you have to factor in that he is operating mentally at the age of about ten.'

'So you don't believe your daughter was seeing Ethan Jenson?'

He set his jaw. 'She told you herself, she met him once or twice.'

'So you don't think she was sleeping with him?'

He frowned at her darkly. 'What sort of question is that?' he asked. 'Of course she wasn't sleeping with him.'

'Had she been sleeping with Robert Polgrean?'

You're taking way too long to answer, Lachlan thought as Eloise's gaze penetrated his.

He hated to think of his little girl becoming intimate with anyone. Robert was about the only person he could envisage as a potential son-in-law but not until years had passed. But most fathers would feel the same about their daughters, he realised. Poppy was sixteen. Sure, she looked and acted a whole lot older but she was still—in his eyes at least—a little girl.

His little girl.

'No,' he said firmly.

Eloise gave a little snort of derision. 'Do you realise most teenage girls these days have had sex by the age of fourteen?'

'I know the statistics, Dr Hayden, but I also know my daughter,' he said. 'She's not the sleep-around type.'

'That's what every parent says. No one wants to think of their son or daughter being sexually active too early but hormones make it virtually impossible for most young people to resist temptation.'

'What about you, Dr Hayden?' he asked with a mocking smile. 'How are you at resisting temptation?'

Eloise tightened her mouth. 'We're not talking about me, Chief Inspector D'Ancey,' she clipped out. 'We're talking about your daughter. You say she's at a friend's house this evening, but what if she isn't? What if she lied to you so she could meet someone in secret, someone you might not approve of, such as Ethan Jenson?'

'Ethan Jenson is dead.'

Her chin came up. 'I know, but he wasn't a little over a week ago, was he?'

His brown gaze burned like a furnace, his expression nothing short of incredulous. 'Are you suggesting *I* had something to do with Ethan Jenson's death?'

'Kate Althorp told me there were a lot of fathers of teenage girls in the district who would be very glad he was out of the way. You could easily be one of them, irrespective of your standing in the community.'

'Those are very serious accusations,' he said. 'If I were you, I would be very careful who I voiced them to, otherwise you could find yourself in very deep water.'

Her eyes glinted challengingly as she held his heated gaze. 'Interesting choice of words, Chief Inspector, don't you think?'

His mouth flattened into a thin white line. A little flutter of alarm disturbed the lining of Eloise's stomach as he stepped towards her. She made to move backwards but came up against the pantry door, the small round knob of the handle digging into the middle of her back.

Then his eyes locked down on hers, glittering with sparks of anger, but there was something else that was far more dangerous.

Male desire…

CHAPTER SEVEN

'W-WHAT are you doing?' Eloise croaked as his body loomed closer.

'What do you think I'm doing?' he asked.

She swallowed and her wobbly belly did another little tumble turn as his chest almost but not quite brushed against hers. 'Stop it immediately.'

He raised his hands in the air. 'I'm not even touching you.'

She ran her tongue over the dryness of her lips. 'I can feel your body heat… That's…that's touching in my book.'

'I haven't read that particular book,' he said, his warm breath caressing her face as his hands came to rest either side of her head on the pantry door. 'Is it worth reading?'

Eloise was having trouble keeping focused on what he was saying. In fact, she was having trouble stringing two thoughts together in her head. All she could focus on was his mouth—his beautifully shaped mouth with its fuller bottom lip that she knew would be nothing short of sensual heaven pressing against hers. This close she could see each masculine pinpoint of dark stubble over his top lip, and the skin of her face began to tingle in anticipation of feeling its abrasiveness against the softness of her face. Her breasts felt tight and tender at the same time, their nipples suddenly aching for the press of his hands, the exploration of his fingers, the heat and fire of his tongue, and the primitive and enthralling scrape of his teeth.

She felt like her body was on fire. Flames were leaping between her legs, sending spot fires to every part of her body. Her brain was zinging with images of their bodies locked together in passion, his hard maleness buried in her feminine softness, the rocking motion of their sexual union making her femininity weep with desire to feel it for real instead of just imagining it.

She arched her back away from the pantry doorknob and her whole body jolted with sensual shock as her body came into full contact with his, from chest to pelvis.

His eyes fastened on hers.

Her heart came to a shuddering halt before kick-starting again with a series of out-of-beat heavy thuds.

Her mouth went dry.

His mouth was close, so close she could feel his breath moving over the achingly sensitive surface of her lips like an invisible feather being brushed along them.

'*You're* touching me,' he said, his voice sounding as if it had been scraped over a rough surface.

'It's the doorknob…' She hitched in a jagged breath. 'It was digging a hole in my back.'

He smiled crookedly. 'And here I was thinking you were coming onto me.'

'I wasn't coming onto you,' she said, knowing it was nothing but a bare-faced lie. She had never wanted a man to kiss her more in her entire life. Her lips burned with the need to feel the hard searching pressure of his. Surely he could see it? How could she hide her longing? It thrummed in her veins like a fast-flowing river of need, the pulse of it so strong it threatened to break through the tender barrier of her skin.

His eyes went to her mouth. 'Are you sure?'

She moistened her lips again. 'P-pretty sure...'

His smile widened. 'So you're in two minds about taking this one step further, are you, Dr Hayden from Australia?'

Eloise swallowed again, her throat feeling far too narrow and dry. 'You know what they say about mixing business and pleasure, Chief Inspector D'Ancey,' she said in a breathless whisper.

'What do they say?' he asked, bringing his mouth to just above hers.

'It's...it's dangerous...'

He cocked one brow. 'Dangerous? How so?'

'It makes things hazy...you know...it colours your judgement until you can't think straight. It's not very...er... professional...'

He very slowly reached to brush a wayward strand of her hair back from her mouth, and gently tucked it behind her ear. 'So you don't think we should continue with this?' he asked.

She compressed her lips just once to see if the tingling sensation would go away, but if anything it made it even worse. 'Um...' *Oh, God, why did he have to have such a kissable mouth?* she thought. It was so strong and yet so soft and so very close to hers.

Way too close.

And his hands were so long fingered and masculine and yet gentle at the same time. She could almost imagine them skating over her naked skin, touching her, shaping her until she was a mindless pool of need.

'Are you usually so indecisive, Dr Hayden?' he asked with another bone-melting smile.

'I'm not sure...'

He laughed and stepped back from her. 'I promised you

dinner. I'd better get on with it. What do you fancy? I have some fresh fish Timmy Ennor dropped in earlier or I can rustle up an omelette.'

Eloise blinked once or twice to reorient herself. *He was talking about food at a time like this?* Wasn't he the least bit affected by that little interlude? Her heart was still doing star-jumps in her chest while he was preparing to toss a salad.

Men!

Who could make them out? They must have some sort of on-off switch when it came to desire. Hers was still silently smouldering, threatening to blow the circuit board of her body every time he looked her way.

'Um…whatever is fine…' she mumbled.

She watched as he began assembling ingredients on the kitchen counter, her heart rate still struggling to find its normal rhythm.

She had never met anyone like Lachlan D'Ancey before. He made her feel like an incompetent junior colleague one minute and a melting female wanton the next. She wondered if he was leading her on deliberately, toying with her to see how far he could go. She knew plenty of men who were like that. They saw female colleagues as easy targets, someone to pass the time with, a supposedly harmless affair to break the boredom of routine investigations. It wouldn't be the first time two colleagues thrown together on a case ended up intimately involved with each other. Emotions ran high during certain investigations. Life-and-death situations often triggered the most primal of all responses which later on, when things cooled down, were nearly always seriously regretted. She knew of at least three marriages that had broken up as a result of such affairs that on a different day might not have occurred.

Her life was complicated enough as it was. She had plans

for her future that held little room for intimate attachments. And even though a secret part deep inside of her longed for the security of a loving long-term relationship, the thought of bringing a child or two into the world that held so many dangers terrified her. What if she had a little Jessica, for instance?

A vision of Jessica's mother's grief-stricken face swam before her eyes.

Lachlan turned around from the refrigerator to see Eloise looking vacantly into space, her expression haunted with shadows he could see reflected in her china-blue eyes.

'So why did you take on this particular case?' he asked, handing her the glass of wine she'd abandoned earlier. 'It wasn't just about the prospects of a promotion, was it?'

She appeared to give herself a mental shake as she took the wine from him. She looked into the contents of the glass for a moment before answering in a soft tone. 'No, not really, although I do want to move up the career ladder. I had a tough case I had to deal with some months ago. I haven't found it easy to move on.'

'Do you want to talk about it?'

She gave him a rueful smile. 'If I thought talking would bring back to life a not quite two-year-old girl and hand her back to her totally devastated mother then, yes, I'd talk until the cows came home, but it won't, will it?'

Lachlan placed a bowl of salad to the table. 'I had to head the investigation of a case of two missing twelve-year-old boys a few years back. It was the biggest search with over four hundred officers involved. It went on for over a month and covered several counties.'

'Did you find them?'

He gave her a grim look. 'A junior officer eventually found them inside a concrete bridge pylon. They had obviously fallen in the day they were reported missing. No one heard their cries for help.'

'Oh, God...'

He blew out a ragged sigh. 'The forensics team had a hard time of it. The younger one working on the case later committed suicide. He couldn't handle the images in his head from being at the scene.'

Eloise gulped back a swallow. 'How do you handle it? The images of what you have to see and do?'

He pulled out a chair for her to sit down. 'I do what most other police officers do. We have a drink and a debriefing chat that at some point usually involves some sort of black humour before returning home to our homes and pretending everything's normal.'

'But it isn't, is it?' she asked softly. 'It can never be normal.'

'No, but if we allow it to invade our every waking moment, we'd all end up like that young forensics guy. We have a job to do and, yes, it's not always pretty or even very rewarding at times, but it has to be done.'

Eloise sat on the chair and laid her serviette across her lap. 'Did you ever consider any other career?' she asked.

He smiled as he placed a salad on the table. 'I think for a time my parents hoped I'd follow in my father's footsteps but I was never really interested in becoming a doctor.'

'Why was that?'

'I had a slight run-in with a cop when I was fifteen,' he said. 'It was nothing serious—it was just a bit of a lark on my part. He could have hauled me over the coals for it but instead he sat me down at the station and talked to me about choices, how the choices we make in our youth seal our fate in adulthood. It really made an impression on me. If he'd ranted and raved and threatened jail, it wouldn't have been half as effective.'

'Is that why you have a reputation for being fairly easy-going?' she asked. 'Kate Althorp said you were greatly admired in the community.'

'I uphold the law but I don't hit people over the head with it unless it's warranted,' he said. 'Brian, for instance, the kid who was in the alley with Robert? He's not a bad kid. He's got a rough sort of background. His father's a drunk who comes and goes when he feels like it and his mother struggles periodically with depression. Brian doesn't need detention, he needs attention, he's crying out for it. That's why he hangs around with Gary Lovelace's gang of youths. He longs to belong somewhere to someone, even if they're less than desirable.'

Eloise couldn't help feeling impressed with his take on things. So many of her male colleagues relished in brandishing the power their position afforded them. Lachlan, however, seemed to really understand the issues in young people's lives, perhaps because he was the father of a teenager himself.

'What about you?' he asked. 'Do you have a sure-fire way of dealing with things?'

She toyed with her wineglass as she thought about it. 'I exercise a bit, walking mostly. I've never been much of a gym bunny, I'm afraid. I like to be alone to process things.'

'Sounds good to me. I do the same. There are some great walks through the farming districts. The roads are narrow but there's not much traffic.'

She gave him another wry smile. 'I don't suppose your daughter has a pair of walking shoes in my size she could lend me till my luggage arrives?'

He smiled back. 'My daughter's idea of sport is lying on the beach, looking at the surfers. I'm not even sure if she owns a pair of trainers. If she does, I can assure you they've never been used.'

'She's very beautiful.'

'She takes after her mother.'

A pang of something that felt like jealousy suddenly stabbed at Eloise's insides. She knew she wasn't exactly in danger of stopping any clocks or anything but neither did she consider herself model material. Her figure was trim and her features classical enough to be considered attractive, but she never felt comfortable without a bit of make-up on. She wasn't sure why she felt that way. Her foster-mother thought it was vain and frowned in disapproval at the very hint of lip-gloss but Eloise had stuck to her guns and used both make-up and perfume to remind herself she was still a woman, even if she was working in what was still considered predominately a man's world.

'Would you like more wine?' Lachlan asked, holding up the bottle.

Eloise twisted her mouth. 'You know what they say about wine, Chief Inspector D'Ancey.'

He grinned at her. 'I do, actually. Erasmus said it. "*In vino veritas*" —in wine there is truth.'

She smiled. 'I'm impressed. I didn't know you were a Latin scholar.'

'I studied it at school,' he said. 'You mentioned you went to a convent school. What was that like?'

'It was strict but the nuns were generally very nice. I had a favourite, Sister Patricia. She was younger than the others and, while not exactly progressive, she always made me feel as if I was special in some way.'

'I am sure you were and still are special.'

Eloise felt her cheeks grow warm. 'She also warned me about men like you,' she said, looking at him from beneath her lashes.

He lifted his eyebrows in a guileless manner. *'Moi?'*

'You're a natural flirt, Chief Inspector D'Ancey and I'm not going to fall for it,' she said primly.

'You think I'm flirting with you?'

She tried her best to frown at him. 'Aren't you?'

He smiled that boyish smile again. 'I'm probably horribly out of practice but, yes, I am and I'm enjoying it immensely. You blush like a schoolgirl every time I look at you.'

She looked down at her plate rather than meet his eyes. 'I'm a bit out of practice, too,' she admitted. 'I really don't mean to give you the wrong impression. I told you before, I'm not here to have a quick fling.'

'If you change your mind, put me at the top of the list of potential candidates.'

She rolled her eyes at him. 'You really need to work on your pick-up lines,' she said. 'That was totally pathetic.'

'Was it?' He chuckled as he handed her the salad dressing. 'I thought that was going to have you fall for me before dessert for sure.'

'Dessert?' Her blue eyes began to sparkle. 'Now, that *is* a pick-up line. What did you have in mind?'

'I'm not sure if I should tell you,' he said. 'You might think I was coming onto to you.'

'Aren't you?'

'What do you think?'

That was the whole trouble, Eloise thought. She didn't know what to think. Her normally rational-do-it-by-the-book mind had been scrambled ever since she'd set eyes on Chief Inspector Lachlan D'Ancey. He rattled her in every way possible. She had never experienced anything like it before in her life. Her brief encounter with Bill had been nothing compared to this. Bill had not moved her quite the way Lachlan's smiles had done.

And even though she kept telling herself Lachlan was divorced with a teenage daughter who, according to Eloise's gut feeling, was somehow involved in the case she was supposed to be investigating, all that seemed to be secondary to what was going on between them now.

She felt it like a pulse in the room. The air was thick and heavy with it.

Attraction.

Male and female.

Uncontrollable.

Forbidden and dangerous.

Irresistible.

'I have some raspberries from Rona Troon's farm,' he said breaking the tension. 'And some wickedly sinful clotted cream from the Hendry dairy farm. Are you tempted?'

'I'm seriously tempted,' Eloise said, but somehow she felt sure that Chief Inspector D'Ancey knew she wasn't talking about raspberries and cream.

CHAPTER EIGHT

'WOULD YOU LIKE a coffee, Dr Hayden?' Lachlan asked as he began to clear their dessert plates from the table.

'No, thank you, and, please, call me Eloise,' she said.

'But not Ellie, right?'

She frowned and rose to help him with clearing the table. 'No...'

'Is that what your mother called you?'

Her hand froze on the glass she had reached to lift from the table. She took a steadying breath and lifted her eyes back to his. 'I just prefer Eloise.'

'Too many bad memories?'

'Now who's playing detective?' she asked with a sharp edge to her tone.

His eyes met hers in a challenge. 'You're a closed book, Eloise Hayden, and I don't like closed books.'

'Tough,' she said with a toss of her head. 'I'm not here to tell you my life story. I'm here to investigate Ethan Jenson's death.' She reached for her purse and key to Trevallyn House. 'Thank you for dinner. I think it's probably time for me to get back to the guest-house.'

'I'll walk you back and don't waste your breath arguing with me.'

'I don't need an escort,' she threw back. 'It's barely four blocks from here.'

'It might only be four streets away but you are a single woman in a village you don't know.'

'I'm trained in self-defence.'

His mouth tilted mockingly. 'You're what? Five foot six and weigh about a hundred and ten pounds, if that. You wouldn't have a hope of fending off an attacker bigger than you.'

She pulled her shoulders back, her eyes glinting with determination. 'All right,' she said. 'I'll prove it. Try and get me in a head lock.'

He looked at her incredulously. 'You're surely not serious?'

She lifted her chin. 'Go on, Chief Inspector. Give it to me. I'll show you how I can—*Oomph!*'

Eloise realised later she'd really had no hope of getting out of *that* particular hold. She didn't even think of trying. As soon as Lachlan's mouth came down and captured hers, every single self-defence manoeuvre was wiped from her brain like a virus did to a computer hard drive.

His lips moved over the surface of hers with almost lazy intent, as if he had all the time in the world and he knew no one—least of all her—was going to stop him. His tongue stroked for entry, just the once, and her lips opened on a sigh, her belly quivering at that first deliciously intimate intrusion. She felt each delve and dive of his tongue as it searched every corner of her mouth before mating with her tongue, stabbing at it, stroking it, sucking on it, sweeping over it until she was sagging against him with legs that refused to hold her upright.

His hands moved from the tops of her shoulders to her waist, pulling her closer so she could feel the hard surge of his body against her.

It had been *so* long since she had felt a man's response to her and it both thrilled and terrified her. She wasn't ready for this. This wasn't supposed to be happening. Not now. Not here. Not in Cornwall when she was working on what could turn out to be the biggest case of her career. She was supposed to be in control. She wasn't supposed to go all weak and watery at the knees just because a very attractive man decided he wanted to prove a point. Although he was proving it rather convincingly, she had to admit. Her mouth felt as if someone had set it alight. Fireworks were going off in her head and her body was melting like ice cream left out in the hot midday sun.

His tongue did another round of her mouth, but this time his hands moved from her waist and cupped her bottom and tugged her even closer to his hardness. She had no hope of resisting that little manoeuvre either. She rubbed herself up against him, her inner thighs trembling at the thought of him driving between them and exploding with the blistering passion she could feel was banked up in him.

'I hate to interrupt, but can you do that somewhere else?' Poppy's voice sounded from the doorway leading into the kitchen. 'It's totally gross.'

Eloise sprang out of Lachlan's arms so quickly she almost fell over. She clutched at the nearest surface and steadied herself, but she had no hope of controlling the rapid tide of red-hot colour that stormed into her cheeks.

Lachlan ran a hand through his hair but unlike Eloise he seemed totally at ease with the situation, which made Eloise wonder how many women he'd brought home before.

'I thought you were staying overnight at Fiona's?' he said. 'You should have called and I would have picked you up. I hope you didn't walk home alone.'

'*Da-ad.*' Poppy rolled her eyes. 'I do know how to protect myself, you know.'

'Well, I certainly hope you aren't considering taking self-defence lessons from Dr Hayden,' he quipped, with a teasing glance in Eloise's direction.

Eloise glared back at him. 'You took me by surprise, that's all,' she said hotly.

He gave her a playful grin. 'You didn't even put up a token fight.'

'I didn't want to hurt you,' she said, scowling at him. 'I could have blackened your eye or broken your wrist or something.'

'While you two get on with pretending you're not seriously attracted to each other, I'm going to bed,' Poppy announced.

Lachlan frowned as he noticed how pale his daughter looked. 'Are you all right, sweetheart?' he asked gently.

Poppy's eyes began to water but she quickly brushed at them with the back of her hand. 'I wanted to talk to Mum,' she said. 'I called her earlier but she was busy and hasn't bothered to call me back.'

'Honey, you know how hard she works,' Lachlan said. 'She probably got tied up with some important clients or something.'

'You don't have to pretend with me,' Poppy said churlishly. 'I know you hate her so there's no point in playing the understanding ex-husband.'

'I do *not* hate your mother,' Lachlan insisted. 'We've been through all this before, Poppy. I know it's hard getting used to living with just me instead of both of us but you have to move on. We both do. Your mother and I are not getting back together. We weren't even together all the years we lived here, not in the real sense.'

'I know…' Poppy's shoulders slumped as she turned away. 'I'm going to bed.'

'You could at least say goodnight to Dr Hayden,' Lachlan said.

'It's fine,' Eloise said. 'Let her be, Chief Inspector.'

Poppy turned to face Eloise. 'You called him Chief Inspector. Don't you know his name?'

'Yes, I do but I—'

'If you're going to sleep with him, you should at least know his first name,' Poppy cut her off rudely.

'I wasn't planning on sleeping with your father,' Eloise said with deliberate firmness. 'I only met him for the first time earlier today.'

'That didn't stop you from kissing him.'

'He kissed me,' Eloise said somewhat defensively. 'I had no intention of—'

'Was he any good?' Poppy cut her off again.

'Poppy, I hardly think—' Lachlan began.

Eloise lifted her chin and held the young girl's challenging brown gaze. 'Yes, he was, actually,' she said. 'Better than good.'

Poppy's eyes went wide. 'Really?'

'Yes,' Eloise answered. 'Up there with the best, actually.'

Poppy turned to her father. 'Are you going to have an affair with her?' she asked.

'I'm seriously considering it,' he answered with a tilt of his mouth.

'Ahem…' Eloise gave them both a pointed look. 'I think I might be the one to decide that.'

'Have you decided?' Poppy asked.

'No, and I don't think I—'

'If you do happen to sleep with my father, don't assume we're going to be best friends or anything,' Poppy said. 'I don't need another mother—I have a perfectly good one of my own.'

'Lucky you,' Eloise said. 'I don't have a mother or a father.'

Poppy's expression visibly softened in contrition. 'Oh… sorry… I didn't realise…'

'It's fine,' Eloise said. 'I learned to accept it a long time ago.'

'You must think I'm a spoilt brat,' Poppy said, shifting from foot to foot.

'I understand that you are dealing with some pretty heavy stuff right now,' Eloise said. 'The divorce of your parents and the unexpected death of an acquaintance is hardly a walk in the park.'

Poppy chewed at her bottom lip without answering, but Eloise observed how the young girl's cheeks had heightened in colour at the mention of Ethan Jenson's death.

Lachlan bent down to kiss his daughter on the cheek. 'I'm just going to walk Dr Hayden back to the guest-house. Will you be OK while I'm gone?'

Tears shone in Poppy's eyes as she looked up at her father. Eloise saw the way the girl's throat moved up and down and the way her body began to tremble.

Lachlan enveloped her in his arms and held her close. 'What is it, Poppy? Has someone upset you? Or hurt you in some way?'

She shook her head against his chest. 'No, I'm just a bit emotional right now. Everyone's talking about Ethan Jenson's death. There are rumours going about that he was murdered.' She lifted her head and looked up at him. 'He wasn't, was he, Dad?'

'You know I can't discuss police business with you, sweetheart,' he said gently. 'But so far the verdict is death by drowning.'

'Drowning is bad enough,' Poppy sniffed. 'But murder is much worse. It means someone is out there who wanted him dead. What if they want someone else dead? Who is going to stop them?'

'Do you want to go and stay with your mother for a few days until things settle down?' he asked.

Poppy gnawed at her bottom lip again, looking more like a child of six than a well-developed sixteen-year-old. 'No,' she said on the back end of a sigh. 'I want to spend some time with Robert. I sort of promised him we'd go on a picnic to the smugglers' caves.'

'I thought you weren't seeing him any more?' Eloise said before she could stop herself.

Poppy frowned as she turned to look at her, her expression colouring again. 'Did he tell you that?'

Eloise nodded. 'Your father and I spoke with him earlier this evening. He had a slight altercation with some youths in the alley behind the Penhally Arms.'

Poppy looked worried. 'Is he all right?'

'He's fine,' Lachlan answered. 'Nick Tremayne had to give him a couple of stitches but apart from that he'll be as good as new in the morning.'

Poppy's shoulders drooped with exhaustion as she headed for the stairs. 'Sorry for disturbing you. You can get back to what you were doing now. I'm going to bed.'

'We weren't doing anything,' Eloise felt compelled to say.

Poppy's mouth stretched into a little smile. 'Maybe I will book in for some self-defence classes with you, Dr Hayden,' she said. 'They look like fun.'

'Go to bed, you obnoxious brat,' Lachlan growled.

Eloise picked up her bag for the second time once Poppy had disappeared upstairs. 'I really must go,' she said. 'Beatrice Trevallyn will think I've come to a perilous end, like the last Australian to visit the village.'

Lachlan opened the door for her. 'Can you swim?' he asked. 'I don't mean the English Channel but enough to save yourself.'

'Of course I can swim,' she answered. 'I can assure you,

Chief Inspector D'Ancey, that I am in absolutely no danger of drowning.'

'That's good to know,' he said as he led the way down the path to the street. 'The last thing this place needs is another accidental death.'

She waited until they had walked a few paces before speaking again. 'Poppy seemed very upset. Do you think it was just about the rumours about Ethan Jenson's death?'

He took a moment to answer. 'I think everyone is upset about Ethan Jenson's death, rumours notwithstanding. The sooner this case is wrapped up, the better.'

Eloise couldn't help thinking he was keen to get rid of her, irrespective of his kiss. It might not take him long to forget about her once she was back in Sydney behind her cluttered desk, but she knew it would very likely take her the rest of her life to forget how it felt to have his mouth on hers.

'About that kiss...' he said into the silence broken only by the whisper of the silvery sea as it stroked against the shore in lace-fringed waves.

'I've forgotten all about it,' she said.

'Liar.'

'You only did it to prove a point.'

'It was extremely enjoyable.'

She turned to glance at him. 'The kiss or proving the point?'

He grinned down at her. 'No harm in a little bit of both, don't you think?'

She narrowed her eyes at him. 'I felt extremely embarrassed in front of your daughter.'

'Don't worry. She's used to it.'

Her disapproving frown increased. 'Used to you proving a point or bringing home strange women and kissing them senseless in your kitchen?'

He stopped and smiled down at her. 'Did I kiss you senseless?'

She pursed her lips. 'I'm not going to answer that.'

He chuckled and began to move on, taking her by the elbow with the cup of his palm. 'If you didn't send out all those sexy signals all the time, I wouldn't dream of kissing you.'

She snorted derisively. 'That is just so typical of men like you. You think because a woman comes over for a drink or a meal it means they want to hop into bed with you. I haven't hopped into bed with a man for longer than I can remember and I'm not going to do it just because you're…you're…'

He grinned down at her. 'I'm what? Single and available?'

'Single and attractive.'

'You think I'm attractive?'

'You know you are,' she said. 'You're tall and dark and handsome. I know it's a cliché but a lot of women really go for that look.'

'Anything else?'

'You care about people—your daughter, for instance. I don't even know who my father is and he's certainly made no effort to find me in the last thirty-two years of my life, so in my book you rate pretty high on the good father monitor.'

'What else?'

She turned to look up at him again. 'You're divorced from your wife but you've never once said a bad word about her. I admire that in a man. So many of the men I've met take every opportunity to vilify their ex-partners.'

'Wow, praise indeed from the uptight Dr Eloise Hayden from Australia.'

She frowned at him. 'You think I'm uptight?'

'I think you need to chill out a little, Eloise,' he said.

'I suppose by chilling out you mean I should have a full-on fling with you while I'm here to make things really interesting.'

His brown eyes twinkled at her. 'It would certainly make things very interesting for the locals.'

'I don't want to be the subject of local gossip.'

'You've definitely come to the wrong place if you want to avoid that,' he said. 'It will be all over the village by morning that we had dinner together. Most people will assume our dinner led to other more satisfying activities.'

She frowned at him sourly. 'Because of your womanising reputation?'

'No,' he said, running his gaze over her stained vest top and close-fitting jeans. 'Because you don't fit the stereotype of the career-woman at all.'

'I look completely different when I'm dressed in a suit.'

'I'd prefer to see you in nothing at all.'

Eloise's jaw dropped open. 'Chief Inspector D'Ancey you are being *highly* inappropriate.'

'I know, but I enjoy seeing you blush,' he said with a teasing smile. 'That was some kiss, though, wasn't it?'

She had to look away from his dancing-with-merriment eyes. 'It was all right, I guess.'

'All right?' He made a sound of affronted pride. 'I gave it my best shot. If Poppy hadn't turned up when she did, I think we might have taken it a step further.'

She gave him a schoolmistress sort of look from beneath her brows. 'You think.'

He gave her a tiny tap on the end of her uptilted nose with one finger. 'I know, Dr Hayden,' he said with a confident smile. 'I know.'

CHAPTER NINE

ELOISE'S INABILITY to fall into a decent sleep had nothing whatsoever to do with her lingering jet-lag, she decided as she tossed and turned till dawn. Lachlan had delivered her to the door of the guest-house and under the cover of darkness had pressed a barely-there kiss to her mouth before leaving her standing there aching for more.

She gave the pillow another hard thump and groaned in frustration. Her lips still felt tingly and her body restless and the sound of Mr Price's laptop computer being pecked at in the early hours of the morning certainly hadn't helped her to relax.

Peck. Peck. Peck. Peck.

It reminded her of Lachlan's pen as he'd sat opposite her...had it really only been a few hours ago? So much seemed to have happened since then.

The pecking of the computer finally stopped and she closed her eyes, willing herself to sleep, when she heard Mr Price speaking into what she assumed was a Dictaphone.

'The killer had stalked the victim relentlessly for months, day and night, like a shadow of evil cast over her, always

there, always invisible but always there. She knew it. She felt it. She sensed it. She even smelt it.'

Eloise buried her head under another pillow and gave another groan.

The County Coroner's Office was located in part of the police headquarters complex in Wadebridge. Eloise had declined Lachlan's offer the night before to drive her there as she wanted to familiarise herself with the area. She also felt the need to re-establish her professional persona. Spending so much time with him the day before had upended her normally rigidly adhered-to priorities.

Dr Peter Middleton, the chief pathologist of Wadebridge County, greeted Eloise as she arrived and introduced her to his assistant, Dr Grant Yates.

'I am sure you have been sent on a bit of a fool's errand, Dr Hayden,' Peter Middleton said as he led the way to the autopsy room. 'I found nothing to suggest anything other than death by drowning.'

'I'm not necessarily here to prove you and Dr Yates wrong,' Eloise said. 'The family deserves to have a second opinion, even if it proves in the end to be the same as yours.'

'I am very sure it will be,' Peter Middleton said with the type of arrogance Eloise loathed seeing in a colleague. 'Morning, Chief Inspector,' he added, as Lachlan peeled himself away from the wall where he had been waiting for them to arrive. 'This is wasting your valuable time as well.'

'That remains to be seen,' Lachlan said, exchanging a quick glance with Eloise.

Eloise pressed her lips together and followed them into the autopsy room where Peter handed them both theatre scrubs.

'You can show Dr Hayden where the change rooms are,' he said to Lachlan.

'Come this way,' Lachlan said and led her to the corridor outside. 'It's the first door on the right. I'll wait for you here.'

Eloise changed into the scrubs and left her things on the hooks behind the door. She allowed herself one quick glance in the mirror and then wished she hadn't. She looked younger than Poppy with no make-up on, her hair flat and her eyes shadowed with tiredness.

She blew out a little breath and went back out to the corridor, where Lachlan was standing dressed in scrubs, again leaning against the wall in that lazy, I've-got-all-the-time-in-the-world manner of his.

'Ready?' he asked, with a little smile of reassurance.

She nodded briskly but inside her stomach was already churning. As much as she loved her work, she hated doing autopsies on young people. It was hard enough doing one on an older person, but when it was someone who hadn't had a chance to live even a quarter of their life it struck at the very heart of her. She felt for the families, the agony of loss they would go through for the rest of their lives, every birthday, every Christmas, and worst of all the anniversary of their loved one's death.

When they re-entered the autopsy room the body had already been wheeled in and placed on a stainless-steel bench in the centre of the room. The overhead lights were switched on, as was the camera to record the autopsy. The microphone Eloise was to use to record her comments was set up and ready to go.

She automatically looked up to the side of the light assembly where a sign in Latin was routinely placed in autopsy rooms across the globe. Somehow it comforted her to find it there.

Hic locus est ubi mors gaudet succurrere vitae. Here a place where death gladly teaches the living.

Around the outside of the room were the usual benches with empty specimen jars, chemical containers, a microscope and a large collection of surgical instruments.

Donning gloves, plastic apron, mask and eye shield, Eloise clicked a button on the floor and started dictating into the overhead microphone, Grant Yates moving forward to help her turn the body as needed.

'External examination,' she began. 'Body of a Caucasian male aged twenty-seven, blonde hair, no external marks of trauma. Incisions from previous autopsy consist of midline thoracoabdominal incision and circumferential scalp incision, both closed with silk sutures. External evidence of prolonged immersion in water from skin wrinkling.'

She took a deep breath and tried to rid her mind of images of that young strong body riding some of the toughest waves the world's oceans could throw up. He had been a good-looking young man, his sun-bleached blond hair, tanned skin and leanly muscled form no doubt a huge drawcard for women across the globe.

She couldn't help wondering if Poppy D'Ancey had indeed experienced a brief fling with him. He had been a lot older than her, of course, but Eloise knew young girls were often attracted to older men. Poppy was a mixture of little girl and sultry siren so it seemed likely Ethan Jenson would have taken what was on offer, in spite of what Lachlan thought.

She looked up to see him watching her, those brown eyes steady on hers, that same reassuring look he'd sent her earlier softening his gaze even more. After their first disastrous encounter she never for one moment would have thought she'd be glad he was here with her. But she was.

'Dr Middleton, I noted from your report that the lungs were full of seawater but that there was no pulmonary oedema from your biopsy. Can you show me from where you took the biopsy?'

The previously removed lungs had been replaced in the thoracic cavity, which was now being spread apart by a retractor inserted by Dr Middleton.

'Yes,' he said. 'From the base of the left lung. There's the incision.'

'Tell me, Dr Middleton, was there anything in the main airways when they were opened?' she asked.

'Seawater, full of seawater, and lots of it.'

'Was there any froth in the airway?' Eloise asked.

In her extensive experience with drowning victims from Australian beaches, usually the victim struggled in the last minutes to get breath. As seawater mixed with mucus in the airway it tended to froth, making breathing even harder and often accelerating the drowning process.

'No froth, just seawater.'

'I wonder if we could take some samples near the end of the bronchi?' she asked. 'I want to see if any foreign material has been aspirated.'

'Foreign material?' Peter Middleton looked at her scathingly. 'What on earth do you think you might find? A school of fish?'

Eloise tightened her mouth without responding and continued with her work. Having taken several more samples of lung tissue for histological examination, she then turned her attention to the diatom testing.

'Dr Middleton, those diatom samples from the lungs—could you tell me how you collected those?' she asked.

'Well, from that briny water in the trachea, of course. I examined them myself. Why, do you think they are wrong?'

'There are a couple of curious features about them, that's all,' she replied, trying to be polite in spite of his brusque manner. 'Did you prepare the sample yourself for microscopy?'

There was a small pause before he answered. 'No, as a matter of fact, I think in this case one of the *deiners*—Michael, I think it was, may have got the samples ready. He's unfortunately not with us now. His mother, who lives in Canada, had a stroke and he's taken leave.'

'Well, from your description of the diatoms, it seems like there may have been freshwater contamination of the samples, maybe from washing or some other slip-up in sample preparation. I'd like to try and get more of that water out of the lungs, and also take a range of samples from other body tissues for diatom analysis. And I'd also like to do a quantitative analysis. Chief Inspector D'Ancey is organising some samples from the drowning site for comparison.'

Eloise looked up at that point and found Lachlan's gaze on her. He gave her a glimmer of a smile as if to reassure her.

She turned back to the body of the young man and began taking multiple tissue samples from several organs. She then worked with Peter Middleton and his assistant to prepare slides and the diatom samples for microscopy, all under her direct supervision.

In addition, she collected blood from the inferior vena cava for carbon monoxide analysis. The lab possessed a gas analyser, so all the testing could be completed within a few days.

Finally the body was sewn back together, using basketball stitch, and returned to the drawer where it had been stored.

'Time for a break,' Peter Middleton said, stripping off his

gloves. 'Grant, can you organise some coffee? I just need to make a couple of calls.'

Lachlan came over to where Eloise was tidying up. 'How are you holding up?' he asked.

She straightened her shoulders. 'I'm perfectly fine. Why do you ask?'

'You looked upset.'

'I can assure you I'm not.'

'Then you should be,' he said. 'Every death is upsetting, none more so than when it's a young person.'

'I seem to remember you saying last night that police officers had to remain clinically detached, or words to that effect,' she said stubbornly, refusing to show that she was indeed feeling emotionally drained.

'You can't shut down completely, Eloise,' he said. 'It's neither healthy nor normal.'

She gave him a direct look. 'So you're admitting to shedding a tear or two behind your mask for Ethan Jenson, are you?'

'I'm admitting that death in a young person is always a tragedy, no matter who they are,' he said. 'Have you arranged to meet his parents yet?'

'No, they haven't requested it so I thought I would wait until the results are in.'

'They will want to see you well before that, Dr Hayden,' he said, and turned away, leaving her standing there alone with the scent of death lingering in the air.

Eloise spent an hour with Ethan Jenson's parents at their request the following day, her heart aching for what they were going through. The pain of their loss was etched on their faces, their eyes red and swollen from endless crying and their cheeks hollowed out with anguish. She expressed her sympathy and did her best to reassure them that the tests she had conducted would hopefully provide them with some sort of closure during such a harrowing time.

'Thank you for coming all this way,' Hugh Jenson said as Eloise prepared to leave. 'We really appreciate the effort you've made to find out the truth about our son's death.'

Eloise took each of their hands in turn. 'As soon as we find out the results of the tests, the chief inspector will contact you,' she said. 'It may take another day or two. I'm sorry you've had to wait so long. I know how hard it makes it, having things drawn out like this.'

'We just want to know the truth,' Jeanne Jenson said, wiping at her eyes. 'I know Ethan wasn't an angel but people are saying things about him that are very upsetting. I won't be able to rest until I know for sure if someone…you know…' she choked over another sob '…did away with him.'

Eloise spent the next few days exploring the local countryside as she waited for the lab tests to be processed. She didn't hear from Lachlan, although she saw him once or twice in the distance, talking to one of the local fishermen by the harbour. On one occasion he lifted his hand in a wave when he caught her staring at him but she quickly turned on her heel and pretended she hadn't seen him. She felt she needed these few days to make some sort of sense of the ambiguity of her feelings towards him and it would only confuse her even more to spend time interacting with him. But avoiding him only made her think of him all the more. She lay awake at night, listening to the pecking of Mr Price in the room next door, and wondered what Lachlan was doing. She walked along the sandy shore each day, listening to the smacking and sucking of the waves, and wondered if he was thinking of how her mouth had felt beneath the heated pressure of his.

Stop it, she remonstrated as she stomped back towards the café on the Harbour Front at the end of the week. She had to stop thinking about a man who was probably just toying with her for a bit of fun. What could he offer her in terms of a relationship anyway? He lived on the opposite side of the globe, for one thing, and the other was…well, she didn't want to fall in love with anyone, much less a recently divorced single dad who had a troubled teenager on his hands.

She had not long been served her coffee when she looked up and saw Poppy come into the café with a friend.

Poppy's red-rimmed eyes briefly met Eloise's gaze before falling away. She murmured something to the girl beside her then they both turned around and left without so much as a greeting.

Eloise could understand Lachlan's reluctance to have his young daughter involved in this case, and while she understood the protocol that prevented her from interviewing witnesses or suspects, she couldn't help sensing something was amiss and would have loved a quiet moment or two—off the record—with the chief inspector's daughter.

Her mobile phone rang just as she drained the last of her coffee and Peter Middleton's voice informed her, 'I have the results from Forensics Services, Dr Hayden. They came in a few moments ago. I thought you might like to meet me at the lab and see them for yourself.'

An hour or so later, Eloise looked up from her microscope. Peter Middleton was sitting next to her, still looking down the second eyepiece of the lab microscope.

'Well, Dr Hayden, this certainly changes things, doesn't it?' he said after a moment.

'It appears so, Dr Middleton,' she said. 'What we have here

now are clear signs of foul play. The diatom test is negative for all tissues, only positive for the water in the lungs. There is clearly foreign matter, looking remarkably like feathers, in the peripheral airways, and the carbon monoxide levels are very high. I would say Ethan Jenson was well and truly dead by the time he hit the water—dead from a combination of smothering and carbon monoxide. He was in the water for at least six hours, but he didn't die from drowning. I'd say he was put into the water about midnight, if he was found around six a.m. the next morning.'

Dr Middleton took off his glasses and leaned back in his chair, his normally curt, no-nonsense manner disappearing completely. 'I guess I have an apology to make.'

'You don't need to apologise, Dr Middleton,' Eloise said with a gracious smile. 'I've had this same experience myself. You make unconscious assumptions and do what seem to be the appropriate investigations—they lead to what seem like reasonable conclusions and then someone comes in from outside, takes a fresh look, and says, "What about this or that?" and suddenly your assumptions look shaky. We've had some famous cases in Australia that have blown up on the basis of external reviews of the evidence, leading to charges being laid or, in one notorious case, a quashed conviction.'

'Well, it looks like this case has just "blown up", as you put it. I appreciate your review, and the fresh angles you've provided,' he said. He gave an audible sigh and confessed, 'On reflection, I feel I should have conducted far more extensive tests in the first place. We usually do with anyone high profile, but there had been a nasty vehicle accident the day before. A hit and run...' He wiped his forehead with his handkerchief and shifted his eyes away from hers.

'I understand how difficult it is,' Eloise said softly.

'Forensic Services are under constant pressure to produce results in a hurry. It's the same back home.'

Peter Middleton's gaze went back to the two signed copies of laboratory results in front of them. 'The family will need to be informed and Chief Inspector D'Ancey,' he said in a weighted tone.

'Yes.'

'I'll take you to his office,' he said, getting to his feet. 'It's a short walk from here.'

Eloise followed him out of the laboratory, wondering what Lachlan was going to say when he heard what she had uncovered.

Lachlan stared at his daughter in shock. 'Are you sure?' he asked, 'absolutely, totally, without a doubt sure?'

Poppy nodded miserably. 'I saw Dr Tremayne a few days ago. He confirmed it. I'm six…' She gulped and continued, 'Almost seven weeks along.'

Lachlan let out a stiff curse and then, seeing the crestfallen look on his daughter's face, came around to where she was sitting and gathered her in his arms.

'I'm so sorry, Dad,' she choked. 'I don't know how I'm going to tell Mum. It's taken me all this time to tell you. I know she'll kill me.'

Lachlan swallowed back his emotion. 'No, she won't,' he said. 'We'll talk to her together and discuss your options.'

Poppy lifted her head away from his chest and looked up at him. 'You mean…get rid of it?'

He swallowed deeply again. 'If that is what you decide to do then I will support you through it,' he said. 'But I don't want you to rush into anything you might later regret. There's a lot to take into consideration—your age, for one thing. I know you feel all grown up, sweetheart, but you're still a child yourself.'

'I know...' she gulped again, and fumbled for a tissue.

Lachlan handed her his handkerchief. His chest felt tight at the sound of her blowing her nose. That simple action reminded him of the hundreds of times over the years he had mopped her tears as a little girl.

But she was no longer a little girl.

She was going to be a mother.

Margaret was going to kill *him*, not Poppy, he thought with a sickening clench of his insides. He should have been more vigilant in checking she was on the Pill, but he had foolishly thought his ex-wife had seen to that.

'Have you told Robert?' he asked once Poppy had stopped sniffing.

'No...I c-can't...' She began to cry all over again.

He frowned and reached for her again, tipping up her chin like he'd been doing ever since she'd been a toddler. 'Why not, Poppy? Surely he has the right to know?'

Her slim throat moved up and down in anguish. 'Because I—I'm not sure if it's his...'

It took Lachlan a good ten seconds or more to register what she had just said. He stood staring down at her, his heart beginning to thud unevenly as a thought crept into his mind like a shadow slipping underneath a door.

'Who else's could it be?' he asked in a cracked whisper that sounded nothing like his normal voice.

She looked at him through tear-glazed eyes and said, 'Ethan Jenson's.'

CHAPTER TEN

THE intercom suddenly buzzed on Lachlan's desk. 'Yes?' he clipped out.

'There's a Dr Eloise Hayden here to see you,' the junior constable said. 'Shall I send her in?'

'Can you ask her to wait a minute or two?' he asked, looking at Poppy who was still pale and trembling.

'Will do.'

Lachlan shoved a hand through his hair as he came back to where his daughter was standing. 'Do you want me to tell your mother for you?' he asked gently.

She bit her lip. 'I want to tell her myself. I phoned her earlier and asked her to come and pick me up and take me back with her for a few days. She was a bit iffy to start with but then she agreed to meet me this afternoon here in Wadebridge. You don't mind, do you, Dad?'

'No, not at all,' he said thinking of the very intuitive Eloise Hayden sniffing around. The sooner Poppy was out of town, the better. 'Have you told anyone else—one of your friends, for instance?'

She shook her head. 'No, only you and Dr Tremayne know. He insisted I tell you.'

'Good. Let's keep it that way for now,' he said. After a little pause he added, 'Did you have strong feelings for Ethan or was it just a little fling to make Robert sit up and take notice?'

Poppy gave him a shamefaced look. 'It was a stupid mistake to get involved with him,' she said. 'I was trying to make Robert jealous after we had that horrible argument a few weeks back. Ethan flirted with me and I enjoyed the attention but then it sort of got out of hand.'

Lachlan felt every hair on the back of his neck lift in apprehension. 'He didn't force you, did he?'

'No, of course not,' she answered glumly. 'I was just too stupid to see him for what he is…I mean was. He slept with three other girls that same week, including Molly Beale of all people. She's so slutty. I feel disgusted with myself for falling for his charm like that.'

He gave her shoulder a gentle squeeze. 'We all make mistakes, sweetheart,' he said.

'I'm so sorry, Dad,' she said again. 'You must be so disappointed in me.'

He pressed a soft kiss to the top of her head. 'I'm disappointed in myself for not seeing the potential for this happening. I feel I've let you down by not protecting you. I guess I've been too distracted, dealing with the divorce.'

'It's not your fault,' she said. 'I know you and Mum weren't happy together. I've known it for years. I've been such a pain, I'm sorry. I just wanted Mum to put me first for once.'

'She does her best,' he said. 'It's been hard for her. She didn't really want to be tied down with a husband and child so young.'

'What about you?' she asked. 'Did you ever resent me being born?'

He smiled at her tenderly. 'What sort of question is that? Of course I haven't resented or regretted it, not for a moment. You are my daughter and I can't imagine life without you.'

She smiled a watery smile and reached up to plant a kiss on his cheek. 'I'd better get going. The bus will be here any minute and I don't want to miss Mum. You know how impatient she is.'

'Do you want me to wait with you? My meeting with Dr Hayden won't take long.'

Poppy gave him a probing look. 'Are you falling for her, Dad?'

He looked at her incredulously. 'In a little over a week? Don't be ridiculous.'

'She's very attractive.'

'She's also very career-driven.'

'I think she likes you.'

'Yes, well, she's going to hate me if she finds out just how involved you were with Ethan Jenson and that I deliberately withheld the information from her,' he said with a deepening frown.

'You're not going to tell her, are you?'

He let out a sigh. 'Not right now, no.'

'Will you get into big trouble, Dad?'

Lachlan looked at his daughter's anxious face and let out another sigh. 'Not if I can help it.' He opened the door and led her out. 'Come on, sweetheart. I'll walk you to the back entrance.'

'He's free now,' the constable informed Eloise a few minutes later. 'It's the first door on the left.'

'Thank you,' Eloise said, and made her way to where she had been directed.

She gave the door a single knock and he issued a command to come in. He was sitting behind his desk, a mound of paperwork on either side of him, but he rose to his feet as she came in.

'I take it you've received the results?' he asked.

'Yes.'

He couldn't help being pleased to see her, but Lachlan didn't like the sound of that curt one-word answer. 'Take a seat,' he said, and once she had sat down he resumed his own seat behind the desk, forcing himself not to reach for his pen to click.

He schooled his features into indifference and asked, 'What did you find?'

'Ethan Jenson was murdered, Chief Inspector,' she stated bluntly. 'He was dead before he hit the water, a combination of smothering and carbon-monoxide poisoning. Feather particles were found in the lung biopsies I took.'

He leaned back in his chair and began to drum his fingers on the desk. 'The family will have to be informed at some point.'

'Yes,' she said. 'And everyone who knew or was associated with Mr Jenson will have to be interviewed. Chief Inspector, that includes your daughter.'

His eyes hardened as they held hers. 'How many times do I have to tell you she has nothing to do with any of this?'

'Are you saying that because you hope it's true or because you're absolutely certain?'

'My daughter is not capable of murder.'

'Perhaps not, but one of her friends or acquaintances could be,' she pointed out. 'As far as I'm concerned, she's a valuable witness for this investigation.'

He shook his head. 'Looking at the criteria you're using, just about everybody in the whole of Cornwall would be just as valuable.'

'You're obviously too close to the investigation to make rational decisions,' she said. 'I'm going to suggest to the superintendent that you step aside and let someone else take charge.'

His expression darkened. 'That won't be necessary. I'm

heading this investigation, Dr Hayden and no one else. I'll make sure all avenues are investigated. Do you understand?'

She lifted her chin. 'And I want to be informed of each and every development along the way, have you got that?'

He got to his feet. 'You will be notified of anything of significance as per standard procedure. You know the angle we take on this. If we go out to the community and suddenly announce to all and sundry that Jenson was murdered, the culprit will know we're on to him and disappear into the woodwork.'

'I realise the delicacy needed in handling cases such as this. It's always a bit of a balancing act,' she said.

The intercom buzzed on Lachlan's desk again and he turned back to lean over his desk to answer it. 'Yes?'

'Chief, Dr Tremayne called a few moments ago. He said he was going to be ten minutes late.'

Lachlan felt a tremor of unease pass through him. 'Oh…right… Give me a buzz when he arrives. Dr Hayden is just leaving.'

Eloise looked at him quizzically. 'Getting rid of me, Chief Inspector? What if I want to speak to Dr Tremayne about my findings?'

'You can book an appointment with him some other time. This is a personal visit.'

'And yet you sounded surprised to know he was coming here,' she observed.

'Did I?' he asked guilelessly.

'Yes.'

'I forgot he said he might be dropping past.'

'Just like you forgot which day it was you were supposed to take your daughter to her friend's house?' she questioned.

He sent her a disarming smile. 'Not much escapes your notice, does it?'

'Not if I can help it.'

He came to stand right in front of her. 'Well, then, clever little Dr Hayden from Australia, maybe I'm just a little forgetful sometimes. Or perhaps I'm distracted by the fact I am struggling to keep my hands off you,' he said in a low sexy drawl.

Eloise felt her body quiver in reaction. She looked up into those brown eyes and felt that cold and hard feeling she'd carried inside her chest for so long melt, its warmth flowing through each and every one of her veins. Her heartbeat increased, her mouth began to tingle and her belly flip-flopped as he came one step closer. 'Um…you're changing the subject…' she said, running her tongue across her lips. 'I didn't notice…er…that…'

He picked up a strand of her hair and looped it around his finger. 'Can we meet up later tonight?' he asked. 'Say about nine?'

'I'm not sure I should say yes,' she said, still staring at his mouth. 'I mean, I'm not really sure what I'm saying yes to.'

'How about we have a walk along the shore and take things from there?' he suggested.

She looked back into his eyes and felt her normally rigid resolve melt and slip away even further. 'Is it wise for us to do that?'

Lachlan took a moment to answer. Of course it wasn't wise, certainly not now with things as they were, but something about Eloise pulled him like a magnet. In spite of the danger she represented, he wanted to have her, even if it was only for a few weeks. He wanted to break through that tough exterior she carried around like a suit of armour and have her purring like a sensual cat instead. She was a passionate woman—he could feel it every time he looked at her or touched her.

'Are you worried about what people might say?' he asked.

'To some degree, yes,' she said. 'I like to keep my private life private. I guess that's hard to do in a small village like this.'

Tell me about it, Lachlan thought wryly. How he was going to keep his daughter's teenage pregnancy quiet for as long as possible was already starting to worry him. Although things had changed over the years, there were still some conservative members of the community who would shun her, which would make a difficult situation intolerable.

'It is hard but not impossible,' he said. 'Anyway, people will expect us to spend time together as part of the investigation.'

'What about your daughter?' she asked.

'What about her?'

'Will you tell her you're…you know…seeing me?'

'*Are* you seeing me, Dr Hayden from Australia?' he asked with another one of his irresistible smiles.

She screwed up her mouth at him. 'Must you keep calling me that?'

'Eloise, then.'

'That's better.'

'Your turn.'

She looked at him in confusion. 'My turn for what?'

'For saying my name,' he said. 'You can't keep calling me Chief Inspector, especially if we end up in bed together.'

'I didn't say I was going to sleep with you,' she said through prim lips.

'You didn't have to,' he said. 'I can see it in your eyes. You want me just as much as I want you. It's called sexual chemistry.'

She gave him one of her prudish schoolmistress-type looks. 'That's nonsense.'

He smiled and opened the door for her. 'I'll meet you at Trevallyn House at nine.'

She sent him a pert glance as she brushed past him in the doorway. 'What if I change my mind?'

'That's entirely up to you,' he said. 'Just give me a call to let me know.'

Eloise wasn't so sure she liked his take-it-or-leave-it attitude. 'I might get a better offer,' she said, with a haughty lift of her chin.

'You might but then again you might not.' His eyes twinkled. 'You know what they say about a bird in the hand and all that.'

Eloise left with a roll of her eyes, but his chuckle filled her head for the remainder of the afternoon, and every time she looked at her watch the hands seemed to be crawling at a snail's pace towards nine p.m.

CHAPTER ELEVEN

'POPPY told me her news,' Lachlan said gravely as soon as Nick Tremayne sat down in his office. 'I can tell you I'm not looking forward to Margaret finding out. Poppy's going back to London with her as we speak.'

'Margaret's not the only one who needs to know,' Nick said. 'Dr Hayden should be informed as well.'

Lachlan jerked upright in his chair. 'No. No way.'

Nick frowned. 'You're not going to tell her?'

'I don't want Poppy's name dragged through the mud. She's just a kid, for God's sake.'

'Peter Middleton spoke to me on the way in,' Nick said. 'Off the record, of course, but as I was the attending doctor he thought I should know the change of verdict. I think you have a professional responsibility to tell Dr Hayden that your daughter had an intimate relationship with Ethan Jenson and that as a result of that relationship she is now pregnant.'

'You seem convinced it is Jenson's baby,' Lachlan said.

'We won't know with any certainty unless we conduct a paternity test. Poppy will have to decide if she wants to know for sure but there are risks involved.'

'What sort of risks?'

'Miscarriage, for one,' Nick answered. 'There's only about a one per cent chance but it still needs to be considered.'

Lachlan shoved a hand through his hair. 'I know it may come across as unfeeling, but right now a miscarriage is sounding pretty good to me.'

'Yes, well, I can understand how you feel and I have discussed Poppy's options with her, but the final decision will have to be hers,' Nick said. 'She will need both yours and Margaret's support during this difficult time.'

'I realise that. That's why I want her kept out of the spotlight until this all dies down.'

'You realise this puts me in a difficult position, don't you?' Nick asked. 'I can't breach patient confidentiality by disclosing Poppy's condition to Dr Hayden. That is your job as her father and Chief Inspector heading the investigation.'

'I will tell her when I think she needs to know,' Lachlan said. 'I just want some time to get my head around it all.'

'She's coming to the clinic at six this evening to see me,' Nick said. 'Do you have any leads on who might be responsible for Jenson's murder?'

Lachlan rubbed his hand over his face in weariness. 'No, but if Dr Hayden hears my daughter's pregnant by the victim she's going to put me right at the top of that list, isn't she?'

Nick narrowed his eyes. 'You're not responsible, though, are you?'

Lachlan scowled at him. 'You know me better than that, Nick. I'm one of the good guys, remember?'

Nick gave him a rare smile. 'Sorry. Had to ask.'

'It's OK. I would have asked you the same question if the tables were turned.' He let out a heavy sigh and, leaning forward, put his head in his hands. 'God I just wish this would all go away.'

'It's a nasty business, that's for sure,' Nick agreed.

Lachlan lifted his head and leaned back in his chair. 'So how are things with you and Kate these days?'

Nick frowned. 'That was a bit out of left field. What makes you ask?'

'Eloise Hayden picked up some sort of a vibe when she was talking to Kate at the clinic. She asked me if you and Kate were an item.'

'Kate and I are friends, as we have been for years,' Nick said. 'You know that.'

Lachlan gave a little shrug. 'I wouldn't have asked but from what I've seen so far, Eloise is pretty switched on.'

'So you're on a first-name basis with her now, are you?' Nick asked. 'Does this mean there's something going on between the two of you?'

'I'm more than thinking about it,' Lachlan admitted. 'I haven't felt like this about anyone before, not even Margaret in the early days.'

'It's about time you put the divorce behind you,' Nick said. 'Although I can't help thinking you're asking for trouble, getting involved with an international colleague. Long-distance relationships never work and you couldn't get much further away than Australia.'

'Don't worry, Nick, I'm not going to fall in love with her,' Lachlan said, although he wondered if was being entirely honest with his friend or even himself.

Nick got to his feet. 'You know what they say about tempting fate.'

Lachlan smiled wryly. 'You're starting to sound like me, rattling off well-worn adages all the time.'

'Yes, well, don't say I didn't warn you.'

'She's a career-woman, Nick. Been there, done that and packed away the T-shirt long ago.'

Nick glanced at his watch. 'I'd better get moving. I've got to call in on Henry Ryall before I head back to the clinic. It sounds like a strep throat.'

'James Derrey was out there yesterday, investigating an alleged theft.'

Nick's brows rose. 'Alleged?'

Lachlan gave a nod. 'Henry's lonely. He's looking for excuses for company.'

'I haven't got the time to waste on people who aren't unwell when I have so many to deal with who are,' Nick growled.

'A cup of tea and a stale biscuit won't hurt you,' Lachlan said. 'If I didn't have this case hanging over my head, I'd go out there myself.'

'You know, you might want to think about having a little chat to Robert Polgrean,' Nick said as he strode towards the door. 'If anyone has a motive for getting rid of Ethan Jenson, it's him.'

Lachlan frowned. 'I will interview everyone I think is connected to the case, but Robert already has a rock-solid alibi for the night in question. I checked that out days ago.'

Nick frowned again. 'But I thought you were convinced it was a simple case of drowning. Why did you feel the need to check out Robert's movements that night?'

'I've been in this business long enough to know things are not always as they seem,' Lachlan said. 'Until Peter Middleton announced his verdict of death by drowning, I was keeping an open mind.'

'Kate told me Dr Hayden was concerned about your reluctance to do another autopsy.'

'Come on, Nick, you've met the victim's parents,' Lachlan said. 'I know they were the ones behind the request but I didn't want to put them through any more agony unless it was absolutely necessary.'

'Have you told them yet?'

'Not yet.'

'They're going to be devastated.'

'Yes, I know,' Lachlan said, sending his hand back through his hair again. 'Drowning is hard enough to accept, but murder is another thing entirely.'

Eloise smiled at Sue, the receptionist at the clinic. 'Hello, Sue, I know I'm a bit early for my meeting with Dr Tremayne but I thought I'd come along anyway.'

'That's fine, Dr Hayden,' Sue said. 'Dr Tremayne is on his way back from a house call but it might be ten or fifteen minutes before he returns. But Kate Althorp is upstairs in Chloe the midwife's office, if you'd rather wait there. Chloe's doing a home visit so you won't be disturbed. I'll let Kate know you are here.'

Eloise waited while Sue contacted Kate via the intercom and within half a minute Kate came downstairs to meet her. 'Has your luggage arrived yet?' she asked as she led the way upstairs. 'Bea told me about your little hiccup.'

'No. Can't you tell?' Eloise said ruefully, as she pointed to the very basic outfit she had bought at St Piran a couple of days previously. 'I called the airline a short time ago. Thankfully they've located it and are shipping it by courier, but I'm not sure when it's going to arrive.'

'I can lend you some things to tide you over,' Kate said as she opened the office door. 'I'm a bit taller than you but I have a few things that might do. I'll bring them round or, even better, you could come to my place for dinner in a day or two. Jem would like to meet you. He's very fond of Lachlan. He thinks it's really cool to be a police officer.'

'I used to think that until I started working alongside the

force,' Eloise admitted wryly. 'Now I sometimes wonder why I put my hand up.'

Kate smiled. 'I feel the same about this place. Nick can be so demanding. I've felt like walking out many times, I can tell you.'

'So why do you stay?'

Kate gave a little shrug. 'I care about the patients...and Nick, of course...'

Eloise let the little silence continue, knowing from years of observing police at work that confessions usually followed.

Kate looked up from the papers she was pretending to be rearranging on the desk. 'I've loved him for years. He's the only man I've ever loved in the true sense of the word.'

'What about your late husband?' Eloise asked.

Kate sighed. 'I loved James in the way you would love a close friend or brother. I knew I couldn't have Nick. He fell in love with Annabel on the first day of university. They had to get married when she became pregnant with their twins. I settled for James and loved him in my way. He was a good man. I missed him terribly when he died but he wasn't the love of my life. My soul mate, if you like.'

'Does such a thing exist?' Eloise didn't realise she had asked out loud what she had been thinking until Kate answered.

'I believe so. Although having said that, I still think you can find someone with similar goals and morals and have a pretty decent life together, but love that lasts a lifetime is rare and it's worth waiting for.'

Eloise felt inclined to agree with her but didn't say so. She was still trying to make sense of her totally uncharacteristic reaction to Lachlan. He affected her like no other man had ever done. She could barely think when she was near him; her body seemed to be on high alert, cutting off the circuit to her brain and every gram of rationality she possessed. She didn't feel like a career-focused professional woman around him, more like a love-struck young girl.

Kate gave her a smile of embarrassment. 'Listen to me,' she said self-deprecatingly. 'It must be peri-menopausal hormones or something.'

'Please, don't apologise,' Eloise said sincerely. 'I feel honoured you felt safe enough to share your feelings with me.'

'I'm not usually the share-my-heart type. I guess it's because you're such a good listener. I sense that you are a deeply sensitive person, Dr Hayden.'

'Please, call me Eloise.'

'Eloise. It's such a pretty name. Does anyone ever shorten it to Ellie?'

'No,' Eloise said. 'Only my mother called me that and since she died I can't quite cope with anyone else doing so. It seems silly really, seeing as was so long ago.'

'The loss of your mother is a huge hurdle to overcome, especially in a woman's life,' Kate said. 'Is your father still alive?'

'I have no idea,' Eloise said. 'I've never met him. I'm not even sure my mother knew who he was.'

Kate suddenly tensed and shifted her gaze slightly. 'How have you dealt with that over the years?'

'I've just accepted it,' Eloise said with an indifferent shrug. 'My mother was pretty loose with her morals. I'm not even sure I would want to know who my father was, to tell you the truth.'

Kate turned to face her. 'Do you think every father—no matter who he is—deserves the right to know he has fathered a child, even if he had no idea at the time it had happened?'

'I guess I do in principle, but what if telling the father was going to be destructive to the child or even to the mother?' she asked. 'I think it's one of those case-by-case scenarios where individuals have to decide what is the best course of action, given the circumstances.'

'What would you do if you found you were pregnant?' Kate asked.

'That would entirely depend on who I was pregnant by,' Eloise answered. 'If I felt the man was to be trusted as a worthy father to my child, I would tell him.'

'What if by telling him you would be threatening his relationships with everyone he held dear?' Kate asked.

Eloise thought about it for a moment, thought too about why Kate was asking such pointed questions. Perhaps she knew someone who was facing exactly that dilemma. Penhally Bay was a small community, the medical practice was busy and Kate had at one time been the practice manager. She would have intimate knowledge of everyone's ailments and circumstances.

'I think I would try and do the right thing by the child and the father,' Eloise answered. 'If my child would benefit from knowing who his or her father was, I would definitely tell him. After, all it's his child, wanted or not.'

Kate let out a sigh. 'You're right, of course. I've thought the same for years but still...'

'Are these questions hypothetical or personal?' Eloise asked after a tiny pause.

Kate met her gaze. 'Personal.'

'I see.'

Another little silence passed.

Kate got to her feet and looked out of the window, her arms crossed in front her chest. 'I want to tell him but I don't know how to go about doing so. You know...bringing up the subject.'

'Do you mean with your son or his father?'

'Both.'

Eloise let another small silence slip by before she asked, 'So what you're saying is your husband wasn't Jem's father?'

Kate slowly turned around to face her. 'James was sub-fertile. We didn't tell anyone about it in the village. We went to London to see a specialist when I failed to fall pregnant. We were both checked out but when the results came back James was devastated, as any man would be. He would have loved a child, a son in particular, but it wasn't to be.'

'But being sub-fertile doesn't mean totally unfertile,' Eloise pointed out. 'The chances of a pregnancy are much lower, of course, but it could have still happened.'

Kate shook her head. 'I know Jem is not James's son. I've known it from the beginning.'

'And you have no doubt who the actual father is?'

'I have no doubt at all.'

'It's Nick Tremayne, isn't it?' Eloise asked.

Kate nodded, anguish clearly written on her features. 'We had one brief…time together…the night of the storm. It should never have happened. We were both in a highly charged emotional state and I let my heart rule my head. Nick did, too, if it comes to that. We've had trouble speaking of that night since…I mean the intimate part of it. We both felt so guilty and ashamed of what we did that ever since we've both tried to pretend it didn't happen. We've been carrying on as we always have—as friends. But a few weeks ago that all changed. Nick finally brought the subject up, only I was so shocked I didn't take the opportunity to talk to him about it like I should have done.'

'What has stopped you telling him Jem is his?' Eloise asked.

'You've met Nick,' Kate said with a rueful set to her features. 'He's not exactly the easiest person to talk to at times. I've wanted to tell him for years but I'm frightened it will destroy the friendship we have. We've known each other since we were teenagers. I'm the one he turns to when he has issues with his kids or the practice. I don't want to jeopardise that.'

'You're going to have to discuss it some time or other,' Eloise advised. 'Your son is nine now but as he grows older he may begin to look more and more like his father. What if Nick somehow guesses it for himself?'

All of a sudden Kate's expression became stricken as the shadow of two large feet appeared at her closed door. Her face paled as she put a trembling hand up to her throat and whispered, 'Oh, no…'

There was a brisk knock and Nick's curt tone clipped out, 'Kate? Have you got Dr Hayden with you?'

Kate's throat moved up and down, making her reply come out slightly strangled. 'Y-yes I have.'

The door opened and Eloise saw the livid expression on Nick Tremayne's face, which meant he must have overhead part if not all of their conversation. The blistering glare he sent in Kate's direction more or less confirmed it.

He turned to Eloise. 'I'm free to see you now, but briefly,' he said crisply. 'I have another rather urgent issue to deal with, as I am sure you'll understand.'

'Yes, yes, of course,' Eloise replied, with a quick glance in Kate's direction.

Kate returned her look with an apprehensive grimace, sat back down at the desk and shuffled some papers with hands that weren't quite steady.

Nick was already striding away, barking at Eloise to follow him downstairs.

He closed the door of his room a few moments later and frowned at her from behind his desk. 'Chief Inspector D'Ancey has already informed me of your findings. I hope you're not going to accuse me of incompetence because I failed to correctly identify the cause of death.'

'No, of course not,' she said. 'Anyway, it wasn't your responsibility in this case to declare the cause of death. You did nothing wrong. Under the circumstances it would be easy to assume he died as a result of drowning.'

He scraped a hand through his salt-and-pepper hair. 'What I just overheard downstairs…' he said, as he levelled his gaze at her. 'I must insist you refrain from discussing it with anyone in Penhally Bay.'

'Of course,' she said. 'How much did you hear of my conversation with Kate?'

His eyes were still blazing with anger and Eloise didn't envy Kate's next meeting with him. 'I am not prepared to discuss or have my private life discussed with virtual strangers,' he bit out.

'If Jem is your son, he needs to know it, and soon,' she said. 'He deserves to know the truth.'

Nick looked at her and gave her a twisted smile, but there was no trace of humour in it. 'You know Lachlan D'Ancey was right about you,' he said. 'You're not just a pretty face.'

Eloise could feel her face growing warm. 'I'm only here for the duration of the investigation,' she said. 'I wouldn't want anyone to get any wrong ideas about Chief Inspector D'Ancey and myself.'

'He's a good man, Dr Hayden. He needs some support right now, especially with this situation with his d—'

Eloise tilted her head quizzically at his abrupt cutting off of his sentence. 'What situation, Dr Tremayne?'

Nick looked at her for a second or two beat before continuing, 'His divorce. It hit him hard. It came right out of the blue.'

'I understood from Chief Inspector D'Ancey that his

divorce was a mutual decision they had been considering for years. He told me that himself.'

Nick Tremayne glanced at his watch and got to his feet. 'Is that all, Dr Hayden?' he asked. 'I need to speak to Kate and I have several patients to see before I go home for the day.'

Eloise rose from her chair. 'That will be all, Dr Tremayne.' She paused then added, 'For now.'

CHAPTER TWELVE

'YOUR luggage has arrived!' Beatrice announced excitedly as soon as Eloise got back to the guest-house. 'Davey's just this minute taken it upstairs to your room.'

'That's the best news I've heard all day,' Eloise said with a relieved sigh.

Beatrice bustled over to the hall table and picked up a sheaf of papers tied with string. 'Oh, and Mr Price left this for you.' She handed it to her. 'It's his manuscript. It's ever so kind of you to offer to read it for him.'

I didn't exactly offer, Eloise thought as she took the thick wad of paper with a strained smile. 'Thanks. I'll read it tonight.'

'Not going out this evening, then?'

'I might go for a walk later,' Eloise said, holding the papers to her chest. 'I have some paperwork to see to first.'

Beatrice checked that no one was about before leaning closer. 'I heard a rumour that you found out that young man didn't drown after all. Is it true?'

Eloise was momentarily taken aback. As far as she knew, the parents of the victim hadn't been formally informed so how anyone else had found out was completely beyond her. 'Where did you hear that?' she asked.

'At the hairdresser's,' Beatrice said. 'Vicki Clements told

me there were suspicious findings to do with the case. She heard one of the other clients talking about it. I think someone the client knows works in the police station at Wadebridge.'

'I'm not at liberty to discuss my findings with anyone other than the police investigating the case.'

'I suppose you mean Chief Inspector D'Ancey,' Beatrice said. 'Davey said he saw you and the chief inspector down at the Penhally Arms the other night.'

Eloise felt like sinking through the ancient floorboards. It seemed that Davey Trevallyn saw a great deal and yet she still hadn't met him. 'We were discussing official business,' she said. 'We have to work together on this case.'

There was a footfall on the stairs and a bulky man in his middle to late forties appeared, his round cheeks and innocent, childlike look immediately identifying him as Beatrice's son, Davey.

'Ah, Davey, my love, finally you get to meet our important guest,' Beatrice said. 'This is Dr Hayden. You remember I told you about her coming all this way from Australia to find out the truth about that surfer's death?'

Davey blinked once or twice and mumbled something in reply, but Eloise couldn't understand a word of it.

'Don't be shy,' Beatrice scolded him fondly. 'I know you don't like meeting strangers but Dr Hayden's a nice lady. She's going to help Mr Price get published. She's reading his book for him. Isn't that nice of her when she's already so busy?'

Davey smiled a nervous smile and backed away, turning the nearest corner and disappearing from sight.

Beatrice tut-tutted and turned back to Eloise. 'I don't know what's got into him. He's always been a bit on the shy side but lately he seems to be even worse. Perhaps it's because Molly upset him by leaving so suddenly. He was quite fond of her, even though she was a bit cruel to him at times.' She let out a little sigh and added as she bustled off, 'It takes all types, though, doesn't it?'

Eloise agreed politely and was halfway up the stairs when she met Mr Price coming down.

'Ah, Dr Hayden, just the person I was hoping to see,' he said with a broad smile. 'I have some suggestions for you for the case you're currently working on.'

She blinked at him once or twice. 'You do?'

'Oh, yes,' he said eagerly. 'I was thinking about it all evening. It's a classic case of a cover-up. He was murdered somewhere else and his body dumped to appear like a drowning. Brilliant, don't you think?'

'Er…yes…'

'I think you need to narrow down your suspects,' he went on. 'You know, the people Mr Jenson was seen associating with in the last hours of his life.'

'That's the job of the local police, Mr Price,' Eloise informed him. 'I'm a forensic specialist called on to give evidence to the coroner. I am not responsible for interviewing witnesses or suspects.'

'Oh…' He looked momentarily deflated but rallied quickly. 'Well, then, you could always do your own investigations, you know, on the sly, or get someone to do them for you.' He puffed out his chest. 'Like me, for instance.'

Eloise had to fight not to roll her eyes in front of him. 'Thank you for your very generous offer but I think it's best if we leave it to the local authorities to deal with,' she said. 'We might end up getting in the way.'

'I can be very discreet.'

She smiled stiffly. 'I'm sure you can, but in this case I think it's best to stay out of it.'

Mr Price began sniffing the air. 'Can you smell that?' he asked.

Eloise suddenly became aware of a faint smell of gas. 'Yes, I can. Has someone left an outlet on or something?' she asked.

'I'll speak to Davey about it,' Mr Price said. 'It happens now and again. There must be a leak somewhere.'

A gas leak?

Eloise began to do the sums in her head.

Ethan Jenson died of a combination of carbon monoxide poisoning and smothering...

Mr Price was already moving past her on the stairs when she swung back around and grasped his arm. 'Mr Price?'

He turned and looked at her. 'Yes, Dr Hayden?'

'Do you know if Ethan Jenson ever came to Trevallyn House? To stay, I mean.'

'I'm not sure but surely Mrs Trevallyn is the one to ask,' he said. 'She knows each and every one of her guests. She makes a point of it. After all, it's her and Davey's home they are renting rooms from. She likes to know exactly who is here and when.'

Eloise quickly excused herself and went in search of Beatrice, who she eventually located sitting in the front room, watching television and eating from a very large box of chocolates.

She closed the lid somewhat guiltily and stuffed them under a cushion when she saw Eloise.

'You won't tell Dr Tremayne, will you?' she asked in a beseeching tone. 'It's my cholesterol. I'm supposed to be cutting down. I allow myself two a day but I just ate five.'

Eloise smiled. 'No, I won't tell. Anyway, I've heard dark chocolate is good for you.'

Beatrice brightened and pulled out the box from beneath the cushions. 'Would you like one? I have peanut brittle or chewy caramel. I'm afraid I've eaten all the soft ones. They're my favourites.'

Eloise took a peanut brittle from the almost empty box. 'I'm a bit of a cupboard chocolate eater, too,' she confessed. Thinking of her mother, she added, 'My thinking is there are worse things to be addicted to, right?'

'Yes, indeed,' Beatrice said. 'My sister was married to a compulsive gambler. He sold everything from under her to feed his addiction—even the toaster and the clock radio went.'

'Oh, dear,' Eloise said. 'That must have been some addiction.'

'It was, but she moved on. She's married to a lovely man now. He's a bit boring but that's neither here nor there.'

'Mrs Trevallyn, I was wondering if you had ever had Ethan Jenson as a guest at Trevallyn House,' Eloise asked once she'd chomped through her chocolate.

Beatrice straightened indignantly on her softly cushioned sofa. 'As if I would allow such a man to sleep in one of my beds!' she said. 'I have very high standards here, as I'm sure you've noticed, Mr Price and yourself being a case in point. I have nothing against surfers, but that young man was a roving tomcat if ever I saw one.'

'So as far as you know he never once came here?'

'No, absolutely not,' Beatrice insisted. 'I don't encourage younger guests anyway. I like the more mature guest. They're far more reliable and never complain about the service.'

Eloise suddenly felt terribly middle-aged and boring.

'Would you like another chocolate?' Beatrice thrust the box under her nose.

'Thanks,' she said, and took two. 'I will.'

The evening was warmer than the night before and the sea breeze only slight. Eloise lifted her face to the air and breathed in deeply. It felt good to be back in her own clothes. She felt safer somehow, as if her armour was back on. She looked down at her dark blue trousers and white linen shirt. They weren't exactly haute couture but they were comfortable and made her feel professional and in control again.

She walked down the steps of Trevallyn House with the intention of avoiding Lachlan before he arrived to collect her, but as if he had sensed her intention, he suddenly appeared at the foot of the stairs.

'Am I too early?' he asked, a little too innocently for her liking.

She gave her head a little toss. 'I was hoping to avoid you.'

He cocked one brow. 'Oh, really? Why was that?'

She gave him a churlish look. 'You know why not.'

He smiled that boyish smile again. 'So I need some work on my pick-up lines. You can coach me through them while we have supper together. I've made a casserole to die for.'

'I wasn't planning on dying tonight.'

'I wasn't planning on killing you.'

Eloise looked up at him. 'Have you talked to anyone about the forensic results?'

He frowned at the gravity of her tone. 'Not apart from my colleagues and Nick Tremayne. Why?'

'There are rumours circulating in the village. I'm concerned that Ethan Jenson's family will hear of the new verdict secondhand.'

He rubbed at his jaw for a moment. 'I was hoping for a bit more time. I'm running with a couple of lines of enquiry but perhaps I'd better talk to the family first. They went to London for a few days but will be back tomorrow, or so I've been told.'

Somehow Eloise fell into step with him along the pathway. 'What are the leads you're working on?' she asked.

'Your findings showed that Jenson was dead prior to being placed in the water. He was seen having a drink with a group of young women at the Anchor Hotel at seven-thirty p.m or thereabouts. The women have all been interviewed and they all said the same thing. Jenson left alone soon after and wasn't seen again until he showed up dead. You said he was in the water by midnight so that leaves approximately four and a half hours in which he was murdered before his body was dumped.'

Eloise glanced up at him. 'So no one knows where he went or who he was with during those hours?'

His forehead was etched in lines of concentration as he continued walking. 'It's as if he disappeared off the face of the earth.'

'Someone must have seen him but they're not telling because they're somehow involved or are worried they might be implicated,' she said.

'That's true enough.'

She stopped walking to look at him again. 'But?'

A sigh whistled out from between his lips. 'But there's something about this that doesn't quite add up,' he said. 'I keep thinking I've missed something along the way. You ever had a case like that?'

'Chief Inspector, they are *all* like that,' she remarked wryly. 'That's what we're paid to do—to make sure things do add up.'

'You can call me Lachlan,' he said with a smile. 'We're off duty, remember?'

'We are?'

'Of course,' he said, reaching for his keys as they approached his house. 'We're just two colleagues sharing a casserole.'

'As long as that's all we'll be sharing.'

'What about a bottle of wine?' he asked as he closed the door. 'Is that allowed?'

'Yes.'

'What about information pertaining to the case?' he added. 'Are we allowed to share that?'

'You know we are,' she said. 'That is, if no one else is listening. Will your daughter be home?'

Lachlan busied himself with opening the wine and finding two glasses. 'She's visiting her mother for a few days.'

Eloise took the glass from him and frowned. 'Did you send her away deliberately?'

'No, it was her idea, actually,' he said. 'Poppy's, that is. She wanted to spend a few days shopping with her mother.'

'I can't help feeling there's something you're not telling me,' Eloise said watching his expression closely.

'I'm getting a little tired of telling you Poppy has got nothing to do with this case,' he said with a little clench of his jaw.

'Where was she the night Ethan Jenson died?'

'She was at home with me.'

She hesitated, then went on. 'Can you prove it?'

'Yes, I can, actually. I had dinner with her about eight and she went upstairs to her room and listened to music until she went to sleep.'

'Did you check on her?'

'I don't usually check on her, but the phone rang at about two in the morning. It was a call from one of the constables working on a case with me in Wadebridge. Poppy woke up then and used the bathroom. We spoke briefly on the landing and she went back to bed.'

'Are you sure she didn't leave the house after that?'

'She was still in bed when I got the call about Ethan Jenson at six a.m.'

Eloise reluctantly backed down. 'All right, I believe you.'

He came over to where she was standing and, using two fingers, slowly lifted up her chin and looked into her eyes. 'You don't like trusting people, do you, Eloise?'

'Every time I have trusted someone they have let me down,' she said in a softened tone.

'So you keep something of yourself back just in case, don't you?' he said. 'You close off the part of yourself that is vulnerable, but in doing so you're not living a full life. It's half a life.'

She stepped out of his hold. 'But it's *my* life.'

'But you're not happy.'

'How do you know I'm not happy?' She looked up at him defensively. 'What right have you got to comment on my private life? How do you know what or who I am?'

'I know because when I kissed you something happened.'

'Nothing happened. You kissed me. I kissed you back. End of story.'

He reached for her, pulling her close to the heat and temptation of his body. 'But it's *our* story, Eloise,' he said, looking down at her mouth with fierce intent. 'It began just over seven days ago and each day is another chapter. Don't you want to see what happens next?'

'I know what happens next,' she said. 'I've read this sort of story before. It's not a novel, it's a short piece of prose. You wave me goodbye in a couple of weeks' time and I never hear from you or see you again.'

'Not according to the version I have,' he said, still looking at her mouth.

'Go on,' she said with a roll of her eyes. 'Tell me what your version is.'

He brought his mouth closer, the movement of his smile against her lips catching on them ever so slightly. 'This is my version,' he said, and covered her mouth with the searing temptation of his.

CHAPTER THIRTEEN

ELOISE wondered much later if she should have at the very least put up token resistance. The thought had crossed her mind but only briefly for as soon as his mouth set fire to hers she was swept away on a rushing tide of need that drove every bit of common sense right out of her head. His tongue danced and darted around her mouth until she was clinging to him, her body screaming out for more.

She kissed him back with escalating excitement, her tongue duelling with his, her stomach leaping and kicking in response as he tugged her even closer to his aroused body. She rubbed against him without inhibition, his low growl of pleasure inciting her to do it again and again.

He backed her into the sitting room towards the sofa, his mouth locked on hers while his hands dealt with her clothes with more haste than care.

Eloise did the same to his, the wild abandon of hearing buttons ping to the floor at their feet thrilling her. Her hands skated over his broad chest as she uncovered it, her fingers exploring the dusting of dark hair before going lower to unfasten his trousers.

His body leapt against her feather-like touch and Eloise wondered if it had been even longer for him than it had for her since the last time he had made love.

She pulled her mouth away from his to anoint his neck and shoulders with teasing kisses, her tongue darting in and out to taste and tantalise him, every movement she made against his skin bringing another guttural sound from his throat.

His pleasure delighted her in a way no one had ever done before. She felt so alive and vibrant, and so very feminine in his arms. Her body pulsed against his, her need matching his as the final barriers of her bra and knickers were tossed to one side.

He looked down at her hungrily, his pupils dilating as he took in her breasts and flat stomach and the gentle curves of her hips. 'I was right,' he said low and deep. 'You look much better without your clothes.'

She gave him a sultry smile as she peeled away his black briefs. 'So do you.'

Lachlan swallowed deeply as she moved down his body in a series of exquisitely tempting kisses, over each of his flat nipples, his sternum, the cave of his belly button and then even further...

He sucked in a breath as she tasted him, her tongue lapping at him in a cat-like manner that lifted every single hair on his scalp. The sensations rose in him with every movement of her mouth on him, the raw intimacy of it taking his breath away.

He pulled away before it was too late and brought her upright to suckle each of her beautiful breasts. He bent his mouth to the right one, drawing delicately on the engorged nipple before increasing the pressure as she clutched at his head and writhed against him.

He moved to the left breast and suckled her, delighting in the whimpering sounds she was making. He moved down her body as she had done to him, lingering over her belly button before moving to the secret heart of her.

She jerked at his first touch, as if it had been a long time since she had felt a man's fingers exploring her neat soft curls. He brought his mouth to her, tasting the sweet honey of her body.

Eloise couldn't believe the impact on her senses at that first intimate stroke of his tongue against her neediness. Her whole body felt as if it was shaking from the inside out, each nerve and pulse sizzling with energy. The first flutters of release came and went, to be replaced by stronger and stronger waves of tension that built to a crescendo until finally she was there, in paradise, her body rocking and rolling with each thunderous wave of pleasure.

She came back to earth with a heavy thud of self-consciousness. Shame coursed through her like a red-hot tide as she met his gaze.

'No,' he said, suddenly straightening and taking her by the upper arms. 'Don't do that.'

'Don't do what?' she asked, trying vainly to tug herself out of his hold.

'Don't go all shy and repressed on me,' he said, frowning at her. 'You enjoyed that. Why should you feel ashamed?'

Tears came to her eyes, which made her both angry and frustrated. 'Because I don't do this sort of thing! I *never* do this…with anyone, or at least not this soon.'

'That makes two of us,' he said sliding his hands down her arms to encircle her wrists. 'I haven't exactly been painting the town red or anything lately. I've been paying lawyer's bills and learning how to be a single dad. I'm ashamed to admit how long it's been. I don't even have a packet of condoms in the house.'

Something loosened in her chest at his gruff confession. 'Oh…'

He gave her a rueful smile. 'Pathetic, don't you think? I'm letting the male side down. I should be out there, having fun every night like everyone else, but until now I haven't even felt the need.'

Eloise ran her tongue across her lips. 'I don't know what to say...'

'I don't suppose you have a condom or two in your purse?' he asked, with another one of those stomach-tilting grins.

'If I have, they'd be well and truly out of date,' she said with a wry twist to her mouth. 'I can't even remember the last time I had sex.'

'Are you on the Pill?'

'Yes, but not for the usual reason,' she confessed. 'I only use it to keep myself regular.'

'So what would you say if we moved to my bedroom and wrote another chapter of our story?'

'I'd say if my foster-parents saw me right now, they would both have myocardial infarcts.'

He laughed as he swept her up in his arms. 'I won't tell if you don't.'

'Put me down, I'm too heavy,' she protested feebly.

His eyes twinkled as he looked down at her. 'Is that a "put me down I don't want to sleep with you" or a "put me down I'm having a fat day"?'

Eloise couldn't help giggling in response. 'It's a "no one's ever swept me off my feet before."'

'Do you like it?'

She gazed into his warm brown eyes and sighed with deep pleasure. 'I love it.'

He carried her through to his room, kicking open the door in such an essentially masculine way she felt her stomach do another somersault.

He laid her on the bed before joining her, his strong thighs draped across hers as he began to kiss her all over again, his mouth wreaking havoc on her already shattered senses.

'You have such a beautiful body,' he said, as he cupped her right breast in his hand, his thumb rolling back and forth over the tight nipple. 'So full and yet so neat.'

'So you *do* think I'm fat.'

He grinned at her mock pout and leaned over to kiss it away. 'I think you're gorgeous, even though you try and hide it all the time.'

She kissed him back and then asked in a musing tone, 'Why am I doing this with you? I feel like I've turned into someone else—someone reckless and shameless and totally wanton.'

He kissed her shoulder and then moved up to her neck, before nibbling on her ear lobe as he said, 'I like the sound of you being reckless and shameless and wanton, especially while you're with me.'

Eloise shivered as his erection brushed against her thigh. Reaching down with her hand, she stroked him boldly, enjoying the satin strength of him against the pads of her fingers.

'Mmm...' he groaned.

'You like that?'

He pressed her back into the mattress and nudged for entry. 'I want you so much I don't think I will last. I'm trying to count backwards and think of sad things to distract myself, but it's not working.'

She smiled and when he looked at her she felt her heart contract. 'You really are a very special lady, Dr Eloise Hayden from Australia. You are so warm and generous under that do-it-by-the-book exterior.'

She wrinkled her brow at him. 'You think I'm uptight and a total control freak, don't you?'

'To be perfectly honest with you, I'm not doing too much thinking at all right at this very moment,' he confessed as he moved against her again.

She lifted her hips slightly and held his gaze. 'I want you to make love to me, Lachlan. *Now*.'

'Is that an order, Dr Hayden?' he asked, with a dancing spark of mischief in his eyes.

'Ye-es,' she said on a swiftly indrawn breath as he surged into her honeyed warmth. 'It is…ohh'

'Am I going too fast?'

'No…no…it's perfect…' she said, on a breath of wonder.

Her body was soaring again, each muscle tightening all over again as she was pitched forwards into oblivion. She clutched at him as she panted her way through it, her skin shivering in reaction as she felt him let finally let go, the sheer force of it pinning her to the bed as he emptied himself.

She stroked his back and shoulders with her hands, exploring him in intimate detail, each knob of his vertebrae, the well-defined muscles that indicated he was a competent swimmer. She went lower to his buttocks, massaging the trim tautness of him before coming back up to his head, her fingers going to his thick curly dark hair, playing with it lingeringly.

'Mmm…' He nuzzled against her neck. 'That's nice.'

'Are you falling asleep on me?' she asked.

He propped himself up on his elbows and looked down at her. 'You know what they say about men who fall asleep after they've made love, don't you?'

She tried to purse her mouth but it turned into a smile instead. 'No, Chief Inspector D'Ancey, what do they say?'

He gave her a playful grin. 'I have absolutely no idea,' he said, and brought his mouth back down to hers.

* * *

Eloise rolled over to her stomach a long time later and idly played with Lachlan's long lean flank lying close to her.

He gave a little shudder. 'That tickles.'

She moved her hand to cup him intimately. 'Does this?'

He stretched like a well-fed jungle cat, even the deep growl that came from his throat sounding primal. 'You're asking for trouble, Dr Hayden. I'm going to pounce on you any minute if you don't stop doing that.'

'I'm hungry.'

He smiled at her. 'For love or for food?'

She let her hand fall away, her expression falling slightly. 'Isn't it a bit soon to be talking of love?' she asked, without looking at him.

He rolled onto his side and turned her face back towards him, his gaze very intense as it held hers. 'I don't know. Is it?'

Eloise felt every second of the pulsing silence as she struggled to think of a suitable answer. She was wary about revealing her feelings but uncomfortable too with allowing him to think she would fall into bed with just anyone to satisfy a physical need.

It was much more than that for her. She hadn't realised how much more it meant to her to be in love with her sexual partner until that moment. It transformed the act into something spiritual and deeply moving.

She moistened her lips. 'I'm not sure…I do know I haven't felt like this before. I'm not sure if it's love or…or something else.' She touched his face with her hand. 'I've never met anyone like you before. I can't believe I'm even lying here with you. It's so out of character for me.'

He kissed the centre of her palm. 'You don't like living in the moment, do you?'

'No…not really.' She gave a little sigh. 'It stems from my

background, I guess. I lived too many days and nights in fear, and eventually those fears were realised. You don't get over that sort of thing in a hurry.'

He brushed her hair back from her face. 'But burying yourself in work isn't going to help you recover, you know. You can't run away from personal demons because they have a habit of coming up behind you and snapping at your heels when you're least expecting it.'

'I know, but I don't want to make the same mistakes my mother made. She hooked up with totally unreliable men. It was almost like another addiction. She just couldn't seem to help herself. I've always sworn I would never take a risk like that.'

'Don't you worry that you will reach the age of forty-five and feel you've missed out on marriage and babies?' he asked.

Her gaze fell away from his. 'I try not to think about it. I would hate a child of mine to suffer some of the things I have seen.' She raised her eyes back to his. 'I just couldn't bear it.'

He brushed her mouth with his lips, softly. 'I know how you feel. Every time I was on a case of child molestation I would be paranoid about Poppy. I drove Margaret mad, telling her never to let her out of her sight. But after a while you realise you can only do so much to protect them. In a perfect world no child would live in danger or poverty, but we don't live in a perfect world.'

'I know, but how wonderful it would be to be able to relax and let go for a while,' she said. 'I feel like I've been living holding my breath for so long. I'm unconsciously waiting for the next phone call telling me of yet another tragic death.'

'Do you ever wonder how different your life would have been if you'd chosen some other career?' he asked.

'Many times, but I can't see myself doing anything else. I try to but I just can't.'

'I'm the same,' he said. 'I love the challenge of a hard-to-solve case. I love that feeling you get when you finally close the file.'

Eloise smiled. 'I've had an offer of help to solve this particular case.'

'Oh, really? From whom? Beatrice Trevallyn?'

'No, but you're close,' she said. 'One of her guests is a wannabe crime writer. He even asked me to read through a couple of his chapters.'

'That would be Mr Price,' he said with a smile. 'He's been coming to Cornwall for years, ten at least. I got roped into reading five chapters of his last novel. I thought it was pretty good, actually. I didn't realise he was already here. He normally comes in July when the weather's more settled.'

'He alerted me to the smell of gas at Trevallyn House,' Eloise said. 'It seems it's a common problem there. I wondered if Ethan Jenson had been there the night he died but Beatrice was adamant he hadn't been. She gave me the whole spiel about men with loose morals never darkening her doorstep and all that.'

Lachlan frowned as something began to niggle at the back of his mind, but before he could figure out what it was the phone rang by the bedside. He had to reach over Eloise to answer it and winked at her playfully as he did so. 'Lachlan D'Ancey.'

A female voice shrieked from the other end of the line, 'How dare you send our daughter back to me pregnant? Poppy said that surfer who died is responsible. What on earth's been going on?'

CHAPTER FOURTEEN

ELOISE froze as the shouted words reverberated around the room. She turned to stare at Lachlan, but he had already risen from the bed and was walking out of the room, carrying the cordless phone with him.

She got up and, stripping the top sheet off the bed, used it to wrap around herself as she went in search of her clothes.

She was so stiff with anger she could barely get her spine to bend low enough to gather her clothes from the sitting-room floor. She dressed haphazardly, not even caring that her white linen shirt was horrendously crumpled.

He came into the sitting room a few minutes later dressed in his trousers, his chest still bare, the phone nowhere in sight. 'I can explain—' he began.

Her eyes flashed livid blue flames of wrath at him. 'Don't bother. I don't want to hear your paltry excuses for withholding such information from me. You do realise what this means, don't you?'

He dragged a hand through his already disordered hair. 'I know it looks bad but—'

'Bad?' This time it was her turn to shriek. 'It's worse than bad, Chief Inspector. You are now the number one suspect. Do you realise that?'

He frowned at her. 'That's totally ridiculous. I had nothing to do with Jenson's death.'

She glared at him. 'How on earth do you expect me to believe a word you say? You have lied to me from the beginning. You insisted Poppy barely knew Ethan Jenson and yet apparently she's carrying his baby. Come on, Chief Inspector, give me some credit for having a bit of grey matter between my ears.'

'I don't want Poppy's name destroyed by gossip and innuendo,' he said, still frowning heavily. 'She's too young to cope with this. It would be bad enough if it was just a simple case of a teenage pregnancy, but this is the sort of scenario that could ruin her life.'

Eloise sent him a flinty glare. 'So you conveniently got rid of the culprit.'

Anger flared in his gaze as it warred with hers. 'No, I did not, and I resent you implying that I did.'

She arched her brows. '*You* feel resentful? Hah! What about what I'm feeling? I feel betrayed. Totally betrayed by a man I had grown to admire and trust.'

'I'm sorry, Eloise. I would have told you but I knew you would immediately think I was responsible. Nick Tremayne begged me to tell you but I wanted to wait until I saw how things lay.'

Her eyes widened in outrage. '*Nick Tremayne knows about this?*' she choked.

He gave her bleak look. 'Yes.'

Fury lit her gaze. 'That's two of you I can't trust. I should have known. I had a feeling both of you were holding something back, but I disregarded it at the time, thinking I was being over-sensitive.'

'He was in a difficult position,' Lachlan said. 'He didn't feel he could breach patient confidentiality.'

'He broke it with *you*.'

'No, because Poppy gave him permission to speak to me,' he said. 'She is my daughter and—'

'But this is now a murder investigation!' she railed at him furiously. 'The person responsible is probably laughing at the performing monkeys of the police force.'

His jaw tightened. 'That's an insulting thing to say.'

She cocked one eyebrow accusingly. 'You think I'm being insulting? What about what you just did?'

'I take it you mean the intimacy we shared.'

'Intimacy?' she scoffed. 'Let's tidy up the terminology, shall we, Chief Inspector? Intimacy is where two people connect both physically and spiritually. There is usually an element of trust in the relationship and mutual respect. What we just shared was a cheap roll in the hay, to use a crude expression, although I can think of numerous cruder ones.'

'I understand how upset you must be. But there are instances in life where the rule book doesn't apply.'

She made an impatient sound at the back of her throat. 'Oh for God's sake, I can't believe I'm hearing this from a top-level officer. Don't you have a police manual any more or do you just make it up as you go along?'

His eyes communicated his growing anger. 'There are times when people have to be put before protocol,' he argued. 'Sometimes the bigger picture has to be taken into account. You'd do well to think about that a bit, Eloise. You're so intent on doing everything by the book you're in danger of riding roughshod over people. You came stomping into the village, expecting everyone to stand up and take notice, but you didn't once consider the real victims in all of this.'

Eloise refused to be sent off course by his criticism, even though she felt a sneaking suspicion it might be warranted.

'You deliberately withheld information from me,' she said. 'We're supposed to liaising on this case. How can I trust you after this?'

'This is an unusual situation,' he argued. 'I didn't want to destroy my daughter's life. You surely must understand that?'

'I understand you were after a bit of fun to put me off the scent,' she bit out. 'Nice work, Chief Inspector D'Ancey. While you've been busy seducing me, the person responsible for Ethan Jenson's murder is probably in another country by now. Well done. Another case with "Unsolved" stamped across it.'

'This case is not going to be unsolved,' he said with implacable resolve. 'I have officers working round the clock.'

She snatched up her purse and threw him a filthy look. 'Then I won't waste any more of your time in case there's a remote possibility you take it on yourself to join them,' she said, and stalked out of his cottage.

Lachlan decided against following her. He'd promised to ring Margaret back when she'd calmed down enough for them to talk through Poppy's situation. That had to be his priority for now, but it didn't rest easy with him that Eloise was so angry.

Not after what they had experienced together. He had hoped... Well, that wasn't going to happen now so he may as well get over it.

He let out a jagged sigh, reached for the nearest phone extension and began dialling.

Eloise didn't bother making an appointment to see Nick Tremayne the following morning. Instead, she stormed to the clinic before the consulting hours had begun and demanded the practice manager Hazel inform Dr Tremayne that she was there to see him and would not be taking no for an answer.

He came in a short time later and before Hazel or Sue could even open their mouths to warn him, Eloise had risen from her chair and stalked over to him. 'I have some important questions to ask you, Dr Tremayne,' she said in a don't-mess-with-me tone.

He didn't dissemble but led the way to his office and closed the door once they were both inside.

Eloise went into full swing. 'Chief Inspector D'Ancey informed me somewhat vicariously last night that his daughter is pregnant.'

Something flickered in his dark brown gaze. 'I see.'

'I understand that the father is the late Ethan Jenson,' she went on.

'That has yet to be established,' Nick said.

Eloise's forehead creased in a frown. 'You mean Poppy isn't certain?'

'Her boyfriend Robert Polgrean could just as easily be the father,' he said. 'They've been dating for four years.'

'Have they had a sexual relationship during the whole of that time?'

His eyes hit hers. 'Dr Hayden, their sexual relationship and Poppy's age are issues you will have to take up with Robert Polgrean or Poppy's father. I prescribed a low-dose pill for Poppy a few months back. As to whether she has taken them as prescribed I can't tell you. I do, however, know she only once had intercourse with Ethan Jenson. It's my feeling it's unlikely to be his child, looking at the dates, but she is naturally very upset that it might be.'

'I'm just trying to do my job, Dr Tremayne,' Eloise said. 'But it's not been easy with people hiding important information from me. I realise your dilemma on the issue of patient confidentiality but this is now a murder investigation and Lachlan D'Ancey the officer heading the investigation, is the one—in my opinion—with the biggest motive for killing the victim.'

'I warned him you would immediately jump to that conclusion, but I can assure you Lachlan D'Ancey is not the culprit. He loves his daughter but he would never do anything to jeopardise his career as that would backfire on Poppy. He works damn hard to provide for her.'

'Thank you for the character reference but I will make up my own mind over the authenticity of Lachlan D'Ancey's integrity.'

He shifted his tongue inside his mouth as he surveyed her tightened features. 'You're the first woman he has even looked at since his divorce.'

She put up her chin. 'So he's desperate and dateless. That's not my problem.'

He frowned. 'He's nothing of the sort. Many women have been keen to date him. He's just not been interested. Avoiding a rebound relationship, as far as I can tell. Up till now he's just been concerned about being a good father to Poppy.'

'And what's your excuse, Dr Tremayne?' she asked.

He scowled darkly. 'I told you before I am not going to discuss my private life with you or anyone. I am absolutely furious with Kate that she spoke to you—a person she hardly knows—about something she should have told me years ago.'

'Maybe she was worried you'd react in exactly the way you're reacting now,' she said. 'It's easy for you to judge but you have no idea of what it's like for a woman caught in that situation.'

'Don't tell me what I do and don't know, Dr Hayden,' he bit out. 'I have personal experience of an unplanned pregnancy. Unlike most men, I stuck around and I never once regretted it.'

'Kate obviously cares very deeply for you,' Eloise said. 'The least you could do is take the time to listen to her. It must have been hard, living a lie for all these years.'

He glared her determinedly. 'Thanks for the counselling session, Dr Hayden, but I will handle this in my own way and in my own time.'

Eloise seriously wondered why Kate was even bothering with Nick Tremayne. She had never met a more prickly and arrogant man in her life. 'I am sorry to have taken so much of your precious time,' she said, and hitched the strap of her bag over her shoulder. 'I will be in touch if there are any other questions I need you to answer.'

He didn't respond but as she closed the door behind her Eloise heard him thump his fist on his desk as he swore rather viciously.

'Eloise?' Kate's whispered call sounded from behind her, and she turned to see Kate standing on the stairs leading to her office. 'Can I see you for a minute?'

Eloise smiled and stepped towards her. 'Of course.'

'Not here,' Kate said, and moved down the stairs to join her. 'I need some fresh air. Have you got time for a short walk?'

'I'd like that very much.'

Eloise noticed how Kate seemed to almost tiptoe past Nick Tremayne's consulting room but she visibly relaxed once they were outside in the fresh warm summer morning air.

'I was going to call you to come to my place for dinner this evening. Are you free?' Kate asked.

'I love to come if that's not too much trouble.'

Kate gave her a sideways glance. 'You can bring Lachlan with you if you like. A little bird told me you and he were an item.'

Eloise shifted her gaze. 'Chief Inspector D'Ancey and I are nothing of the sort,' she said crisply.

'Oh...I must have been misinformed.'

Eloise whooshed out a breath and stopped to look at Kate. 'I am so mad at him right now I can barely think straight.'

'Is it about Poppy?'

Eloise hesitated. She wasn't sure how much Kate knew and neither did she want to make Poppy's situation any more difficult than it already was.

'It's all right,' Kate said. 'I know about her pregnancy. I know I'm not really supposed to discuss patient details but in this case I think it's warranted.'

'What a pity Chief Inspector D'Ancey and Dr Tremayne didn't share your view.'

'If it's any consolation to you, Nick was pretty insistent that Lachlan tell you, but he refused. Nick and I discussed it together that day.'

Eloise released a sigh. 'I feel caught in an impossible situation,' she said. 'Lachlan is the first man I've ever felt had something to offer me in terms of a relationship but this has ruined everything. I can't trust him.'

'Don't throw away a once-in-a-lifetime chance at happiness,' Kate said. 'Men like Lachlan don't come along every day. He's a decent man and a very loving father.'

'I'm supposed to be investigating a suspicious death, not on a mission to find a husband,' Eloise said regretfully.

Kate smiled sadly. 'Don't end up like me, Eloise. I am quite a bit older than you and the only man I love is too angry to even speak to me.'

'Hopefully he'll come to terms with it soon,' Eloise offered although from what she'd seen so far she had her doubts. 'It's been a bit of a bombshell and with circumstances as they are with his older children, it's understandable he'd be finding it a bit hard to deal with.'

'Are you going to give Lachlan another chance?' Kate asked after they had walked a little way further.

Eloise looked out to sea, thinking of her apartment so many thousands of kilometres away. 'I have a job to go home to,' she said.

'You can find a job here, Eloise. You're free to do what your heart tells you to do.'

'I'm not sure what my heart is telling me,' Eloise confessed after another few paces. 'I haven't listened to it for a long time.'

Kate gave her arm a gentle squeeze. 'Don't leave it too late, Eloise,' she said, and they walked back to the clinic in silence.

CHAPTER FIFTEEN

'How did your meeting with Ethan Jenson's parents go?' James Derrey asked Lachlan as he came in from another call.

'It was pretty harrowing, as you might expect,' Lachlan answered. 'I took Gaye Trembath with me. She stayed on to sit with Mrs Jenson. We both felt she needed a bit of support.'

'Nasty business,' James said. 'What's next?'

'I want feather samples taken from the Anchor Hotel, where Ethan Jenson was staying, as well as any other place he was known to have spent a night or several hours,' Lachlan said. 'I'll get both Peter Middleton and Dr Hayden to examine them to see if they match the feathers from the lung biopsy Dr Hayden took.'

'Yes, Chief. Anything else?'

'Yes,' he said. 'I want you to find out where Molly Beale is.'

James lifted his brows. 'Isn't she staying at Trevallyn House?'

'No, apparently she left the day Dr Hayden arrived. She didn't leave a forwarding address.'

'You think she's got something to do with this?' James asked.

Lachlan drummed his fingers on the desk for a few seconds. 'I don't know. I know Molly's done a runner before but I want to know if her bank account has been accessed.'

'Have you checked with her mother?'

'I spoke to Maisie Beale earlier,' Lachlan said. 'She threw her daughter out of the house a couple of months ago. Apparently she found Molly in bed with Maisie's new boyfriend.'

James grimaced. 'That must have gone down a treat.'

'It sure did. Maisie insists she never wants to see her daughter again.'

'You don't think…?'

'Molly took her belongings with her when she left Trevallyn House. She didn't have much, mind you, but it always pays to keep an open mind. Our Molly had a bit of reputation with the lads, as I'm sure you know.'

'Did she have a fling with Ethan Jenson, do you think?' James asked.

Lachlan recalled his daughter's distress at hearing Molly Beale had been one of Jenson's conquests so soon after her. 'Yes, I have reason to believe she did.'

James Derrey came back to the station a couple of hours later and took the seat opposite Lachlan.

'Chief, Molly Beale hasn't accessed her bank account or any of her credit cards for over a week,' he said. 'The cards are all up to the max in any case. No one seems to know where she went. She didn't have many friends—I suppose no one trusted her with the silver, not to mention their husbands or boyfriends.'

'I'll go and speak to Beatrice Trevallyn,' Lachlan said. 'It sounds like she was the last person to see her. She might be able to tell me something. You'd better come with me.'

They drove the short distance to Trevallyn House but as they got out of the car the first person to greet them was Arnold Price, who was coming back from a stroll.

'Ah, Chief Inspector, just the person I was hoping to see. How's the investigation going?' Mr Price said with a beaming smile. 'Have you found a suspect yet? I have some suggestions if you haven't. You see, I have this theory—'

'Hello, Mr Price.' Lachlan smiled to take the sting out of his interruption. 'We're here to see Mrs Trevallyn, actually. Do you know if she's about?'

'I think she might be having a nap. I haven't seen her for a couple of hours but, then, I've been out walking thinking through my plot,' he said. 'Shall I get Davey to fetch her? I think he's usually in the garden at this time of day.'

Eloise turned into the gate of Trevallyn House just then to see Lachlan and a junior constable talking to Mr Price, her heart sinking when all three men turned to face her.

'Dr Hayden.' Mr Price was the first to speak. 'How delightful you are all here at the same time. This is absolutely marvellous for my research. Chief Inspector D'Ancey wants to interview Mrs Trevallyn.' He turned to look at Lachlan and added entreatingly, 'I don't suppose I could listen in?'

Lachlan shook his head. 'Sorry, Mr Price. Although this is a routine enquiry, I'm afraid it will have to remain closed to the public.'

'I'll see if I can find Davey,' Mr Price said with another affable smile. 'I don't like to go to Mrs Trevallyn's room on my own. She's bit old-fashioned that way.'

'I understand,' Lachlan said, and once the elderly gentleman had gone round the side of the house he turned to Eloise. 'Dr Hayden, this is PC James Derrey. James, this is Dr Eloise Hayden from Australia.'

Eloise shook the younger man's hand. 'It's nice to meet you, James.' And with a little glittering glance cast in Lachlan's direction she turned back to James and added, 'And you can drop the Dr and the bit about coming from Australia. I prefer to be called Eloise.'

'Oh...right, then,' James said, looking a little flustered as he took in the silent exchange between his chief and their international guest.

'What did you want to see Beatrice about?' Eloise asked Lachlan after a short, tense pause.

'I want to interview Molly Beale, the cleaning maid who worked here previously. So far we haven't been able to locate her.'

'You think she's somehow involved in this?' Eloise asked, not realising she was practically repeating verbatim with what James had asked not half an hour earlier.

'It's too early to say,' Lachlan answered. 'I would like to know her movements on the night in question and take it from there.'

'You'd better come in and wait in Beatrice's sitting room,' she said, unlocking the front door, but as soon as she stepped inside she reeled backwards from the strong smell of gas.

Lachlan had smelt it too and dragged her backwards and called out for James to call the fire service.

'What if Beatrice is inside?' Eloise asked, frowning in concern.

'Stay here and I'll check,' he said.

'No, I'm a trained doctor,' she said. 'She might be unconscious.'

'We'll all be unconscious if we don't take care. Now, stay here.'

Eloise stood her ground, whipping her hand out of his iron hold. 'No, I will not stay here. If she and Davey are unconscious, they'll need to be moved, and you can't do that on your own. We can put handkerchiefs over our mouths and see where they are.'

Mr Price came up the front steps, puffing heavily. 'I can't

find Davey and the back door is locked.' He sniffed the air and frowned. 'Is that gas?'

'Yes, it is. Please, stay well back until the fire crew gets here,' Lachlan ordered. 'Eloise, take this handkerchief and double it over your mouth. If at any stage you feel faint or nauseous, you are to leave the building immediately—is that understood?'

She nodded, folded the cloth over her mouth and followed him into the guest-house.

Lachlan checked each room, opening every window he came to while keeping a close watch on Eloise a step behind him.

They found Beatrice first. She was lying on the floor of one of the smaller rooms upstairs. Lachlan rushed to the window while Eloise dropped to her knees and checked for a pulse. 'She's alive,' she said.

Lachlan found Davey the other side of the single bed, still with tools in hand in front of the faulty outlet.

'Davey's over here,' he said, and bent down to examine him. 'He was obviously trying to fix the leak when he lost consciousness.'

Eloise came over and examined Davey quickly, relieved to find a pulse, although it was a little thready. 'We need to get them both to hospital or the clinic at least in order to give them oxygen.'

James appeared at the door with a couple of firemen, who had already turned off the gas at the mains.

The patients were soon transported to the clinic and after Nick Tremayne had assessed them, they were given oxygen until the ambulance arrived to transport them to St Piran Hospital.

Kate came over to where Eloise was awaiting a final decision by the fire crew about the safety of staying at Trevallyn House.

'I'm afraid they're going to close it down temporarily,'

Kate said. 'It seems the gas pipes have needed replacing for years but poor Bea never had the money. You can stay with me. Jem will love it.'

'That's very kind of you,' Eloise said. 'What about Mr Price?'

'Lachlan's taken care of that,' she said. 'He's got a spare room.'

'Mr Price will be beside himself,' Eloise said with a wry look in Lachlan's direction, where he was still speaking to Nick.

Lachlan turned as if he'd felt the weight of her stare and came over to speak to her. 'Dr Hayden, I've organised for some pillows from the Anchor Hotel and a couple of other places, as well as Trevallyn House, to be tested for a match with the feathers found in Ethan Jenson's lungs.'

'Thank you, Chief Inspector,' she said in a crisp, professional tone. 'I was just about to suggest we take some samples from the guest-house.'

One of his brows lifted in surprise, or was it admiration? Eloise couldn't really tell. 'Were you, now?' he asked.

'Yes,' she said. 'I smelt gas the other day and it occurred to me there might be a connection, but so far I haven't been able to establish one. Not unless Molly Beale secretly took Ethan Jenson up to her room. Beatrice Trevallyn was adamant he had never been there but that's not to say…'

He glanced at Kate, who was hovering near by. 'Let's leave our discussion till you examine the samples,' he suggested. 'Give me a call when you're done at the lab.'

'Right.'

He strode away with a brief nod and smile at Kate on his way past.

Kate whistled through her teeth as she came back to Eloise. 'I'd say he was done like a dinner.'

Eloise frowned. 'What on earth do you mean?'

'The way he looked at you just then,' Kate said with a knowing smile. 'I'd say you'd better organise for the rest of your things back home to be sent over straight away. That man is in love.'

'That man is a jerk,' Eloise said irritably. But she couldn't help glancing in his direction when she hoisted her bag over her shoulder and made her way outside to her car.

Dr Middleton looked up from the lab's microscope some hours later. 'They found a match,' he said. 'Have a look and see what you think.'

Eloise came over and examined the samples carefully for several minutes and eventually came to the same conclusion. 'You're right, Dr Middleton. The sample from Trevallyn House exactly matches the feather particles I took from the lung biopsy. We'll ask them to do a cross-check to make sure, but I think it's starting to add up.'

After a series of cross-checks were done and the results documented, Eloise called Lachlan on his mobile and arranged to meet him in his office. Her tone was matter-of-fact but inside she was a jangling mess of nerves, hurt and heartache.

When she arrived at his office, she stood outside his door for several moments, trying to get her chest to loosen enough to breathe. *You can do this*, she reminded herself sternly.

She clenched her hand into a fist and raised it to the door's surface, but it suddenly opened and her hand landed on Lachlan's chest with a little thump.

'Maybe I should think about getting a doorbell,' he said with a twisted smile.

Eloise's hand dropped back to her side but she could still feel the warmth of his chest against her knuckles and her chest gave another flutter.

'I have a match,' she announced briskly, once they were both seated. 'Trevallyn House—in fact, the very pillow from the bed Molly Beale used.'

'I thought you might.'

She looked at him closely. 'Have you found out what happened yet?'

'Davey woke up a couple of hours ago,' he said. 'He told us everything. It seems Molly asked him to distract Beatrice so she could bring Ethan Jenson up to her room that night. It hadn't been the first time either. The arrangement was that Ethan would wait upstairs in her room while Molly finished the dinner things downstairs. Then she would come up and they would presumably have sex and then with Davey's help Ethan would be escorted off the premises, all without Beatrice finding out.'

'Did he tell you what happened that particular night?' she asked.

'Yes he did. Poor chap. He's distraught, of course, but Molly threatened him so much he did what she suggested. He was terrified his mother's home and livelihood would be taken from her. You remember I told you about a salmonella outbreak a while ago?'

She nodded.

'Well, Davey was frightened he might have to be institutionalised or something if his mother could no longer keep the guest house going. You have to remember he thinks like a young child.'

'Yes, I realise that. It's very sad.'

'Apparently the arrangement went as planned. Ethan Jenson left the Anchor Hotel around seven-thirty and Davey let him in and locked the door to Molly's room with Jenson inside. That was to stop other guests inadvertently opening the wrong door apparently. Jenson waited upstairs but Molly got held up with some extra work. When she got to her room

Ethan was lying face down on the bed and there was a strong smell of gas. She told Davey she quickly turned off the gas at the wall and opened the window before she tried to find a pulse, but when she couldn't find one she hatched a plan to get them both off the hook.'

'Clever of her,' Eloise remarked cynically.

He gave a shrug. 'Molly isn't exactly a rocket scientist and certainly Davey wouldn't have been much help. Why they didn't call an ambulance at that point I guess we'll never know. Ethan might have been able to be resuscitated. He may have only just lost consciousness.'

Eloise inwardly winced at the thought of Ethan's parents being informed of the possibility their son might not have died if help had come sooner. 'What happened next?' she asked.

'Molly told Davey if he didn't get rid of Jenson's body he would be charged with murder because he was the one who brought him into the house and locked him in the room. So that's what Davey did. He took Ethan down under cover of darkness and dumped him in the ocean.'

Eloise frowned as she tried to take it all in. 'And no one saw him? Ethan Jenson was five eleven and of average weight. It would have been hard to disguise him as something else.'

'Davey is often seen about at odd hours carrying old bits of rubbish about the place. He does some gardening jobs for a couple of retired folk down near the harbour. If anyone saw him, they'd think nothing of it. He's often got a sack of some kind on his back.'

'But what about the smell of gas at Trevallyn House?' Eloise asked. 'Surely Beatrice would have been able to smell it that evening if not some of the other guests.'

'Beatrice Trevallyn has no sense of smell. She had a mini-stroke a couple of years ago and as a result lost her ability to smell. As for the other guests staying there...well, there weren't any at that time. Mr Price hadn't yet arrived and you didn't come until early June. The place is often empty as it's a bit run-down. Davey did his best but really he should have contacted the gas people much earlier. One can only assume he was worried about the expense of refitting the pipes.'

'Have you located Molly Beale to get a statement?'

'Yes, she was found about an hour ago in Glasgow. She gave a frank and full confession. She was lying low, hoping things would settle down. That was why she left the day you arrived. When she heard a police doctor was coming from Australia she knew she had to get away, and fast, and not leave a trail. She used what cash she had on her but, of course, it eventually ran out. We got her on her first cash-card transaction.'

'She was taking a very big risk, trusting Davey to keep quiet,' Eloise commented.

'Davey's been infatuated with her for years,' he said. 'He would do anything for her. It's my guess she played on it for all she was worth.'

A silence swirled around them for several long seconds.

'Will charges be laid against both of them?' she asked.

'I would hazard a guess that Davey won't be charged on the basis of his disability. Molly will be charged with perverting the course of justice. She's already pleaded guilty. The coroner's going to reopen the inquiry at short notice on account of you being here from abroad. He'll need you to present your findings. I think the inquiry will be in about ten days' time.'

'So we were both wrong,' Eloise said after another small pause. 'You thought it was drowning and I thought it was a straight case of murder.'

'Yes,' he said, looking at her mouth. 'We were both wrong.'

Eloise swallowed as another protracted silence thickened the air.

'Eloise, there's something I want to ask you.'

'No, please,' she said, forcing herself to meet his gaze. 'Don't.'

He frowned at her. 'You don't want to even consider the possibility that we could have a relationship, do you?'

'I live in Sydney, you live in Penhally Bay.'

'You could move.'

She tightened her mouth. 'Why don't *you* move?'

His frown deepened. 'Because I have a daughter and an ex-wife who expects to see her reasonably regularly, that's why. I also have a grandchild on the way. I can't move...or at least not right now.'

'And yet you expect me to drop everything and take up with you—for how long? Six months, a year?'

'I hadn't got as far as putting a time frame on it,' he said. 'We've known each less than two weeks.'

Eloise wondered if he was having a dig at her for falling into bed with him so readily. She hoped not. She *desperately* hoped not. 'Lachlan...' She moistened her lips and tried to get her voice to co-operate by sounding normal instead of choked up with emotion. 'I think I made a mistake... I mean, I *know* I made a mistake by sleeping with you. I gave you completely the wrong impression. It was a mistake, one of my biggest, actually.'

He frowned at her. 'The biggest mistake you'll ever make is walking out that door without giving me a chance to put things right between us.'

'You can't put things right that were wrong from the word go,' she said, steeling herself for his counter-attack, which she knew was going to undo her completely unless she kept her emotions under tight control. 'I was a fool to be tempted. I'm ashamed of my weakness. It's totally unprofessional and it could have jeopardised the whole investigation.'

'But it didn't, Eloise,' he said. 'We solved this case working together, looking at it from different angles. We could make a great team. Please, take the time to think about it. You have to stay around for the coroner's inquiry in any case.'

Eloise felt as if her heart was being clamped by a huge vice. She wanted to say yes to everything, but how could she know it would work out? He had just ended a miserable marriage. It would be unfair of her to expect him to jump straight into a new one if, in fact, he had the intention of asking her, which she very much doubted.

She would be risking everything she had worked so hard for—her career, her professional reputation, and the one thing she had protected so guardedly for so long. Her heart.

'Please, Eloise,' he said. 'At least think about it for a week or two. Don't you owe me that?'

Eloise felt as if every part of her was being stitched into a tight knot of pain deep inside her. Her chest felt weighted, as if a stone had settled there, pushing her heart to one side so it couldn't work properly. 'I don't owe you anything, Lachlan,' she said in the same controlled tone, even though she was as close to tears as she had ever been. 'We had a brief fling and as far as I'm concerned that's the end of it.'

'I'm not going to make a fool of myself, begging you to change your mind,' he said. 'Neither am I going to tell you I love you because I'm not sure if what I feel is the real thing, but it sure as hell feels like it.'

'You're still getting over your ex-wife,' she said, even as her heart gave a sudden leap of hope before settling down again. 'You're vulnerable right now. Any man would be.

Especially with Poppy in the situation she is in. You're not able to think clearly.'

He let out a sigh and sent a hand through his hair. 'Maybe you're right,' he said, giving her a wry smile. 'I'm not exactly doing this the textbook way, am I?'

She gave him a small smile in return. 'Maybe you should book in for some lessons or read a book or something.'

'*Dating for Dummies*. Now, that just might be the way to go,' he said with one of his disarming grins.

She reached up and kissed him on the cheek before her common sense muscled in to stop her. 'You're a good man, Chief Inspector D'Ancey. There are a lot of women out there who would give an arm and a leg to be with you.'

His mouth twisted ruefully. 'But not you?'

She let out a heartfelt sigh. 'What you need is a hearth-and-home type, someone to have your dinner ready when you come home from another tough day at the station. Not someone who is slaving over blood splatter samples and lying awake most nights, having nightmares about the victims' last moments of life.'

He reached out and touched her softly on the cheek with the back of his knuckles. 'You take care of yourself, Dr Eloise Hayden from Australia,' he said softly.

She swallowed back the emotion rising in her throat and gave him a stiff little smile. 'I will,' she said. Moving out of his embrace, she left the room and closed the door quietly but firmly behind her.

CHAPTER SIXTEEN

'How do you feel now the coroner's inquiry is over?' Kate Althorp asked close to three weeks later.

Eloise slumped as she sank into the nearest sofa chair. She had been staying with Kate and Jem since Trevallyn House had been closed for the repairs to the gas system to be completed. Beatrice and Davey had both recovered and had gone to recuperate with Beatrice's sister and her husband in Devon. Beatrice had decided to sell the guest-house and move into something smaller with Davey, which seemed a good solution all round.

'I'm fine. I feel a bit sorry for Molly Beale, however,' Eloise answered. 'When she goes to court she'll probably get three years for perverting the course of justice, but she might get out earlier if she behaves herself. She might even benefit from being inside for a short time. No charges were laid against Davey. A psychiatrist declared him unfit to stand trial.'

'What about Ethan Jenson's parents? How did they seem to handle it all?' Kate asked.

Eloise puffed out a sigh and laid her head back on the sofa cushions. 'I've talked to them a few times,' she said. 'As you can imagine, it's agonising for them. They can't help thinking that if only Molly or Davey had stopped and called for help when they first discovered him, Ethan might be alive today.'

'Everyone is wise in hindsight,' Kate said. 'But I guess they panicked at the time.'

'Yes, that's true, although he was definitely dead when he hit the water. At least he didn't suffer. Drowning is not a pleasant way to die, although I guess it's better than some other ways.'

Kate fiddled with her watch for a moment. 'I thought you might like to know Lachlan is back from London. He brought Poppy with him.'

Eloise gave her an offhand glance. 'I don't see what that has to do with me.'

'She had a miscarriage while she was in London with her mother,' Kate said. 'That's why Lachlan wasn't at the inquiry. He sent a signed affidavit instead.'

Eloise had assumed he had taken leave to avoid running into her at the inquiry where she had been called to present her evidence. She hadn't thought for a moment there might be some other reason he hadn't shown up. She'd been so angry that he hadn't even bothered to phone her, but now she realised he would have been totally preoccupied with his daughter, offering his support and trying to help her get over an extremely traumatic time.

'Is Poppy all right?' she asked.

'Physically, yes, but a bit fragile emotionally, or so Lachlan said. No one in the village knows about it, of course, apart from Nick and Robert, who has been a real sweetheart to her. I'm only telling you because she wants to see you before you leave tomorrow.'

Eloise looked at Kate in surprise. 'She wants to see me? But what on earth for?'

'I don't know, but she called a few minutes ago, before you came home. I think Robert is driving her over right now.'

Eloise chewed at her lip and frowned.

'Are you going to see Lachlan before you leave tomorrow?' Kate asked into the silence.

Eloise shifted her gaze. 'I don't really see the point.'

Kate gave her a lengthy look. 'Are you sure you're doing the right thing by leaving with things so up in the air between you?'

Eloise got to her feet and began to pace the room. 'I can't stay here without some sort of commitment from him, Kate. I don't know what he's told you, but we had a brief fling. It was little more than a one-night stand,' she said, trying to convince herself that was all it had been.

'He didn't speak of it in quite those terms,' Kate said.

Eloise swung around to look at her. 'What did he say?'

'Not much. He didn't betray any confidences or anything. He just said how much he had enjoyed being with you and that he was going to miss you. Also that you made him realise what he had been missing out on in his marriage to Margaret.'

Eloise frowned. 'Nothing else?'

Kate shook her head. 'Why, were you expecting something else?'

Eloise whooshed out a breath and crossed her arms over her chest. 'I don't know... I guess a marriage proposal might have made me think twice about leaving.'

Kate's eyes went wide. 'I thought you were a career-woman to the backbone? No marriage, no kids—or have I got it wrong somewhere?'

'Yes, well, I was totally career focused until I met Chief Inspector Lachlan D'Ancey,' Eloise confessed. 'Ever since then I keep having these crazy thoughts about a white dress and a long veil and...and...'

'And?'

Eloise scowled. 'Never mind. It's stupid anyway. My flight's booked and I'm almost packed.'

'You can always cancel the flight and unpack your bag.'

'I could but I won't.' The doorbell rang and Eloise added as she went to answer it, 'Kate, you've been so kind over the last couple of weeks. I really appreciate it, especially as you've got your own issues to deal with right now.'

'They've waited several years,' Kate said resignedly. 'I guess they can wait a little longer.'

Poppy was standing on the doorstep looking pale and thin, nothing like the surly street-wise teenager Eloise had met four weeks ago.

'Hello, Dr Hayden,' she said with a wavering smile. 'I hope this isn't an inconvenient time for you?'

'No, it's fine. I wasn't doing anything special tonight, just packing.'

'You're leaving tomorrow, right?' Poppy asked, her brown eyes containing a flicker of worry.

'That's the plan.'

Poppy shifted from foot to foot. 'Um…are you free to come for a little walk? Robert's waiting in the car for me. It won't take long.'

Eloise looked to where Robert was sitting behind the wheel of his run-down car. He lifted his hand in a small wave and turned back to the car magazine he was reading. 'Sure. Why not?' she said. 'You lead the way.'

Poppy led the way to the bay past the lifeboat station and down onto the sand. 'I always like to take my shoes off on the sand, don't you?' she asked. 'I like the feel of it squishing between my toes.'

'Yes,' Eloise said, wondering what this was all about. Poppy seemed as if she wanted to get something off her chest and although Eloise hadn't been expecting any last-minute friendly overtures, she thought that as the young girl had been through a rather traumatic time, she at least deserved a hearing.

Poppy took off her sandals and looked at them for a moment. 'I have a huge apology to make,' she said, dragging her gaze up to meet Eloise's. 'I was so rude to you the first time I met you. And that day at the café when I totally ignored you. I know you probably think I'm a horrible person, but really I'm not. I was just very confused and upset.'

Eloise smiled. 'You're a teenager, Poppy. Sixteen is a tough age. I remember it all too well. You're not quite an adult but you want to be one.'

'I had a taste of being an adult and I can tell you I'm not quite ready for it,' Poppy said, biting down on her lip. 'I'm not sure if you know, but I had a miscarriage. I made Dad promise not to tell anyone. Only Mrs Althorp and Dr Tremayne know...and Robert, of course...'

Eloise saw the glisten of moisture in the young girl's eyes and placed a gentle hand on her arm. 'Do you want to talk about it? It sometimes helps to talk to someone other than a family member.'

Poppy sniffed and wiped her nose on the back of the sleeve of her light cotton shirt. 'It's OK. Dad's been great,' she said. 'Mum's been better since...since...I...lost it. She was so angry at me. I wanted her to hold me and tell me things were going to be OK, but all she could do was shout at me for wasting my life and throwing my career options away. She wanted me to have an abortion. She kept pressuring me. She even made me an appointment at a clinic. I was so confused. I just wanted to turn back the clock and make it all go away... And then I started to bleed...'

'You poor darling,' Eloise said softly.

Poppy gave her a wobbly smile. 'I wish you would stay a little longer and give my father a chance. He pretends he's OK but I know he's not. It's my fault, isn't it? If I'd been nicer to you from the start, maybe you wouldn't be flying back to Australia tomorrow.'

'Poppy, it's not your fault at all,' Eloise insisted. 'Things just…just didn't work out.'

'Why? Don't you like him or something?' Poppy asked, looking at her intently.

Eloise gave her a crooked smile touched with regret. 'I like him, Poppy,' she said. 'I like him a lot.'

'Enough to marry him?'

'That's a completely hypothetical question.'

'Because he hasn't asked you?'

Eloise let out a breath in a slow but uneven stream. 'No, no, he hasn't.'

'Would it make a difference if he did?' Poppy asked.

'Listen, Poppy, your father's just come out of his marriage to your mother. The last thing he needs right now is a new wife.'

Poppy poked at a bit of seaweed with her big toe. 'It'd be all right with me, you know…if he did ask you, I mean. I know I said I didn't want another mother but I like you. You make my dad smile. I love my mum and all that, but I can see now why they couldn't make a go of things. Mum's too driven. She can't stop and look at the big picture. She's really happy with Roger. They're both as career mad as each other. Dad loves his work, he would never have gone as far as he has without some sort of dedication and ambition, but he still always finds time for me. When he heard I was losing the baby, he dropped everything to come to me, even though the inquiry had just started.'

'You're a very lucky girl to have such a wonderful

father,' Eloise said, feeling wretchedly guilty for misjudging him so badly.

Poppy smiled. 'I think so, too. I just want him to be happy. He's only thirty-nine, that's not really old.'

'No, it's not.'

Another little silence passed, broken only by the whisper of the water lapping gently at the shore.

'I feel so guilty about the miscarriage,' Poppy said after another few paces. 'Guilty but relieved.' She stopped and looked at Eloise again. 'Do you think that's terribly wrong of me?'

'No, of course it's not wrong to feel that way,' Eloise answered. 'It must have been such a difficult time for you. You need to put it behind you now and get on with your life.'

'Yes...that's what Robert said.'

They walked a little further in silence until Poppy looked down at the sand near her toes. 'Hey, look,' she said. 'Someone's written a message on the sand with shells.'

Eloise looked at the first couple of letters and wrinkled her brow. 'It doesn't make sense. What does *aila* mean?' She peered a little closer and asked, 'Is that next letter to it *r* or *n*?'

Poppy looked down. 'It's definitely *r*,' she said, and then, visibly brightening, added, 'Hey, this is fun. Robert and I used to do this. We'd leave coded messages for each other on the beach. Here's another one. I think that's *t*—or is it *f*?'

Eloise crouched down. 'I'm not sure. I think someone's walked across that section.' She straightened and walked a bit further to where the shells began again and started reading the rest of the letters out loud. '*Susmorf...*' She looked up at Poppy again with a puzzled expression. 'What does *susmorf* mean?'

'Um...I think there's meant to be a gap between the *s* and the *m*,' Poppy said, suddenly biting her lip.

Eloise frowned again. 'It still doesn't make sense.'

'There's more over here,' Poppy said. 'Look.'

Eloise looked, her eyes narrowing slightly. 'Hang on a minute...' She leant down a little closer. *'nedyaH...esiolE.'* She straightened and met Poppy's gaze. 'That's my name spelt backwards.'

'Oh, yes.' Poppy looked back at her with big innocent brown eyes. 'So it is.'

'And there's an *r* and D for Doctor.' Eloise looked at Poppy again. 'What's going on?'

Poppy gave her a sheepish look. 'Maybe we should have started at the other end,' she said. 'I think I might have got Dad's directions wrong.'

Eloise's eyes narrowed even further. *'Your father wrote this?'*

Poppy nodded and started to walk quickly back the way they had come. 'I think I can hear Robert calling me,' she called over her shoulder. 'I'll meet you back at the car.'

Eloise would have gone after her but the need to read the rest of the message was too great. She walked along and mentally rotated the words so they made sense. *'Question mark...me...marry...you...will...'* She stopped when she came to a large pair of bare feet and slowly looked upwards into a pair of whisky-brown eyes.

'Someone went for a jog over the last bit,' Lachlan said with a rueful smile. 'I'm not sure if it makes sense any more.'

Eloise blinked at him, her heart starting to race and her legs feeling as if they were as soggy and waterlogged as the sand at the water's edge a few feet away.

He stepped closer and took both of her hands in each of his. 'Will you marry me, Dr Eloise Hayden from Australia?' And with a boyish grin added, 'Or is it Ausfnalia?'

She laughed and threw herself into his arms, her heart feeling as if it was going to burst with joy. 'I don't care what or where it is—I'm staying here with you.'

He swept her off her feet and swung her around, the shells of his proposal crunching under his feet. 'Do you mean it? Do you really mean it?' he asked.

'Yes.' She was crying and laughing all at the same time. 'Of course I mean it. I know it's crazy and too soon for you and too soon for me and my career is probably going to take a nosedive, but I love you. I think I've been fighting it from the start, but I can't stop how I feel any more.'

'I love you too, darling,' he said. 'I should have told you earlier but I only realised it today. The thought of you getting on that plane and never coming back was too much to bear. I suddenly realised I was in love with you, *really* in love with you, which meant I had to find a way to ask you to marry me in a hurry.'

She hugged him around the neck and showered his face and mouth with kisses. 'That was a very creative way to propose.'

'Actually, it was Poppy who gave me the idea,' he said. 'And all was going well until that wretched jogger went past. He had feet like planks.'

'Just as well the tide didn't come in,' she said, smiling at him delightedly.

'I had already covered that contingency, although I must confess I had a bit of trouble locating enough shells. There must have been a few kids down here today, collecting them.'

'At least I saw it and answered it,' she said with a heartfelt sigh. 'That's all that matters.'

His brown eyes twinkled. 'Yes, but do you know what they say about messages written in the sand, Dr Hayden?'

She grinned from ear to ear. 'I don't know. What *do* they say, Chief Inspector?' she asked.

He smiled at her tenderly. 'They say they last for ever,' he said, and brought his mouth down to hers.

* * * *

*Virgin Midwife,
Playboy Doctor*

MARGARET McDONAGH

Margaret McDonagh says of herself: 'I began losing myself in the magical world of books from a very young age and I always knew that I had to write—pursuing the dream for over twenty years, often with cussed stubbornness in the face of rejection letters! Despite having numerous romance novellas, short stories and serials published, the news that my first "proper book" had been accepted by Mills & Boon for their Medical Romance™ line brought indescribable joy! Having a passion for learning makes researching an involving pleasure, and I love developing new characters, getting to know them, setting them challenges to overcome. The hardest part is saying goodbye to them, because they become so real to me. And I always fall in love with my heroes! Writing and reading books, keeping in touch with friends, watching sport and meeting the demands of my four-legged companions keeps me well occupied. I hope you enjoy reading this book as much as I loved writing it.'

Joanne, Sheila and Jenny, for inviting me to be part of this exciting project and for all their hard work and encouragement

Shelley of Web Crafters for designing me such a great website!

And D, BB and B from T…
(you know who you are!)
Thanks for making this such a
moving experience!!

CHAPTER ONE

'SOMETHING'S WRONG, isn't it?'

Midwife Chloe MacKinnon unwrapped the blood-pressure cuff from around Avril Harvey's arm and tried to offer the anxious woman a reassuring smile. 'Your blood pressure is rather high,' she admitted, masking her own growing concern as she re-checked the notes and previous readings.

'What about the other things?' Tears glistened in Avril's pale blue eyes, while her swollen fingers nervously shredded a paper tissue. 'I've always suspected things weren't right but the people at my previous practice in Birmingham told me not to worry. They said they were normal signs of pregnancy.'

Chloe took one trembling hand in hers and squeezed gently before returning to her chair. This was the first time she had seen Avril. The woman had moved to the small Cornish town of Penhally Bay in the last couple of weeks with her husband, Piers, both determined that their longed-for child would grow up in a better environment than the inner city. But this was Avril's first baby. And at thirty-nine, being short in stature, underweight and with a history of migraines, she had a few of the risk factors that warned Chloe to be on her guard. Add in the symptoms she had presented with that morning, and Chloe was worried about Avril's well-being as well as for that of her baby, suspecting that she had developed pre-eclampsia.

'I always saw my GP at my old practice as well as the midwife.' Avril paused and bit her lip. 'Could I see one of the doctors here today?'

'We're more midwife-led here…' Chloe hesitated as fresh tears spilled down the mother-to-be's cheeks.

'I don't want to be a nuisance, and I don't mean to doubt your expertise. It's just that I don't know anyone and I don't know what to think. I'm so scared.'

Chloe smiled, wanting to put her at ease. 'I understand, Avril, don't worry. I'll ask one of the doctors on duty to see you.'

The GPs left straightforward cases to Chloe and her colleague, Kate Althorp, but if it would set the distressed woman's mind at rest to have the second opinion, Chloe wasn't going to be awkward about it. Avril was alone in a strange place and feeling vulnerable, clearly on edge, her pale skin sallow, her short blonde hair lank. Time was of the essence. All that mattered was the safety of both mother and baby.

'Thank you, Chloe.' Avril gave a weary sigh, pressing the fingers of one hand to her temple. 'I wish my husband was with me.'

'Would you like me to call him for you?'

'No, it's all right. After dropping me here, Piers had to make the half-hour drive to St Piran for a meeting at the secondary school. He's an art teacher and he'll be working there when the new term begins,' she explained tearfully. 'We were looking forward to the summer to settle into our new home first and prepare for the baby. He won't be back for another couple of hours.'

Nodding, Chloe reached for the phone and keyed in the extension number for Reception. She watched as Avril turned her head to stare sightlessly out of the window of the room on the first floor of the expanding Penhally Bay Surgery. Chloe had tilted the blinds to keep out the full effects of the merciless July sunshine and was grateful for the coolness inside the building.

'Hello, Sue,' she said when her call was answered by the head receptionist. 'I'm with Avril Harvey for her antenatal appointment. Would you ask one of the doctors to pop upstairs for a few minutes? Thank you.'

The tone of Sue's reply assured Chloe that the woman had grasped the seriousness of the situation and would respond swiftly to the request. Hanging up, Chloe returned her attention to Avril.

'What made you choose to settle in Penhally Bay?' she asked, trying to distract the woman from her worries.

'We've been here several times for weekends and holidays—we even spent our honeymoon here ten years ago.' A reminiscent smile lightened Avril's expression. 'We both love the friendly, peaceful atmosphere, and Piers finds inspiration here for his painting.'

'Cornwall has always drawn artists. One of my friends, Lauren, is physiotherapist here, and she's an avid painter, too. Some of her work hangs on the wall in the waiting area downstairs.'

Interest momentarily chased the shadows from Avril's eyes. 'I noticed those. She's very good. Piers's paintings are more abstract. He's hoping to have time to develop and sell his work alongside the teaching.'

'So your move was both personal and professional?' Chloe encouraged.

'It seemed ideal when the job came up in St Piran. We never expected to have a child after such a long wait, but when we discovered I was pregnant, we both wanted a different kind of life for our family. I don't know what I'll do if anything happens to my baby.' A sob escaping, she rested one palm over her stomach.

Rising to her feet, Chloe pulled another tissue from the box she kept handy, then rounded the desk, squatting down to put a comforting arm around Avril's thin shoulders. 'Try not to imagine the worst-case scenarios. Even if there is something amiss, it doesn't mean you won't have a perfectly healthy baby. We're going to do all we can to help you,' she said reassuringly, handing over the fresh tissue.

'Thank you.' Avril blew her nose and dabbed at her tear-stained cheeks. 'I'm sorry to be so silly.'

'You're not being silly. It's an emotional and worrying time.'

Before she could continue, a brief knock sounded and the door opened. Chloe glanced up, barely suppressing a groan as Dr Oliver Fawkner strode into the room with his customary swagger, exuding self-confidence and blatant sex appeal. Oh, no! Why did it have to be him? Dressed in dark grey chinos and a crisp white shirt, he looked cool and unruffled, the shirt's short sleeves showing off tanned, olive-toned skin and leanly muscled forearms dusted with dark hairs. Straightening, Chloe stepped round the far side of her desk, self-consciously putting a solid barrier between them.

Oliver had been working as an extra GP at the practice since mid-June as cover for the surgery's increasing workload, the busy holiday season and while Lucy Carter continued her maternity leave. No one could deny what an excellent doctor Oliver was. But for reasons she couldn't explain, he made her feel acutely nervous. He was just too…everything. Too masculine, too much the playboy, too outrageous, too sure of himself. And far too devastating in the looks and charm departments for any woman's peace of mind. Especially a woman like her. One who shied away from male attention and anything that made her feel uncomfortable.

Nothing and no one made her feel more uncomfortable than bad boy Oliver Fawkner.

'Chloe. I heard you wanted me.'

The rough-edged, smoky voice sent a shiver rippling down her spine. Despite being five feet seven, Chloe had a long way to look up Oliver's ruggedly athletic six-foot-three-inch frame before she met the gleam of amused devilment in brown eyes as sinful and dangerous to the health as the finest chocolate. Chloe forced herself not to react when he sent her a cheeky wink. The man was a rogue. And he never missed an opportunity to tease her, flirt with her, disturb her, which only made her more tongue-tied and feeling like a gauche country bumpkin.

'Dr Fawkner, this is Avril Harvey,' she said, trying to hide her uneasiness and maintain her cool professionalism as she gave Oliver the personal details he needed about their patient's age and circumstances.

Stepping forward with his trade-mark smile, Oliver shook the woman's hand. 'Hello, Avril, it's good to meet you.'

'Th-thank you, Doctor.' Avril managed a teary smile in response. 'I'm sorry to be a bother, asking to see you.'

'You are not a bother. What seems to be the problem?' he asked, and Chloe tensed as that warm, molten gaze held her captive once more.

Clearing her throat, she dragged her gaze free and stared down at the notes. 'This is Avril's first appointment with us after moving to Penhally with her husband. She is in her thirty-second week, and until now has been attending her previous practice in Birmingham for her antenatal checks.'

'They said I was worrying for nothing,' Avril commented, continuing to shred the tissue, revealing her anxiety.

'Avril's been experiencing headaches, which are not uncommon for her with her history of migraines, but she has also had episodes with her vision, including floaters. Then there is the oedema—and lack of weight gain,' Chloe explained, meeting Oliver's gaze again, glad to see he was now in full doctor mode and all signs of teasing had vanished. 'I did the routine checks today and there is some protein in Avril's urine. Her blood pressure has spiked, too. The notes show it has been irregular in the past, but while the last reading recorded was 145 over 85, two weeks ago, today it was 190 over 110, the highest ever.'

Oliver frowned with concern, squatting down beside the mother-to-be, talking quietly to her as he examined her hands and assessed the level of swelling in her legs and ankles. Gently he rested a hand on her belly, and Chloe suspected that the smallness of the baby and Avril being underweight had not escaped his attention. He was very good with patients. Chloe just wished she felt as secure and untroubled when working with him as she did with the other male doctors in the practice, none of whom affected her the way Oliver did. Her awkwardness around him disturbed her as it was not something she had ever experienced before.

'Avril, I don't want you to worry unduly,' Oliver told the woman, continuing to hold her hand. 'But I agree with Chloe that your symptoms are more serious than your previous practice believed.'

'Oh! I knew it. What's wrong with me, Doctor? Is it the stress of the move?'

Oliver glanced up and Chloe nodded for him to continue. She wasn't territorial about her role when a second opinion was beneficial, and she worked well in partnership with the GPs to deliver the best possible care to her patients. As Avril was new and nervous, and seemed to trust Oliver, Chloe was happy to take a back seat for now.

'We suspect you have a condition called pre-eclampsia,' Oliver explained, and Chloe, impressed again with his patient care, noticed how he was respectful to include her and not take over completely.

'That's dangerous, isn't it?' Avril's voice rose with alarm. 'Is my baby going to die?'

Oliver was swift to reassure her, without scaring her unduly, about the dangers to her own health, which Chloe knew was of concern at this point. 'Not if we can help it, Avril. Pre-eclampsia affects about one in ten pregnancies and is caused by a defect in the placenta.' He glanced up and sent Chloe a quick smile, inviting her to participate.

'That's right. The baby receives nutrients and oxygen from the mother through the placenta,' she explained to Avril. 'That's why it is so important to have regular antenatal checks because the symptoms don't always show up in the early stages. Today we've seen signs that you could be affected. You have protein in your urine, your blood pressure is considerably elevated, and you have swelling in your hands, legs and feet, plus the headaches and visual problems. If we catch things straight away, there is every chance that both you and your baby will come through this without further ill-effects.'

Avril was clearly struggling to absorb all the information. She turned her anxious gaze back to Oliver. 'What will happen? Can you give me something to make it go away?'

'No, I'm sorry, Avril, but there isn't a medical cure as such.'

'But my baby!'

Chloe handed over another tissue, which the woman took in her free hand, the other one still clasped within Oliver's. 'I know it's distressing, but you need to keep as calm as you can. Chloe will refer you to the hospital in St Piran and—'

'Is that really necessary?' Avril interrupted.

'I'm afraid it is.' Oliver's tone was firm but gentle. 'They'll monitor your symptoms, keep a close eye on your blood pressure and the levels of protein in the urine. It may be that after a day or two you can go home on strict bed rest, but they will advise you what is best.'

'Once you are lying down, especially on your left side, it is possible that your blood pressure will come down. It's a question of how effectively they can keep you settled and stable,' Chloe added.

'And if they can't?' Avril fretted.

Oliver remained calm and persuasive. 'They'll do some

tests, check your blood, and they'll listen to your baby's heart with a foetal monitor. You'll also have an ultrasound to check on the condition of your baby. Depending on what they find, they may suggest you have a steroid injection to help the baby's lungs, and you may have some other drugs for your blood pressure, and maybe some magnesium. Ultimately, the best way to protect you both would be to carry out a Caesarean and deliver your baby straight away, but that is something your doctor and midwife at the hospital will discuss with you.'

'Oh, my goodness.' Tears trickled from Avril's eyes as she sat back on the chair. 'I'm only thirty-two weeks along.'

'Everything will be done in the best interests of your baby's health and your own,' Chloe reassured her.

Oliver released Avril's hand and rose to his feet. 'Can your husband come and collect you to drive you to the hospital?'

'He's already gone to St Piran. I don't know what to do,' Avril cried.

'I can take you.' Chloe glanced up from writing a note to the midwife and doctor at the hospital. 'I'm free until after lunch when I have a couple of house calls to make before my afternoon clinic. One of those calls is halfway between here and St Piran, so it won't be a problem. We can phone your husband, Avril, and have him meet you at the hospital.'

The woman sank back in relief. 'That is so kind of you. I wouldn't like to go on my own in a taxi or something. Are you sure you don't mind?'

'Not at all,' Chloe assured her with a smile.

Her nerves tingled as she felt Oliver watching her, and her gaze was drawn to his against her will. Dark eyes focused intently on her making her shift uneasily on her chair. How did he do that? What was it about this man that made her so edgy? Thick, lustrous, over-long dark hair brushed the collar of his shirt and framed a face that was far too handsome. The straight, well-proportioned nose, sensual mouth and chiselled, masculine jaw, combined with those wicked chocolate eyes to complete the playboy package...the wealthy, devil-may-care doctor who, according to rumour, loved to surf and live the high life. A life totally opposite from her own. Shaking her head to rid herself of her unwanted thoughts about him, she mustered her reserves and kept her voice controlled.

'Thank you for your assistance, Dr Fawkner.'

A knowing smile curved his mouth. 'Always a pleasure, Chloe. I'll organise an outside line so Avril can contact her husband while you write your notes for the hospital. Then I'll help her downstairs.'

Chloe wanted to decline, to send him away, but she had to place Avril's needs above her own. 'All right,' she conceded, her evident reluctance widening Oliver's smile, a boyish dimple appearing in his left cheek.

Focusing on her task, she tried to ignore the masculine rumble of his voice, followed by Avril's tearful but brief conversation as she explained developments to her husband.

'He's going directly from the school to the hospital,' Avril confirmed, once again holding Oliver's hand as he helped her to her feet.

'That's good news. Chloe, I'll take Avril down in the lift and meet you by your car.'

'Thanks.'

Chloe gathered up her things and hurried down the stairs, stopping at Reception to explain what was happening and to collect the notes for her home visits. She was ready to head outside when the lift doors opened and Oliver gently guided Avril towards the exit. Once Avril was settled in the car, her seat belt in place, Chloe walked round to the driver's side, disconcerted when Oliver followed her. She opened the door, but the light touch of his fingers on her bare arm made her jump, and she paused, looking at him in confusion, alarmed at the way her skin burned from his touch.

'Let me know how things turn out?' he asked, and his genuine concern warmed her.

'Of course. I can check in with you later.'

'I'll look forward to it.' He hesitated a moment and Chloe fought not to reveal her discomfort when he leaned across her, making her all too aware of him as he ducked his head through the open door to talk to their patient. His body brushed against hers, and she sucked in an unsteady breath, only to find herself inhaling his unfamiliar, earthy, male scent. 'Good luck, Avril. I wish you and your husband a healthy baby. Now I'll leave you in Chloe's capable hands. She's a terrific midwife—you can trust her to give you the very best care and advice.'

Chloe was still reeling from Oliver's praise when he straightened, held her gaze for an endless moment, then stroked one finger across the tip of her nose. 'Drive carefully, babe,' he instructed, his voice soft but husky, before he stepped back to let her slide behind the steering-wheel and close the door.

Fighting down a fresh welling up of confusion, trying to ignore the way her nose prickled and her arm still tingled from the caress of his fingers, Chloe strapped on her seat belt with shaky hands and started the car. She backed out of her parking space and eased onto Harbour Road. As she headed towards the curve of the seafront and the turning to Bridge Street in the centre of town, which would take her along the side of the river and out towards the St Piran road, she glanced back one last time in her rear view-mirror.

The image that stayed with her was of Oliver, hands thrust into his trouser pockets as he stood outside the surgery, watching her go.

Despite a busy surgery, the afternoon dragged by and Oliver had a tough time concentrating and putting invasive thoughts of Chloe MacKinnon from his mind.

'Keep off that leg as much as possible for the next few

days, Linda,' he advised the young tourist, having strapped up her sprained ankle.

'I will,' she promised with a rueful smile. 'No dancing for me for a while.'

Oliver handed a prescription for some painkillers and anti-inflammatories to the girl's companion, reminding them again of the best course of action. 'Rest, ice, compression and elevation. If you have any problems don't hesitate to phone or come back and see me.'

'Thanks, Doctor.' The young man grinned at him, appearing to relish his role of nursemaid to his pretty girlfriend, helping her out of the room as Oliver opened the door and followed them through Reception.

'The pharmacy is the next building along Harbour Road.' Oliver stood with them outside the surgery entrance and pointed them in the right direction. The late afternoon heat radiated off the tarmac and sunlight shimmered on the waters in the harbour opposite where fishing boats and assorted pleasure craft bobbed on the gentle swell. 'They'll sort out the medication while you wait.'

Oliver watched for a moment as his final patient of the day hobbled along beside her boyfriend, then he went back inside and, after exchanging a few words with the receptionists, he returned to his desk in the consulting room that had been made available for his use while he was there. The previous occupant, Lucy Carter, married to Ben, an A and E consultant at St Piran, and daughter of the surgery's senior partner, Nick Tremayne, was on maternity leave.

Sighing, he set about the task of updating his patient notes and dealing with the ever-present pile of paperwork, but his attention wandered in a predictable direction. To Chloe. Whose room was immediately above his own. His gaze lifted, as if somehow by staring at the ceiling he could see her, will her presence. She was all he seemed to think about these days. And she scarcely appeared to know he was alive. It was a novel and not very pleasant experience.

He had only been in Penhally Bay a short time, but he had been drawn to Chloe from the moment they had met on his first day in his new job. And he meant what he had said earlier. Chloe was an excellent midwife…the best he had worked with. He admired her skill, her kindness, the way she always went that extra mile for the mums-to-be who meant so much to her. Like today, accepting Avril's need for another opinion and putting herself out to drive the obviously panicked woman to hospital. Perhaps he had been working too long in an impersonal big city practice. His time back in Cornwall had opened his eyes again to the true meaning and enjoyment of proper community medicine.

London had been a blast. At first. He'd had the brains to breeze through medical school, had enjoyed a successful career and an active social life since qualifying and, thanks to his family's success, he'd had the money to live life to the fullest. A cynical smile tugged his mouth. There had been good times, but his lifestyle had had its downsides, too. He was tired of those who were impressed by the family name, the bank balance, the exaggerated reputation. Tired of being used. He wanted to be seen for himself, the person he was, and not for the added trappings or as a prop to give someone else a good time. He had become mistrustful, dubious of people's—women's—motives.

He had grasped the opportunity to come back to Cornwall, his home county. His family was here, although thankfully far enough away from Penhally to allow him privacy. He loved them. They loved him. They had just never understood him. Never understood his need to make his own way and not be swallowed up in Fawkner Yachts like his grandfather, his parents, his brother and his sister. It had always been medicine that had drawn him, excited him, not the family business.

Being back in Cornwall had added benefits. He could indulge his passion for surfing and jet-skiing on an almost daily basis. And already he felt reconnected, enjoying his work in a way he had not done in the cut-and-thrust impersonal world London had become for him. Having made a conscious decision to change his life, the plan had been to settle in Penhally Bay and lie low while he established himself. He had no experience of long-term relationships, had never lived with a woman, but it was one of the things he most wanted...to find a nice girl, to settle down, to have a family. Eventually. What he had not anticipated had been meeting anyone who interested him so soon. And Chloe MacKinnon more than interested him.

She was unlike anyone he had ever known. He had never felt like this about a woman before and he was wary, unsure of venturing into the unknown. In the future, he wanted something different, some*one* different, and from all he had seen and heard so far, Chloe fitted the bill in every way. Just thinking about her made him smile and sent the blood pumping faster through his veins, a curl of heat flaming in his gut.

Chloe was the cutest thing he'd ever seen. Wholesome, in the nicest way, she had an earthy, natural beauty, something she seemed completely unaware of. She seldom wore make-up—she didn't need it. Her skin was smooth, almost translucent, while her eyes, a stunning moss green, shone between long, dusky lashes. Luscious, rosy lips begged to be kissed. At work she kept the luxuriant waves of her long ebony hair restrained in a braid, knot or ponytail, but he ached to see it loose in all its wild glory, to run his fingers through it, bury his face in it, to breathe in the lingering scent of fresh apples and sunshine that always clung to her.

Restrained was a word that could apply to Chloe in general. Serene and intelligent, she had a quiet humour that appealed to him and a sense of fun that came to the fore when she was relaxed with her friends. He had seen how she devoted all her energies to her mums-to-be and to the newborns she appeared to love with passion. She would make an amazing mother. But it was her other passions that sparked his interest and made him curious. From what he had discovered, Chloe's life outside work was a closed book—aside from her loyalty to her female friends and the evenings out she spent with them, he had no idea where she went, what she did, or who she did it with.

No doubt about it, Chloe intrigued the hell out of him. She seemed so together, so content, but she was a very private person and he had found it an uphill struggle to get close to her. At first he had assumed she must have a husband or boyfriend, for sure, but he had been amazed to discover that Chloe had no one special in her life. Furthermore, she was content that way. Why? It didn't make sense that someone so lovely and smart would be alone. But it left the field open for him. Not that he was making any headway. Chloe kept her distance from him and his own uncertainties about the timing and his suitability for a relationship made him cautious about pushing too fast.

Completely without artifice, Chloe had an air of innocence about her, one that surprised him, yet soothed his jaded spirit. He was used to women flaunting themselves and making obvious advances—it came with the territory. The Fawkner name and money drew women like iron filings to a magnet. For a time he hadn't minded. Hell, he had been young and carefree, and he had made the most of the opportunities that had come his way. But he wanted something different now—he wanted Chloe MacKinnon. He just hadn't expected it to happen so soon and wasn't sure he was ready. Yet he wasn't able to keep away from her.

Not that it had got him very far. For the first few days Chloe had treated him with the same friendly professionalism she bestowed on all her colleagues, but when he had made his personal interest in her known, she had been endearingly and puzzlingly shocked. He might have found her reaction amusing had it not led to her cooling noticeably, turning formal and businesslike, and clamming up more tightly than a bank vault.

Shaking his head, he ran his fingers through his hair, an image of Chloe vivid in his mind. She had a body to die for, but she had no notion how sexy she was. Even in the short-sleeved white tunic and loose navy blue trousers she wore to work, she turned him on as no other woman ever had. Her figure was stunning. A classic hourglass shape, with lush, full, feminine curves…soft and mouth-watering. His fingers itched to touch, his mouth to taste. But he could never get within a foot of the skittish Chloe and that was beginning to frustrate him no end.

It was a new experience for him to have to work so hard to gain a woman's attention, to get her to even speak to him outside work, let alone go out with him on a date. But despite her reserve and his own caution about getting involved with someone so soon, he wanted her more and more each day. The simmering desire nagged at him, refusing him respite, and he couldn't get her out of his head. Which meant that he somehow had to find a way past those prickly defences. Especially if he ever hoped to take her to bed. The very thought of having her naked, laid out for him, those long, inky-black tresses tumbled over his pillows, that voluptuous body arching under him as he loved her, was enough to make him harder than he'd ever been and so burning with frustration he thought he might go up in flames.

A knock on his door made him jump. For a moment he imagined it was Chloe—longed for it to be her—even if she had just come to tell him how things had gone with Avril at the hospital.

'Come in,' he called, his voice rough with desire, his heart racing in anticipation.

His gaze was fixed on the door as it slowly opened and he

almost couldn't breathe as he waited for Chloe to enter his room. When he saw, instead, that his visitor was senior partner Nick Tremayne, he struggled to swallow the wash of bitter disappointment.

'Oliver, do you have a few moments?'

'Of course, Nick.' He summoned up a smile. 'What can I do for you?'

In the short time he had been in Penhally, Oliver had come to admire the older man. He was an excellent doctor, knowledgeable if a bit aloof, but there were tensions he had yet to understand, especially between Nick and Kate Althorp, the former practice manager who had returned to her career in midwifery and now worked alongside Chloe in the practice. He suspected that Nick was a difficult man to get to know, one who felt deeply but who found it hard to share those feelings, a man who shut himself off and stuck stubbornly to a rigid point of view. Thankfully, Oliver had rubbed along well with his enigmatic boss…so far.

Exuding impatience, Nick strode across the room to gaze silently out of the window before he turned and moved back to the desk. Looking troubled, Nick folded his tall frame to sit in a chair opposite, his dark hair showing signs of grey, his gaze restless as it darted around the room.

'Is something wrong, Nick?' Oliver probed after a moment.

'What?' The older man looked up in surprise, as if disturbed from his private thoughts. 'Oh, no. No, just a lot on my mind. How are things with you? Settling in all right?'

Oliver leaned forward and folded his arms on the desk. 'Very much so. I'm enjoying my time here immensely.'

'Good. I'm glad,' he murmured, drifting again as if considering something.

Waiting patiently, Oliver reflected on the snippets of gossip he had heard. He didn't know the history between Nick and Kate, but it was clear that something had happened between them recently as they were barely speaking. At least, Nick was barely speaking to Kate, Oliver amended. Kate looked stressed and unhappy, while the tension whenever the two were near each other was palpable.

'So, Oliver,' Nick said, apparently having come to a decision. He rubbed his palms together and shifted on the chair. 'I have a favour to ask of you.'

'I'll be pleased to do what I can to help.'

Nick nodded, sitting back, his expression serious. 'I noted from your CV that you've had a special responsibility for antenatal services in a previous practice.'

'That's right,' Oliver confirmed, wondering where this was going.

'I have some extra duties coming up in the next weeks, working with the town committee regarding the twinning of Penhally with a small town in Normandy. It would be of great assistance to me if you could take over my antenatal role. Just for the time being.'

Regarding his boss closely, Oliver wondered if the twinning committee thing was a ruse. He suspected Nick wanted an excuse to avoid Kate. Frowning, he considered the request. While he didn't want to become embroiled in practice politics or take sides in whatever dispute had occurred between Nick and Kate, he couldn't deny that taking on the extra duties had an appeal. Saying yes would mean more time working closely with Chloe. And the more time he could spend with her, getting to know her, easing past her defences and deciding if there was something worth pursuing, the better as far as he was concerned.

'No problem, Nick.' There was no way he was going to turn down an opportunity to be near Chloe. 'I'll be happy to cover for you.'

The older man's relief was evident. 'Excellent. Thank you, Oliver. I'll fill you in on things and if it's not too short notice, perhaps you could start by attending the next meeting with the midwives?'

'Sure.' Oliver pulled his diary towards him and opened it. 'When is it?'

'Actually, it's in about half an hour. I, um, have to leave early,' he finished, having the grace to look uncomfortable at the lame explanation.

Hiding a smile, Oliver nodded. 'Don't worry about it.'

He listened and made notes as Nick went through the salient points he needed to know, a shiver of anticipation fluttering inside him at what lay ahead. The prospect of breaking the news to Chloe and Kate that he would be replacing Nick for the immediate future was an unappealing one. He imagined that each woman would have her own reasons to be unsettled by the change. But he wasn't going to shy away from the challenge. This unexpected turn of events could work in his favour. He was wary about the timing, unsure where any relationship might go, but instinct told him there could be something interesting between them. And desiring her as he did, he now had the perfect chance to try to woo Chloe MacKinnon.

CHAPTER TWO

CHLOE watched Kate check her watch for the tenth time in as many minutes. Kate was quite a few years her senior but they had always got on well together. The friendship had deepened further since Kate had returned to work alongside her as a midwife after giving up her job as practice manager and taking a refresher course so she could resume her previous career.

'Kate, are you all right?'

Uncharacteristically fidgety, her companion glanced up and attempted a half-hearted smile. 'Fine. Fine.'

'You realise you're holding that file upside down?' Chloe asked with calm concern.

'Oh!' Kate stared at the offending object in her hands and closed it, setting it on top of the pile in front of her. 'Sorry, Chloe, I'm as jumpy as anything.'

'Nick?'

'Who else?' Kate's wry laugh was brief and without humour.

Chloe smiled in sympathy. Having only very recently been privy to details of the latest turmoil between Kate and the senior partner at Penhally, she was worried about her friend and couldn't help but be annoyed at Nick's behaviour. True, it had to come as a shock to learn by chance that he was the father of Kate's nine-year-old-son, Jem, but to her mind his reaction had been excessive and his treatment of Kate inexcusable. Given the tension that now existed between the two of them, it was unsurprising that Kate was nervous at the prospect of their weekly antenatal meeting. The previous meetings since Nick had learned of Jem's paternity had been fraught and awkward.

'Would you rather I took the meeting on my own and brought you up to date on Monday?' Chloe offered, wanting to spare her friend and colleague further distress.

Kate shook her head. 'No, my love, thank you. I have to face him and I'm not going to run away. I've known him a long time and he has his own way of dealing with things. He can be so stubborn,' she added with a sad, resigned smile.

'If there's anything I can do…'

'Actually…' Kate straightened, a frown of consideration creasing her brow. 'I hate to impose, but are you busy tonight?'

'No, I've nothing special planned.'

'You're not going out with the girls?'

Chloe shook her head. 'Not this Friday. I'm meeting Lauren at the farmers' market tomorrow morning before my lunchtime parents' class, then we're getting together with Vicky in the evening. What did you have in mind?'

'I think I should see Nick away from work, explain things from my point of view, and leave him to mull the situation over on his own.' Kate paused as if uncertain of her plan. 'It may not work, but I feel I have to try. If you don't mind me dropping Jem off at your place for an hour or so—he does so love seeing you and playing with your cats—then I could go and talk to Nick.'

'That would be fine,' Chloe agreed as they arranged a convenient time.

Chloe hoped Kate knew what she was doing. As the older woman had rightly said, Nick could be extremely stubborn and difficult. She didn't want to see Kate hurt even more. Before she could express her concerns, the door swung open and Chloe saw that Kate's surprise matched her own when it was Oliver and not Nick who walked into the room. He was carrying a tray, and Kate hurried to clear a space on the desk so he could put it down.

'I brought refreshments,' he explained with a smile, handing around mugs of tea before passing Chloe the sugar bowl and a spoon, clearly having noted her sweet tooth. She wasn't sure what to make of that. Removing the tray, he replaced it with a biscuit tin. 'I snaffled the last of Hazel's Cornish fairings, too!'

Kate smiled at him, ever gracious and polite. 'Thank you, Oliver, this is very welcome.'

Hooking a spare chair towards him with one foot, Oliver sat and reached for his own mug. He was far too close. Her stomach tightening, her pulse racing alarmingly, Chloe drew in a ragged a breath and battled the urge to edge her own chair further away. What was he doing here? And why did he always make her feel so strange?

'Any news on Avril?' Oliver asked, opening the tin and taking out one of the delicious ginger spiced home-made biscuits.

'Yes. I was going to tell you but you were still with patients.' Chloe bit her lip cursing her defensiveness. Oliver's gaze met hers, a smile playing around his mouth, and she looked away, setting her mug down to mask her trembling fingers. 'They are monitoring Avril but it is looking increasingly likely that a Caesarean will be necessary. Probably on Monday…if she remains stable over the weekend. I'll let you know when I hear anything.'

'Thanks, I'd appreciate that. Let's hope mother and baby are both fine.'

Chloe nodded, noting how Kate sipped her tea and glanced anxiously towards the door. Her friend met her gaze and then looked at Oliver. 'Nick's not coming, is he?' she asked, undisguised hurt in her brown eyes.

'No, Kate, I'm afraid he isn't. I'm sorry.' Oliver sounded sincere and understanding. 'He's asked me to stand in for him with the antenatal work for the next couple of weeks because he has extra responsibilities on the town twinning committee.'

'I see.'

Kate's smile was strained and Chloe wasn't sure which she wanted to do more...hug her friend or give Nick a piece of her mind. This was a public slap in the face for Kate but Chloe had to admit she had been surprised by and grateful for Oliver's sensitivity. It sounded as if he thought Nick's behaviour was wrong and the town twinning work an excuse, but he was polite enough not to say so. She met his warm gaze, a confused mix of emotions swirling inside her. At the moment, however, she was too worried about how Kate was feeling to concern herself with the prospect of having to work more closely with Oliver.

With evident effort and fierce determination, Kate raised her chin. 'Shall we get on, then? We have quite a bit to cover and I don't want to be late home for Jem. I have plans this evening,' she added, meeting Chloe's gaze.

'Of course,' Chloe agreed after a moment of hesitation, still concerned at the thought of Kate going to confront Nick. 'If you're sure.'

'Positive,' Kate insisted firmly.

Oliver put his mug on her desk and took out a notebook, seemingly unaware of the undercurrents. 'OK, ladies. Be gentle with me!' His cheeky wink made Kate smile, and for that Chloe was grateful. If only she herself didn't feel so awkward around him.

'We've covered Avril Harvey, one of our new patients. There's nothing more we can do there until we hear from the hospital,' Chloe began, opening the file and making her own notes. 'All being well, mother and baby will come home safely in the days ahead.'

'We'll keep an eye on them for a few weeks before handing them over to the health visitors,' Kate agreed.

Oliver concurred. 'Fine. Who's next?'

For a while they discussed their ongoing cases, including local vet, Melinda, married to GP Dragan Lovak, who was five months pregnant and maintaining excellent health.

Kate selected the next file and filled them in on one of her cases. 'I'm regularly seeing Stephanie Richards. All is going well with her pregnancy but she's twenty-two and nervous about having this baby on her own. Her boyfriend left her and isn't interested in being a father. Stephanie's in a rented flat in Bridge Street, and there's not much help from her own family so she needs extra support from us. Her baby is also due at the end of October—the same as Melinda's.'

'As far as potential problems are concerned, I have one mother showing signs of possible placental abruption,' Chloe informed them, waiting while Oliver made a note of the name and details. 'Angela Daniels had some discomfort and spotting. She was checked out at St Piran where they did an ultrasound and full blood count, plus a Kliejaur test to detect the presence of foetal red cells in maternal circulation. It was determined that the problem was mild and Angela was sent home on bed rest once the bleeding had stopped. She's in her twenty-ninth week now.'

'So we keep a close eye on her,' Oliver commented, busy with his notebook.

'Absolutely. She's on my list and she has my pager and mobile numbers in case of an emergency.' Chloe informed him. 'Angela's also having more regular checks with the consultant at the hospital. Likewise Susan Fiddick. Didn't you see her yesterday, Kate? What is the update on her?'

Her concern for the young woman evident, Kate referred to

her file. 'The breech was spotted at her thirty-six-week appointment and they tried to turn the baby at the hospital this week, the thirty-eighth. It wasn't successful and the procedure was abandoned. St Piran is predicting difficulties and have offered Susan an elective Caesarean next week. However, Susan and her husband want her to have the baby at home by vaginal delivery. While we're all for keeping things natural whenever possible, I've advised them to reconsider…there could be problems in the next week or two,' Kate warned them.

'We'll give you any help you need,' Chloe promised.

Kate smiled. 'Thanks. Let's hope they make the decision for themselves. Now, what about our new babies?'

'I understand there's a detailed newborn screening programme in operation throughout the region.' Oliver glanced up at Kate, his gaze moving to linger on Chloe until she shifted uneasily. 'Nick mentioned it now covers cystic fibrosis?'

Chloe nodded. 'Yes, CF is now included in the screen along with sickle cell disease, phenylketonuria and congenital hypothyroidism. We do a heel-prick test on the babies when they are between five and eight days old and the samples are sent to the Newborn Screening Laboratory Service in Bristol. They test the blood for immunoreactive trypsinogen. In babies with CF, this is increased in the first few weeks of life. If IRT is found, they do DNA tests. Sometimes they require a second sample when the baby is three or four weeks old.'

'So far our babies have been clear, thank goodness,' Kate added, 'but an early diagnosis means early treatment and the prospect of a longer, healthier life.'

'I've just sent samples in for three babies, including little Timmy Morrison.' Chloe paused and gave an affectionate smile. 'Beth and Jason have been waiting years for their first child.'

'Is he the baby you delivered at their home in the early hours last Friday?' Oliver asked, returning her smile.

'Yes. They were over the moon, it was very emotional.' Embarrassed, knowing how involved she became with her mums-to-be and their babies, she dragged her gaze from Oliver's warmly knowing one and focused her attention back on the files in front of her. 'Kate, what about the Trevellyans?'

'They are having a break from IVF for a month or two, but we're keeping in regular contact while they decide what to do. I want to follow this journey through with them but...'

'What's wrong?' Oliver frowned when Kate paused.

Kate sighed, wrestling with her thoughts. 'Fran and Mike are Nick's patients. So are Susan and Darren Fiddick. I'm not sure what to tell them about the new arrangements. No offence, Oliver, but some patients are going to want to stay with Nick.'

'None taken, I assure you.' Chloe couldn't doubt the sincerity in his voice. 'The patients' needs are the most important thing and somehow we'll sort this out so that they don't have to lose either you or Nick. Don't worry, Kate. I'll have a word with Nick on Monday. I'm sure that me taking over his duties is only a short-term measure.'

Kate looked hopeful, but Chloe felt less reassured that Nick would see sense. She was grateful to Oliver for trying, however. Smiling to convey her thanks, she was confused by the flare of something hot and intense in his eyes. Her alarm increased as he shifted closer. Reaching out for another ginger biscuit, his arm brushed against hers and caused an inexplicable prickle of sensation to shoot along her nerve endings. Disconcerted, she leaned away to fuss with the files again, wondering why it was suddenly hard to breathe and uncomfortably warm in the room.

'Other than the new couples booked in for preliminary appointments next week, and anything unforeseen that comes up, I think that's it for now,' she said, her voice less steady than normal.

The others agreed, and Chloe was relieved when Oliver

gathered up the tea things and biscuit tin, putting them all back on the tray and leaving the room. She immediately felt calmer and more settled with him gone.

'I'll see you later, then, Chloe,' Kate murmured, stacking her files.

'OK.' She bit her lip. 'You still think this is a good idea?'

A mix of inner pain and fierce determination shone in the older woman's eyes. 'I think this meeting proved what needs to be done. I can't let patients suffer because of Nick's displeasure with me personally. Not that Oliver isn't a great doctor, he is, but people like the Trevellyans and the Fiddicks deserve better from Nick. They trust him to come through for them. He can't abandon them because of me.'

'Just be careful.'

'I will.' Smiling, Kate patted her arm. 'Thank you for caring. Now, I'm going to put these files away and collect my things from the staffroom.'

Chloe watched her go, sighing as she rose to her feet and made her own preparations to leave. With luck, she'd have time to go home, feed the cats, shower, change and have a snack before Kate dropped Jem off. It had been another long, busy week and she was tired. She loved her job but it could be very demanding on her time and energy, and she never knew when she could be called out by one of her mothers during the night or at a weekend. Babies didn't follow a nine-to-five, five-day-a-week schedule! Smiling to herself, she gave her room a final check and then turned to leave, shocked to find Oliver blocking her doorway.

Oliver leaned against the doorframe and watched as Chloe finished tidying her desk, a smile on her face as she turned towards him. He regretted the way that smile faded, to be replaced by wary uncertainty as her footsteps faltered and she hesitated just out of his reach. Knowing faint heart never won fair lady, he pressed ahead with his plan to ask her out.

'Hi.'

'Hello.' She looked puzzled as her gaze met his then flicked away again. 'Is something wrong?'

As nervous as a teenager, he summoned a smile and tried to look more confident than he felt. 'No, not at all. I was just wondering... Would you like to come out for a drink or something tonight?'

'Me?' Amazement shone in her green eyes before she ducked her head.

'Yes, you!' He couldn't help but laugh, shaking his head at her total lack of self-awareness. Surely guys asked her out all the time? 'Why not you?'

She regarded him in silence, apparently devoid of an answer. Closing the distance between them, he couldn't resist brushing a few wayward strands of hair that had escaped her ponytail back behind her ear. This close to her, he saw the tiny network of faint scars that crisscrossed the side of her neck and dipped to her left shoulder. He'd not noticed them before. As his fingertips trailed over the series of narrow white lines, he felt the shiver that rippled through her at his touch before she froze as if in shock.

Concerned at the thought of her being hurt in any way, his voice dropped to a husky whisper. 'What happened, babe?'

'Nothing.' Beneath his fingers he detected the rapid and irregular beat of her pulse. 'An old childhood mishap.'

Oliver didn't believe her. He could tell from her evasive tone, not to mention the shadow of remembered pain clouding her eyes, that there was much more to the event that had left these marks on her satin soft-skin than she had divulged. He was alarmed because he had never felt this intensely about a woman before. Why Chloe? What was it about her that drew him? He was impatient to know all about her, but he sensed her skittishness and knew he needed to take his time with her.

'So,' he said, getting them back on track and reluctantly removing his hand from her skin, 'about tonight…'

'I'm sorry, I can't.' Her voice sounded less steady and assured than before. 'We can talk more about any patient queries you have next week.'

She thought he was asking her out to talk about patients? Frowning, he shook his head. 'No, that's not it.' Frustrated that she didn't seem to understand his intentions, he thrust his hands in his pockets to stop himself reaching for her again. 'Chloe.'

She shifted uneasily, looking ready to flee. 'I already have plans, Oliver. I need to go.'

'Sure.' He was still puzzled by her reaction but he let it go…for now. Knowing she often met up with physiotherapist Lauren Nightingale and some of their other friends, he smiled again. 'Girls' night out?'

'No. Not this time.'

'You have a date?' Bitter disappointment and a wave of jealousy coursed through him. Had his caution meant he had missed his chance? Had some other man beaten him to Chloe?

She edged around him towards the door, her movements jerky. 'Excuse me. I'll, um, be late.'

'Of course.' Swallowing a curse, he reluctantly stood aside to let her by. 'Maybe another time.'

Scowling, unsure of himself, wondering what the hell he was doing chasing after the woman when he wasn't sure he was ready to get involved, he watched Chloe hurry to the stairs and disappear from view. He had been positive she wasn't seeing anyone. Her rejection left a sour taste in his mouth and an ache inside him. Not to mention the fact she had seemed so surprised that he would ask her out at all. Why was the idea so strange to her? What was wrong with him? Did Chloe just see him as some feckless playboy, like so many other people did?

Why was he even torturing himself over her? There had always been women who wanted to be with him, but he hadn't been interested in any of them. All he could think about, all he wanted, was Chloe. Something about her drew him in. In some inexplicable way, just being around her centred him, calmed him, made him feel real. There was so much about her he had yet to discover and he sensed there was something mysterious she held inside. He wanted to know her. Wanted Chloe to trust him, to open up to him. The prospect of an evening alone wondering where she was, what she was doing…and, dammit, who she was doing it with…was distinctly unappealing.

'Oliver?'

Glancing round in surprise, he saw Kate hovering at the staffroom door. He moved to join her, thankful to discover they were alone.

'How are you doing, Kate?' he asked, concerned that she had looked pale and stressed since the upset with Nick.

'I'm fine.'

He wasn't taken in by the brave smile she sent him. 'You can talk to me. If you ever need to.'

'Thanks.' He saw her knuckles whiten as she gripped her hands tightly together.

'I'm sorry about today. About Nick ducking out of the antenatal meeting.'

'It's not your fault.' She tried another smile, no more successful than the last. 'Nick and I have to work this out between us, Oliver.'

'OK.' He'd back off…for now. But he'd be keeping his eye on her just the same.

Kate's expression lightened as she watched him. 'How about you?'

'Me?'

'I've noticed you seem smitten with our Chloe.'

'Yeah.' That was one way of putting it. Oliver sent Kate a rueful smile. 'Not that I'm getting very far. Chloe treated me with the same friendliness she does everyone else for the first few days I was here but now she's cooled and it's almost impossible to get close to her.'

Now Kate's smile was genuine. 'I think it dawned on her that you were seeing her in a way that the other doctors don't.'

'I was interested from the first moment I met her.'

'Chloe wouldn't have realised that,' Kate commented, surprising him.

'Why not? She's a beautiful woman. Men must beat a path to her door.'

Kate shook her head. 'Hardly.'

'What are you trying to tell me?'

'Just that Chloe really is as unaware and innocent as she seems.' Kate paused and rested a hand on his arm. 'Tread carefully with her, Oliver.'

He was sure there was more here than Kate was saying. 'Tell me about Chloe.'

The older woman's expression contained a mixture of amusement and caution. 'What do you want to know?'

'Everything. Anything.' He ran a hand through his hair, his frustration showing. 'I just asked her out. She turned me down flat. She seemed to think I wanted to discuss work, but…I don't know. I gather she has a date tonight, anyway.'

'Actually, she's watching my son for me while I run an errand.'

'She is? Why didn't she say so?' Oliver stared at her in bemusement. 'I know you're friends, Kate. What do you think I should do? I didn't plan on getting involved with anyone when I came here,' he admitted, sitting down and resting his elbows on his knees. 'But…well, I hadn't counted on meeting Chloe.'

Kate frowned, taking a chair next to his. 'Chloe is…'

'What?' he prompted after she paused and the silence lengthened.

'She's not like the kind of women you're probably used to mixing with.'

He raised an eyebrow at that, irritated by the way so few people saw beyond the image. Sure, he enjoyed life, he liked to have a good time, indulge in the things he could afford and which gave him pleasure and relaxation away from the pressures and responsibilities of his work, things like surfing and jet-skiing. That didn't mean he was a jerk.

'I wanted time to settle, for the community to accept *me*, not judge on rumour and gossip or the family name.' He paused, reining in his disgruntlement. It wasn't Kate's fault. He needed to earn a new reputation, a true one. 'I've noticed you and Lauren are very protective of Chloe.'

Kate's expression softened. 'Chloe is special. Be patient, Oliver. Go slowly. Don't scare her.'

'She's frightened of me?' Shocked, he stared at Kate in disbelief. He respected women, would never cause anyone harm. 'I don't understand. I'd never hurt her.'

'Not intentionally, maybe.'

'But—'

'Chloe puts up a lot of barriers and not many people get to know the real woman,' Kate explained. 'Her work is her life and that has always suited her.'

'She doesn't date?'

'No.'

Confused, Oliver studied Kate's face. 'But why? She's intelligent, beautiful, funny.'

'I know.' The older woman's smile was filled with affection and a hint of sadness. 'You'll have your work cut out to persuade Chloe. It won't be easy. But I think you'd be good for her.' She hesitated a moment, biting her lip as she considered him. 'I can't break a confidence, Oliver, and Chloe is one of my best friends. I don't know everything, but I do know that she has issues.'

'Issues?'

'I can't say more. I would if I could—and I encourage you to persevere.'

He mulled over the information. 'Issues from her past? With men?' Was that why Chloe was so skittish?

'Only Chloe can explain…if she trusts you enough.'

So, if he really wanted to take things further, he had to keep working hard to earn Chloe's trust. Patience wasn't his strong suit, not when he wanted something badly enough…and he did want Chloe. To her friends she was special. Hadn't he sensed that, too? There was something different about her. Wasn't that why he was still interested when a relationship so soon had never been on his agenda? For some reason he couldn't yet fathom, Kate saw something in him, and was encouraging him not to give up on Chloe. He had no idea where the journey would end, but for now he was along for the ride.

'Oliver, I think you should talk to Lauren. She knows much more than I do about Chloe's past…not that she'll divulge any secrets. But she might have some better advice on how to gain Chloe's confidence.' Kate hesitated, her gaze assessing. 'If you're serious about this. Chloe's not a temporary kind of girl.'

'I know that.' Oliver frowned, seeking a way to explain feelings he scarcely understood himself. 'I came here to begin a different life, Kate, to settle down. This is new to me, but I'd like the chance to get to know Chloe, to see what develops. She affects me in ways I've never experienced before.'

'Then I think you'll find Lauren and I will do all we can to help.'

A slow smile curved Oliver's mouth as hope flared inside him. He didn't imagine wooing Chloe was going to be easy, not from the subtle, mysterious hints Kate had given him. He wasn't even sure of himself, of what he was getting into. But giving up on Chloe was not an option.

Kate stood outside Nick's imposing stone built house, situated at the opposite end of the village to her own whitewashed cottage. Was she doing the right thing? She had managed to sound confident when she told Chloe of her plans, but much of that bravado had evaporated. It was impossible to explain how hurt she was. Nick had genuine cause to be angry at the way he had found out about Jem—overhearing her confidential confession to Eloise that day at the surgery must have been a shock—but she didn't feel it excused his behaviour towards her since. Today he had taken the easy way out in his eagerness to avoid her, but in doing so he had drawn Chloe, Oliver and a host of patients into their personal disagreement, and that wouldn't do.

Having worked up a fresh head of indignation, she walked along the path to the single-storey extension where the top half of the yellow-painted stable door stood open. Inside the expensively fitted kitchen, all wood and granite and steel, Nick stood at the island unit, his back to her. Before she lost her nerve, she rapped on the door. Nick swung round in surprise, his face creasing in a scowl of displeasure, the expression in his eyes cooling, leaving her in little doubt that she was not welcome. Tough.

'What do you want?' he demanded, voice harsh.

'We need to talk, Nick.'

He folded his arms across his chest, withdrawing into himself. 'We have nothing to talk about.'

'You're wrong.' As he turned and left the room without another word, she reached over the lip of the door and opened the bottom half, swinging it open and following him into the main part of the house, finding him in the airy sitting room. 'Don't walk away from me!'

'You're trespassing.'

'For goodness' sake!' Usually slow to ire, Kate wanted to shake the man. 'How long are you going to keep this up? It isn't going to go away by ignoring it.'

Nick faced her, his scowl deepening. 'I've told you, I don't want to talk about it. I feel betrayed, I—'

'*You* feel betrayed? That's rich. For once in your life stop and think how other people might feel. How *I* might feel.' Her hands clenched to fists at her sides. 'What we did, Nick, we did together. It was a terrible time, we needed each other. Then we both admitted it was wrong and we never spoke of it again. I had the guilt of betraying James while he was out there, dying, his body never found. How do you think it was for me, coming to terms with losing my husband, discovering I was pregnant from my one night of comfort with you? What was I supposed to do? Come and tell you and Annabel about it? Or would you rather I had sprung it on you a few years later while you were going through your own desperate grief at losing your wife? When would have been the "right time", Nick?'

He looked surprised at her outburst but no more approachable. 'I don't know. I don't have any answers. What do you expect of me?'

'Nothing. Nothing at all,' she shot back, knowing she had long ago given up expecting anything from the man she had always loved but who had chosen another woman over her, a woman for whom he was still grieving.

'What about Lucy, Jack and Edward?' he demanded, naming his grown-up children. 'What do you think this will do to them?'

'I have no idea. All I do know is that they are adults, exceptional people who have their own lives and responsibilities. You can tell them or not, as you think fit. What really worries you? That they'll think less of you?'

Shoving his hands in his pockets, Nick turned away to stare

out of the window. 'My relationships with all three of them haven't been easy.'

'No.' Kate resisted pointing out that he was largely to blame for that. It wouldn't help the current situation. 'The person who most concerns me is Jeremiah. He's only a child. I don't want him hurt.'

'I repeat, what *do* you want?' he challenged, swinging back to face her, his expression fierce.

Kate held her ground. 'I have no intention of making demands on you, or of publicly outing you as Jem's father. If you would like to spend more time getting to know him until you decide what you want to do, that's fine with me, but I won't have him hurt, used or tossed aside if it gets too much.' Taking advantage of Nick's continued silence, she pressed on. 'At work, I want you to at least be civil. It isn't fair on the other staff, or the patients, that you treat me like a pariah. Today was embarrassing for everyone, especially Chloe and Oliver. And it isn't right for people like the Trevellyans and the Fiddicks that you put our personal business before their medical needs. They are *your* patients, Nick. We have to see their journeys through with them, even if you cut back some of your other antenatal work for patients not on your list. We're adults. We made adult decisions, adult choices, adult mistakes. We have to bear the consequences like adults,' she finished, the fight draining out of her.

A muscle pulsed along Nick's jaw and he evaded her gaze. They stood in tense silence for several moments until Kate could bear it no longer. Her shoulders slumped. She knew him well enough of old to know he wasn't about to unbend, not until he had time to think things over for himself. If only she didn't still care for him, if she didn't still love him, despite all their ups and downs and all that had happened in their years of friendship.

'Think about it, Nick,' she advised quietly. 'I'll see myself out.'

She was shaking, her pulse racing from the fraught encounter, as she walked back towards the centre of the village. Finally she was passing the library and approaching the cluster of six cottages known as Fisherman's Row, which occupied the last of the space before the harbour bridge and the turning to Bridge Street. Forcing back the threat of tears, she stopped outside one of the colourful old cottages and rang Chloe's doorbell.

With Jem safely occupied, kicking a ball around the small enclosed garden at the rear of her cottage, Chloe dried her hands and went to answer the front door.

'Hi,' she greeted, stepping back to let Kate enter, noticing the glisten of unshed tears in her brown eyes and the paleness of her face, presumably evidence of her recent encounter with Nick. 'Come on in. I've just made some fresh lemonade.'

'OK.'

'Jem's out at the back. He's been fine. He wore Pirate and Cyclops out in no time,' Chloe chattered on, gesturing to the two cats curled up asleep side by side in an armchair.

Kate managed a smile. 'Thanks, Chloe. For everything.'

'No problem.' Returning the smile, she poured two glasses of the ice-cold, tangy drink and handed one to her friend. 'Would you like to sit a while?'

'That would be good.'

They chose chairs by the open doors, watching Jem play outside. Chloe curbed her nosiness but couldn't help wondering what had happened when Kate had visited Nick. It seemed clear that Kate didn't want to talk about it, however. Nick was a wonderful doctor, but he could be difficult, and he was known to be rigid in his opinions. Chloe ached for her friend and the predicament she now found herself in.

Kate had recently taken her into her confidence about Nick being Jem's father and, whilst she didn't know the circumstances of how it had all come about, she knew how much her friend fretted over it and felt guilty. Chloe could understand how Nick felt at not being told before, but she could also understand Kate's point of view. Although Kate had always been staunch in her friendship and support, Nick often appeared to take her for granted and not appreciate all she did, for the practice and for him. If both of them had felt guilty for their aberration all those years ago, and then both had needed to deal with bereavement at different times, it couldn't have been easy for Kate to know what to do for the best.

'Chloe?'

'Hmm?' Feeling relaxed, she leaned back in the chair and sipped her drink.

'Why did you let Oliver think you had a date tonight?'

Surprised at Kate's question, Chloe faced her. 'I'd made arrangements with you.'

'I could easily have changed my plans.'

'But why?' She frowned in confusion. 'Oliver probably just wanted to talk about work after our meeting. I told him we'd discuss it next week.'

Kate laughed. 'That's not at all what he wanted, Chloe!'

'It isn't?'

'No, my love!' Shaking her head, Kate reached out and patted her arm with amused tolerance. 'Oliver's interested in you.'

A prickle of breathless apprehension rippled through Chloe. 'Excuse me?'

'As a woman. Chloe...' She sighed, her smile reflecting both affection and a hint of exasperation. 'I know you don't think of yourself that way, but you *are* a woman. A beautiful woman. And Oliver has noticed.'

'He can't have!'

Laughing again but kindly, Kate finished her lemonade. 'Oliver reminds me of my late husband, James, when he was that age. The whole sexy surfer image and the warm charm, but with that underlying kindness and honesty.'

'But what am I going to do?' Chloe fretted, with increasing alarm.

'It's a new experience for you, I know, but why not try it?' Surprisingly calm in comparison to her own raging emotions, Kate's voice was gentle with understanding. 'Spend time with Oliver. Get to know him. You might find you enjoy being with him.'

With the heavy weight of her past preying on her mind, holding her in chains, Chloe stared at her friend, speechless with shock. How could Kate even suggest such a thing?

'Oh, Chloe, my love!' Chuckling, Kate set down her empty glass. 'You should see your face!' Sobering, the older woman reached out and took her hand. 'I know a little about your past, but maybe this is the perfect time for you to finally put it behind you. I hate to see you missing out on such a big part of life. Outward images can be deceptive. There's so much more to Oliver. Don't judge him on rumour. He could be the perfect man to teach you to be a woman in the fullest sense of the word—the real woman you are inside—if only you would let him.'

CHAPTER THREE

'HELLO, Oliver.'

At the sound of the female voice behind him, Oliver turned from scanning the crowds at Penhally's Saturday morning farmers' market and met Lauren Nightingale's slate-grey gaze. Tall, athletic and curvy, she was attractive, with an engaging smile, her long, light brown hair glowing lighter under the summer sunshine. Excellent at her job, the thirty year old was renowned for building rapport with her patients—and, he had discovered, affectionately teased for her inherent clumsiness. Oliver had only heard good things about her, and following the interactions he had already had with her through work, he liked her immensely.

'Hi, Lauren.'

Unable to help himself, his gaze strayed past her, eager for a glimpse of Chloe, whom Kate had hinted would be here with her friend today. He felt deflated when he could find no sign of her.

'Kate was right, you do have it bad!'

'Sorry?' The teasing in Lauren's tone had him switching his attention back to her. A frown creased his brow. 'What did you say?'

Grey eyes sparkling with mischief, Lauren linked her arm through his and led him towards a haphazard collection of tables and chairs. 'Sit for a few minutes. We'll have something to drink and discuss a strategy.'

'A strategy?' Feeling he had stepped into some kind of twilight zone, Oliver's frown deepened, but he did as instructed and sat down.

'About Chloe.' A dimpled smile appeared as Lauren faced him. 'I assume she is the reason you are here?'

'You assume correctly,' he admitted, returning the smile.

Accepting a chilled fruit smoothie, he began to relax as it dawned on him that Kate must have told Lauren about their talk, and that the younger woman was possibly not averse to the idea of him dating Chloe. At least, he hoped that was what Lauren meant by planning a strategy. Again his gaze strayed around the shifting crowds of tourists and locals examining the stallholders' wares.

'I'm afraid Chloe won't be joining us,' Lauren told him, correctly reading the direction of his thoughts. 'She was paged this morning to attend a pregnant tourist staying at the Anchor Hotel.'

Trying to mask his disappointment, Oliver nodded and decided to get straight to the point. 'So Kate's spoken of my interest in Chloe?'

'She has. And however daft it sounds, I feel as protective of Chloe as some old Victorian aunt.' The warning was softened by the smile and the laughter in her eyes, but was there nonetheless.

'That's OK. I'm glad Chloe has such good friends looking out for her,' he answered calmly, hoping to allay any fears Lauren might have. 'This isn't a game for me, Lauren. I don't know what you might have heard about my past, but—'

She raised a hand and forestalled his words. 'I'm not much of a one for heeding rumour and gossip, Oliver. I take people as I find them. And I'm a pretty good judge of character. You may not have been with us long, but I like you, so does Kate, and we both think you could be just what Chloe needs. But things are not going to be straightforward,' she finished, and this time her warning sounded more serious.

'Kate mentioned there were issues, but I don't know what they are.' He met Lauren's gaze, his own sincere. 'You and Kate both say I should keep trying. What is it you think Chloe needs? And why me?' he asked, his uncertainty showing, unsure himself whether he, who had never had a steady relationship, was able to deliver what her friends believed he could. 'What can you tell me that I need to know if I'm to begin to win Chloe's trust?'

Lauren took a sip of her tangy drink, her expression thoughtful. 'First of all, Chloe doesn't date.'

'You mean she isn't dating anyone right now?' Oliver clarified, but Lauren was shaking her head.

'No, I mean she doesn't date. Full stop.'

'Ever?' For a moment he was sure he had misunderstood but then remembered Kate had said something similar the night before. 'Chloe never dates at all?'

'That's right.'

'But why?'

Lauren's grey gaze was sombre as she faced him. 'It's a long story, Oliver, and it isn't mine to tell. I won't break Chloe's confidence, no matter how much I support what you are trying to do.'

'I wouldn't expect you to. So where do I go from here?' he persisted, puzzled.

'You'll have your work cut out for you.' Lauren's words again echoed Kate's and her smile was just as sad. 'Be Chloe's friend, don't take away her choices, don't push too hard too soon.'

A heavy knot of suspicion tightened his gut. 'Someone hurt her in the past? Physically? Emotionally? Or both?' Lauren didn't reply but, then, she didn't have to. The shadows clouding her eyes as she withdrew her gaze answered his questions more effectively than words.

They were answers he found hard to come to terms with. At some time in the past someone had abused Chloe. Pain lanced through him at the unpalatable knowledge. And anger at the unknown person who'd hurt her. Various scenarios, each more disturbing than the last, played through his mind. The new knowledge explained why Chloe devoted herself to her work, ignoring her beauty and her sexuality, friendly and warm, yet always trying to remain professional, keeping up some invisible barrier. No wonder her close friends were so protective of her.

He wanted to protect her, too, but he also felt daunted. It was a big responsibility to shoulder. Was he the right man to gentle Chloe back to life? Wary and anxious, he sat back and finished his drink, a succession of thoughts running through his mind. He doubted himself, yet Chloe's closest friends had chosen to believe in him, to trust him. After his experiences in the past, it was a heady feeling, and the start of what he had come here to find…being recognised and accepted for himself.

Everything led back to Chloe, the woman who had filled his waking moments and fired his sleeping ones with erotic dreams since the moment he had met her. The idea of any other man claiming her was unthinkable. His mind was made up. He would do all he could to earn Chloe's trust and learn her secrets. To awaken her sensuality. To show her what it was like to be loved and cherished. A step at a time.

'I'll be seeing Chloe tonight,' Lauren told him, drawing him from his thoughts. 'Kate and I will do our best to encourage her to give you a chance, but the hard work will be up to you.'

'Thanks, Lauren. I'll do all I can to live up to your faith in me, to not let Chloe down.' He hoped he was up to the task, that he wouldn't fail her.

Smiling, Lauren drained her drink. 'I believe you. So, what are you doing this weekend?' she asked, and Oliver assumed the talk of strategies for wooing Chloe was over.

'Luckily I'm off duty. Today it's surfing if the waves are right, otherwise jet-skiing. Tomorrow I thought I might take the bike out and explore. I don't know this part of Cornwall very well.'

Lauren's gaze sharpened. 'You have a motorbike?'

'Yeah. My main indulgence…along with my surfboard and jet-ski,' he admitted with a rueful smile.

'I've never ridden myself, but I know a couple of popular places where riders meet up. You might want to check them out early tomorrow morning, get some tips. It would be worth your while.'

'Great. Thank you.' Surprised at Lauren's insistence, Oliver jotted down the names of the hangouts she mentioned, marking one in particular that she recommended. 'I'll take a run out there.'

'I hope you meet up with a kindred spirit tomorrow.' For a moment, her eyes gleamed with something Oliver couldn't interpret, then she was turning away and gathering her things. Rising to her feet, she brought their chat to an end. 'See you, Oliver. Good luck.'

'Bye, Lauren. Thanks again.'

Oliver watched Lauren walk away, his mind full of thoughts and fledgling plans to win Chloe round and prove to her that he could be her friend…and more, in time.

'How did things go today? Everything OK with the mother and baby at the hotel?'

In her kitchen, opening a bottle of red wine, Chloe looked up at Lauren's question and smiled. 'Thankfully both are doing fine. They're staying in St Piran Hospital overnight as a precaution as there was some postpartum bleeding. Nothing major. The baby boy is fit and healthy. Eight pounds two ounces. There is also one very scared, very confused but very proud father.'

'Did the woman really not know she was near term?' her friend asked, an incredulous expression on her face.

'No. She didn't keep her antenatal appointments or scans because her mother told her she'd done well enough in her day and she didn't believe in a lot of interference.' Chloe grimaced, pouring the wine and handing Lauren a glass.

'Thanks.' They walked out to the tiny patio at the back of Chloe's cottage and sat to enjoy the warmth of the evening. 'All's well that ends well. I'm sure she'll be more careful with antenatal care if she has another baby.'

'I hope so. She did have a bit of a shock. So did the staff and residents of the Anchor Hotel!' Chloe chuckled, then took a sip of her wine. 'Do you want any nibbles before Vicky gets here with the pizzas?'

'No, I'm fine. Thanks.'

Chloe enjoyed meeting up with her friends. Often, like tonight, they got together at each other's houses, or they went out for a meal or to the cinema, or sometimes went dancing at one of the nightclubs in nearby Rock. With Lucy, Melinda and Eloise all wrapped up with their new husbands and, in some cases, babies or pregnancies, it was Lauren, Vicky Clements and herself who most regularly met up now. Vicky, an old school friend of Lauren's, worked at her mother's hair and beauty salon in Penhally. Chloe was three years younger than both of them, and although they hadn't been close during their school days, they had known each other all their lives in the village. Their friendships had grown in adulthood. Vicky was good fun, but she was also a terrible gossip, and Chloe was careful to guard her secrets around her. Apart from Kate at work, Chloe was closest to Lauren. And Lauren and Kate were the only people who had any inkling about her past...and the way that past impacted on her present and her future.

'There must have been something in the Penhally water this last year or so,' Lauren commented after a short silence, reclaiming Chloe's attention.

'How do you mean?'

'So many people falling in love, getting married, having babies...' Lauren looked at her and laughed. 'And not necessarily in that order!'

It had certainly been a busy time for the village and its residents. Among the many happy events to take place had been the marriage of vet Melinda Fortesque to GP Dragan Lovak. Chloe and Lauren had been bridesmaids at the wedding. Former neighbours in Fisherman's Row, Dragan and Melinda had recently moved into their dream home on the outskirts of the village and were awaiting the arrival of their first baby in October.

However, it hadn't all been people getting together and living happily ever after. Lauren herself had broken up with Martin Bennett, her long-term boyfriend. Not that she seemed upset about the split, far from it. Lauren had been more contented and freer these last weeks. Which surely lent weight to Chloe's view that you should be responsible for your own happiness and you didn't need a man. She said as much to Lauren now.

'It's true that things didn't work out with Martin. We were drifting for a long time and we never would have worked, but that doesn't mean I don't want another relationship. I'm certainly not going to be celibate for ever. I'm just taking a breather because I was with Martin so long, on and off, and I want to be sure where I am and where I am going before I meet someone else...hopefully in the months ahead. I enjoy sex, Chloe. Most people do. I know you had a terrible experience and example with your parents, but it isn't always like that. Far from it.'

Chloe bit her lip. 'I know you and Kate think I'm missing out, but how can I miss what I've never known? I'm happy with my life. What more do I need?'

Her thoughts automatically turned to Oliver. She couldn't believe he had asked her out. Not that it meant anything to him. Kate had to be wrong about that. Rumour had it that he could have his pick of women—beautiful, available, experienced women. Women who were the antithesis of her. Why on earth would Oliver be interested? And why did she find him so unsettling, so challenging? She had never reacted to any other man the way she did to him.

'I saw Oliver today.' Lauren's words, echoing her own thoughts, had Chloe's gaze jerking up in surprise. 'He really likes you, Chloe. I think you should give him a chance to show you how good a relationship can be.'

Chloe shook her head. 'I'm not designed or destined to be with anyone.'

'Nonsense.'

'But Oliver…?' Confused, Chloe took a hasty gulp of her wine, a swirl of unknown and frightening emotions rampaging inside her. Her voice was mocking when she spoke again. 'The virgin midwife and the playboy doctor? I don't think so, Lauren. I'm not the sort of person to hold Oliver's interest for a second, not if he knew about me. He'd either laugh or be bored in five minutes.'

'You're underestimating him.'

'I—'

'Why not let Oliver decide for himself?' Lauren's smile was understanding, even as her words challenged all Chloe's preconceived notions. 'He might surprise you.'

Chloe remained silent for several moments, wrestling with

uncertainty. 'I'm scared, Lauren,' she finally admitted, her voice shaky.

'I know.' Her friend leaned over and gave her a gentle hug. 'But I agree with Kate. I hate to see you only living half a life. There is so much out there for you…if you would just allow yourself to take a chance. If you don't, you're allowing your father to win, to control your life from the grave just as surely as he did before.'

Chloe sat back, lost in thought, trying to convince herself that Lauren and Kate were wrong. Her life was fine the way it was—she had a career she loved, good friends, hobbies she enjoyed. How could she need more? Need something she had never known and never wanted? She had never felt sexual desire and she had no conception of missing anything. All desire and sex and love meant to her was what she had seen her father do to her mother…along with the way he had also controlled her from a young age. In her experience, giving herself to a man meant pain and domination and humiliation, just as she and her mother had endured for years.

No one knew the full horror of it. Lauren knew part of her story. She had been there to help her all those years ago when she had needed someone. Chloe would never forget the debt she owed her friend. As for Kate, Chloe had confided the basic details, but she suspected the older woman had read more between the lines. But asking her to step outside her comfort zone, to consider something she had always rejected, to awaken a part of her she didn't even know she had…? Racked with indecision, she met Lauren's gentle grey gaze.

'I don't know what to do, Lauren.'

'Take things slowly. Get to know Oliver better. Spend time with him,' her friend advised. 'How do you feel when you are with him at work?'

'He makes me confused, jumpy, on edge. I don't understand it,' she admitted.

Lauren smiled. 'That's good.'

'It is?'

'Sure. It means you're aware of him, connecting.' Lauren paused a moment, her voice serious when she spoke again. 'Nothing can change what happened in the past, Chloe, but you can change the hold that past has on your future. Think about it. You have tomorrow to yourself. Get out in the country, like you planned.' She reached out and took her hand. 'Knowing what I do about you and your past, do you think I would encourage you to let Oliver close if I didn't trust him to take care of you? He's a good man, Chloe. Nothing like your father. Let him prove it.'

Before Chloe had the chance to reply, the sound of Vicky's shrill call reached them. 'Yoo-hoo! Anyone home?'

'We're out here,' Lauren called back, giving Chloe a moment to compose herself.

Chloe watched as Lauren moved to place her empty glass on the table, but she misjudged the distance and the glass hit the edge before toppling to the ground.

'Damn!' Lauren exclaimed as the glass shattered. 'I'm sorry, Chloe.'

'Don't worry about it. I'll clear it up. Mind you don't cut yourself.'

Tutting, irrepressible Vicky Clements, short and thin and sporting a different hair colour every week—today it was bright red—stepped outside. 'Well done, Lauren, as clumsy as ever, I see!'

Chloe shared a sympathetic smile with Lauren, infamous for her mishaps, and went to fetch the dustpan and brush. Part of her was relieved Vicky had arrived, curtailing further uncomfortable discussion, but another part of her knew it was not going to be anywhere near so easy to banish the welter of thoughts churning in her mind—all of which featured the disturbing presence of wickedly attractive Oliver Fawkner.

* * *

Early on Sunday morning, Oliver rode out of Penhally Bay, past the headland, where the church and lighthouse sat, and up Mevagissey Road to the cliffs above the beach where he had surfed the day before. He always felt an intense freedom and peace when he was out alone on his bike, and this early there were few people about to intrude on his solitude.

He had scarcely thought of anything but Chloe in the last hours, turning over all Lauren had said, worrying about what she *hadn't* said but had implied about Chloe's troubled past. Preoccupied by trying to formulate a plan to gain Chloe's confidence, he followed the directions Lauren had given him as he passed the Smugglers' Inn, then turned into the country. A short while later he was surprised to find a motorbike hire and repair place called Addison's Yard in a secluded wooded setting, then it was behind him and he rode on to the hidden beauty spot Lauren had recommended. It was beautiful. A high point on a rocky promontory, it overlooked the surrounding coast and countryside.

From Lauren's description, he had expected to find a group of bikers gathering here before heading out for a day's ride, but as he pulled off the road, he could only see one other bike. The powerful Yamaha engine idled beneath him as he pondered whether to approach the rider, who sat astride an impressive-looking red Ducati, apparently enjoying her privacy.

There was no doubt that the rider was female, given the way she filled out the lightweight black and red leathers. Oliver slowly approached, wondering why the woman had her helmet on and her visor down. Surely both must hinder her enjoyment of the view and the weather. Cruising up beside her, he switched off his bike and took off his own helmet and gloves.

'It's fantastic up here,' he commented, but his opening gambit earned him only a brief nod of the head. Anxious to ensure that the woman didn't feel uncomfortable alone with him, he decided to focus on their shared interest. 'That's a great bike.'

'Mmm.' A noncommittal grunt sounded from behind the visor.

OK. Shaking his head, wondering if Lauren was wrong about the helpfulness of fellow enthusiasts, Oliver tried again. 'I'm new to the district. I was told this was the place to come to learn of some good places to ride.' His frown deepened as his companion grunted some unintelligible reply. 'Sorry, I missed that.'

The woman shrugged. Oliver looked her over, admiring her lush curves. She almost looked like… He snapped off the ridiculous thought. Of course not. His mind was playing tricks on him. But as he studied her more closely, he noted the way a curl of dark hair had escaped from under her helmet. And then he saw the tiny feather of scars on her neck below her ear, visible above the collar of her leathers. He leaned closer and a faint hint of fresh apples teased him on the breeze. No way! He rocked back, unable to believe it. Lauren had to have known! She had sent him here to find his kindred spirit, he remembered. Hot damn!

'Chloe!' He heard a muffled yelp from inside her helmet and laughed aloud. 'I know it's you, babe. Your secret is out.'

She flipped up her visor, familiar green eyes sparking with indignation and annoyance. 'How did you know it was me?'

'I'm coming to know you—and several things gave the game away.' Reaching out, he traced the web of scars on her neck with one fingertip, feeling the tremble of her flesh beneath his touch. Pausing a moment to leisurely peruse her stunning body, his gaze rose and caught the blush that stained her cheeks before teasing, 'You look fantastic. I never would have pegged you as a biker chick, though.'

Green eyes clouded before she glanced away. 'You may believe you know me, Oliver, but I'm not at all what you think.'

And from the sound of her voice she imagined he wouldn't want to know her if he learned the truth. She couldn't be more wrong. Anger at whoever had stripped her of her confidence in herself as a woman rose inside him like an unstoppable tide. He took one of her hands in both of his. Her skin was so soft, her hand strong but gentle, fitting perfectly into his larger ones. He meant the touch to be reassuring, but even this simple contact fired his blood and sent desire fizzing through his body, reminding him he had to keep a tight rein on his self-control…at least for the time being.

'Chloe?' He waited until she drew in a ragged breath and allowed her wary gaze to return to his. Then he laid his cards on the table, honestly and sincerely. The only thing he kept back was how badly he wanted to take her to bed, knowing she was nowhere near ready to hear that yet. 'I want to know you, all of you, and to be your friend. Nothing you can tell me will make me care any less about you, or not want to know you.'

She gave a shaky laugh, her anxiety obvious. 'I don't know.'

'I'm not running away, Chloe. This isn't some passing fad to me. But I'm happy to go slowly, for us to take our time getting to know each other until you feel comfortable.' Raising her hand, he pressed a brief kiss to her palm and released her, putting some space between them so she wouldn't feel crowded. 'So, how about today? Can we take a ride together?' He cursed himself for the phraseology. The double entendre hung between them but she seemed refreshingly and innocently unaware of the kind of ride he really wanted to share with her. Banishing his erotic thoughts, he kept his voice soft and cajoling. 'I'd love to see your favourite parts of Cornwall. Will you show me?'

She debated for an inordinate amount of time, indecision evident in those expressive green eyes. Tense, she finally nodded, her smile nervous. 'All right.'

It was such a minor victory, and yet Oliver felt as elated at this one small achievement as he would winning the World Rip Curl Super Series surfing title or the Isle of Man TT bike race. Silently thanking Lauren for pointing him in the right direction, he pulled his gloves and helmet back on, waiting for Chloe to be ready. He was still overwhelmed and delighted to discover her unexpected adventurous spirit and love of bikes. It proved that they had more than work in common—and that the fledgling feelings he'd had for Chloe from the first were worth exploring. There was so much he wanted to share with her but he had to move cautiously, both to gain her trust and to work through his insecurities about his own past. Today he had the chance to begin that process. He couldn't wait.

Far too conscious of Oliver beside her, Chloe readied herself for their ride, silently cursing Lauren whom she imagined had been the traitor who had tipped Oliver off about where to find her that morning. Her friend had been clever, she'd give her that. Oliver had been surprised when he had recognised her. She was still amazed he had done. Hell's bells, she'd nearly fainted in shock when he'd rolled in on his impressive-looking black Yamaha and taken off his helmet!

After a fun evening with Lauren and Vicky, she had gone to bed, her rescued cats, Pirate and Cyclops, curled up near her feet, but all her dreams had been filled with images of the playboy doctor who had knocked her life out of kilter in a few short weeks. Not to mention Lauren's and Kate's combined advice to give Oliver a chance.

Sunday had dawned promising another hot, sunny day, and she had left early for Addison's Yard. With little space and no offroad parking at her cottage in Fisherman's Row, she garaged her Ducati with the enthusiastic couple who owned the bike business. After a cup of coffee with early birds Roger and Jean Addison, she'd embraced the freedom her bike afforded her and had ridden the short distance to one of her favourite secluded places to think and plan her day. To discover she shared her secret passion for motorbikes with Oliver brought another rush of confused emotions.

Feeling that sinful dark gaze focused on her, she glanced up. The way he looked at her was like a caress...not that she knew what the caress of a man felt like. But Oliver always made her feel unsettled yet strangely alive. Her palm still tingled from the kiss he had so unexpectedly and shockingly placed there. She felt gauche, out of her league. There had to be any number of experienced women keen to be with him—she wasn't so blind or stupid that she didn't realise Oliver was incredibly good-looking—so why was he interested in someone like her? Maybe if he found out about her past his interest would cease, no matter what he said to the contrary.

A smile curved his mouth and she had the unnerving feeling he knew what she was thinking. 'One step at a time, babe. Let's enjoy our day. OK?'

'OK.' Chloe heard the doubt in her own voice and knew he'd heard it, too.

She flipped down her visor, cutting off his view of her face so he couldn't read her expressions any more. Filled with nervous anticipation, she started her bike and led the way into what, for her, was the unknown...spending time with a sexy, attractive man who made his interest in her abundantly and frighteningly clear. Quite what she was going to do about that, if anything, remained to be seen.

Chloe couldn't believe how quickly the day sped by, or how disappointed she was that her time with Oliver was nearly over. They'd ridden miles along the coast and inland, spending time on Bodmin Moor with its wild landscape, granite tors, standing stones and unique history. She had imagined Oliver as a typical beach boy, interested only in surfing and women, but he'd proved to be a fascinating companion, keen to learn things, sharing unexpected bits of information and, most surprisingly of all, keeping her laughing all day. They had shared a picnic lunch on the moor, spent the afternoon exploring on both bike and foot, then had enjoyed an early fish-and-chip supper along the coast before making their way home. By evening they were back in Penhally, Oliver having followed her home after she had left her bike in its secure garage at Addison's Yard.

As she opened her front door, conscious of Oliver behind her, Chloe couldn't remember when she had last enjoyed herself so much. Usually, getting out on the bike was her escape and she liked to be alone to relax and unwind, but sharing things with Oliver today had made everything even better...special. Which was a bit scary in itself. She hadn't expected to relax with him, to enjoy being with him, for him to be so thoughtful and smart and funny. But she had—and he was.

He hadn't pressed her for details about her own life but he'd been open in telling her about himself, his childhood, the pluses and minuses of growing up in a well-known and wealthy family. The self-deprecating humour with which he had related tales of his scrapes and mishaps had brought tears of laughter to her eyes. All the while, though, she'd felt sad that she had nothing similar to offer about her own time growing up. A time dominated by her father's anger, his fists, his vicious tongue.

'What are you thinking?'

Oliver's husky voice broke through her reverie. Manufacturing a smile, she shook her head. 'Nothing.'

'You look sad.' His voice gentle, he crossed the living room, closing the gap between them.

'No.' Her memories were sad but she didn't want the past

spoiling this magical day, one she had never expected to have. 'I'm fine.'

But the thoughts, having intruded, were not so easy to banish. Was Lauren right? Was she allowing her father to control her life now as much as he had when he'd been alive? Not for the first time, she wondered what Oliver would think if she was ever able to confide in him about her father's mental, verbal and physical abuse. No matter what he had said about accepting anything she told him, she felt ashamed and embarrassed about her past. And she was sure he would laugh when he found out about her complete lack of experience with men.

She knew that her years of conditioning at home with her father had caused her to shut down one whole side of herself, but she hadn't felt she had been missing anything, had genuinely never felt interest in or desire for a man. It was Oliver who was awakening those kinds of feelings within her. And she was scared. Scared to open herself up to hurt, scared Oliver would either despise her or ridicule her for her past.

She was startled from her introspection when Oliver took both her hands in his. Uncertain, she looked up and met his dark, intense gaze, aware of the way her pulse raced and her skin tingled from his touch as his fingers stroked the sensitive insides of her wrists.

'Thank you for today, Chloe.'

His smoky voice increased the feeling of intimacy and made her skittish. 'I had a good time,' she admitted truthfully, earning herself a boyish smile.

'I'm glad. I really enjoy being with you, and I'd like us to spend much more time together.'

'Why?' She couldn't hide her confusion. 'You could have anyone.'

A chuckle rumbled from his chest. 'I don't want *anyone*. I want *you*.'

'I'm no good at this.'

'You mean letting a man get close to you?' he asked, no hint of judgement in his tone.

'I don't know how to be what you want me to be.'

For a moment his fingers tightened on hers, then he released them, but only so he could cup her face, drawing her gaze to his. Dark brown eyes looked deeply into hers. His touch was warm, sure but gentle, making her quiver from head to toe. Her chest felt tight and she wasn't sure she could remember how to breathe.

'Chloe, I never want you to be anything or anyone but yourself.' He was serious, intent, sincere. 'I like you just the way you are.'

'But—' Her words were silenced as he brushed the pad of his thumb across her lips.

'I'm not going to hurt you. We'll take things as slowly as you want,' he promised, and despite her wariness and doubt she felt warm deep inside, her heart thudding against her ribs. 'Give me a chance, babe…give *us* a chance. I want you to feel comfortable, to know you can trust me with anything.'

She finally managed to draw in a ragged breath. 'Oliver…'

'Shh. One step at a time. OK?'

'OK,' she finally agreed, not at all sure she knew what she was doing, but when he smiled at her like that she took leave of her senses, and the thought of more days like today was too tempting to resist.

'Thank you.' She saw him take a deep breath of his own, as if he was relieved or something. His thumbs stroked softly across her cheekbones, his eyes darkening as he stared at her mouth. 'May I kiss you goodnight?'

Chloe's eyes widened. 'You want to kiss me?'

'I do. Very much.' The chuckle rumbled out again, his smile deepening, bringing the dimple to his cheek. 'Is that so bad?'

he teased, eyes twinkling with amusement. 'Or such a surprise? You look like you've never been kissed before!'

'I haven't.'

He laughed, clearly disbelieving her, then his expression sobered as he continued to study her face. 'Damn,' he groaned, his body tensing. 'You're serious.'

Oliver's shock was only what she had expected. She had known he wouldn't understand. How could he think she was anything but an oddity? Chloe ducked her head as an astonished silence stretched between them. At least he knew part of the truth about her now, even though it was bound to drive him away and cool his interest in a single moment. She tried to step back but his hold tightened. He tilted her head up, but she resolutely closed her eyes so she wouldn't see the mocking derision she was sure must be in his.

'Chloe…look at me.'

'No,' she murmured, hands clenched to fists at her sides.

Oliver's hands slid along her neck to burrow into her hair, his thumbs grazing the line of her jaw, tipping her chin up further. 'Open your eyes, babe,' he insisted softly, his voice persuasive, a husky whisper that seemed to reach all her nerve endings.

Biting her lip, she mustered some bravado and forced herself to meet his gaze, surprised to find nothing but kindness and caring and honesty.

'Did you think I was going to make fun of you, or walk away?'

'I don't know.' Chloe shrugged. 'Maybe. Yes.' Frowning, she searched his gaze. 'I'm not like the kind of women you must have dated.'

'No, you're not,' he agreed, and for a moment her heart sank and a surprising wave of disappointment washed through her. 'But they're in the past. They don't interest me. You're different, Chloe. In a good way. And I'm *not* walking away.' Her heart started thudding again. She opened her mouth to protest, but the fingers of one hand brushed across her lips, silencing her. 'I'm serious when I say I don't want anyone but you. I meant it when I told you we'd take things at your pace. When you feel ready to talk, to tell me about your past and why it has held you back from experiencing your full potential as a desirable woman, I'm here to listen. Until then we'll spend more time together, get to know each other, whatever you want.'

She had no idea why, but she believed him. And she felt a crazy sense of nervous excitement she had never experienced before. Trying to block out the warnings of her past, she thought of Lauren's and Kate's advice, and especially of Oliver, this day they had shared, and took a tentative step out on a limb. 'Yes.'

'Yes?'

Oliver looked puzzled and she smiled. 'Yes, you may kiss me goodnight,' she whispered, her nervousness bringing a tremble to her voice.

Chocolate eyes turned dark and fiery as her words sank in. Again his hands moved to cup her face and her own hands rose to his chest, resting there uncertainly. Even through the soft leather she could feel the rapid beat of his heart, and when she breathed in, she inhaled the subtle masculine fragrance of him. She liked it. Her whole being shook as his head lowered and her eyes fluttered shut, the breath leaving her in a rush as his mouth met hers, his lips moving gently…warm, sure and seductive. Unable to help herself, she leaned into him. The kiss lasted no more than ten seconds. It wasn't enough. Already she wanted more, wanted to do it again, wanted it to go on for ever, and she barely suppressed a whimper of protest when he slowly pulled back.

Confused, she opened her eyes, saw Oliver's smile. Then he was letting her go, and she swayed, leaning against the sofa for support as she watched him walk away. Speechless, she pressed a hand to her mouth where the imprint of his still lingered. She licked her lips, tasting a teasing hint of the unfamiliar flavour of him. At the door, Oliver stopped and looked back at her, his eyes dark and unfathomable, his voice smoky with promise.

'Goodnight, Chloe. I'll see you tomorrow. Sweet dreams, babe.'

CHAPTER FOUR

OLIVER spent a couple of moments between patients updating his notes and preparing a referral letter to the cardiac consultant at St Piran. He was troubled by the worsening angina of the woman he had just seen, who smoked, had high blood pressure, high cholesterol and a family history of heart problems. Frowning, he concisely explained his concerns and requested the consultant's opinion.

It was Wednesday afternoon, and he was still shocked by the discoveries he had made on Sunday...the amazing day he had spent with Chloe. She was everything he had imagined and so much more. But absorbing the reality that she was twenty-seven-years old and had never even been kissed was taking some time.

Knowing she was in the room above, taking an antenatal clinic, his gaze strayed upwards. So near and yet so far. She was beyond innocent. How? Why? He had told her he would give her the time she needed to trust him, and he meant it, but that didn't mean he wasn't eager to understand why someone so beautiful and together had absolutely no idea about her own body, about need and pleasure and sexual fulfilment. Chloe wasn't being coy or shy or playing a game. She was genuine— and for some reason she had never had or explored sexual feelings.

At first, from the things Lauren and Kate had implied, he had assumed Chloe had been hurt by a previous boyfriend. But that was clearly not the case. Something much more fundamental must have happened in her earlier years to have caused her to shut off a whole part of herself. She had feared on Sunday that learning the truth of her inexperience would drive him away, make him lose interest. The opposite was the case.

Far from putting him off, Chloe's innocence brought a wave of affection and a rush of possessive satisfaction that no other man had touched her. *He* wanted to be the one to awaken her desires and teach her about the pleasures of her body, to show her how beautiful and sexy she was. But he couldn't banish the flickers of doubt that nagged at him. Was Chloe right for him? Was *he* the right man for *her*? Lauren and Kate appeared to believe so and claimed to see beyond the playboy stereotype he sought to escape. Did Chloe?

Nothing in his past had prepared him for a woman like her. Yes, he was wary, but he couldn't now imagine not having her in his life. With Chloe it would be all or nothing. He needed to go on seeing her, to win her trust and friendship, but he would have to be very sure of himself and his plans for the future before he took things beyond a few simple kisses. He was getting too far ahead of himself. For now he would spend as much time as he could with her outside work…which wasn't as easy as it sounded.

As well as being on call to her expectant mothers, Chloe had several out-of-hours ante- and postnatal groups, plus a parenting class for new mothers and fathers, in which she gave general support and advice on anything from care of the newborn to breast-feeding problems. Then there was the well-woman clinic where she helped with a range of issues, including family planning and pre-conception advice. Aside from a few snatched work-related conversations at the practice, including news of the safe delivery by C-section of Avril

Harvey's baby daughter on Monday, there had been little chance to see her at all.

But tonight, all being well, Chloe was his…for a few hours, at least. And he planned on making the most of them, talking, learning more about each other, just being together so she would feel more at ease and begin to trust him. He frowned, realising how involved his emotions were becoming with this woman. Perhaps it was time to stop doubting himself, to stop worrying that this was all happening sooner than he had planned and just see where the road ahead might lead…for them both.

Oliver glanced at his watch. He loved his job, gave one hundred per cent to his patients at all times, but he was longing to be alone with Chloe and he had another half an hour to go before both their clinics ended and he could take her home. With a resigned sigh, he pressed the buzzer and prepared to welcome his next patient.

'Let me take him for you,' Oliver offered with a smile, rising to his feet to help the harassed-looking young woman who struggled to manoeuvre a double buggy into the consulting room, one child aged about two strapped in and complaining noisily, a baby of a few months held in her free arm.

'Thanks so much.' The woman gratefully handed over the baby to Oliver's care, her answering smile rueful. 'Whoever said having the two so close together was a good idea wants their head examined.'

Chuckling, Oliver balanced the baby against his chest. 'Take your time,' he advised, waiting while she parked the buggy, sat down and endeavoured to quiet the fractious two-year-old.

'Sorry about that.' She brushed a few strands of mousy hair back from her overheated face.

'No problem.' Oliver glanced at the notes, familiarising himself with the Anker family's names. 'What can I do for you today, Juliet?'

'It's Leo,' she informed him, referring to the baby he was still holding. 'He has a cold—in this weather, can you imagine!—and he seems to have trouble breathing sometimes.'

'Let me have a look at him. How long have you noticed the problem?'

Juliet bared Leo's chest so Oliver could listen to his lungs. 'Just a couple of days. I'm probably worrying about nothing, but…'

'It's always better to be safe than sorry.' Oliver gave her a reassuring smile before resuming his thorough examination. 'His lungs are clear,' he told her a short while later, looping his stethoscope round his neck. 'Everything sounds fine. And his temperature is normal. When is Leo's breathing worse?'

'Mostly when he's trying to feed.'

Oliver checked the notes once more. 'And are you still breast-feeding?'

'Yes. I really wanted to. I had trouble managing it with William, but Chloe was wonderful, helping me through both pregnancies and supporting me afterwards. I had no problems at all feeding Leo,' she explained proudly, dressing the baby again.

'Chloe's an excellent midwife.' Oliver was all too aware of how his heart had leapt at hearing Chloe's name. With an effort he forced his mind back to the matter at hand. 'The best thing to do with Leo is to put a couple of saline drops in each nostril before feeding. That will help to thin and disperse any congestion, and he should find feeding much easier. You can also try holding him in a more upright position until he is over the cold.'

A relieved smile stripped the worry from Juliet's rosy face as she strapped Leo into place beside his now silent, watchful brother. 'That's great. Thank you so much, Dr Fawkner.'

'No trouble. You have two fine sons.' He held the door open and helped Juliet guide the buggy out of the room. 'Let me know if Leo's cold doesn't clear in another couple of days, or if you have any other concerns.'

His next patient was a middle-aged man with recurrent muscular pain in his back. After prescribing some analgesia, he recommended that the man see Lauren Nightingale for some gentle physiotherapy to help strengthen his back.

'I'm willing to try anything, Doctor,' he agreed with a wan smile.

Smiling in sympathy, Oliver made a couple of notes. 'I'll see to the referral and Lauren will contact you directly. Any problems, come back and talk to me.'

As the man made his uncomfortable departure, Oliver reflected on another mixed afternoon surgery while he waited for his final patient of the day to come through. The summer influx of tourists and surfers brought an upsurge in minor injuries and illnesses. He had been taken on at the practice to assist his new colleagues in covering the additional cases on top of the usual workload of local families, farmers and fishermen. In the weeks he had been in Penhally, he had seen everything from surfboard collisions to scrapes on the rocks, weaver and jellyfish stings, fractures, sprains, cuts that needed stitching, and had given what seemed a never-ending series of tetanus injections.

Oliver looked up and smiled as a knock on the door announced the arrival of Rachel Kenner. He had seen from the notes that the local vicar's daughter seldom visited the surgery, but one look at her frightened blue eyes told him that something serious and troubling had brought her there today. Gently he sat her down and tried to put her at ease. Slender and shy, with short blonde curls and a nervous manner, she looked younger than her seventeen years and very vulnerable.

'Hello, Rachel. Take your time and make yourself comfortable,' he said encouragingly as she shifted restlessly on the chair. 'What can I do to help you today?'

Clasping shaking hands together in her lap, she stared at him in silence for several long moments and then burst into tears.

Chloe had just shown her last mum-to-be of the afternoon out of the room when the phone rang. She returned to her desk, grimacing at the sight of the pile of paperwork awaiting her, and picked up the receiver.

'Sorry, Chloe, am I interrupting?' Sue, the head receptionist apologised.

'No, Sue, it's fine. Mrs George has just left. Is there a problem?'

'Oliver asks if you could pop down to his consulting room as soon as you are free,' Sue continued and Chloe's heart skittered at the sound of his name and at the request. She was still gathering her wits as Sue continued. 'He has Rachel Kenner with him.'

Surprise jolted Chloe from her wayward thoughts about the man whose all-too-brief kiss three days ago still left her jittery, ridiculously excited and confused. 'Rachel? OK, I'm on my way down.'

Wondering why Reverend Kenner's shy, studious daughter might need her, Chloe hurried down the stairs to the suite of consulting rooms, frowning as she knocked on the door of what had been Lucy's room but which Oliver was now using.

'Come in.'

Stepping inside, Chloe felt another burst of nervous anticipation, then she met Oliver's darkly sinful gaze. Warmth stole through her whole being. For just a moment something intense and deeply personal burned in his eyes, and a small smile played at his mouth, then he was back in professional mode, as if the private connection had never happened.

'Thanks for coming down, Chloe.'

'No problem.' She dragged her attention away from the man who had hijacked all her thoughts of late and focused on the girl who sat by the desk, tear tracks marking her pale cheeks, a pile of soggy tissues clutched in her shaking hands. Chloe's heart went out to her, and she moved to her side, slipping an arm around her slim shoulders. 'Hello, Rachel, my love. Whatever has happened?'

Her question set off another burst of sobbing. Chloe held Rachel while she cried, raising a querying gaze to Oliver who looked on with sympathetic concern.

'Rachel's come to see us because she has a problem she's not sure how to handle,' he explained after a moment, choosing his words with care. 'I said we'd do all we can to help.'

'Of course we will,' Chloe agreed robustly, giving Rachel an encouraging smile.

Oliver hunkered down on the other side of the distraught girl and offered her a fresh tissue. His kindness touched Chloe's heart. 'Rachel, do you want to explain to Chloe, or would you like me to tell her?'

'You d-do it. P-please.' Sniffing, Rachel wiped her face and blew her nose.

'OK.' Oliver moved back, giving the teenager some space. His voice was matter-of-fact and without judgement or drama. 'Rachel had a short relationship with a boy whom she thought cared about her. Now she fears she's pregnant and she's worried about telling her father.'

Chloe couldn't have been more surprised. Rachel was the very last person she would ever have imagined being in this difficult situation. Not just because she was the vicar's daughter, or even because she was shy, but because she had been so focused on her education and her dream to be a teacher. As for Rachel's father, Chloe knew how close he and Rachel were, especially since her mother had died some years ago, leaving them alone. Reverend Kenner was a kind-hearted, generous and understanding person, and Chloe knew he would stand by Rachel no matter what. Those were bridges that could be crossed after they had determined whether the teenager *was* pregnant.

'First things first, then,' Chloe decided, following Oliver's no-nonsense approach. 'We'll do some checks to make sure, but what makes you believe you are pregnant? Have you done a home test, my love, or are you guessing because you've missed some periods?'

'Both,' Rachel admitted. The crying had stopped for now, but her voice sounded thick with tears.

Chloe gave her shoulders a reassuring squeeze. 'And how far along do you think you are, Rachel?'

'F-four months.' She hiccupped, smiling gratefully when Oliver crossed the room, returning with a cool glass of water for her. 'Thank you,' she whispered, taking a few sips. 'It only happened the once. He s-said it would be all right.'

Oliver looked resigned and Chloe smothered a sigh. How many times had they heard a tale like this one? Once was all it took. 'You don't think the father of the baby will stand by you?'

'I know he won't,' she scoffed, full of hurt and scorn.

'Can you tell us what happened?'

Rachel raised her head. Her blue eyes were red-rimmed and her lower lip trembled. 'I couldn't believe he had even noticed me. I should have known better. But he told me he cared, and he was nice to me when we went out a few times. I was stupidly flattered. I'd never had a boyfriend before. They tend not to notice me because I am shy and bookish, not to mention being the vicar's daughter,' she added with a touch of cynicism.

'But this boy did notice you?' Oliver encouraged.

'So I thought...at the time.' Rachel took another drink of water and drew in a ragged breath, fresh tears spilling from between her lashes and trickling down her pale cheeks. 'But it was all lies, just to get what he wanted. He didn't force me to have sex, I wanted to by then, but it wasn't what I expected.

I didn't enjoy it.' More tears slipped free. 'He wasn't caring at all. It really hurt.'

Chloe gave her another hug and waited until the girl calmed again. 'Who was it, Rachel?'

'G-Gary Lovelace.'

Somehow Chloe bit back a retort. Damn those Lovelaces. They were a well-known problem family in Penhally, the father in prison, not for the first time, and the mother left alone with several difficult children. Gary, the eldest at seventeen, was good-looking but lazy and always in trouble. Thrown out of school, he was now unemployed and following in his father's unsavoury footsteps. That Rachel had become one of Gary's targets was more than upsetting. Judging by Oliver's expression, he hadn't yet come into contact with the Lovelace family during his first weeks at the practice. Checking that Rachel wasn't watching, Chloe shook her head and mouthed to Oliver that she would explain later. His brief nod confirmed his understanding.

'Gary never came near me again,' Rachel continued, her shoulders shaking as she sobbed. 'I tried to talk to him, to tell him about the b-baby, and he just laughed. He said being with me had been a joke, payback to my father for his do-gooding ways.'

'Oh, Rachel,' Chloe soothed, seeing the murderous look on Oliver's face, knowing he would like a few minutes alone with wretched Gary Lovelace, just as she would.

They took some time to gentle Rachel through the necessary tests and health check, confirming the pregnancy.

'Have you given any thought to what you want to do?' Oliver asked gently as he sat back down at his desk.

'Not really.' Rachel bit her lip. 'For a while I tried to pretend none of it was happening. I have so many plans for my life. I desperately want to be a teacher. But how am I going to manage with a baby? I do know that I can't get rid of it, no matter what the circumstances or why it's here.'

Drawing up another chair, Chloe sat beside her. 'We'll do everything we can to support you, Rachel, but I honestly think you need to tell your father.'

'Oh, but I can't!' the teenager all but wailed.

'Rachel, I agree with Chloe,' Oliver announced in support. 'I know it must be scary to face these things, but your father is a good man and he'll stand by you.'

Rachel ducked her head, her shoulders shaking. 'He'll be so disappointed in me. He's so wrapped up in his community work, I hardly see him any more.'

'He loves you dearly. And you love him.' Chloe rested a reassuring hand on Rachel's arm. Her thoughts strayed for a moment and she wondered what it must be like to have a good, caring father, as Rachel did, a man so different from her own. Suppressing a shiver, she pushed her memories away. 'You're going to need his support, Rachel. This isn't something you can hide from him.'

'I just don't know how to tell him.'

Chloe opened her mouth to make a promise, then closed it again and glanced at Oliver. He smiled, a glint in his eye, as if he knew what she had been about to say.

'Would you like Chloe and me to come home with you and help explain things to your father?' Oliver offered, and Chloe smiled at him in gratitude, knowing he had somehow been in tune with her train of thought.

'You'd do that?' Rachel looked from her to Oliver and back again. 'Really?'

'Of course. If you think it would make things easier for you.'

Looking young and scared, Rachel nodded. 'Yes, please.'

'All right.' Glancing at Oliver, Chloe rose to her feet. 'I'll just pop upstairs and fetch my things, then I'll be ready to go.'

Rachel clutched her hand before she could leave. 'Thank you. Thank you both, so much.'

'Do you think Rachel will be all right?'

Hearing the worry in Chloe's voice, Oliver reached for her hand and linked his fingers with hers. So much for his plans to have her to himself for the evening, he thought wryly, given the hour or more they had spent at the vicarage after driving Rachel home. Not that he begrudged helping the teenager smooth things over with her father, or answering their endless questions. He didn't. He was just impatient to have Chloe to himself as their time alone together was precious.

'Your judgement was perfect,' he reassured her now. 'Yes, Rachel's father was shocked and upset, but he's devoted to his daughter and it's obvious he's going to stand by her. The plan to involve the aunt and uncle who live in Plymouth, and who are experienced and regular foster-parents, sounds an excellent one.'

'It would be wonderful if they agree to help Rachel care for the baby when the time comes, while she continues her A levels and does her teacher training at Plymouth university,' she agreed, sounding more hopeful.

'Exactly. And in the meantime, Rachel has her father…and us.'

The smile Chloe bestowed on him turned his heart over and sucked the air out of his lungs. 'Yes. She does. Thank you for being so good with her.'

'It wasn't me, it was you.' It was no good. He couldn't wait another moment. Coming to a halt, he drew her to face him, his free hand cupping her cheek. Slowly, carefully, he placed an all-too-brief, all-too-chaste kiss on her lips. 'You're pretty special, Chloe MacKinnon.'

A becoming blush pinkened her cheeks. 'I am not.'

'Now, we could argue about that for the rest of the

night…and I'd most definitely win,' he teased, starting them walking again.

Back at her car, Chloe opened the doors. 'Do you want me to drop you at the surgery so you can collect your own car?'

'No, it's OK. I'm not on call tonight and I can easily walk to work in the morning.' He didn't intend to waste another second of time with Chloe. 'How about we pick up something to eat?'

'That sounds nice. But I have some chicken and things for a salad in the fridge. It won't take me long to put something together. If you'd like that?' she finished doubtfully.

Did she believe such a plan might be too homely for a supposed playboy like him? He'd soon disabuse her of that worry, but that she might think it brought a sting of disappointment. The shallowness and false impressions were things he had come to Penhally Bay to escape. It mattered to him that Chloe saw the real man.

'Perfect.' He stroked one finger along her bare forearm, feeling her shiver in reaction, seeing confusion and awareness darken her eyes. He smiled and withdrew his touch. 'Thank you for asking me. I'd love to spend some quiet time at home with you.'

As she turned away and started the engine, he noticed that her hand wasn't entirely steady and she sounded more than a touch breathless. 'OK.'

Back at her cottage in Fisherman's Row, Oliver insisted on helping her put the impromptu meal together. 'Tell me about Gary Lovelace,' he requested, smiling at Chloe's unladylike exclamation.

His smile faded, however, when he learned about the reputation of the family and the endless problems they seemed to cause.

'Eve Dwyer knows more about them than I do. She's a practice nurse who lives in the village, but she's currently on an agency placement in Newquay until a vacancy becomes available back here,' Chloe explained, taking some tomatoes from the fridge and beginning to chop them. 'According to Eve, Tassie, the ten-year-old girl, is the only decent one in the Lovelace family. I don't know the whole story, but the mother, Amanda, just can't cope, and Eve is involved doing what she can to help Tassie. Gary is the main troublemaker and is leading his younger brothers astray. It sounds as if he played poor Rachel ruthlessly in one of his games. I can just imagine his sick thrill at getting the vicar's daughter in trouble.' The knife sliced through the juicy tomatoes with vigour and Oliver winced at the symbolism. 'I'd like a few moments to have my say to that boy.'

'Join the queue.'

Chloe made a murmur of agreement. 'I think most in Penhally feel the same way. Oh, blast,' she finished, setting down the knife and raising her finger to her mouth.

'Have you cut yourself?'

'It's nothing.'

Concerned, he took her hand, holding it under the cold tap for a few moments. 'Have you got any plasters?'

'In that drawer.' She pointed across the other side of the kitchen and he soon found what he needed. 'I'm getting as bad as Lauren in the clumsy stakes!'

'What is it with her?' he asked, moving back and carefully drying Chloe's cut finger on some clean absorbent kitchen roll, applying pressure to stem a fresh welling of blood.

'Lauren's always been accident-prone. Why?'

Oliver shrugged. 'I just noticed she doesn't judge distance well when she's reaching for something, and she trips over or walks into things that are in shadow.'

'You think there's something wrong?'

'Probably not if she's always been like it,' he soothed, regretting having caused Chloe any concern about her friend. Bu something nagged at him about Lauren's clumsiness. Pushing the thought from his mind, he gently applied the plaster over Chloe's cut. As he finished, she went to pull her hand away, but he held on. 'Wait. I haven't kissed it better yet.'

'Oh!'

Cradling her left hand, pale and delicate-looking against his darker skin, he slowly raised it, enjoying the feel of her soft skin. He placed a feather-light kiss over the injured spot, lingering a moment, his gaze holding hers, before he released her.

'There we go, babe.'

'Right. Thanks.' She looked adorably flustered. Swallowing, she turned back to the counter. 'Um, did I tell you Avril Harvey might be well enough to bring her baby home on Friday?'

Oliver hid a smile at her unsubtle change of subject. 'You did. It's good news that mother and daughter are doing well. Her husband must be relieved.'

'Yes, he is.' Placing the cold chicken on plates, Chloe drizzled dressing over the fresh salad. 'And I gather you spoke with Nick.'

'He's agreed to take back his own cases, including the Trevellyans and the Fiddicks, but I'll handle any other antenatal work not on his list for the time being,' he clarified, taking the cutlery and a jug of iced water to the table.

'Thank you. Kate will be pleased. At least Nick is being civil to her at work again—if not friendly.'

Oliver would have liked to ask what the issue was about but he didn't want to intrude on a private matter between Kate and Nick, and he also didn't want to spend this time with Chloe talking about work. He steered the conversation back to more personal things and they discussed books and music, films and motorbikes while they ate their chicken salads with soft granary rolls warmed in the oven.

'That was great,' Oliver praised when they had finished.

'Would you like some ice cream?'

Carrying the plates back to the kitchen to wash them, Oliver smiled. Chloe and her sweet tooth! 'Please.'

After drying up, he leaned against the counter, watching as she spooned out two bowls of hazelnut meringue ice cream. The uniform she still wore failed to mask her womanly curves. She was so beautiful, with her clear skin, luxuriant dark hair and those stunning green eyes. His body tightened with desire. To resist reaching for her and spoiling all his good intentions to take things slowly and let Chloe set the pace, he walked into the cosy living room. Sitting on the sofa, he familiarised himself with her two rescue cats. He knew the ginger one who had lost an eye was called Cyclops, while the all-white cat with a black patch over one eye was called Pirate.

'How did you do that?' Chloe asked a few moments later, eyes wide with surprise as she watched him stroke the cats.

'Do what?'

'Make friends with Pirate. He's very wary of trusting people, especially men. He didn't have a very happy start in life.' Her words ended abruptly and shadows clouded her eyes, as if she realised that she could have been talking about her own past. Looking uncertain, she handed him a bowl and spoon. 'Here.'

'Thanks, babe.'

Before she could move away, Oliver caught her free hand and encouraged her to sit beside him on the sofa. Sensing her unease, he kept things light, giving her time to relax again. The ice cream was excellent and he said so.

'It's from the Trevellyans' herd of pedigree Guernseys,' Chloe told him, savouring every spoonful of her treat in a way that tightened his gut more by the second. Smiling, she set her empty bowl aside. 'Mike and Fran, along with Mike's brother and sister-in-law, Joe and Sarah, produce some wonderful things. I love their blue cheese. They have a great farm shop and also sell at the weekly farmers' market.'

Oliver turned to face her, using the pad of one thumb to brush across her lips and the corner of her mouth. 'Stray ice cream,' he murmured, raising the thumb to his own mouth and sucking it.

'Oliver…'

He heard the uncertainty in her voice, but also the edge of arousal, which was matched by the darkening of her eyes. As much as he needed his next breath in order to survive, he *had* to kiss her, but he didn't want to rush her or push her too far too soon. Slowly, he leaned closer, giving her every opportunity to stop him, to move away, to say it was not what she wanted. Needing to touch her, but careful not to scare her by pulling her against him and wrapping his arms around her as he so longed to do, he closed one hand loosely around her wrist. He could feel the rapid beat of her pulse, and he loved the feel of her soft skin beneath the light caress of his fingertips. His gaze fixed on the lushness of her lips. Chloe swayed towards him. He closed the last of the distance, brushing his mouth lightly across hers, feeling and hearing her gasp as he used the tip of his tongue to clean any remaining ice cream from her skin. She was so sweet, so pure. Being with her felt so right. He longed for the day he could kiss and lick her all over.

'You taste delicious, Chloe.'

With a soft moan, she pressed her lips to his, unskilled but enthusiastic…not that he was complaining. Far from it. Used to obvious women who knew what they wanted and how to play the game, Chloe was a refreshing change. He felt protective of her. Everything about her was different. He had never felt for another woman as he did for Chloe. Had never been prepared to spend so long wooing a woman. And it had never been so important to gain someone's trust and friendship.

Oliver pulled back. Raising his free hand, his fingers traced the shape of her face. Moss-green eyes opened, fringed by sooty lashes, and she surprised him by following suit, her own fingers exploring the contours and textures of his face. Just that simple touch from her set him on fire. Catching her exploring hand, he brought it to his mouth, focusing his gaze on hers, watching her reactions as he teased her palm with his lips and tongue tip, nibbling the mound by her thumb with his teeth, making her moan.

'Oliver?'

'Mmm?' Feeling the tremor run through her, hearing the huskiness in her voice, he licked tiny circles in the centre of her palm with his tongue tip, 'You like that?'

'Yes. But…'

Responding to her nervousness, he stilled, seeing her flush and glance away. 'But?' he encouraged, his heart in his mouth as he waited to hear what she was going to say, hoping it wasn't to ask him to stop.

Chloe sucked in a ragged breath. She had never known feelings of desire and need before, and she found it hard to understand what was happening to her body. When Oliver touched her and kissed her, even looked at her with that melting dark gaze, she felt strange. Tingly and warm. Excited but nervous. Needy. He brushed his fingers over her skin and her flesh burned. He kissed her, lightly, briefly, and her body quivered in a way she had never experienced before. Deep inside she felt a knot of tension, a restlessness, an ache she wasn't sure how to assuage.

Oliver had never laughed at her or made her feel stupid. Amazingly, he still seemed to want her. And he was so patient, so gentle…undeniably sexy. Her past may have caused her to shut down that part of herself, but she didn't get to be a twenty-seven-year old midwife in the twenty-first century without understanding the mechanics of sex. She talked about it every day without embarrassment. Doing anything in practice was another matter entirely, and now she had Oliver here, had discovered how much she was enjoying being with him, she didn't have a clue what to do. A self-deprecating smile curved her lips.

'Chloe?'

His husky voice drew her from her thoughts and she realised he was still waiting for her to answer his question. His fingers stroked the sensitive flesh along the inside of her forearm and she couldn't halt the quiver that rippled through her. Could she ask? Would he mind?

'I want—' Again her words halted and she cursed herself for being so nervous.

'Tell me what you want, Chloe.' He rested his hand along the side of her neck, his thumb caressing her skin, and she leaned into his touch, seeking more. 'Never be scared to say what you need. You can always ask me anything, tell me anything. OK?'

She nodded, then sucked in a deep breath. 'I like you kissing me,' she finally admitted, bringing a dimpled smile to his handsome face.

'It's going to get even better.'

'I don't know what to do. I want…' She bit her lip, seeing his gaze drop back to her mouth. She remembered how his had felt moving teasingly over hers. It wasn't enough. 'Will you show me how to kiss properly?'

'You can count on it, babe,' he promised roughly, something hot and primal flaring in his eyes, filling her with excited anticipation and a new burst of wariness as she couldn't entirely let go of the memories of her past.

Edging closer, she tentatively rested a hand on his shoulder. 'What would lesson one be?' She was surprised at her own boldness. Surprised, too, by the inner realisation that she was coming to trust Oliver to be careful with her, to not harm her.

'Chloe…' He tensed, and for a horrible moment she thought she had misread the situation and made a fool of herself. She went to pull back, but he stopped her. 'Wait.' His eyes were impossibly dark and she discovered with amazement that his hand was unsteady as he moved to brush some wayward strands of hair back from her face. 'Are you sure?'

'Yes.' Her answer was a bare whisper, a curious mix of certainty and uncertainty churning inside her.

'Slow and easy,' Oliver murmured, almost to himself, she thought. His tongue tip peeped out as he moistened his lips, and her stomach jolted in response, but he paused again, holding her gaze. 'Any time you want to stop, we stop. OK?'

Chloe nodded, sure she was going to burst with impatience if she didn't feel his mouth against hers again…now. And then he was moving, his hand slipping round to the back of her head, his fingers sinking into her hair, his head lowering to hers. She tried to breathe and found it was almost impossible. Her heart pounded in her chest. She felt his warmth, scented his enticing masculine aroma. Then his mouth met hers, firmer this time as it moved rhythmically, knowing and arousing.

She gasped as he nibbled her lower lip, then he gently sucked on it, and she thought she was going to melt. Her hand tightened on his shoulder as she tried to balance herself. The urge to draw him closer, to press herself against him was overwhelming, but he deftly took charge, retreating when she impatiently wanted to move on, keeping her on the edge, desire spiralling more and more, leaving her feeling heady and out of control.

When his tongue teased the seam of her lips, they instinctively parted for him. She momentarily froze as she tasted him, sweet but rawly male, for the first time. Clinging to him, a whimper escaped as he changed the angle, deepening the slow, thorough, strength-sapping kiss. The tip of his tongue stroked around the insides of her lips, teasing her, before dipping inside, making her want more. But when her own tongue ventured forward to meet his, he retreated, denying her quest. Far, far too soon, the kiss was over. Chloe moaned a protest when she felt Oliver withdrawing from her, breaking contact, pulling back.

Confused, dazed, she finally managed to force her eyes open and focus on his face. His small smile was pure wickedness and gave another kick to her fluttering stomach, but she was gratified to hear that his own breathing was ragged. Realising how she was clutching him, one hand gripping the fabric of his shirt on his shoulder, the other having become entangled with his, their fingers locked together, she forced herself to relax her hold. She had no idea what to say. All she wanted to know was when they could do it again. It had been amazing.

Oliver's hand slid free of her hair, grazing across her cheek before his fingertips traced her mouth which felt swollen and sensitised from their kiss. His eyes were even darker than before, heated, watchful. She wondered what he was thinking, whether the kiss had meant anything at all to him…a kiss that had completely blown her away.

Before either of them could speak, the sound of her pager intruded on the intimate, electrically charged silence. To her regret, Oliver set her further away and released her. She felt bereft without his touch. Pulling herself together, knowing someone needed her, she fumbled for her pager with unsteady hands, anxiety gripping her when she saw who the urgent plea was from.

'What's wrong?' Oliver asked, as if reading her sudden tension.

'It's Angela Daniels. My mother-to-be on bed rest with placental abruption.' She met Oliver's dark, concerned gaze. 'She's haemorrhaging.'

CHAPTER FIVE

THE THREE hours since the call to Angela Daniels's emergency had passed in a blur. Chloe sat huddled in the passenger seat of the car and glanced across at Oliver, absorbing his strong, handsome profile in the shadows of the night. He had been a tower of strength. Having insisted on accompanying her, they had arrived at the house to find Angela's husband, Will, in a state of shock and panic, while Angela herself had collapsed on the bedroom floor and was in a bad way. Chloe had focused all her attention on Angela. Oliver had summoned the air ambulance, and then had taken charge of calming Will before coming to assist her in trying to stabilise Angela's deteriorating condition.

Seeing the woman on the floor and all that blood had brought back a terrible nightmare and for a moment Chloe had frozen, fearing that the outcome of this event would be the same as the one years ago. She had been scared that she wouldn't be good enough, competent enough. But thanks to Oliver, and the rapid dash by air ambulance to St Piran in the gathering dusk, both Angela and her baby were alive. For now. Chloe doubted whether either would have survived had they been forced to make the half-hour journey to hospital by road. As it was, the helicopter had delivered them there in minutes. Whether Angela would pull through after the amount of blood she had lost, as well as crashing twice in Resus before her baby was delivered by Caesarean, remained to be seen. Having gone along in the helicopter, Chloe now felt exhausted after the drama of the evening, drained both physically and emotionally.

Walking out to the hospital waiting area, covered in blood and battered by distressing memories, she had been amazed, relieved and more grateful than she could say to find that Oliver had followed by car to St Piran and was waiting to collect her. He had taken one look at her face and said nothing at all. He'd just been there, which was what she had needed, the look in his dark eyes one of concern and compassionate understanding. When he had slipped an arm around her, she had stiffened momentarily, but then she'd remembered that this was Oliver, and for reasons she couldn't explain, she felt safe with him. Again, he had seemed to instinctively judge her reaction, and he'd kept her close as he'd led her to the car, without ever making her feel threatened or restrained.

They were nearly back in Penhally Bay now. All she wanted was to get home. Have a shower. Face her demons. After parking the car, Oliver locked up and followed her to her front door. It was nearly midnight and the street was almost deserted, just a few tourists walking along the seafront. At the end of the eastern wall of the harbour, on the promontory beyond the church, stood the lighthouse. In the darkness of night, its beam arced out across the water, warning of the dangerous rocks where the wreck of the *Corazon del Oro* lay, the infamous seventeenth-century Spanish treasure ship which still drew tourists and divers to Penhally. Turning their backs on the village, Oliver took the keys from her shaky fingers and guided her inside her cottage. Resting his hands on her shoulders, he ushered her towards the stairs.

'Up for a bath or shower, then into bed, babe,' he instructed, his voice soft but brooking no argument. 'I'll make you a drink.'

She felt she had to attempt a token protest. 'You don't have to do that.'

'I know. But I want to. Now go,' he finished, dropping a kiss on the top of her head.

Too tired and shaken to manage further disagreement, she walked slowly up the stairs, feeling Oliver's gaze on her all the way.

Oliver watched Chloe head upstairs, a frown of concern creasing his brow. He wasn't sure what but something had happened. Something other than the emergency with Angela Daniels. Chloe had been amazing with the terrified mother-to-be—calm, professional, reassuring and skilfully efficient—but there had been a shadow in her eyes, such inner pain it had rocked him. No way was he leaving her until he knew she was all right. And, hopefully, he could encourage her to talk it out, to share whatever burden she had carried tonight.

He headed for the kitchen and hunted out the necessary ingredients for hot chocolate. It wasn't the weather for it as the night was sultry after another sweltering July day, but Chloe needed something comforting. And as he couldn't take her to bed and love her into a state of pleasured oblivion, the hot chocolate would have to do for now. Waiting for the drink to heat, hearing the shower running upstairs, he leaned against the counter and thought back over the evening.

Chloe's innocent eagerness to experiment, her shy boldness in asking for what she wanted, had both delighted and encouraged him. And it had been increasingly difficult to keep a rein on his desire as he had kissed her—less chastely than before. She had been nervous but she had enjoyed it, and he had been careful to call a halt before she had been ready to stop, leaving her disappointed and wanting more. He couldn't wait for the day he could kiss her freely, letting loose all the passion and hunger he had for her. But it was too soon. That had been reinforced by the way Chloe had tensed when he had put his arm round her at the hospital. Apparently kissing was one thing, being held was something else entirely. Something he would have to work on gently now he knew of her anxiety. Now he had admitted to himself that, whatever his doubts, no way could he walk away from this woman. Chloe needed someone to coax her out of her inner prison. He wanted to be that man. To be good enough for her. He wanted to discover what it was that haunted her and to try to make it right.

Tonight wasn't the time to ask, but he did hope to learn what had affected her so deeply with Angela. By the time the hot chocolate was ready, the shower had stopped. He found a container of tiny marshmallows and dropped a couple into her mug to melt, then headed upstairs, unexpectedly meeting her emerging from the bathroom. He stopped, unable to move, scared he'd drop the drinks or go into meltdown like a marshmallow himself at the sight of her dressed only in a soft, figure-hugging, sleeveless vest top and a flimsy pair of cotton boxers that revealed the length of her legs.

Great legs. Not too slender, but shapely and well curved. He could imagine all too clearly how they would feel wrapped around him as he... No, he couldn't afford to think erotic thoughts right now. He dragged his gaze upwards, only to halt at the delectable view of her full, firm breasts. Oh, hell. To torment him even further, pebbled nipples pressed out the thin cotton fabric of her top. His mouth watered. His hands craved to be free to fill themselves with her tempting flesh. Instead, his fingers tightened round the mugs in desperation and he valiantly sought to ignore the clamour of his own body as it responded to the sight of hers.

He cleared his throat, his voice gruff. 'Bed.' For a moment he closed his eyes. If only he could join her there.

Chloe, apparently innocently unaware both of the image she presented and his reaction, complied without comment. He followed her into her room, knowing he had to have taken leave of his senses...and that a cold shower was going to do little to stave off the state of his raging desire for Chloe tonight. Painfully aroused, he watched as she moved to the bed, sliding beneath the single light sheet that was her only covering for the heat of the summer night. Handing her the mugs, Oliver toed off his shoes. Propping himself next to her, on top of the sheet, he accepted his mug and then took her free hand in his, waiting for her to relax before even thinking of drawing her closer.

For a while they sipped their drinks in silence. He could feel her tension—it almost vibrated off her—and it was there in the tautness of her face reflected in the glow of the single lamp on the bedside chest next to her.

'You did a great job tonight, Chloe.'

Setting her empty mug aside, she shrugged. 'It was touch and go. I was grateful for your help. I know Angela wanted to be at home but, given the signs on her last scan, it may have been wiser had she stayed in hospital.'

'That was the consultant's call. Not yours.'

'Yes. I know.'

OK, so she wasn't blaming herself for the sudden deterioration in Angela's condition, which had been one of his fears. If that wasn't the issue, what was it that had upset her? Careful not to scare her by holding her down, he leaned across her to put his mug next to hers. Moving back into place, he slid an arm around her shoulders and drew her closer, cradling her head against his chest. With one hand he stroked the loose locks of her glossy, ebony hair.

Chloe held herself stiffly against him, but he didn't move, just waited, offering comfort, revelling in being able to hold her for the first time. The fact that she hadn't immediately pulled away was a major breakthrough. Even if she wasn't actively participating.

'Relax,' he murmured, keeping his voice low. His heart clenched when she drew in a ragged breath, only for it to shudder out of her. 'You're shaking. Don't you like being hugged?'

He thought she wasn't going to answer, but when she finally spoke, he had to strain to hear her whispered words. 'I'm not used to it.'

'I hope to be doing it a lot...if you'll let me,' he told her softly, careful to keep his hold loose so she didn't feel restrained.

He wanted answers but knew he had to be calm and patient, however frustrating it might be. Until he knew what had happened in her past, he didn't know what he was working against, what could alarm her or having her backing off. He felt like he was walking on eggshells.

'You are an incredible midwife, Chloe,' he praised, returning to their former conversation.

'Thank you.' He heard the surprise and pleasure in her voice at his compliment.

'I've worked with many people in different places who "do midwifery" but you are a proper midwife for all the right reasons and in all the right ways. I admire your desire to let things develop naturally for both mother and baby, using as little intervention as possible and putting the mother first. The care here is very patient-led and holistic. It's refreshing. And it's a real pleasure to work with you and Kate. You really believe in what you are doing. It's not just a job.'

'Not to me. I enjoy what I do.'

'It shows.' He continued stroking her hair. 'What made you choose midwifery as a career?' he asked, knowing when he felt her stiffen that he had touched something raw inside her. 'Chloe?'

A deep painful sigh escaped her but she didn't pull away.

He waited, hoping she was coming to trust him enough to confide in him about something important to her.

'I came home from school one day to find my mother lying on the floor, bleeding.'

The words cut through him and he smothered a groan as it dawned on him what seeing Angela must have meant to Chloe. 'Tonight made you remember.'

'Yes. For a moment I froze, and it was as if I was reliving it.' A tremor ran through her and he instinctively cuddled her closer. 'I was ten. My mother was six months pregnant.' Her voice was flat but the underlying emotion was obvious and Oliver ached for her. 'I called the ambulance but it seemed to take ages to come. The person on the phone told me what to do, and I tried...tried to keep calm and help. My mother survived, but it was hopeless for the baby.'

So she had become a midwife, needing to do all she could to help others as she hadn't been able to help her mother? 'It wasn't your fault, Chloe,' he reassured her, his voice rough.

'I couldn't do anything. I let my little brother die.' A sob of guilt was barely suppressed at her confession.

'Chloe, you were a child. You were not responsible, not to blame,' he insisted, wanting to ease the pain she had buried all this time and which had come back to haunt her after finding Angela in a similar situation. 'With the knowledge you now have, you know that even the best professional could not have saved your brother. Sometimes these things happen, a fluke of nature.'

'He killed him.'

Oliver hesitated, not sure if she knew what she was saying, or whether the trauma the ten-year-old child had endured had made her confused. 'Who did?' He moved his fingers under her hair to soothingly massage the back of her neck.

'My father.' She sucked in a ragged breath, still tense in his arms. 'He'd gone off on one of his rages. He hit her, she fell...and he kicked her in the stomach. That's why she miscarried. He said he never wanted the baby anyway. He left her to bleed to death, wanted them both to die, and he went out fishing. If I hadn't come in and found her... Later he blamed me for saving her.'

'God, Chloe.'

This was the first real confidence she had ever shared with him. Instinctively he gathered her unprotesting form closer still, breathing in the fresh apple scent of her hair and skin. What she had told him was shocking enough, but the way she had recounted it, as if such violence at home had been nothing unusual, made him feel sick. What must it have been like to grow up in that kind of environment? And then it occurred to him that he may have unwittingly discovered the root of the problem. Was the dark spectre in Chloe's past her father? If so, it made sense that she never wanted to speak of her childhood. It seemed that every time he came closer to an answer, all he found were more questions.

Oliver couldn't bear the thought of Chloe being hurt in any way. Yet someone *had* hurt her. And the prime suspect was her father. It tore at him that she had been emotionally and physically dominated by someone who should have loved and cared for her. No wonder she didn't trust those emotions. Or men. Despite everything she had been through, she had survived and triumphed, at least in terms of her career, her friendships, her hobbies. But she had closed her mind and her heart to love, men and sex. He had yet to find out the full details of what had happened, but he desperately wanted to teach Chloe that she could trust him not to hurt her or control her, that it was safe to experience with him all the things she had banished from her life until now.

'I'm sorry,' she murmured, making him frown.

'There's nothing whatever for you to apologise for.'

She relaxed more against him. 'Thank you for being here this evening.'

'I'll always be here for you, babe.'

As he spoke the words, he knew how much he meant them. While part of him was scared of what he would be taking on by pursuing things with Chloe, he recognised that he was in too deep, his emotions and his desires ensnared, to back away and let her down. Lost in his own thoughts, he dropped a kiss on the top of her head, his free hand moving to whisper up and down her bare arm.

Something had happened to him the day he had met Chloe. Her friends said she was special and the more he came to know her the more he knew that was true. From the first moment he had been drawn to her. He thought back over the pleasant but meaningless relationships he had been involved in over the years. Most had been brief and temporarily satisfying, but had never filled a hidden void he had never allowed himself to acknowledge until recently, when the urge for a different and settled life had brought him back to Cornwall.

With Chloe, the smallest, most seemingly insignificant progress felt like the greatest victory of his life, and just being with her made him happy. Yes, he wanted to make love to her, but what he felt with Chloe, what he *needed* with her, was about so much more than sex. For the first time in his life he wanted a woman for more than a mutually enjoyable but short-lived affair. Chloe was more. So much more in every way. Yet the responsibility of all that meant weighed heavily on him. He didn't doubt his steadfastness. He wanted to settle down, to have a family of his own, and he knew that when he found the right woman, he would be loyal and faithful and loving, in for the long haul. *Was* Chloe the one? Could she see beyond the Fawkner name and the old reputation to the person he was inside?

With his mind occupied, Oliver held Chloe until she fell

asleep. Nothing would please him more than to slide under the sheet and stay with her all night, but he knew what small communities were like and he wasn't prepared to make her the subject of unwitting gossip. He wanted people here to see him for what he was now. If and when Chloe asked him to stay of her own free will...well, that was a different matter entirely. Regretfully, he eased away and slipped on his shoes. Making sure she was comfortable, he watched her sleep, his chest tight with longing and his growing feelings for her.

Turning away, he used the pad and pen Chloe kept on the bedside chest to write her a note. Leaving his message where she would find it when she woke up, he bent and kissed her lightly on the forehead before switching off the lamp and leaving her room. After checking that her cottage was secure, and that the two cats had fresh water, he took Chloe's spare keys, let himself out and locked the door after him.

He walked the short distance up Bridge Street to the flat Nick had arranged for him to rent until the end of July. Soon he would have to make more permanent plans. But even knowing he wasn't going to spend many of the few hours left of the night asleep, he couldn't think about anything now. His mind was too full of Chloe.

'I hear you had an eventful night,' Kate commented with a sympathetic smile when Chloe arrived at work the next morning.

'That's one way of putting it.' Yawning, Chloe sat down at her desk. 'Angela Daniels got out of bed to visit the bathroom, had a dizzy spell, fell to the floor and caused the already damaged placenta to rupture. It was only thanks to the air ambulance that we arrived at the hospital in time. I'm going to ring and see how she's doing.'

Kate gestured to the desk. 'Oliver left a message for you. He said he knew you would be worried, so he phoned St Piran first thing. Angela had a stable night and she's doing well. The baby is fine. It's all in the note.'

'Thanks.'

Tears stung Chloe's eyes and she looked away from Kate's knowing gaze. Oliver had been wonderful the previous evening. She hadn't felt at all scared when he had held her. Far from it, actually. She had felt safe and secure, so much so that she had confided to him about her mother's miscarriage. Oliver had been so understanding and supportive. And then she had fallen asleep in his arms! She couldn't believe it. Despite only having a few hours of rest, she had awoken feeling relaxed…and strangely disappointed to find herself alone. Opening her eyes to the sun-filled room, her gaze had fallen at once on the note he had left for her.

I hope you slept well. I made sure all was safe and secure before I left—and both Cyclops and Pirate were fine. Thank you for sharing part of your past with me. I'm always here for you when you feel ready to tell me the rest. You are a terrific midwife and an amazing woman. I'll see you later, babe. Call me if you need anything.
Love, Oliver x

It made her smile just thinking of him. He was nothing like she had first imagined him to be when he had joined the practice. Lauren and Kate were right. There was so much more to him than the sexy surfer image. He was smart and funny, kind and thoughtful…all qualities that came naturally to him. But always there was that underlying thread of intimacy, of warmth and caring, that made her feel both nervous and giddily excited.

Remembering how he had signed the note made her think of claiming the kiss he had left her. Which made her think of kissing in general. After her lesson the previous evening, when he had shown her how magical and arousing it could be, how wonderful he tasted, how incredible he made her feel, she could kiss Oliver for ever. She felt hot and tingly just thinking about it and she couldn't wait to do it again. Funny that she had never been interested before, had never spent a second considering it, and now, thanks to a few hours and a couple of kisses with Oliver, she could think of little else.

Chloe worried that Oliver saw more than he should. He was frighteningly attuned to her, the only person who saw deeper than the surface veneer she had worn for more years than she could remember. She had a few close friends, including Kate, but it was Lauren who knew more about her than anyone. Yet even from her she kept back an awful lot. That Oliver saw the person inside both scared her witless and made her feel secure, cared for, warm.

Although Oliver was aware of her inexperience, and now knew about her mother losing the baby—and why—she was worried that if she did bring herself to confide more about the nature of her childhood, she would drive him away. He had said he wanted to know, that nothing would change how he felt, but she wasn't so sure. She was ashamed of her past, of her father and the legacy his brand of abuse had bestowed on her, and she wasn't sure she could handle the emotions that might flood out if she unlocked things she had kept hidden so deeply inside her for years.

'Oliver told me he'd sorted things out with Nick about the antenatal work.' Kate's comment drew her from her reverie. She looked up, saw her friend's brave smile, and knew the situation with Nick still hurt her. 'I think the compromise will suit everyone—and our Friday meetings should be more comfortable.'

'I hope so. Have you spoken to Nick?'

Kate averted her gaze. 'Only in passing—about work. That's an improvement, anyway.'

'Kate...'

'I know, my love. But Nick has to come round to things in his own time. He's not ready yet to consider letting Jem into his life.' She sighed, sipping her coffee. 'I know people see Nick as being aloof, and he can be, but I've know him a long time, known the losses and disappointments he has endured, the responsibilities he's shouldered. He finds it hard to address his feelings—to open himself up to more hurt and loss.'

Chloe nodded. It was true that there was much she didn't know about Nick, or his relationship with Kate. She just thought her friend deserved someone who would make her happy rather than bring her so much angst and uncertainty.

'How are things going with you and Oliver?' Kate asked, changing the subject.

Again Chloe fought a blush. 'OK.'

'You've been seeing him?'

'Yes.' Closing the file in front of her, Chloe folded her arms and leaned on the desk. 'He's been very patient, very kind. I've really enjoyed his company.'

'That's wonderful!' Kate smiled in delight, a twinkle in her eyes. 'He's a very genuine man. Not to mention an exceedingly handsome one!'

Chloe couldn't deny that, even if she did still wonder why he wanted to be with her when any number of women would be after him. She met Kate's gaze and felt warmth stain her cheeks. 'He kissed me.'

'And?'

'I liked it,' she admitted.

She had more than *liked* it. She was impatient to kiss him again. And, she realised, she was coming to more than *like* Oliver, too.

'I'm really pleased for you, Chloe. You deserve to find happiness.' Kate paused, her expression turning serious. 'If you feel something for Oliver, if he is awakening you to the things you have missed and never known before, don't be too scared to go for it. He's a good man. He'll look after you.'

'That's what Lauren said. But what if he is just passing through? What if he leaves Penhally when his contract ends and I'm nothing but a diversion?' she asked, acknowledging and voicing her fears aloud for the first time.

'I believe Oliver is far more serious about you than that. Have you asked him why he came back to Cornwall?'

Chloe shook her head. 'No. We haven't discussed that.'

He had told her all about his childhood, funny tales from medical school, snippets about his London life, but he had never said if he was back in Cornwall for good. She was scared to ask, scared to be told he would be leaving soon.

'Don't lose this chance, my love. See Oliver for the man he is. Something special, some*one* special, doesn't come around very often.' Kate paused, a sadness and depth of experience in her eyes that made Chloe believe her friend was thinking about Nick. 'Ask yourself what you want most, how you feel when you are with him—and how you would feel if he *did* leave and you had never taken that risk.'

The phone rang then, announcing that her first patient had arrived, bringing an end to her conversation with her friend.

Kate gathered up her things. 'I'm off on my home visits. If I have time, I'll call in at the Trevellyans' farm. Fran was sounding down last time we spoke and I'd like to check up on her. My first visit is to Susan Fiddick.'

'I thought she went to the hospital yesterday.'

'She did…and the scan shows the baby is still breech. But she insisted on coming home, ignoring St Piran's advice for the Caesarean.' Kate looked concerned. 'I'm hoping to talk her round—and Nick said he would speak to her as well.'

Chloe offered a sympathetic smile. However natural they tried to keep the whole pregnancy and birthing process, sometimes it wasn't easy matching the woman's wishes with the safest care. Not when nature intervened and things didn't go according to plan.

'Good luck. I hope everything works out.'

'Thanks.' Kate paused on her way to the door. 'I hope things work out for you, too. With Oliver. Think about what I said, my love.'

And think she did. Throughout a morning busy with appointments at the surgery, followed by an afternoon of home visits around the district, Oliver was never far from her mind. When she arrived back in Penhally, she was running late, with time only to sort out her paperwork and grab a quick snack before her evening duty at the well-woman clinic. Things were winding down in the surgery when she went in, but Sue was behind the reception desk and waved her across.

'Everything all right?' Chloe asked with a smile.

'It's been manic.' Looking stressed, Sue grimaced. 'Kate is in St Piran. She was called back out a couple of hours ago when Susan Fiddick went into labour. *Now* she's finally agreed to intervention.'

Chloe shook her head. Poor Kate. And poor Susan. 'What about Jem?'

'He's staying over with a school friend.' Sue shuffled her messages. 'Here we go. These are for you. And Oliver has asked you to see him before you head off for the clinic. He's finished his patient list.'

'OK.'

Chloe's stomach filled with butterflies and her heart skittered. Why did Oliver want to see her? Was it about work…or something else? Feeling breathless, she hurried up the stairs to drop off her things and put her patient files away, then headed back down to the consulting rooms. Oliver's door stood ajar and she paused a moment watching him, noting the uncharacteristic frown on his face as he studied some papers.

She tapped on the door. Their gazes met and she was surprised at the serious expression in those devilish brown eyes. 'You wanted to see me?'

'Chloe, hi.' The smoky tones of Oliver's voice did curious things to her insides.

'Is there a problem?'

'Come in a minute.' He rose to his feet and crossed to meet her, closing the door before dropping a brief kiss on her lips. 'Take a seat.'

He perched on the edge of the desk near her and a very different fluttering, this time of unease, knotted her stomach. 'What's wrong?'

'It's about the Morrisons,' he told her.

'Baby Timmy?' She rubbed suddenly damp palms on her trousers. 'Oliver?'

A ragged sigh escaped. 'The results have come back from the heel-prick tests.'

'Already? And?'

'Chloe…the test for cystic fibrosis is positive.'

Her fingers clenched around the arms of the chair, her knuckles white as she battled away the unprofessional sting of tears. She knew she became too involved with her mums and their babies. She couldn't help it. Her job meant the world to her. Beth and Jason had tried so long for their baby and had suffered two miscarriages before little Timmy had come along this summer. There had been nothing in their history to suggest cystic fibrosis was a worry, no family incidence. But they must both be carriers and the one in four chance had hit them.

'Chloe?'

'Have you told them?' Somehow she forced the words out, pushing the image of Timmy from her mind.

'Not yet. And not without you. I didn't want you finding out alone, seeing the report left on your desk.' He paused, reaching out to take one of her hands in his. 'Maybe you would like it if we break the news to them together?'

His thoughtfulness touched her and she quelled a fresh threat of tears, unconsciously curling her fingers with his. 'Yes. Thank you. The test isn't conclusive,' she added, grasping at straws.

'No. There will be much to discuss with Beth and Jason, and further investigations to authenticate the results with a DNA test for the delta F508 gene. If CF *is* confirmed, we can bring Lauren in as soon as possible to help with physiotherapy needs.'

'Yes.' Chloe nodded, scarcely able to take it in.

'You know early diagnosis means much more successful treatment and longer life expectancy. We start treatment and physio before there is lung damage, and refer to a specialist CF centre.'

Knowing she wasn't going to hold on much longer, she withdrew her hand from his and rose unsteadily to her feet, unable to meet his all-seeing gaze. 'Thanks for the information. Let me know when to be available to see the Morrisons.'

She turned and walked to the door, one hand pressed to her lips to hold in the sob that fought to escape. Her free hand fumbled with the doorhandle. Just when she managed to open it, desperate to be alone, she felt Oliver behind her, his hand reaching past her to hold the door closed and then lock it. She froze.

'Chloe…'

The gentleness in that husky voice threatened to undo her. 'I need to go.'

'No. Come here, babe.'

Hands settled on her shoulders and turned her to face him. Her eyes widened in confusion, tears shimmering on her lashes, and she tried to blink them back, but a couple escaped, dropping onto her cheeks. He cupped her face, his thumbs brushing the moisture away. A shiver ran through her, and she felt uncertain when he drew her closer, tucking her head against his chest with one hand, his other arm curling around her.

'Oliver?' She held herself stiffly in his embrace.

'You're upset. Take a few moments. Let me cuddle you.'

Being held like this should have spooked her—would have done had it been any man but Oliver. Wrapped in his embrace she felt both anxious yet safe. Beneath her cheek she could feel the steady, calming beat of his heart. To her surprise, she began to relax, allowing her hands to rest at his waist, her fingers feeling the play of muscle beneath firm flesh through the thin fabric of his shirt. Another few moments and instinct had her leaning into him, her arms sliding around him, while his free hand stroked her back, and his husky, whispered words soothed her. She had no idea how long they stayed that way, but gradually she felt calmer, stronger.

Although he relaxed his hold, Oliver didn't let her go, but he pulled back far enough to look down and meet her gaze.

Embarrassed, Chloe bit her lip. 'I'm sorry.'

'Never apologise for caring.'

'I'm a professional, I—'

'You are also human. And you're so good at your job because of how you feel about the mums and their babies.' Sincerity and understanding shone in his brown eyes. 'It's been a difficult couple of days. This news about Timmy, on top of the emergency with Angela, was bound to affect you. The day it doesn't is the day any of us should stop doing this job.'

Aware he was still holding her close, that her body was responding in unfamiliar ways, Chloe found the strength to place some much-needed distance between them. His nearness addled her senses and turned her brain to mush. She more than liked him, was coming to trust him, but she still felt nervous of all the new and unknown sensations assailing her.

'I'm OK now.'

Oliver frowned, unconvinced, but he allowed her to retreat. 'Are you sure?'

'Yes. Thanks.' She managed a smile, grateful for his support. 'I have to get ready for the well-woman clinic.'

Something she didn't recognise crossed his expression as he looked down at her. 'All right. I'll talk to you later, babe,' he promised, tucking a stray wisp of hair behind her ear, his fingers lingering for a moment before he dropped a firmer kiss on her mouth, then stepped back.

Chloe let herself out of the room, jogging up the stairs to her own office where she sank into her chair, one fist pressed against her chest. Why did she feel so strange? Yes, she was upset about the news of Timmy Morrison's positive test, but Oliver had been empathetic, helping her over the initial shock, and he had managed to ground her again. He had been right— she would have hated to find the report on her desk, cold, with no warning. Sharing it with him, knowing he cared too, had made it easier. What she found less easy to understand were the raging emotions she felt when she was with him, the way her body reacted when he touched her.

Somehow she got through the evening, grateful that the clinic was busy. Oliver had been right, it had been a hell of a week. He had understood her, but she knew she took things too personally with her mums and babies. She couldn't help it. She became so involved in them and their lives, but it often cost her emotionally. Unfortunately her duty at the clinic meant she couldn't see Oliver, or Lauren, that evening. She would have liked to have talked to someone, she reflected as she walked home along the harbour front to her cosy cottage in Fisherman's Row.

She liked her home. It was the first place she'd been able to call her own. The first place where she felt safe and settled. After greeting Pirate and Cyclops, she fed them, then went upstairs to shower, washing the stresses of the day away before changing into a cool top and shorts. Padding back down to the kitchen, she made herself a sandwich, then sat in the living room with the patio doors open and tried to relax.

She went to bed early, but felt restless and edgy, as well as uncomfortably warm. Her window was open, but there was scant breeze off the harbour to ease the sultry night air. When the phone rang, startling her, she picked up the receiver, hoping none of her mums-to-be had a problem.

'Hello. Chloe MacKinnon.'

'Hi, babe.'

The throaty voice sent a prickle along her spine. 'O-Oliver! Is something wrong?' She propped herself up against the pillows, frowning with confusion.

'I wanted to see how you were feeling,' he explained. 'Did I wake you?'

'No, it's too hot to sleep. I can't stop thinking about little Timmy,' she admitted after a pause, something about the dark and the connection she felt with Oliver making it easier to admit her worries.

'I know. Sometimes things are horribly unfair.' She could tell by his voice that he genuinely cared. 'We'll find a time between our appointments tomorrow when we're both free and we'll talk to Beth and Jason together.'

'Thank you.'

They discussed the Morrisons a while longer, then moved away from work, talking comfortably about anything and everything. Chloe snuggled down, relaxing, a smile on her face as Oliver's husky voice and rumbly laugh sounded in her ear.

'I missed seeing you tonight,' he told her softly some time later.

Biting her lip, Chloe gripped the receiver tighter, affected by the warm intimacy of his voice, longing for him knotting her stomach. 'Me, too.'

'Yeah?' She heard the smile in his voice, thought she also

heard the faint rustle of a sheet. Was he in bed, too? The image made her even hotter. 'We'll do something nice together at the weekend.'

'I'd like that,' she agreed, all too quickly, the prospect of spending time with him bringing a rush of excited anticipation.

'Do you think you can sleep now?'

She *did* feel languorous and at ease. Just talking with him had done that for her. It had been what she had needed without even knowing it. But Oliver had. 'Yes, I think so. Thank you for ringing.'

'No problem. I've enjoyed it,' he assured her.

'Me, too.' So much so she didn't want it to end. 'Goodnight, Oliver.'

'Goodnight, babe. Sweet dreams. I'll see you in the morning.'

When the click sounded in her ear, indicating that Oliver had hung up, she felt stupidly alone, but also had a warm, fuzzy, fluttering inside her tummy.

She had only known him a few weeks, but she was discovering how much she had misjudged him at the beginning. He wasn't the fast-living playboy gossip had suggested, but an instinctive, fantastic doctor, and a man who treated her with infinite patience, caring and sensitivity. She had never once felt threatened, pressured or unsafe. And as for his kisses… Oh, my! Oliver made her feel things she had never felt before, stirred things inside her that she wasn't sure how to handle. She just knew she didn't want them to stop.

CHAPTER SIX

'I'M SORRY. I'd forgotten about today.' As Chloe glanced up, Oliver saw regret in her eyes. 'We don't have to stay long, but I promised Eloise I'd come by.'

'Don't worry about it, babe. We've had a great weekend...and I have plans for later,' he added, his voice dropping as he murmured in her ear, close enough to feel her quiver in response.

Dressed in denim shorts and a loose cotton shirt knotted at the waist, which left her midriff bare, Chloe looked good enough to eat. His hunger for her only increased with every passing day. Resting one hand at the small of her back, enjoying the feel of her super-soft skin under his palm, Oliver guided her along the beach towards the spot where the informal barbecue party was well under way.

'Remind me again what we're celebrating.'

Chloe smiled up at him. 'Eloise Hayden and Lachlan D'Ancey's engagement.'

'He's the local police chief?' Oliver asked, his gaze scanning the gathering for people he knew.

'He lives in Penhally but he's based at the station in Wadebridge,' Chloe explained. 'He met Eloise, an Australian forensic pathologist, when she came over last month to give a second opinion on a surfer's death.'

Oliver nodded. 'I heard the talk, but I've never met Lachlan or Eloise.'

'They are really nice. There's Eloise, talking to Kate. Shall we say hello?'

'Sure.'

As Chloe led the way, he reflected on the last couple of days. Friday had been difficult, meeting the Morrisons and breaking the news about Timmy's results. But Beth and Jason had been strong, drawing on the support and encouragement Chloe had given them. He knew better than anyone how the news had affected Chloe, and he was so proud of the care and compassion she offered to her patients. If the next round of tests confirmed that Timmy did have cystic fibrosis, he knew that the family would have first-class support from Chloe, Lauren and himself, as well as whatever specialist advice could be offered to them.

After the success of his Thursday night phone call, speaking to each other last thing before they went to sleep had become a habit. Even if he had only just parted from her, they still talked for a few moments on the phone. It was special…and increased even more his growing need to be with her, to not have to leave her at all.

On Saturday, after morning appointments, he and Chloe had gone for a ride on their motorbikes, then had spent the evening cuddled up at her cottage, watching a DVD, talking, drinking wine and doing a lot of kissing. They were winding up the intimacy and the passion, with deeper, hotter kisses and some tantalising, teasing touches. He made sure he left her wanting more, but it also drove him insane with his own desire for her. Faced with Chloe's increasing confidence and eagerness, it was becoming ever more difficult to keep a tight rein on his control. But he wanted her to be ready, to ask for what she wanted, to need him as much as he needed her.

He had never been that into kissing before. It was too

intimate somehow, and past relationships had been more about instant gratification—on both sides. The full joy of devoting time to kissing, without rush and pressure, had passed him by. Until now. He could kiss Chloe for hours, days...for ever. Knowing he had to take things slowly with her brought everything back to basics, to endless hours of foreplay and hot, sexy, incredibly intimate and satisfying kisses. It was like nothing he had ever known before. There was no demand to perform, no haste for fulfilment. The drawn-out loving, leading to the blossoming of Chloe's sensuality, was reward in itself. For now. If he felt this charged from kissing her, he'd probably combust when he finally made love to her.

Plans for today had changed when Chloe had remembered the beach barbecue. Oliver was just content to be with her, whatever the circumstances. It was a major advance that she was unconcerned at them being seen in public as a couple. He cared about her and he wanted people to know that. In staking his claim, he was taking a risk, putting himself on the line, but, as he discovered more every day, Chloe was worth it.

After being introduced to Eloise and talking with her, Kate and Chloe for a few minutes, Oliver accepted Eloise's invitation to head to the barbecue buffet table and fetch some refreshments for himself and Chloe.

'I'll catch up with you in a few minutes,' he promised, leaving her with her friends.

Chloe watched Oliver saunter with deceptive lazy grace across the sand towards the food table where Lachlan was in charge of the barbecue. Oliver looked equally stunning in the faded jeans and body-hugging T-shirt he wore today as he did in the smart clothes he wore for work. She turned back to find Kate and Eloise watching her, knowing smiles on their faces. Chloe fought a blush.

'Any improvements in the situation with Nick?' Eloise

asked, and, although thankful to have escaped questions about Oliver, Chloe felt sorry for Kate. Eloise was the only other person who knew about Jem's real father.

'Things have settled down a little at work.' Kate managed a smile, her gaze straying to Jem, who was playing beach cricket with some friends. 'But Nick isn't ready to face the reality that Jem is his son. I don't know if he ever will be.'

Chloe looked around the assembled group. 'Is Nick not here?'

'No.' Kate's disappointment was obvious. 'He's gone to France for the weekend with the twinning committee. They have meetings in Normandy.'

They chatted for a few moments, then other people claimed Eloise's attention. Kate went to talk with Lucy and Ben, smiling as she cuddled their baby daughter, Annabel, whom she had delivered in difficult circumstances last Christmas. Chloe wished her friend could be as content in all aspects of her life. Turning away, she looked for Oliver, seeing he was still at the food table, talking with Lachlan, Dragan and Melinda. As she headed in that direction, she bumped into Eve Dwyer.

'Hello, Chloe, good to see you.'

'And you, Eve. How are things?' she asked the older woman.

'I'm fine. A bit tired of the commute to Newquay,' she admitted. 'I'll be so glad when a practice nurse vacancy comes up here in Penhally.' Eve paused a moment, glancing around to check they were not being overheard. 'Is the rumour about Rachel Kenner and Gary Lovelace true?'

Frowning, Chloe nodded. 'I'm afraid so. Poor Rachel. Gary treated her terribly.'

'How is she coping?' Eve asked, ever the compassionate nurse.

'She was very frightened, especially about facing her

father,' Chloe admitted. 'But you know how lovely Reverend Kenner is, and how much he cares for Rachel.'

Eve nodded, looking distracted. 'So he's supporting her?'

'Very much so. I'm seeing her regularly and she's determined to keep the baby while still following her dream to be a teacher,' she told her, explaining about the aunt and uncle in Plymouth.

'That's good.'

Chloe caught an edge in Eve's tone and realised the other woman looked pale and strained. 'Eve, are you all right?'

'I'm fine.' Her gaze slid away and she redirected the conversation. 'That family. Tassie is the only one with any goodness in her.'

'She's lucky to have your care and support,' Chloe praised, admiring of all Eve was trying to do for the troubled young girl.

'Tassie's not had much of a start in life. But even at ten she plans to be different from the rest of them, to use her brains to make a good life for herself. I want to help her.'

Eve still looked troubled and again Chloe voiced her concern. 'Are you sure you're OK?'

'Don't worry, Chloe. Just a shadow from the past,' the older woman murmured cryptically.

Before Chloe could question her further, Oliver arrived at her side, handing her a plate of food and a drink. 'Here we go, babe.'

'Thanks.' Chloe introduced him to Eve. The other woman seemed eager to leave, so Chloe had to let the subject drop. 'That was strange.'

Distracted, Oliver took a bite of his fish. 'Hmm?'

'Nothing,' Chloe murmured, watching Eve walk away, her shoulders hunched as if she carried the weight of the world on them.

Her worry about Eve dissipated as she and Oliver talked while enjoying their food. Afterwards, they mingled for a short time, and Chloe was supremely conscious of Oliver beside her, touching her, one hand at the hollow of her back, warm against her bare skin. The pad of his thumb dipped under the waistband of her shorts and traced tiny circles at the base of her spine...devastating, enticing, strength-sapping touches. So simple, yet so seductive. Her legs felt shaky and there was a heavy knot in her stomach. All she could think about was how wonderful the weekend had been, how amazing it was to kiss him, how much she wanted to be alone with him again, how special it had become that his voice on the phone was the last thing she had heard the last three nights before she had fallen asleep.

'Ready to leave, babe?'

His voice was a husky whisper in her ear, his warm breath fanning her skin, sending tingles of awareness through her whole body. She met his sinful dark gaze, feeling hotter than ever, and nodded. 'Yes.'

He bestowed on her the kind of smile that always made her breathless, then took her hand, linking their fingers. After they had said their goodbyes, he led her back along the harbour front to his car and before long they were heading out of town.

'Why are we here?' she asked a while later as Oliver pulled into the parking area at a watersports centre a short way along the coast from Penhally.

'Knowing how you love motorbikes, I have an adventure planned.'

'What kind of adventure?' Anxiety gnawed in the pit of her stomach.

He slanted her a glance, dark eyes sparkling with mischief. 'I'm taking you jet-skiing.'

Chloe forced herself to climb out of the car. Part of her wanted to experience the thrill of riding a jet-ski, but she couldn't get beyond the fear that gripped her. She didn't want her past to keep impinging on the rest of her life. In the time she had known Oliver she had faced many of her demons but...

Her footsteps slowed, her heart thudded under her ribs. What was she going to do? How could she tell Oliver?

It took a few seconds before Oliver realised that Chloe was no longer walking with him towards the beachfront office where they would pick up the two-seater jet-ski he had hired. If Chloe enjoyed their outing, he planned to buy her a present—a single-person machine like his so they could go out on the water together. He turned round, noting the paleness of her face, the shadow of fear in her wary green eyes. Hell. He'd done something wrong. Walking back, he took both her hands in his.

'What's happened?' He searched her gaze, could feel her shaking. 'Talk to me, babe. Tell me whatever it is you're feeling.'

'I—I'm scared. Of the water. I nearly drowned once.'

'Damn, I'm sorry.' Oliver wanted to kick himself. Instead, he wrapped her in a gentle hug. 'I had no idea.' He pulled back enough to look into her eyes, seeing the uncertainty in their green depths. 'I didn't mean to upset you.'

'You haven't. It's not you. It's *him*.'

Confused, he lightly rubbed his hands up and down her bare arms. 'Him?' he queried, trying to make sense of what she was saying.

'My father.'

When she exhaled a ragged breath, he led her off the path towards a low wall. Sitting next to her, he slipped an arm around her, his free hand holding one of hers. 'Tell me.'

'I was about seven. I never understood why he went into rages, what put sudden ideas in his head, but this day he marched me down to the rocks.' Her fingers tightened on his and Oliver cuddled her closer, feeling icy cold despite the heat of the day. 'I'd never swum. My mother was always scared and kept me away from the water, and though I loved the beach, I suppose her fear rubbed off on me. Something set my father off, and he said I could learn to swim or drown.' Chloe's voice wavered. 'He picked me up and tossed me in. I did nearly drown. A couple of nearby fishermen pulled me out. They threatened to tell the police but my father insisted it had been an accident and persuaded them to keep quiet.'

Horrified, he didn't know what to say. 'God, Chloe.'

This was another confidence, another sign of her coming to trust him. But it was also another piece in the jigsaw that her father was responsible for the horrors of her childhood. He hated it that he had made her face something upsetting when all he had wanted was for her to have fun this weekend.

'I'll cancel the booking. We'll go somewhere else,' he reassured her, startled when she pushed against him, her head shaking vigorously.

'No!'

'Chloe?'

She turned to face him, grasping his hand. 'I don't want to let him win, Oliver. I don't want to be afraid of things because of him for the rest of my life. You've opened my eyes to so much recently. You must think I'm really stupid,' she finished on a whisper, ducking her head.

'That's the very last thing I think of you.' His heart swelled with emotion. He couldn't bear to imagine all she had been through, couldn't bear to consider what else her father had done to her, what more he still had to learn about her childhood. Holding her close, he stroked her hair. 'I think you're amazing. And I'm so proud of you. Whatever you want to do, I'm here to help. Whenever you're ready to talk, I'm here to listen.'

She raised her head, disbelief and hope warring in her eyes, a shaky smile hovering at her mouth, making him want to kiss her senseless. 'Oliver?'

'Yes, babe?' He cleared his throat, his voice sounding raw to his own ears.

'Take me jet-skiing.'

* * *

She had to be crazy. Chloe choked down a nervous laugh. Here she was in a wetsuit and impact buoyancy vest about to face one of her nightmares. She was frightened. But she trusted Oliver—and what she had told him was true. She didn't want to spend the rest of her life being afraid, didn't want what Lauren had said to be true…that her father was still ruling her life from the grave. Oliver had changed her. He gave her strength and courage. She *was* scared, had no idea where all this might lead, but she was tired of living in the shadows.

'Chloe, look at me.' He cupped her face, raising her gaze to his. 'You can change your mind at any time.'

Her chest was tight and she felt sick, but she shook her head. 'No.'

'We're going *on* the water, not *in* it. There is no way on this earth that I would let anything bad happen to you.'

'I know.' She believed it, believed the earnest sincerity in his dark eyes as they looked deeply into her own.

'Trust me.'

Feeling this was now about far more than a ride on jet-ski, she tentatively placed her hand in his, immediately feeling enveloped by his gentle strength. Oliver sat her in front of him, his arms reaching round her to the controls, cocooning her in his protective embrace.

'OK?'

She nodded, trying to bank down her fear of the water, relaxing a little as he nuzzled her, pressing a kiss to the sensitive hollow below her ear. They started slowly, easing out from the shore, the water calm and smooth along this stretch of coast, for which she was heartily thankful. It didn't take her long to get used to the unfamiliar motion and, to her surprise, she began to enjoy it, feeling incredibly safe with Oliver watching over her. After a while he drew to a halt and they drifted for a few moments, the engine idling as they looked back towards the spectacular Cornish coastline.

'All right, babe?'

Nodding, she glanced round to smile at him. 'I'm fine. Thank you.'

'Thank *you*—for trusting me.' Before she could say anything, his mouth met hers in a brief but stirring kiss. 'Ready to move on?'

Sensing that there was more than one meaning to his words, Chloe's insides fluttered in nervous excitement. 'Yes,' she told him shyly, earning herself the kind of dimpled smile that would have weakened her knees had she not already been sitting down.

'Faster?'

'Faster,' she agreed, feeling warm and giddy with happiness at his carefree laugh and the glowing approval in his eyes.

They had a fun time. It was exhilarating, riding with Oliver, the spray hitting their faces. And always she felt safe, never sensing he was taking risks or trying to play the macho showoff. When they finally arrived back at the shore, Oliver slipped off, holding her steady and seeing her gently onto dry land. Then she did something she had never done in her life. She spontaneously hugged him, carried along by pure joy and emotion, the freedom from a part of her past that had held her back for so long. Could she now move on and let go of the other chains that bound her?

She couldn't think about that now because Oliver's arms closed around her, holding her close, making her all too aware of him, the strength of his athletic body pressed against her, the heady masculine scent of him. Her smile faded at the look in his eyes…intense, fiery hunger. Then his head lowered, his mouth taking hers, and she surrendered to the magic of his kiss.

'I hear you're something of a hero.'

Oliver's eyes opened at Chloe's words and he smiled tiredly. 'Hardly.'

He'd been more relieved than ever to leave work, dash to the flat for a quick shower and change of clothes, and then meet up with Chloe to enjoy a quiet meal at her cottage before relaxing on the sofa. Taking her hand, he shifted his position and drew her towards him, encouraging her to sit on his lap facing him, her legs straddling his. Grateful to hold her close, he breathed in the familiar scent of sunshine and fresh, fruity apples, feeling settled and grounded with her in his arms. Meeting her gaze, he saw the concern in her green eyes as she brushed a wayward fall of hair back from his face before resting her hands on his shoulders. He was encouraged that she was so comfortable with the new intimacy that had continued to build after their passionate kiss following their jet ski outing several days ago.

'I came back from house calls—one of which was to Avril Harvey, by the way, and she and her daughter are doing fine— to hear you'd had a run-in with Nick,' she prompted.

'That's good news about the Harveys.' His smile faded as he answered the other part of her comment. 'As for Nick, he didn't want me going out to see Henry Ryall, said we'd wasted enough time on the man, that there was nothing wrong with him.'

Chloe frowned. 'That doesn't sound like Nick. He can be difficult, but he puts patients first.'

'I know.' Oliver's frown mirrored Chloe's. Nick was still stressed and edgy. Clearly the problem with Kate had not been resolved. 'Anyway, he's been out to Henry's farm more than once in the last month, so have Dragan and Adam. No one found anything wrong with him. They'd all done everything by the book, there was no reason to believe that Henry was sick,' he admitted, recalling Nick's arguments. 'The consensus of opinion was that Henry was sad and lonely having recently lost his wife...'

'But?' Chloe raised an eyebrow, as if knowing that wouldn't be good enough for him.

'I don't like writing people off too soon. And I can't explain it, but I had a hunch, one I didn't want to ignore. Nick told me to go and waste my time if I wanted to.'

'You were right, though, and it wasn't a waste of time.'

Sighing, Oliver ran his hands down her back to her delectable rear end, pulling her even closer. 'It was a complete fluke that I happened to be there at that precise moment.'

'Having weak tea and stale biscuits,' Chloe teased, making him smile. He'd discovered Henry's infamous idea of 'refreshments' for himself.

'I'd checked Henry's notes, spoken with Dragan, Adam and Nick. Henry had reported banging his head twice in the same place in the last weeks, but they'd all done the right examinations and checks and could find nothing wrong with him,' he explained, the fingers of one hand finding the gap between the waistband of her jeans and the bottom of her shirt, enjoying the feel of satiny skin. 'Henry couldn't give a clear picture of what was wrong, just that things weren't right, that he felt foggy and was still having headaches. He seemed fine when I first got there and I thought maybe Nick was right and I *was* wasting my time.'

'But you weren't?'

'No. I did the same examinations, checked the reaction of his pupils, tested if he could balance on one leg, walk in a straight line, could touch the end of his nose with one finger with his eyes shut…all the usual things. I monitored his blood pressure and gave him a thorough health check. There was no sign of anything amiss.'

Looking puzzled, Chloe sat back and watched him. 'So what happened?'

'We were talking, I was getting ready to leave, and suddenly Henry's mouth was moving but no sound was coming out.' He shook his head, still unable to believe the timing of it, wondering what would have happened had Henry been alone and unable to raise help. 'One moment he was speaking normally, the next he was looking bemused and frightened, unable to speak.'

'Wow.' Chloe's eyes widened in amazement.

Smiling, Oliver tucked a strand of hair that had escaped her braid back behind her ear. 'It was bizarre. But something I'd seen before. I took Henry straight to hospital, they did a CT scan and discovered a small bleed in his brain. He's having an operation to repair it and he should make a good recovery.'

'How could that happen?'

'Sometimes with a head injury you can have this slow, tiny bleed that causes no outward symptoms for a time. It didn't help that Henry hit his head twice in the same place in rapid succession. No one could have known. There was nothing to alert Dragan, Adam or Nick, no reason for them to send Henry for further tests. As I said, it was pure chance I happened to be there.'

Chloe dropped a kiss on his mouth. 'I'm glad you were. Lucky Henry. And I hope Nick was apologetic.'

'He was.' Oliver couldn't resist giving her another kiss before he continued. 'To be fair, he waited on at the surgery for me to get back from St Piran to talk about it. That's why I was late.'

'I'm just glad Henry is going to be all right.'

'Me, too.' He raised his free hand to cup her face. 'And I'm glad to be here with you now.' Brushing the pad of his thumb along the fullness of her lower lip, he held her gaze. 'I desperately want to kiss you.'

Creamy cheeks turned rosy as she flushed and her voice was breathy. 'Do you?'

'Oh, yeah!'

'OK.' She smiled, sinking against him. Her mouth was honey sweet, so eager and welcoming that he was instantly lost, his control on the ragged edge.

* * *

Chloe couldn't hold back a whimper of needy excitement as she lost herself in the taste and feel and scent of Oliver. They had spent every moment they could together since the jet-ski outing on Sunday, and she was feeling closer to him than ever. As well as increasingly frustrated when he kept calling a halt to their ever more passionate kisses before she wanted to stop. She was impatient for more…she just wasn't sure what *more* was, or how to persuade Oliver she was ready. He was so determined to take things slowly. She was also unsure what all this meant to him. His care seemed genuine but, as she had mentioned to Kate, was she just a diversion for Oliver? Did he plan to stay in Penhally Bay?

Reluctantly, she pulled back from the kiss, seeing his eyes darken with a desire that matched her own. One of his hands rested on her back under her shirt, sending heat permeating throughout her body. She wanted his hand to move. Wanted to touch him, too. Licking her lips, noting the flare of response in his eyes as he watched her, she shifted even closer, bringing their bodies more intimately into contact. Her own eyes widened as she felt the undeniable evidence of his arousal. Nervous, not sure how far she wanted to take this, she hesitated.

'Chloe?' Oliver's voice was rough and she was excited that she could affect him like this.

'About my lessons.'

A smile dimpled his cheek but the hungry look in his eyes didn't fade. Her pulse skittered as his fingers began a gentle caress up and down her spine. 'You're not enjoying them?'

'You have to know I am,' she protested, unable to prevent herself pouting at him.

A chuckle rumbled from his chest. 'But?'

'I'm ready to move on to a more advanced level.'

'I see.' The fingers on her back stilled for a moment. 'And what do you expect the next steps to be?'

Faced with the intensity of his gaze and the smoky roughness of his voice, some of her nerve deserted her. 'Um...I don't know. I just feel...'

'Tell me what you feel, babe,' he encouraged when she paused, distracting her by nibbling along her jaw.

'When you kiss me and touch me, I feel all tingly and achy and heavy.' Long, thick lashes lifted and she couldn't look away from the heat in his dark gaze. She swallowed, searching for the right words to explain. 'I don't want you to stop as soon as you do. I need you to touch me in other places...and I want to touch you, too.'

She was surprised and pleased when Oliver drew in a ragged breath. 'Are you sure?'

'Yes.'

Sinking her fingers into the thickness of his hair, she kissed him with eager enthusiasm, unable to get enough of him. When he sucked on her tongue, drawing her into the hot sweetness of his mouth, it was so erotic and inflaming that she feared she would explode, need tightening almost painfully inside her. Pulling back a few inches, she looked down, her fingers shaking as she began to inch up the fabric of his T-shirt, exposing a flat stomach with a narrow trail of dark hair disappearing beneath the waistband of his jeans. She pushed the fabric higher, revealing a toned abdomen and broad chest...olive-hued skin, supple flesh and hard muscle. Helping her, he pulled the T-shirt over his head and for a moment she just studied him, heat prickling along every nerve ending. He was beautiful. There was no other word to describe the masculine perfection of him. Hesitating, she spotted the dark ring encircling the bicep of his left arm.

'You have a tattoo.' Surprised, she investigated the narrow barbed band usually hidden by his clothes.

'I have two,' he told her.

Her gaze met his, seeing the amused mischief in his dark brown eyes. 'Where's the other one?'

'You can look for it another time.'

Disappointed, she frowned at him. 'Why not now?'

'Because my control is finite,' he warned her with a wry smile. 'And if I'm going to survive this next lesson, no way are you going anywhere near my other tattoo.'

Her heart skittered, her mind racing as she wondered just where it was. 'Oliver…'

'No, babe. Not now.' He shifted as if uncomfortable, again making her aware of his arousal. 'Today we both keep above the waist.'

Capturing her wrists, his gaze holding hers, he slowly brought her hands to his chest. She closed her eyes, savouring her first feel of him, warm and firm, his heartbeat under her palm as rapid as her own. Her lack of expertise didn't appear to bother him and he deftly tutored her, guiding her natural responses, showing her how he liked her to touch him. Soaking up every new experience, each new texture, she brushed her fingertips over the brown orbs of his nipples, shocked at his reaction, his stifled groan, the way his body tightened.

'That feels good,' he told her huskily, allowing her to explore him at will but stopping her if she tried to dip below his waist. 'May I touch you, too?'

Her whole body quivered with nervous anticipation. Unable to find her voice, she nodded, her breath catching, her heart racing as Oliver slowly but surely undid the buttons of her shirt one by one. The backs of his fingers brushed against her skin, setting off little fires of sensation. Shaking, she bit her lip as he peeled the shirt away, sliding it down her arms, his breath catching as he took in the sight of her full breasts encased in a green lacy bra. She enjoyed wearing nice underwear. Like growing her hair long, it was a throwback to her youth and her father's control, a way of thumbing her nose at him, refusing to let him dominate everything in her life. The clasp at her back parted with a deft flick of Oliver's fingers and a mix of embarrassment, fear and excitement churned inside her as he slowly drew the straps down her arms, baring her to his view.

'You're perfect, Chloe,' he praised, his voice raw.

As his fingertips skimmed her ribs, his tanned skin looked exotic against the creamy paleness of her own. He leaned in to kiss her, lingering a while before his lips grazed away from her mouth to trail down her throat. His hands rested on her sides, while her own grasped his shoulders as she trembled, on the brink of something she didn't understand, yearning for his touch, yet scared, too.

'Oliver?'

'Slow and easy, babe,' he whispered, his voice seductive, low and husky, his breath warm against her skin as he nibbled round her neck. She started as his tongue tip tickled across the web of faded scars that fanned down to her shoulder. 'Did your father do this?'

Too lost in the moment to care what else she was revealing, she curled into his touch. 'He hit me and I fell through a glass door,' she whispered, feeling the sudden tension in Oliver's body, aware of his simmering anger on her behalf before he took a steadying breath and gentled again.

He raised his head to meet her gaze. 'Chloe...'

'Let's not talk about it now.' She didn't want to spoil this incredible moment with thoughts of her father.

After a pause, Oliver nodded, but his reluctance was clear and she knew they would have to talk at some point. Later. Much later if she had her way. She sighed as his fingers began to whisper over her skin, feather-light touches that teased and tingled and aroused.

'Your skin is impossibly soft, so warm and silky and smooth,' he told her, his voice dropping to a husky murmur. 'I love touching you.'

When his thumbs brushed the undersides of her plump, firm breasts, Chloe thought she would never breathe again. Then his hands covered her flesh fully for the first time and she was sure she had died and gone to heaven. She bit back a cry, her fingers tensing on his shoulders as she instinctively arched to his touch.

'Any time you say stop, Chloe, I'll stop.'

His murmured promise registered through the hazy fog of pleasure enveloping her, but she didn't want him to stop. Not yet. Not when this felt so fantastic. She closed her eyes, unable to focus on anything but the caress of his hands as he shaped her, his questing fingertips exploring nipples that had peaked to hard, sensitive crests. A moan escaped. She had never known anything like this. She couldn't believe the way her body was reacting, the way her breasts felt fuller and heavier, every sensation spearing deep inside her. And when Oliver touched her with his lips, lightly lapping his warm tongue around and over one nipple before he gently suckled it inside his mouth, she jolted, her body writhing in his arms.

It was so overwhelming, so new and scary and wonderful, that she pulled back. 'Stop.' Her voice was thready, mixed with confusion and doubt, yearning and desire.

Oliver immediately withdrew, and at once she regretted that the word had been pulled from her so unexpectedly. She hadn't meant it. Not really. Now she missed his touch. Surprising them both, she wrapped her arms around him, relishing the closeness, the feel of her breasts pressed against his bare chest. His hands stroked her back and she buried her face against his neck, breathing in his masculine scent, unconsciously rubbing herself against him.

'Chloe.'

She ignored the warning in his rough voice. This felt so good. The ache she had told him about had intensified between her legs and she instinctively pressed herself against his hardness. Oliver groaned and put some distance between them.

'Enough now, babe.' He sounded tense, and she raised her head to look at him, seeing colour flush across his cheekbones, strain etched on his handsome features.

'Did I do something wrong?'

'Hell, no. But this is getting out of hand. It's too soon for you...and my control is at breaking point.'

Intrigued, she smiled at him. 'Really?'

'You're wicked!'

That seemed not to be an entirely bad thing as he was laughing. However, he gently but firmly eased her away from him, drawing her shirt back up her arms, unsteady fingers refastening her buttons before he pulled his own T-shirt back over his head. All too soon, he was lifting her off his lap and rising to his feet.

'I think it's time I said goodnight.'

Chloe heard the regret in his voice, felt her own sense of sinking disappointment, but at the same time she knew he was right. She wasn't yet ready to ask him to stay. There were things she had to come to terms with inside herself before she was free to move on, and she knew she had to open her past to Oliver and confide in him before she took the irrevocable step of letting him take her to bed.

Her body alive and buzzing, she walked him to the door, enjoying a last, lingering, passionate kiss before he left. Sighing, Chloe locked the door and leaned back against it, unable to comprehend how her life had changed so drastically in the few short weeks since she had met Oliver.

Slipping into bed some time later, she lay back against the pillows, disinclined to pick up her book. Would Oliver ring as he had done every night for the last week? How did he really feel about her? She couldn't believe how selfless he was, how patient, but was that because he really cared or because he wasn't that affected? He'd certainly felt aroused that evening.

Just thinking about touching him, having him touch her, sent a wave of heat washing through her. She couldn't help but wonder what it would be like to go further—what would have happened if she hadn't had a second of nervous panic at the overwhelming but unknown sensations and stopped him. Her body still tingled, her breasts felt sensitive, her blood was still zinging through her veins, but she felt a restless tension, an ache deep inside that needed fulfilment.

She was so lost in reliving all the new experiences that she jumped when the phone rang. Smiling, she snuggled down and reached for the receiver, welcoming the prospect of hearing Oliver's voice one more time before she slept.

CHAPTER SEVEN

'COME in young man. Let me get a look at you.'

Hiding a smile at the barked command, Oliver walked further into the neat-as-a-pin living room of the bungalow in Gull Close, situated on the other side of the river from Bridge Street. Occupied by Gertrude Stanbury, the former headmistress of the local school, whom everyone had warned him was a tyrant, the home had a small garden beyond the open patio doors and a view of the water. Squatting down to eye level with the rotund figure propped on the sofa by a multitude of pillows, and one each under the knees that were giving her such trouble, he introduced himself.

'Hello, Ms Stanbury, I'm Dr Oliver Fawkner, the new GP.'

'Humph.' One small arthritic hand shook his with a surprisingly strong grip, while sharp grey eyes gave him the once-over. 'You need a haircut. Never would have tolerated that in my school. But you're a handsome devil, I'll say that for you. Are you any good as a doctor?'

The smile he had been trying to hold in escaped. 'Thankfully my other patients seem to think so,' he told her, still holding her hand, taking immediately to the bullish, white-haired lady who was clearly sharp and shrewd and, if the glint in those eyes was anything to go by, had a sense of humour lurking under the surface bluster.

'I suppose you're here to prod and poke me about.'

'And to tell you that we've heard from the hospital. Your operation for the first knee replacement has been brought forward to the third week in September.' Gently, he checked the sixty-seven-year-old over, pleased to find her blood pressure was stable. Aside from the arthritis, which severely reduced her mobility and caused her considerable pain, she appeared to be in good health. 'The consultant will write to you directly but you can always call on us if you need more information or if there is anything else we can do.'

The tyrant-in-disguise patted his hand. 'I'll be glad to get it over and done with.'

'Once you are home again, Lauren Nightingale will be by to help you with some gentle physiotherapy to get you moving and mobile until they can do the second knee,' he explained, sitting back on his heels, taking his time to ensure there was nothing else she needed.

'Talented girl, Lauren,' she muttered with a frown. 'Always good at art. Clumsy as a mule, though, and as stubborn with it. No doubt she'll try and bully me.'

Oliver chuckled. Gertrude Stanbury was priceless! He could just imagine her as the formidable headmistress ruling her school with an iron hand and caring heart. 'Lauren's very good at her job. She'll take care of you. Now, is there anything else I can do for you today? How's the pain?'

'Bloody awful. How do you think?' the woman riposted, but her eyes gleamed and he could tell she was enjoying having someone to spar with.

'I'll take a look at the medications you're on and see if there's anything else that will make you more comfortable until the operation.' Taking both her hands in his, he turned them over and carefully inspected them. 'Any more deterioration with your hands or wrists?'

She looked down, hiding her eyes, but he'd seen the flash of worry in them. 'I get by.'

'We want you to do better than that. I'll investigate some alternative ideas to help you keep active and reduce the pain,' he promised, jotting himself a note on her file. He'd mention it to Lauren, too.

'Would you mind bringing me a fresh jug of chilled water?'

The question was polite but the command was clear nevertheless. 'No problem.' Smiling, Oliver rose to his feet and took the empty jug from the table nearby.

'My daily will have left another one ready in the fridge. Bring yourself a glass. I want to talk to you.'

Checking his watch, Oliver headed to the kitchen. He had one more house call to make before returning to the surgery for his afternoon list and a mountain of paperwork, and while lingering with Ms Stanbury would mean he'd miss lunch, he didn't mind. Having discovered from Lauren that the girls were planning a night out to see some film or other, he'd persuaded Chloe to go and enjoy herself. He'd miss her like crazy, but it was important that she keep up with her own circle of friends.

After last night, when he'd nearly lost the last remnants of his composure, it might be a good idea to cool things for an evening to give him a chance to shore up his ragged self-control before faced with the temptation of Chloe in the flesh again. At least he could look forward to talking with her on the phone at bedtime. Tomorrow, Friday, he was planning a beach picnic after work and the weekly midwifery meeting. If sea conditions permitted, he could do some surfing while Chloe relaxed, then they could eat and talk before he walked her home.

As for the weekend—well, he hoped to spend as much of that with her as possible. Whatever few lingering doubts remained about what he was getting into so soon after his return to Cornwall, he had come too far with Chloe to back off now. Aside from the ever-present physical desire, he genuinely liked her. She made him happy. The more he knew her, the more he agreed with her friends that Chloe was special. When he was with her he felt contented, whole, alive and charged with a buzz of excitement he had never known with anyone else. And he wanted to help her overcome her past.

He took the full jug from the fridge, refilled the empty one and set it in the coolest part to chill before returning to the living room.

'Anything else I can get for you while I'm here, Ms Stanbury?' he asked, handing the woman a glass of fresh, cold water.

'Call me Gertie. And do sit down, young man.'

Oliver grinned. 'Thanks. What did you want to talk to me about?'

'Word has it you're seeing our Chloe.' Shrewd grey eyes assessed him. 'I hope you're not going to break her heart.'

'So do I, Gertie.' Given how deeply he was becoming involved and how little he knew of Chloe's own feelings, he hoped *she* wasn't going to break *his* heart either. Pushing the niggling concern aside, he met Gertie's gaze. 'I shall do everything I can to never hurt Chloe in any way at all.'

The elderly woman gave a satisfied nod. 'I can see you mean it. Good. What that girl needs is someone to cherish her.'

'Do you know Chloe from school?' he asked, unable to resist some gentle prying.

'Yes, indeed. She was a first-class student.' A reminiscent look crossed her face. 'I was so glad to discover how well she had done for herself. When she ran away…'

The words trailed off, but Oliver's gut tightened, his attention sharpening. 'Chloe ran away?'

Gertie paused for a moment, sipping her drink, and Oliver

remained silent, tense and unsettled as he waited, impatient to hear what the woman had to say.

'I don't think anyone knows the extent of what went on in that house.' A shiver ran through her and Oliver felt chilled as the implications of her words sank in. 'I so feared for that poor child. And for her mother. Chloe's father was an evil man.'

'Why did no one do anything?' It was a struggle to keep hold of his temper and disgust at the thought of Chloe and her mother being left at the hands of such a bully.

'There was never any evidence. Chloe's mother denied everything, refused to leave him…Chloe herself would never talk. Too scared to, I suppose, poor mite. Everyone was frightened of him. You hardly ever saw Chloe or her mother outside the house. Thank goodness she was allowed to attend school.' Gertrude shook her head sadly. 'I tried to take an interest in Chloe. As I said, she was an avid learner but she had such a reserve about her and she didn't mix well with people. She ran away when she was sixteen, after her exams. I never knew what happened to her, never expected to see her again, but she must have kept in touch with her mother somehow—I guess through Lauren.'

Sitting forward, Oliver rested his forearms on his knees. 'When did she come back to Penhally?'

'After her father died, four years ago, Chloe returned to care for her mother. She worked locally as a midwife, then joined the surgery when Dr Tremayne and his then partner, Dr Avanti, opened the practice here,' Gertie continued, setting her glass aside, grimacing as she shifted her arthritic body into a more comfortable position. 'When her mother died eighteen months ago, Chloe sold the old house and bought the cottage in Fisherman's Row. I don't know how many people had any inkling back then what went on behind closed doors, or what that girl's life was like. It was well hidden. But I saw enough every day at school to be concerned. My biggest regret is that, although I tried, I couldn't make a difference. Now…well, I am just so proud of Chloe for making a success of herself. She deserves to be happy.'

Oliver felt sick to his stomach. He wanted to tear Chloe's father apart piece by piece—would have done had the man still been alive. Yet even from the grave her father cast a shadow over Chloe's life, one Oliver desperately wanted to lift. He needed Chloe to trust him enough to tell him about her childhood herself. Only then could he really reach her, really begin to help her put the past behind her.

Meeting Gertie's gaze, seeing the understanding in her eyes, he nodded. 'If it's in my power, Gertie, I shall do all I can to make sure Chloe's future is a happy one.'

'A quick word with everyone if I may,' Nick announced, standing in the staffroom doorway at the end of a busy Friday.

Oliver had left the surgery some while ago to answer an emergency call from the lifeguards to attend an injured tourist on the beach, so Chloe sat next to Lauren. She'd been looking forward to heading home as soon as the midwifery meeting was over, but had been delayed with Rachel Kenner. The girl had needed reassurance and Chloe was trying to see her as often as necessary to give support and advice. Her father was busy with arrangements for the annual remembrance service in August, when the town gathered by the lighthouse in memory of the victims of the storm that had claimed so many lives, Nick's father and brother and Kate's husband James among them.

Chloe was meant to be joining Oliver on the beach for a picnic supper. Given that she had been out with Lauren and Vicky yesterday evening, and today had been so hectic, she had hardly drawn breath, much less spoken with Oliver, she was more than eager to see him. Their phone conversation last night had been brief. She had been late home and sleepy, while he had sounded distracted.

'As you know,' Nick said, his words diverting her from her thoughts, 'I went to France with the twinning committee last weekend. It was a successful visit and things are moving on apace. It should be an excellent venture for Penhally, especially for tourism and business connections. For our part, Dr Gabriel Devereux will be joining us in the practice for a year, and although he won't be able to begin work until autumn, he is coming over shortly for a couple of days to look around. I hope everyone will make him welcome.'

There was some general muttering, but it was one of the practice nurses, Gemma Johnson, who spoke up. 'Have you met him? Does he speak English?'

'His English is perfect—he did some of his training in London—and from all I've heard, he's a highly respected doctor,' Nick confirmed.

His gaze swept the room. Chloe noted how he looked longest at Kate, a frown creasing his brow, the shadows in his eyes suggesting he was still having problems coming to terms with the enormity of the news about her son Jeremiah. *His* son, as it turned out. Chloe wished for a happy ending for them all.

'Dr Devereux will stay with me on this visit, but I've agreed to help him find somewhere suitable to rent. I know Oliver has been comfortable in the flat in Bridge Street, but that was for the short term,' Nick continued, and the reality that Oliver's stay in Penhally might be over all too soon sent a shock wave of alarm and disappointment through Chloe's body. 'If anyone has any ideas, I'd welcome them.'

Lost in thought, Chloe was only half listening as Lauren spoke up. 'What about the Manor House?'

'Isn't that already occupied?' Nick queried.

'Only until the end of August,' Lauren confirmed. 'But the Bartons are going to be away in South Africa for another two years at least. I've heard nothing about new tenants—and given that I live in the Gatehouse Cottage at the end of the drive and have the spare keys, the solicitor always keeps me informed and asks me to check on things. The house is comfortable, furnished, not too grand, and conveniently situated. I'm sure the Bartons would welcome renting it to someone on a year-long let. Especially someone recommended by and attached to the surgery. They are more interested in the quality of the tenant and keeping the house occupied and in good order than in asking for some ridiculously high rent.'

Nick offered a rare smile. 'Thank you, Lauren, that sounds excellent. Could you let me have the contact details for the solicitor? If it can be arranged, and if the house is available, perhaps Dr Devereux can have a look while he is here to see if it will suit his needs.'

'Yes, of course.' Frowning, Lauren reached for her bag and fumbled through it to find her address book. 'I have it here...somewhere.'

'Thank you, everyone,' Nick said. 'Have a good weekend.'

People rose and began filing out, talking among themselves, but Chloe waited for Lauren as they had planned to walk back to town together. Lauren was going to meet Vicky, while Chloe wanted a quick shower and to change her clothes before heading to the surfing beach to find Oliver...and the picnic he had promised her. She was so hungry.

When Lauren was finished and had handed over the details Nick wanted, Chloe turned to leave, noticing Kate ahead of her. She was about to say goodnight when Nick spoke again.

'I appreciate this, Lauren.' His took the piece of paper, then his voice firmed. 'Kate, could you wait a moment? I'd like to have a word.'

Chloe saw the shimmer of wariness in her friend's eyes. 'Yes, of course.'

Hesitating as Lauren went on ahead, Chloe searched Kate's

gaze, feeling anxious about leaving the older woman. But Kate smiled and nodded imperceptibly, and she had no option but to say goodnight and follow Lauren downstairs. Even so, her worry for Kate remained.

Kate tried to appear unconcerned as she was left alone with Nick. True, since she had confronted him at home he had been civil to her at work, but the tension remained between them. Their old friendship was in tatters. She tried so hard to understand him; despite all the upset, blame and guilt over Annabel's death, Kate was sure that Nick had still not properly grieved for his wife. On top of which he had found out about Jem in the worst of ways. She wished that had never happened but it was too late to turn back the clock. And however unrequited her love, however hopeless the situation seemed, she could not regret having Jem in her life.

Meeting Nick's watchful gaze, she struggled for composure. 'You wished to talk to me,' she prompted, managing to keep her voice level.

'Yes. Sit, please.' She did as she had been bidden, while Nick closed the door and then sat opposite her, looking uncomfortable. Legs braced, he rested his elbows on his knees, his hands clenched together. 'I know it's rich of me to ask, given the recent difficulties between us, but you have been—and still are—invaluable to the practice.'

'Thank you.'

The praise surprised her. Nick was not often one for compliments or showing his feelings. That he had said anything, especially in the current circumstances, created a warm glow inside her.

'I know your role here has changed since you ceased being practice manager and returned to midwifery, but I would be grateful if you would be among the few to come for lunch to meet Dr Devereux, to welcome him and help familiarise him with the practice and Penhally Bay.'

Kate swallowed her disappointment. She should have known Nick would only want to talk with her about work. 'I see. Who else will be there?'

'I was thinking of asking Dragan and Melinda. As incomers themselves, and originally from continental Europe, I thought they might have useful insights for Gabriel.'

'That's a good idea,' she acknowledged, realising how hard Nick was trying, that this was important to him—and maybe important to them in the longer term.

'Lucy and Ben will be coming, too, and bringing baby Annabel. I want to keep it informal. A barbecue, I thought. I…' The hesitation lengthened, then he raised his head, the expression in his eyes cautious. 'I have no objection if you wish to bring Jeremiah.'

Kate sat back, considering his words. Jem would attend as *her* son—she read that much between the lines. Part of her was downhearted, and yet she recognised the gesture for what it was…an olive branch of sorts. She couldn't expect too much too soon. Maybe if Nick saw Jem again in a social setting he would feel some draw, even if he was far from ready to acknowledge him as his son. It was less than she had dreamed of, but more than she had hoped for in recent weeks, so she accepted the hesitant step forward.

'All right, Nick,' she agreed, calling herself all kinds of a fool for allowing his answering smile to affect her so. 'We'll be happy to come and meet Gabriel.'

'Thank you, Kate, I appreciate it. I'll let you know when I have confirmation for the date of his visit.'

The edge of relief in his tone and the slight relaxing of his tension gave her a measure of hope that the future might not be as bleak as she had feared.

* * *

Chloe sat on the sand, her arms around her drawn-up knees, enjoying the early evening sunshine and the sight of Oliver surfing. Even though the beach was still busy and many people were in the water, she had picked him out straight away, instinctively drawn to him, admiring even from this distance the impressive athleticism of his six-foot-three inch frame, his supple movements, as if he were at one with the waves. The swell wasn't huge, but he caught the next crest, twisting, turning, weaving, as he rode the board back towards the shore. Moments later, he was wading through the shallows, his board tucked under his arm, his free hand pushing wet strands of hair back from his face.

Oh, my! Chloe thought she might self-destruct at the sight of him. All that bare, olive-toned skin over lean muscle dotted with water droplets. Strong shoulders, broad chest with a light dusting of dark hair arrowing down in a narrow line over an impressive abdomen, tight belly and disappearing under the low-slung, body-moulding, wetsuit shorts he wore. And she could glimpse part of the second tattoo he had mentioned. Sited off-centre, below his navel and over his right hipbone, the top of it peeped out from the waistband of his shorts. She couldn't distinguish what it was but, remembering how wonderful it had been to touch him two nights ago, she was filled with an eagerness to explore that body further.

Finding it hard to draw breath, Chloe struggled to swallow the lump lodged in her throat when her gaze clashed with his. His lips parted, his eyes darkened, and then he smiled. That slow, sexy, dimpled smile that melted her insides and made her forget her own name. He dropped to his knees beside her and leaned in to give her a lingering kiss.

'Hi, babe.'

'Hi.' He smelt of sea, sun and man. 'Sorry I'm late. Nick held us all back to talk about the twinning thing. Some French doctor is coming over in a few months to work in the practice for a year.'

'Yeah?'

Oliver seemed interested but not concerned, and her fertile imagination conjured up reasons why the arrival of an extra doctor didn't bother him. Was there room at the surgery for both Oliver and Gabriel? Was Oliver planning to extend his current contract? She had taken Kate's advice and had asked Oliver about his return to Cornwall. He'd been open about his desire for a different kind of life, his need to settle, and she had hoped that had meant he would stay in Penhally itself.

She had also been surprised and moved that someone as self-assured and confident as Oliver had insecurities about himself. He'd explained how he had never been able to shake off the playboy reputation or the family name, that people judged him on those rather than the person he was. She had felt guilty because that was exactly how she *had* first seen him. Now, though, she thought of him very differently. And she didn't want him to leave. As she was struggling with her confused emotions, her stomach gave an audible rumble and Oliver laughed, rising to his feet again.

'Sounds like I need to feed you,' he teased, picking up his surfboard. 'The car is nearby so I'll head back to fetch the cooler. I won't be long.'

'OK.'

Chloe watched him go, admiring his rear view. Sighing, she dropped her head on her knees, thinking about comments made by Vicky last night when they had been out at the cinema. Comments she had tried to banish from her mind.

'I sometimes wonder if there's any oestrogen in your body,' Vicky had complained.

Taken aback, Chloe had frowned. 'What do you mean?'

'Well, you have the scrumptious Oliver Fawkner panting after you and you don't seem to be doing anything about it.'

Warming to her theme—subtle and tactful not being in her vocabulary—Vicky had continued. 'A holiday fling is what you need. No commitment, just some fun with a guy who knows how to please a woman. I'll have him if you don't want him!'

Vicky's words upset her now as they had last night. Lauren had intervened, and had later taken her aside and told her to take no notice. 'You know what Vicky is like. She doesn't mean any harm. And she doesn't know about your past.'

Which was true, Chloe acknowledged now. But she didn't want to think of her relationship with Oliver as some meaningless fling, and she was worried because she had no idea how *he* viewed their time together. She had no experience of this kind of thing, her feelings were so new and beyond her understanding. After Vicky's comments, and now with the news that Gabriel Devereux would be coming from France, she couldn't shake off the nagging fear that Oliver might not be serious about her, that he might move on. From her if not from Penhally itself.

'What's wrong?'

She glanced up, so lost in thought she had been unaware of Oliver's return. 'Nothing,' she answered, managing a smile, her gaze travelling over him.

He had changed out of his wetsuit into ordinary cut-off denims, topped with a short-sleeved shirt he had left unbuttoned, allowing her a glimpse of his delectable torso. Her hands itched to explore him again. Her own body yearned to feel his touch. Setting the cooler down, he sat beside her and began taking out an impressive array of food. The sight of the treats in store, including some of the Trevellyans' blue cheese she loved so much, had her stomach rumbling again.

She felt a new edginess, a tension, as if they had reached a turning point. But maybe that was inside herself. She had decisions to make, and she knew if she wanted to take things further with Oliver she needed to face up to the demons that held her back. For now, though, she would enjoy his company and their picnic…time enough later to gather the courage to confront her memories of her father and confide in Oliver about her past.

The picnic had been a success and, as always, he adored being with Chloe. But Oliver sensed something had been different this evening. At times she had seemed distracted, focused inward, and a flicker of unease gripped him as he followed her inside her cottage. For a moment she stood with her back to him, looking out of the window, and he couldn't wait any longer to hold her. Closing the distance between them, admiring her curves in her sleeveless, knee-length dress, he slid his arms around her waist, nuzzling her neck as he drew her back against him.

'You're very quiet tonight, babe.'

'Just a bit tired,' she murmured. 'It's been a hectic week.'

He frowned, not entirely convinced by her explanation. 'Do you want me to go home and let you get an early night?' He'd be disappointed to cut short his time with her but he didn't want her fatigued.

'No.' She wriggled in his hold, turning to face him, taking him by surprise when she wrapped her arms around his waist and buried her face against him, her words muffled. 'No, don't go.'

Something wasn't right. He tightened his hold, raising a hand to stroke her hair. 'I missed this last night.'

'Me, too.'

'But you had a good time?' he asked, hearing an edge in her voice.

She burrowed closer against him. 'It was fine.'

'Did someone upset you?'

'No.' He didn't believe her but she changed the subject before he could question her further. 'What have you been up to the last couple of days?'

'Actually, I met an old friend of yours,' he told her, deciding to take a chance and offer her an opening to confide in him.

She pulled back to look up at him. 'You did? Who?'

'Gertie.'

'Gertie?' He smiled because her puzzled frown looked so cute. 'I don't know a Gertie.'

'Gertrude Stanbury. Your old headmistress.'

This time he laughed aloud at the expression on Chloe's face, her eyes widening, her mouth dropping open in shock. 'You called Ms Stanbury *Gertie*?'

'She asked me to. She likes me.'

'Obviously.' Chloe shook her head, a genuine smile curving her mouth. 'You're such a charmer!'

He manufactured a hurt look. 'What did I do?'

'We were so in awe of her at school,' she reflected with a reminiscent frown. 'Her rule was law. Nothing got by her.'

'She did say I should have a haircut.'

'I bet!'

Oliver regarded her for a moment. 'You think I should cut my hair?'

'No!' She sounded horrified at the prospect, but his smile faded as her fingers sank into the thick strands at his nape, tightening his gut and increasing his arousal. 'I like it. I just meant Ms Stanbury would have commented on it.'

'Yeah, she had quite a bit to say for herself. She's very fond of you,' he added, watching her carefully, controlling his own emotions as he recalled the tale the older lady had related.

'Really?'

'Mmm.' He slipped his hand under the fall of her hair and trailed his fingers over her silken skin. 'She said she used to worry about you, and she's very proud of your success.'

A welter of emotions chased across Chloe's green eyes, ranging from alarm to surprise. 'Oh. What else did she say?'

she queried, a new wariness in her voice, her body tensing in his hold, her arms loosening from around him.

'She told me how much she regretted being unable to help you, to make a difference. She said you ran away.'

'Yes.' He could feel her trembling before she moved away from him, wrapping her arms around herself. 'No one could have helped.'

Oliver was disappointed by her withdrawal, even though he had expected it. He felt nervous himself, concerned he was pushing too fast, unsure how best to reach Chloe, to encourage her to open up to him, to convince her it was safe to do so. Taking her hand, he led her to the sofa and sat down. Expecting her to keep her distance, he was relieved and delighted when she cuddled up against him.

'My father was a controlling, vindictive man.' Oliver held his breath as Chloe began speaking, wanting to protect her, hoping he was strong enough to help her through what was to come. Cradling her head on his shoulder, he kissed the top of her head. 'I don't know what had turned him that way but he was paranoid about things and he had very set rules and ideas. Nothing was ever good enough for him. The slightest thing would send him into a rage.'

'Was he an alcoholic?'

Chloe shook her head, turning more fully into him, her hand resting on his chest. 'No. He didn't need a drink to lose his head, to be violent. He did have a drink, on occasion, but not often. He had cut my mother off from her family and friends before I was even born. I don't know if I have grandparents, cousins or anything.'

'Why did he do that?' he asked when she paused, his fingers tracing soothing circles on the back of her neck.

'Like I said, it was all about control. He brought her here when they married. She knew no one, wasn't allowed to work, to go out without him, to have friends. He had to be in charge of her whole life. And mine when I came along,' she added, a quiver in her voice, and Oliver closed his eyes. 'He was physically, emotionally and verbally abusive to us both...sexually abusive to my mother.'

'But not to you?' He didn't know how to get the words past the painful lump in his throat.

'Not to me. Not that,' she confirmed softly.

A sigh of relief escaped him. Not that the rest she had suffered hadn't been bad enough. He couldn't bear to think of Chloe left vulnerable at the hands of such a man—her own father who was meant to protect and nurture her.

'What happened, Chloe?'

'Sometimes, when I was very young, if he decided I'd been bad, he'd lock me in a cupboard, often for hours. Later he'd use his fists,' she admitted, and he could hear the remembered fear and pain behind her words.

'Didn't your mother do anything to protect you?' Despite seeing cases during his medical career, knowing of people who stayed with their abusers for various reasons, he didn't have his rational doctor head on now because this was Chloe and personal, and he felt angry, aching for her. 'Why didn't she leave him?'

Chloe drew in a ragged breath and he shifted them so they were lying on the sofa and he could hold her more securely, keeping her close and safe. 'I feel bad, guilty, because I often hated her, blamed her for staying,' she whispered, and he felt the wetness of her tears seep through his shirt.

'No, babe,' he protested, desperate to get through to her, to not have her carry this burden. 'They were the adults. Their responsibility, their duty, was to care for you. You have nothing to feel guilty about.'

For a few moments a tense silence stretched, and he wondered if she would continue, if he could bear it if she did. They had not turned the light on and, as dusk fell, the darkening room gave a privacy that appeared to encourage the sharing of secrets.

'I think my mother was so brainwashed, her self-esteem so shattered, that she couldn't think for herself,' Chloe explained, a deep sigh torn from her. 'She said she loved him once, that it was her duty as his wife, that you made allowances, even that he didn't mean it. But he *did* mean it.' Anger and disgust rang in her voice. 'He enjoyed the control, the domination. His rules were strict and often contradictory. He demanded that my mother remain feminine and attractive for him, yet he criticised her for her appearance and accused her of trying to attract other men.' Almost by instinct, she pressed closer, as if seeking the comfort he was so desperate to give her. 'Once I became a teenager, his anger focused more on me, on putting me down, challenging me, finding fault. Apart from school, I wasn't allowed out. I couldn't have friends, wear nice clothes, make-up, jewellery, perfume. Then he started accusing me of flaunting myself for men, of being just like my mother.'

'Chloe...' Her name escaped as a groan. He felt helpless, unable to imagine the horror her life had been, furious that no one had helped her. And he could see how the groundwork had been laid to make Chloe subconsciously deny her sexuality and attractiveness—and mistrust men. 'Was there no one you could talk to?'

She shook her head. 'He had us so well isolated. And he made it clear what he would do if we ever told anyone. I hated him, Oliver, and while I felt sorry for my mother, wanted to stop her pain, I began to hate her, too, to disrespect her for not doing anything. And yet I did nothing myself, was just as cowardly and afraid of him.'

'What could you have done on your own? As a child, with no adults stepping in to care for you?' he interjected. 'Don't blame yourself, babe, please. It is not your fault. And you most definitely were not, and are not, a coward.'

He understood now why Chloe's past experiences made her wary and cynical about relationships, love, marriage, men. Frightened, she had protected herself by shutting down the part of her that would allow desire, believing it led to hurt and abuse and the surrendering of control, of her very self. He was angry and distressed at all she had endured, but so proud of her for all she had achieved despite it, for having the courage to face it, to share it with him, to let him close to her. It was a special gift, one he hoped he deserved. To know he was the first man she had ever trusted, had ever allowed to kiss her, hold her, touch her... It was humbling, overwhelming.

'What happened to make you run away?' he asked, his voice rough with emotion.

He felt her shaking and hated himself for causing her any further upset. 'It was after my exams, when I was sixteen. I came home from school to find my father waiting for me. He started accusing me, saying he had seen me flirting with a man outside school. It was crazy. I'd spoken to a boy, a classmate, about an exam for less than a minute, but nothing I said made a difference. You didn't answer back, didn't challenge his perception of things. He...' She halted, her voice breaking.

'It's OK,' he whispered, his chest tight, stroking a hand up and down her back. 'You don't have to tell me.'

'I do. I need to.' Oliver's own shuddering breath mirrored hers. 'He said I had to be taught a lesson.' Again she paused and he heard the determination in her voice. Turning more onto his back he drew her on top of him and she pressed her face into his neck. 'It was Lauren who found me hiding after I had escaped his attack. She and Vicky were three years ahead of me at school, so not really friends with me then. Lauren had left home after A levels, moving away to do her physiotherapy training, but she was back for a week's break. I was a mess. Bleeding and bruised. He'd hacked all my hair off with scissors. I was so scared, so angry. I felt guilty leaving my mother, but I knew I could never go back there. I believed he'd kill me one day.'

'God, Chloe.' Shocked, his hold tightened and he wished he had been around to protect her, get her away.

'Lauren took me to her home. Thankfully her parents were out. Did you know she was adopted?' she asked, confusing him for a moment with the change of tack.

'No,' he admitted, getting his head together. 'I didn't know that.'

'Anyway, Lauren cleaned my cuts, found me clothes, fed me, got part of the story out of me. Then she gave me money, made some phone calls to a women's group she knew through college, and found me a safe place to stay away from Penhally. No one else knew where I had gone, at least to begin with, but I kept in touch with Lauren and she passed on news about my mother. The shelter helped me get on my feet and find a way to pursue my goal to be a midwife. When I was twenty-three, I heard my father had died and that my mother needed someone. I came back and felt strangely detached. I couldn't grieve for him, and I had confused, ambivalent feelings for her, but I needed to do it, needed the closure. She was a broken woman, her mind was scattered, hardly in touch with reality. We never talked about what happened. As for Lauren, I returned the money eventually, but I can never repay her for all the rest.'

'You are amazing, babe. Strong and brave.'

'No, it was just self-preservation,' she refuted, sounding sad. 'Years ago my mother told me I'd understand one day. But I'm never going to be like her, never going to endure what she did for love.'

Her words troubled him and showed him the journey was not yet over. Cupping her face with his hands, he tried to see her in the darkness, to give her his strength, assure her he was sincere, prove to her she could trust him.

'That wasn't love, Chloe. Not at all. You're not your mother...and I'm not your father.'

She didn't answer, but neither did she pull away. Instead, she rested her head on his chest and slipped her arms around him. He held her long into the night, seeking guidance for the best way to help her, stunned, overcome, even more in awe and in love with her than he had been before she had trusted him with the horrors of her childhood.

For a moment he froze, realising what he had just admitted to himself. He hadn't planned it, hadn't expected it to happen so soon, but this whole gamut of feelings and emotions had grown and deepened over the weeks and he was in love with Chloe MacKinnon. In some ways he was stepping into the unknown as much as she was, experiencing all this for the first time. Chloe deserved the best—he prayed that could be him.

He felt the full weight of responsibility for what he was taking on, for what this meant for Chloe's sake. But he knew with an utter certainty and finality that he didn't just want to be the first man Chloe let into her life, he wanted to be the *only* man. The man to claim her heart, the man to cherish her and love her and care for her...for ever.

If only she would let him.

CHAPTER EIGHT

HER Saturday lunch-time parents' class over, Chloe headed out to Lauren's cottage and wandered around her studio, admiring the selection of paintings her friend had available for sale. When she decided which one she wanted, there would be the usual good-natured debate about the cost, an argument Chloe was always determined to win, convinced that Lauren should not make over-generous allowances for her friends. In truth, she loved all Lauren's work, but this painting had to be extra-special because it was for Oliver.

Just thinking about him made her warm and tingly, although thoughts of last night, of facing up to the past and revealing the full extent of her father's cruelty, had a chilling effect. Confiding in Oliver had been one of the most difficult things she had ever done. Not because of the way Oliver had reacted. Far from it. He had been wonderful...tender, considerate, protective and supportive. She had felt his anger, but it had been *for* her, and she had never felt anything but safe with him.

For the second time she had fallen asleep in his arms, only to wake up that morning to find herself alone on the sofa, a light throw tucked around her, a pillow under her head, and his note propped on the coffee-table, waiting for her. She'd had appointments and her lunchtime class, while Oliver had had morning surgery, so she had not seen him yet today, but she had done a lot of thinking.

That he believed in her made her feel good, and thinking of his words, his reasoning, had helped ease her long-buried guilt. Oliver was right. None of it had been her fault. Her parents had failed in their responsibilities to protect her. She had not been to blame for her father's anger, or for her mother's choices. Sharing the burden with Oliver, telling him things she had never told anyone else, not even Lauren, had brought unexpected but welcome inner peace, a letting go. She refused to allow her father any more influence on the rest of her life.

She wanted to do something for Oliver to show her appreciation. Something tangible that, should he decide to leave, would be a reminder of her and his time in Penhally. That he might go was too painful to consider. It would soon be his birthday and, knowing how he admired Lauren's work and loved the local landscape, it had seemed an excellent idea to buy one of her paintings for him.

'Have you found something you like?' Lauren asked with a smile, handing her a glass of chilled fruit juice.

'Thanks.' Chloe took a sip of the drink and turned back to the array of work with a sigh. 'I love them all. That's the trouble.'

Her friend laughed. 'I appreciate the compliment. Perhaps I can help. Where are you going to hang it?'

'Actually, I'm not. It's a present…for Oliver,' she admitted, blushing.

'Really?' Lauren's smile widened. 'That's great. I'm so pleased for you, Chloe.'

'It's his birthday in two weeks' time. I want to thank him—and I want him to have something to remember me by if he leaves Penhally.'

Lauren frowned. 'What makes you think he might leave? He wants to settle down, doesn't he?'

'He's said nothing about staying or extending his contract at the surgery.' Sitting down, she confided her fears to her friend. 'I told him about Gabriel Devereux arriving from France in the autumn, and Oliver wasn't the least bothered.'

'The surgery is getting busier all the time, especially with the ongoing expansion, and could easily carry another GP or two. Lucy is still on maternity leave and Dragan will be cutting back when Melinda has the baby. And with Ed and Maddy having recently chosen hospital work in St Piran over staying at the practice, there is space for Oliver and, later, the French doctor for his year's placement. Probably another nurse, too. You're really smitten with Oliver, aren't you?' Lauren added after a pause, sitting beside her.

'Yes.' Chloe met her friend's gaze. 'But I don't know how he feels. And I have no experience of this sort of thing. What if Vicky's right and this is just a fling?'

Lauren waved her comment aside. 'Vicky was talking nonsense, and you know it. Oliver cares about you, Chloe. We can all see it. And we can all see the difference in you, too. You're blossoming. It's fantastic. You've come such a long way in the last days and weeks. Don't get cold feet and turn back now. Oliver is good for you—and believe me, you're good for him. See where it takes you, go for what you want.'

'I don't know.'

'Hasn't he shown you how different he is? Has he ever pressured you, scared you, tried to change or control you? Has he ever said he's leaving?'

Confused, Chloe shook her head. It was true that Oliver made her feel things she had never felt before. Things that were so unfamiliar but which made her heart beat with excitement and brought incredible sensations to her body. But he had always left the choice to her, had respected her, never pressured her.

'What I feel is scary…but exciting,' she admitted.

'You are learning what it is to be a woman, desired by a sexy man. Go with it. You won't be sorry,' Lauren reassured. 'Now, about this picture.'

Dragging her thoughts back to the matter at hand, Chloe stood up again and returned her attention to the canvases. 'Are you trying some new techniques?' she asked, noting subtle differences in Lauren's new work compared with older pictures.

'No, why?'

Surprised at the edge in her friend's voice, Chloe glanced round and saw Lauren frowning in puzzlement, almost squinting as she looked at her own work. A flicker of unease curled inside her as she remembered Oliver's questions about Lauren's clumsiness. Could there really be something wrong? Unwilling to consider it, sure her friend would say something if there was a problem, Chloe tried to set her disquiet aside. Perhaps she was seeing changes in the paintings that weren't there.

'All the pictures are amazing, Lauren. But with Oliver's love of the sea, I'll settle on this magnificent coastal landscape,' she decided, preparing herself for the battle ahead to ensure Lauren took enough money for her work.

Oliver glanced at his watch and wondered when Chloe would be home. He hadn't seen her since last night, when leaving her had been almost impossible. After a busy morning at the surgery, when his clinic had overrun he had sent her a text and discovered she was with Lauren for the afternoon and having a meal with her friend. Having told her he was home if she wanted to meet up, all he could do was wait. And worry. He understood if she was feeling awkward after last night's talk about her past and knew she might need some space. But he wanted to be with her. He still felt shaky, sick about all she had suffered, angry that no one had helped her. Until Lauren. Thank goodness she had been there to help Chloe get away to safety.

As for his own feelings for Chloe, well, he loved and wanted her more every day. He had never spent so much time with a woman, being with her, getting to know her, talking, laughing, dating...all without sex getting in the way. He enjoyed it. Because it was Chloe. Not that he didn't want to make love with her. He did. He ached for it, and hoped they'd get there before he expired from unfulfilled desire. In the meantime, everything about her fascinated him, and the slow build-up of the physical side of things was exciting, and heightened the anticipation.

That she had been completely unaware of her own body's needs and desires was amazing, but awakening her to intimacy, sharing the journey with her, was the most incredible experience of his life, an honour and a privilege. He could kiss and touch Chloe for ever. Yearned to do so. It took every atom of self-control he had not to rush things. Tamping down his desire, his urgent need to know her fully, wasn't easy, but he was determined to do this the right way for Chloe. Nothing had ever felt this special. Being with Chloe made his world a better place. He wanted her, needed her. But it was too soon to tell her. He had to be sure of her feelings for him and where she saw this going before he made a public commitment. What scared him was that Chloe might never be ready to consider love, marriage and for ever.

He paced the small rented flat. In a week or so he would have to vacate it, make long-term plans about work and living arrangements. He glanced at his watch again. Was Chloe home yet? Should he ring her? He dragged his fingers through his hair, caught in an agony of indecision yet knowing the next move had to be hers.

Chloe stored Oliver's painting safely in her spare room. The end of July was approaching. She hoped he would stay, but what would happen if he didn't? What if he left and she never experienced being with him in the fullest sense of the word because she had been too cautious, too cowardly to take a chance and go for what she knew deep down inside she wanted?

She couldn't imagine ever feeling like this about anyone else. Couldn't imagine ever allowing any other man into her life the way she had Oliver. Because she trusted him. Trusted him not to be like her father, not to hurt her, control her, abuse her. If she gave herself to him now, he would take a big piece of her heart and soul if he left, and she might never be the same again. But if she didn't... Lauren was right. No one knew what tomorrow would bring. And she would forever regret this missed opportunity if she didn't take it.

Her mind made up, she left her cottage, thankful not to meet anyone as she made her way to Oliver's flat. As she walked, she thought over the last weeks, the way she had grown in confidence thanks to Oliver's patient care. They had progressed from those first awkward kisses, when she hadn't known what to do, to the most amazingly erotic, deep, drugging kisses that knocked her senseless and set every part of her aflame. Then there had been some pretty serious petting. She felt hot and achy just thinking about his touch... and being able to touch him.

Despite rejecting Vicky's ridiculous suggestion that she use Oliver for sexual experimentation, Chloe *was* curious. Not because she wanted to see what sex was like on a general level, and certainly not to use Oliver. She could never do that. This was about Oliver himself, the need she felt for him alone. The thought of stepping into the unknown was scary. But she had reached the point where she was even more scared *not* to explore where this might go. He had awakened a long-dormant part of her. It was him she wanted. Badly.

Shaking with nerves, she hesitated outside Oliver's door, reaching out to ring the door bell before her remaining courage deserted her. It was several moments before she heard the turn of the lock, then the door opened. She had been on the point of walking away, losing her nerve, but she froze, her gaze locked on Oliver, taking in the wonder of the man. She looked slowly up long, tanned, muscled legs to where a pair of skimpy, faded denim shorts hung low on narrow hips, the button unfastened. The tattoo above one hip bone was almost fully visible—vaguely it registered that it depicted a lone wolf. Her gaze followed the narrow line of dark hair from the gaping waistband, up over a taut belly and toned abdomen to the perfectly contoured chest, broad and muscled, olive skin marked by the two orbs of bronze nipples.

Slowly, he raised one arm and braced it on the doorframe above his head, the rippling play of muscles and the tattoo banding his bicep distracting her. She felt hot enough to melt into a puddle at his feet and couldn't drag enough air into her lungs. Biting her lip, she forced her gaze to continue up the strong column of his throat, over a jaw darkened with the shadow of a day's stubble, past sensual lips that held such sexy promise until her gaze clashed with his. Rich brown eyes...sinful, liquid, hot with a sexual need that both excited and frightened her. Part of her wanted to run away. The rest of her couldn't move, wanted to stay, needed to touch him.

'Chloe?'

The smoky voice pushed her over the edge. She pressed a closed fist to her sternum, terrified she was going to hyperventilate or faint or do something equally embarrassing in front of him. A ragged breath shuddered through her.

'Is something wrong, babe?'

She shook her head, unable to speak. Vulnerable, she tried to convey through her eyes why she was here. Her heart rate doubled as awareness stilled him. His own eyes darkened impossibly, his expression growing hotter, even more intense, and his lips parted a fraction as if in silent invitation and anticipation. He said nothing, just lowered his arm and held out his hand to her. Trembling so badly she could barely command her limbs to obey, she took a jerky step forward and placed her hand in his, sealing her fate.

Warm, strong fingers closed over hers and drew her inexorably closer. She stepped over the threshold, deafened by the pulse racing in her ears, drawn by the unquenchable ache deep inside her. The sound of the door closing and the lock turning was loud in the electrically charged silence.

Helpless to halt her own fate, Chloe surrendered herself to Oliver's will.

Oliver couldn't believe that Chloe was there, that she had come to him, but he read the need in her eyes, felt it in the quiver of her body, the frantic race of her pulse. He wanted her as he had wanted no other woman. He ached with it, ached to back her up to the wall and take her, hot, hard and desperately. But he knew he couldn't do that. Not yet. Somehow he had to get a grip on his raging desire before it slipped out of control. This was Chloe's first time, and whatever it cost him to wait and go slowly, so be it. He was going to make this as special and memorable an experience for her as he could. Later there would be time to indulge in more carnal, urgent pursuits and introduce her to exciting new experiences. Later…

Not yet breaking the silence between them, he led her to his bedroom, more than grateful he'd stocked up on some condoms in the last few days in the hope that this precious event might happen. His hand held hers lightly. He wanted her to join him of her own free will, to make the decision herself. As much as he longed to sweep her up in his arms and tumble her to his bed to ravish her, this had to be Chloe's choice. The first time had to be right. Halting beside the bed, he turned to face her, his heart swelling with affection at the look in her eyes…a sliver of fear mixed with determination and longing. He was so damn proud of her.

'Are you sure this is what you want, Chloe?'

'Y-yes. If you do.'

'Hell, yes!' Feeling raw with need, he gave a rough laugh at her doubt. 'You have no idea how badly. But this time is for you, babe. If I do anything you don't like, you tell me. If you want me to stop, you say so. OK?'

She gave a shaky nod. 'OK.'

Holding her gaze, he released her hand and slowly began to undo the buttons down the front of her sleeveless, multi-coloured sundress. 'First we'll get this off you. I can't wait to see you properly. You're so beautiful, Chloe. I want to touch you and taste you all over. You always remind me of food,' he murmured, brushing his lips along her neck.

'Food?'

'Mmm.' He nuzzled against her, his tongue flicking out to sample her skin. 'You smell like green apples, sunshine and fresh air. Your skin is as smooth and pure as cream, you taste as sweet as honey, and your mouth and nipples are as succulent and juicy as strawberries. I want to eat you all up, Chloe. I hunger for you…and it's never going to stop. You are a feast I shall never have my fill of.'

'Oliver…' Her whole body trembled in reaction to his words.

'Let me love you, babe. Let me show you how beautiful you are, how special desire and passion and making love will be between us.'

'Yes.'

She whimpered, swaying as he peeled off the dress and discarded it, revealing her lush curves covered only in lacy green bra and panties. Heat seared through him. His nostrils flared. Sucking in a strangled breath, he fought to keep to the plan, despite how painfully hard and desperate he was for her. To distract himself and boost her confidence, he kept talking to her, praising her. His own hand shook as he reached out and traced the outline of her bra and panties with his fingertips, watching and feeling the reactions of her body to the light touches. A flush of arousal warmed soft, ivory skin, her nipples hardened further, pushing anxiously against their lace covering, and her flesh rippled as she shivered in anticipation.

'You can touch me, too, Chloe. I want you to. I long to feel your hands and mouth on me.'

Guiding her palms to his chest, he left her to explore, loving her curious, enthusiastic touch. He reached round to unfasten her bra, allowing the perfection of her breasts to spill free. Full, firm but soft, they filled his hands and she moaned as he shaped them, his thumbs grazing over the tight, swollen, sensitive peaks. She arched towards him in response, her own fingers tightening on his flesh.

Chloe was so reactive to his touch. He couldn't wait to turn weeks of seductive kisses and lingering foreplay into the real thing, imagining how much pleasure he could bring her. Resisting the temptation to linger on her breasts just yet, he knelt in front of her, sliding his hands down her hips. Leaning in, he nuzzled the rounded swell of her belly, breathing in the scent of her. His heart thudded, his body tightened even further. Slipping his hands round to cup her delicious rear, he held her still to him as he explored her navel with lips, teeth and tongue. She gasped, squirming against him, and he felt her legs giving way. Supporting her, he eased down her panties, his gaze drawn to ivory thighs and the apex of them where a triangle of soft dark curls arrowed down to the core of her femininity. He laid her gently on the bed, moving to straddle her, his knees on either side of hers, keeping his shorts on to maintain some much-needed distance so he remembered this was for Chloe and didn't end things in an instant.

Running his hands up her body, he leaned in to kiss her, giving her more of his weight, rubbing his chest across her breasts as she wrapped her arms around him and opened her mouth for his tongue. She tasted amazing. His own body shook as her hands tentatively explored, her nails grazing down his spine, threatening to tip him over the edge. He drew back, concentrating on her needs.

His fingers stroked the baby-soft skin of her thighs, sliding higher as they parted for him, dipping between, feeling her heat and growing excitement. Her hold on him tightened and he drew his head back to watch her, seeing the flush of arousal colour her face, her eyes turning darker and unfocused. Her breaths were rapid and ragged as he brushed his fingers over her, getting her used to the sensations before touching her more intimately. She felt incredible. He sucked in his own shuddering breath, sure he was going up in flames at any moment.

'Oliver?'

She sounded uncertain at what she was feeling. 'Easy, babe,' he soothed, taking his time as he stroked her, slowly parting her and exploring deeper.

Unbelievable. She was perfect. So hot and wet. And tight, he discovered as he carefully pressed one finger inside her. He used the pad of his thumb to circle and brush across her sensitive clitoris, and she gasped, squirming on the bed, clutching at him.

'What...? What's happening?' she cried on a half-sob.

'Trust me. Just let go.' She was so close. He could feel it in her, the building tension. Carefully he added a second finger, rhythmically stroking inside her. 'Go with it, Chloe. Let it happen. It feels good, doesn't it?'

'Yes! Please...Oliver!'

She tightened round his fingers and he took her through the release that gripped her, holding her close, revelling in the cries pulled from her as she clung to him, surrendering to what he knew was the first climax she had ever experienced. He made sure to extend and prolong the sensations for her.

Watching her pleasure was incredible. It overwhelmed him to share this with her, to know he was the one to make her feel good, to make her come apart. And this was just the beginning.

Easing his fingers from her, he softly stroked her trembling thighs and belly, brushing kisses across her flushed face. 'You were amazing, babe. Did you like it?'

Nodding she turned her face into his neck, hiding, her arms wrapping around him.

'Don't be shy with me.' Her flesh quivered as his fingers resumed their light stroking along her inner thighs. 'What you felt that time will only get better, Chloe. When I use my mouth on you. When I'm inside you and we come together.'

He gave her a few moments to adjust, then he began kissing her again, building up her arousal a step at a time as he slowly inched his hands and his mouth down her body, worshipping every part of her, lingering at her breasts before continuing his journey to her navel, then lower. She froze in shock the first time he touched his mouth to her most intimate flesh but he gentled her through, encouraged by the responses of her body, her sighs and moans, the way she writhed beneath him.

'You can't,' she gasped in shocked delight.

Oliver chuckled. 'Sure I can.' And he proceeded to show her how.

'Oh, my! Oliver!'

'Come for me, babe.'

He kept her on the brink for as long as his patience could bear it, then led her over the edge to her second orgasm, this one even stronger and more intense than the first. He kept his tongue and fingers moving, intensifying her pleasure, loving her cries, her uninhibited responses. As after-shocks rippled through her, he released her long enough to shrug out of his shorts and reach for a condom, cursing his shaking fingers as he wrestled to extract it and roll it on. Soon it would be time.

He'd needed Chloe to climax a couple of times, wanted her

so hot and wet and needy that she would be relaxed and boneless enough that she wouldn't have the time to worry or the strength to tense herself when he took her virginity. He was scared. He'd never been anyone's first man before. He didn't want to hurt her, ever, and he'd tried everything he could think of to make it as easy and good for her as possible. She had been so tight to his fingers and he shook with wanting, imagining how it would feel to be inside her. Chloe was so special. Looking down at her, limp and replete, a small smile curving her mouth, he knew it was now or never.

Chloe struggled to open her eyes as she felt Oliver's hands lift her sated body and slide a pillow under her hips before gently setting her down again. Why was he doing that? His fingers stroked her thighs, parting them before he eased between them. She felt languid, every part of her quivering with sensation after the indescribable pleasure of two amazing orgasms, and it took an effort to raise her hand and run her fingers up his chest and throat to cup his jaw. The faint rasp of stubble was an exciting caress against her skin. His earthy male scent teased her, aroused her. Heat shimmered off him and she met his gaze, saw the intent in his eyes, the flare of colour across his cheekbones.

Oh, help. It was going to happen.

She wanted it, but she was scared.

Before she could voice her concerns, his mouth took hers in a searing kiss, deep, seductive, hotter than hot, dragging her back into oblivion. Nothing existed but Oliver and the way he made her feel. His hands and mouth brought her back up to full arousal. Every part of her was straining for release. She felt achy, empty, needy. Oliver sank the fingers of one hand in her tousled hair, meeting her gaze, his eyes hot with desire. He moved to her and, as she felt him poised for the first time, her hands instinctively grasped at him.

'Relax, Chloe.' His voice was hoarse. He teased kisses at the corners of her mouth, his tongue tip stroking her bottom lip. 'Trust me.'

Slowly, so slowly, he entered her. She felt the unfamiliar pressure. It went on and on as he pressed inexorably forward. Her breaths were coming in ragged gasps, her heart racing madly. For a moment he paused, but before she could tense or prepare herself, he thrust forward again, firmer, surer. The pressure intensified and she felt a sense of impossible fullness. She'd expected pain but there was nothing more than a brief sting before it was gone.

He paused to allow her body to accommodate him. 'Are you OK, babe?'

'Yes,' she managed, although 'OK' didn't seem to cover the magnitude of it.

'Is it uncomfortable for you?'

She shook her head in response to his rough, raw question. The sensations were amazing. His own breathing was as ragged as her own, then he groaned, his hold tightening as he began to move, slowly at first, and then with less restraint. The friction was exquisite. Her fingers dug into the slick flesh of his back. Sobbing, unable to help herself, she curled around him, her hips rising to match his rhythm. Oh, this was fantastic! She loved it. She wanted more. And something far greater than she had already experienced was clamouring inside her.

'Please, Oliver. Please…'

Oliver fought to retain control, to go slowly, to make this first time right for Chloe. But it was impossible not to react to the way she responded so naturally and eagerly to him. Her scent, her taste, the feel of her opening to him, accepting him, welcoming him into her body, was the most incredible thing that had ever happened to him. She fitted him like a glove. He couldn't hold on. He had to move. As she clutched at him, pleaded with him, instinctively wrapped her legs round him and tilted her hips, sending him deeper still, she pushed him over the edge. His control snapping, he upped the tempo, unable to hold back any more. He bound her to him and gave himself up to the unbelievable bliss of making love with Chloe MacKinnon. She met and matched his every demand, crying out as he took her higher and higher, until the moment when she flew with him over the precipice, freefalling into the abyss as her release triggered his and unimaginable pleasure shot him spiralling into oblivion.

He had no idea how long it was before he managed to stir himself. He had to be crushing her. Keeping her with him, he carefully rolled them to the side, tightening his hold, needing her close. Always. He had to be dead. He couldn't breathe, his heart was thundering far too fast. Only it wasn't enough. Not nearly enough. For ever wouldn't be enough with Chloe.

Forcing his eyes open, he focused on her flushed face, wiping tears from her cheeks with unsteady fingers. 'Chloe, are you all right? Did I hurt you?'

'No. Not at all. It was… Wow!' A naughty smile sparked her green eyes and curved lips rosy and swollen from his kisses. 'I loved it,' she admitted with a shy laugh. 'Can we do it again?'

Ecstatic, he hugged her and gave a mock groan. 'Help me. I've created an insatiable monster!'

'If you don't want to, I understand.'

'What?' Alerted by the uncertainty in her voice, he rolled them over, cupping her face in his hands. 'Not want to? Are you crazy?'

She bit her lip, making him want to do the same, to taste her again—all over. 'I just thought…'

'Thought once would be enough? Hell no, babe. You can unthink that idea. No way am I ever going to have my fill of you or do all the things I want to do with you.'

* * *

Oliver's words fired new arousal through a body she thought must surely be sated. She couldn't believe she was here with him, that after so many years of locking her sensual side away, Oliver had breezed into her life and so easily broken down the walls of her prison—a prison she hadn't even consciously known existed. Now she knew what she had been missing, but she also knew it wasn't sex per se, it was Oliver himself. She wanted to travel this erotic journey with him for ever.

'Don't move,' he instructed, rolling off her.

'I don't think I could.'

Smiling, she watched as he left the room, presumably to dispose of the condom. She closed her eyes, trying to capture and relive every moment of the most earth-shattering experience of her life. She felt exhilarated, charged, buzzing with life and yet deliciously spent. Her eyes opened as Oliver came back into the room, unselfconscious about his nakedness, and she revelled in being able to look at him in all his naked glory. He was superb. When he knelt on the bed beside her and she realised what he was going to do, she tensed, feeling embarrassed.

Leaning down, he kissed her. 'Let me take care of you, babe.'

A blush stained her cheeks and she closed her eyes, surrendering to him as he used a warm, wet flannel to wash between her thighs. She felt tender, but not unpleasantly so. When he had finished, he surprised her again, lifting her up in his arms and carrying her from the room.

'Where are we going?' she murmured, feeling sleepy.

'I've run a warm bath for you. I don't want you getting stiff and sore.'

Touched by his kindness, she pressed a kiss to his cheek. He set her on her feet beside the bath, cupping her face to bestow a lingering kiss on her lips.

'You get in. I won't be a minute, then I'll scrub your back!'

Smiling, Chloe pinned up her hair and lowered herself into the fragrant bubble bath, the lavender scent relaxing her. Oliver soon returned and slipped into the bath behind her, wrapping his arms around her. For a while she enjoyed resting back against his chest, disinclined to talk. As the water began to cool, Oliver reached for the sponge, soaped it, and took his time working over every inch of her.

'What about my turn?' she complained when he rose and stepped out of the bath.

'Next time.' The devilish smile he sent her as he shook out a towel and held it ready for her made her glow inside with renewed desire. 'I have other plans for you now.'

When he led her back to the bedroom, she discovered he had changed the sheets and again felt a mixture of embarrassment and gratitude for his thoughtfulness. She gasped as he tipped her onto the bed and followed her down, relishing the feeling that this was Oliver let off the leash of the self-control he had maintained until now. He was an amazing man and it hit her for the first time that she'd fallen completely in love with him. Oh, hell. But she didn't have time to fret over the revelation because Oliver's hands and mouth were taking her back to paradise.

In the days that followed, Chloe spent every spare moment she could with Oliver—and every night with him in his bed or hers. Lauren and Kate had noticed the difference in her, claiming she was glowing. Oliver was certainly teaching her things she had never imagined and she was a more than willing pupil, growing in confidence to explore his body and give him pleasure in return.

As she waited for her next patient to arrive, she couldn't stop her mind drifting to Oliver. It always did. The last month had changed her life. *Oliver* had changed her life. She had never been so happy, never felt so free, so content, so whole. But she was scared it wouldn't last. Nothing had been said about any kind of future. Oliver had never discussed his plans for when this contract ended or his flat lease expired, and he had never said how he felt about her, not in words, even while he loved her with his body. She had been equally careful not to betray her own feelings for him, but she very much feared she had given Oliver more than her body. She had given him her heart and her soul.

She had gone into this with her eyes open, so she had no one to blame but herself for falling in love with him—something she had claimed she would never do. But until Oliver, she had never known what love was. Now she did…and it just might break her heart.

CHAPTER NINE

'A QUICK word before you go out to your house calls?'

Oliver looked round at Nick Tremayne's words, halting on his way towards the front entrance of the surgery. 'Of course.'

Puzzled by the request, wondering what Nick wanted to talk to him about, Oliver followed the older man to his consulting room and closed the door.

'Sit down, Oliver.' The senior partner's relaxed manner and rare smile eased Oliver's wariness. 'You're probably aware there are changes afoot in the practice,' Nick began. 'My daughter, Lucy, headed up the plans for expansion before she went on maternity leave. When the alterations are finished we'll have a broader capability to treat minor injuries, plus there will be X-ray facilities and a plaster room. Various other services will be more in-house, including Lauren having a better physiotherapy space to see more patients here.'

'Everyone's very excited about the new facilities,' Oliver agreed.

'Good, good. The workload is continuing to increase for us all, and not just during the tourist season. Initially, your contract was temporary, but your experience suits our needs and will benefit us even more when the expansion is complete.' The older man paused, his gaze assessing as he sat forward and rested his elbows on the desk. 'How would you feel about staying on in Penhally Bay? You've fitted in here, the patients like and trust you, and the staff find you a pleasure to work with. Lucy may not come back to work full time for some time, and Dragan would like to be flexible and reduce his hours when Melinda has their baby. Even with Gabriel Devereux coming over from France for a year in the autumn, we'll need another doctor. We've discussed things, Oliver—myself, Lucy, Dragan and Adam—and we'd like to offer you a full-time post and a junior partnership.'

He felt dumbstruck! When he had first decided to come back to Cornwall, he had hoped to settle down, and the opportunity to stay on permanently suited him down to the ground. Possibilities ran through his mind. Part of him wanted to accept Nick's offer on the spot, knowing he had finally found a place to call home, one that offered the kind of community-based medicine he loved. But another part of him urged patience and caution. He needed to share this with Chloe, to have some sense of what the future held in store for them, and if he had a chance with her long term. If Chloe didn't want him, he wasn't sure he could stay here, to see her, work with her but not touch her and be with her.

For the first time in his life he was in love. He had laid himself bare to Chloe, was totally vulnerable in a way he had never been before. Physically, things just got better and better between them, and she was an avid learner, eager and enthusiastic to experience everything. Emotionally, he felt on shaky ground. For him it was serious. But he had no clue about Chloe's feelings. She had never spoken of them, had never asked about his own. Neither had she asked him about his plans. So many times he had wanted to tell her he loved her but he had held back, scared of her rejection.

Old hurts and doubts nagged at him and he couldn't help but remember the way he had been used so often before. He had never been so uncertain, or so dependent on another person for his happiness, his very existence. Did Chloe see beyond the playboy image to the person he was inside? Could she get over her past and come to love him? He needed answers before he could give Nick a decision.

'Think about it and let me know in a few days,' Nick said now, clearly taking his silence for reticence.

'I will. Thank you, Nick. I'm overwhelmed—but delighted.' Rising to his feet, he shook his boss's hand. 'I just need to be sure of a couple of things before saying one hundred per cent yes.'

A knowing glint appeared in Nick's eyes. 'I understand.'

As he headed out to complete his house calls, Oliver already knew what he wanted. To accept the position, to put down roots in Penhally and make a life with Chloe. To love her, marry her and cherish her. For ever. What would she say when he told her he loved her? Could she care for him as he did for her? Or was he making a mistake in pinning all hopes for the future on her?

'How did the barbecue go?' Chloe asked when she met up with Kate for a quick cup of tea before the final antenatal clinic of the day began.

'It was good.' Kate smiled, helping herself to one of Hazel's home-made biscuits. 'I have to say that Gabriel Devereux, the French doctor, is absolutely *gorgeous*! Dark skin, dark hair, dark eyes. Charm personified. And that accent!'

Chloe smiled. 'Sounds like you're smitten.'

'Unfortunately I'm fifteen or twenty years too old.' Kate chuckled. 'Lucky Lauren, though, having him as a neighbour when he arrives for his year's placement. He loved the Manor House and Nick is making the arrangements for the long-term let.'

'That's good. And what about Jem? Was everything all right?' Chloe asked, concealing how much she had worried about Kate and her son attending Nick's welcoming event for the French GP.

Sitting back in her chair, propping her feet up, Kate looked thoughtful. 'It actually went well. Nick has always known Jem, of course, just not that he's his father,' she explained, lowering her voice even though the staffroom was empty. 'At one point Jem fell over, grazing his knee, and it was Nick who took him indoors to bathe it. I was desperate to go, too, but thought it best to leave well alone. Neither of them said anything but, with at least four other doctors in attendance, I took it as a step forward that Nick wanted to do it himself.'

Chloe hoped Kate was right. It would be good if Nick did come round. Even if he decided not to publicly claim Jem as his son, he could have a friendly relationship with the boy, be an influence in his life as a role model. And she knew Kate would be happy if her own friendship with Nick could return to its former footing, even if her love ultimately remained unrequited.

'How about you and the lovely Oliver?' Kate queried, her eyes twinkling.

Fighting a blush, Chloe thought again of how special he was, how her life had changed because of him. 'It's good. More than good.'

'Why do I sense a but?' Kate sat forward again, a frown creasing her brow. 'What's worrying you, my love?'

'We've just not talked about anything. You know, whatever this is between us. Not beyond taking things a day at a time. I'm terrified he'll move on soon and this brief interlude will be over,' she admitted, her stomach tightening.

'Oh, Chloe. Perhaps Oliver is being cautious because he knows what a big step this is for you,' she suggested, and it was Chloe's turn to frown as she considered her friend's words. 'This is new for him, too. Maybe he needs to hear how *you* feel.'

Chloe thought over what Kate had said as she returned to her room and prepared to greet her first patient of the afternoon.

If only she had some idea how Oliver felt about her, if he planned to stay, she might have the courage to take that extra step and confess how much she loved him.

Never willing to stint on patient care, Oliver forced himself to set his thoughts about his own future aside, but he longed to return to the surgery and see Chloe. The afternoon seemed to drag, but he was soon on his final home visit.

Edith Jones, one of Lucy's patients, lived in a bungalow in Polkerris Road. In her seventies, Edith had endured a tough year. On top of her heart problems and suffering a minor stroke, she had fallen in her home and split her kneecap in two. Since she had returned home from the hospital after initial rehabilitation, the district nurses and a GP visited her regularly, and Lauren was involved in her care, helping her remain as mobile as possible. Oliver had visited Edith a couple of times and was thankful the elderly lady was maintaining Lucy's original advice to change her diet and reduce her salt intake.

'Anything else I can do for you today, Edith?' he asked, packing away his things, satisfied with the results of his examination.

'No. Thank you, Dr Oliver.' She sent him a gentle smile. 'It's a bit of a struggle, but I'm coping, and everyone is very kind. I'm relieved to be able to stay in my own home with my own things around me. Sarah Pearce, my neighbour, is an angel. And I have my cat for company.'

'Call any time if there is anything you need.'

Reassured that Edith was settled, he took his leave. The journey back to the surgery was short and, when he pulled his four-by-four into the car park he saw Lauren getting out of her Renault.

'Hi, Lauren,' he greeted her, balancing his pile of patient notes and his medical bag while locking the door.

'Hello, Oliver.'

'I've just seen Edith Jones. She seems to be doing well.'

Walking with him towards the entrance, Lauren nodded. 'Yes, she is. I'm going in twice a week at the moment.'

They walked into the reception area to be greeted by Sue, the head receptionist. Oliver smiled and set his notes down on the counter for them to be filed away, then accepted the bundle of phone messages Sue handed him.

'Thank you. Anything urgent, Sue?' he asked, flicking through them.

'No, I don't think so. I do have one urgent call for you, though, Lauren,' she continued, handing over the message. 'Can you call back straight away?'

Lauren frowned at the note. 'Of course. I'll do it now.'

'Vicky is here—she said she was meeting you. She's upstairs, talking with Chloe,' Sue explained.

'I'm going up,' Oliver told Lauren, eager to see Chloe himself. 'I'll let Vicky know you're back.'

'Thanks, Oliver.'

Filled with urgency and a sense of purpose, Oliver left his medical bag and his phone messages in his consulting room then headed for the stairs. At the top, he rounded the corner. Chloe's door was open, but as he heard her and Vicky talking he hesitated outside, frozen to immobility, unable to believe what he was hearing. Blindly, he put out a hand to brace himself, feeling as if his heart was being dug out of his chest with a blunt spoon, leaving him bleeding and battered.

'Is that beard rash on your neck?' Vicky grinned, perching on the desk and leaning closer.

'No.' Chloe fought a blush, determined to hide the truth from Vicky. It was just as well she couldn't see the other places on her body that carried the faint mark of the delicious caress of Oliver's stubbled jaw. 'I was in the sun too long.'

Vicky's grin widened. 'Sure you were! So you and Oliver

are finally doing the wild thing, like I told you to. I knew my plan would work. Having him around for a few weeks was bound to liven up your boring sex life.'

'Thanks.' Her ironic riposte was lost on Vicky.

'What's the stud muffin like in bed? I wouldn't mind finding out for myself when you've finished with him...if he sticks around long enough.'

Chloe's hands clenched to fists in her lap as she tried to hide her anger, wishing Lauren would hurry back and rescue her from this torture. The very thought of Oliver with anyone else twisted her insides with pain and jealousy. She liked Vicky...usually. The woman wasn't spiteful, but she was incredibly tactless, leaping in without thinking. No way was Chloe going to leave herself or Oliver open to Vicky's brand of loose talking. And no way did she want Vicky anywhere near Oliver.

'You haven't been stupid enough to fall in love with him, have you, Chloe?' Vicky continued, flicking her fringe—today her hair was green—away from her eyes.

'Of course not,' she lied.

'Well, that's a relief. We all know he's not that kind of man, so it's no use you starting to think wedding bells or anything. That's why he was so perfect for your summer fling.'

'So you said.' Chloe ducked her head to hide her hurt, wanting to yell that Vicky had no idea what kind of man Oliver was. She knew there was no point in explaining, the other girl would never understand how wrong she was. 'Let's forget it, Vicky. It's not important.'

She just wanted Vicky to go. She knew how sensitive Oliver was about people falsely labelling him as a playboy and she was disappointed and cross with Vicky for doing the same thing. She wanted to protect Oliver, to stand up for him, but at the same time she didn't want Vicky spreading rumours and gossip around Penhally about her relationship with Oliver. And she certainly wasn't going to confide to Vicky how she truly felt about him, not until she had told Oliver himself and knew what his plans were and if she stood any chance with him. Vicky knew nothing of her past and would never comprehend what a huge step she had taken in trusting Oliver and finding love with him. It wasn't something she wanted talked about or mocked, however well meaning the teasing might be.

Oliver leaned against the wall, a tight band around his chest preventing him from breathing. Something inside him died and a void opened up. A dark, cold void where just moments ago there had been hope and love and the feeling that maybe this once he had met someone who saw beyond the playboy exterior. He had thought Chloe was different. Apparently not. He stepped into the room, bitter hurt and betrayal swirling inside him, mingling with anger at himself for being such a fool and at Chloe for not being all he had thought she was.

He had tried not to worry that Chloe had said nothing about her feelings, had not wanted to spoil the perfection of their days and nights together by pressing her too soon, by revealing his love for her. He had worried that she might never get beyond her past, and yet he had still gone ahead and laid himself bare to her, committing himself body and soul, leaving himself more vulnerable than ever before.

That Chloe had discussed him with her friends, had been using him as a temporary playboy for some sex education and a holiday fling, hurt more than he believed possible. He was devastated. All his dreams and plans, fledgling ones that had taken real flight after Nick's offer earlier, now crumbled to dust around him.

In the moment before Chloe or Vicky noticed his presence, he drank in the sight of the woman he had so wanted to believe in but who had hurt him beyond bearing. She glanced round then, shock and guilt in her expressive eyes when her gaze met his.

'Oliver! I—'

'Vicky, Lauren is waiting for you downstairs,' he interrupted, somehow managing to force the words past the tightness in his throat.

'Oops! Didn't see you there.' With an irritating giggle, Vicky slid off the edge of Chloe's desk. 'Thanks. I'll see you later.'

A tense silence followed her departure. Feeling as if the floor had been pulled out from under him, he thrust his hands in his pockets and forced himself to look at Chloe. 'Nick offered me a permanent job in Penhally.'

He watched as her face lost colour and renewed shock widened moss-green eyes. Clearly this wasn't the pleasant surprise he'd wanted it to be and she'd meant what she'd said to Vicky—she didn't love him, had never expected more than a few nights in his bed before he moved on.

'You're thinking of staying here?'

'Of course, that doesn't fit in with your plans, does it, babe?' Hurt brought a sarcastic edge to his voice. 'You and Vicky had it all figured out. I was a not entirely repulsive *stud* you thought you could use to satisfy your curiosity about sex for a night or two because it wouldn't matter to me.'

Chloe stared at Oliver in horror. The icy chill of his voice was matched by the expression in his eyes, eyes devoid of their normal life and warmth.

'That's not—'

'I heard what you said.'

'Oliver!' Hazel's urgent call from the direction of the landing prevented Chloe making a rebuttal. 'We have an emergency outside. Can you come?'

'Of course.' He cast Chloe one searing look before turning away. 'I'm done here.'

The finality of the words cut Chloe to the quick. 'But—'

Chloe watched through a film of tears as Oliver strode away, his footsteps retreating down the stairs as he followed Hazel. Slumping against her desk, her whole body shaking in reaction, Chloe wrapped her arms around herself. Damn Vicky. Just how much of their conversation had Oliver heard? It must have sounded bad. And on top of that, instead of responding with the joy and hope she felt at the thought of Oliver staying, the shock and confusion of the last moments had made her reaction slow and lukewarm.

What was she going to do? So inexperienced at this kind of thing, she had made a mess of everything. Because of her past, she hadn't believed she could be happy, that what she felt for Oliver was real, that it could work. Had not believed he could love her. But his pain had been obvious. She would never forget the look in his eyes. The knowledge that he now believed she had used him stung.

'Chloe, what the hell is going on?' Lauren demanded, rushing into the room and closing the door behind her.

Tears trickled down her cheeks and her voice shook. 'Oliver's gone. It's over.'

'Vicky told me what happened. She's an idiot.' Lauren handed her a tissue and slid an arm around her shoulder. 'So will you be if you let Oliver go. Damn it, Chloe! You have to go after him.'

'No.' A sob escaped. She thought she had known what pain was like but this was worse, much worse. 'I can't. He'd never believe me now.'

Lauren cursed. 'I was there when he followed Hazel downstairs. He was devastated. I've never seen anyone look so broken. You love him, Chloe, I know you do. Don't let it end like this. It's too important, for both of you. He doesn't know what Vicky is like, he didn't understand you were trying to protect him from gossip. He's not a mind-reader. You have to explain.'

'I've been too scared to tell him I love him.' Chloe's throat closed and her chest crushed with hurt. 'Now it's too late. I let him down.'

'*Tell* him.'

'What if he won't talk to me?' she whispered through her tears, scared she had driven Oliver away for good.

'You won't know until you try. Make him listen,' Lauren advised. 'He's hurting now because he loves you. You love him. What have you got to lose?'

Nothing, Chloe realised as her friend left her alone to think. She had already lost everything that mattered to her. A fierce mix of need and hurt and anger swirled inside her. She was angry with herself for handling things so badly, angry with Vicky for interfering, angry and disappointed that Oliver hadn't given her the chance to explain. It hurt that he hadn't believed in her enough. But why should he? She'd never told him how she felt, had taken everything he had given her these last weeks but had still doubted. After what he had overheard, followed by her reaction, what else was he to think?

Lauren was right. She was the only one who could change that. Oliver was worth fighting for. She gathered up her things and hurried down the stairs, upset to discover that Oliver had left. The emergency had been a suspected heart attack and he had gone along in the ambulance to St Piran with the critically ill patient. No one could tell when he might be back.

Unwilling to hang around the surgery, she went home to shower and change her clothes. After feeding the cats, she paced her small living room. Several times she phoned Oliver's flat but there was no reply, and his mobile was switched off. When her phone rang, she jumped and rushed to answer, hoping it was Oliver, swallowing her disappointment when she discovered it was not. It was Kate.

'Are you all right, Chloe? What's going on with you and Oliver?'

'I don't know.' Her voice trembled with tears. 'He overheard me talking to Vicky this afternoon. She can be so persistent and thoughtless. I told her a few fibs. I was trying to stop her gossiping, but now Oliver thinks I have just been using him. It isn't true!'

'I know that, my love. So will Oliver when he's calmed down,' Kate reassured her, but Chloe knew it wasn't that simple.

'He told me that Nick had offered him a permanent post. Oh, Kate, I was so shocked, so stunned to discover he had heard me and Vicky, that I reacted badly. I didn't get the chance to explain, and now he believes there's nothing between us, that I don't care. And that's my fault, too, because I was too scared to tell him.'

A heartfelt sigh from Kate increased her anxiety. 'He's going, Chloe. I was here at the surgery when he came back from the hospital fifteen minutes ago. He told Nick he didn't want the job, that there was nothing for him to stay for.'

'No!'

'Go to him, my love. It doesn't matter who is more at fault, you are both hurting and you need each other. If you don't talk to him, you will always regret it,' Kate counselled, reinforcing Lauren's advice. 'Make it right, Chloe...before it's too late.'

Knowing there was a wealth of meaning behind Kate's words, empathising with her friend's difficult situation with Nick, the man she had loved for so long, Chloe made her decision.

Oliver tossed clothes into his bags, trying to use anger to mask the bitter lance of terrible pain. How could he have been so stupid? Chloe wasn't different at all. Like everyone else, she had seen the outer package, the reputation, and not the man inside. His gut ached at the knowledge she had used him as some kind of sex tutor. And he would never forget the look of shock on her face when he had told her he was staying. Clearly she didn't want him. He had read everything wrong and now there was nothing for him in Penhally Bay.

A furious pounding on the door had his head snapping up. He hesitated. He wasn't on duty. Indeed, he had a few days off to decide if he even wanted to see out his contract here. But what if someone was in trouble? Hell. He ran a hand through his hair and stalked towards the door. Throwing it open, he froze when he saw who waited outside. Chloe. Her hand, raised to knock again, fell to her side. Before he could react, she pushed past him.

'What do you want, Chloe, another quick tumble in bed before the playboy leaves town?' He hated himself for the words and tried to close his mind to the hurt clouding her green eyes.

'No. That wouldn't be enough.' She folded her arms across her chest and fixed him with a glare. 'I'm here because you didn't give me a chance to explain and I'm not going to let you judge me and leave without me saying my piece.'

Unwanted amusement and affection welled inside him at her bravado. He'd never seen her so riled before. It was cute. No, he— Before he could formulate his thoughts and raise his defences again, she launched into her attack.

'Do you seriously think, with my background and having waited until the age of twenty-seven, that I would suddenly turn into some kind of sexpot who is going to sleep with anyone for the sake of it? Yes, Vicky made some stupid comment when she found out you were interested in me that I should go for it. But that's Vicky. She doesn't know about my past. She certainly doesn't know me if she thought I could ever do such a thing.' She paused a moment, dragging in a lungful of air. 'And neither can you if you believe it, even for a moment. I didn't come on to you, chase you. You courted me. And it was only when I came to know you, to like you, to trust you, that I began to wonder if maybe you were someone special, someone who made it worth my while to confront things that terrified me and open myself up to experiences I had shut out of my life because I was so scared. You think I would have just jumped into bed with anyone?'

She was shaking with rage and hurt. All the fight went out of him as every word she said hit home and he acknowledged how badly he had behaved, how horribly he had treated her. Yes, he did know her better. He just hadn't allowed himself to believe it could be true that he had found his perfect soulmate, that she could ever come to love him back, that there could be a happy ever after. Just when it had all been falling into place, everything had been shaken up and he had allowed his own insecurities to get the better of him, to believe the worst of her.

'Chloe…' He tried to swallow past the lump in his throat and find his voice. 'I'm sorry.'

'So am I.'

Tears shimmered on long sooty lashes as he closed the gap between them. 'I was so dumb.'

'Me, too.'

'Can you forgive me, babe? Please?'

'Oliver—'

He rested the fingers of one hand over her lips, not wanting her to reject him as he deserved, needing to say his own piece while he had the chance. 'I should never have paid heed to what I heard. I was just so stunned, so hurt when you told Vicky you didn't love me.'

'Vicky means well, but she's the biggest gossip in Penhally, Oliver, and she has zero tact. I didn't want her telling all and sundry our private business. I was angry with her for judging you, for being so shallow, but I knew she would never listen, never understand, so I let her ramble on. No way was I going to tell Vicky, of all people, about my feelings—not when I hadn't even had the courage to tell you.'

'Chloe,' he murmured, stepping closer, a glimmer of hope challenging the darkness inside him. 'When I came back to Cornwall, I was jaded, fed up with people using me because of the family name, the money, my so-called playboy lifestyle. Sure, I liked to have a good time, to enjoy myself, but no one saw *me*. The person inside. Not until you. I was drawn to you from the first and the more I came to know you, the more I knew you were special, and I dared to allow myself to believe.' He cupped her face, breathing in her fresh apple scent. 'Nick sprang the junior partnership on me and immediately I had all these plans and wanted to share them with you. But I had no idea how you felt. When I heard you talking and it seemed to have all been some grand scheme for a fling between us, I let the hurt and fear get in the way of my common sense and all I knew about you. I was scared because I thought I had been a fool to think someone like you could possibly care about someone like me.'

'Someone like you?' she challenged, her own hands lifting to grasp his wrists. 'A fantastic, caring doctor, adored by his patients, young and old, male and female? Someone like you, who is good and kind, funny and intelligent, selfless and giving? Someone like you who saw *me* when no one else had, and who cared enough to wait, to gain my trust, to spend so much time getting me through the scary moments and awakening me to all I was missing by not setting the past behind me where it belongs? Someone like you, who changed my life…who made me really feel alive for the first time? That someone like you?'

'Yeah.' Love and desire glowed inside him at the sincerity of her words.

'Oliver, I don't care about your bank balance. I don't care about Fawkner Yachts. It wouldn't matter to me who your family were as long as they loved you and were proud of you. I'm proud of you. And I love you. I should have told you before, but I was scared, too. Scared you would leave soon and I'd never see you again. Scared none of this meant to you what it did to me. You stole my heart, you made me believe in romance and love and for ever. You even made me like sex,' she added with a shy laugh, a blush staining her cheeks.

'Chloe…'

Her eyes full of vulnerability, she stepped back a couple of paces and pulled the tie holding the fabric of her floaty dress together. She let it drop, revealing barely-there silk and lace bra and panties. Every part of him sprang to attention. OK. Any moment now he would remember how to breathe. That or pass out. Dear God…

'I've never seduced a man before.'

He filled his lungs on a ragged gasp. 'You're doing one hell of a good job,' he managed, his voice hoarse with love and admiration and desire.

'Am I?'

'Oh, yeah.' Given how hard he was and how close to embarrassing himself. 'Don't move.'

He reached for the phone, his fingers shaking as he felt for the keys and dialled a number, his gaze never leaving Chloe's.

'Nick? It's Oliver Fawkner. If the offer for the junior partnership still stands, I'd like to accept. Thank you. Yes, I'm sorry about that, it was a misunderstanding. I've just discovered that I have everything to stay for. All I'll ever need is right here in Penhally Bay.'

As he replaced the receiver, he saw joy dance in Chloe's beautiful green eyes, along with a whole host of feelings that mirrored his own. To think he had been so foolish to risk throwing this away. 'Now, you said something about seducing me.'

'Yes. That.'

'Don't let me stop you,' he invited, his fingertips brushing across the rounded swell of her breasts over the top edges of her bra, enjoying the tremor that rippled through her.

'I was kind of hoping you might take over at this point.'

'I don't know. You're doing so well.'

'Really?'

'Don't you know you had me on my knees from the moment we met?'

She shook her head, looking shy yet bold, sexy yet uncertain as her fingers began to undo the buttons of his shirt. 'I only know you didn't give up on me, didn't let my past and my fears chase you away.'

He moaned as she freed his shirt, leaned forward and closed her mouth over one sensitive nipple. Not wanting to be left out, he deftly unhooked her bra and tossed it away, filling his palms with her firm, full, soft flesh.

'How about we do the seducing together?' he suggested hoarsely.

'Good idea.'

'We'll do everything together, Chloe, for the rest of our lives. I'll do all I can to make you happy and I'll love you for ever. If you'll let me.'

'Yes.' She whimpered as his thumbs brushed over taut nipples. 'I will. If you'll let me love you for ever, too.'

'I think I can manage that.'

Her fingers fumbled with the fastening of his jeans. 'Starting now?'

'Hell, yes!' He kissed her, long and hard and deep. 'What say we shock Vicky and make it another wedding for Penhally before the year is out?'

'Lauren is right. There definitely must be something in the water!'

He nipped her earlobe. 'Is that a yes?'

'Of course it's a yes!'

'I already have a present for you,' he told her with a teasing smile, thinking of the jet-ski he'd ordered.

Green eyes sparkled with mischief as she looked at him. 'Funny. I have a present for you, too. It's at home. I hid it in the spare room. It's for your birthday, but I was going to give it to you if you left...to remember me by.'

'As if I could ever forget you.' He groaned, pulling her close. 'And I'm never leaving, babe.' As curious as he was about what she had bought him, amazed and touched that she had done such a thing, he had other things on his mind right now. 'Presents can wait until later.'

'Whatever did you have in mind?'

Laughing, he swung her up in his arms and carried her to the bedroom. He set her back on her feet, grimacing when he saw her pained expression as she looked at his half-packed luggage.

'Like I said, I was dumb.'

'You can still pack.'

He froze at her words. 'What do you mean?'

'Your lease here runs out any day.' Shy invitation shone in her eyes. 'I was thinking... Maybe you'd care to move in with me?'

'I'd love to. And down the line, when we decide about a family, we can find a new home together that we can grow into. With the cats, of course.'

'Perfect.'

'No. You're perfect.' He tipped her on to the bed and stripped off the rest of his clothes. 'Do you think, knowing you—and your background—that I ever would have embarked on a relationship with you if all I had wanted was a quick, meaningless tumble before I moved on again? You're not a quick tumble kind of woman, Chloe. If I'd only wanted one night, I would never have touched you. I would have walked away. But I came here to settle down, to meet the right woman for me, and

I soon knew you were the one. You are a forever kind of woman. My forever woman. It's happened quickly, but I love you. And I've never said that to anyone before. I know this is all new to you. If you need time to be sure, that's fine, I understand. But I'm only going to love you more each day.'

Tears filled her eyes, threatening to spill past her lashes. 'I am sure. I love you, too. So much. I just can't believe I'm enough for you.'

'Babe, you are everything.' He joined her on the bed, dipping his head to steal a hot kiss. 'And it'll be my pleasure to prove it to you every day for the rest of our lives.'

She wriggled out of her panties. 'Starting now.' It was half question, half demand, her voice throaty with arousal.

'This very second.'

He fulfilled his promise, as he planned to fulfil all his promises to her, now and for all the years that lay ahead of them. How could he be this lucky? He was the happiest man alive, and if he had his way, Chloe was going to be the most satisfied woman in Penhally Bay. Hell, the whole world!

Linking his fingers with hers, holding her gaze, he united them, starting them on their journey to paradise together, joining not just their bodies, but their hearts and their souls…for ever.

*\ *\ *\ *

Special Offers
In the Village Collection

Welcome to Penhally Bay—
a Cornish coastal town with a big heart!

On sale	On sale	On sale
2nd December 2011	6th January 2012	3rd February 2012

Collect all 3 volumes!

Save 20%
on all Special Releases

Find out more at
www.millsandboon.co.uk/specialreleases

Visit us Online

MILLS & BOON

Book of the Month

MARION LENNOX
Sydney Harbour Hospital: Lily's Scandal

ALISON ROBERTS
Sydney Harbour Hospital: Zoe's Baby

2 in 1 GREAT VALUE

We love this book because...

This fabulous 2-in-1 introduces Medical Romance's fantastic new continuity—set in the high-octane, gossip-fuelled world of Sydney Harbour Hospital. Brace yourself for eight helpings of sizzle, scandal and heart-wrenching emotion!

On sale 3rd February

Visit us Online

Find out more at
www.millsandboon.co.uk/BOTM

0112/BOTM

Don't miss Pink Tuesday
One day. 10 hours. 10 deals.

PINK TUESDAY IS COMING!

10 hours...10 unmissable deals!

This Valentine's Day we will be bringing you fantastic offers across a range of our titles—each hour, on the hour!

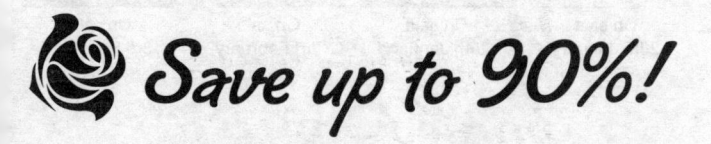

Save up to 90%!

Pink Tuesday starts
9am Tuesday 14th February

Find out how to grab a Pink Tuesday deal—register online at **www.millsandboon.co.uk**

Visit us Online

0212/PM/MB362

Special Offers

Every month we put together collections and longer reads written by your favourite authors.

Here are some of next month's highlights— and don't miss our fabulous discount online!

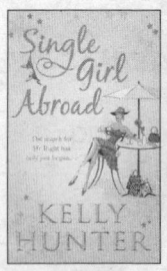

Single Girl Abroad — KELLY HUNTER	 COURTNEY MILAN — *Trial by Desire*	 BE MY VALENTINE VAMPIRE	Lynne GRAHAM — Playboys
On sale 20th January	On sale 20th January	On sale 3rd February	On sale 3rd February

Save 20% on all Special Releases

Find out more at
www.millsandboon.co.uk/specialreleases

Visit us Online

0212/ST/MB359

Special Offers
Escape For... Collection

We guarantee these four volumes will shower you with pure indulgence and escapism

Collect all 4 volumes!

Escape for New Year — On sale 16th December

Escape for Valentine's — On sale 20th January

Escape for Mother's Day — On sale 17th February

Escape for Easter — On sale 16th March

Save 20% on Special Releases Collections

Find out more at
www.millsandboon.co.uk/specialreleases

Visit us Online

0112/10/MB356

FREE Online Reads

Visit
www.millsandboon.co.uk
today to read our
short stories online—FOR FREE!

- Over 100 short stories available
- New reads updated weekly
- Written by your favourite authors, including…Lynne Graham, Carol Marinelli, Sharon Kendrick, Jessica Hart, Liz Fielding and MANY MORE

You can start reading these FREE Mills & Boon® online reads now just by signing up at www.millsandboon.co.uk

Visit us Online

Sign up for our FREE Online Reads at **www.millsandboon.co.uk/onlinereads**

Have Your Say

You've just finished your book. So what did you think?

We'd love to hear your thoughts on our 'Have your say' online panel
www.millsandboon.co.uk/haveyoursay

- Easy to use
- Short questionnaire
- Chance to win Mills & Boon® goodies

Visit us Online
Tell us what you thought of this book now at
www.millsandboon.co.uk/haveyoursay

YOUR_SAY

Mills & Boon® Online

Discover more romance at
www.millsandboon.co.uk

- **FREE** online reads
- **Books** up to one month before shops
- **Browse our books** before you buy

...and much more!

For exclusive competitions and instant updates:

Like us on **facebook.com/romancehq**

Follow us on **twitter.com/millsandboonuk**

Join us on **community.millsandboon.co.uk**

Visit us Online — Sign up for our FREE eNewsletter at **www.millsandboon.co.uk**

WEB/M&B/RTL4